D1094450

A FIRESIDE BOOK

OF

Yuletide Tales

☆

Edward Wagenknecht: A Bibliography

ABRAHAM LINCOLN: HIS LIFE, WORK, AND CHARACTER (1947)
CAVALCADE OF THE AMERICAN NOVEL (IN PREPARATION)
CAVALCADE OF THE ENGLISH NOVEL (1943)
THE CHIMES, BY CHARLES DICKENS (INTRODUCTION BY E. W.) (1931)
THE COLLEGE SURVEY OF ENGLISH LITERATURE (WITH OTHERS) (1942)
THE FIRESIDE BOOK OF CHRISTMAS STORIES (1945)
THE FIRESIDE BOOK OF GHOST STORIES (1947)
THE FIRESIDE BOOK OF ROMANCE (1948)
A FIRESIDE BOOK OF YULETIDE TALES (1948)
GERALDINE FARRAR, AN AUTHORIZED RECORD OF HER CAREER (1929)
A GUIDE TO BERNARD SHAW (1929)
JENNY LIND (1931)
JOAN OF ARC, AN ANTHOLOGY OF HISTORY AND LITERATURE (1948)
LIFE ON THE MISSISSIPPI, BY MARK TWAIN (INTRODUCTION BY E. W.) (1944)
LILLIAN GISH, AN INTERPRETATION (1927)
THE MAN CHARLES DICKENS, A VICTORIAN PORTRAIT (1929)
MARK TWAIN, THE MAN AND HIS WORK (1935)
SHAKESPEARE, A MAN OF THIS WORLD (1947)
SIX NOVELS OF THE SUPERNATURAL (1944)
THE STORY OF JESUS IN THE WORLD'S LITERATURE (1946)
UTOPIA AMERICANA (1929)
VALUES IN LITERATURE (1928)
WHEN I WAS A CHILD (1946)

"And you anon shall by their noise
Perceive that they are merry"

GEORGE WITHER

A FIRESIDE BOOK OF YULETIDE TALES

Edited by EDWARD WAGENKNECHT

WITH ILLUSTRATIONS BY
WARREN CHAPPELL

The Bobbs-Merrill Company, Publishers
INDIANAPOLIS & NEW YORK

Printed in the United States of America

FIRST EDITION

TO

LILLIAN GISH

WIE EINST IN MAI

Contents

Introduction xi

I. ONCE IN ROYAL DAVID'S CITY

THE STABLE OF THE INN: *Thomas Nelson Page* 3

FRANKINCENSE AND MYRRH: *Heywood Broun* 15

INASMUCH: *Heywood Broun* 17

WE, TOO, ARE BIDDEN: *Heywood Broun* 19

THE SAD SHEPHERD: *Henry van Dyke* 22

WHITE SHAWL FROM ALEXANDRIA: *Frederic Mertz* 40

TO COME UNTO ME: *Robert Nathan* 44

MIDNIGHT IN THE STABLE: *Elizabeth Goudge* 47

II. CHRISTMAS LEGENDS

ON HANGING A STOCKING AT CHRISTMAS: *Charles S. Brooks* . . 75

THE FIR-TREE: *Hans Christian Andersen* 85

A CHRISTMAS LEGEND OF HAMELIN TOWN: *Coningsby Dawson* . 94

THE LEGEND OF THE CHRISTMAS ROSE: *Selma Lagerlöf* 106

TWINKLE: *Harold Leonard Bowman* 122

MRS. BARBER'S CHRISTMAS: *Martin Armstrong* 125

THE STATE VERSUS SANTA CLAUS: *Arthur Stringer* 132

THE ESCAPE OF ALICE: *Vincent Starrett* 139

III. FRANKLY SENTIMENTAL

A CHRISTMAS DREAM, AND HOW IT CAME TRUE: *Louisa May Alcott* 157

AN EMPTY PURSE: *Sarah Orne Jewett* 172

THE GIFT OF THE MAGI: *O. Henry* 180

IT HAPPENED AT WILD CAT: *Frederick Landis* 186

CHERISHED AND SHARED OF OLD: *Susan Glaspell* 194

THE LITTLE CHRISTMAS TREE: *Stella Gibbons* 204

DAVID'S STAR OF BETHLEHEM: *Christine Whiting Parmenter* . 217

IV. SOME CHRISTMAS ASPIC

CHRISTMAS EVERY DAY: *W. D. Howells* 233

DOWN PENS: *Saki* 242

OLD FOLKS' CHRISTMAS: *Ring Lardner* 247

THE CHRISTMAS CARD: *James Bridie* 258

THE CHRISTMAS CARP: *Vicki Baum* 272

CHRISTMAS FORMULA: *Stella Benson* 284

V. CHRISTMAS AT HOME AND ABROAD

CHRISTMAS IN MAINE: *Robert P. Tristram Coffin* 295

WHAT AMELIA WANTED: *Elsie Singmaster* 303

MR. KAPLIN AND THE MAGI: *Leonard Q. Ross* 313

A LITTLE RAIN: *Brendan Gill* 321

THE CHRISTMAS TREE SHIP: *Harry Hansen* 325

STAR IN THE EAST: *Fred Ward* 330

ST. ANTHONY'S FIRST CHRISTMAS: *Wilfred Thomason Grenfell* 333
A SOMERSET CHRISTMAS: *Llewelyn Powys* 340
CHRISTMAS DAY AT KIRKBY COTTAGE: *Anthony Trollope* . . 345
THE MAGIC TREE: *Elisabeth Neilson* 378
THE HALLELUJAH CHORUS: *Pierre van Paassen* 388

VI. CHRISTMAS ADVENTURES

MERRY CHRISTMAS: *Herman Melville* 397
THE SEVEN POOR TRAVELLERS: *Charles Dickens* 402
A STRANGER KNOCKED: *Joseph Shearing* 429
TWILIGHT OF THE WISE: *James Hilton* 446
CHRISTMAS HONEYMOON: *Howard Spring* 456

VII. WHAT IS THE CHRISTMAS SPIRIT?

WHAT CHRISTMAS IS AS WE GROW OLDER: *Charles Dickens* . . 479
CHRISTMAS IN POSSESSION: *M. E. Braddon* 484
CHRISTMAS EVE—POLCHESTER WINTER PIECE: *Hugh Walpole* 508
A PINT OF JUDGMENT: *Elizabeth Morrow* 524
COUNTRY CHRISTMAS: *Paul Hoffman* 537
ONCE ON CHRISTMAS: *Dorothy Thompson* 548

Illustrations

Frontispiece

FACING PAGE

The Stable of the Inn 8

The Legend of the Christmas Rose 138

The Gift of the Magi 170

Down Pens 266

Christmas in Maine 298

Merry Christmas 426

What Christmas Is As We Grow Older 458

Introduction

This book, a companion to *The Fireside Book of Christmas Stories* (Bobbs-Merrill, 1945), which now exists in more than 500,000 copies, differs from the other volume in a number of ways. In the earlier anthology the material was arranged under four heads, and though the last two of these were wide enough to admit a considerable variety, it is still true that I was obliged to reject many excellent stories for no better reason than that they would not fit into the framework which I had designed. I am not in any sense apologizing for this: there are advantages as well as disadvantages in the use of a comparatively rigid scheme. But I am pointing out that having done one thing in *The Fireside Book of Christmas Stories*, I have done something else again in *A Fireside Book of Yuletide Tales*. This time the collection of material came first and the classification afterward. The material has been allowed to classify itself, and I rejected no story that I really wanted. I did not, for example, plan to have a section called "Christmas Adventures"; we have a section called "Christmas Adventures" because that is where some of the stories that I wanted to reprint asked to go. And it is purely an accident that we have our divisions in the form of the lucky number seven, rather than five or eight or thirteen.

As in all my anthologies, I have attempted here a balance of familiar and unfamiliar materials. There are stories whose right to inclusion in a Christmas anthology has long since been established, and which I believe my readers will greet as old friends. There are others, like the selection from *Moby Dick*, which have probably never been thought of before in this connection. "An Empty Purse" is one of Sarah Orne Jewett's least familiar tales, and the pieces by Miss Braddon and Louisa May Alcott may not unfairly be described, to use one of Carl Van Vechten's favorite words, as "excavations." I am very proud of the fact that I have become the "onlie begetter" of a fine story by one of my favorite storytellers, Joseph Shearing: "A Stranger Knocked" was written especially for my book. One other story, "The State versus Santa Claus," by Arthur Stringer, is here printed for the first time; and here, too, the stories by two good Chicagoans, Harold Leonard Bowman and Vincent Starrett, first appear before a general audience.

As in *The Fireside Book of Christmas Stories,* the word "story" has been rather loosely defined. There were a few essays in the earlier book, and there are some here. Moreover, a number of the best *narratives* in the book are factual, not fictional, material. I might discourse long upon this theme: the English novel began by masquerading as "history," and there is still, surely, much history in it. In a day and a milieu in which naked imagination was as terrifying to the *bourgeoisie* as the sight of the naked body, Defoe attempted to mislead his readers upon this point; Swift, like modern fictionists—see, in this collection, Howard Spring's ending for "Christmas Honeymoon"—merely attempted, by the use of the same methods, to achieve verisimilitude. Yet contemporaries did not make nice distinctions, and a bishop denounced *Gulliver's Travels* as a wicked imposture, having been unable to find Lilliput on a map.

I. *Once in Royal David's City.* Christmas began at Bethlehem, and so far as modern Christmas stories concern themselves with the religious aspects of Christmas they must begin at Bethlehem too. The Biblical narratives themselves were not available for this book, since I had already used them in *The Fireside Book of Christmas Stories,* and it was a rule that nothing that had been used there should be repeated here. It was fortunate, therefore, that Thomas Nelson Page should have been willing to go to Bethlehem for us, to retell the Bethlehem story, faithfully so far as adherence to its narrative outlines is concerned, with deep reverence for its spirit, yet with all the grace and charm of a modern man of letters.

"The Stable of the Inn" is followed in Section I by three of Heywood Broun's imagined episodes of the first Christmas and by

Henry van Dyke's story of how the Babe of Bethlehem, anticipating his life's work, brought healing to a sick soul. It is followed too by a brief tale much more in the modern idiom, "White Shawl from Alexandria," in which Frederic Mertz renews the old story for us and freshens its appeal by viewing it from a novel and unfamiliar angle.

The "modern" spirit of this story helps to bridge the gap between what precedes it and the two stories which follow. Here we move away from royal David's city and the first Christmas, geographically, chronologically—not, I think, in spirit. Miss Elizabeth Goudge, always at her best when writing of children and of her beloved Channel Islands, takes her point of departure from one of the oldest and sweetest legends of the Nativity, while Robert Nathan, a writer always mindful of man's continued need, amid all his new playthings, of the old spiritual sustenance, has dared to place the divine simplicities of Christmas against the background of the glamour capitol of the world. It is interesting that both writers find it advisable to call upon the imagination of children to bridge the gap between past and present.

It may also be interesting to remark in passing that while most of the distinctively religious stories are included in Section I, the epigraphs printed at the beginning of each section remain distinctively religious throughout the book. This device will help, I hope, to keep readers mindful of the real meaning of the Christmas festival.

II. *Christmas Legends*. Section II leaves, one might say, the realm of faith for the realm of fancy: here is a varied group of Christmas legends. We open with an essay from *Chimney-Pot Papers*—"On Hanging a Stocking at Christmas"—and from here we pass to three richly imaginative tales, all steeped in the storied past of our race. There are not many stories of our own time that we can confidently think of as classics in their kind, but "The Legend of the Christmas Rose" is such a story. "The Fir-Tree," quite naturally, needs no introduction. And the best Christmas story Coningsby Dawson ever wrote tenderly embroiders one of the loveliest bits of medieval tradition.

Clearly of our own time, on the other hand, though the action involves a world which lies outside of time altogether, is Dr. Bowman's story of the mischievous angel. So, too, though in a much more serious vein, is Martin Armstrong's tale of the old lady who went home on Christmas day. Arthur Stringer gaily reminds us of the one for whom we hang our stockings, and Vincent Starrett brings the section to a close with his pastiche on a book which only very unfortunate children have never found under the tree.

III. *Frankly Sentimental.* This is not the place to write a history of the word "sentimental." Is a sentimental story a story which appeals to human emotion? Or is it a tale in which the emotional appeal is forced? Or is it merely a tearful story?

There is no virtue, surely, in insensibility—no more than in impercipience. On the other hand, there is no virtue in lachrymosity either.

As it is difficult to achieve a definition of the word "sentimental" which will satisfy everybody, so, by the same token, it would be unreasonable to expect all readers to react to any given specimen of the sentimental tale in the same way. There can be no doubt that Christmas is one of the outstanding subjects which, by any definition, tend to inspire sentiment, and I am not aware that anybody has ever tried to put together a book of Christmas stories with no "sentimental" tales in it.

There are few absolute standards anywhere in the field of literary criticism: about all I can say of the stories I have chosen is that I hope they will please as many people as possible.

A few genuine old-fashioned stories seem to be desirable in a Christmas book. In *The Fireside Book of Christmas Stories,* Louisa May Alcott was represented by the familiar Christmas story from *Little Women.* Wanting Miss Alcott again, I have presented her this time in terms of a long-forgotten story—a kind of child's variation of Dickens' *Christmas Carol*—which will come to most present-day readers with a sense of novelty. The spirit of old New England lives again in the Jewett tale, and "The Gift of the Magi," which is almost the type-tale for modern stories of Christmas sentiment, is here reprinted both because it is a fine story and for the special benefit of those who wondered audibly why it had been left out of my earlier book.

The other stories in this section are all more recent. They are, I hope, sufficiently varied in their appeal to make a good bouquet when they are tied together, and I intend no disrespect toward any of them when I leave them without further, individual comment.

IV. *Some Christmas Aspic.* But if you want sweets with your Christmas dinner, you also want some aspic. Not too much, but enough. So we come to Section IV, in which it is hoped that the reader will find just what he needs to balance the other courses, but not so much as to give him an excuse to forget that Christmastime is a festival season.

William Dean Howells' long-beloved tale concerns itself with some of the disadvantages which would result from trying to celebrate Christmas every day. Saki deals wryly with a nonidealistic aspect of the festival which we have all encountered, but Ring Lardner's theme is of a monstrous type of young American for whose existence we have only our own weak folly, in a traditionally opulent and acquisitive society, to blame. Prosperity and all its problems are far away from the personages of "The Christmas Carp," which seems to me, in its mingled humor and pathos, a small masterpiece and one of the finest stories in the book. And the author's last sentence shows her to be well aware that it contains implications which carry far beyond the story or even the Christmas festival itself.

The other two stories both partake of the fantastic. James Bridie has given us a delightfully "zany" tale; Stella Benson offers a terrifying glimpse of the "Brave New World." "It can't happen here!" This surely must have been the spontaneous exclamation of most of the author's readers, whether in England or in America, when the story first appeared. I hope not, I am sure. But it makes me uneasy to recall that not many years have passed since we would all have made exactly the same remark about many of the decrees which bureaucrats and brass hats have passed down since, all too many of which have been supinely accepted.

V. *Christmas at Home and Abroad.* The fifth section offers a kind of Baedeker of Christmas celebrations. We begin in New England with Robert P. T. Coffin, move to Pennsylvania with Elsie Singmaster, to New York with Leonard Ross (and Hyman Kaplan!), to the South with Brendan Gill, to old Chicago with our good friend Harry Hansen, and 'way out to Montana with Fred Ward. In so vast and varied a country as this, no complete "coverage" can be attempted, and the regions to be represented had to be governed by limitations of space and availability of material.

The most unfortunately named of all Americans at the present time may be presumed to be those who carry the name of Kilroy, but the Kaplans too have had their trials. During the war, an acquaintance of mine registering, under that name, for a course at Oxford was immediately asked whether he were related to Hyman, to which he promptly replied that he himself carried but one pencil and one fountain pen.

With the great missionary-hero, Sir Wilfred T. Grenfell, yarning for us out of his own experience, we make Labrador a steppingstone on our way to the Old World. Llewelyn Powys and good old Anthony Trollope take us to England. In these days of our happy Trollope revival, it is good to be able to print such a sound, characteristic, and comparatively unfamiliar Trollope tale. Mrs. William Allan Neilson reminds us of a Germany where children were warm and secure, with no Hitler poisoning their young minds and no American airmen raining death upon them from the skies; and it is surely heart-warming to end with Pierre van Paassen's record of what must surely be one of the most eloquent and inspiring protests ever made against those who would destroy the joy of Christmas through blasphemous travesties of the spirit of Him in whose honor the festival was established.

VI. *Christmas Adventures.* Compared to the stories in, say, Section I, for example, it might be said that the tales in Section VI are less "Christmas stories" than stories with a Christmas setting. The term "Christmas story" is often used rather differently in England from the way we use it in America. For us a Christmas story is generally a story which deals with specifically Christmas happenings and expresses the spirit of Christmas. The English often think of a Christmas story as merely a traditional tale—all the better if there be a few ghosts in it—of the kind that Englishmen have loved to tell for many generations, to give themselves delightful shivers before the warm and comfortable Christmas fire. Henry James, for example, creating a story with an English setting, began "The Turn of the Screw" with the words: "The story had held us, round the fire, sufficiently breathless, but except the obvious remark that it was gruesome, as on Christmas Eve in an old house a strange tale should essentially be. . . ." and went on from there to one of the greatest ghost stories in the English language, but one which no American reader, surely, has ever thought of as eminently suited for Christmas.

I have not gone nearly so far as that in Section IV. Every tale printed here has a Christmas setting, and most have, I think, the "feel" of Christmas. Certainly this is eminently true of Mr. Hilton's, which reminds us that he understood the implications of his own Shangri-La. But all four of the British stories have the British literary tradition behind them. Now that Herman Melville has at last come into his own, I think many readers will enjoy the Christmas sailing of the *Pequod* from Nantucket, in quest of Moby Dick—surely one of the half-dozen most momentous voyages in literature.

VII. *What Is the Christmas Spirit?* Of Section VII there is not a great deal that needs to be said. I have sought to close with a section varied in subject matter, each of whose selections should pre-eminently breathe the spirit of Christmas. This is about all that the selections printed under this heading have in common, but in their variations they recapitulate the main themes of the anthology.

So we have wise reflections on the meaning of Christmas by Charles Dickens—without whom any Christmas book must be not merely incomplete but ridiculous. We have also a long, delightful, old-fashioned tale of Christmas adventure by the author of *Lady Audley's Secret* (surely dirty old Jiffins is a strangely un-Victorian variation of the Christmas angel); a characteristic episode from a favorite novel by Hugh Walpole; a delightful story about children at Christmastime by Mrs. Morrow; and two charming reminiscential pieces in which we get as close, I fancy, to what Christmas in America means—to what the Christmases of our childhood mean, as they are carried in memory, by the present generation of Americans—as paper and ink can take us.

The Editor and the Publishers of this volume express their gratitude to the many authors, agents, publishers, and other proprietors who have co-operated in clearing the permissions involved in this book. I am indebted to my friend, Mrs. Elsie Singmaster Lewars, not only for assisting me in making a selection from her own rich treasure-trove of Christmas stories but also for calling my attention to the fine story by Pierre van Paassen. Mr. Joseph Kinsey Howard, editor of *Montana Margins*, published by the Yale University Press, extended courtesies in connection with my use of Fred Ward's "Star in the East," and both Dr. Ray E. Smith, of Indianapolis, and Mr. Claude Billings, of Akron, Ohio, have been helpful in connection with Frederick Landis' story, "It Happened at Wild Cat."

I must not forget to thank the editors of the book review journals—*The Saturday Review of Literature*, the *New York Herald Tribune Weekly Book Review*, *The New York Times Book Review*, and the *Chicago Sunday Tribune Magazine of Books*, who ran my "card"—nor the people who wrote to me about it. Some asked me to use stories I had already decided upon; some first called my attention to stories that are printed here; some asked for tales which, for one reason or another, it has not seemed practicable to use. But I am equally grateful to them all.

I am inevitably grateful, too, to Mr. D. L. Chambers, president of The Bobbs-Merrill Company, who wanted to publish this book, and to Mr. Herman Ziegner, Mr. John L. B. Williams, Mr. Allen C. Rearick and other members of The Bobbs-Merrill staff, in Indianapolis and New York, who have co-operated generously in getting the book ready under unusual difficulties. And surely no author or editor needs to say that he is very thankful to have been associated with one of the most accomplished illustrators in America, Mr. Warren Chappell.

The following persons, all except one of whom were students of mine last year in the College of Liberal Arts or the Graduate School of Boston University, have generously assisted me in preparing copy: Mr. Robert F. Delaney, Mrs. Eunice B. Lockhart, Miss Virginia M. Murphy, Mr. Theodore Pearce, Mrs. William Hunter Perry, Miss Kathleen Sheehan, and Miss Shirley J. Stanwood. My son, Robert Edward Wagenknecht, has again assisted me in copyreading.

EDWARD WAGENKNECHT

West Newton, Massachusetts

I

ONCE IN ROYAL DAVID'S CITY

Dim-berried is the mistletoe
With globes of sheenless grey,
The holly mid ten thousand thorns
Smoulders its fires away;
And in the manger Jesu sleeps
    This Christmas Day.

WALTER DE LA MARE

The Stable of the Inn

THOMAS NELSON PAGE

IT WAS in the twenty-seventh year of the reign of Augustus Caesar or, as some say, in quite another year—in what was known simply as the tenth month, or, by another account, at the beginning of the eighth month. Toward the eventide of a calm day, two travellers of the peasant class, a man and a young woman—the latter riding an ass, beside which the man walked—toiled slowly up the rough highway that climbed the rocky hills a little to the southward of the ancient capital of Judea where Herod now reigned. The top of the pass in the range toward which their faces were set was crowned with a small town, whose walls, lifted above the straggling olive trees, gleamed white and pink in the light of the declining sun. The wayfarers had journeyed all day, and the woman was faint with fatigue. At length she spoke to the man. He bowed his head and, as they reached a convenient point, turned out of the rough and dusty highway, and at a little distance came to a halt in a sloping, bare field to one side, in which, on an outjut of rock, stood an old and rude tower, lifted above the folds along a ledge of the hill—the tower of Eder. On the lower hills beyond the far edge of the field some shepherds were minding their flocks as they grazed their way slowly homeward along the sides of the rocky ravines which seamed the range.

Moving far enough into the field to be beyond the dust and noise of the highway, and, if necessary, to seek refuge in the tower, the man helped the woman to dismount with more gentleness than was usually shown by people of their class. Behind them streamed the mingled traffic of a road that led to a great city. Men on foot or mounted on asses or camels passed along; truckers with loads of produce packed in immense panniers on their beasts or bearing on their heads bundles so huge that it was a wonder they were not crushed beneath them; drovers with herds of dusty cattle or flocks of sheep and goats on the way to market; travellers of a better degree, with servants and attendants following their horses or chariots; long lines of camels swinging slowly by in single file like great flocks of gigantic four-legged birds, the dust spurting in clouds from their lagging feet at every step. And now and then a body of soldiers swung clanking by, taking the best part of the road and with imperious voices ordering every one out of their way.

The man was already past middle age and, though of the peasant class, his face was strong and his features good, like so many of his race. The woman, young enough to be his daughter, might have been taken for his wife, save for a certain distance in his manner toward her. A young Roman noble who passed them that day, on his way to Herod's court, observing them, and noting, with an eye for beauty, the delicate features of the young woman, disclosed by her veil's slipping for a moment, concluded that the woman was some Jewish girl of station, and that her attendant was her father's steward escorting her home. She was, indeed, treated by her companion with a distinction approaching reverence. Having helped her down, he spoke softly and spread his robe on the ground for her to sit upon.

From a little distance floated upward the bleating of sheep, and presently the flocks began to appear, winding up from the lower slopes, led by their shepherds toward the folds built on the sides of the hills. To the woman's sigh of fatigue the man replied soothingly that they would soon be at their journey's end—at Bethlehem.

"Little Bethlehem!" murmured the young woman.

" 'And thou Bethlehem, in the land of Juda, art not the least among the princes of Juda,' " quoted the man. " 'For out of thee shall come a governor that shall rule my people Israel.' But thou art faint. The bottle is dry. The child that cried to us for water took the last drop. I will try to get thee some. The shepherds yonder will have it." She said something of her fear for him if he went among strange men, for the road from Jericho, which they had lately crossed, was infested with robbers—and the shepherds were a wild and reckless class. He reassured her and left her. Bearing the leathern bottle in his hand, he crossed the field and went over to one of the sheepfolds near by, where he talked to one of the shepherds, an elderly man, bearded to the eyes. When he returned a little later, he bore in his hand a bottle of milk and a piece of the coarse bread that the shepherds eat. Not long afterward the shepherds themselves came over, one after one; plain; bearded; beaten by the weather; tanned by the sun; men of the field, with their stout staves, their sheepskin coats and goat-skin leggings, and their bags, or scrips, hung over their shoulders. At their approach the young woman, who was soon to be a mother, shyly drew about her her veil, which was ample enough to cover her from head to foot. The man as quietly moved forward and, interposing between her and the strangers, greeted the leader. But they were friendly. They wanted to talk.

"Thou art from Galilee?" queried the shepherd in the lead, a rough, grizzled man with eyes that burned deep under his shaggy brows. "Thy speech is Galilean?"

The other man bowed.

"Of Nazareth."

"Can any good thing come out of Nazareth!" jeered a voice from the rear.

"As good as from Kerioth," answered another, at which his companions laughed. The speaker turned to the traveller.

"Thy name is—what?"

"Joseph, son of Jacob."

"Thou knowest my uncle, Zebedee, the fisherman? He hath a fine son——"

"I know him and his son James, and young Simon from the Rock who fishes with him."

"I know them not," said the shepherd; "but Zebedee is my mother's brother, and Judas the Zealot——"

"His wife is half-sister to her," said the traveller, with a movement of the head toward the young woman.

The connection made an impression on all around and the men drew closer together.

"Dost thou know Judas the Zealot?"

Joseph bowed.

"Hast thou seen him lately?"

"But the other day he came up from the sea to my shop to get a sheath put to his fish-knife."

"I know that knife," said the shepherd, glancing around at his companions with pride. "He had it of one of the Sicarians. The Romans did not get it."

The other shepherds laughed hoarsely.

"It hath done other work in its time," continued the shepherd. "I heard my uncle tell of it. When Judas's father was slain, one of his captains flung himself over the cliff, and my uncle found the knife later at the foot of the cliff when he was drying his net."

"When didst thou see him last?" asked Joseph, as if to change the subject.

"He came to the Passover and sought me out. He wanted me to go and be a fisherman, but I told him that I knew the hills better than the water and I would stay here. Dost thou look for the coming one?"

Joseph bowed.

"Whither goest thou?" asked the shepherd. "Jerusalem is behind thee."

"To Bethlehem, to meet the tax, and be enrolled."

"Ah! The tax! The tax! It is always the tax," exclaimed the shepherd, while the others growled their assent. "Why should they enroll us! To slay us? Did not King David try it! And how many men did it cost! Would that we had more like Judas! Art thou of Bethlehem?" he added.

"Yea, of the tribe and lineage of David. Both of us."

He glanced around to where the young woman sat.

The speech evidently made a further impression on the shepherds.

"Would that we had another David! That would be better yet!"

"Aye, aye!" echoed the others. "And he was a shepherd! He would see us righted and not let them carry us off to the war and leave our sheep without a shepherd."

"But there is no war, now, nor rumor of war," said Joseph, "and the ploughshare is better than the sword and the pruning-hook than the spear."

"Dost thou know Joachim?" asked the shepherd suddenly.

"Yea," said Joseph; "well."

"He was once a shepherd here, fifteen or twenty years ago."

Joseph listened with interest.

"It was when the high-priest drove him from the altar because his wife was barren. He came here and lived with me. And 'tis said his wife knew not where he was and feared him dead. And he prayed always, always, and one night a vision came to him. An angel said to him: 'Was not Sara long barren? And Rachael? And yet she bore Joseph who was lord of Egypt—stronger than Samson and holier than Samuel.' And he bade him leave and go to Jerusalem and enter by the Golden Gate. And I have heard that his wife met him there and that she bore him a daughter?"

"It is true," said Joseph; "she is there."

The shepherd stopped and gazed long and curiously at the figure on the ground.

"So!" he murmured. "Zebedee said there was talk of strange things at Nazareth; he said that word had come that again a barren woman had borne a child—a woman as old as our mother Sara, and that her husband had seen a vision—his name was Zachariah, was it not? Hast thou heard of it?" His voice sank and his eyes sought the traveller's eyes. The other shepherds listened intently.

The young woman on the ground drew her veil yet closer about her. It was as if a white morning-glory had withdrawn within itself at the approach of evening.

"I have heard so," said Joseph briefly.

"Can it be that the time draws nigh?" asked the old shepherd tremblingly.

"Who knoweth the times and the seasons?" replied the other, as if to avoid the gaze fixed upon him.

"But it is said that a virgin must bear a child, and he shall be called Emmanuel. Can it be? Does it mean that we are never to see the rising again of Israel?"

"Is the Lord's arm shortened that it cannot save?" replied Joseph quietly. "Or is His ear dulled that He cannot hear?" He turned to where the young woman sat on the ground.

"But I grow old," said the shepherd. "I had a son once, but the Romans——" He broke off. "We have scores to settle."

"Aye, that we have," came in chorus from the others.

"Wait on the Lord," said Joseph. The young woman rose from the ground and Joseph lifted her gently to her saddle.

"Have a care of thy wife," said the shepherd. "She is young and the soldiers——"

"I have no fear," said Joseph calmly.

"They fear not God, nor regard man. To them an Israelite is a dog."

"We have no fear," said Joseph firmly.

"The place will be full. There is but one inn, and it will be crowded. They have been passing since sunrise. Clouds of dust on the road all day. We could see it from the hills."

The others assented.

"God will provide for us," said Joseph, as, bidding the shepherd adieu, he turned the ass's head toward the road.

The shepherds stood and watched them as they moved slowly upward until they were lost in the shadows on the highway, and then turned back to their flocks. What they said, it was, perhaps, well that no soldiers were near to hear; for the older man's words had stirred them deeply, and prophecy after prophecy was recounted pointing to the overthrow of Roman power.

For two hours nearly the travellers plodded onward up the mountain. The village on its shoulder above them turned pink, then white as alabaster; and then the white faded to an icy blue; once more flushed to a saffron hue, and gradually died until by the time the travellers reached the nearest houses down the slope all was

"The shepherds approached softly, and there in the manger, wrapped in swaddling-bands, lay the young child."

THE STABLE OF THE INN

Story on page 3

dusk, and with the darkness had come the cold. Once they paused at a turn in the road, and rested while they gazed across the dark valley to the eastward to where some miles away gleamed many lights. "There it is," said Joseph. "There is Jerusalem. The Temple."

"I have had many happy hours there," said his companion softly. As they moved on, between them and the sky on a hill beside the road, a cross lifted itself. "Look the other way," said Joseph quickly; but he was too late. The young woman shuddered and bowed her head low. "Some robber, perhaps, but he is dead," explained Joseph. The young woman's only answer was a moan.

When they arrived at the village itself, they found what the shepherds had said to be true. The village was quite full and the only inn there had no place for them.

When they reached the gate-way of the entrance court, travellers were being turned away, and a number of them were consulting together as to whether they should remain in the street all night or should go back toward Jerusalem. The gates would be shut; but they might find a lodging place in some other village.

It was dark, for the moon, though nearly full, was not yet risen above the hills, and it was too late to seek shelter elsewhere. Joseph went boldly to the gate and knocked. For some time there was no answer; but he continued to knock. Jeers broke out from the group in the street behind him; but he paid no heed. He kept on knocking. After a while the bar was drawn on the inside, and the porter partly opened the gate. When, however, he saw only a plain man with a woman mounted on an ass, he spoke shortly and told him that there was no room for them in the inn. Joseph made known his situation. His wife could go no farther and could not remain in the street all night. This did not avail. The porter spoke with contempt. "Better than you have been turned away tonight."

"Than me?—Yes," said Joseph; "but not better than that I bring." He took from his scrip an official paper and added that he had come "under Caesar's order."

"You trouble me much," growled the porter. But he admitted them, and told Joseph that he might spend the night in the stable if he could find a place there.

"In the stable!" said Joseph.

"Yes, and you'd better be glad to get that," growled the porter. "The other night we had to put up a man that a dog of a Samaritan had found on the road from Jericho, naked and half-dead. He must needs bring him here and order the best room for him. A priest and a Levite were here that night, and a pretty fuss they made too—they wanted him put in the stable; but the Samaritan's money was good, so the master took him in."

Joseph said that he was glad to have the stable, and, leading the ass inside the gate, he followed the direction of the porter. He picked his way carefully across the dim court, amid the camels and asses crowded therein, and crossed over to the side to which the porter carelessly waved him, where, hollowed in the rock, were the rough caves used as stables for the inn.

Here in a stall which had, perhaps, been kept vacant in the hope that some guest of quality might come who would pay for it, and would bring honor to the inn, Joseph placed his wife, using such means as he could to make her comfortable.

The inn itself was full of life and movement; lights flared and failed and flared again, as busy servants bustled about attending to the wants of the numerous guests who ate and drank, sang, danced, and slept as they listed.

Across the court, where the camels and other cattle ruminated or slumbered, all was dark and still—as dark and still as it must have been when darkness was upon the waters before the dawn of the first creation, when God said, "Let there be light," and there was light.

Far away, across the sea, on her seven hills, Rome glittered with her myriad lights, innumerable as the stars of heaven, and in his imperial palace ruled Augustus Caesar, master of the world, whose decree had gone out that all the world should be taxed—ruled in such splendor that the greatest men of their time proclaimed him a god—ruled with such power that a simple carpenter in a little town in a far-away province across the seas could not be overlooked and left at home; but must make a long and perilous journey with his wife to be taxed in the city of his fathers, where he was a up and complained that they had awakened him. "Thou st soundly, then, thou of Kerioth," they said. But Judas de- l that they had disturbed a dream he had. "I dreamt of silver," aid; "a garden like one I know near Jerusalem and a great sure there—a man on his knees and I arrested him—and gave n up, and found thirty great pieces of silver. Oh! I felt rich—as h as that Zaccheus men talk of—and then you waked me up; I uld hang myself." His companions, however, paid little atten- on to him. They were too wonderstruck—and presently they egan to say one to another, "Let us now go even to Bethlehem and see this thing which is come to pass, which the Lord hath made known unto us."

In a few moments they were ready to start.

"If we are going," said the leader, "we might as well take with us some milk. We may come across our friends, Joseph and his wife, and they will find it hard to get anything in that crowded place." He went off, and in a little while came back with a bottle of milk.

"What is the use of that?" growled the one who had had his dream disturbed. "They will have enough. Better save and sell it, and let me give the money to the poor."

"Judas, thou art ever prating of giving, yet givest naught," said the man with the bottle of milk. "Come with us."

"I am not going," said the man of Kerioth. "I shall stay and see that no one troubles the sheep."

"See that thou trouble them not thyself," said one of his fellows, at which the others laughed.

"Come on," said the leader. And they set forth in haste, followed by the gibes of the one left behind.

Out in the dusty road they filed, one behind the other, and by the moonlight began to ascend the winding, rocky road which led up toward the hills above them. Stumbling over the rocks in the dusk with their ill-shod feet; passing the commonplace wayfarers coming or going with their asses or on foot, it was hard to believe that but now they had seen and heard Heavenly messengers—as Abraham and Jacob and Daniel had seen them.

stranger, and in which when he arrived l
in the inn, and was fain to lodge in the in
tle, as little considered as they.

None but the lowly shepherds in the fie
them. To them happened a strange thing tha

It must have been about midnight. The mo
up the sky and flooded the hills with light. The
herds was on watch, while the others slept. Many t
his mind—the promises to Abraham and to his se
words of peace that the traveller from Nazareth had
through his memory. He began to dream. And the fi
struck him was the strange behavior of the sheep in the
rose from the ground and, facing toward the mountai
lambs kneel at their mothers' sides. But they were all sti
as if carved of stone. And while he wondered, suddenly the
near him—so suddenly that it was as if he had dropped down
him—a presence. He had no time to question—a light—a glor
imaginable—brighter than the moon—more glorious than the su
like the glory of the Lord. It awoke some of the others. It was rou
about them, and they were sore afraid. Then a voice sounded i
their ears—and the angel said unto them: "Fear not; for behold I bring you good tidings of great joy, which shall be to all people; for unto you is born this day in the city of David, a Saviour, which is Christ the Lord, and this shall be a sign unto you: ye shall find the babe wrapped in swaddling-clothes, lying in a manger."

Astonished and still terrified—stunned beyond thought—the shepherds lay as they had been found—and suddenly there was with the angel a multitude of the Heavenly host, praising God, and saying, "Glory to God in the Highest, and on earth peace to men of good-will." Then they went away upward—up into the Heaven—and only the shepherds were left on the earth with their flocks. When they recovered their courage and looked up, the sky was as usual on clear and cloudless nights—and only the moon was shining down, flooding the fields with light. They began to talk in low tones of what they had seen and heard, and to wonder what it all meant. One of the younger men who had not spoken before

"Well we shall know when we get there. If the babe be there—we shall know," said the leader.

It was near day when they reached the town. They came at length to the gate of the inn. In the twilight of the dawn it was just being opened by the sleepy and gruff porter as they arrived, and he stood in the open gate-way yawning. He heard their inquiry in dull silence.

He pondered a moment. "What is it ye want?" he asked sullenly.

"We want to know if two travellers who came here late last night found shelter?"

"Two travellers? Nearer two hundred. Look at the court-yard. So full that one cannot walk across it. And the house is packed."

"Two who came late? A man and a young woman—he was much older than she—she——"

"Oh! Aye. Two came late—too late——"

"What became of them?"

"There was no place for them in the inn——"

"And you turned them away?"

"Who said I did? Am I a dog to do that?"

"What became of them?"

The porter half turned.

"Go look in there." He pointed toward the stable. "I gave them shelter there for the young woman—and none too soon. There are three of them there now, I judge, from what I heard but now."

The shepherds gave an exclamation and, passing across the court-yard to the stable, paused at the opening that led into the dusky recess. A woman's voice, low and soft, yet jubilant, was heard. She was speaking in the tone of gladness of a young mother:

"My soul doth magnify the Lord. And my spirit hath rejoiced in God my Saviour."

The shepherds approached softly, and there in the manger, wrapped in swaddling-bands, lay the young child.

It was, then, not a dream. This was the sign unto them.

"His mercy is on them that fear Him, from generation to generation," crooned the young mother as the shepherds drew near. "He hath put down the mighty from their seats and exalted them of low degree." It was the hymn of the poor.

The shepherds entered softly. The morning light stole into the recess and fell on the group, and the shepherds sank to their knees to gaze on the babe in wondering awe. So, in the stable began the first worship of Him who came to save the world—Christ the Lord.

That day it was noised abroad—that wonders had happened in the city of David, and in the country round about. It reached the ears of the authorities, and an investigation was made. In the time of the taxing all rumors were looked into. Theudas and Judas were the proof of how serious such rumors might be. But this report was traced to a few poor shepherds who, returning to the fields from a village, told a strange story of a babe born in a stable and of angels appearing and preaching peace and good-will to all men. No one paid any attention to them at the time. Only Mary, the young mother, kept all these things and pondered them in her heart.

Caesar Augustus in Rome was celebrating his world-wide peace, and Herod Ascalonita was too busy with his dreams of power to pay attention to such talk. When some months later it recurred and some Eastern travellers brought it again to his attention, with the story of an old prophecy from the Hebrew writings, referring to Bethlehem, he disposed of the matter finally by sending soldiers and slaying all the babes born in the village mentioned from two years old and under, including among them, it is said, even one of his own children, who was born there. But by this time, says the sacred record, Joseph, having been warned by God in a dream, had taken the young child and his mother and departed into Egypt.

Three Christmas Episodes

HEYWOOD BROUN

FRANKINCENSE AND MYRRH

ONCE there were three kings in the East and they were wise men. They read the heavens and they saw a certain strange star by which they knew that in a distant land the King of the World was to be born. The star beckoned to them and they made preparations for a long journey.

From their palaces they gathered rich gifts, gold and frankincense and myrrh. Great sacks of precious stuffs were loaded upon the backs of the camels which were to bear them on their journey. Everything was in readiness, but one of the wise men seemed perplexed and would not come at once to join his two companions, who were eager and impatient to be on their way in the direction indicated by the star.

They were old, these two kings, and the other wise man was young. When they asked him he could not tell why he waited. He knew that his treasures had been ransacked for rich gifts for the King of Kings. It seemed that there was nothing more which he could give, and yet he was not content.

He made no answer to the old men who shouted to him that the time had come. The camels were impatient and swayed and snarled. The shadows across the desert grew longer. And still the young king sat and thought deeply.

At length he smiled, and he ordered his servants to open the great treasure sack upon the back of the first of his camels. Then he went into a high chamber to which he had not been since he was a child. He rummaged about and presently came out and approached the caravan. In his hand he carried something which glinted in the sun.

The kings thought that he bore some new gift more rare and precious than any which they had been able to find in all their treasure rooms. They bent down to see, and even the camel drivers peered from the backs of the great beasts to find out what it was which gleamed in the sun. They were curious about this last gift for which all the caravan had waited.

And the young king took a toy from his hand and placed it upon the sand. It was a dog of tin, painted white and speckled with black spots. Great patches of paint had worn away and left the metal clear, and that was why the toy shone in the sun as if it had been silver.

The youngest of the wise men turned a key in the side of the little black and white dog and then he stepped aside so that the kings and the camel drivers could see. The dog leaped high in the air and turned a somersault. He turned another and another and then fell over upon his side and lay there with a set and painted grin upon his face.

A child, the son of a camel driver, laughed and clapped his hands, but the kings were stern. They rebuked the youngest of the wise men and he paid no attention but called to his chief servant to make the first of all the camels kneel. Then he picked up the toy of tin and, opening the treasure sack, placed his last gift with his own hands in the mouth of the sack so that it rested safely upon the soft bags of incense.

"What folly has seized you?" cried the eldest of the wise men. "Is this a gift to bear to the King of Kings in the far country?"

And the young man answered and said: "For the King of Kings

there are gifts of great richness, gold and frankincense and myrrh.

"But this," he said, "is for the child in Bethlehem!"

INASMUCH

ONCE there lived near Bethlehem a man named Simon and his wife Deborah. And Deborah dreamed a curious dream, a dream so vivid that it might better be called a vision. It was not yet daybreak, but she roused her husband and told him that an angel had come to her in the vision and had said, as she remembered it, "Tomorrow night in Bethlehem the King of the World will be born." The rest was not so vivid in Deborah's mind, but she told Simon that wise men and kings were already on their way to Bethlehem, bringing gifts for the wonder child.

"When he is born," she said, "the wise men and the kings who bring these gifts will see the stars dance in the heavens and hear the voices of angels. You and I must send presents, too, for this child will be the greatest man in all the world."

Simon objected that there was nothing of enough value in the house to take to such a child, but Deborah replied, "The King of the World will understand." Then, although it was not yet light, she got up and began to bake a cake, and Simon went beyond the town to the hills to get holly and made a wreath. Later in the day husband and wife looked over all their belongings, but the only suitable gift they could find was an old toy, a somewhat battered wooden duck that had belonged to their eldest son, who had grown up and married and gone away to live in Galilee. Simon painted the toy duck as well as he could, and Deborah told him to take it and the cake and the wreath of holly and go to Bethlehem. "It's not much," she said, "but the King will understand."

It was almost sunset when Simon started down the winding road that led to Bethlehem. Deborah watched him round the first turn and would have watched longer except that he was walking straight

---

toward the sun and the light hurt her eyes. She went back into the house and an hour had hardly passed when she heard Simon whistling in the garden. He was walking very slowly. At the door he hesitated for almost a minute. She looked up when he came in. He was empty-handed.

"You haven't been to Bethlehem," said Deborah.

"No," said Simon.

"Then, where is the cake, and the holly wreath, and the toy duck?"

"I'm sorry," said Simon, "I couldn't help it somehow. It just happened."

"What happened?" asked Deborah sharply.

"Well," said Simon, "just after I went around the first turn in the road I found a child sitting on that big white rock, crying. He was about two or three years old, and I stopped and asked him why he was crying. He didn't answer. Then I told him not to cry like that, and I patted his head, but that didn't do any good. I hung around, trying to think up something, and I decided to put the cake down and take him up in my arms for a minute. But the cake slipped out of my hands and hit the rock, and a piece of the icing chipped off. Well, I thought, that baby in Bethlehem won't miss a little piece of icing, and I gave it to the child and he stopped crying. But when he finished he began to cry again. I just sort of squeezed another little piece of icing off, and that was all right, for a little while; but then I had to give him another piece, and things went on that way, and all of a sudden I found that there wasn't any cake left. After that he looked as if he might cry again, and I didn't have any more cake and so I showed him the duck and he said 'Ta-ta.' I just meant to lend him the duck for a minute, but he wouldn't give it up. I coaxed him a good while, but he wouldn't let go. And then a woman came out of that little house and she began to scold him for staying out so late, and I told her it was my fault and I gave her the holly wreath just so she wouldn't be mad at the child. And after that, you see, I didn't have anything to take to Bethlehem, and so I came back here."

Deborah had begun to cry before Simon finished his story, but when he had done she lifted up her head and said, "How could you do it, Simon? Those presents were meant for the King of the World, and you gave them to the first crying child you met on the road."

Then she began to cry again, and Simon didn't know what to say or do, and it grew darker in the room and the fire on the hearth faded to a few embers. And that little red glow was all there was in the room. Now, Simon could not even see Deborah across the room, but he could still hear her sobbing. But suddenly the room was flooded with light and Deborah's sobbing broke into a great gulp and she rushed to the window and looked out. The stars danced in the sky and from high above the house came the voice of angels saying, "Glory to God in the highest, and on earth peace, good will toward men."

Deborah dropped to her knees in a panic of joy and fear. Simon knelt beside her, but first he said, "I thought maybe that the baby in Bethlehem wouldn't mind so very much."

WE, TOO, ARE BIDDEN

THE angel of the Lord said to the shepherds, "And this shall be a sign unto you: Ye shall find the babe wrapped in swaddling clothes, lying in a manger."

They made haste to go to Bethlehem to see the thing which had come to pass. "For unto you," the angel said, "is born this day in the city of David a Saviour, which is Christ the Lord."

But as they journeyed to Bethlehem they fell into a discussion as to just how they should find the place where the infant lay. The shepherds were not folk familiar with the town, even though it lay a short journey from the fields in which they tended their flocks. Besides, they knew that many from the country roundabout had gone to Bethlehem in compliance with the decree of Caesar Augustus that all the world should be taxed. Indeed, one of the

---

group grumbled, "In Bethlehem there be many mangers, and how are we to find the one?"

And the youngest shepherd said, "It will be made known to us."

The night was bright with stars and the way more easy than they had expected. In spite of the late hour many walked in the narrow streets of Bethlehem, and from all the houses there came a clatter. The shepherds stood for a moment in some perplexity as to the appointed place. The noises of the town were confusing to men who had been standing silent under starlight.

And suddenly the volume of voices increased, and down the street there came a caravan of camels. Upon the backs of the beasts sat great bearded men, and with them they brought sacks of precious stuffs and huge treasure chests from distant kingdoms. The air was filled with the pungent tang of spice and perfume.

The startled shepherds stood against the wall to let the cavalcade of the mighty pass by. And these wise men and kings seemed to have no doubt as to their destination. They swept past the inn and dismounted at the door of a stable. Servants took the burdens from the backs of the camels, and the kings and the wise men stooped and went in through the low door of the stable.

"It is there the child lies in the manger," said one of the shepherds and made as if to follow, but his fellows were abashed and said among themselves, "It is not meet that we should crowd in upon the heels of the mighty."

"We, too, are bidden," insisted the youngest shepherd. "For us, as well, there was the voice of the angel of the Lord."

And timidly the men from the fields followed after and found places near the door. They watched as the men from distant countries came and silently placed their gifts at the foot of the manger where the child lay sleeping. And the shepherds stood aside and let the great of the earth go out into the night to take up again their long journey.

Presently they were alone, but as they had no gifts to lay beside the gold and frankincense they turned to go back to their flocks. But Mary, the mother, made a sign to the youngest shepherd to come closer. And he said, "We are shepherds, and we have come suddenly from the fields whence an angel summoned us. There is naught which we could add to the gifts of wise men and of kings."

Mary replied, "Before the throne of God, who is a king and who is a wise man, you have brought with you a gift more precious than all the others. It lies within your heart."

And suddenly it was made known to the shepherd the meaning of the words of Mary. He knelt at the foot of the manger and gave to the child his prayer of joy and of devotion.

The Sad Shepherd

HENRY VAN DYKE

I

OUT OF the Valley of Gardens, where a film of new-fallen snow lay smooth as feathers on the breast of a dove, the ancient Pools of Solomon looked up into the night sky like dark, tranquil eyes, wide-open and motionless, reflecting the crisp stars and the small, round moon. The full springs, overflowing, melted their way through the field of white in winding channels, and along their course the grass was green even in the dead of winter.

But the sad shepherd walked far above the valley, in a region where ridges of gray rock welted and scarred the back of the earth; and the solitude was desolate; and the air was keen and searching.

His flock straggled after him. The sheep, weather-beaten and dejected, followed the path with low heads swaying from side to side, as if they had travelled far and found little pasture. The black, lop-eared goats leaped upon the rocks, restless and ravenous, tearing down the tender branches and leaves of the dwarf oaks and wild olives. They reared up against the twisted trunks and crawled and scrambled among the boughs. It was like a company of gray downcast friends and a troop of hungry little black devils following the sad shepherd afar off.

He walked looking on the ground, paying small heed to them. Now and again, when the sound of pattering feet and panting breaths and the rustling and rending among the copses fell too far behind, he drew out his shepherd's pipe and blew a strain of music, shrill and plaintive, quavering and lamenting through the hollow night. He waited while the troops of gray and black scuffled and bounded and trotted near to him. Then he dropped the pipe into its place again and strode forward, looking on the ground.

The fitful, shivery wind that rasped the hill-tops, fluttered the rags of his long mantle of Tyrian blue, torn by thorns and stained by travel. The rich tunic of striped silk beneath it was worn thin, and the girdle about his loins had lost all its ornaments of silver and jewels. His curling hair hung down dishevelled under a turban of fine linen, in which the gilt threads were frayed and tarnished; and his shoes of soft leather were broken by the road. On his brown fingers the places of the vanished rings were still marked in white skin. He carried not the long staff nor the heavy nail-studded rod of the shepherd, but a slender stick of carved cedar battered and scratched by hard usage, and the handle, which might have been of precious metal still more richly carved, was missing. He was a strange figure for that lonely place and that humble occupation—a fragment of faded beauty from some royal garden tossed by rude winds into the wilderness—a pleasure-craft adrift, buffeted and broken, on rough seas.

But he seemed to have passed beyond caring. His young face was frayed and threadbare as his garments. The splendor of the moonlight flooding the wild world meant as little to him as the hardness of the rugged track which he followed. He wrapped his tattered mantle closer around him, and strode ahead, looking on the ground.

As the path dropped from the summit of the ridge toward the Valley of the Mills and passed among huge broken rocks, three men sprang at him from the shadows. He lifted his stick, but let it fall again, and a strange ghost of a smile twisted his face as they gripped him and threw him down.

"You are rough beggars," he said. "Say what you want, you are welcome to it."

"Your money, dog of a courtier," they muttered fiercely; "give us your golden collar, Herod's hound, quick, or you die!"

"The quicker the better," he answered, closing his eyes.

The bewildered flock of gray and black, gathered in a silent ring, stood staring while the robbers searched their master.

"This is a stray dog," said one, "he has lost his collar, there is not even the price of a mouthful of wine on him. Shall we kill him and leave him for the vultures?"

"What have the vultures done for us," said another, "that we should feed them? Let us take his cloak and drive off his flock, and leave him to die in his own time."

With a kick and a curse they left him. He opened his eyes and lay still for a moment, with his twisted smile, watching the stars.

"You creep like snails," he said. "I thought you had marked my time to-night. But not even that is given to me for nothing. I must pay for all, it seems."

Far away, slowly scattering and receding, he heard the rustling and bleating of his frightened flock as the robbers, running and shouting, tried to drive them over the hills. Then he stood up and took the shepherd's pipe, a worthless bit of reed, from the breast of his tunic. He blew again that plaintive, piercing air, sounding it out over the ridges and distant thickets. It seemed to have neither beginning nor end; a melancholy, pleading tune that searched forever after something lost.

While he played, the sheep and the goats, slipping away from their captors by roundabout ways, hiding behind the laurel-bushes, following the dark gullies, leaping down the broken cliffs, came circling back to him, one after another; and as they came, he interrupted his playing, now and then, to call them by name.

When they were nearly all assembled, he went down swiftly toward the lower valley, and they followed him, panting. At the last crook of the path on the steep hillside a straggler came after him along the cliff. He looked up and saw it outlined against the sky. Then he saw it leap, and slip, and fall beyond the path into a deep cleft.

"Little fool," he said, "fortune is kind to you! You have escaped.

What? You are crying for help? You are still in the trap? Then I must go down to you, little fool, for I am a fool too. But why I must do it, I know no more than you know."

He lowered himself quickly and perilously into the cleft, and found the creature with its leg broken and bleeding. It was not a sheep but a young goat. He had no cloak to wrap it in, but he took off his turban and unrolled it, and bound it around the trembling animal. Then he climbed back to the path and strode on at the head of his flock, carrying the little black kid in his arms.

There were houses in the Valley of the Mills; and in some of them lights were burning; and the drone of the mill-stones, where the women were still grinding, came out into the night like the humming of drowsy bees. As the women heard the pattering and bleating of the flock, they wondered who was passing so late. One of them, in a house where there was no mill but many lights, came to the door and looked out laughing, her face and bosom bare.

But the sad shepherd did not stay. His long shadow and the confused mass of lesser shadows behind him drifted down the white moonlight past the yellow bars of lamplight that gleamed from the doorways. It seemed as if he were bound to go somewhere and would not delay.

Yet with all his haste to be gone, it was plain that he thought little of where he was going. For when he came to the foot of the valley, where the paths divided, he stood between them staring vacantly, without a desire to turn him this way or that. The imperative of choice halted him like a barrier. The balance of his mind hung even because both scales were empty. He could act, he could go, for his strength was unbroken; but he could not choose.

The path to the left went up toward the little town of Bethlehem, with huddled roofs and walls in silhouette along the double-crested hill. It was dark and forbidding as a closed fortress. The sad shepherd looked at it with indifferent eyes; there was nothing there to draw him.

The path to the right wound through rock-strewn valleys toward the Dead Sea. But rising out of that crumbled wilderness a mile or two away, the smooth white ribbon of a chariot-road lay upon the flank of a cone-shaped mountain and curled in loops toward its peak. There the great cone was cut squarely off, and the levelled summit was capped by a palace of marble, with round towers at the corners and flaring beacons along the walls; and the glow of an immense fire, hidden in the central court-yard, painted a false dawn in the eastern sky. All down the clean-cut mountain-slopes, on terraces and blind arcades, the lights flashed from lesser pavilions and pleasure-houses.

It was the secret orchard of Herod and his friends, their trysting-place with the spirits of mirth and madness. They called it the Mountain of the Little Paradise. Rich gardens were there; and the cool water from the Pools of Solomon plashed in the fountains; and trees of the knowledge of good and evil fruited blood-red and ivory-white above them; and smooth, curving, glistening shapes, whispering softly of pleasure, lay among the flowers and glided behind the trees. All this was now hidden in the dark. Only the strange bulk of the mountain, a sharp black pyramid girdled and crowned with fire, loomed across the night—a mountain once seen never to be forgotten.

The sad shepherd remembered it well. He looked at it with the eyes of a child who has been in hell. It burned him from afar. Turning neither to the right nor to the left, he walked without a path straight out upon the plain of Bethlehem, still whitened in the hollows and on the sheltered side of its rounded hillocks by the veil of snow.

He faced a wide and empty world. To the west in sleeping Bethlehem, to the east in flaring Herodium, the life of man was infinitely far away from him. Even the stars seemed to withdraw themselves against the blue-black of the sky till they were like pin-holes in the vault above him. The moon in mid-heaven shrank into a bit of burnished silver, hard and glittering, immeasurably remote. The ragged, inhospitable ridges of Tekoa lay stretched in mortal slumber along the horizon, and between them he caught a glimpse of the sunken Lake of Death, darkly gleaming in its deep bed. There was no movement, no sound on the plain where he walked, except the soft-padding feet of his dumb, obsequious flock.

He felt an endless isolation strike cold to his heart, against which he held the limp body of the wounded kid, wondering the while, with a half-contempt for his own foolishness, why he took such trouble to save a tiny scrap of worthless life.

Even when a man does not know or care where he is going, if he steps ahead he will get there. In an hour or more of walking over the plain the sad shepherd came to a sheep-fold of gray stones with a rude tower beside it. The fold was full of sheep, and at the foot of the tower a little fire of thorns was burning, around which four shepherds were crouching, wrapped in their thick woollen cloaks.

As the stranger approached they looked up, and one of them rose quickly to his feet, grasping his knotted club. But when they saw the flock that followed the sad shepherd, they stared at each other and said: "It is one of us, a keeper of sheep. But how comes he here in this raiment? It is what men wear in kings' houses."

"No," said the one who was standing, "it is what they wear when they have been thrown out of them. Look at the rags. He may be a thief and a robber with his stolen flock."

"Salute him when he comes near," said the oldest shepherd. "Are we not four to one? We have nothing to fear from a ragged traveller. Speak him fair. It is the will of God—and it costs nothing."

"Peace be with you, brother," cried the youngest shepherd; "may your mother and father be blessed."

"May your heart be enlarged," the stranger answered, "and may all your families be more blessed than mine, for I have none."

"A homeless man," said the old shepherd, "has either been robbed by his fellows, or punished by God."

"I do not know which it was," answered the stranger; "the end is the same, as you see."

"By your speech you come from Galilee. Where are you going? What are you seeking here?"

"I was going nowhere, my masters; but it was cold on the way there, and my feet turned to your fire."

"Come then, if you are a peaceable man, and warm your feet

with us. Heat is a good gift; divide it and it is not less. But you shall have bread and salt too, if you will."

"May your hospitality enrich you. I am your unworthy guest. But my flock?"

"Let your flock shelter by the south wall of the fold: there is good picking there and no wind. Come you and sit with us."

So they all sat down by the fire; and the sad shepherd ate of their bread, but sparingly, like a man to whom hunger brings a need but no joy in the satisfying of it; and the others were silent for a proper time, out of courtesy. Then the oldest shepherd spoke:

"My name is Zadok the son of Eliezer, of Bethlehem. I am the chief shepherd of the flocks of the Temple, which are before you in the fold. These are my sister's sons, Jotham, and Shama, and Nathan; their father Elkanah is dead; and but for these I am a childless man."

"My name," replied the stranger, "is Ammiel the son of Jochanan, of the city of Bethsaida, by the Sea of Galilee, and I am a fatherless man."

"It is better to be childless than fatherless," said Zadok, "yet it is the will of God that children should bury their fathers. When did the blessed Jochanan die?"

"I know not whether he be dead or alive. It is three years since I looked upon his face or had word of him."

"You are an exile then? he has cast you off?"

"It was the other way," said Ammiel, looking on the ground.

At this the shepherd Shama, who had listened with doubt in his face, started up in anger. "Pig of a Galilean," he cried, "despiser of parents! breaker of the law! When I saw you coming I knew you for something vile. Why do you darken the night for us with your presence? You have reviled him who begot you. Away, or we stone you!"

Ammiel did not answer or move. The twisted smile passed over his bowed face again as he waited to know the shepherds' will with him, even as he had waited for the robbers. But Zadok lifted his hand.

"Not so hasty, Shama-ben-Elkanah. You also break the law by

judging a man unheard. The rabbis have told us that there is a tradition of the elders—a rule as holy as the law itself—so that a man may deny his father in a certain way without sin. It is a strange rule, and it must be very holy or it would not be so strange. But this is the teaching of the elders: a son may say of anything for which his father asks him—a sheep, or a measure of corn, or a field, or a purse of silver—'it is Corban, a gift that I have vowed unto the Lord'; and so his father shall have no more claim upon him. Have you said 'Corban' to your father, Ammiel-ben-Jochanan? Have you made a vow unto the Lord?"

"I have said 'Corban,'" answered Ammiel, lifting his face, still shadowed by that strange smile, "but it was not the Lord who heard my vow."

"Tell us what you have done," said the old man sternly, "for we will neither judge you, nor shelter you, unless we hear your story."

"There is nothing in it," replied Ammiel indifferently. "It is an old story. But if you are curious you shall hear it. Afterward you shall deal with me as you will."

So the shepherds, wrapped in their warm cloaks, sat listening with grave faces and watchful, unsearchable eyes, while Ammiel in his tattered silk sat by the sinking fire of thorns and told his tale with a voice that had no room for hope or fear—a cool, dead voice that spoke only of things ended.

II

"In my father's house I was the second son. My brother was honored and trusted in all things. He was a prudent man and profitable to the household. All that he counselled was done, all that he wished he had. My place was a narrow one. There was neither honor nor joy in it, for it was filled with daily tasks and rebukes. No one cared for me. I was a beast of burden, fed only because I was useful, and the dull life irked me like an ill-fitting harness. There was nothing in it.

"I went to my father and claimed my share of the inheritance. He was rich. He gave it to me. It did not impoverish him and it made me free. I said to him 'Corban,' and shook the dust of Bethsaida from my feet.

"I went out to look for mirth and love and joy and all that is pleasant to the eyes and sweet to the taste. If a god made me, thought I, he made me to live, and the pride of life was strong in my heart and in my flesh. My vow was offered to that well-known god. I served him in Jerusalem, in Alexandria, in Rome, for his altars are everywhere and men worship him openly or in secret.

"My money and youth made me welcome to his followers, and I spent them both freely as if they could never come to an end. I clothed myself in purple and fine linen and fared sumptuously every day. The wine of Cyprus and the dishes of Egypt and Syria were on my table. My dwelling was crowded with merry guests. They came for what I gave them. Their faces were hungry and their soft touch was like the clinging of leeches. To them I was nothing but money and youth; no longer a beast of burden—a beast of pleasure. There was nothing in it.

"From the richest fare my heart went away empty, and after the wildest banquet my soul fell drunk and solitary into sleep. Then I thought power is better than pleasure. If a man will feast and revel let him do it with the great. They will favor him, and raise him up for the service that he renders them. He will obtain a place and authority in the world and gain many friends. So I joined myself to Herod."

When the sad shepherd spoke this name his listeners drew back from him as if it were a defilement to hear it. They spat upon the ground and cursed the Idumean who called himself their king.

"A slave!" Jotham cried, "a bloody tyrant and a slave from Edom! A fox, a vile beast who devours his own children! God burn him in Gehenna."

The old Zadok picked up a stone and threw it into the darkness, saying slowly, "I cast this stone on the grave of the Idumean, the blasphemer, the defiler of the Temple! God send us soon the Deliverer, the Promised One, the true King of Israel!" Ammiel made no sign, but went on with his story.

"Herod used me well," he continued, "for his own purpose. He welcomed me to his palace and his table, and gave me a place among his favorites. He was so much my friend that he borrowed my money. There were many of the nobles of Jerusalem with him, Sadducees, and proselytes from Rome and Asia, and women from everywhere. The law of Israel was observed in the open court, when the people were watching. But in the secret feasts there was no law but the will of Herod, and many deities were served but no God was worshipped. There the captains and the princes of Rome consorted with the high priest and his sons by night; and there was much coming and going by hidden ways. Everybody was a borrower or a lender, a buyer or a seller of favors. It was a house of diligent madness. There was nothing in it.

"In the midst of this whirling life a great need of love came upon me and I wished to hold some one in my inmost heart.

"At a certain place in the city, within closed doors, I saw a young slave-girl dancing. She was about fifteen years old, thin and supple; she danced like a reed in the wind; but her eyes were weary as death, and her white body was marked with bruises. She stumbled, and the men laughed at her. She fell, and her mistress beat her, crying out that she would fain be rid of such a heavy-footed slave. I paid the price and took her to my dwelling.

"Her name was Tamar. She was a daughter of Lebanon. I robed her in silk and broidered linen. I nourished her with tender care so that beauty came upon her like the blossoming of an almond tree; she was a garden enclosed, breathing spices. Her eyes were like doves behind her veil, her lips were a thread of scarlet, her neck was a tower of ivory, and her breasts were as two fawns which feed among the lilies. She was whiter than milk and more rosy than the flower of the peach, and her dancing was like the flight of a bird among the branches. So I loved her.

"She lay in my bosom as a clear stone that one has bought and polished and set in fine gold at the end of a golden chain. Never was she glad at my coming or sorry at my going. Never did she give me anything except what I took from her. There was nothing in it.

"Now whether Herod knew of the jewel that I kept in my dwelling I cannot tell. It was sure that he had his spies in all the city, and himself walked the streets by night in a disguise. On a certain day he sent for me, and had me into his secret chamber, professing great love toward me and more confidence than in any man that lived. So I must go to Rome for him, bearing a sealed letter and a private message to Caesar. All my goods would be left safely in the hands of the king, my friend, who would reward me double. There was a certain place of high authority at Jerusalem which Caesar would gladly bestow on a Jew who had done him a service. This mission would commend me to him. It was a great occasion—suited to my powers. Thus Herod fed me with fair promises, and I ran his errand. There was nothing in it.

"I stood before Caesar and gave him the letter. He read it and laughed, saying that a prince with an incurable hunger is a servant of value to an emperor. Then he asked me if there was nothing sent with the letter. I answered there was no gift, but a message for his private ear. He drew me aside and I told him that Herod begged earnestly that his dear son, Antipater, might be sent back in haste from Rome to Palestine, for the king had great need of him. At this Caesar laughed again. 'To bury him, I suppose,' said he, 'with his brothers, Alexander and Aristobulus! Truly, it is better to be Herod's swine than his son. Tell the old fox he may catch his own prey.' With this he turned from me and I withdrew unrewarded, to make my way back, as best I could with an empty purse, to Palestine. I had seen the Lord of the World. There was nothing in it.

"Selling my rings and bracelets I got passage in a trading ship for Joppa. There I heard that the king was not in Jerusalem, at his Palace of the Upper City, but had gone with his friends to make merry for a month on the Mountain of the Little Paradise. On the hill-top over against us, where the lights are flaring to-night, in the banquet-hall where couches are spread for a hundred guests, I found Herod."

The listening shepherds spat upon the ground again, and Jotham muttered, "May the worms that devour his flesh never die!" But Zadok whispered, "We wait for the Lord's salvation to come out of Zion." And the sad shepherd, looking at the firelit mountain far away with fixed eyes, continued his story:

"The king lay on his ivory couch, and the sweat of his disease was heavy upon him, for he was old, and his flesh was corrupted. But his hair and his beard were dyed and perfumed and there was a wreath of roses on his head. The hall was full of nobles and great men, the sons of the high priest were there, and the servants poured their wine in cups of gold. There was a sound of soft music; and all the men were watching a girl who danced in the middle of the hall; and the eyes of Herod were fiery, like the eyes of a fox.

"The dancer was Tamar. She glistened like the snow on Lebanon, and the redness of her was ruddier than a pomegranate, and her dancing was like the coiling of white serpents. When the dance was ended her attendants threw a veil of gauze over her and she lay among her cushions, half covered with flowers, at the feet of the king.

"Through the sound of clapping hands and shouting, two slaves led me behind the couch of Herod. His eyes narrowed as they fell upon me. I told him the message of Caesar, making it soft, as if it were a word that suffered him to catch his prey. He stroked his beard softly and his look fell on Tamar. 'I have caught it,' he murmured; 'by all the gods, I have always caught it. And my dear son, Antipater, is coming home of his own will. I have lured him, he is mine.'

"Then a look of madness crossed his face and he sprang up, with frothing lips, and struck at me. 'What is this,' he cried, 'a spy, a servant of my false son, a traitor in my banquet-hall! Who are you?' I knelt before him, protesting that he must know me; that I was his friend, his messenger; that I had left all my goods in his hands; that the girl who had danced for him was mine. At this his face changed again and he fell back on his couch, shaken with horrible laughter. 'Yours!' he cried, 'when was she yours? What is yours? I know you now, poor madman. You are Ammiel, a crazy shepherd from Galilee, who troubled us some time since. Take him away, slaves. He has twenty sheep and twenty goats among my flocks at the foot of the mountain. See to it that he gets them, and drive him away.'

"I fought against the slaves with my bare hands, but they held me. I called to Tamar, begging her to have pity on me, to speak for me, to come with me. She looked up with her eyes like doves behind her veil, but there was no knowledge of me in them. She smiled into the red eyes of Herod, and threw a broken rose in my face. Then the silver cord was loosened within me, and my heart went out, and I struggled no more. There was nothing in it.

"Afterward I found myself on the road with this flock. I led them past Hebron into the south country, and so by the Vale of Eshcol, and over many hills beyond the Pools of Solomon, until my feet brought me to your fire. Here I rest on the way to nowhere."

He sat silent, and the four shepherds looked at him with amazement.

"It is a bitter tale," said Shama, "and you are a great sinner."

"I should be a fool not to know that," answered the sad shepherd, "but the knowledge does me no good."

"You must repent," said Nathan, the youngest shepherd, in a friendly voice.

"How can a man repent," answered the sad shepherd, "unless he has hope? But I am sorry for everything, and most of all for living."

"Would you not live to kill the fox Herod?" cried Jotham fiercely.

"Why should I let him out of the trap," answered the sad shepherd. "Is he not dying more slowly than I could kill him?"

"You must have faith in God," said Zadok earnestly and gravely.

"He is too far away."

"Then you must have love to your neighbor."

"He is too near. My confidence in man was like a pool by the wayside. It was shallow, but there was water in it, and sometimes a star shone there. Now the feet of many beasts have trampled through it, and the jackals have drunken of it, and there is no more water. It is dry and the mire is caked at the bottom."

"Is there nothing good in the world?"

"There is pleasure, but I am sick of it, for it betrays its lovers. There is power, but I hate it, for it crushes its servants. There is wisdom, but I mistrust it, for it outwits the simple. Life is a game and every player is for his own hand. Mine is played. I have nothing to win or lose."

"You are young, you have many years to live."

"I am old, yet the days before me are too many."

"But you travel the road, you go forward. Do you hope for nothing?"

"I hope for nothing," said the sad shepherd, "yet if one thing should come to me it might be the beginning of hope. If I saw in man or woman a deed of kindness without a reason, and a proof of love gladly given for its own sake only, then might I turn my face toward that light. Till that comes, how can I have faith in God whom I have never seen? I have seen the world which he has made, and it brings me no faith. There is nothing in it."

"Ammiel-ben-Jochanan," said the old man sternly, "you are a son of Israel, and we have had compassion on you, according to the law. But you are an apostate, an unbeliever, and we can have no more fellowship with you, lest a curse come upon us. The company of the desperate brings misfortune. Go your way and depart from us, for our way is not yours."

So the sad shepherd thanked them for their entertainment, and took the little kid again in his arms, and went into the night, calling his flock. But the youngest shepherd Nathan followed him a few steps and said:

"There is a broken fold at the foot of the hill. It is old and small, but you may find a shelter there for your flock, where the wind will not shake you. Go your way with God, brother, and see better days."

Then Ammiel went a little way down the hill and sheltered his flock in a corner of the crumbling walls. He lay among the sheep and the goats with his face upon his folded arms, and whether the time passed slowly or swiftly he did not know, for he slept.

He waked as Nathan came running and stumbling among the scattered stones.

"We have seen a vision," he cried. "A wonderful vision of angels. Did you not hear them? They sang loudly of the Hope of

Israel. We are going to Bethlehem to see this thing which is come to pass. Come you and keep watch over our sheep while we are gone."

"Of angels I have seen and heard nothing," said Ammiel, "but I will guard your flocks with mine, since I am in debt to you for bread and fire."

So he brought the kid in his arms, and the weary flock straggling after him, to the south wall of the great fold again, and sat there by the embers at the foot of the tower, while the others were away.

The moon rested like a ball on the edge of the western hills and rolled behind them. The stars faded in the east and the fires went out on the Mountain of the Little Paradise. Over the hills of Moab a gray flood of dawn rose slowly, and arrows of red shot far up before the sunrise.

The shepherds returned full of joy and told what they had seen. "It was even as the angels said unto us," said Shama, "and it must be true. The King of Israel has come. The faithful shall be blessed."

"Herod shall fall," cried Jotham, lifting his clenched fist toward the dark peaked mountain. "Burn, black Idumean, in the bottomless pit, where the fire is not quenched."

Zadok spoke more quietly. "We found the new-born child of whom the angels told us wrapped in swaddling clothes and lying in a manger. The ways of God are wonderful. His salvation comes out of darkness, and we trust in the promised deliverance. But you, Ammiel-ben-Jochanan, except you believe, you shall not see it. Yet since you have kept our flocks faithfully, and because of the joy that has come to us, I give you this piece of silver to help you on your way."

But Nathan came close to the sad shepherd and touched him on the shoulder with a friendly hand. "Go you also to Bethlehem," he said in a low voice, "for it is good to see what we have seen, and we will keep your flock until you return."

"I will go," said Ammiel, looking into his face, "for I think you wish me well. But whether I shall see what you have seen, or whether I shall return, I know not. Farewell."

III

The narrow streets of Bethlehem were waking to the first stir of life as the sad shepherd came into the town with the morning, and passed through them like one walking in his sleep.

The court-yard of the great khan and the open rooms around it were crowded with travellers, rousing from their night's rest and making ready for the day's journey. In front of the stables half hollowed in the rock beside the inn, men were saddling their horses and their beasts of burden, and there was much noise and confusion.

But beyond these, at the end of the line, there was a deeper grotto in the rock, which was used only when the nearer stalls were full. At the entrance of this an ass was tethered, and a man of middle age stood in the doorway.

The sad shepherd saluted him and told his name.

"I am Joseph the carpenter of Nazareth," replied the man. "Have you also seen the angels of whom your brother shepherds came to tell us?"

"I have seen no angels," answered Ammiel, "nor have I any brothers among the shepherds. But I would fain see what they have seen."

"It is our first-born son," said Joseph, "and the Most High has sent him to us. He is a marvellous child: great things are foretold of him. You may go in, but quietly, for the child and his mother Mary are asleep."

So the sad shepherd went in quietly. His long shadow entered before him, for the sunrise was flowing into the door of the grotto. It was made clean and put in order, and a bed of straw was laid in the corner on the ground.

The child was asleep, but the mother was waking, for she had taken him from the manger into her lap, where her maiden veil of white was spread to receive him. And she was singing very softly as she bent over him in happiness and wonder.

Ammiel saluted her and kneeled down to look at the child. He saw nothing different from other young children. The mother waited for him to speak of angels, as the other shepherds had done. The sad shepherd said nothing, but only looked, and as he looked his face changed.

"You have had great pain and danger and sorrow for his sake," he said gently.

"They are past," she answered, "and for his sake I have suffered them gladly."

"He is very little and helpless; you must bear many troubles for his sake."

"To care for him is my joy, and to bear him lightens my burden."

"He does not know you, he can do nothing for you."

"But I know him. I have carried him under my heart, he is my son and my king."

"Why do you love him?"

The mother looked up at the sad shepherd with a great reproach in her soft eyes. Then her look grew pitiful as it rested on his face.

"You are a sorrowful man," she said.

"I am a wicked man," he answered.

She shook her head gently.

"I know nothing of that," she said, "but you must be very sorrowful, since you are born of a woman and yet you ask a mother why she loves her child. I love him for love's sake, because God has given him to me."

So the mother Mary leaned over her little son again as if she were alone with him; and Ammiel went out very quietly.

Joseph was waiting outside the door.

"How was it that you did not see the angels?" he asked. "Were you not with the other shepherds?"

"No," answered Ammiel, "I was asleep. But I have seen the mother and the child. Blessed be the house that holds them."

"You are strangely clothed, for a shepherd," said Joseph. "Where do you come from?"

"From very far away," replied Ammiel; "from a country that you have never visited."

"Where are you going?" asked Joseph.

"I am going home," answered Ammiel, "to my mother's and my

father's house in Galilee. It is a long journey. Will you not wish me a safe home-coming?"

"Go in peace, friend," said Joseph.

And the sad shepherd took up his battered staff, and went on his way rejoicing.

White Shawl from Alexandria

FREDERIC MERTZ

She awoke with the merchant Jebal's hand shaking her shoulder and in her ears the thin whimpering of a baby somewhere in the dark. Behind the flame of the earthen lamp, the short-bearded brown face of the merchant Jebal had a grim look. But his voice held something besides resentment. Fear.

"Put on your cloak and sandals," Jebal said in a low and hurried voice. "Those three who rode in from the desert yesterday to our camp outside Sychar——I have been watching them in secret all night. Desert raiders, palming themselves off as holy men——"

He paced away down the narrow inn room, checking over its clutter of boxes and bales. "We push on as soon as the inn gates are opened," he said. "And I make a vow never to bring any camel train of mine through Judea again."

The girl sat up, drawing the long white shawl about her shoulders. Even in that harassed hour the merchant Jebal felt an instant's hot pride in his ability to find and bargain for beautiful things. He had picked out this girl in smoky torchlight, behind the shutters of a house close by the brawling wharves of Tyre. Her shawl he had snapped up long before, one breath-choking noon in Alexandria. He had known that sometime he would bring them together—two treasures held for no profit except his own subtle enjoyment. He looked at them now, fingers hardening over the hilt of his knife. There were some possessions he did not intend to give up without a fight.

The Tyrean girl's young mouth smiled a little, though her eyes had grown still and attentive. She said, "Those three are holy men."

His lips twitched under the beard. "How do you know?"

"All this day when they rode with you, not one of them looked at me. Not one of them was even thinking about me. These are things a woman notices."

She spoke so quietly that some of the unease went out of him.

"A while back," he said, "down in the courtyard, those three stood aside and talked together. Then they took the merchandise they had bought from me into the stable. Perfumes and a gold chain into a stable! Does that make sense? Not after yesterday, when they greeted me with the story that they were commanded by the stars to choose royal gifts. What else was that tale but a trick to make me show them my goods?"

"Did they not pay you for those gifts?"

He brushed the question impatiently aside. "If they plan to ambush me, they expect to steal back their own coin along with everything else. And unless they plan robbery, this is surely the beginning of some rebellion. They have bought my spices and gold chain for an upstart chief of theirs, who has come in secretly from the hills. If he lies hidden with his men at arms in the stable of this inn, Herod's soldiers are certain to get wind of him by sunrise. And my goods will be found in the stable, to bear witness that I was implicated."

The Tyrean girl stood up. The merchant Jebal made an unexpected, fumbling move that cupped her chin in the hollow of his hand. He said, "I would not exchange you, as you stand here, for Egypt's richest emerald. And by all the gods I do not intend to lose you!"

His fingers were swift and harsh, covering the cloudy gleam of her shawl with a dark cloak. He went to the door and signaled two of his porters, stationed to guard this end of the passage. For such big-bodied men they moved softly, transporting boxes and bales. But to the Tyrean girl it seemed that all around them the air was restless, as if the merchant Jebal's words had stirred up a rustling of great wings.

She drew near to him, the Alexandria shawl held closely about her. This hour before the dawn was cold and exceptionally quiet, save for the wailing infant near by, refusing to be stilled. "You will see," she whispered to Jebal. "Those three may yet be holy men, with no plans except to follow the signs they read in the heavens."

He made a warding gesture with two fingers of his right hand. "These nights the stars come too close in the heavens of Judea. I tell you, this is haunted country."

They found a dim stairway leading down into the courtyard. She stood against the inn wall, watching Jebal and his men dip in and out of shadow, like shapes in a dream. There seemed to be no sound in the world except the whimper of a baby.

The crying came from across the courtyard. Over there, a straggling lean-to served as entrance to the hillside cave that was the inn stable. A strange place for a young child. She stood listening while that small, valiant stubbornness went on with its complaint. And all at once she knew that she might use this crying to set at rest the doubts of the merchant Jebal. A woman could walk easily and naturally into that stable, to help another woman whose infant refused to be comforted.

She crossed through lantern light spilling across the stable doorway. Another lantern beyond it made a dusty, bright smudge on the earthen floor. From the far side of that lighted circle, two faces watched her come toward them—a weatherbeaten-looking man, and a young woman with a troubled gentleness in her eyes. She held a whimpering baby under a coarse and shabby cloak.

Bewilderment was what the Tyrean girl read in the look of those two who bent above the crying child. And not because of its crying. For beside them, on the wide edge of the manger where straw was still hollowed to the shape of a little body, rested the gifts that the three strangers had bought yesterday from the merchant Jebal. Those two caskets, one of myrrh and the other of frankincense, were unmistakable. And the gold chain lay between them.

Some look of recognition in the Tyrean girl's face must have prompted the man to guess that she had seen those things before.

In his soft, provincial patois he began to explain matters that he himself seemed to find in want of explanation. She could not understand the Judean dialect, and there was no need that she should understand it. For she was remembering again those three who had ridden in from the desert, their eyes austerely fixed on far horizons. They had not noted her, for they were busy spelling out a secret written in the stars. So they had come upon an infant fretting in a drafty cave used for a stable. And from what they had done then, the Tyrean girl knew that these were not men to lie in ambush for a passing camel train. She could go back with this assurance to Jebal.

But first there was something to do here. The white shawl was warm against her shoulders. She slid it out from under her cloak, and in its soft splendor she enfolded the mother and child. The woman spoke some breathless word of thanks. In the sudden stillness, the baby lay quieted.

The merchant Jebal was waiting, eyes alert. He said at once, "You have lost your shawl."

She shook her head. "It was a gift I left. Was that too high a price to pay for knowing that we ride in peace?"

He looked intently at her. "You have found out something?"

She smiled. "Those were holy men and wise," she said. "Their thoughts were on nothing except the stars. And the stars may tell wise men what gifts to make ready for a king. But it takes a woman to know what is needful for a baby crying in the cold."

To Come Unto Me

ROBERT NATHAN

THAT year there were very few houses for rent anywhere; and people lived wherever they could. Only the rich were able to buy an entire house, with wood and plaster walls, a rose garden and a bathroom. Nevertheless on Christmas Eve both rich and poor enjoyed the spirit of the season; for the rich gave each other gifts and the poor were delighted with the sight of the Christmas trees which, painted white, blue, and even green, and decorated with colored lights, twinkled everywhere along the public highways.

At the house of a very famous man a party was in progress. Since this man was the president of a motion picture studio, his guests were for the most part motion picture actors and actresses, which is to say that they were the most beautiful and famous people in the world. This did not make them as happy as might have been expected; and they joined in the singing of Christmas carols with hearts no less lonely and empty than those of poor people who also wished to be loved.

Among these famous and beautiful people were two children, named Henry and Lettice. Everybody in the world knew what they looked like, what they talked like, what their favorite games were, what they wore and what they liked to eat. But what no one knew was what was in their hearts, because their hearts were the hearts of children.

And so, while the fiddles scraped, while the great singers sang, and while the footmen passed about among the guests with glasses of champagne and punch, and little sandwiches in the shape of snowflakes and crescent moons, and gingersnaps for the children, Lettice went tiptoeing to Henry in one corner of the great room and asked him, "What are you doing?"

To which Henry replied, "Nothing."

However, nothing to a child is so crowded with dreams as *nothing*. And so, when Lettice said, "I know a wonderful secret," Henry followed her out of the room and down the long hall and out into the garden, prepared for all the beautiful things without a name which he had been dreaming about.

But all he saw at the end of the garden was a kind of stable, with a little light over the door.

"I don't think that's so wonderful," said Henry.

"That's because you don't know," said Lettice.

"Don't know what?" asked Henry.

In answer, Lettice opened the door of the stable. And there, lying in a crib made of an old manger, was a baby.

"Now what do you think?" said Lettice triumphantly.

"I don't think it's wonderful at all," said Henry.

"Do you think maybe it's Baby Jesus?" asked Lettice.

"I don't know," said Henry. "I never saw it before."

"I wish it was Baby Jesus," said Lettice, "because then we could pray."

"You can pray if you want to," said Henry, "on account of you wouldn't know who it was till afterward anyhow."

"I can say 'Now I lay me' and the Lord's Prayer," said Lettice.

"All right," said Henry. "I don't mind."

So the two children knelt on the floor of the tool shed, in front of the baby, whose father and mother, having no other place to live at the moment, were helping the cook at the big house wash dishes in return for a roof over their heads.

"Our Father which art in Heaven," said Lettice. "Hallowed be Thy name. . . ."

And all around them as they knelt, the invisible air was peopled with the unseen faces of the past, with saints and captains, beggars and kings, with the smiling children, the dreaming children into whose hands, year after year, God had delivered His world, into whose hearts, endlessly renewed, He had put His love, into whose keeping He had given His Son.

For it is in the hands of the children that all things are placed, both good and evil, the poem and the sword, the knowledge of distant worlds, the hope of peace and the fruitfulness of earth.

"I pray the Lord," said Henry, "my soul to keep."

In the big house they sang "O Little Star of Bethlehem" and Lettice's mother and Henry's father wondered where they were. And in the kitchen the two new helpers smiled at each other across the soapy water. They did not expect very much for their child. Perhaps he might grow up to be a good carpenter.

Midnight in the Stable

ELIZABETH GOUDGE

I

IT WAS the snow that made that Christmas such an extra special one. They did not often see snow in the Channel Islands, and never before in the children's memory had it come at Christmas. It began two days before Christmas Day, soft white flakes drifting down out of an iron-gray sky, and by Christmas Eve, when the sky cleared and the sun appeared again, it had spread over their familiar home a beauty so new and so exciting that they could scarcely contain themselves.

The old rose-red roof of the weather-worn farmhouse where they lived was flecked with white, as though someone had scattered an armful of white flowers over it, and on each of the windows the frost had traced delicate outlines of ferns and grasses. The garden and courtyard were hidden beneath a spread coverlet of gleaming white, and under the bright sunshine and the deep blue sky each frosted twig on bush or tree shone like silver wire. The farm's name of Bon Repos suited it in this weather. A great reposeful silence gripped the world; there was nothing to be heard but the faint murmur of the sea beyond their garden and the chirping of the robins about their door.

The children fed these robins to bursting point, and it was the sight of the little red-breasts bobbing about on the snow like lighted lanterns, and chirping so cheerfully in the intervals of refreshing themselves, that gave Colin du Frocq his bright idea. "Let *us* have lanterns, Girls," he said to his four sisters, "and go out carol singing."

"Carol singing in the snow on Christmas Eve!" cried golden-haired Peronelle, jigging for joy. "Good idea, Colin!"

"Would it interfere with hanging up our stockings?" asked Jacqueline anxiously.

"No," said Colin. "We'd hang them up, go to bed, say good night to the parents, and then get up again."

"But would the parents approve?" asked Michelle, the bespectacled eldest, a little primly.

"Can't say," said Colin. "Better not ask them. We've never been told *not* to go carol singing."

But little Colette, the baby of the family and the only one who still believed in Father Christmas, waxed a little tearful. "If he comes and finds us gone," she wailed, "he won't put anything in our stockings!"

"Leave it to me, darling," consoled Peronelle. "*I'll* see to it. We'll write a note to Father Christmas. 'Dear Sir, The du Frocqs are out but will be returning shortly. Please leave the customary seasonable gifts. Yours truly, the du Frocqs.' "

It was after the mid-day dinner, and the five of them stood outside the front door in the old cobbled courtyard, rosy-cheeked and radiant and apparently entirely oblivious of the cold that had fallen like a blight upon shivering grown-ups. Michelle and Peronelle, who were both in their teens, had gone so far as to put on thin coats over their dark blue serge skirts and red jerseys, and Jacqueline's pretty face was framed in the green knitted scarf she had thrown over her dark curls as an opening flower is framed in its calyx, but the wicked bright-eyed Colin had burdened himself with no outdoor garments, and fat little Colette, wrapped so snugly in layer upon layer of soft dimpled flesh, quantities of flannel petticoats and vests, with a sky-blue woolen frock smocked in scarlet over all, would by the addition of an overcoat have been rendered too hot to move. They were all five so young that newly lit life tingled to the end of every finger tip and sprang and sparkled in hair and eyes; there was as yet no slackening of its flame or fading of its warmth.

"We'll spend the afternoon in the stable," said Colin. "No one hears us in the stable. We'll practice the carols there and make ourselves lanterns out of the mangel-wurzels. . . . Listen, is that the bus?"

"The bus!" yelled Colette in triumph, and trundled hastily across the courtyard to the doorway leading into the lane, the others following helter-skelter.

At that time, the end of the nineteenth century, a few farms and a fishing hamlet were the only human habitations in the wild and beautiful part of the Island where they lived, and their one link with the town of Saint Pierre, a few miles away, was the daily horse bus. Its arrival was at all times an excitement, for it brought them their visitors, groceries, newspapers and shellfish. Absolutely anything might arrive off that bus, anything from a visiting uncle to a crab for dinner, and at Christmas time, when presents from admiring friends were to be expected, the arrival of the bus became not only an interesting event but a world-shaking cataclysm.

The children, cantering like young ponies, reached the bus stopping place, where four lanes met just beyond their farmhouse, just as Jean the bus driver reined in his two ancient horses and brought the clattering old vehicle to a standstill.

"Anything for us?" they yelled to Jean, their eyes going to the box beside him where the parcels were piled.

"Not today, praise be," said Jean, winking one eye at them. "I've had my bus so weighed down with parcels for you youngsters this last week that the springs is broke. Today, I thank le bon Dieu, I've traveled light."

"Oh!" chorused the children sadly. "Beast!" they continued good humoredly. "Merry Christmas!"

"Merry Christmas!" echoed Jean, and then, turning his head over his shoulder, "This is where you get out, Mamselle."

The children turned their attention from the parcels outside the bus to the passengers inside. They knew most of them: a couple of old fisher wives from the hamlet of Breton Bay, the woman from the Post Office and the traveling tinker; but they did not know the girl whom Jean addressed as Mamselle.

Yet, as they stood beside the bus watching her get out, they wished they did know her, for in spite of the clothes that she wore, the clothes of a beggar maid, she was attractive. Her dark eyes had the softness of black pansies in her white heart-shaped face, and the hair that escaped from under the shawl that she wore over her head clung round her forehead in enchanting brown curls. Not even her broken black button boots, her frayed black skirt, her rusty shawl, and the disreputable carpet bag she carried could hide her slender beauty. She was like a flower, a snowdrop or a Christmas rose or a white camellia, and when she stumbled a little in getting out of the bus, for she had the carpet bag in one hand and was holding something large and heavy in the folds of her shawl with the other, the children rushed to help her as though she had been the Queen.

"*Merci, mes enfants,*" she said laughing. If you had not helped me I might have bumped my baby."

"Have you a baby?" they chorused in joy. "A baby? Quick! Let's see!" And they in their fresh young beauty closed in upon hers like the petals of a flower about the golden heart. The bus turned and rolled away again, the other passengers took their ways home with backward glances of amusement, but the six worshiping the baby were too absorbed to notice.

And certainly it was an enchanting baby, as enchanting as its mother. It was round and fat, and deliciously creased and dimpled. Its eyes were dark, and solemn with the deep solemnity of the very new, but young as it was it had already learned to be amused, for it laughed when Colette was lifted up to kiss it, and its kicking feet and brandished fists were busy establishing contact with a world that seemed good to it. It had no hair at all upon its head but this, somehow, seemed to the children an added attraction. . . . A nice baby.

"A boy?" asked Peronelle, holding out a slim forefinger to be gripped by engaging dimpled fingers with nails so tiny that they made her heart miss a beat.

"Of course," said the girl in the slightly superior tone adopted by the mothers of sons.

"Isn't he good!" whispered Jacqueline, clasping a booted foot.

"He never cried the whole way over," triumphed his mother.

"Over?" asked Michelle. "Where have you come from?"

"From France, Mamselle," said the girl. "I have just landed."

"But where are you going?" demanded Colin. "Who are you?"

The girl's soft face suddenly hardened. "That is my affair, little M'sieur," she said. "And now I must ask you to let me go on my way."

"We'll take you," said Colin gallantly. "I'll carry your bag."

"No," said the girl firmly. "Do you live here? In this farmhouse? Your mother would not like you to be out in this bitter cold with so little on to keep you warm. I will watch you run home."

At the door into the courtyard they turned round to wave and saw her still standing at the place where the four lanes met. "Good-by," they shouted. "Merry Christmas!"

"Merry Christmas!" she called back, and nodded and smiled as they turned in and were hidden from her sight.

"She was very anxious to get rid of us, wasn't she?" said Jacqueline, aggrieved.

"I don't think she wanted us to see which way she was going," said Peronelle, a little puzzled.

"Clever!" mocked Colin. "She was just being grown-up and officious. She hasn't been grown-up for very long, either, and those new grown-ups are always the worst."

Further argument was quenched by an explosion of tears from Colette that for its suddenness, noise, and wetting quality was like the bursting of a cistern.

"I want a baby!" she wailed. "I want a baby, too!"

"Well, you can't have one," said Michelle firmly. "I expect you'll have lots of babies when you're grown-up, but you can't have one now."

"But I want one now!" roared Colette.

"You can't, duckie," explained Peronelle gently. "It isn't possible."

"Why not?" yelled Colette.

"Because you've got to have a husband before you have a baby, and only grown-up people have husbands."

"But I don't want a husband!" shouted Colette. "I want a baby!"

"Oh, be quiet, do!" implored Michelle. "Blow her nose, someone, for heaven's sake!"

"You're nothing but a baby yourself, Colette," scoffed Colin. "A nasty little red-faced crybaby whose nose wants wiping."

At this, but for Michelle, there would have been a battle. "Stop it!" she commanded, pushing them apart. "Horrid little children! How are we to get those lanterns made if you spend the whole afternoon scrapping?"

They ran across the courtyard, everything forgotten except the night's adventure and the preparations for it. "Come on!" they yelled to each other. "The stable and the mangel-wurzels! The carols! Get the kitchen cushions and the rug from Michelle's bed and come *on!*"

II

The du Frocqs had an even greater capacity than most children for changing in the space of half a minute from demons to angels, and vice versa. There was still a slight suggestion of tails and cloven hoofs about them as they lifted the latch of the stable door, but the moment it had clicked shut behind them they were all wing and halo. Their eyes beamed softly in the dim light, and they smiled at each other as though family disagreement was a thing unknown.

This happy transformation could perhaps partly be attributed to the influence of the stable itself, for a stable is a delightful place at any time, but on Christmas Eve it moves quietly from its usual position on the fringe of human life and becomes the hub of the world.

The moment they had shut the door behind them the children knew that some strange change had come over their stable as well as over themselves. Outwardly it looked just the same, with its raftered cobwebby roof from which hung a lantern and bunches of dried herbs, and those lovely orange seed pods that children call Chinese lanterns, its uneven floor of rounded cobbles, its little square window through which the sunshine shone slantwise like a golden sword, and its dark velvety shadows that were not frightening shadows, like those in the lanes at midnight, but deep cool wells of comfort and friendliness. And it smelt just the same; of the sweet fresh hay in the mangers, of oats and clean horses and dried herbs; a smell of field and gardens that almost set high summer blazing in mid-winter.

And the animals looked as usual: Lupin, the old fat horse who pulled the family carriage; Mathilde, the sprightly piebald person who did the milk round in the mornings; Albert, Grandpapa's little donkey who had been lent to them over Christmas; Olivia, the lovely little fawn-colored Jersey cow, who had not been well lately and so had been promoted from the cow byre to the stable; Maximilian, their plumy black mongrel dog; and Marmalade the cat, who was ensconced in a box beneath Lupin's manger with a family of six ginger kits.

And yet it was all quite different. The motes of dust in the golden beam of sun were dancing in ecstasy, the hay in the manger was whispering and rustling as though it had secrets to tell, and the comfortable shadows had mysteries in their depths.

And the animals were in a queer mood; aloof, even a little patronizing. The night-black eyes of Lupin and Mathilde were as mysterious as the shadows, and Albert the donkey, usually so meek, was brandishing his tail and stamping his hoofs as though he, and not the lion, were the king of beasts. Maximilian, though he lay quite still with his nose on his extended paws and his silky black lids a little lowered over his lustrous eyes, was yet quivering with excitement, and the yellow eyes of Marmalade, sitting royally among her squirming kits, shone like lamps.

The children, with Michelle's rug over them, settled themselves comfortably on the cushions and a pile of hay in the one empty stall, with their backs turned to the empty manger, and set to work on their mangel-wurzels, making little windows in their sides with their pocket knives and scooping out places in the middle for the candles to stand. As they worked they sang, Peronelle beating time and leading them in a voice that had a blackbird's sweetness but unfortunately not a blackbird's capacity for sticking to the right note. Regarded as a musical performance their carol singing was hardly a success, for they none of them had an ear for music and each sang in a different key, but the stable liked it. . . . The hay stopped whispering to listen, the shadows crept a little closer, and the animals looked up over their shoulders with softly beaming eyes. . . . They sang "Good King Wenceslas," "Noel" and "While Shepherds Watched," and they sang too, in their Island patois, some of the old cradle songs that had been crooned to them when they were babies, and the French carols they had learned in the nuns' kindergarten where they had gone when they were little.

It was not until they had finished singing that they commented to each other upon the strangeness of the stable, and then only very tentatively, each afraid that the others would laugh at what they all were feeling.

"It's a nice old legend," said Michelle airily.

"What?" asked Peronelle, though she knew quite well what Michelle was thinking of.

"That all stables are changed and sacred on Christmas Eve. That at midnight, in every stable all over the Island, the animals kneel down and worship the manger."

This was an old belief on the Island, and had lasted for hundreds of years. The peasants and little children believed it, and the grown-up intellectuals, smiling tolerantly, were careful not to smudge it with the breath of their own disbelief.

"Wouldn't it be fun," said Colin, "to be here at midnight, in our own stable, and see what happens?"

"No! No!" cried Jacqueline in horror. "You know quite well, Colin, that any human being who dares to look at the animals at midnight falls down dead."

Though this also was part of the legend they all, except Colette, who was busy playing some game of her own in the shadows, roared with laughter at her, so that she hung her head in rosy shame. . . . Only the animals did not laugh. Lupin and Mathilde, looking over their shoulders again, whinnied softly and warningly, and Albert, flinging up his head, ee-hawed like a trumpet blast.

"What ever's the matter with Albert?" asked Colin. "You'd think he owned the whole place."

"Donkeys are always conceited on Christmas Eve," explained Peronelle softly. "You see, one of them carried Mary when she rode to Bethlehem."

"I wonder what Albert will do tonight at midnight," mused Colin. "It's all nonsense about falling down dead. I say, you Girls, let's get back from the carol singing when midnight is striking and look."

"Ye-es," said Michelle doubtfully. "Perhaps just *after* midnight."

"Yes," decided Peronelle briskly. "After midnight. It's a pity to run unnecessary risks. Though there's nothing in it, of course."

"Oh, nothing," said Michelle airily. "Surely we've done enough lanterns now? It must be tea time. Come on. Where's Colette?"

So absorbed had they been in their mangel-wurzels that they had not noticed that Colette had left them. Now, turning round, they saw her behind them at the empty manger.

She had filled it with fresh hay and decorated it all round the edge with herbs and orange Chinese lanterns that she had pulled from low-hanging bunches, and now she had climbed right inside it and was pressing the hay with her fat hands and her dimpled knees to make a soft place in the middle. The last of the afternoon sun, shining full upon her, illumined her blue frock and touched her golden curls to a flaming aureole.

"She's like a bird preparing a nest, isn't she?" whispered Michelle. "Little birds sit inside their nests like that and press them with their bodies to make them round."

"She's like a little angel," said Peronelle softly, and felt a pang at her heart, for there were times when her little sister seemed to her so saintly that she was afraid she would spread her wings and fly away back to heaven.

But Colin had no such illusions.

"Tea time, Colette," he roared at her.

Colette's round face popped up over the edge of the manger. "What's for tea?" she demanded.

"Muffins," said Colin. "Toasted. . . . Mother told me . . . and goche."

Goche was a particularly ravishing kind of Island cake much beloved by Colette. She rolled over the edge of the manger like a cherub falling from heaven, picked herself up, and trundled eagerly toward the door.

"Come on," she cried to the others, standing on tiptoe to lift the latch. "Goche. Muffins. Come *on*."

Reassured, they came on, taking their noise and laughter with them across the snow-covered courtyard to the old farmhouse, where the lamp was already lit behind the kitchen window, and the kettle was singing beside the hearth. . . . The stable was left to a silence so deep that the rustle of the hay and the soft rhythm of the animals' breathing were only audible as heartbeats throbbing at the center of the world.

III

It was moments such as this one, thought Rachell du Frocq, the mother of the children, as she lifted the old silver teapot in her beautiful hands, that justified life. . . . It was moments like this that made it worth while. . . . Her eyes passed caressingly over the bright heads of the munching children and met those of André, her husband, sitting opposite to her at the old kitchen table, and he nodded, reading her thought.

They were an attractive couple. Rachell, beautiful, strong-willed, tall and proud, with dark hair coiled on her shapely head like a coronet and black eyes whose indomitable fire neither sickness, sorrow, nor hardship had ever been known to quench; and André, thin, bearded, deprecating, a dreamy idealist who put his ideals into practice in private life with such success that his gentle unselfishness more than made up to his family for his complete lack of any practical ability whatsoever.

Their eyes, having met and greeted each other, looked lovingly at the room where they sat, an old room that had absorbed the joy and peace of some three hundred Christmas Eves into the pulse of its life. The log fire was burning brightly in the great chimney enclosure, with its stone seats one on each side and its bread oven built in the thickness of the wall. It flickered its dancing light over the whitewashed, raftered ceiling, the *jonquière* or day bed, the willow pattern china on the old oak dresser, and the rich red and blue and gold of Rachell's best French tea set that was used only at festivals and birthdays. . . . A lovely room, warm and companionable and, just for this once, for the children never spoke when muffins and goche were on the table, silent.

But silence never lasts long on a farm, and this one was shattered by the sudden, clattering entrance of Matthieu Torode, their milkman and mainstay on the farm, come to wish them good night before he tramped off to his lonely cottage on the cliffs. He was a nice person, was Matthieu, young and tall and broad-shouldered, with clod-hopping feet that could yet tread very gently when a cow was sick, and large ugly hands that could milk with a swiftness and skill unrivaled on the Island. He was an inarticulate person, but what little he did say was always rich with the courtesy of the Island peasant, and his bright dark eyes and sudden smile were as vividly alive as water flashing beneath the sun.

"Good night, M'sieur, M'dame, Mamselles," he said. "*Dieu vous garde.*"

"Good night!" they cried. "Merry Christmas, Matthieu, merry Christmas!"

"Merry Christmas!" he echoed, his dark eyes suddenly somber, and bowing he left them rather abruptly, banging the door.

"So lonely in that cottage of his!" murmured Rachell compassionately. "That wretched girl!"

For two years ago Matthieu, so large and capable and seemingly full of common sense, had allowed himself to be made a fool of by a slip of a girl whose head did not even reach to the top of his shoulder. She was Denise Marquand, the granddaughter of the eccentric, savage old farmer who owned Blanchelande, the desolate farm upon a clifftop not two miles from them, and when Matthieu triumphantly announced his betrothal to her Rachell shook her head in gloomy prophecy. She did not know Denise, who had only a few weeks before come from her convent school in France to live with her grandfather, but the name Marquand was an ominous one on the Island, for the Marquands were no good. They had never been any good, and their farm had for centuries been shunned by the Islanders. The present owner of it, and the last man to bear the name of Marquand, old Alexander Marquand, returned the compliment. . . . He set his dogs upon any but his own laborers who ventured near Blanchelande. . . . He was not even neighborly with the du Frocqs, though friendship between Bon Repos and Blanchelande was an old tradition. In business matters he had for years been rewarding André's fair play with double dealing, and his friendly greetings with black looks, and gradually all intercourse between the two had wilted and died. So no one from Bon Repos except Matthieu, who had wooed her on the cliffs when the gorse was out in the spring and the primroses were turning every sheltered hollow into a cup of sweetness, had ever set eyes on Denise when she eloped to France with some idle, handsome, holiday-making Frenchman whom she met down on the sands below her home.

Strange stories were told of the old man's rage, of the vow he had made to set the dogs on her too if she ever dared to show her face at Blanchelande again, but no corroboration of them could ever be got out of Matthieu. . . . He never mentioned the name Marquand again. . . . He gave all his tenderness and strength to the farm animals, no doubt finding, like many another man before him, that the more he saw of loquacious human beings the more he preferred dumb animals.

"He's not got over it," said Rachell to André, recalling Matthieu's somber look and sudden exit.

"Surely," said André. "It was two years ago."

"Two years," said Rachell, "though they may pass like two centuries, do not heal a wound."

"No," agreed André sadly.

"May we get down?" asked Colin, uninterested by this discussion. "We've eaten everything and we have several important things to do."

"Of course," smiled Rachell. "There is silver paper and ribbon for tying up the presents in my bottom drawer."

IV

It was when the children had gone, and she and André sat one on each side of the glowing fire, that the knock came at the front door. They went together to open it, expecting it to be some friend come to wish them a happy Christmas, and together they stared in astonishment at the slim girl with her baby in her arms.

"Can you give me some food?" she demanded, and her clear, imperious voice was in such contrast to her beggar-maid clothes that for the moment they were rooted to the spot. She swept past them, across the hall and into the lighted kitchen, where she dropped down on one of the benches within the chimney enclosure and unwound her shawl from her sleeping baby.

"I've enough money left to pay for a night's lodging," she said, when her hosts had pulled themselves together sufficiently to follow her, "but I'd like food and a rest before I look for it. I'm tired. I crossed from France today."

The shawl had fallen back from her beautiful little head and showed her white face drawn with fatigue, with the dark eyes deeply shadowed but as indomitable as Rachell's own.

"Oh, and could you lend me a needle and thread," she went on. "My skirt's torn."

On one side it hung in jagged rents round her ankles, and Rachell exclaimed at the sight of it. "You fell?" she asked.

"No," said the girl briefly. "At the place where I went some dogs were set on me," and brushing André's ejaculations of horror contemptuously aside she reached eagerly for the food that he brought her.

While Rachell nursed the adorable baby she ate as greedily as a little child, now and then vouchsafing them a little information between her eager mouthfuls.

"I chose this house to come to because I liked your children," she said.

"You saw the children?" asked André.

"I met them in the lane this afternoon. Nice children. The children of good parents."

"This baby," said Rachell, rocking her knee, "has a good parent. I've never seen so clean a baby."

"Almost the last of my money," smiled the girl, "went on soap and baby powder."

Rachelle looked up, her eyes on the black clothes. "You are widowed?" she asked gently.

"Yes, Madame," replied the girl. "But that is not a matter of condolence."

The sudden hardness of her tone, and the defiant fling back of her head, made André wince. They opened a door upon a blackness of sordid disillusion upon which one hated to look on Christmas Eve. "That is past," he said hastily. "That is past."

"Thank God," said the girl, and reached for another piece of cake.

It was when she had finished it, and was preparing for departure, that there began between Rachell and André one of those wordless battles of the will which their differences of temperament made amusingly frequent. . . . For André was one of those idealists who stick at nothing; he would have given his last shilling to a beggar at the door and gone to bed perfectly happy in the conviction that God would provide for his starving family in the morning. . . . Rachell, on the other hand, believed that charity began at home; she would have given the half of her last shilling to the beggar at the door and gone to bed happy in the conviction that at least she had sixpence left for the children's breakfast should it turn out that, after all, there is no God.

So now André, with a flicker of his left eyelid, a half gesture of his head toward the *jonquière,* and a whole gesture of his right thumb toward the ceiling, suggested to Rachell that Colin should be put to sleep in the kitchen tonight and his little room given to this mother and child.

But Rachell received these hints with no signs of enthusiasm. . . . She knew nothing about this girl. . . . She was not going to have her in the house with her innocent daughters. . . . With a swift, cool glance she put André in his place and turned back to the girl.

"They will give you a bed at a fisherman's cottage I know of at the hamlet of Breton Bay," she said kindly, but with the utmost firmness. "The woman is an old servant of mine and I will write a note saying that I have sent you. Tomorrow I will come down and see you, and you will tell me how I can help you."

Obediently, though her face was a little sullen, the girl rose, holding out her arms for her baby.

André tried once more. . . . He coughed, poked the fire, laid a gentle hand upon his wife's shoulder. . . . All no good.

"You will find the way quite easily," continued Rachell evenly, just as though he had neither coughed nor poked. "Take the lane to the right at the crossroads and go straight on."

"I know the way," said the girl proudly. . . . So proudly that André knew she did not want, beggar maid though she was, to stoop to the humility of seeking for shelter at Breton Bay.

"That's right," said Rachell heartily. "Sit down again, my dear, while I write the note, and wrap up a few comforts for you and the babe."

André, beaten and sorrowful, turned and went out. As he slammed the front door behind him, and stood in the snowy courtyard looking up at the blazing stars, a voice tolled over and over again in his brain, "There was no room for them in the inn."

V

Slowly he crossed the courtyard to the stable, for it was time he lit the oil stove that kept his beloved animals warm through the night. His thoughts reached out to them in a glow of affection, for according to the Island legend tonight was their hour of glory of which no man might defraud them.

With a little thrill at his heart he lifted the latch and walked in. The silver starlight softly illumined the stable and showed him the patient shapes of the animals, their breath hanging like incense in the fragrant air. Maximilian, running to him, kissed his hand and folded an affectionate black body round his right leg.

"So you're here, old chap, are you?" said André, pulling the silky ears. "Why aren't you in the house? Why are you neglecting your family on Christmas Eve?"

Maximilian squirmed his body apologetically, and André suddenly remembered that he always did leave the house for the stable on Christmas Eve. . . . Their dogs always had. . . . Odd.

Dismissing the oddness he fumbled for matches and bent to light the oil stove that stood in the empty stall. It was good to see its soft golden light creep tentatively out into the mysterious shadows, laying caressing fingers of light on the animals' satiny backs and—what was that?—lighted candles set around the empty manger?

He started and came nearer, then stood gazing, not ashamed of a pricking behind his eyelids as he looked at Colette's Chinese lanterns, set like tapering flames about the manger where her hands had pressed the hay to make the nest within it soft and round.

Half in play and half in earnest, a little ashamed but yet enjoying himself, he set to work to complete the preparations that she had begun. He tidied the stable, sweeping up the scattered hay and putting in a tidy pile the rug and cushions that the children had left in disarray when they stampeded off to tea, and finally he lighted the lamp so that it swung like a star from the raftered ceiling. Then, with one long last look round, he went softly out into the courtyard and neglected, purposely, or in forgetfulness, he hardly knew which, to lock the door behind him.

A beam of lantern light, shining out from the stable door before he closed it, showed him a figure standing in the shadows beside the doorway to the lane. . . . So she was too proud, after all, to obey

Rachell and seek shelter with a fisherman's wife? . . . He crossed the snowy courtyard hastily, yet when he got to the door he found he had been mistaken, for there was no one there.

"Has the poor girl gone, dear?" he asked Rachell when he returned to the kitchen.

"Ages ago, darling," replied Rachell cheerfully. "You've been an unconscionable time in that stable. . . . It was quite impossible, dearest, for me to have a girl like that in the house with the Girls. . . . I know best in these matters."

André gave the little dignified gesture of the head with which his side of an argument always ended; a gesture that admitted the right of her stronger will to its own way but kept his own opinion unaltered. Then, gently changing the subject, he began to tell her about Colette's manger.

VI

Some hours later, in the snowy lane, the children stood together in a little group, palpitating with excitement. Everything had worked out according to plan. They had gone obediently to bed, and then they had got up again and left the house by way of Peronelle's bedroom window and the back-door porch. They stood now lighting the candle ends in their lanterns, and exclaiming in delight as the points of flame steadied into glowing petals of gold that spread their radiance over the strange world of glistening snow and silvered trees whose tops were lost in the blackness of the night.

"Where are we going first?" asked Michelle.

"Blanchelande," replied Colin promptly.

He had expected an outcry from the Girls, for the farm of Alexander Marquand was "out of bounds." . . . Rachell, though she thought it likely that the grim stories told about the old man had in them more falsehood than truth, was yet taking no chances for the children. . . . But there was no outcry, only a quickly drawn breath of excitement. The Girls, apparently, thought as he did, that in this magical starlit night their destination must be a fairy-tale one; if not Aladdin's cave then an ogre's castle; and no place has a greater fairy-tale quality than a forbidden house where fear dwells.

The only dissentient voice was Peronelle's. "Won't it be too far for Colette?" she asked a little anxiously.

"If it is you Girls can carry her," said Colin.

At this the Girls looked a little askance at Colette, for the addition of two coats, gaiters, and a woolen muffler to her already immense collection of underclothes had made her broader than she was long, and correspondingly heavy. Moreover she had had to be awakened from sleep to be brought on this expedition and was still drowsy with it, her golden head in its red tam-o'-shanter so heavy with dreams that it was lolling on her neck like an overweighted dahlia.

"Carry her yourself," said the Girls indignantly to Colin.

"Not me," said Colin.

"Not going to be carried," lisped Colette indignantly between two yawns. "Colette walk."

"Come on, then," said Colin. "Step out. It's a goodish way."

It certainly was, but so wonderful a way that no one grumbled. They chose the cliff path to Blanchelande, where they were out in the open, rather than the inland lane where who-knew-what lurked in the shadows under the trees. It took them past Matthieu Torode's little cottage, tucked away cozily in a hollow where in spring the gorse and the broom were a blaze of gold, and on along the clifftop, with the sea murmuring against the rocks far down below them, and over their heads a great sky set with blazing stars, and a round white moon whose light made a glittering pathway over the sea and illumined the fallen snow with points of sparkling fire.

It had not been a heavy fall, and it did not clog their footsteps; it was a white crisp coverlet that smoothed their path for them and beckoned them on and on for the sheer joy of printing their footsteps in its whiteness, waiting for them as the virgin page waits for the imprint of the poet's mind upon it.

"Look what we've written!" said Jacqueline, with a backward glance over her shoulder. "What does it say?"

"Peace and good will," said Peronelle softly. "Look! Here is Blanchelande."

The farm was true to its name on a night like this. Between the white moonlight and the white snow its gaunt granite walls gleamed like white marble. It stood foursquare to the winds, with no trees to shelter it and no creepers veiling the hardness of its outlines. There were no lights in the windows and no smoke rising from the chimney, and behind it the farm buildings crouched like frightened animals. . . . It might have been a house where only the ghosts were alive.

If the children's hearts failed them a little they gave no sign. Resolutely they made their way to the front of the house, where a door of such strength and grimness that it seemed to defy all entry faced a courtyard littered with garbage and untidy boxes and barrels.

"Now," said Peronelle. "Do we sing out here, or knock at the door and ask to go in?"

But no one answered her question, for suddenly, as though the gates of hell had been opened, pandemonium broke out in such a fury of barking and baying and snarling as the children had never heard. . . . They had forgotten the Blanchelande dogs. . . . They came streaking out from behind the house, and from the shadows of the courtyard, their leaping, gliding bodies dark against the snow. . . . There were at least a hundred of them.

"Steady, you chaps," said Peronelle's quiet, courageous voice. "Stand together with Colette in the middle. Keep your heads and remember that dogs always like us and we like dogs."

Dogs? But were these dogs? They seemed more like wolves. Though their heads were up and they would sooner have died than run away the heart of each child turned to water within it.

"There are only four," said Peronelle, counting. "Speak to them very politely and hold out your fists for them to smell."

"Good dogs," murmured the du Frocqs courageously. "A merry Christmas. Peace and good will. We're only carol singers and we don't mean any harm," and they bravely held out their doubled fists to the snarling jaws.

The dogs lifted their inquiring noses to the fists and smelled them, they lowered them to the hems of the children's coats and smelled those, they cocked their ears to the sounds of the children's voices and gazed with deep absorption at their boots. They were satisfied. These were good children. They smelled courageous and sounded kindhearted, and their boots were respectable boots. Four pink tongues curled out to caress and four tails were raised in welcome.

"Hi! You get out of there!"

The door had been flung open, and a harsh voice was shouting at them from the dark cavern within.

"We're carol singers," explained Peronelle. "We're coming inside to sing to you."

"Oh, are you?" inquired the voice grimly. "Not if I know it. You get along home, or I'll set the dogs on you."

"You can't," said Colin. "The dogs like us."

The voice materialized into a tall stooping figure that came out into the moonlight and confronted them, and for the first time the children looked up into the face of the hated Alexander Marquand. He was an old man, fierce-eyed, gray-bearded, with a lean weather-beaten face that seemed to have been carved in keen fierce lines out of a piece of dark wood. . . . Yet the children, who had never yet met cruelty in any form, felt no fear of him. . . . They smiled engagingly.

"Let us in," they pleaded.

Hands in pocket he surveyed them, the moonlight and lantern light illuminating for him their glowing pink cheeks and bright eyes and delightfully bunchy figures, and the dogs standing round them with sterns aquiver and eyes raised beseechingly to their master's face. . . . Let these children in, they said, for they smell right.

But it was Colette, tired out by the walk along the cliff, who clinched the matter. Both her father and her grandfather had gray beards, and the very sight of one recalled to her mind strong arms that in her babyhood had lifted her off her inadequate legs—Colette's legs had never been equal to her weight—and a personality from whom emanated all the good things of this life. She ran to Monsieur Marquand, clasping him with her fat hands, her cherubic face raised to him, imploring warmth, shelter, and an opportunity of sitting down. "My legs ache," she said.

Before he realized what he was doing he had picked her up and carried her into his dark, stone-floored kitchen, the dogs and the other children following pell-mell at his heels, and set her down before the dying fire, staring at the lot of them in comical bewilderment.

But the children knew quite well what to do. They pushed Monsieur Marquand into his fireside chair and gave him Colette to hold upon his knees, they flung wood upon the dying embers and lit the oil lamp that hung from the rafters. They took chestnuts from their pockets—chestnuts were a very important part of Christmas fare on the Island, and every child's pocket was full of them—and set them to roast upon the hearthstone, and then sitting down cross-legged before the fire they began to sing.

The years rolled away from Alexander Marquand. All his bitterness and hatred, his inheritance from a line of savage forbears and fostered in him by years of misfortune and bereavement, seemed to be going with the smoke up the chimney. The kitchen that a short while ago had seemed cold, empty, and dark was filled with warmth and light, singing, and the cheerful sound of popping chestnuts. Old memories awoke and peopled it with ghosts; the figures of his childhood, the brothers and sisters who more than a half century ago had sung these very same French carols; his own dead children, who had roasted their chestnuts at this hearthstone; his little granddaughter who used to sit upon his knee as Colette was sitting now. . . . A bitter memory this last one. His pride would never forgive her for the disgrace she had brought upon his name.

"I think we ought to be going now," said one of the children suddenly, after a long while. "You see, we want to be home by midnight, so as to look in the stable afterward and see if the animals are still kneeling down."

Monsieur Marquand started and looked up. For how long had

he been sitting here, eating chestnuts, listening to carols, dreaming dreams, and seeing visions? The child, he was astonished to find, was now asleep in his arms, her golden head on his shoulder. So bewildered was he that he was not quite certain what child it was; one of his own out of the past or some cherub out of the carols the children had been singing; in either case he was reluctant to let it go.

"I'll come with you," he said. "And carry the child."

VII

The homeward journey was as magical as the outward one, perhaps more magical because of the tremendous waiting silence that gripped the world. . . . The sea was hardly whispering now, and the blaze of the stars seemed a little veiled, as though they had hidden their eyes. . . . The old man and the children plodded on, the four dogs at their heels, and none of them spoke until they were nearly home and saw three figures with a swinging lantern coming to meet them.

"Mother and Father and Matthieu Torode!" ejaculated Michelle. "But how did they know where we were?"

"They went up to fill our stockings and found us gone," said Peronelle. "Idiots that we were not to think of that!"

"They fetched out Matthieu to help them and tracked our footsteps through the snow!" exclaimed Colin. "Well done, them! Hullo, Father! Hullo, Mother!"

"You naughty children!" cried Rachell, thoroughly exasperated now that her anxiety was relieved. "I'd like to spank the lot of you."

"You have made your Mother very anxious," reproved André mildly.

Suddenly Matthieu, who had been grinning jovially and swinging the lantern, saw who it was who carried Colette. "Monsieur Marquand!" he ejaculated, and the smile was wiped off his face and his lantern became rigid.

"Monsieur Marquand?" asked André and Rachell, and gazed in

astonishment at the man who for years had so unreasonably counted himself their enemy.

Monsieur Marquand made a move as though to put Colette into her mother's arms. "May I restore your property to you, Madame?" he said coldly. "And then bid you good night."

"No, Marquand!" said André sharply. "You have done us a service tonight, and you will come home and have a drink with me."

Monsieur Marquand hesitated, and made another effort to dislodge Colette, but she was comfortable where she was and wriggled closer. With a curt, abrupt nod he yielded.

VIII

The first stroke of midnight, borne very faintly on the still air from the distant town of Saint Pierre, rang out as the cavalcade entered the courtyard. It was followed by bell after bell, as all the different church clocks in the town began to strike, so far away that the tiny sounds seemed like tinkling drops of water falling into the deep well of the gripping silence. The little group of human beings halted, as though a hand had been laid on them to quiet their shuffling feet and wagging tongues, but the four Marquand dogs went like a streak of lightning across the snowy courtyard, and the foremost one, making a little crying noise like an eager child, pushed his nose against the door; it must have been unlatched because it opened a little way, letting out a beam of light that stretched right across the snow to the feet of the watching humans, and the four dogs went in.

The last stroke of midnight sounded from the last of the Saint Pierre churches, there was a pause, and then, still so faint and far away that it sounded as though they were ringing under the sea, the Christmas bells rang out in silvery peals that seemed to the listeners to be the twinkling frost and the sparkling stars made audible in music.

"Now," said Colin softly, and with the fully awakened Colette close at his heels he ran across to the stable door and flung it open.

He was not surprised, of course, and neither was Colette, though it was even lovelier than they had expected, but to all the others what they saw inside the stable had the quality of one of those blinding visions that change the whole course of a man's life forever.

All the animals had gathered round in a semicircle; the horses, the cow, the little donkey, the five dogs, and the golden cat. They were not kneeling down now, though Colin stoutly declared afterward that he had heard them get up from their knees when he opened the door. The dogs were lying with their noses on their paws, and the other animals were standing quietly brooding, their wide dark eyes fixed on the baby who lay in the decorated manger, curled round fast asleep in the soft place that Colette's hands had pressed out. His pretty mother had been sleeping among the cushions that André had arranged so tidily on the hay, but she was sitting up now and rubbing the sleep out of her eyes. As they stood there watching she let her hands drop and looked up at them, smiling, her eyes dark with mystery in her flowerlike face. The light of the lantern, swinging overhead, illumined the scene with a glowing softness that seemed strangely to come from the manger itself. . . . Each stalk of hay seemed a line of golden light and Colette's Chinese lanterns glowed round the crib like petals of flame. . . . The deep stillness in which they watched lasted for a few more minutes whose brief span seemed like eternity, and through it the bells threaded their silver chain of sound.

IX

It was these minutes that the children remembered ever afterward. It was this vision that was reality and not the swift tumult of following events that seemed to them to have the confusion of a dream and to be as little worthy of attention. . . . Yet a few details of the dream stuck in their memory: Matthieu's cry of "Denise! Denise!" a cry so full of grief and longing that it pierced them as though an arrow had gone through their bodies; Denise's face raised to his, white with her mute passion of penitence; old Monsieur Marquand most unaccountably bursting into tears and being patted on the back by their father; Denise's clear voice, restored to her at last, saying over and over again, "Forgive me. Forgive me, Madame; I did not want to go down to Breton Bay and so I crept into the stable instead. Forgive me, Grandfather. Please, Matthieu, forgive me. . . ." Monsieur Marquand asked no one to forgive him, though goodness knew, thought the children afterward, his behavior in setting the dogs on Denise when she had tried to go back to her home had been atrocious enough; but then perhaps his tears, the first he had shed for sixty years, so he said later, were a rich ransom for his evil deeds.

So many things were ransomed by the events of that night: the ancient friendship between Bon Repos and Blanchelande; the old affection between Monsieur Marquand and his granddaughter; the old love between Matthieu and Denise that born again transformed her into Madame Torode, a rosy-cheeked matron who lived in the little cottage in the gorse-filled hollow on the cliffs, and watched her son grow to strength and vigor on an Island of peace and good will set like a jewel between sun and sea.

But to the children Denise and her baby were not to be identified with the mother and child they had seen in the stable. No. These were eternal, unchanging figures. . . . A mother who would never grow old and a child who would never grow up. . . . The children would probably never see them again; but the animals would. Every Christmas Eve, when the church clocks of Saint Pierre struck midnight, the animals would kneel down and worship what they saw.

II

CHRISTMAS LEGENDS

Some say that ever 'gainst that season comes
Wherein our Saviour's birth is celebrated,
The bird of dawning singeth all night long:
And then, they say, no spirit can walk abroad;
The nights are wholesome; then no planets strike,
No fairy takes, nor witch hath power to charm;
So hallow'd and so gracious is the time.

HAMLET

II

CHRISTMAS [illegible]

[illegible]
[illegible]
[illegible]
[illegible]
[illegible]
[illegible]
[illegible]

On Hanging a Stocking at Christmas

CHARLES S. BROOKS

As Christmas is, above all, a holiday for children, it is proper in its season to consider with what regard they hold its celebration. But as no one may really know the secrets of childhood except as he retains the recollection of his own, it is therefore in the well of memory that I must dip my pen. The world has been running these many years with gathering speed like a great wheel upon a hill, and I must roll it backward to the heights to see how I fared on the night and day of Christmas.

I can remember that for a month before the day I computed its distance, not only in hours and minutes but even in seconds, until the answer was scrawled across my slate. Now, when I multiply 24 x 60 x 60, the resulting 86,400 has an agreeable familiarity as the amount I struck off each morning. At bedtime on Christmas Eve I had still 36,000 impatient seconds yet to wait, for I considered that Christmas really started at six o'clock in the morning.

There was, of course, a lesser celebration on Christmas Eve when we hung our stockings. There were six of them, from mother's long one to father's short one. Ours, although built on womanish lines, lacked the greater length and they were, consequently, inferior for the purpose of our greed; but father's were woefully short, as if fashioned to the measure of his small ex-

From *Chimney-Pot Papers*, by Charles S. Brooks, by permission of Yale University Press, publishers.

pectancy. Even a candy cane came peeping from the top, as if curiosity had stirred it to look around.

Finally, when the stockings were hung on the knobs of the mantel, we went up the dark stairs to bed. At the landing we saw the last glimmer from the friendly sitting-room. The hall clock ticked solemnly in the shadow below with an air of firmness, as much as to say that it would not be hurried. Fret as we might, those 36,000 seconds were not to be jostled through the night.

In the upper hall we looked from a window upon the snowy world. Perhaps we were too old to believe in Santa Claus, but even so, on this magic night might not a skeptic be at fault—might there not be a chance that the discarded world had returned to us? Once a year, surely, reason might nod and drowse. Perhaps if we put our noses on the cold glass and peered hard into the glittering darkness, we might see the old fellow himself, muffled to his chin in furs, going on his yearly errands. It was a jingling of sleigh bells on the street that started this agreeable suspicion, but, alas, when the horse appeared, manifestly by his broken jogging gait he was only an earthly creature and could not have been trusted on the roof. Or the moon, sailing across the sky, invited the thought that tonight beyond the accustomed hour and for a purpose it would throw its light across the roofs to mark the chimneys.

Presently mother called up from the hall below. Had we gone to bed? Reluctantly now we began to thumb the buttons. Off came our clothes, both shirts together tonight for better speed in dressing. And all the night pants and drawers hung as close neighbors, one within the other, with stockings dangling at the ends, for quick resumption. We slipped shivering into the cold sheets. Down below the bed, by special permission, stood the cook's clock, wound up tight for its explosion at six o'clock.

Then came silence and the night. . . .

Presently, all of a sudden, Brrr—! There arose a deafening racket in the room. Had the reindeer come afoul of the chimney? Had the loaded sleigh crashed upon the roof? Were pirates on the stairs? We awoke finally, and smothered the alarm in the pillows. A match! The gas! And now a thrill went through us. Although it was still as black as ink outside, at last the great day of all the year had come.

It was, therefore, before the dawn that we stole downstairs in our stockings—dressed loosely and without too great precision in our hurry. Buttons that lay behind were neglected, nor did it fret us if a garment came on twisted. It was a rare tooth that felt the brush this morning, no matter how it was coddled through the year.

We carried our shoes, but this was not entirely in consideration for the sleeping house. Rather, our care proceeded from an enjoyment of our stealth; for to rise before the dawn when the lamps were still lighted on the street and issue in our stockings was to taste adventure. It had not exactly the zest of burglary, although it was of kin: nor was it quite like the search for buried treasure which we played on common days: yet to slink along the hallway on a pitch-black Christmas morning, with shoes dangling by the strings, was to realize a height of happiness unequaled.

Quietly we tiptoed down the stairs on whose steep rail we had so often slid in the common light of day, now so strangely altered by the shadows. Below in the hall the great clock ticked, loudly and with satisfaction that its careful count was done and its seconds all despatched. There was a gurgle in its throat before it struck the hour, as some folk clear their throats before they sing.

As yet there was not a blink of day. The house was as black as if it practiced to be a cave, yet an instinct instructed us that now at least darkness was safe. There were frosty patterns on the windows of the sitting-room, familiar before only on our bedroom windows. Here in the sitting-room arose dim shapes which probably were its accustomed furniture, but which to our excited fancy might be sleds and velocipedes.

We groped for a match. There was a splutter that showed red in the hollow of my brother's hand.

After the first glad shock, it was our habit to rummage in the general midden outside our stockings. If there was a drum upon the heap, should not first a tune be played—softly lest it rouse the house? Or if a velocipede stood beside the fender, surely the restless creature chafed for exercise and must be ridden a few times around the room. Or perhaps a sled leaned against the chair (it but rested against the rigors of the coming day) and one should feel its runners to learn whether they are whole and round, for if flat and fixed with screws it is no better than a sled for girls with feet tucked up in front. On such a sled, no one trained to the fashions of the slide would deign to take a belly-slammer, for the larger boys would cry out with scorn and point their sneering mittens.

The stocking was explored last. It was like a grab-bag, but glorified and raised to a more generous level. On meaner days shriveled grab-bags could be got at the corner for a penny—if such mild fortune fell your way—mere starvelings by comparison—and to this shop you had often trotted after school when learning sat heaviest on your soul. If a nickel had accrued to you from the sale of tintags, it was better, of course, to lay it out in pop; but with nothing better than a penny, there was need of sharp denial. How you lingered before the horehound jar! Coltsfoot, too, was but a penny to the stick and pleased the palate. Or one could do worse than licorice. But finally you settled on a grab-bag. You roused an old woman from her knitting behind the stove and demanded that a choice of grab-bags be placed before you. Then, like the bearded phrenologist at the side-show of the circus, you put your fingers on them to read their humps. Perhaps an all-day sucker lodged inside—a glassy or an agate—marbles best for pugging—or a brass ring with a ruby.

Through the year these bags sufficed, but the Christmas stocking was a deeper and finer mystery. In the upper leg were handkerchiefs from grandmother—whose thoughts ran prudentially on noses—mittens and a cap—useful presents of duller purpose—things that were due you anyway and would have come in the course of time. But down in the darker meshes of the stocking, when you had turned the corner of the heel, there were the sweet extras of life—a mouth-organ, a baseball, a compass and a watch.

Some folk have a Christmas tree instead of hanging their stockings, but this is the preference of older folk rather than the preference of children. Such persons wish to observe a child's enjoyment, and this is denied them if the stocking is opened at the dawn.

Under a pretense of instruction they sit in an absurd posture under the tree; but they do no more than read the rules and are blind to the obscurer uses of the toys. As they find occasion, the children run off and play in a quieter room with some old and broken toy.

Who can interpret the desires of children? They are a race apart from us. At times, for a moment, we bring them to attention; then there is a scurry of feet and they are gone. Although they seem to sit at table with us, they are beyond a frontier that we cannot pass. Their words are ours, but applied to foreign uses. If we try to follow their truant thoughts, like the lame man of the story we limp behind a shooting star. We bestow on them a blind condescension, not knowing how their imagination outclimbs our own. And we cramp them with our barren learning.

I assert, therefore, that it is better to find one's presents in the dawn, when there is freedom. In all the city, wherever there are lights, children have taken a start upon the day. Then, although the toys are strange, there is adventure in prying at their uses. If one commits a toy to a purpose undreamed of by its maker, it but rouses the invention to further discovery. Once on a dark and frosty Christmas morning, I spent a puzzling hour upon a coffee-grinder—a present to my mother—in a delusion that it was a rare engine destined for myself. It might have been a bank had it possessed a slot for coins. A little eagle surmounted the top, yet this was not a sufficient clue. The handle offered the hope that it was a music-box, but although I turned it round and round, and noises issued from its body quite foreign to my other toys, yet I could not pronounce it music. With sails it might have been a windmill. I laid it on its side and stood it on its head without conclusion. It was painted red, and that gave it a wicked look, but no other villainy appeared. To this day as often as I pass a coffee-grinder in a grocer's shop I turn its handle in memory of my perplexing hour. And even if one remains unschooled to the uses of the toys, their discovery in the dawn while yet the world lies fast asleep is far beyond their stale performance that rises with the sun.

And yet I know of an occurrence, to me pathetic, that once attended such an early discovery. A distant cousin of mine—a man really not related except by the close bond of my regard—was brought up many years ago by an uncle of austere and miserly nature. Such goodness as this uncle had once possessed was cramped into a narrowing and smothering piety. He would have dimmed the sun upon the Sabbath, could he have reached up tall enough. He had no love in his heart, nor mirth. My cousin has always loved a horse and even in his childhood this love was strong. And so, during the days that led up to Christmas when children speculate upon their desires and check them on their fingers, he kept asking his uncle for a pony. At first, as you might know, his uncle was stolid against the thought, but finally, with many winks and nods—pleasantries beyond his usual habit—he assented.

Therefore in the early darkness of the day, the child came down to find his gift. First, probably, he went to the stable and climbing on the fence he looked through the windows for an unaccustomed form inside the stalls. Next he looked to see whether the pony might be hitched to the post in front of the house, in the manner of the family doctor. The search failing and being now somewhat disturbed with doubt, he entered his nursery on the slim chance that the pony might still be there. The room was dark and he listened on the sill, if he might hear him whinny. Feeling his way along the hearth he came on nothing greater than his stocking which was tied to the andiron. It bulged and stirred his curiosity. He thrust in his hand and coming on something sticky, he put his fingers in his mouth. They were of a delightful sweetness. He now paused in his search for the pony and drawing out a huge lump of candy he applied himself. But the day was near and he had finished no more than half, when a ray of light permitted him to see what he ate. It was a candy horse—making good the promise of his uncle. This and a Testament had been stuffed inside his stocking. The Testament was wrapped in tissue, but the horse was bitten to the middle. It had been at best but a poor substitute for what he wanted, yet his love was so broad that it included even a sugar horse; and this, alas, he had consumed unknowing in the dark. And even now when the dear fellow tells the story after these many years have passed, and comes to the sober end with the child crying in the twilight of the morning, I realize as not before that there be no Christmas kept unless it be with love and mirth.

It was but habit that we hung our stockings at the chimney—the piano would have done as well—for I retain but the slightest memory of a belief in Santa Claus; perhaps at most, as I have hinted, a far-off haze of wonder while looking through the window upon the snowy sky—at night a fancied clatter on the roof, if I lay awake. And therefore in a chimney there was no greater mystery than was inherent in any hole that went off suspiciously in the dark. There was a fearful cave beneath the steps that mounted from the rear to the front garret. This was wrapped in Cimmerian darkness—which is the strongest pigment known—and it extended from its mouth beyond the furthest stretch of leg. To the disillusioned, indeed, this cave was harmless, for it merely offset the lower ceiling of the bathroom below; yet to us it was a cave unparalleled. Little by little we ventured in, until in time we could sit on the snug joists inside with the comfortable feeling of pirates. Presently we hit on the device of hanging a row of shining maple-syrup tins along the wall outside where they were caught by the dusty sunlight, which was thus reflected in on us. By the light of these dim moons the cave showed itself to be the size of a library table. And here, also, we crouched on dark and cloudy days when the tins were in eclipse, and found a dreadful joy when the wind scratched upon the roof.

In the basement, also, there was a central hall that disappeared forever under an accumulation of porch chairs and lumber. Here was no light except what came around two turns from the laundry. Even Annie the cook, a bold venturesome person, had never quite penetrated to a full discovery of this hallway. A proper approach into the darkness was on hands and knees, and yet there were barrels and boxes to overcome. Therefore, as we were bred to these broader discoveries, a mere chimney in the sitting-room, which arose safely from its fenders, was but a mild and pleasant tunnel to the roof.

And if a child believes in Santa Claus and chimneys, and that his presents are stored in a glittering kingdom across the wintry hills, he will miss the finer pleasure of knowing that they are hidden somewhere in his own house. For myself, I would not willingly forego certain dizzy ascents to the topmost shelves of the storeroom, where, with my head close under the ceiling and my foot braced against the wall, I have examined suspicious packages that came into the house by stealth. As likely as not, at the ringing of the door-bell, we had been whisked into a back room. Presently there was a foot sounding on the stairs and across the ceiling. Then we were released. But something had arrived.

Thereafter we found excitement in rummaging in unlikely places—a wary lifting of summer garments laid away, for a peek beneath—a journey on one's stomach under the spare-room bed—a pilgrimage around the cellar with a flaring candle—furtive explorations of the storeroom. And when we came to a door that was locked—— Aha! Here was a puzzle and a problem! We tried every key in the house, right side up and upside down. Bluebeard's wife, poor creature,—if I read the tale aright,—was merely seeking her Christmas presents around the house before the proper day.

The children of a friend of mine, however, have been brought up to a belief in Santa Claus, and on Christmas Eve they have the pretty custom of filling their shoes with crackers and scraps of bread by way of fodder for the reindeer. When the shoes are found empty in the morning, but with crumbs about—as though the hungry reindeer spilled them in their haste—it fixes the deception.

But if one must have a Christmas tree, I recommend the habit of some friends of mine. In front of their home, down near the fence, is a trim little cedar. T—— connects this with electric wires and hangs on it gayly colored lamps. Every night for a week, until the new year, these lights shine across the snow and are the delight of travelers on the road. The Christmas stars, it seems, for this hallowed season have come to earth.

We gave the family dinner. On my mother fell the extra labor, but we took the general credit. All the morning the relatives arrived—thin and fat. But if one of them bore a package or if his pockets sagged, we showed him an excessive welcome. Sometimes there was a present boxed and wrapped to a mighty bulk. From this we threw off thirty papers and the bundle dwindled, still no gift appeared. In this lay the sweetness of the jest, for finally, when the contents were shriveled to a kernel, in the very heart of it there lay a bright penny or a common marble.

All this time certain savory whiffs have been blowing from the kitchen. Twice at least my mother has put her head in at the door to count the relatives. And now when the clock on the mantel strikes two—a bronze Lincoln deliberating forever whether he will sign the Emancipation Bill—the dining-room door is opened.

The table was drawn out to prodigious length and was obliquely set across the room. As early as yesterday the extra leaves had been brought from the pantry, and we had all taken part in fitting them together. Not to disturb the larger preparation, our supper and breakfast had been served in the kitchen. And even now to eat in the kitchen, if the table is set before the window and there is a flurry of snow outside, is to feel pleasantly the proximity of a great occasion.

The Christmas table was so long and there were so many of us, that a few of the chairs were caught in a jog of the wall and had no proper approach except by crawling on hands and knees beneath it. Each year it was customary to request my maiden aunt, a prim lady who bordered on seventy and had limbs instead of legs, to undertake the passage. Each year we listened for the jest and shouted with joy when the request was made. There were other jests, too, that were dear to us and grew better with the years. My aunt was reproved for boisterous conduct, and although she sat as silent as a mouse, she was always warned against the cider. Each year, also, as soon as the dessert appeared, there was a demand that a certain older cousin tell the Judge West story. But the jest lay in the demand instead of in the story, for although there was a clamor of applause, the story was never told and it teases me forever. Then another cousin, who journeyed sometimes to New York, usually instructed us in the latest manner of eating an orange in the metropolis. But we disregarded his fashioned instruction, and peeled ours round and round.

The dinner itself was a prodigious feast. The cook-stove must have rested and panted for a week thereafter. Before long, Annie got so red bringing in turkeys and cranberry sauce—countless plates heaped and toppling with vegetables and meats—that one might think she herself was in process to become a pickled beet and would presently enter on a platter.

In the afternoon we rested, but at night there was a dance, for which my maiden aunt played the piano. The dear good soul, whose old brown fingers were none too limber, had skill that scarcely mounted to the speed of a polka, but she was steady at a waltz. There was one tune—bink a bunk bunk, bink a bunk bunk—that went around and around with an agreeable monotony even when the player nodded. There was a legend in the family that once she fell asleep in the performance, and that the dancers turned down the lights and left the room; to her amazement when presently she awoke, for she thought she had outsat the party.

My brother and I had not advanced to the trick of dancing and we built up our blocks in the corner of the room in order that the friskier dancers might kick them over as they passed. Chief in the performance was the Judge West cousin who, although whiskered almost into middle age, had a merry heart and knew how to play with children. Sometimes, by consent we younger fry sat beneath the piano, which was of an old square pattern, and worked the pedals for my aunt, in order that her industry might be undivided on the keys. It is amazing what a variety we could cast upon the waltz, now giving it a muffled sound, and presently offering the dancers a prolonged roaring.

Midway in the evening, when the atrocities of dinner were but mildly remembered, ice-cream was brought in. It was not hard as at dinner, but had settled to a delicious softness and could be mushed upon a spoon. Then while the party again proceeded, and my aunt resumed her waltz, we were despatched upstairs.

On the bed lay our stockings, still tied with string, that had been stuffed with presents in the dawn. But the morning had now sunk into immeasurable distance and seemed as remote as Job himself. And all through the evening, as we lay abed and listened to the droning piano below, we felt a spiritual hollowness because the great day had passed.

The Fir-Tree

HANS CHRISTIAN ANDERSEN

OUT in the woods stood a nice little Fir-tree. The place he had was a very good one; the sun shone on him; as to fresh air, there was enough of that, and round him grew many large-sized comrades, pines as well as firs. But the little Fir wanted so very much to be a grown-up tree.

He did not think of the warm sun and of the fresh air; he did not care for the little cottage-children that ran about and prattled when they were in the woods looking for wild strawberries. The children often came with a whole pitcher full of berries, or a long row of them threaded on a straw, and sat down near the young Tree and said, "O, how pretty he is! What a nice little fir!" But this was what the Tree could not bear to hear.

At the end of a year he had shot up a good deal, and after another year he was another long bit taller; for with fir-trees one can always tell by the shoots how many years old they are.

"O, were I but such a high tree as the others are," sighed he. "Then I should be able to spread out my branches, and with the tops to look into the wide world! Then would the birds build nests among my branches; and when there was a breeze, I could bend with as much stateliness as the others!"

Neither the sunbeams, nor the birds, nor the red clouds which morning and evening sailed above him, gave the little Tree any pleasure.

In winter, when the snow lay glittering on the ground, a hare would often come leaping along, and jump right over the little

Tree. O, that made him so angry! But two winters were past, and in the third the Tree was so large that the hare was obliged to go round it. "To grow and grow, to get older and be tall," thought the Tree; "that, after all, is the most delightful thing in the world!"

In autumn the wood-cutters always came and felled some of the largest trees. This happened every year; and the young Fir-tree, that had now grown to a very comely size, trembled at the sight; for the magnificent great trees fell to the earth with noise and crackling, the branches were lopped off, and the trees looked long and bare: they were hardly to be recognized; and then they were laid in carts, and the horses dragged them out of the wood.

Where did they go to? What became of them?

In spring, when the Swallows and the Storks came, the Tree asked them, "Don't you know where they have been taken? Have you not met them anywhere?"

The Swallows did not know anything about it; but the Stork looked musing, nodded his head, and said, "Yes; I think I know; I met many ships as I was flying hither from Egypt; on the ships were magnificent masts, and I venture to assert that it was they that smelt so of fir. I may congratulate you, for they lifted themselves on high most majestically!"

"O, were I but old enough to fly across the sea! But how does the sea look in reality? What is it like?"

"That would take a long time to explain," said the Stork, and with these words off he went.

"Rejoice in thy growth!" said the Sunbeams, "rejoice in thy vigorous growth, and in the fresh life that moveth within thee!"

And the Wind kissed the Tree, and the Dew wept tears over him; but the Fir understood it not.

When Christmas came, quite young trees were cut down; trees which often were not even as large or of the same age as this Fir-tree, who could never rest, but always wanted to be off. These young trees, and they were always the finest looking, retained their branches; they were laid on carts, and the horses drew them out of the wood.

"Where are they going to?" asked the Fir. "They are not taller than I—" there was one indeed that was considerably shorter—"and why do they retain all their branches? Whither are they taken?"

"We know! we know!" chirped the Sparrows. "We have peeped in at the windows in the town below! We know whither they are taken! The greatest splendor and the greatest magnificence one can imagine await them. We peeped through the windows, and saw them planted in the middle of the warm room, and ornamented with the most splendid things—with gilded apples, with gingerbread, with toys, and many hundred lights!"

"And then?" asked the Fir-tree, trembling in every bough. "And then? What happens then?"

"We did not see anything more: it was incomparably beautiful."

"I would fain know if I am destined for so glorious a career," cried the Tree, rejoicing. "That is still better than to cross the sea! What a longing do I suffer! Were Christmas but come! I am now tall, and my branches spread like the others that were carried off last year! O, were I but already on the cart! Were I in the warm room with all the splendor and magnificence! Yes; then something better, something still grander, will surely follow, or wherefore should they thus ornament me? Something better, something still grander, *must* follow—but what? O, how I long, how I suffer! I do not know myself what is the matter with me!"

"Rejoice in our presence!" said the Air and the Sunlight; "rejoice in thy own fresh youth!"

But the Tree did not rejoice at all; he grew and grew, and was green both winter and summer. People that saw him said, "What a fine tree!" and towards Christmas he was one of the first that was cut down. The axe struck deep into the very pith; the Tree fell to the earth with a sigh: he felt a pang—it was like a swoon; he could not think of happiness, for he was sorrowful at being separated from his home, from the place where he had sprung up. He well knew that he should never see his dear old comrades, the little bushes and flowers around him, any more; perhaps not even the birds! The departure was not at all agreeable.

The Tree only came to himself when he was unloaded in a court-yard with the other trees, and heard a man say, "That one is splendid! we don't want the others." Then two servants came in rich livery and carried the Fir-tree into a large and splendid drawing-room. Portraits were hanging on the walls, and near the white porcelain stove stood two large Chinese vases with lions on the covers. There, too, were large easy-chairs, silken sofas, large tables full of picture-books, and full of toys worth hundreds and hundreds of crowns—at least the children said so. And the Fir-tree was stuck upright in a cask that was filled with sand: but no one could see that it was a cask, for green cloth was hung all round it, and it stood on a large gayly-colored carpet. O, how the tree quivered! What was to happen? The servants, as well as the young ladies, decorated it. On one branch there were hung little nets cut out of colored paper, and each net was filled with sugar-plums; and among the other boughs gilded apples and walnuts were suspended, looking as though they had grown there, and little blue and white tapers were placed among the leaves. Dolls that looked for all the world like men—the Tree had never beheld such before—were seen among the foliage, and at the very top a large star of gold tinsel was fixed. It was really splendid—beyond description splendid.

"This evening!" said they all; "how it will shine this evening!"

"O," thought the Tree, "if the evening were but come! If the tapers were but lighted! And then I wonder what will happen! Perhaps the other trees from the forest will come to look at me! Perhaps the sparrows will beat against the window-panes! I wonder if I shall take root here, and winter and summer stand covered with ornaments!"

He knew very much about the matter! But he was so impatient that for sheer longing he got a pain in his back, and this with trees is the same thing as a headache with us.

The candles were now lighted. What brightness! What splendor! The Tree trembled so in every bough that one of the tapers set fire to the foliage. It blazed up splendidly.

"Help! help!" cried the young ladies, and they quickly put out the fire.

Now the Tree did not even dare tremble. What a state he was in! He was so uneasy lest he should lose something of his splendor, that he was quite bewildered amidst the glare and brightness; when suddenly both folding-doors opened, and a troop of children rushed in as if they would upset the Tree. The older persons followed quietly; the little ones stood quite still. But it was only for a moment; then they shouted so that the whole place re-echoed with their rejoicing; they danced round the Tree, and one present after the other was pulled off.

"What are they about?" thought the Tree. "What is to happen now!" And the lights burned down to the very branches, and as they burned down they were put out one after the other, and then the children had permission to plunder the Tree. So they fell upon it with such violence that all its branches cracked; if it had not been fixed firmly in the cask, it would certainly have tumbled down.

The children danced about with their beautiful playthings: no one looked at the Tree except the old nurse, who peeped between the branches; but it was only to see if there was a fig or an apple left that had been forgotten.

"A story! a story!" cried the children, drawing a little fat man towards the Tree. He seated himself under it, and said, "Now we are in the shade, and the Tree can listen too. But I shall tell only one story. Now which will you have; about Ivedy-Avedy, or about Klumpy-Dumpy who tumbled downstairs, and yet after all came to the throne and married the princess?"

"Ivedy-Avedy," cried some; "Klumpy-Dumpy," cried the others. There was such a bawling and screaming!—the Fir-tree alone was silent, and he thought to himself, "Am I not to bawl with the rest?—am I to do nothing whatever?" for he was one of the company, and had done what he had to do.

And the man told about Klumpy-Dumpy that tumbled down, who notwithstanding came to the throne, and at last married the princess. And the children clapped their hands, and cried out, "O, go on! Do go on!" They wanted to hear about Ivedy-Avedy too, but the little man only told them about Klumpy-Dumpy. The Fir-tree stood quite still and absorbed in thought: the birds in the wood had never related the like of this. "Klumpy-Dumpy fell downstairs, and yet he married the princess! Yes, yes! that's the way of the world!" thought the Fir-tree, and believed it all, because the man who told the story was so good-looking. "Well, well! who knows, perhaps I may fall downstairs too, and get a princess as wife!" And he looked forward with joy to the morrow, when he hoped to be decked out again with lights, playthings, fruits, and tinsel.

"I won't tremble to-morrow!" thought the Fir-tree. "I will enjoy to the full all my splendor! To-morrow I shall hear again the story of Klumpy-Dumpy, and perhaps that of Ivedy-Avedy too." And the whole night the Tree stood still in deep thought.

In the morning the servant and the housemaid came in.

"Now then the splendor will begin again," thought the Fir. But they dragged him out of the room, and up the stairs into the loft; and here in a dark corner, where no daylight could enter, they left him. "What's the meaning of this?" thought the Tree. "What am I to do here? What shall I hear now, I wonder?" And he leaned against the wall lost in reverie. Time enough had he too for his reflections; for days and nights passed on, and nobody came up; and when at last somebody did come, it was only to put some great trunks in a corner out of the way. There stood the Tree quite hidden; it seemed as if he had been entirely forgotten.

" 'Tis now winter out-of-doors!" thought the Tree. "The earth is hard and covered with snow; men cannot plant me now, and therefore I have been put up here under shelter till the spring-time comes! How thoughtful that is! How kind man is, after all! If it only were not so dark here, and so terribly lonely! Not even a hare. And out in the woods it was so pleasant, when the snow was on the ground, and the hare leaped by; yes—even when he jumped over me; but I did not like it then. It is really terribly lonely here!"

"Squeak! squeak!" said a little Mouse at the same moment, peeping out of his hole. And then another little one came. They snuffed about the Fir-tree, and rustled among the branches.

"It is dreadfully cold," said the Mouse. "But for that, it would be delightful here, old Fir, wouldn't it?"

"I am by no means old," said the Fir-tree. "There's many a one considerably older than I am."

"Where do you come from," asked the Mice; "and what can you do?" They were so extremely curious. "Tell us about the most beautiful spot on the earth. Have you never been there? Were you never in the larder, where cheeses lie on the shelves, and hams hang from above; where one dances about on tallow candles; that place where one enters lean, and comes out again fat and portly?"

"I know no such place," said the Tree. "But I know the wood, where the sun shines, and where the little birds sing." And then he told all about his youth; and the little Mice had never heard the like before; and they listened and said,

"Well, to be sure! How much you have seen! How happy you must have been!"

"I!" said the Fir-tree, thinking over what he had himself related. "Yes, in reality those were happy times." And then he told about Christmas Eve, when he was decked out with cakes and candles.

"O," said the little Mice, "how fortunate you have been, old Fir-tree!"

"I am by no means old," said he. "I came from the wood this winter; I am in my prime, and am only rather short for my age."

"What delightful stories you know!" said the Mice: and the next night they came with four other little Mice, who were to hear what the Tree recounted; and the more he related, the more plainly he remembered all himself; and it appeared as if those times had really been happy times. "But they may still come—they may still come. Klumpy-Dumpy fell downstairs, and yet he got a princess!" and he thought at the moment of a nice little Birch-tree growing out in the woods: to the Fir, that would be a real charming princess.

Who is Klumpy-Dumpy?" asked the Mice. So then the Fir-tree told the whole fairy tale, for he could remember every single word of it; and the little Mice jumped for joy up to the very top of the Tree. Next night two more Mice came, and on Sunday two Rats, even; but they said the stories were not interesting, which vexed the little Mice; and they, too, now began to think them not so very amusing either.

"Do you know only one story?" asked the Rats.

"Only that one," answered the Tree. "I heard it on my happiest evening; but I did not then know how happy I was."

"It is a very stupid story! Don't you know one about bacon and tallow candles? Can't you tell any larder-stories?"

"No," said the Tree.

"Then good-by," said the Rats; and they went home.

At last the little Mice stayed away also; and the Tree sighed: "After all, it was very pleasant when the sleek little Mice sat round me and listened to what I told them. Now that too is over. But I will take good care to enjoy myself when I am brought out again."

But when was that to be? Why, one morning there came a quantity of people and set to work in the loft. The trunks were moved, the tree was pulled out and thrown—rather hard, it is true—down on the floor, but a man drew him towards the stairs, where the daylight shone.

"Now a merry life will begin again," thought the Tree. He felt the fresh air, the first sunbeam, and now he was out in the court-yard. All passed so quickly, there was so much going on around him, that the Tree quite forgot to look to himself. The court adjoined a garden, and all was in flower; the roses hung so fresh and odorous over the balustrade, the lindens were in blossom, the Swallows flew by, and said, "Quirre-vit! my husband is come!" but it was not the Fir-tree that they meant.

"Now, then, I shall really enjoy life," said he, exultingly, and spread out his branches; but, alas! they were all withered and yellow. It was in a corner that he lay, among weeds and nettles. The golden star of tinsel was still on the top of the Tree, and glittered in the sunshine.

In the court-yard some of the merry children were playing who had danced at Christmas round the Fir-tree, and were so glad at the sight of him. One of the youngest ran and tore off the golden star.

"Only look what is still on the ugly old Christmas tree!" said he, trampling on the branches, so that they all cracked beneath his feet.

And the Tree beheld all the beauty of the flowers, and the freshness in the garden; he beheld himself, and wished he had remained in his dark corner in the loft: he thought of his first youth in the wood, of the merry Christmas Eve, and of the little Mice, who had listened with so much pleasure to the story of Klumpy-Dumpy.

" 'Tis over—'tis past!" said the poor Tree. "Had I but rejoiced when I had reason to do so! But now 'tis past, 'tis past!"

And the gardener's boy chopped the Tree into small pieces; there was a whole heap lying there. The wood flamed up splendidly under the large brewing copper, and it sighed so deeply! Each sigh was like a shot.

The boys played about in the court, and the youngest wore the gold star on his breast, which the Tree had had on the happiest evening of his life. However, that was over now—the Tree gone, the story at an end. All, all was over; every tale must end at last.

A Christmas Legend of Hamelin Town

CONINGSBY DAWSON

CHRISTMAS Eve in Hamelin Town—the first since the children had been stolen! Had you plodded through Hamelin's crooked streets, snow-carpeted as if by the drift of angels' feathers, you could still have espied faded posters offering gold to the Piper's heart's content if he would only restore the little people. You might even have met the town-crier going his rounds, stopping every few hundred yards to ring his bell and announce:

"O, yes! O, yes! Whereas a certain gipsy musician, who calls himself the Pied Piper and is famed for his skill in rat-catching, hath lured away our children, let it be known that for their return will be paid whatever ransom he demands, even to our last guilder. Proclaimed by order of the Mayor and Corporation."

He did not add, as would have been customary, "All's well on a frosty night. And merry Christmas to everybody!"

Nothing had been well since the children's sudden exodus, which had taken place in spring-time, when fruit-trees were a mist of blossom. Since then months of thwarted hope had elapsed. Every evening bereaved mothers had climbed to empty nurseries, promising themselves, "They will be here tomorrow." They had folded back coverings from cots, so that everything might wear an aspect of welcome. More than ever, this night, they missed the patter of tiny feet. From habit, and in an effort to deceive themselves, they had hung up little stockings. The Widow Swartz was the only mother who had performed the Christmas ritual knowing that her presents would give pleasure.

Her little boy, Carl, who hobbled on a crutch, was the sole survivor of the vanished children's army. He lived down a side-street near the river, in the humblest quarter of the town. His mother took in washing, which she scrubbed on the river bank. When there were banquets, she helped in kitchens of the wealthy. Before the catastrophe the citizens of Hamelin had spoken of Widow Swartz as a deserving case and had pitied her because her son, even if he grew to manhood, could never be of much support to her. Since the spring, as the only mother whose child had been spared, she had become an object of envy.

Of course, you remember how the catastrophe had occurred. Hamelin had been infested with rats, which had grown so bold that they had fought the dogs and killed the cats and bitten the babies in the cradles. The citizens had gone in a body to the Mayor, threatening to fling him out of office if he didn't find a remedy. The wretched man, who was immensely fat from over-indulgence at public dinners, was at his wits' end when, seemingly from nowhere, up had sprung a quaint fellow offering to destroy the pests for the sum of a thousand guilders. No sooner uttered than his bargain was accepted. Producing a pipe, he had blown three shrill notes. There had followed a grumbling, which had swelled to a mighty rumbling; out of houses and cellars the rats had come tumbling. Frisking over and round him, they had swarmed in a crowd. He had led them as far as the River Weser, where they had promptly drowned.

The miracle had been performed too easily. The Mayor had scoffed at the miracle-worker's claim to receive the bounty he had stipulated. In revenge the Pied Piper had played a second tune, more merry, more melodious. The Hamelin children, snatching their baby sisters and brothers, had come running. The same magic that had made them dance as round a May-pole, had held their elders speechless and rooted. Fathers and mothers had been compelled to watch their darlings dance away through the grave, old town to the Weser's banks, across the bridge and out into the blowy country, where they had completely vanished.

No one would ever have learned what had become of them, had it not been for Carl, the little lame boy. On his crutch he had striven to keep pace with the frolicking procession. Bertha, his playmate, and next-door neighbor, had tried to help him, as she had always done since the time when he had been too small to handle a crutch. As the music had swelled more maddeningly, she had capered ahead till her conscience had reproached her. She had danced ahead again when, all of a sudden, the green side of the Koppelberg Mountain had opened. Hobbling with all his might, Carl had shouted:

"Wait for me. Please wait for me."

All the children save himself had entered. Slowly, as though unwilling to shut him out, the mountain was closing. At the last moment Bertha had glanced across her shoulder and started back that she might drag him through in time. Too late. The mountain had rolled into place. He had found himself solitary, the music dwindling fainter; then no sound save a distant cuckoo calling.

As he was wandering home disconsolately, he had been met by the hue-and-cry: men riding cart-horses, laborers armed with scythes, women shaking broomsticks. Where was that thieving rogue, the Pied Piper? When Carl had told his story, no one had believed him. Who had ever heard of a mountain opening? The chief constable had cuffed him, advising him not to tell lies. The pursuers had pushed farther afield, leaving him to hobble wearily back to his mother. Even she had refused to credit him.

"You're not lying, Carl, I know that. You're imaginative. But please don't repeat it. It's hard enough to earn a living; you'll set folks against us."

Meanwhile couriers had ridden far and wide. Not until the first excitement had quieted did the Mayor and Corporation remember that the children's army had left a survivor. Having questioned him, they had armed the town-guard with picks and shovels and ordered the boy to guide them to the very spot where he had imagined he saw the gateway. For a week the guard had dug. However deeply they had penetrated, they had discovered nothing but stones and earth opposing them. So opinions had become divided regarding Carl's truthfulness. He might have mistaken the spot on the mountain. He might have been the victim of magic. In default of a better explanation, his elders had at last conceded that probably something such as he described had happened.

It seemed extraordinary to Carl how being the only child in Hamelin had increased his value. In former days people had speculated as to why he had been born lame—whether the sin had been his dead father's or his mother's. Now they acted quite differently—as though his lameness was a proof of virtue. They were outspoken in saying they wished their children had been lame. Had they been cripples, like Carl, they, too, would have lagged behind and been too late to enter the mountain.

Changed sentiment transformed his mother from a woman to be blamed into a mother to be venerated. She was the only mother who had a child. All the childless mothers came to visit her in her side-street, that they might bribe her to lend them Carl that they might fondle him. The Mayoress came. Wives of members of the Corporation came. The proudest and most disdainful beauties humbled themselves to court her. Carriages and men-servants thronged the side-street of Widow Swartz, as though her ramshackle cottage were a shrine and her lame boy a saint.

"What a cherub!" They tried to pick him up. "What an angel's face! He has fair hair like my little Wilhelm's."

When they mentioned Wilhelm, or Gretchen, or Hans, they wept unrestrainedly.

From a small person who had been less than nothing, Carl had bloomed into a celebrity. Gentlemen, prancing by on horses, dismounted to pat his head. The daintiest ladies delayed their steps to make a fuss over him.

But Carl wasn't happy. Streets were too empty. Grown-ups might show themselves kinder; he longed for the little people.

On this first Christmas Eve since the children had been stolen, the Widow Swartz sat cuddling Carl on her lap. Sparkling embers of a never-too-prosperous fire were dying. She had been recounting the Bethlehem story. The room was growing chilly.

"I'll have to be tucking you in bed," she whispered. "Father Christmas mustn't find us awake. If you could tell him the desire you covet most, what would you ask him?"

"I'm tired of playing alone, Motherkins. I want Bertha. I would ask that the children might come back."

Outside in the heavy snow they heard a crunching. The light from a passing lantern flashed. Was the traveler Santa Claus, the Pied Piper, or a robber?

Fears were laid to rest as his bell sounded, followed by the hoarse grumbling of his voice:

"O, yes! O, yes! Whereas a certain gipsy, famed for his skill in rat-catching, hath lured away our children . . . whatever ransom he demands. By order of the Mayor and Corporation."

"Do you think he will come, Mother?"

"Who?"

"Santa Claus."

"I haven't a doubt."

"I have." He dug his face into her bosom. "I have. He must have heard about Hamelin. He's too busy. Just for me, he won't trouble to drive his reindeer to our town."

"He will."

"I don't think so, Mother." Carl shook his curly head. "And I don't think something else. I don't think there'll be a Christmas tomorrow. This year there weren't any toys in the shops. All the toy-merchants have moved to places where there are children."

"The toy-trade's been bad," she admitted. "But that's the more reason why Santa Claus should remember you."

"Do you remember last year," the boy persisted, "the hundreds of Christmas trees that were lighted—one in every window? And the big one that the Mayor set up in front of the church, hung with thousands of candles?"

"How could I forget, darling?"

"I was wondering, Mother, whether Bertha and Gretchen and Hans have Christmas trees in that other land."

"But are you sure, Carl, that you did truly see that other land? Isn't it possible that you just imagined it?"

"I saw it, Mother." He reached up his arms, drawing her face down. "Haven't I shown you the very spot on the mountain where they entered?"

"Yes. But you said there was a gateway. There was nothing but grass. Even the grass will be covered with snow tonight."

"But, listen, Mother. Because it's Christmas, don't you think if we went and called to them, the children might hear us?"

She shook her head. "The fire's nearly out. We mustn't let Santa Claus surprise us."

"He won't surprise us, Mother. He won't come, unless—unless we manage to get the other children."

When Carl had said his prayers and was snuggled beneath his blankets, the Widow Swartz did not undress. She sat beside him, watching how as sleep claimed him his seriousness relaxed and his face dimpled into smiling. She could guess what he was dreaming, for he dreamed it every night. He was peering again through the gateway in the mountain, seeing a land where everything was diminutive and lovely, full of flowering woods and doll's-house huts. In his sleep he began to murmur. She pieced together the scene. He hadn't been too late. He had scurried through the gateway in the mountain just in time. He was with Bertha, preparing for Christmas, decorating with mistletoe and holly. Now they'd hung up their stockings and were snuggling in their beds, squeezing their eyes tightly that Santa Claus might arrive sooner. In that other land he had no doubts concerning Santa Claus; it was only here in Hamelin that his lonely heart grew skeptical.

But what if he didn't—if Santa Claus should fail to come? If he didn't through considering one child not worth his while, Carl would never again believe in Christmas. Something must be done to bring Santa Claus. What could an unprotected widow do at this late hour on a snow-bound night?

Rising softly, she crept to the leaded panes. Her own solitariness gaped back at her. What a different Christmas Eve! How deserted! Snow lay untrodden, save by feet of the town-crier. Windows stared blank and spectral. Yet over all, in the frosty sky, the Bethlehem star was shining.

She glanced across her shoulder at Carl. Did she dare desert him? If she were to go to Koppelberg Mountain and call, would the children hear her? Anything was worth trying. If she could persuade them to forsake their other land and accompany her, Santa Claus would be sure to visit Hamelin. Carl would have a real Christmas. As long as he lived, he would believe in Christmas. He would awake tomorrow to find gladness in the streets—children. It was the night of the infant Jesus. Faith could remove mountains.

Stealing a last look at her child, she crept down the creaking staircase. How cold it was outside! The night was bitter. Blank walls of houses, their eaves dripping icicles, seemed hostile to her errand. But far above, the bright eye of the Bethlehem star was cheerful.

Snow had drifted into banks. Past the Mayor's house she sped—the fat old Mayor who since the tragedy had become unpopular. No one spoke to him. No one attended his banquets. No one pitied him the loss of his three blond children.

"Serve him right," they said. "Our homes wouldn't be empty if he hadn't been too mean to pay the Piper."

The bridge across the Weser seemed built of glass. The Weser far below was solid.

Ahead loomed the Koppelberg Mountain. It looked so altered by shifting shadows that she doubted whether she could find the spot that Carl had indicated. There was a stream ran by it, she remembered, and a coppice to the right.

Several times she missed her direction. Her feet and hands were numb. Wind swept the ice-bound country with a brittle sigh.

"Children! Children!" She knelt, sobbing. "Come home. It's Christmas."

To her amazement, beneath the snow-blanketed surface, she heard the shout of joyous voices.

"Children! Children! It's Christmas."

The mountainside bulged. In the twinkling of an eye a gateway had formed. Peering through it, the Widow saw tiny huts in a diminutive woodland, precisely as Carl had described. In the window of each hut was a tree which glittered with candles. Pouring out came the children, small feet pattering, wooden shoes clattering, little hands clapping, little tongues chattering—all the noisy boys and girls, with rosy cheeks and flaxen curls, sparkling eyes and teeth like pearls. They weren't a day older and were dancing just as merrily as when they had so heedlessly followed the Piper.

"Christmas! Christmas!" they sang. "Look, Hans! Look, Gretchen! Hurray for Christmas! It's been snowing."

Bertha was first to notice the ill-clad woman who knelt as in prayer.

"Why, you're Widow Swartz! How kind of you to fetch us!"

The other sprites joined hands, forming a ring about her and chanting, "Did you hang up our stockings?"

Bertha divined the Widow's terror. Clasping her, she breathed into her face and eyes.

"We're not dead. If we were dead, I couldn't hug you."

"But, children," the Widow gasped, recovering her senses, "you'll catch cold. You're not dressed for Winter."

"We shan't. We never catch cold," they chorused.

"Oh, come," she implored, still dreading the Pied Piper. "Hurry home before your fathers and mothers waken."

"Home! Home!"

What a bedlam of shrill voices! Pell-mell they started like a pack of excited puppies. They remembered the road. The boys and girls with no baby brothers and sisters to carry went scampering down the mountainside scuffling the snow so that it rose in a silver cloud.

Skies were growing gray; stars were waning. At a bend the jutting roofs and old-world towers of Hamelin leaped to sight. Across the bridge, caked with ice, which spanned the Weser, the children pelted. By the time Widow Swartz caught up, they were rattling knockers on the doors of their homes. Windows were popping up; night-capped heads popping out. Of a sudden churchbells began to peal and chime. The air rocked with music.

Long before she had reached her cottage in the side-street every urchin had escaped her. What did that matter? She had brought them back. After days of mourning it was Christmas in Hamelin. As she entered Carl's room, he was sitting up.

"Santa Claus has been, Mother."

She caught him to her breast.

"A merry Christmas, darling."

"A merry Christmas, Mother!"

"Quickly—dress quickly. I've a most wonderful secret."

But at that moment Bertha burst in on them, rosy-cheeked and starry-eyed.

"Carl, you ought to have been with us. I tried to drag you through the gateway."

They were locked in each other's arms.

So many questions to be asked.

"Was he kind to you?"

"Who?"

"The Pied Piper?"

"We never saw him after the door had closed behind us."

"But what did you do? Tell me. Every night I've dreamed of you."

"Played. But don't waste time, Carl. What have you found in your stocking?"

Once more streets were full of laughing sprites, sliding, romping. Enmities were forgotten. Even the Mayor was forgiven. He spent most of the morning with anybody's children in the public square, building a snowman.

Carl, wandering with Bertha, was happy and unnoticed. The pretty ladies passed him, driving in their sleighs. Why should they notice him? Seated beside them, wrapped in furs, they had their own recovered darlings. As twilight fell, windows glowed with candles. From attics and cellars last-year's toys had been raked out.

"You do believe in Christmas?" Widow Swartz urged her son.

For the thousandth time he assured her.

"But how did it happen, Mummy?"

"I called to them, and the side of the mountain opened."

"They were waiting to be called." The little boy nodded.

"Waiting! Yes, they seemed to be. I expect they were."

Later she asked him,

"Do you mind not being so important?"

"How do you mean, not so important, Mummy?"

"Not having everybody stop to speak to you, the way they did when you were the only child."

"Why should I? I have Bertha."

What happiness! Fires in nurseries. Gossiping voices. Then the bed-hour. Little people in long nightgowns, praying against their mothers. Soft faces cushioned on white pillows.

"God bless you, darling."

"And you, Mummy."

Tiptoeings down the stairs. No one asked how the children had returned. The Pied Piper seemed an evil better not mentioned. And yet how often the parents stole back to those nurseries! First the father peered in, then the mother.

"Still sleeping," he whispered.

And she, "Still sleeping."

It was a miracle incredible that they should ever have left them.

"Why did they? They seem as fond of us as ever."

"Fonder."

"Tomorrow, when they're more used to us, we'll ask them."

But in the morning the alarm spread from house to house.

"Where's Gretchen? Where's Hans? Where's Wilhelm?"

In every nursery it was the same. Bedclothes were tossed back. Dents made by little heads were still fresh on the pillows. At an unguarded hour between midnight and dawning the mountain must have called; the children had vanished—all except the lame boy whom the mountain had rejected.

So in Hamelin the three hundred and sixty-four days, which stretched like a wilderness between Christmas and Christmas, scarcely counted. Its citizens lived for the sacred eve when, with the hanging up of stockings, if a mother went alone to the Koppelberg Mountain, the child spirits would return. Year in, year out, the miracle continued, till another crop of children were born and themselves became parents.

When Carl himself grew up, he became a toy-merchant, married, and became a father. The finest doll he manufactured in any year he always reserved for Bertha.

"But why for Bertha?" His wife would protest.

"She was kind to me when I was helpless."

It was strange with what eagerness, each Christmas, he would wait for her. She was never a day older—a flaxen little girl who treated him like a child.

One Christmas he waited in vain. He was Mayor of Hamelin by then and nearly eighty. His grandchildren, clambering up his knees, strove to console him.

"What does Bertha matter, Grandpa? Who wants the other children? You have us."

Struggling from his chair, he summoned the Town Council. Its members assembled glumly. Things had reached a pretty pass, they said, when fathers of families couldn't stay in their homes on a holiday. Enquiring the reason for the absence of the other children, the old Mayor was informed that the last of the mothers whom the Pied Piper had robbed had died. As a consequence there had been no mother sufficiently interested to visit the mountain to call the lost children. They were too much occupied decorating trees and hanging mistletoe for living children. As a parting thrust the Council hinted that the Mayor was too hide-bound by tradition. If he reverenced the future instead of the past, Hamelin's trade-conditions might show improvement.

Next Christmas Eve, when his household was sleeping, old Carl let himself into the night. As his mother had done before him, he set out hobbling on his crutch in search of the Koppelberg Mountain. He never reached it. Where the road leaves the bridge for Koppelberg and the open country, he was found next morning sprawled in the snow, with the loveliest doll he had ever fashioned beside him.

They gave the doll to his youngest granddaughter. Hamelin would miss him, but he had grown too childish to cope with the modern rush. After that the story of the Pied Piper and the old sadness, as so often happens with past griefs, became a legend.

But because of Carl, the lame boy, and his mother, the world has learned to believe that little children are never really lost—nor, for that matter, any one who has been loved by some one who remembers. On Christmas Eve they come back, even though we may not see them. They come hoping and expecting to find their stockings hanging beside the familiar fireplace. If they find them, they know that they still are wanted—that they're kept alive by living people's loving. Which is probably the reason we hang up stockings and dream of Bethlehem; for as long as we have faith, nothing ever dies.

The Legend of the Christmas Rose

SELMA LAGERLÖF

ROBBER MOTHER, who lived in Robbers' Cave up in Göinge Forest, went down to the village one day on a begging tour. Robber Father, who was an outlawed man, did not dare to leave the forest, but had to content himself with lying in wait for the wayfarers who ventured within its borders. But at that time travellers were not very plentiful in Southern Skåne. If it so happened that the man had had a few weeks of ill luck with his hunt, his wife would take to the road. She took with her five youngsters, and each youngster wore a ragged leathern suit and birch-bark shoes and bore a sack on his back as long as himself. When Robber Mother stepped inside the door of a cabin, no one dared refuse to give her whatever she demanded; for she was not above coming back the following night and setting fire to the house if she had not been well received. Robber Mother and her brood were worse than a pack of wolves, and many a man felt like running a spear through them; but it was never done, because they all knew that the man stayed up in the forest, and he would have known how to wreak vengeance if anything had happened to the children or the old woman.

Now that Robber Mother went from house to house and begged, she came one day to Övid, which at that time was a cloister. She rang the bell of the cloister gate and asked for food. The watchman let down a small wicket in the gate and handed her six round bread cakes—one for herself and one for each of the five children.

While the mother was standing quietly at the gate, her youngsters were running about. And now one of them came and pulled at her skirt, as a signal that he had discovered something which she ought to come and see, and Robber Mother followed him promptly.

The entire cloister was surrounded by a high and strong wall, but the youngster had managed to find a little back gate which stood ajar. When Robber Mother got there, she pushed the gate open and walked inside without asking leave, as it was her custom to do.

Övid Cloister was managed at that time by Abbot Hans, who knew all about herbs. Just within the cloister wall he had planted a little herb garden, and it was into this that the old woman had forced her way.

At first glance Robber Mother was so astonished that she paused at the gate. It was high summertide, and Abbot Hans' garden was so full of flowers that the eyes were fairly dazzled by the blues, reds, and yellows, as one looked into it. But presently an indulgent smile spread over her features, and she started to walk up a narrow path that lay between many flower-beds.

In the garden a lay brother walked about, pulling up weeds. It was he who had left the door in the wall open, that he might throw the weeds and tares on the rubbish heap outside.

When he saw Robber Mother coming in, with all five youngsters in tow, he ran toward her at once and ordered them away. But the beggar woman walked right on as before. She cast her eyes up and down, looking now at the stiff white lilies which spread near the ground, then on the ivy climbing high upon the cloister wall, and took no notice whatever of the lay brother.

He thought she had not understood him, and wanted to take her by the arm and turn her toward the gate. But when the robber woman saw his purpose, she gave him a look that sent him reeling backward. She had been walking with back bent under her beggar's pack, but now she straightened herself to her full height.

"I am Robber Mother from Göinge Forest; so touch me if you dare!" And it was obvious that she was as certain she would be left in peace as if she had announced that she was the Queen of Denmark.

And yet the lay brother dared to oppose her, although now, when he knew who she was, he spoke reasonably to her. "You must know, Robber Mother, that this is a monks' cloister, and no woman in the land is allowed within these walls. If you do not go away, the monks will be angry with me because I forgot to close the gate, and perhaps they will drive me away from the cloister and the herb garden."

But such prayers were wasted on Robber Mother. She walked straight ahead among the little flower-beds and looked at the hyssop with its magenta blossoms, and at the honeysuckles, which were full of deep orange-colored flower clusters.

Then the lay brother knew of no other remedy than to run into the cloister and call for help.

He returned with two stalwart monks, and Robber Mother saw that now it meant business! With feet firmly planted she stood in the path and began shrieking in strident tones all the awful vengeance she would wreak on the cloister if she couldn't remain in the herb garden as long as she wished. But the monks did not see why they need fear her and thought only of driving her out. Then Robber Mother let out a perfect volley of shrieks, and, throwing herself upon the monks, clawed and bit at them; so did all the youngsters. The men soon learned that she could overpower them, and all they could do was to go back into the cloister for reinforcements.

As they ran through the passage-way which led to the cloister, they met Abbot Hans, who came rushing out to learn what all this noise was about.

Then they had to confess that Robber Mother from Göinge Forest had come into the cloister and that they were unable to drive her out and must call for assistance.

But Abbot Hans upbraided them for using force and forbade their calling for help. He sent both monks back to their work, and although he was an old and fragile man, he took with him only the lay brother.

When Abbot Hans came out in the garden, Robber Mother was still wandering among the flower-beds. He regarded her with astonishment. He was certain that Robber Mother had never before seen an herb garden; yet she sauntered leisurely between all the small patches, each of which had been planted with its own species of rare flower, and looked at them as if they were old acquaintances. At some she smiled, at others she shook her head.

Abbot Hans loved his herb garden as much as it was possible for him to love anything earthly and perishable. Wild and terrible as the old woman looked, he couldn't help liking that she had fought with three monks for the privilege of viewing the garden in peace. He came up to her and asked in a mild tone if the garden pleased her.

Robber Mother turned defiantly toward Abbot Hans, for she expected only to be trapped and overpowered. But when she noticed his white hair and bent form, she answered peaceably, "First, when I saw this, I thought I had never seen a prettier garden; but now I see that it can't be compared with one I know of."

Abbot Hans had certainly expected a different answer. When he heard that Robber Mother had seen a garden more beautiful than his, a faint flush spread over his withered cheek. The lay brother, who was standing close by, immediately began to censure the old woman. "This is Abbot Hans," said he, "who with much care and diligence has gathered the flowers from far and near for his herb garden. We all know that there is not a more beautiful garden to be found in all Skåne, and it is not befitting that you, who live in the wild forest all the year around, should find fault with his work."

"I don't wish to make myself the judge of either him or you," said Robber Mother. "I'm only saying that if you could see the garden of which I am thinking you would uproot all the flowers planted here and cast them away like weeds."

But the Abbot's assistant was hardly less proud of the flowers than the Abbot himself, and after hearing her remarks he laughed derisively. "I can understand that you only talk like this to tease us. It must be a pretty garden that you have made for yourself amongst the pines in Göinge Forest! I'd be willing to wager my soul's salvation that you have never before been within the walls of an herb garden."

Robber Mother grew crimson with rage to think that her word was doubted, and she cried out: "It may be true that until today I had never been within the walls of an herb garden; but you monks, who are holy men, certainly must know that on every Christmas Eve the great Göinge Forest is transformed into a beautiful garden, to commemorate the hour of our Lord's birth. We who live in the forest have seen this happen every year. And in that garden I have seen flowers so lovely that I dared not lift my hand to pluck them."

The lay brother wanted to continue the argument, but Abbot Hans gave him a sign to be silent. For, ever since his childhood, Abbot Hans had heard it said that on every Christmas Eve the forest was dressed in holiday glory. He had often longed to see it, but he had never had the good fortune. Eagerly he begged and implored Robber Mother that he might come up to the Robbers' Cave on Christmas Eve. If she would only send one of her children to show him the way, he could ride up there alone, and he would never betray them—on the contrary, he would reward them, in so far as it lay in his power.

Robber Mother said no at first, for she was thinking of Robber Father and of the peril which might befall him should she permit Abbot Hans to ride up to their cave. At the same time the desire to prove to the monk that the garden which she knew was more beautiful than his got the better of her, and she gave in.

"But more than one follower you cannot take with you," said she, "and you are not to waylay us or trap us, as sure as you are a holy man."

This Abbot Hans promised, and then Robber Mother went her way. Abbot Hans commanded the lay brother not to reveal to a soul that which had been agreed upon. He feared that the monks, should they learn of his purpose, would not allow a man of his years to go up to the Robbers' Cave.

Nor did he himself intend to reveal his project to a human being.

And then it happened that Archbishop Absalon from Lund came to Övid and remained through the night. When Abbot Hans was showing him the herb garden, he got to thinking of Robber Mother's visit, and the lay brother, who was at work in the garden, heard Abbot Hans telling the Bishop about Robber Father, who these many years had lived as an outlaw in the forest, and asking him for a letter of ransom for the man, that he might lead an honest life among respectable folk. "As things are now," said Abbot Hans, "his children are growing up into worse malefactors than himself, and you will soon have a whole gang of robbers to deal with up there in the forest."

But the Archbishop replied that he did not care to let the robber loose among honest folk in the villages. It would be best for all that he remain in the forest.

Then Abbot Hans grew zealous and told the Bishop all about Göinge Forest, which, every year at Yuletide, clothed itself in summer bloom around the Robbers' Cave. "If these bandits are not so bad but that God's glories can be made manifest to them, surely we cannot be too wicked to experience the same blessing."

The Archbishop knew how to answer Abbot Hans. "This much I will promise you, Abbot Hans," he said, smiling, "that any day you send me a blossom from the garden in Göinge Forest, I will give you letters of ransom for all the outlaws you may choose to plead for."

The lay brother apprehended that Bishop Absalon believed as little in this story of Robber Mother's as he himself; but Abbot Hans perceived nothing of the sort, but thanked Absalon for his good promise and said that he would surely send him the flower.

Abbot Hans had his way. And the following Christmas Eve he did not sit at home with his monks in Övid Cloister, but was on his way to Göinge Forest. One of Robber Mother's wild youngsters ran ahead of him, and close behind him was the lay brother who had talked with Robber Mother in the herb garden.

Abbot Hans had been longing to make this journey, and he was very happy now that it had come to pass. But it was a different matter with the lay brother who accompanied him. Abbot Hans was very dear to him, and he would not willingly have allowed another to attend him and watch over him; but he didn't believe that he should see any Christmas Eve garden. He thought the whole thing a snare which Robber Mother had, with great cunning, laid for Abbot Hans, that he might fall into her husband's clutches.

While Abbot Hans was riding toward the forest, he saw that everywhere they were preparing to celebrate Christmas. In every peasant settlement fires were lighted in the bath-house to warm it for the afternoon bathing. Great hunks of meat and bread were being carried from the larders into the cabins, and from the barns came men with big sheaves of straw to be strewn over the floors.

As he rode by the little country churches, he observed that each parson, with his sexton, was busily engaged in decorating his church; and when he came to the road which leads to Bösjo Cloister, he observed that all the poor of the parish were coming with armfuls of bread and long candles, which they had received at the cloister gate.

When Abbot Hans saw all these Christmas preparations, his haste increased. He was thinking of the festivities that awaited him, which were greater than any the others would be privileged to enjoy.

But the lay brother whined and fretted when he saw how they were preparing to celebrate Christmas in every humble cottage. He grew more and more anxious, and begged and implored Abbot Hans to turn back and not to throw himself deliberately into the robber's hands.

Abbot Hans went straight ahead, paying no heed to his lamentations. He left the plain behind him and came up into desolate and wild forest regions. Here the road was bad, almost like a stony and burr-strewn path, with neither bridge nor plank to help them over brooklet and rivulet. The farther they rode, the colder it grew, and after a while they came upon snow-covered ground.

It turned out to be a long and hazardous ride through the forest. They climbed steep and slippery side paths, crawled over swamp and marsh, and pushed through windfall and bramble. Just as daylight was waning, the robber boy guided them across a forest meadow, skirted by tall, naked leaf trees and green fir trees. Back of the meadow loomed a mountain wall, and in this wall they saw a door of thick boards. Now Abbot Hans understood that they had arrived, and dismounted. The child opened the heavy door for him, and he looked into a poor mountain grotto, with bare stone walls. Robber Mother was seated before a log fire that burned in the middle of the floor. Alongside the walls were beds of virgin pine and moss, and on one of these beds lay Robber Father asleep.

"Come in, you out there!" shouted Robber Mother without rising, "and fetch the horses in with you, so they won't be destroyed by the night cold."

Abbot Hans walked boldly into the cave, and the lay brother followed. Here were wretchedness and poverty! and nothing was done to celebrate Christmas. Robber Mother had neither brewed nor baked; she had neither washed nor scoured. The youngsters were lying on the floor around a kettle, eating; but no better food was provided for them than a watery gruel.

Robber Mother spoke in a tone as haughty and dictatorial as any well-to-do peasant woman. "Sit down by the fire and warm yourself, Abbot Hans," said she; "and if you have food with you, eat, for the food which we in the forest prepare you wouldn't care to taste. And if you are tired after the long journey, you can lie down on one of these beds to sleep. You needn't be afraid of oversleeping, for I'm sitting here by the fire keeping watch. I shall awaken you in time to see that which you have come up here to see."

Abbot Hans obeyed Robber Mother and brought forth his food sack; but he was so fatigued after the journey he was hardly able to eat, and as soon as he could stretch himself on the bed, he fell asleep.

The lay brother was also assigned a bed to rest upon, but he didn't dare sleep, as he thought he had better keep his eye on Robber Father to prevent his getting up and capturing Abbot Hans. But gradually fatigue got the better of him, too, and he dropped into a doze.

When he woke up, he saw that Abbot Hans had left his bed and was sitting by the fire talking with Robber Mother. The outlawed robber sat also by the fire. He was a tall, raw-boned man with a dull, sluggish appearance. His back was turned to Abbot Hans, as though he would have it appear that he was not listening to the conversation.

Abbot Hans was telling Robber Mother all about the Christmas preparations he had seen on the journey, reminding her of Christmas feasts and games which she must have known in her youth, when she lived at peace with mankind. "I'm sorry for your children, who can never run on the village street in holiday dress or tumble in the Christmas straw," said he.

At first Robber Mother answered in short, gruff sentences, but by degrees she became more subdued and listened more intently. Suddenly Robber Father turned toward Abbot Hans and shook his clenched fist in his face. "You miserable monk! did you come here to coax from me my wife and children? Don't you know that I am an outlaw and may not leave the forest?"

Abbot Hans looked him fearlessly in the eyes. "It is my purpose to get a letter of ransom for you from Archbishop Absalon," said he. He had hardly finished speaking when the robber and his wife burst out laughing. They knew well enough the kind of mercy a forest robber could expect from Bishop Absalon!

"Oh, if I get a letter of ransom from Absalon," said Robber Father, "then I'll promise you that never again will I steal so much as a goose."

The lay brother was annoyed with the robber folk for daring to laugh at Abbot Hans, but on his own account he was well pleased. He had seldom seen the Abbot sitting more peaceful and meek with his monks at Övid than he now sat with this wild robber folk.

Suddenly Robber Mother rose. "You sit here and talk, Abbot Hans," she said, "so that we are forgetting to look at the forest. Now I can hear, even in this cave, how the Christmas bells are ringing."

The words were barely uttered when they all sprang up and

rushed out. But in the forest it was still dark night and bleak winter. The only thing they marked was a distant clang borne on a light south wind.

"How can this bell ringing ever awaken the dead forest?" thought Abbot Hans. For now, as he stood out in the winter darkness, he thought it far more impossible that a summer garden could spring up here than it had seemed to him before.

When the bells had been ringing a few minutes, a sudden illumination penetrated the forest; the next moment it was dark again, and then the light came back. It pushed its way forward between the stark trees, like a shimmering mist. This much it effected: The darkness merged into a faint daybreak. Then Abbot Hans saw that the snow had vanished from the ground, as if some one had removed a carpet, and the earth began to take on a green covering. Then the ferns shot up their fronds, rolled like a bishop's staff. The heather that grew on the stony hills and the bog-myrtle rooted in the ground moss dressed themselves quickly in new bloom. The moss-tufts thickened and raised themselves, and the spring blossoms shot upward their swelling buds, which already had a touch of color.

Abbot Hans' heart beat fast as he marked the first signs of the forest's awakening. "Old man that I am, shall I behold such a miracle?" thought he, and the tears wanted to spring to his eyes. Again it grew so hazy that he feared the darkness would once more cover the earth; but almost immediately there came a new wave of light. It brought with it the splash of rivulet and the rush of cataract. Then the leaves of the trees burst into bloom, as if a swarm of green butterflies came flying and clustered on the branches. It was not only trees and plants that awoke, but cross-beaks hopped from branch to branch, and the woodpeckers hammered on the limbs until the splinters fairly flew around them. A flock of starlings from up country lighted in a fir top to rest. They were paradise starlings. The tips of each tiny feather shone in brilliant reds, and, as the birds moved they glittered like so many jewels.

Again, all was dark for an instant, but soon there came a new light wave. A fresh, warm south wind blew and scattered over the forest meadow all the little seeds that had been brought here from southern lands by birds and ships and winds, and which could not thrive elsewhere because of this country's cruel cold. These took root and sprang up the instant they touched the ground.

When the next warm wind came along, the blueberries and lignon ripened. Cranes and wild geese shrieked in the air, the bullfinches built nests, and the baby squirrels began playing on the branches of the trees.

Everything came so fast now that Abbot Hans could not stop to reflect on how immeasurably great was the miracle that was taking place. He had time only to use his eyes and ears. The next light wave that came rushing in brought with it the scent of newly ploughed acres, and far off in the distance the milkmaids were heard coaxing the cows—and the tinkle of the sheep's bells. Pine and spruce trees were so thickly clothed with red cones that they shone like crimson mantles. The juniper berries changed color every second, and forest flowers covered the ground till it was all red, blue, and yellow.

Abbot Hans bent down to the earth and broke off a wild strawberry blossom, and, as he straightened up, the berry ripened in his hand.

The mother fox came out of her lair with a big litter of black-legged young. She went up to Robber Mother and scratched at her skirt, and Robber Mother bent down to her and praised her young. The horned owl, who had just begun his night chase, was astonished at the light and went back to his ravine to perch for the night. The male cuckoo crowed, and his mate stole up to the nests of the little birds with her egg in her mouth.

Robber Mother's youngsters let out perfect shrieks of delight. They stuffed themselves with wild strawberries that hung on the bushes, large as pine cones. One of them played with a litter of young hares; another ran a race with some young crows, which had hopped from their nest before they were really ready; a third caught up an adder from the ground and wound it around his neck and arm.

Robber Father was standing out on a marsh eating raspberries.

When he glanced up, a big black bear stood beside him. Robber Father broke off an osier twig and struck the bear on the nose. "Keep to your own ground, you!" he said; "this is my turf." Then the huge bear turned around and lumbered off in another direction.

New waves of warmth and light kept coming, and now they brought with them seeds from the star-flower. Golden pollen from rye fields fairly flew in the air. Then came butterflies, so big that they looked like flying lilies. The bee-hive in a hollow oak was already so full of honey that it dripped down on the trunk of the tree. Then all the flowers whose seeds had been brought from foreign lands began to blossom. The loveliest roses climbed up the mountain wall in a race with the blackberry vines, and from the forest meadow sprang flowers as large as human faces.

Abbot Hans thought of the flower he was to pluck for Bishop Absalon; but each new flower that appeared was more beautiful than the others, and he wanted to choose the most beautiful of all.

Wave upon wave kept coming until the air was so filled with light that it glittered. All the life and beauty and joy of summer smiled on Abbot Hans. He felt that earth could bring no greater happiness than that which welled up about him, and he said to himself, "I do not know what new beauties the next wave that comes can bring with it."

But the light kept streaming in, and now it seemed to Abbot Hans that it carried with it something from an infinite distance. He felt a celestial atmosphere enfolding him, and tremblingly he began to anticipate, now that earth's joys had come, the glories of heaven were approaching.

Then Abbot Hans marked how all grew still; the birds hushed their songs, the flowers ceased growing, and the young foxes played no more. The glory now nearing was such that the heart wanted to stop beating; the eyes wept without one's knowing it; the soul longed to soar away into the Eternal. From far in the distance faint harp tones were heard, and celestial song, like a soft murmur, reached him.

Abbot Hans clasped his hands and dropped to his knees. His face was radiant with bliss. Never had he dreamed that even in this life it should be granted him to taste the joys of heaven, and to hear angels sing Christmas carols!

But beside Abbot Hans stood the lay brother who had accompanied him. In his mind there were dark thoughts. "This cannot be a true miracle," he thought, "since it is revealed to malefactors. This does not come from God, but has its origin in witchcraft and is sent hither by Satan. It is the Evil One's power that is tempting us and compelling us to see that which has no real existence."

From afar were heard the sound of angel harps and the tones of a Miserere. But the lay brother thought it was the evil spirits of hell coming closer. "They would enchant and seduce us," sighed he, "and we shall be sold into perdition."

The angel throng was so near now that Abbot Hans saw their bright forms through the forest branches. The lay brother saw them too; but back of all this wondrous beauty he saw only some dread evil. For him it was the devil who performed these wonders on the anniversary of our Saviour's birth. It was done simply for the purpose of more effectually deluding poor human beings.

All the while the birds had been circling around the head of Abbot Hans, and they let him take them in his hands. But all the animals were afraid of the lay brother; no bird perched on his shoulder, no snake played at his feet. Then there came a little forest dove. When she marked that the angels were nearing, she plucked up courage and flew down on the lay brother's shoulder and laid her head against his cheek.

Then it appeared to him as if sorcery were come right upon him, to tempt and corrupt him. He struck with his hand at the forest dove and cried in such a loud voice that it rang throughout the forest, "Go thou back to hell, whence thou art come!"

Just then the angels were so near that Abbot Hans felt the feathery touch of their great wings, and he bowed down to earth in reverent greeting.

But when the lay brother's words sounded, their song was hushed and the holy guests turned in flight. At the same time the light and the mild warmth vanished in unspeakable terror for the darkness and cold in a human heart. Darkness sank over the earth, like a coverlet; frost came, all the growths shrivelled up; the animals and birds hastened away; the rushing of streams was hushed; the leaves dropped from the trees, rustling like rain.

Abbot Hans felt how his heart, which had but lately swelled with bliss, was now contracting with insufferable agony. "I can never outlive this," thought he, "that the angels from heaven had been so close to me and were driven away; that they wanted to sing Christmas carols for me and were driven to flight."

Then he remembered the flower he had promised Bishop Absalon, and at the last moment he fumbled among the leaves and moss to try and find a blossom. But he sensed how the ground under his fingers froze and how the white snow came gliding over the ground. Then his heart caused him ever greater anguish. He could not rise, but fell prostrate on the ground and lay there.

When the robber folk and the lay brother had groped their way back to the cave, they missed Abbot Hans. They took brands with them and went out to search for him. They found him dead upon the coverlet of snow.

Then the lay brother began weeping and lamenting, for he understood that it was he who had killed Abbot Hans because he had dashed from him the cup of happiness which he had been thirsting to drain to its last drop.

When Abbot Hans had been carried down to Övid, those who took charge of the dead saw that he held his right hand locked tight around something which he must have grasped at the moment of death. When they finally got his hand open, they found that the thing which he had held in such an iron grip was a pair of white root bulbs, which he had torn from among the moss and leaves.

When the lay brother who had accompanied Abbot Hans saw the bulbs, he took them and planted them in Abbot Hans' herb garden.

He guarded them the whole year to see if any flower would spring from them. But in vain he waited through the spring, the summer, and the autumn. Finally, when winter had set in and all the leaves and the flowers were dead, he ceased caring for them.

But when Christmas Eve came again, he was so strongly reminded of Abbot Hans that he wandered out into the garden to think of him. And look! as he came to the spot where he had planted the bare root bulbs, he saw that from them had sprung flourishing green stalks, which bore beautiful flowers with silver white leaves.

He called out all the monks at Övid, and when they saw that this plant bloomed on Christmas Eve, when all the other growths were as if dead, they understood that this flower had in truth been plucked by Abbot Hans from the Christmas garden in Göinge Forest. Then the lay brother asked the monks if he might take a few blossoms to Bishop Absalon.

And when he appeared before Bishop Absalon, he gave him the flowers and said: "Abbot Hans sends you these. They are the flowers he promised to pick for you from the garden in Göinge Forest."

When Bishop Absalon beheld the flowers, which had sprung from the earth in darkest winter, and heard the words, he turned as pale as if he had met a ghost. He sat in silence a moment; thereupon he said, "Abbot Hans has faithfully kept his word and I shall also keep mine." And he ordered that a letter of ransom be drawn up for the wild robber who was outlawed and had been forced to live in the forest ever since his youth.

He handed the letter to the lay brother, who departed at once for the Robbers' Cave. When he stepped in there on Christmas Day, the robber came toward him with axe uplifted. "I'd like to hack you monks into bits, as many as you are!" said he. "It must be your fault that Göinge Forest did not last night dress itself in Christmas bloom."

"The fault is mine alone," said the lay brother, "and I will gladly die for it; but first I must deliver a message from Abbot Hans." And he drew forth the Bishop's letter and told the man that he was free. "Hereafter you and your children shall play in the Christmas straw and celebrate your Christmas among people, just as Abbot Hans wished to have it," said he.

Then Robber Father stood there pale and speechless, but Robber Mother said in his name, "Abbot Hans has indeed kept his word, and Robber Father will keep his."

When the robber and his wife left the cave, the lay brother moved in and lived all alone in the forest, in constant meditation and prayer that his hardheartedness might be forgiven him.

But Göinge Forest never again celebrated the hour of our Saviour's birth; and of all its glory, there lives to-day only the plant which Abbot Hans had plucked. It has been named CHRISTMAS ROSE. And each year at Christmastide she sends forth from the earth her green stalks and white blossoms, as if she never could forget that she had once grown in the great Christmas garden at Göinge Forest.

Twinkle

HAROLD LEONARD BOWMAN

Twinkle was a mischievous little angel who loved to play in the streets of Heaven. There were many happy cherubs there, but Twinkle had a bubbling boyishness, which made him popular with his friends. There was a glint of playfulness in his eyes which won him his name. He was known occasionally to play tricks that disturbed some of the older and more sedate angels. Sometimes at a serious moment he would lift his eyes and wink at some sober, elderly angel who, in spite of himself, could not help smiling back at the little fellow with his downy wings. Twinkle had a lovely little silver halo which he usually wore tilted a bit to one side—as no proper angel should.

One day word went around Heaven that a great event was to occur on a distant star called "the earth" and that a company of angels was going on a journey to celebrate this important occasion. Twinkle did not understand what it was all about, but when a crowd gathered he was always there. So now Twinkle tagged along.

The angels flew rapidly to the earth and delivered their message, announcing the birth of a child who was to be a Saviour, a Lord of Good-will, a Prince of Peace. As the angelic chorus sang, little Twinkle fluttered about on the edge of the cherubic host.

Their mission performed, the angels started back to Heaven. But Twinkle was a curious little fellow and he wanted to see what this was about which the angels were so excited. So he decided to find out. Instead of returning with his friends, he settled down to the dark hillside and, keeping well in the shadows, he followed the shepherds who were going to investigate the news the angels had brought.

Twinkle saw the shepherds go into a near-by town and then into a stable. A little frightened by these dark and unfamiliar surroundings, Twinkle kept out of sight until the shepherds emerged and returned to their flocks on the hillsides.

Then very quietly Twinkle tiptoed over to the door of the stable, gently pushed it open and stepped inside without a sound. At first he was puzzled. What was so wonderful about this? Just a woman holding something in her arms. She looked up and saw this chubby little angel standing there. Partly through embarrassment and partly because he was the kind of angel he was, Twinkle winked at the woman. She smiled—a gracious, gentle smile it was, that encouraged him; so he came closer and then he saw the little baby in her arms—the most beautiful little babe that Twinkle had ever seen, so helpless but so dear. So this was to be a Saviour; this infant was one whose advent Heaven was celebrating. The twinkle in the little angel's eyes brightened. He reached up to his silver halo—it was tilted on the side, as usual—and took it off and, reaching it out, placed it on the head of the babe. Again the child's mother smiled, in gratitude. She reached out her hand to touch Twinkle, but he, startled by his daring, turned and fled into the night.

He was out of breath and his wings were worn when he finally reached the gates of Heaven.

Hearing his clamor for admission, St. Peter opened the portal and greeted him with a stern reproof. "Twinkle, where have you been? And what have you done with your halo? Have you got into trouble again?" Twinkle slipped in without answering. But the story soon spread and everyone wondered how Twinkle had lost his lovely silver halo. Such misbehavior as this must be brought to the attention of the good Father who ruled in Heaven. So when all the celestial company was gathered about the great white throne, little Twinkle came and stood alone amid the reproachful looks of the other angels.

"Father," he said, "forgive me for losing my halo. I gave it to the little babe in the manger in Bethlehem." A murmur of disapproval swept through the host of angels—that one of their number should think so little of his halo as to give it away.

But the Father looked at Twinkle and smiled. "You have done well," he said. And then the angels who were watching Twinkle were amazed to see shining above his face a new halo, brighter than the other, for this one was of purest gold. Twinkle felt it on his head; he reached up to touch it with his hand, to make sure it was real; it was. He gave it a slight tilt to one side—for that was the jaunty sort of angel Twinkle was.

Mrs. Barber's Christmas

MARTIN ARMSTRONG

OLD MRS. BARBER sat alone in her wooden chair whose arms, gripped by the hands of three generations of grandmothers and grandfathers, were smoothed and worn till they looked like polished bones. The blinds were drawn, the lamp lighted, and a merry fire crackled in the grate where the kettle was just beginning to sing. At first its songs were far-off and sad—thin ghosts of songs forgotten, but soon they settled to a warm homeliness like the comfortable purred song of a cat. And the two together—the sadness and the homeliness—soothed old Mrs. Barber till she really felt quite well again. That uncomfortable, dazed feeling in her head had gone and she settled down into a blurred, peaceful mood in which, like a spool unwinding itself, her mind effortlessly reproduced the doings of the day. Yes, on the whole she had enjoyed herself, and anyhow she was glad she had gone: Lizzy would have been hurt if she had not turned up for dinner on Christmas Day. Four miles each way was a long walk but—well—she was glad she had gone, even though the walk back had almost been the death of her. Yes indeed, and if it hadn't been for Mr. Robson, the Lord knows what would have become of her. Directly she left Lizzy's to walk home again, she had felt it was going to be too much for her, and by the time she had done two miles she was feeling really bad. What a mercy that Mr. Robson in the cart had overtaken her and given her a lift for the rest of the way. And even

From *The Bazaar and Other Stories,* by Martin Armstrong, by permission of Jonathan Cape, Limited, publishers.

then how ill she had felt: at one moment she really believed she was going to die in the cart, and when they stopped at her cottage Mr. Robson had to lift her down just as if she were a child again. Then she couldn't find her key, in fact she was feeling too ill to bother about it. All she wanted was to lie down, and if Mr. Robson had not held her up she actually would have lain down—just where she was, in the road. "Let me lie down. Let me lie down," she had whispered, and it was only after Mr. Robson had pretended to be angry with her that she had managed to pull herself together enough to remember where she had put the key. Then Mr. Robson had propped her against her door and forbidden her to lie down while he fastened his horse's reins to the railings, and after that he had unlocked her door and put her into her chair, and not only that but he had even made a fire for her and filled the kettle. Yes, he was a good fellow, was Robson, to bother so much about an old woman.

Once in her chair, she felt all right, she said, and so he had left her, promising to send his girl in an hour or two to see if she wanted anything.

And now she really did feel all right. The warmth of the fire seemed to be going right through her as though she were a pane of glass. It was grand. Mr. Robson certainly knew how to make a fire. . . . Yes, he was a good fellow, was Robson, to bother so much about an old woman. Sometimes a little shiver ran down her spine and the fire went blurred for a moment and seemed to recede from her, but that was rather nice, for it seemed to increase the sensation of tired well-being which had taken possession of her and rose sometimes on a little wave of ecstasy to a delicious feeling of numbness in her legs. As soon as the kettle boiled she would make herself a good strong cup of tea: and with a fire like that the kettle wouldn't be long . . . no . . . certainly Mr. Robson knew how to make a fire. . . . Yes . . . he was a good fellow, was Robson, to bother so much about! . . .

The kettle suddenly began spluttering and she roused herself to take it off the fire and fill the teapot.

"After all," said Mrs. Barber to Janie Robson, who had looked in when she was at her second cup, "after all, there's nothing like a good strong cup of tea for putting you right, no matter what's wrong. How anyone could get along without it, beats me. And yet there's the Bible. You won't find a word about tea from beginning to end. Wine, water, and milk, you'll find—'He asked for water and she gave him milk': that was Jael, you know; and then there's 'Wine to gladden man's heart'—but seemingly they didn't go in for tea in those times. Well, there's no accounting for tastes." And then Mrs. Barber remembered again that it was Christmas Day and insisted on Janie running home. "You don't want to be bothered with an old woman on Christmas night, my dear," she said. "And tell your father from me that I'm doing nicely now."

At six o'clock the bells began to ring for the evening service: first one, clear and high in the darkness; then another, a deeper, warmer one; and soon all eight fell into their places in the scale. Over and over they tumbled down the length of the scale until there was no beginning and no ending to it, but just a continuous flow like water down a long waterfall. And then the bells suddenly changed places and wove in and out of one another on a new tune.

Mrs. Barber liked the bells. They produced in her a warm, mysterious, slightly ecstatic feeling, faintly recalling a long line of buried memories. "Dear me," she said to herself, shaking her head wonderingly. "Deary, deary me!" And suddenly she decided that she would go to church. Why not? It was just exactly what she was feeling inclined for. Besides, the distance was nothing, not a quarter of a mile. Well, if she was going she would have to get ready at once, and she got up—dear me, how stiff she was, to be sure!—and put on her bonnet and coat and a warm woollen muffler. Then she placed the matches on the edge of the table where she would be able to lay her hand on them in the dark, extinguished the lamp, and went out.

As she locked the door behind her, she felt as pleased and excited as a child on the brink of a secret escapade. It was a bitter night. She could feel the cold go right down her throat, and she pulled the muffler up over her mouth and nose. The road was like iron:

her steps knocked on it as though she were wearing clogs, and in the clear flinty darkness the grass in the ditches sparkled as if with a new-fallen shower of crystals. Her legs were still a little weak, but then the distance was nothing, not a quarter of a mile, and she would have a long rest in the church . . . an hour and ten minutes at least . . . and coming back would be all downhill . . . besides, the distance was nothing, not a! . . . The porch looked like a cold yellow cave at the end of the path between the tombstones, but when she passed through it and down the step into the church, it was very far from being cold: it was deliciously warm, with a comfortable smell of hot-pipes and paraffin-oil. The crowd that flowed past her up the nave made her feel suddenly nervous and irritable and she took her seat far back among the empty pews where there would be no one to bother her or to notice if she did not stand up during the psalms.

From where she sat, the church looked like a huge softly-shining cavern upon whose floor the congregation was spread in a black, restless mass, out of which the pillars grew up, gradually more and more luminous, into the warm, misty light like the stems of giant lilies. Lamps hung from the arches and, far off in the distant chancel, which appeared as a glowing core of radiance beyond the paler light of the nave, the tall altar-candles shone like a row of stars.

For Mrs. Barber's old eyes the many lamps and candles filled the church with a golden fog, and sometimes the lights receded from her, just as it had happened at home when she was gazing into the fire, or became suddenly blurred and shed clusters of divergent rays downwards to the floor and up into the darkness of the roof, so that the whole cavern seemed full of blazing comets. "Like the blessed stars of Heaven," Mrs. Barber murmured to herself, wondering where the phrase had come from.

Then the organ began, building up out of nothing just such a wonderful world for the ear as the lights and pillars and arches had made for the eyes: and soon there was a quiet stir of white shapes in the chancel and she knew that the choir had come in.

She listened delightedly to the intoning of prayers and the rich, clear chanting of psalms whose words were lost in the warm resonance of the chancel, till the church seemed to brim up with a shimmering lake of sound which washed and soothed her tired brain. Then came the hymn she had known all her life, and as she stood, steadying herself by holding with both hands on to the book-ledge, the lights and the tall pillars and the black, uneven mass of the congregation seemed to sway with the swaying of the music. "O come, let us adore Him! O come, let us adore Him!" said the music, climbing and climbing to the height from which at last it curved so satisfyingly down to the closing chord. The old words surged back into her memory with the music—"God of God, Light of Light . . . Very God, begotten not created"—it had never occurred to her to wonder what they meant: their emotional meaning for her was profound and sufficient and when she sat down again she felt exhausted, more from the intensity of her feelings than from the effort of standing.

Far away in the chancel the monotone of an unheard prayer rose again, but she did not kneel. She felt that she must sit quite still for a while, and then, as she raised her eyes, the lights swam away from her again, hung aloft and remote, and swung back large and blurred, scattering long beams on the cowering congregation. "Like the blessed stars of Heaven," she whispered to herself again. Again the stars swam upwards, up and up and up: it seemed, this time, as if they would never come back. They swam into a circle, then into another, circle above circle—like a crown—like a bride's cake, and Mrs. Barber could see now (so clearly that she wondered that she had failed to notice it before) that every star was a lighted taper held by an angel. There they stood, a calm, stationary whirlpool of angels, ascending whirl above whirl into infinite height.

Suddenly—so suddenly that Mrs. Barber jumped—they burst into song, a great chord of music, basses, tenors, altos, trebles, ringing and vibrating together till the sound of it drew her right out of herself and she saw herself receding upwards. Up and up and up she flew, till she was no more than a minute pin-point of light. Then her light expanded and she became herself again, as it were: and there she was, among the angels—a great crowd of them all facing one way. Their wings towered up before her and on each side of her: she could see every plume in minute detail, soft golden feathers laid perfectly one on another. She could not resist the impulse to put out her hand and stroke the wing in front of her. The angel looked round and his eyes smiled at her, but his mouth did not stop singing. It seemed that they were all expecting some one—Mrs. Barber too felt the expectancy and suddenly their voices burst out again, but right in her ear this time, loud and startling. "Hallelujah! Hallelujah!" they sang, as though for the entrance of a king. And all at once they broke apart in front of her and curved away to the right and left, and she saw that some one was standing in the space which they had made. It was Jesus. He stood like a large, simple giant, twice as large as any of the angels, wrapped in a plain blue cloak. And then, as Mrs. Barber stood gazing at him, Jesus caught sight of her. She felt afraid just for a moment, but then he smiled as though he recognized her—such an extremely pleasant smile that at once she felt at ease. . . . It was nice of him to bother so much about . . . But he was calling her. "Mrs. Barber!" he was saying: and then, much louder, "Mrs. Barber!" and again, alarmingly loud, "Mrs. Barber!" "Yes, sir, yes!" she said, trying in vain to move forward. And then a sudden giddiness came over her and everything was lost in a golden fog. "Come, Mrs. Barber," the voice went on. "Why, I declare: you've been asleep." "O no, sir," laughed Mrs. Barber, struggling to her feet. "Not asleep, sir!" But, all the same, she felt a little confused, a little dazed, because she was back in the church among "the blessed stars of Heaven"—that is, among the lamps and candles—but now, somehow, the church was quite empty and she was going towards the door with the Vicar. How stiff and useless her legs were! It was so much more difficult to walk than to fly. She tried to explain to the Vicar: "It's difficult, you know, sir . . ." she said. "It's difficult after being up there." But though her legs were so helpless she was still glowing with happiness, and as they walked back to her cottage—apparently the Vicar was going to her cottage too—she told him, as well as she could, of the wonderful things she had seen. She wouldn't have told everybody, of course; but the Vicar, being a clergyman, would understand. "And all the angels," she explained, "carried . . . carried . . . bells." Then she paused, perplexed. Surely that wasn't the word? Bells? No, how silly of her! It was tapers. "Yes, all the angels, sir, carried tapers. Wonderful! You've no idea." But the Vicar was asking about her key, and he unlocked her door for her and lit the lamp and would not leave her until she had assured him that she was really quite well and had promised that she would go straight to bed. "O perfectly well, thank you, sir: and very, very happy."

She was too tired to undress: besides, she had promised the Vicar that she would get into bed at once. Yes, he was a good gentleman, was the Vicar . . . or was it Jesus? or Mr. Robson? . . . to bother so much about an old woman. . . . But all the angels were ringing bells . . . and the distance was nothing . . . not a quarter of a mile.

The State versus Santa Claus

ARTHUR STRINGER

THE SHY old man in Turkey red trimmed with rabbit skin began to look worried. He wasn't used to crowds. And the courtroom was warm. And he didn't like the way people kept staring at him. It made him feel a good deal like a polar bear in a zoo.

He was almost glad when he heard a crack-voiced court attendant shout: "Everybody rise!" For that meant, of course, that the Judge was coming out of his chamber and seating himself in the big black chair under the solemn crossed flags.

But the prisoner at the bar, as he mopped a broad red face with his foolish rabbit-fringed sleeve, was a trifle disappointed about the Judge, whom the Prosecutor addressed as Father Time. For that Judge seemed a bit too old for his job. He looked as though he hadn't known a good meal or cracked a smile for half a century. His glance, it's true, was as sharp as a weasel's, but his shoulders sagged and his face looked tired, as though he had heard too many cases and reviewed too many crimes and seen too many prisoners pass out the side door with the iron grille and never come back.

Nor did the portly figure in Turkey red altogether like the appearance of the Prosecuting Attorney. He too was an old man, hard-eyed and gaunt and lean, with a nutcracker profile and an eye that told you he'd be as quick and merciless as a steel trap. His narrow face, in fact, had worn an acid smile of contempt as he glanced about at the rubicund old figure in red, a smile which said as plain as day: "Well, Old Boy, it won't take me long to finish *you* up!"

Santa Claus, as he shifted in his seat, wished there had been a few children about. He seemed to get along better with children. His earlier suspicion that he wasn't among friends even deepened to a conviction as he turned and studied the Jury. He had really hoped for a different sort of Jury, one that could give a chuckle now and then and whisper behind their hands and nudge neighboring ribs and perhaps make a spitball or two and wonder how you wound up Exhibit A on the Prosecutor's table and whether the red paint on Exhibit B actually had the adorable painty smell that all Noah's arks ought to have. But the twelve good men and true on *this* Jury impressed him as twelve dried-up old prunes who wouldn't know anything more about putting a toy airplane together than they'd know about spinning a musical top. And it wasn't only their age he objected to. It was no crime, after all, being old. What he didn't like was the enmity in their rheumy old eyes when they blinked down at the Christmas Tree, marked Exhibit X, on the Prosecutor's table. And Santa Claus wasn't used to enmity. He didn't thrive on it. Those twelve old Jurors, in fact, looked so much like twelve old owls blinking solemnly down on a blighted world that he was glad to turn away and let his eyes rest on the Counsel who'd been assigned to defend him.

But even then the prisoner didn't perceptibly brighten. That lawyer, the Big Policeman downstairs had said, was just the man for him. He'd never lost a case. On the other hand, he'd never won a case, for the simple reason that he always got them so mixed up they never came to an end. He was invariably addressed as "Mr. Folly," being a senior member of the old and established firm of Folly & Youth. But he, too, was plainly too old for his job. When the prisoner had pointed out that they were giving him a decrepit octogenarian in his second childhood, the Big Policeman had sagely wagged his head up and down and said: "That's why you're getting him!" And this thought began to disturb Santa Claus. It disturbed him almost as much as did an inspection of his learned counsel who, instead of paying attention to the court procedure, occupied himself by counting his waistcoat buttons and drawing little pictures on his brief case and trying to balance three pencils at once on the inkwell.

And those court proceedings obviously ought to be paid some attention to, the rotund prisoner suddenly realized, for the Prosecuting Attorney was already on his feet. He was not only on his feet but he was talking about the prisoner, and talking about him in a way which very promptly gave that prisoner gooseflesh. And that prisoner's lawyer, as the tirade went on, merely sat back laughing at the way the Prosecutor's Adam's-apple went up and down with a three-inch plunge as he discoursed. It was no wonder Santa Claus's face lost a little of its ruddiness. Things certainly weren't looking any too well for him. And cases certainly weren't won by laughing at your adversary's Adam's-apple.

"This prisoner," the Prosecutor was proclaiming, "is an impostor. He's more than an impostor; he's an absurdity. And for the good of the People I want him abolished. I want him done away with, just as we did away with Fairy Tales in this state last year, just as we did away with Music the year before. I speak, sir, for Science and Truth. And before we can progress into perfect statehood we must abolish these foolish old myths that are an affront to reason and a confusion to the mind of youth."

"Objection," casually announced the prisoner's attorney as he succeeded in balancing his third pencil on the inkwell cover.

"Objection denied," barked back the stooping old graybeard on the bench.

"This old scoundrel," proceeded the Prosecutor, directing a long and bony finger towards the cowering Santa Claus, "has not only outlived his usefulness—if he ever had any—but has also blocked the highway of progress. He is pagan in ancestry and pagan in spirit. We know, gentlemen, that in this enlightened age we never get anything for nothing. We know that life is struggle and combat, and that to the strong belong the spoils. Yet this old deceiver claims to give us things for nothing. He seeks to delude our children and our children's children with the contention that for one day in the year the ironclad laws of commerce and competition can be dispensed with. He keeps youth credulous and soft-hearted when they should be practical-minded and satisfied with an eye for an eye and a tooth for a tooth. On that one irrational and irresponsible day in a year of reason, he says, the laws of give-and-take can be abrogated and things can come to us unearned. He claims, in other words, that miracles can still be brought about in this workaday world of ours. That claim is not only fraudulent, but this ruddy prisoner is fraudulent in the way in which he presents it. Even his place of abode is fraudulent. He contended, I understand, that his home was in the once conveniently vague neighborhood of the North Pole. But that Pole has now been found and explored, and those explorations have failed to disclose any such home. This is an age of steel and stone, of skyscrapers and towering cities. Yet today, in this age of elevators and steam-heated apartments, this old impostor claims to travel by sled and reindeer and——"

"Objection," said the attorney for the defense, looking up from a locomotive he was drawing on a brief back.

"Objection noted," proclaimed the Bench, rousing himself from what looked suspiciously like forty winks.

"And even here," pursued the blandly smiling Prosecutor, "I shall not only anticipate but I shall elucidate my opponent's objection. Why that sled and reindeer, I ask? Simply because, in the medieval era of his origin, sled and reindeer stood for the fastest means of locomotion known to semicivilized man. But we live in a new age, an age of progress. And any self-appointed peddler of unsolicited charities who can't today travel one-tenth as fast as one of our mail planes is no longer entitled to his job!"

The Prosecutor, on ending that peroration, took a drink of ice water and smiled icily at the murmur of approval that swept through the courtroom. Then he once more directed a lean and accusatory finger at the prisoner.

"There's something else that this old impostor lays claim to. He contends that while on this brief but incredibly active annual pilgrimage of debauching and pauperizing our rising generation he enters their midnight homes by way of the chimney. By the chimney, mark you, by the chimney and under cover of darkness. And that, gentlemen, is as far as I need to go. We may not be versed in Norse mythology; but we all know modern architecture. So I merely ask you, gentlemen of the jury, to take one good look at this old impostor. Study him closely, gentlemen. Note his ample proportions, his potbelly, his obesity doubtlessly due to a life of overindulgence. All I ask of you, gentlemen, is to give him the once-over and then decide for yourselves whether or not a figure of those dimensions could get down a modern chimney flue!"

Again the Prosecutor took a drink of ice water, a murmur of approval swept through the courtroom, and a far-from-happy prisoner mopped his forehead with the rabbit-fringed tail of his Turkey-red surtout.

"But that, gentlemen, is not all," resumed the gaunt and grim-eyed Prosecutor. "This crafty old impostor not only succeeds in deluding youth, he triumphs as well in depraving parenthood itself. He beguiles careless-minded mothers and fathers into a communion of deception. He makes them passive agents in his nefarious enterprises. He prompts them to perpetuate a tradition that is a blot on this nation of truth lovers. And above and before everything, we must have Truth!"

"That's right," suddenly cackled out Juror Number Nine. "Sixty-eight years ago I lied to my step-mother about shovelin' the snow off our well platform, and all I got that Christmas was a stockin' full o' coal. And I've hated Christmas ever since."

It was the infirm Mr. Folly who at this juncture restored the picture puzzle he'd been working over to the table of exhibits and rose blandly to his feet.

"If Your Honor will permit me," he casually observed, "I am prompted to move for a mistrial."

The Judge who looked so disconcertingly like Father Time sat back on the bench, blinking at a window which a court attendant had opened to cool off the overheated room.

"On what grounds?" he finally demanded.

"On the grounds," said Mr. Folly with an unexpectedly stern glance toward the jury box, "that my client is not being tried before a body of his peers."

"That looks like a pretty intelligent jury to *me*," ventured the Judge, "even though Number Nine didn't know enough to keep his mouth shut."

"I'm not attacking their intelligence," pursued the quiet-toned Mr. Folly. "What I'm criticizing is their age."

"Fiddlesticks," retorted the Judge, "every man in this courtroom is an old man, and you know it, sir!"

"All except one, Your Honor," contended the unabashed Mr. Folly.

"What one?" demanded the bench.

"My client, Your Honor," replied the wizened counsel for the man in red, whose color deepened as the eyes of the courtroom were once more directed on his uncomfortable person.

"I can't say that he looks much like a spring chicken," said the Man on the Bench, with a throaty cackle that was unctuously re-echoed by the crowd.

"Appearances, Your Honor, are sometimes deceptive," said Mr. Folly.

"How about those white whiskers?" demanded the irate Prosecutor.

"Your Honor," said Mr. Folly, hobbling closer to the Judge's bench, "I wouldn't care to have it generally known, but this client of mine is a trifle off in the upper story. He's quite child-minded, in fact. And those whiskers are only a disguise. Under them, he's merely a child, a child who refused to grow up. For the foolish old fellow still has a forlorn craving for happiness. He keeps on believing in good-will and kindliness and all that sort of thing. It's a very sad case. And instead of cluttering up the Calendar this way, he really ought to be handed over to the care of his friends."

"Has he any friends?" demanded the Judge.

"Not here," said the astute Mr. Folly.

"Then how are we to know he has any?"

Mr. Folly scratched his bald head in perplexity. "That's not an easy question to answer, Your Honor. But I'd suggest, in the circumstances, that we let the children decide it."

"But there are no children about," demurred the Court.

"Then we might take a ballot," suggested Mr. Folly.

"A ballot? What kind of ballot?" demanded the Judge.

But that question remained unanswered. For the woebegone prisoner himself, who had got unsteadily up from his chair, was crossing to the open window. Through that open window he thrust his two fat arms encased in Turkey red. And a tear ran down his plump but wrinkled cheek as he stared out at the wintry sky that had darkened as the afternoon wore away.

"Children," he cried in a voice tremulous with emotion, "*Children, do you want me?*"

A hush fell over the courtroom. And in that hush three hundred straining ears heard only the sighing of the wind. But as that wind increased in force two objects of white fluttered down and rested on the outstretched and unsteady hands of the wistful old figure in Turkey red. Some people said they were slips of paper; and some people always claimed that they were only especially large snowflakes. But they came in a stream, and then in a cloud. They came so thick that the Big Policeman had to pull down the window to keep them from covering the courtroom floor. But even then they flattened themselves against the panes, and piled up about the outside walls, and grew deeper and deeper, until the room darkened and the hushed watchers looked at one another with childish wonder in their eyes.

"Dear me," said the decrepit old court attendant as he turned on the lights, "if it isn't one of those old-fashioned blizzards again!"

"Looks to me," observed the Big Policeman, blinking up at the gray oblong that had once been a window, "like it's goin' to be worse than that blizzard of 1888!"

"Again, all was dark for an instant, then there came a new light wave"

THE LEGEND OF THE CHRISTMAS ROSE

Story on page 106

The Escape of Alice

VINCENT STARRETT

I

THE RED linen covers opened slightly and a little girl slipped out, leaving behind her a curious vacancy in one of the familiar pictures signed with Mr. Tenniel's initials. She looked about her with bright, alert eyes, hoping no one had been a witness to her desertion, and then carefully began to climb down. She need not have alarmed herself, for she was no bigger than a minute, and clearer eyes than those of the rheumatic old antiquarian who kept the shop would have been needed to note her departure. Fortunately, the shelf onto which she had emerged was not high, and by exercising great caution the little girl was able to reach the floor without accident.

Still watching the old man closely, she reached a hand into the pocket of her print dress and produced a few crumbs of cake, which she hurriedly ate. Almost instantly she began to grow, and, in a moment, from a tiny little mite of two or three inches, she had shot up into as tall a schoolgirl of thirteen as the proudest parent could wish. Her ascent, indeed, was so rapid that before she quite realized what had happened, there was her head on a level with the shelf on which, only an instant before, she had been standing; and there was the prison from which she had escaped: *Alice's Adventures in Wonderland,* read the gold letters over the door.

She plucked the volume from its place, and advanced with it to the proprietor of the bookshop.

Published by arrangement with the author.

"If it is not too much," said Alice, "I think I will take this."

The old bookseller, whose wits had been woolgathering for years, would not for worlds have admitted that he had not heard her enter the shop. He took the book from her hand and peered nearsightedly at the title.

"You choose wisely," he said, and patted the red covers lovingly. "*Alice*—the ageless child! It is one of the greatest compendiums of wit and sense in our literature. There are only two books in the world to match it. You shall have it for fifteen cents, for it is far from new, and I now see that the frontispiece is missing."

"And what are the other two?" asked Alice, eagerly.

"When you are older you will read them," said the old bookman. "They are called *Don Quixote* and *The Pickwick Papers*." He pronounced the strange name "Keehoty" and Alice thought he must be speaking French. It must be a very pretty language, she reflected.

Then suddenly Alice blushed, for she remembered that she could not pay. Timidly she handed the red-covered volume back.

"I'm so sorry," she said, "but I have no money. I don't know why I was so stupid as to come away without any."

"Money!" cried the bookseller. "Did I ask money for this book? Forgive me! It is a habit I have fallen into for which I am sorry. Money is the least important thing in the world. Only the worthless things are to be had for money. Those things which are beyond price—thank God—are to be had for the asking. Take it, child! Tomorrow is Christmas Day. I should be grieved indeed if there were no *Alice* for you on Christmas Day—as grieved as if there were no Santa Claus."

There was something so unearthly about the strange old man that Alice wondered if she were not perhaps still in Wonderland. With a sobriety quite out of keeping with her usually merry disposition, she thanked him and went out into the snow-clad streets.

II

The plethora of Santa Clauses spending the holiday week-end in the city bewildered Alice; and now, after a long afternoon in the hurly-burly of metropolitan life, she was becoming tired. The number of Santa Clauses resident on earth appalled her, and the extravagance of their promises, while pleasant enough, almost frightened her. Without any questions asked—even her address, which would have taxed her wits if it had been requested—they accepted her commissions and guaranteed immediate delivery. The final excursion through the great department stores had been adventurous and diverting, but now (toward nightfall) it was becoming monotonous, what with its profusion of Kriss Kringles and street hawkers, and its babble of eleventh-hour shoppers. It was like seeing a thrilling movie drama for the second time, thought Alice, who had initiated herself into the delights of this form of entertainment for the first time that day, and wondered at its remarkable duplication of events. By five o'clock the little girl knew just what each and every Santa Claus was going to say to her, and what was coming next, and that at least one of the three remaining Santas would want to kiss her. She had been kissed almost to suffocation, as it was, and that was beginning to bore her, too.

It occurred to Alice, who was a shrewd little girl and not one of your bleating lambs, that Santa Claus, despite his profusion—or because of it—might be something of an old fraud. She was certain that not one of him resembled the jolly old saint of her mental picture. The cottony fellow at Wanacooper's was not a bit red and chubby, nor very jovial either; and she hoped the others—at the Emporium, and the Bargain Store, and the Bon Marché—would agree more sympathetically, as to outline, with the merry and very dear old gentleman of her favorite poem.

She repeated the first lines, softly, under her breath:

" 'Twas the night before Christmas,
And all through the house
Not a creature was stirring,
Not even a mouse . . ."

Well, that was not surprising. Obviously, all the creatures who might otherwise have been stirring about the house on the night before Christmas were crowding and jostling each other in department stores, buying useless presents for people they didn't like. Alice thought it odd that this hadn't occurred to her before. It made the beginning of the poem quite clear.

The Santa Claus at the Emporium was entirely surrounded by children, just like all his duplicates, and, in the midst of an alarming racket, was writing long lists of juvenile wants in a big bookkeeper's ledger. The big bookkeeper was nowhere about, and so the old fellow went right ahead, just as if it had been his own ledger, and filled as many columns as a child wished, in the most amiable manner in the world. He was the nicest Santa Claus Alice had yet seen.

He didn't immediately notice Alice, who was neither larger nor smaller than most of the other children shouting around him; but when he did notice her he liked her right away. He liked the old-fashioned way of her, and her last-century clothes, and from the way she looked at him he was sure that she, at least, believed in him, and wasn't dropping round just to see how much she could get out of him. And then he hurried, so he could finish quickly with the others and get around to Alice. It wasn't very long until there she was—right up beside him—with his dear old whiskers tickling her shell-like ears (one of them, anyway), and his pen poised over a perfectly blank page, ready to write down anything Alice asked him to. His voice, too, was very pleasant.

"Now," said this kindly old saint, adjusting his eyebrows with care, for they were slightly moth-eaten and appeared to be falling off—and no wonder, either, for hundreds of boys and girls had been leaning against them all day—"now," said this nice old man, "what do you wish me to bring *you* for Christmas, little Golden-hair?"

There was something charming about the way he emphasized the *you* that put Alice at ease immediately. So she told him all about the lovely doll, and the darling kitten, and the sweet bird she wanted, and had been wanting for a long time, and all about the books she needed to catch up on the world. For she had been locked away so long that she felt a bit out of date, and such phrases as "United Nations" and "Maple Nut Sundae" simply meant nothing to her, while they were the common property of every other girl and boy in the land.

The good-natured old soul wrote them all down carefully, and then kissed Alice just as she had expected he would. He promised faithfully to deliver every one of her orders, in person, and warned her to be sure the hearth fire was extinguished before midnight.

"Because promptly at midnight," he said, "I shall come down the chimley."

Alice giggled at that.

"You mean the chimney, don't you!" she asked.

"Chimney, indeed!" snorted Santa Claus. "After all these years, don't you think I know the difference between a chimney and a chimley? No, sir! I come down a chimley, every time. I'll leave it to everyone here."

Turning to the crowd of boys and girls around him, he asked: "How do I get into the house, children?"

"Down the chimley!" roared the chorus.

"You see?" said Santa Claus.

Alice did see, and felt very much ashamed of her display of ignorance.

"Never mind," said Santa Claus kindly. "But I think," he added, "you had better go along now with my assistant, and be sure we have all these things in stock. He'll be glad to show you around. It's all free, you know. Just look around as long as you like, and if you see anything else you want, come right back and tell me about it."

There was a little boy standing beside Santa Claus, with a metal tag on his collar, and the generous old gentleman turned and asked him to go and fetch his—that is, Santa Claus's—assistant. While Alice was waiting, a lot of other children pushed forward, and Alice was pretty nearly forgotten. But after a while she heard someone say, "He's coming now. He'll be here in just a minute, now," and at the same moment she saw Santa Claus's assistant coming toward her.

He was a sprightly little fellow, and Alice decided to like him. He came up in a sort of blue-green light, which danced all around him, and without the slightest hesitation Alice took his hand and walked away with him.

The little man's fingers were so cold and hard, though, that Alice was surprised, and when she was sure he wasn't looking she looked him over. And when she had done that, she almost screamed, used as she was to queer things in Wonderland. For the little man was made of wood. Everything about him was wood; and there was Alice holding on to his wooden fingers, and he was talking out of his wooden mouth, and the whole affair was the most wooden episode Alice could remember. His remarks concerning some of the books Alice wanted, the little girl thought, were the most wooden thing about him. But the little man's face was rather nice, for it was highly painted in blue and green, and he had bright yellow eyes that fairly sparkled with enamel.

"Let's see now," said the wooden man. "Dolls were first on the list, weren't they? Well, here we are. We call this room 'The Kingdom of Dolls,' although as a matter of fact it is ruled by a Queen, and never did have a King, because the Queen is rather old and nobody will marry her. And as she won't allow any of the other dolls to marry until she finds herself a King, it makes it hard for the younger ones."

"Dear me," said Alice. "Do you suppose I might get a peep at the Queen, without being seen? Please excuse the rhyme."

"Easy enough," said the wooden man. "There she is—that long-haired doll with the purple robe. She likes to be looked at, and I need hardly tell you that her hair is false. She's awfully stuck up, though, and we won't tarry long, for she'd only snub us."

"What a funny crown she is wearing," laughed Alice, turning her head to look back.

"You may well say so," said the wooden man, ironically, "for it is made of kistletoe. She never takes it off!"

"Kistletoe!" said Alice, and then, forgetting her humiliating experience about the chimley, "Don't you mean mistletoe?"

"No, I mean kistletoe," replied the wooden man, impatiently. "Everybody knows what kistletoe is. But then, perhaps you are too young. When you are older, you will know more."

"I'm thirteen," said Alice with dignity.

"Thirteen!" shrieked the wooden man, so loudly that Alice felt sure she had offended him again. "What a dreadfully unlucky number! I should be frightened to death to be thirteen. How long have you been thirteen?"

"Nearly two months now," Alice confessed miserably. Then she brightened. "But everybody has to be thirteen some time. Weren't you ever thirteen?"

"Never!" declared the wooden man firmly. "When my thirteenth birthday approached, I tore off a whole year of the calendar, and passed right into my fourteenth year. Of course, there was a fearful row about it; but it's really just like skipping a grade at school. If you're smart enough you can do it. We have some very nice calendars," he added professionally.

Alice was bewildered, but she had forgotten her wounded dignity. Near by a little boy was pestering his mother to buy him a rabbit, and Alice paused to listen. It was a fine-looking white rabbit made of kid and fur, and it reminded her of an old friend she had made in Wonderland. But it couldn't be, of course, for by this time she knew she had left Wonderland behind her when she ran away from the bookshop.

"Can he talk, Mommy?" the little boy was asking. "I squeeze him and squeeze him and he won't say a word. Make him talk, Mommy!"

"Hush, darling, it isn't a doll," said his mother. "Rabbits can't talk, you know. Whoever heard of a rabbit talking!"

"I did," cried Alice eagerly, and she would have said more if the wooden man hadn't pinched her and made her say, "Ouch!"

He was trying to drag her away from the counter, but Alice refused to budge.

"Rabbits can too talk," she called out again; but just then she looked right into the eyes of the white rabbit and saw one of them close in an unmistakable wink that seemed to say, "Don't give me away, Stupid! My ears and whiskers, you ought to know better than that."

Alice was so ashamed of herself that she bit her lip harder than she intended. In a moment, however, her attention was attracted by a succession of melodious sounds, ending on a queer upward inflection that seemed to leave the phrase unfinished and hanging in the air.

"Do listen!" she exclaimed. "Isn't that too sweet? It sounds like a bird singing."

"Most birds do," said the wooden man dryly. "That's your bird," he added, more politely. "You asked for a bird you know."

"But why does it end its song so abruptly?" asked Alice. "It doesn't seem to finish."

"Confinement," answered the guide briefly. "Its cage is too small. The notes only reach the ceiling, then echo back into its own ears, which naturally surprises it into silence. It's too bad, for it's losing its upper register. It once sang very well."

"I shall let it go when I get it," declared Alice with decision.

"You may do as you please, of course," agreed the wooden man, "but you'll only be wanting another one, next Christmas."

They hurried forward, pressing through the crowd about the cage. It was humorous the way the people fell back on either side of the wooden man's sharp elbows. What they saw, when they reached the cage, was a beautiful yellow bird with black wings and big black eyes, swinging and singing on a perch of gold.

"Wound up too tightly," muttered the wooden man. "One of the monkeys has been monkeying with the key."

With a ferocious glare at the children around him, he reached in a hand, and Alice heard a sharp *click.* The bird stopped singing in the middle of a note. Then the wooden man lifted the little creature from its perch and brought it forth just as if it were made of wood, too.

"Oh!" cried Alice, in distress. "You mustn't hurt the bird. It wasn't *its* fault that somebody monkeyed with the key."

The word *monkeyed* puzzled her, but she supposed it was all right, since that was what the wooden man had said.

But the wooden man only laughed and held the bird out for her inspection. Then Alice saw that it was not a real bird at all; it was made of a thin metal so skillfully painted as only to look real.

"You forget this is Toyland," grinned the wooden man. "This

bird is no more real than I am, than these children are—than you are, for that matter."

"Ain't I real?" asked Alice, in alarm. Quickly correcting herself, she said: "Am I not real?"

"Real enough," said the wooden man carelessly. "A real nuisance," he muttered, under his breath; but fortunately Alice didn't hear this rude remark. More pleasantly he continued: "Oh, the bird is real enough. It just doesn't know what it is singing, or why it is singing, that's all."

"Maybe it's happy," said Alice; but the wooden man said he doubted it, and hustled her away with a gesture of impatience. Alice was getting tired of his bullying manner. "Aren't there any more animals?" she asked after a moment.

"Birds aren't animals," sneered the wooden man, and then he was very much ashamed of himself. "I beg your pardon," he said, contritely. "I had forgotten you are only thirteen." (He shuddered as he mentioned the sinister number.) "Well, yes, there is the Performing Pony, and the Talking Dog, and the Teddy Bear, and the Laughing Hyena, and the Ingenious Ibex, and the Loquacious Lynx, and—— Oh, we have quite a menagerie."

He looked quizzically at Alice, and suddenly began to sing:

"Oh, ferocious and atrocious is the beast they call the lynx;
And fierce his howl, and black his scowl, and red his jowl, methinks. . . ."

"You have a very nice voice," said Alice, as the singer paused.

"I wish you wouldn't interrupt," snapped the wooden man. "First you want to hear about the animals, and then you don't." Then he stopped. "Do you really like my voice?" he asked eagerly.

"I haven't much of a voice myself," mused the little girl, "but I think I could speak a piece."

"Let's hear it," urged the wooden man. And in a moment Alice heard herself reciting:

"I thought I heard a parson swear
Because his eyes were sore;
I turned around, and saw he was
Asleep upon the floor.
'Alas,' I whispered, fearfully,
'That two times two is four!'

"I thought I saw a mastodon
Upon the pantry shelf;
I looked again, and saw it was
A picture of myself.
'O dear,' I said, 'the albatross
Is eating all the pelf!' "

"What's pelf?" demanded the wooden man, critically.

"Pelf is—I think it's something to eat," explained Alice. "But I didn't have to say pelf. I could have said elf, or delf——"

"Or squelf!" jeered the wooden man. "Poetic license is a dangerous thing for a girl of thirteen. I shall see that yours is revoked at once."

Alice began to cry with shame and humiliation.

"There, there," cried the wooden man, ashamed of himself again. "I was only plaguing you. You rhyme beautifully—much better than I do. Now, let's go and see P. D."

"P. D.?" queried Alice, drying her tears. "Who is P. D.?"

"Why, the Plausible Donkey, to be sure," laughed the wooden man. "You said you wanted to see some more animals."

"Why don't you call him D. P.?" asked Alice, after a moment, as they walked toward the menagerie.

"Why?" The wooden man seemed suspicious.

"Democratic Party," giggled Alice; and then she stopped as she caught sight of the wooden man's face, which was contorted with paint. "I beg your pardon," she added hastily.

But the wooden man wouldn't speak another word until they arrived at the Donkey Shelter, when he became cheerful once more.

"Let me introduce you to the Plausible Donkey," he said gallantly.

"Pleased to meet you, Mr. Donkey," said Alice timidly. "What beautiful eyes you have."

"The better to see you with, my child," quoted the Plausible Donkey, just to show that he was not such a donkey as he looked. "What can I do for you today?"

"Can you sing?" asked Alice, innocently.

"Heavens!" groaned the wooden man, in her ear. "Now you've done it! He has no more voice than a crow!"

But the Plausible Donkey was pleased by the question.

"It is not surprising that you do not know my ability in that respect," he smiled, "since this is your first visit. The fact is—" he blushed modestly—"the fact is, I am descended from that notable singer, Maxwelton."

"Maxwelton!" echoed Alice, in surprise. "I thought that was a song."

"It was originally," the Plausible Donkey said, plausibly. "My ancestor was named after the song because his brays were bonnie."

"Oh," said Alice, politely; but the wooden man snickered and spoiled it all.

"You're making fun of me," she cried, with tears in her voice, "and I don't want to hear you sing now."

She hurried away, leaving the wooden man to apologize as best he could for Alice's impoliteness. He was puffing when he overtook her.

"I think we've had enough of animals," he said between gasps. "Let's go over and see the books." It was evident, even to Alice, that he was getting tired of his charge.

They were in the book department before they knew it—before Alice knew it, at any rate. All around them were books—heaps and heaps of them—on tables and shelves, and piled on long counters, and hung up in booths; and in the very center of the immense room was a great American Eagle, made entirely of books, the work of the chief window dresser, who was a very literary man.

"Have you *The Young Visiters?*" asked Alice.

"Young visitors!" echoed the wooden man. "Santa Claus has dozens of them—hundreds—every day. Thousands, I guess!"

"Silly! It's a book," said Alice. "It was written by a friend of mine, Daisy Ashford, when she was only nine years old."

The wooden man looked suspiciously at his charge.

"Nobody could write a book at nine," he said with finality.

"Daisy could, and did," said Alice.

"Nobody could get it published, anyway," sneered the wooden man. "Of course, anybody could *write* one."

"And she had it published, and here it is!" cried Alice, triumphantly. She snatched a book from a long counter, and presented it to her companion.

The wooden man took it cautiously, turned it over, and handed it back.

"Where does it say she is only nine years old?" he demanded.

"In the preface, of course," answered Alice. "She's older now, but she was only nine when she wrote it."

She whirled over the leaves until she found the place.

"There it is! Sir James Barrie himself says so, in the introduction."

"Humph!" said the wooden man. "He probably wrote it himself. And he wasn't nine when he wrote it, either."

"He would at least know how to spell visitors, wouldn't he?"

The wooden man stared at the cover. At sight of the title he was visibly shaken.

"It might be a typographical error," he ventured. "But, if you know this Daisy Ashford, what's her book about?"

"It's about a man who—who was in love with—with a young woman," explained Alice. "He was rather an old man, and——"

"Then Barrie wrote it!" interrupted the wooden man. *"That ends that!"*

"It doesn't end anything," cried Alice, almost in tears.

"Really," admonished the wooden man, "you mustn't get out of temper. You haven't had the chance to keep up on your reading that I have, being right here in the book section. You probably don't even know about a man called Lewis Carroll and a little girl—she wasn't very bright either—who had some peculiar experiences in a foreign land."

Alice was so flabbergasted that she couldn't think of anything to say. She just stood there with her mouth open.

"Well," he continued testily, "we've checked on the doll, and the bird, and the books. There was to be a kitten, I believe. That means we'll have to go back to the menagerie."

"I won't go back to the menagerie," Alice said firmly, "and if the kittens are no more polite than the donkeys, I won't have one."

"You'll have to ask Santa Claus to strike it off the list then, or you'll have it sure tomorrow morning. And we'll have to hustle, too, for the old boy closes at eight o'clock. He went on strike for a shorter day, last month—seven hundred of him—and after eight o'clock he won't do a lick of work."

"Let's hurry," cried Alice breathlessly.

So they hurried back through the teeming aisles, past the Plausible Donkey, who brayed after them jeeringly, past the Singing Bird, which offered to finish its song if they would only tarry, past the stuck-up Queen of the Dolls, who ogled the wooden man shamefully, and arrived at length at the cottony dwelling of Santa Claus. But—alas—the door now was closed, and tacked to the outer panel was a large sign, "Gone to the Races. Back Next Year."

"Oh!" said Alice, "Isn't it provoking! Now I shall have to have a kitten, after all—and I suppose it will eat the bird, and scratch the doll, and tear up the books, and make me angry all day long."

"No doubt," said the wooden man callously.

"But what does he mean by the races?" asked curious Alice.

"The reindeer races," replied the wooden man. "They race annually on Saturn's race track, and the winning Santa Claus is the boss Santa Claus of the year; he makes the rounds on Christmas Eve. It doesn't take a minute to get there, and probably by this time the races are over."

"I hope our Santa Claus won, don't you?" cried Alice.

"What's the difference?" shrugged the wooden man. "They all look alike."

"That's so," said Alice, reflectively, "but this one was very nice."

"They're paid to be nice," said the wooden man, cynically. "I'm paid to be nice. You don't think I've been piloting *you* around all afternoon for fun, do you?"

"Well," said Alice, with spirit, "I like that! I'm sure if I knew who paid you, I'd report you and you wouldn't get a penny. You don't deserve it, for you haven't been nice. I shall leave you, this minute."

"Good-bye," grinned the wooden man, mockingly. "Close the door after you as you go out."

III

"That was a very rude wooden man," thought Alice to herself, as, half blinded with tears, she hurried through the snowy streets. "It is very evident that he tore off his thirteenth year. That is the year when people learn to be polite. And he said I wasn't real. I never knew till I was thirteen how real I was."

Without quite knowing where she was going, unconsciously her footsteps strayed toward the shop of the old bookman, the only friend she had found who seemed to be genuine. The precious volume, which once she had thought a prison, was safe beneath her arm. Well, she knew now what she would do. She would give it back, and if the old man were so kind as to let her, she would creep back into the pages and be happy there forever. . . .

"Poor child," smiled the old bookman, when she had related her adventures, and cried over them. "Indeed he did need his thirteenth year. That is the age at which one best appreciates what reality is. Once learned, it is a lesson never to be forgotten. To the child of thirteen, all things are real if they are beautiful, and all things are unreal that are ugly. Anything is real that we *want* to be real. Sensible writers, like Barrie, learn this at thirteen and tear off *all* the remaining years of the calendar. Time passes, but they remain thirteen; they improve their writing; their appreciation of beautiful things becomes deeper, but at heart they are still children. They have never escaped from their thirteenth year, and they never will—and they are very glad about it."

To this astonishing harangue Alice had no reply, for she understood very little of it; but it sounded interesting, and she liked the look on the old bookman's face as he said it.

"Would you mind, sir," she asked timidly, "if I were to creep back into my book, and hide again on your shelf?"

"Are you quite sure you can manage it?" asked the old man.

"Oh, yes," said Alice, "for I still have a piece of the cake that I brought with me. I had two pieces—one to make me grow, and one to make me small again. Just watch!"

Then she took a few crumbs of cake from her pocket and began to eat them; and the old bookman, standing by, saw her shrink down and down and down, until she was such a tiny little thing at his feet that his eyes could scarcely find her.

He picked her up gently, and opened the book lying on the counter.

"You must find the place," he said. "Do you remember it?"

With a little sigh of happiness, Alice slipped into the right picture, where, to her great joy, she fitted like a glove—and suddenly the picture was complete again, and the old bookman turning the leaves over and over could not find her—there were so many of her, and he did not know which one was *really* Alice.

Suddenly the book fell from his hand, and clattered onto the floor, striking his foot as it fell. At the same instant, of course, he awoke, seated in his chair near the old stove. He smiled a little, but was not surprised, for he was used to dreaming strange and pleasant dreams. As he stooped to pick up the book, a customer entered the store.

"What have you there?" asked the stranger, looking at the volume in the old man's hand. "*Alice in Wonderland!* Charming thing! What do you ask for it?"

"Not this copy," said the old man, firmly. "This is my personal copy. This is one book you cannot buy."

To this astonishing harangue, Alice had no reply, for she understood very little of it, but it sounded interesting, and she liked the looks on the old bookman's face as he said it.

"Would you mind, sir," she asked timidly, "if I were to creep back into my book and hide again on your shelf?"

"Are you quite sure you can manage it?" asked the old man.

"Oh yes," said Alice. "But I did have a piece of the cake that I brought with me. I had two pieces—one to make me grow, and the other to make me small again. Just watch!"

She quickly took a few crumbs of cake from her pocket and began to eat them, and the old bookman, standing by, saw her shrink down and down and down, until she was such a tiny little thing at his feet that his eyes could scarcely find her.

He picked her up gently and rested the book, lying on the counter.

"You must find the place," he said. "Do you remember it?"

With a little sigh of happiness, Alice slipped into the illustration where, a few pages before, she fitted like a glove—and suddenly the picture was complete again, and the old bookman, turning the pages eagerly over, could not find her—there were so many of them, and he did not know which one was really Alice.

Suddenly the book fell from his hand, and clattered onto the floor, striking his foot as it fell. At the same moment someone came to the window, scratched his shoulder, and the old bookman jumped a little, but was not surprised, for he was used to dreaming things, in pleasanted ones. As he stooped to pick up the book, a customer entered the store.

"What have you there?" asked the stranger, looking at the volume on the floor. "Alice's Adventures in Wonderland? Let me see. The same old thing! What do you ask for it?"

"Not for sale," said the old man, quietly. "This is one of my treasures. This is one book you cannot buy."

III

FRANKLY SENTIMENTAL

I sing the birth was born to-night,
The author both of life and light;
  The angels so did sound it.
And like the ravished shepherds said,
Who saw the light, and were afraid,
  Yet searched, and true they found it.

The Son of God, th' eternal king,
That did us all salvation bring,
  And freed the soul from danger;
He whom the whole world could not take,
The Word, which heaven and earth did make,
  Was now laid in a manger.

BEN JONSON

A Christmas Dream, And How It Came True

LOUISA MAY ALCOTT

"I'M so tired of Christmas I wish there never would be another one!" exclaimed a discontented-looking little girl, as she sat idly watching her mother arrange a pile of gifts two days before they were to be given.

"Why, Effie, what a dreadful thing to say! You are as bad as old Scrooge; and I'm afraid something will happen to you, as it did to him, if you don't care for dear Christmas," answered mamma, almost dropping the silver horn she was filling with delicious candies.

"Who was Scrooge? What happened to him?" asked Effie, with a glimmer of interest in her listless face, as she picked out the sourest lemon-drop she could find; for nothing sweet suited her just then.

"He was one of Dickens's best people, and you can read the charming story some day. He hated Christmas until a strange dream showed him how dear and beautiful it was, and made a better man of him."

"I shall read it; for I like dreams, and have a great many curious ones myself. But they don't keep me from being tired of Christmas," said Effie, poking discontentedly among the sweeties for something worth eating.

"Why are you tired of what should be the happiest time of all the year?" asked mamma, anxiously.

"Perhaps I shouldn't be if I had something new. But it is always the same, and there isn't any more surprise about it. I always find heaps of goodies in my stocking. Don't like some of them, and soon get tired of those I do like. We always have a great dinner, and I eat too much, and feel ill next day. Then there is a Christmas tree somewhere, with a doll on top, or a stupid old Santa Claus, and children dancing and screaming over bonbons and toys that break, and shiny things that are of no use. Really, mamma, I've had so many Christmases all alike that I don't think I *can* bear another one." And Effie laid herself flat on the sofa, as if the mere idea was too much for her.

Her mother laughed at her despair, but was sorry to see her little girl so discontented, when she had everything to make her happy, and had known but ten Christmas days.

"Suppose we don't give you *any* presents at all—how would that suit you?" asked mamma, anxious to please her spoiled child.

"I should like one large and splendid one, and one dear little one, to remember some very nice person by," said Effie, who was a fanciful little body, full of odd whims and notions, which her friends loved to gratify, regardless of time, trouble, or money; for she was the last of three little girls, and very dear to all the family.

"Well, my darling, I will see what I can do to please you, and not say a word until all is ready. If I could only get a new idea to start with!" And mamma went on tying up her pretty bundles with a thoughtful face, while Effie strolled to the window to watch the rain that kept her in-doors and made her dismal.

"Seems to me poor children have better times than rich ones. I can't go out, and there is a girl about my age splashing along, without any maid to fuss about rubbers and cloaks and umbrellas and colds. I wish I was a beggar-girl."

"Would you like to be hungry, cold, and ragged, to beg all day, and sleep on an ash-heap at night?" asked mamma, wondering what would come next.

"Cinderella did, and had a nice time in the end. This girl out here has a basket of scraps on her arm, and a big old shawl all round her, and doesn't seem to care a bit, though the water runs out of the toes of her boots. She goes paddling along, laughing at the rain, and eating a cold potato as if it tasted nicer than the chicken and ice-cream I had for dinner. Yes, I do think poor children are happier than rich ones."

"So do I, sometimes. At the Orphan Asylum today I saw two dozen merry little souls who have no parents, no home, and no hope of Christmas beyond a stick of candy or a cake. I wish you had been there to see how happy they were, playing with the old toys some richer children had sent them."

"You may give them all mine; I'm so tired of them I never want to see them again," said Effie, turning from the window to the pretty baby-house full of everything a child's heart could desire.

"I will, and let you begin again with something you will not tire of, if I can only find it." And mamma knit her brows trying to discover some grand surprise for this child who didn't care for Christmas.

Nothing more was said then; and wandering off to the library, Effie found "A Christmas Carol," and, curling herself up in the sofa corner, read it all before tea. Some of it she did not understand; but she laughed and cried over many parts of the charming story, and felt better without knowing why.

All the evening she thought of poor Tiny Tim, Mrs. Cratchit with the pudding, and the stout old gentleman who danced so gayly that "his legs twinkled in the air." Presently bed-time arrived.

"Come now, and toast your feet," said Effie's nurse, "while I do your pretty hair and tell stories."

"I'll have a fairy tale tonight, a very interesting one," commanded Effie, as she put on her blue silk wrapper and little fur-lined slippers to sit before the fire and have her long curls brushed.

So Nursey told her best tales; and when at last the child lay down under her lace curtains, her head was full of a curious jumble of Christmas elves, poor children, snow-storms, sugar-plums, and surprises. So it is no wonder that she dreamed all night; and this was the dream, which she never quite forgot.

She found herself sitting on a stone, in the middle of a great field, all alone. The snow was falling fast, a bitter wind whistled by, and night was coming on. She felt hungry, cold, and tired, and did not know where to go nor what to do.

"I wanted to be a beggar-girl, and now I am one; but I don't like it, and wish somebody would come and take care of me. I don't know who I am, and I think I must be lost," thought Effie, with the curious interest one takes in one's self in dreams.

But the more she thought about it, the more bewildered she felt. Faster fell the snow, colder blew the wind, darker grew the night; and poor Effie made up her mind that she was quite forgotten and left to freeze alone. The tears were chilled on her cheeks, her feet felt like icicles, and her heart died within her, so hungry, frightened, and forlorn was she. Laying her head on her knees, she gave herself up for lost, and sat there with the great flakes fast turning her to a little white mound, when suddenly the sound of music reached her, and starting up, she looked and listened with all her eyes and ears.

Far away a dim light shone, and a voice was heard singing. She tried to run toward the welcome glimmer, but could not stir, and stood like a small statue of expectation while the light drew nearer, and the sweet words of the song grew clearer.

"From our happy home
Through the world we roam
One week in all the year,
Making winter spring
With the joy we bring
For Christmas-tide is here.

"Now the eastern star
Shines from afar
To light the poorest home;
Hearts warmer grow,
Gifts freely flow,
For Christmas-tide has come.

"Now gay trees rise
Before young eyes,
Abloom with tempting cheer;

"Blithe voices sing.
And blithe bells ring,
For Christmas-tide is here.

"Oh, happy chime,
Oh, blessed time,
That draws us all so near!
'Welcome, dear day,'
All creatures say,
For Christmas-tide is here."

A child's voice sang, a child's hand carried the little candle; and in the circle of soft light it shed, Effie saw a pretty child coming to her through the night and snow. A rosy, smiling creature, wrapped in white fur, with a wreath of green and scarlet holly on its shining hair, the magic candle in one hand, and the other outstretched as if to shower gifts and warmly press all other hands.

Effie forgot to speak as this bright vision came nearer, leaving no trace of footsteps in the snow, only lighting the way with its little candle, and filling the air with the music of its song.

"Dear child, you are lost, and I have come to find you," said the stranger, taking Effie's cold hands in his, with a smile like sunshine, while every holly berry glowed like a little fire.

"Do you know me?" asked Effie, feeling no fear, but a great gladness, at his coming.

"I know all children, and go to find them; for this is my holiday, and I gather them from all parts of the world to be merry with me once a year."

"Are you an angel?" asked Effie, looking for the wings.

"No; I am a Christmas spirit, and live with my mates in a pleasant place, getting ready for our holiday, when we are let out to roam about the world, helping to make this a happy time for all who will let us in. Will you come and see how we work?"

"I will go anywhere with you. Don't leave me again," cried Effie, gladly.

"First I will make you comfortable. That is what we love to do. You are cold, and you shall be warm; hungry, and I will feed you; sorrowful, and I will make you gay."

With a wave of his candle all three miracles were wrought—for the snow-flakes turned to a white fur cloak and hood on Effie's head and shoulders; a bowl of hot soup came sailing to her lips, and vanished when she had eagerly drunk the last drop; and suddenly the dismal field changed to a new world so full of wonders that all her troubles were forgotten in a minute.

Bells were ringing so merrily that it was hard to keep from dancing. Green garlands hung on the walls, and every tree was a Christmas tree full of toys, and blazing with candles that never went out.

In one place many little spirits sewed like mad on warm clothes, turning off work faster than any sewing-machine ever invented, and great piles were made ready to be sent to poor people. Other busy creatures packed money into purses, and wrote checks which they sent flying away on the wind—a lovely kind of snow-storm to fall into a world below full of poverty.

Older and graver spirits were looking over piles of little books, in which the records of the past year were kept, telling how different people had spent it, and what sort of gifts they deserved. Some got peace, some disappointment, some remorse and sorrow, some great joy and hope. The rich had generous thoughts sent them; the poor, gratitude and contentment. Children had more love and duty to parents; and parents renewed patience, wisdom, and satisfaction for and in their children. No one was forgotten.

"Please tell me what splendid place this is?" asked Effie, as soon as she could collect her wits after the first look at all these astonishing things.

"This is the Christmas world; and here we work all the year round, never tired of getting ready for the happy day. See, these are the saints just setting off, for some have far to go, and the children must not be disappointed."

As he spoke the spirit pointed to four gates, out of which four great sleighs were just driving, laden with toys, while a jolly old Santa Claus sat in the middle of each, drawing on his mittens and tucking up his wraps for a long cold drive.

"Why, I thought there was only one Santa Claus, and even he was a humbug," cried Effie, astonished at the sight.

"Never give up your faith in the sweet old stories, even after you come to see that they are only the pleasant shadow of a lovely truth."

Just then the sleighs went off with a great jingling of bells and pattering of reindeer hoofs, while all the spirits gave a cheer that was heard in the lower world, where people said, "Hear the stars sing."

"I never will say there isn't any Santa Claus again. Now, show me more."

"You will like to see this place, I think, and may learn something here perhaps."

The spirit smiled as he led the way to a little door, through which Effie peeped into a world of dolls. Baby-houses were in full blast, with dolls of all sorts going on like live people. Waxen ladies sat in their parlors elegantly dressed; black dolls cooked in the kitchens; nurses walked out with the bits of dollies; and the streets were full of tin soldiers marching, wooden horses prancing, express wagons rumbling, and little men hurrying to and fro. Shops were there, and tiny people buying legs of mutton, pounds of tea, mites of clothes, and everything dolls use or wear or want.

But presently she saw that in some ways the dolls improved upon the manners and customs of human beings, and she watched eagerly to learn why they did these things. A fine Paris doll driving in her carriage took up a black worsted Dinah who was hobbling along with a basket of clean clothes, and carried her to her journey's end, as if it were the proper thing to do. Another interesting china lady took off her comfortable red cloak and put it round a poor wooden creature done up in a paper shift, and so badly painted that its face would have sent some babies into fits.

"Seems to me I once knew a rich girl who didn't give her things to poor girls. I wish I could remember who she was, and tell her to be as kind as that china doll," said Effie, much touched at the sweet way the pretty creature wrapped up the poor fright, and then ran off in her little gray gown to buy a shiny fowl stuck on a wooden platter for her invalid mother's dinner.

"We recall these things to people's minds by dreams. I think the girl you speak of won't forget this one." And the spirit smiled, as if he enjoyed some joke which she did not see.

A little bell rang as she looked, and away scampered the children into the red-and-green school-house with the roof that lifted up, so one could see how nicely they sat at their desks with mites of books, or drew on the inch-square blackboards with crumbs of chalk.

"They know their lessons very well, and are as still as mice. We make a great racket at our school, and get bad marks every day. I shall tell the girls they had better mind what they do, or their dolls will be better scholars than they are," said Effie, much impressed, as she peeped in and saw no rod in the hand of the little mistress, who looked up and shook her head at the intruder, as if begging her to go away before the order of the school was disturbed.

Effie retired at once, but could not resist one look in at the window of a fine mansion, where the family were at dinner, the children behaved so well at table, and never grumbled a bit when their mamma said they could not have any more fruit.

"Now, show me something else," she said, as they came again to the low door that led out of Doll-land.

"You have seen how we prepare for Christmas; let me show you where we love best to send our good and happy gifts," answered the spirit, giving her his hand again.

"I know. I've seen ever so many," began Effie, thinking of her own Christmases.

"No, you have never seen what I will show you. Come away, and remember what you see tonight."

Like a flash that bright world vanished, and Effie found herself in a part of the city she had never seen before. It was far away from the gayer places, where every store was brilliant with lights and full of pretty things, and every house wore a festival air, while people hurried to and fro with merry greetings. It was down among the dingy streets where the poor lived, and where there was no making ready for Christmas.

Hungry women looked in at the shabby shops, longing to buy meat and bread, but empty pockets forbade. Tipsy men drank up their wages in the bar-rooms; and in many cold dark chambers little children huddled under the thick blankets, trying to forget their misery in sleep.

No nice dinners filled the air with savory smells, no gay trees dropped toys and bonbons into eager hands, no little stockings hung in rows beside the chimney-piece ready to be filled, no happy sounds of music, gay voices, and dancing feet were heard; and there were no signs of Christmas anywhere.

"Don't they have any in this place?" asked Effie, shivering, as she held fast the spirit's hand, following where he led her.

"We come to bring it. Let me show you our best workers." And the spirit pointed to some sweet-faced men and women who came stealing into the poor houses, working such beautiful miracles that Effie could only stand and watch.

Some slipped money into the empty pockets, and sent the happy mothers to buy all the comforts they needed; others led the drunken men out of temptation, and took them home to find safer pleasures there. Fires were kindled on cold hearths, tables spread as if by magic, and warm clothes wrapped round shivering limbs. Flowers suddenly bloomed in the chambers of the sick; old people found themselves remembered; sad hearts were consoled by a tender word, and wicked ones softened by the story of Him who forgave all sin.

But the sweetest work was for the children; and Effie held her breath to watch these human fairies hang up and fill the little stockings without which a child's Christmas is not perfect, putting in things that once she would have thought very humble presents, but which now seemed beautiful and precious because these poor babies had nothing.

"That is so beautiful! I wish I could make merry Christmas as these good people do, and be loved and thanked as they are," said Effie, softly, as she watched the busy men and women do their work and steal away without thinking of any reward but their own satisfaction.

"You can if you will. I have shown you the way. Try it, and see how happy your own holiday will be hereafter."

As he spoke, the spirit seemed to put his arms about her, and vanished with a kiss.

"Oh, stay and show me more!" cried Effie, trying to hold him fast.

"Darling, wake up, and tell me why you are smiling in your sleep," said a voice in her ear; and opening her eyes, there was mamma bending over her, and morning sunshine streaming into the room.

"Are they all gone? Did you hear the bells? Wasn't it splendid?" she asked, rubbing her eyes, and looking about her for the pretty child who was so real and sweet.

"You have been dreaming at a great rate—talking in your sleep, laughing, and clapping your hands as if you were cheering some one. Tell me what was so splendid," said mamma, smoothing the tumbled hair and lifting up the sleepy head.

Then, while she was being dressed, Effie told her dream, and Nursey thought it very wonderful; but mamma smiled to see how curiously things the child had thought, read, heard, and seen through the day were mixed up in her sleep.

"The spirit said I could work lovely miracles if I tried; but I don't know how to begin, for I have no magic candle to make feasts appear, and light up groves of Christmas trees, as he did," said Effie, sorrowfully.

"Yes, you have. We will do it! we will do it!" And clapping her hands, mamma suddenly began to dance all over the room as if she had lost her wits.

"How? how? You must tell me, mamma," cried Effie, dancing after her, and ready to believe anything possible when she remembered the adventures of the past night.

"I've got it! I've got it!—the new idea. A splendid one, if I can only carry it out!" And mamma waltzed the little girl round till her curls flew wildly in the air, while Nursey laughed as if she would die.

"Tell me! tell me!" shrieked Effie.

"No, no; it is a surprise—a grand surprise for Christmas day!" sung mamma, evidently charmed with her happy thought. "Now, come to breakfast; for we must work like bees if we want to play spirits tomorrow. You and Nursey will go out shopping, and get heaps of things, while I arrange matters behind the scenes."

They were running downstairs as mamma spoke, and Effie called out breathlessly——

"It won't be a surprise; for I know you are going to ask some poor children here, and have a tree or something. It won't be like my dream; for they had ever so many trees, and more children than we can find anywhere."

"There will be no tree, no party, no dinner, in this house at all, and no presents for you. Won't that be a surprise?" And mamma laughed at Effie's bewildered face.

"Do it. I shall like it, I think; and I won't ask any questions, so it will all burst upon me when the time comes," she said; and she ate her breakfast thoughtfully, for this really would be a new sort of Christmas.

All that morning Effie trotted after Nursey in and out of shops, buying dozens of barking dogs, woolly lambs, and squeaking birds; tiny tea-sets, gay picture-books, mittens and hoods, dolls and candy. Parcel after parcel was sent home; but when Effie returned she saw no trace of them, though she peeped everywhere. Nursey chuckled, but wouldn't give a hint, and went out again in the afternoon with a long list of more things to buy; while Effie wandered forlornly about the house, missing the usual merry stir that went before the Christmas dinner and the evening fun.

As for mamma, she was quite invisible all day, and came in at night so tired that she could only lie on the sofa to rest, smiling as if some very pleasant thought made her happy in spite of weariness.

"Is the surprise going on all right?" asked Effie, anxiously; for it seemed an immense time to wait till another evening came.

"Beautifully! better than I expected; for several of my good friends are helping, or I couldn't have done as I wish. I know you will like it, dear, and long remember this new way of making Christmas merry."

Mamma gave her a very tender kiss, and Effie went to bed.

The next day was a very strange one; for when she woke there was no stocking to examine, no pile of gifts under her napkin, no one said, "Merry Christmas!" to her, and the dinner was just as usual to her. Mamma vanished again, and Nursey kept wiping her eyes and saying: "The dear things! It's the prettiest idea I ever heard of. No one but your blessed ma could have done it."

"Do stop, Nursey, or I shall go crazy because I don't know the secret!" cried Effie, more than once; and she kept her eye on the clock, for at seven in the evening the surprise was to come off.

The longed-for hour arrived at last, and the child was too excited to ask questions when Nursey put on her cloak and hood, led her to the carriage, and they drove away, leaving their house the one dark and silent one in the row.

"I feel like the girls in the fairy tales who are led off to strange places and see fine things," said Effie, in a whisper, as they jingled through the gay streets.

"Ah, my deary, it *is* like a fairy tale, I do assure you, and you will see finer things than most children will tonight. Steady, now, and do just as I tell you, and don't say one word whatever you see," answered Nursey, quite quivering with excitement as she patted a large box in her lap, and nodded and laughed with twinkling eyes.

They drove into a dark yard, and Effie was led through a back door to a little room, where Nursey coolly proceeded to take off not only her cloak and hood but her dress and shoes also. Effie stared and bit her lips, but kept still until out of the box came a little white fur coat and boots, a wreath of holly leaves and berries, and a candle with a frill of gold paper round it. A long "Oh!" escaped her then; and when she was dressed and saw herself in the glass, she started back, exclaiming, "Why, Nursey, I look like the spirit in my dream!"

"So you do; and that's the part you are to play, my pretty! Now whist, while I blind your eyes and put you in your place."

"Shall I be afraid?" whispered Effie, full of wonder; for as they went out she heard the sound of many voices, the tramp of many feet, and, in spite of the bandage, was sure a great light shone upon her when she stopped.

"You needn't be; I shall stand close by, and your ma will be there."

After the handkerchief was tied about her eyes, Nursey led Effie up some steps, and placed her on a high platform, where something like leaves touched her head, and the soft snap of lamps seemed to fill the air.

Music began as soon as Nursey clapped her hands, the voices outside sounded nearer, and the tramp was evidently coming up the stairs.

"Now, my precious, look and see how you and your dear ma have made a merry Christmas for them that needed it!"

Off went the bandage; and for a minute Effie really did think she was asleep again, for she actually stood in "a grove of Christmas trees," all gay and shining as in her vision. Twelve on a side, in two rows down the room, stood the little pines, each on its low table; and behind Effie a taller one rose to the roof, hung with wreaths of popcorn, apples, oranges, horns of candy, and cakes of all sorts, from sugary hearts to gingerbread Jumbos. On the smaller trees she saw many of her own discarded toys and those Nursey bought, as well as heaps that seemed to have rained down straight from that delightful Christmas country where she felt as if she was again.

"How splendid! Who is it for? What is that noise? Where is mamma?" cried Effie, pale with pleasure and surprise, as she stood looking down the brilliant little street from her high place.

Before Nursey could answer, the doors at the lower end flew open, and in marched twenty-four little blue-gowned orphan girls, singing sweetly, until amazement changed the song to cries of joy and wonder as the shining spectacle appeared. While they stood staring with round eyes at the wilderness of pretty things about them, mamma stepped up beside Effie, and holding her hand fast to give her courage, told the story of the dream in a few simple words, ending in this way:

"So my little girl wanted to be a Christmas spirit too, and make this a happy day for those who had not as many pleasures and comforts as she has. She likes surprises, and we planned this for you all. She shall play the good fairy, and give each of you something from this tree, after which every one will find her own name on a small tree, and can go to enjoy it in her own way. March by, my dears, and let us fill your hands."

Nobody told them to do it, but all the hands were clapped heartily before a single child stirred; then one by one they came to look up wonderingly at the pretty giver of the feast as she leaned down to offer them great yellow oranges, red apples, bunches of grapes, bonbons, and cakes, till all were gone, and a double row of smiling faces turned toward her as the children filed back to their places in the orderly way they had been taught.

Then each was led to her own tree by the good ladies who had helped mamma with all their hearts; and the happy hubbub that arose would have satisfied even Santa Claus himself—shrieks of joy, dances of delight, laughter and tears (for some tender little things could not bear so much pleasure at once, and sobbed with mouths full of candy and hands full of toys). How they ran to show one another the new treasures! how they peeped and tasted, pulled and pinched, until the air was full of queer noises, the floor covered with papers, and the little trees left bare of all but candles!

"I don't think heaven can be any gooder than this," sighed one small girl, as she looked about her in a blissful maze, holding her full apron with one hand, while she luxuriously carried sugar-plums to her mouth with the other.

"Is that a truly angel up there?" asked another, fascinated by the little white figure with the wreath on its shining hair, who in some mysterious way had been the cause of all this merry-making.

"I wish I dared to go and kiss her for this splendid party," said a lame child, leaning on her crutch, as she stood near the steps, won-

"But she hugged them to her bosom"

THE GIFT OF THE MAGI

Story on page 180

dering how it seemed to sit in a mother's lap, as Effie was doing, while she watched the happy scene before her.

Effie heard her, and remembering Tiny Tim, ran down and put her arms about the pale child, kissing the wistful face, as she said sweetly, "You may; but mamma deserves the thanks. She did it all; I only dreamed about it."

Lame Katy felt as if "a truly angel" was embracing her, and could only stammer out her thanks, while the other children ran to see the pretty spirit, and touch her soft dress, until she stood in a crowd of blue gowns laughing as they held up their gifts for her to see and admire.

Mamma leaned down and whispered one word to the older girls; and suddenly they all took hands to dance round Effie, singing as they skipped.

It was a pretty sight, and the ladies found it hard to break up the happy revel; but it was late for small people, and too much fun is a mistake. So the girls fell into line, and marched before Effie and mamma again, to say good-night with such grateful little faces that the eyes of those who looked grew dim with tears. Mamma kissed every one; and many a hungry childish heart felt as if the touch of those tender lips was their best gift. Effie shook so many small hands that her own tingled; and when Katy came she pressed a small doll into Effie's hand, whispering, "You didn't have a single present, and we had lots. Do keep that; it's the prettiest thing I got."

"I will," answered Effie, and held it fast until the last smiling face was gone, the surprise all over, and she safe in her own bed, too tired and happy for anything but sleep.

"Mamma, it *was* a beautiful surprise, and I thank you so much! I don't see how you ever did it; but I like it best of all the Christmases I ever had, and mean to make one every year. I had my splendid big present, and here is the dear little one to keep for love of poor Katy; so even that part of my wish came true."

And Effie fell asleep with a happy smile on her lips, her one humble gift still in her hand, and a new love for Christmas in her heart that never changed through a long life spent in doing good.

An Empty Purse

SARAH ORNE JEWETT

I

LITTLE Miss Debby Gaines was counting the days to Christmas; there were only three, and the weather was bright and warm for the time of year. "I've got to step fast to carry out all my plans," she said to herself. "It seems to me as if it were going to be a beautiful Christmas; it won't be like any I've spent lately, either. I shouldn't wonder if it turned out for the best, my losing that money I always call my Christmas money; anyway I'll do the best I can to make up for it."

Miss Debby was sitting by the window sewing as fast as she could, for the light of the short winter day was going, mending a warm old petticoat and humming a psalm-tune. Suddenly she heard a knock at the door; she lived in two upstairs rooms, and could not see the street.

"Come in!" she said cheerfully, and dropped her lapful of work.

"Why, if it isn't Mrs. Rivers!" she exclaimed with much pleasure.

The guest was a large woman, fashionably dressed. You would have thought that a very elegant blue-jay had come to make a late afternoon call upon such a brown chippy-sparrow as Miss Debby Gaines. Miss Debby felt much honored, and brought forward her best rocking-chair; and Mrs. Rivers seated herself and began to rock. Her stiff silk gown creaked as if she were a ship at sea.

"What are you doing—something pretty for Christmas?" she asked.

"It may be for Christmas, but it isn't very pretty," answered Miss Debby with a little laugh and shake of the head. "Tell you the truth, I was mending up a nice warm petticoat that I don't have much use for; I thought I'd give it to old Mrs. Bean, at the poorhouse. She's a complaining, cold old creatur', an' she's got poor eyesight and can't sew, and I thought this would make her real comfortable. It's rather more heavy than I need to wear."

"I've been down town all the afternoon, and it's so tiresome trying to get anything in the stores," complained Mrs. Rivers. "They push you right away from what you want time to look over. I like to consider what I buy. It's a great burden to me trying to get ready for Christmas, and I thought I shouldn't do anything this year on account of my health. I've had large expenses this autumn. I had to buy new carpets and a new outside garment. I do like to see the pretty things in the stores, but they were so full of people and so hot and disagreeable this afternoon."

Miss Debby had picked up her petticoat and was holding it close to the window while she sewed on the button with firm linen stitches.

"I haven't been down the street for two or three days," she said. "You'll excuse me for goin' on with my work; it's most dark, and I'll be done in a moment; then we can sit an' talk."

"It does me good to come and see you once in a while," said Mrs. Rivers plaintively. "I thought I'd stop on my way home. Last year you had so many pretty little things that you'd been making."

"There aren't any at all this year," answered Miss Debby bravely. "It wasn't convenient, so I thought I'd just try having another kind of a merry Christmas."

"Sometimes I wish I had no more responsibilities than you have. My large house is such a care. Mr. Rivers is very particular about everything, and so am I." She gave a great sigh, and creaked louder than before, but Miss Debby did not find the right sort of consolation to offer, and kept silence. "You enjoy having your pretty house," she ventured to say after a few moments; "you wouldn't like to do with as little as some,"—and Mrs. Rivers shook her head in the dusk, and went on rocking.

"Presents aren't nothing unless the heart goes with them," said Miss Debby boldly at last, "and I think we can show good feelin' in other ways than by bestowing little pin-cushions. Anyway, I've got to find those ways for me this year. 'Tis a day when we New England folks can speak right out to each other, and that does us some good. Somethin' gets in the air. I expect now to enjoy this Christmas myself, though I felt dreadful bad last week, sayin' to myself 'twas the first time I couldn't buy Christmas presents. I didn't know how interested I was goin' to get; you see I've made my little plans."

Then they talked about other things, and Mrs. Rivers grew more cheerful and at last went away. She always found Christmas a melancholy season. She did not like the trouble of giving presents then, or at any other time; but she had her good points, as Miss Debby Gaines always bravely insisted.

II

Early on Christmas morning Miss Debby waked up with a feeling of happy expectation, and could hardly wait to make her cup of tea and eat her little breakfast on the corner of the table before she got out her best bonnet and Sunday cloak to begin her Christmas errands. It was cloudy and dark, but the sunlight came at last, pale and radiant, into the little brown room; and Miss Debby's face matched it with a quiet smile and happy look of eagerness.

"Take neither purse nor scrip," she said to herself as she went downstairs into the street. There was nobody else stirring in the house, but she knew that the poorhouse would be open and its early breakfast past by the time she could get there. It was a mile or so out of town. She hugged a large package under her shawl, and shivered a little at the beginning of her walk. There was no snow, but the heavy hoar-frost glistened on the sidewalks, and the air was sharp.

Old Mrs. Bean was coming out of the great kitchen, and when her friend wished her a merry Christmas she shook her head.

"There ain't anybody to make it merry for me," she said.

"I wish you a happy Christmas!" said Miss Debby again; "I've come on purpose to be your first caller, an' I'm going to make you the only present I shall give this year. 'Tis somethin' useful, Mis' Bean; a warm petticoat I've fixed up nice, so's you can put it right on and feel the comfort of it."

The old woman's face brightened. "Why, you are real kind," she said eagerly. "It is the one thing I've been wantin'. Oh yes, *dear sakes!* ain't it a beautiful warm one—one o' the real old-fashioned quilted kind. I always used to have 'em when I was better off. Well, that *is* a present!"

"Now I'm goin', because I can come an' set an' talk with you any day, and today I've got Christmas work," and off Miss Debby went to the heart of the town again.

Christmas was on Tuesday that year, and she opened the door of a little house where a tired-looking young woman stood by an ironing-table and looked at her with surprise. "Why, Miss Gaines!" she exclaimed; "where are you going so early?"

"I wish you a happy Christmas!" said Miss Debby. "I've come to spend the mornin' with you. Just through breakfast? No; the little girls are eatin' away yet. Why, you're late!"

"I didn't mean to be," said the young mother; "but I felt so tired this morning, and pretty sad, too, thinking of last year an' all. So I just let the children sleep. Nelly's got cold and was coughing most all night, and I couldn't bear to get up and begin the day. Mother sent for me to come over to spend Christmas, but I couldn't get the courage to start. She said she'd have some little presents ready for the little girls, and now I'm most sorry I disappointed her."

"That's just why I'm here," said Miss Debby gayly, and with double her usual decision. "No, Nelly's not fit to go out, I can see; and you leave her here with me, an' you just get ready and take Susy and go. Your mother'll think everything of it, and I'll see to things here. Ironin'? Why, 'twill do me good. I feel a little chilly, and Nelly and I can have a grand time. Now you go right off an' get ready, and catch the quarter-to-nine train. I won't hear no words about it."

So presently the pale, hard-worked young mother put on her widow's bonnet and started off down the street, leading bright-faced little Susy by the hand; and Miss Debby and her favorite, Nelly, watched them go, from the window. The breakfast dishes were washed and put away in such fashion that Nelly thought it quite as good as doll's housekeeping; and then, while Miss Debby ironed, she sat in a warm corner by the stove and listened to stories and to Miss Debby's old-fashioned ballads, which, though sung in a slightly cracked voice, were most delightful to childish ears. What a Christmas morning it was! And after the small ironing was done, what pleasant things there seemed to be to do! Miss Debby rummaged until she found some little aprons cut for the children; and first she basted one for Nelly to sew, and then she took the other herself, and they sat down together and sewed until dinner-time. The aprons were pink and added to the gayety of the occasion; and they were ready at last to surprise Nelly's mother by being put back in their place in the same roll—all done even to the buttons and buttonholes, for Miss Debby found time to finish Nelly's as well as her own. And they had bread and milk for dinner, and Miss Debby told stories of when she was a little girl. Altogether there never was a happier Christmas Day, and the spirit of Christmas, of peace and good-will, shone brightly in Miss Debby's face. Her quick eyes saw many chances to lend a helping hand to the poor defenceless household. When Nelly's mother came home at night, heartened and cheered by her visit, she found the ironing and mending done; and a day or two later the pink aprons turned up all ready to be put on. And Nelly's tiresome cough, which sounded like the whooping-cough, was quite stilled by some good old-fashioned dose which Miss Debby mixed agreeably with molasses and put to simmer on the stove. There seemed to be no end to the kind and thoughtful things Miss Debby did that day in a neighbor's house.

She had started for home at dusk, just before it was time for young Mrs. Prender to get back, and was walking along the street, a little tired, but very happy.

"Why, it's only half past four o'clock now!" she exclaimed, as she passed the watchmaker's window. "I mean to go and see Mrs. Wallis a little while," and she quickened her steps.

Presently Miss Debby Gaines came to a fine large house, very different from the one she had just left, and took pains to straighten her little black bonnet as she went up the long flight of handsome stone steps. An elderly man-servant opened the door.

"I wish you a happy Christmas!" said Miss Debby. "Can I see Mrs. Wallis, do you suppose, Mr. Johnson?"

"Oh, yes'm," said Johnson with feeling. "I was wishing somebody'd come in, Miss Gaines, now it's beginning to get dark. The young ladies was here this morning, and brought their presents, but they'd made a promise to go out into the country with some young friends, so they aren't coming to dinner, and Mrs. Wallis has been alone all day. She was pleased to have 'em go, though."

By this time Miss Debby had crossed the wide hall to the library, where the kind mistress of the house was sitting alone. She hesitated a moment before she could speak.

"I wish you a happy Christmas!" she said. "It's only me, Mrs. Wallis—Debby Gaines."

"Why, Miss Debby!" and there was something in the tone of this hostess which told at once that she was glad to see a friend. "Why, dear Miss Debby! Come and sit down in this chair by me! I don't doubt you have been trotting about all day," and Mrs. Wallis held out a warm, affectionate hand.

"No, I've been keepin' house for Mis' Prender, so she could go and see her mother," explained Miss Debby quite simply. "I had a nice time with her little girl that's just getting over a cold and couldn't go with the others. I was just on my way home. I thought I'd stop and see if there was anything I could do for you."

"Nothing except to stay a little while and keep me company," said Mrs. Wallis. "My granddaughters are usually here, but they had a very pleasant plan made for them, and I was very glad to have them go. A skating party and a dinner at the Ashtons' country house, and a dance."

"Young folks will be young folks," said Miss Debby. "I should like to hear all about it when they come and tell. Everybody seemed to be goin' somewhere today; 'twas the nice clear weather."

"There are all my pretty presents on the table," said Mrs. Wallis. "Somehow they haven't been very good company; this is the first Christmas in all my life that I have happened to spend quite alone."

Miss Debby might not have done so much without thinking, by daylight, but she drew a little nearer and took hold of Mrs. Wallis's hand.

"You must have had a great many lovely things to remember," she said softly. "But anybody can't help feeling lonesome; I know how 'tis. Everybody misses somebody the world over. There was all of us together once at home, and now I'm a kind of sparrow on the housetops. But I've had a beautiful day so far. I own I was afraid you'd have a sight of company an' I should have to miss askin' to see you."

"I'm glad somebody wanted to see me," said Mrs. Wallis more cheerfully, "and one of the friends I've known longest"; then they went on with much pleasant talk of the old days, and Mrs. Wallis gave Miss Debby an excellent cup of tea, and they had a happy little feast together there in the library before the humble, loving-hearted guest went away, leaving peace and good-will once more in a lonely and troubled heart.

She stopped here and there at the houses of other friends, forgetting in her happiness that she was empty-handed on Christmas Day, and everywhere she left a new feeling of friendliness and pleasant kindness. At one house she comforted a crying child by mending his broken top, and at another she knew just how to help a pretty girl to get ready for her Christmas party, and sat down and took off her big woollen gloves to alter the refractory dress, which had seemed impossible to be worn. She was like a good angel as she sat there, sewing and smiling and putting everybody's mind at ease.

It was late in the evening when this was finished, and she had had a long day; but she stopped, with great bravery, and asked to see the minister, just to tell him how thankful she was for his sermon on Sunday and wish him a happy Christmas. The minister had been a little discouraged for some reason, as ministers often are, and even Christmas kindnesses in the shape of welcome presents from his friends did not cheer him half so much as the sincerity and affection of Miss Debby's visit. He watched the little figure go down the steps with tears in his eyes. So few persons could forget themselves to remember others as this dear parishioner could; it was worth living for, if one could sometimes help and refresh those who are the true helpers; and he went back to his work in the study feeling like a better and busier man than when he had left it.

So Miss Debby came back to her little home again. The fire was out and it was all dark, but she went straight to her small rocking-chair by the window and sat down to rest, and to thank the Lord for such a happy day. Though her purse was empty her heart was full, and she had left pleasure and comfort behind her all along the way.

Presently she lighted her lamp, and then she saw on the table a great package with a note beside it; the note was from Mrs. Rivers.

"Something you said the other day," Miss Debby read, "made me feel differently about Christmas from the way I have before, and I am going right to work to try to make as many people happy as I can. And you must feel that my heart goes with these presents that I send you first. They are some of my own things that I liked, and I send them with love."

Miss Debby's face shone with joy. She had always liked Mrs. Rivers, but she had often pitied her a little; and now the note made her feel as if she had found a new friend in an old one. This was the way that Miss Debby's Christmas came to its happy end.

The Gift of the Magi

O. HENRY

ONE dollar and eighty-seven cents. That was all. And sixty cents of it was in pennies. Pennies saved one and two at a time by bulldozing the grocer and the vegetable man and the butcher until one's cheeks burned with the silent imputation of parsimony that such close dealing implied. Three times Della counted it. One dollar and eighty-seven cents. And the next day would be Christmas.

There was clearly nothing to do but flop down on the shabby little couch and howl. So Della did it. Which instigates the moral reflection that life is made up of sobs, sniffles, and smiles, with sniffles predominating.

While the mistress of the home is gradually subsiding from the first stage to the second, take a look at the home. A furnished flat at eight dollars per week. It did not exactly beggar description, but it certainly had that word on the lookout for the mendicancy squad.

In the vestibule below was a letter-box into which no letter would go, and an electric button from which no mortal finger could coax a ring. Also appertaining thereunto was a card bearing the name "Mr. James Dillingham Young."

The "Dillingham" had been flung to the breeze during a former period of prosperity when its possessor was being paid thirty dollars per week. Now, when the income was shrunk to twenty dollars, the letters of "Dillingham" looked blurred, as though they were thinking seriously of contracting to a modest and unassuming D. But whenever Mr. James Dillingham Young came home and reached his flat above he was called "Jim" and greatly hugged by Mrs. James Dillingham Young, already introduced to you as Della. Which is all very good.

Della finished her cry and attended to her cheeks with a powder-puff. She stood by the window and looked out dully at a gray cat walking a gray fence in a gray back yard. Tomorrow would be Christmas Day, and she had only $1.87 with which to buy Jim a present. She had been saving every penny she could for months, with this result. Twenty dollars a week doesn't go far. Expenses had been greater than she had calculated. They always are. Only $1.87 to buy a present for Jim. Her Jim. Many a happy hour she had spent planning for something nice for him. Something fine and rare and sterling—something just a little bit near to being worthy of the honor of being owned by Jim.

There was a pier-glass between the windows of the room. Perhaps you have seen a pier-glass in an eight-dollar flat. A very thin and very agile person may, by observing his reflection in a rapid sequence of longitudinal strips, obtain a fairly accurate conception of his looks. Della, being slender, had mastered the art.

Suddenly she whirled from the window and stood before the glass. Her eyes were shining brilliantly, but her face had lost its color within twenty seconds. Rapidly she pulled down her hair and let it fall to its full length.

Now, there were two possessions of the James Dillingham Youngs in which they both took a mighty pride. One was Jim's gold watch that had been his father's and his grandfather's. The other was Della's hair. Had the Queen of Sheba lived in the flat across the airshaft, Della would have let her hair hang out the window some day to dry just to depreciate Her Majesty's jewels and gifts. Had King Solomon been the janitor, with all his treasures piled up in the basement, Jim would have pulled out his watch every time he passed, just to see him pluck at his beard from envy.

So now Della's beautiful hair fell about her, rippling and shining like a cascade of brown waters. She did it up again nervously and quickly. Once she faltered for a minute and stood still while a tear or two splashed on the worn red carpet.

On went her old brown jacket; on went her old brown hat. With a whirl of skirts and with the brilliant sparkle still in her eyes, she fluttered out the door and down the stairs to the street.

Where she stopped the sign read: "Mme. Sofronie. Hair Goods of All Kinds." One flight up Della ran, and collected herself, panting. Madame, large, too white, chilly, hardly looked the "Sofronie."

"Will you buy my hair?" asked Della.

"I buy hair," said Madame. "Take yer hat off and let's have a sight at the looks of it."

Down rippled the brown cascade.

"Twenty dollars," said Madame, lifting the mass with a practiced hand.

"Give it to me quick," said Della.

Oh, and the next two hours tripped by on rosy wings. Forget the hashed metaphor. She was ransacking the stores for Jim's present.

She found it at last. It surely had been made for Jim and no one else. There was no other like it in any of the stores, and she had turned all of them inside out. It was a platinum watch-chain, simple and chaste in design, properly proclaiming its value by substance alone and not by meretricious ornamentation—as all good things should do. It was even worthy of The Watch. As soon as she saw it she knew that it must be Jim's. It was like him. Quietness and value—the description applied to both. Twenty-one dollars they took from her for it, and she hurried home with the eighty-seven cents. With that chain on his watch Jim might be properly anxious about the time in any company. Grand as the watch was, he sometimes looked at it on the sly on account of the old leather strap that he used in place of a chain.

When Della reached home her intoxication gave way a little to prudence and reason. She got out her curling-irons and lighted the gas and went to work repairing the ravages made by generosity added to love. Which is always a tremendous task, dear friends—a mammoth task.

Within forty minutes her head was covered with tiny close-lying curls that made her look wonderfully like a truant schoolboy. She looked at her reflection in the mirror long, carefully, and critically.

"If Jim doesn't kill me," she said to herself, "before he takes a second look at me, he'll say I look like a Coney Island chorus girl. But what could I do—oh! what could I do with a dollar and eighty-seven cents?"

At seven o'clock the coffee was made and the frying-pan was on the back of the stove, hot and ready to cook the chops.

Jim was never late. Della doubled the watch-chain in her hand and sat on the corner of the table near the door that he always entered. Then she heard his step on the stair away down on the first flight, and she turned white for just a moment. She had a habit of saying little silent prayers about the simplest everyday things, and now she whispered: "Please, God, make him think I am still pretty."

The door opened and Jim stepped in and closed it. He looked thin and very serious. Poor fellow, he was only twenty-two—and to be burdened with a family! He needed a new overcoat and he was without gloves.

Jim stepped inside the door, as immovable as a setter at the scent of quail. His eyes were fixed upon Della, and there was an expression in them that she could not read, and it terrified her. It was not anger, nor surprise, nor disapproval, nor horror, nor any of the sentiments that she had been prepared for. He simply stared at her fixedly with that peculiar expression on his face.

Della wriggled off the table and went for him.

"Jim, darling," she cried, "don't look at me that way. I had my hair cut off and sold it because I couldn't have lived through Christmas without giving you a present. It'll grow out again—you won't mind, will you? I just had to do it. My hair grows awfully fast. Say 'Merry Christmas!' Jim, and let's be happy. You don't know what a nice—what a beautiful, nice gift I've got for you."

"You've cut off your hair?" asked Jim, laboriously, as if he had not arrived at that patent fact yet even after the hardest mental labor.

"Cut it off and sold it," said Della. "Don't you like me just as well, anyhow? I'm me without my hair, ain't I?"

Jim looked about the room curiously.

"You say your hair is gone?" he said, with an air almost of idiocy.

"You needn't look for it," said Della. "It's sold, I tell you—sold and gone, too. It's Christmas Eve, boy. Be good to me, for it went for you. Maybe the hairs of my head were numbered," she went on with a sudden serious sweetness, "but nobody could ever count my love for you. Shall I put the chops on, Jim?"

Out of his trance Jim seemed to quickly wake. He enfolded his Della. For ten seconds let us regard with discreet scrutiny some inconsequential object in the other direction. Eight dollars a week or a million a year—what is the difference? A mathematician or a wit would give you the wrong answer. The Magi brought valuable gifts, but that was not among them. This dark assertion will be illuminated later on.

Jim drew a package from his overcoat pocket and threw it upon the table.

"Don't make any mistake, Dell," he said, "about me. I don't think there's anything in the way of a haircut or a shave or a shampoo that could make me like my girl any less. But if you'll unwrap that package you may see why you had me going awhile at first."

White fingers and nimble tore at the string and paper. And then an ecstatic scream of joy; and then, alas! a quick feminine change to hysterical tears and wails, necessitating the immediate employment of all the comforting powers of the lord of the flat.

For there lay The Combs—the set of combs that Della had worshiped for long in a Broadway window. Beautiful combs, pure tortoise shell, with jeweled rims—just the shade to wear in the beautiful vanished hair. They were expensive combs, she knew, and her heart had simply craved and yearned over them without the least hope of possession. And now they were hers, but the tresses that should have adorned the coveted adornments were gone.

But she hugged them to her bosom, and at length she was able to look up with dim eyes and a smile and say: "My hair grows so fast, Jim!"

And then Della leaped up like a little singed cat and cried, "Oh, oh!"

Jim had not yet seen his beautiful present. She held it out to him eagerly upon her open palm. The dull precious metal seemed to flash with a reflection of her bright and ardent spirit.

"Isn't it a dandy, Jim? I hunted all over town to find it. You'll have to look at the time a hundred times a day now. Give me your watch. I want to see how it looks on it."

Instead of obeying, Jim tumbled down on the couch and put his hands under the back of his head and smiled.

"Dell," he said, "let's put our Christmas presents away and keep 'em awhile. They're too nice to use just at present. I sold the watch to get the money to buy your combs. And now suppose you put the chops on."

The Magi, as you know, were wise men—wonderfully wise men—who brought gifts to the Babe in the manger. They invented the art of giving Christmas presents. Being wise, their gifts were no doubt wise ones, possibly bearing the privilege of exchange in case of duplication. And here I have lamely related to you the uneventful chronicle of two foolish children in a flat who most unwisely sacrificed for each other the greatest treasures of their house. But in a last word to the wise of these days let it be said that of all who give gifts these two were the wisest. Of all who give and receive gifts, such as they are wisest. Everywhere they are wisest. They are the Magi.

It Happened at Wild Cat

FREDERICK LANDIS

THEY still tell the story of John Winston down at the little town of Wild Cat, particularly around Christmas time, for that is when it all happened, many years ago.

The men and women who knew John Winston have all joined him now in the slab-strewn lot with the tall fir trees and the hedge around it, the lot behind the white church where they all worshiped with that firm faith which was the staff of older days, but the tale still hovers over the town and seems to soften the harsh outline of the hills, once crowned with oaks, then scalped by lumbermen, and now towering, bald and unlovely, above Indian River, resting while it may, as if it knew that in less than half a mile it must plunge in turmoil down deep gorges, surge past great rocks, then leap from a lofty precipice, all this in order that it may form a little pocket of wild beauty in an otherwise tranquil Indiana countryside—a gem of cliffs, ferns, canyons, soaring trees, mirrored waters, spectral shadows, gliding fancies, whispering yesterdays, twilight patience, silent majesty, and far above, up a shimmering ladder of sunlight, the fleecy clouds; a rugged cathedral of Time, with a congregation of ages and a gospel of never-ending peace.

But I started to tell you the story of John Winston——

That was the coldest December in forty years; this was agreed by the old timers who sat, enveloped in several layers of pants and vests, in Jones' store, around the wood-burner with the pipe which meandered all over the place, seeking an exit, before it finally

From *The Hoosier Editor*. Reprinted by permission of Kenesaw M. Landis II.

found one at the rear—and when that disputatious group agreed upon any proposition, it was an epoch in the life of Wild Cat.

Villagers swarmed into Jones' store that Christmas Eve for candy, nuts, fruits, toys; and many a greeting went back and forth, the crest of the yuletide spirit being reached when "Old Skinflint" Snooks, who loaned money at forty percent, gave Henry Prosch, the village shoemaker, one of the two rare Havanas he had purchased for a nickel.

Business was so brisk that Mr. Simeon Jones impressed into the service Mrs. Jones and several minor Joneses to wait upon the jostling throng in the smoke-filled room, and whenever the door opened, there was a wave of mirth and melody from without—shouts of children, silvery sleigh-bells, Christmas carols from the church, over the way.

Yes, it was good to be alive that night!

So thought John Winston as he left his home around nine o'clock, the old spacious red brick house on Signal Hill, the house with the four white columns, the iron letter "S" on its broad chimneys and the white cupola on top.

He was the foremost citizen of Wild Cat, combining with farming the activities of real estate and banking, while on the side, he was the keenest politician in Indiana, a state not without its fair proportion of political impresarios.

He was credited with manufacturing two United States senators and several governors, though never seeking office for himself. As he explained it one night at a love feast of his party, "Some like to play race horses, but to my way of thinking, the finest sport is to pick up some fine young fellow with the points of a thoroughbred, back him and see how far he can go."

He was great of frame, something like six feet-four and built accordingly; there wasn't an ounce of fat loafing on his iron dimensions, for nothing loafed around John Winston.

His was the head of a great mastiff, large and crowned with a thick, white mane, while his face, ruddy as a boy's, was clean and sharp, with high cheek bones, shaggy brows, keen gray eyes, a promontory of a nose and a crag of a chin.

His temper was stormy, but the door of his heart was never locked; he belonged to no church, but felt at home in all of them, for he helped them all.

On occasion he took a drink of liquor that would fell an ox, but never to excess, and down at the state capital it was said he played a game of poker which seldom failed to summon all to repentance, bringing to the furtherance of his art an imperturbability which would dismay an oriental and a penetrating glance sufficient to read the meditations of the sphinx.

He was bluff, direct, impulsive, loyal to the death and a hater-extraordinary; a man of parts, this John Winston!

So he left his home at the edge of Wild Cat that Christmas Eve, making his way down to the village street, plodding cautiously the icy way, with many a jab of his hickory cane; his long blue cape buttoned at the neck and on his head a cap of seal-skin.

Entering Jones' store, he was acclaimed in a manner fitting to his local lordship, and after transacting his business, he paid homage to the spirit of the season by passing cigars to the be-whiskered philosophers arguing around the stove, then took his leave.

Starting home the way he had come, he paused, then obeyed a strange impulse to return by the way of Indian River, just why, he was never quite able to explain to his own satisfaction, for he had not gone that way for years.

The river was frozen so solidly that sleighing parties drove down its crystal sheet from Wild Cat to Georgetown, ten miles away, and as Winston started up the middle of the ice-locked stream, it was so still that as he looked over the town, chimney smoke arose straight to Heaven from houses that were dark; arose calm, un-vexed—like incense from an altar, and all was silent, save when fences cracked, wagon wheels rang in the snow or the whistle of a locomotive wriggled upward in the bitter night, only to drip icicles, then die away.

He thought it was cosmic glory which lured him on, the wild anarchy of it, the challenge of the elemental, the weird beauty, for it seemed a world was dead and covered with a winding sheet, and he alone remained and now was walking through a silvery citadel of desolation.

The King of Winter was on his throne, and that vast throne was white and drenched with more diamonds than kings of earth ever dreamed of—the prodigal gift of a pallid moon, now drifting over all, through clouds of hammered pearl.

Winston breathed deeply, for there was life and power in the air, but this King of Winter was capricious; one instant he thrilled the solitary traveler with frigid wine, then smote his cheek with arctic breath, as with a saber.

So he went along, this man, now nearing his seventieth year, when all at once he saw a black object in the distance, lying on the ice.

He approached, not knowing whether it be man or beast, then found it was the frozen body of a man, and holding his lantern down, he recognized the face of Tom Blake, the village carpenter; not a bad man, this Tom Blake, save to himself.

Pouring wrath upon the head of him who had sold the victim liquor, Winston looked off through leafless trees, up a hillside where a light in a cabin window clutched his heart, for in that cabin a little boy and girl, motherless for a year, awaited for their father's return.

He drew a hand across his eyes, whether from perplexity or something else, and seeing some Christmas trinkets, scattered on the ice, he put them in his coat, then summoning all his strength, lifted the frozen body to his shoulder and carried it back to town.

"Give him a 'white man's funeral'—and send the bill to me!" he told the village undertaker, and then—in the doorway—"Not a word of this until after Christmas—not one word!" Then he returned to Jones' store, strangely indifferent now to the jests of those within, and proceeded to buy more toys than that emporium had often sold to a single customer.

Again he sought the river, but now with a sense of loneliness he had not known since another night long ago when he had stood upon a picket line in Tennessee, and his feet were strangely heavy. As he went along he wondered whether, after all, it had been the weird beauty of the night that lured him on. He found himself measuring the distance to the spot, and once there, he glanced again toward the cabin light, then trudged knee-deep up the snowy hillside.

Reaching the cabin, he looked in at the window, and there in a bed beside the fireplace, lay Bill and Mary, their heads billowed in golden curls, dreaming, he hoped, of Santa Claus.

Gently he pushed open the door; the fire was almost gone, the embers turning from red to gray, an empty stocking hanging on either side.

Going to the wood box, he rekindled the fire, then with a thrill he had not known since his own children were little, opened the bundles from Jones' store, filling the stockings from top to toe. He placed on the hearth a train of cars, a metal top, a sheep on wheels and a hobby horse for Bill; then a book of fairy tales, a string of beads, a bottle of perfumery and a large flaxen-haired doll for Mary.

Next he hung two jumping-jacks, and in his elation, manipulated one of them so loudly that one little head stirred, whereupon he drew a rocking chair before the fire, filled his pipe and gazed into the flame-encircled logs.

Suddenly he sat up, startled, spilling tobacco ashes on his vest—he had not told his wife!—but he could not leave those children now—besides, Martha slept very soundly.

And so John Winston sat and smoked and thought all night until finally the first rays of dawn filtered through the window, when he slipped out of the room.

Mary awoke first and unwilling to believe her widening eyes, shook Bill, and they sat up in bed, then ventured forth to see whether it could be real. With overflowing ecstacy they pounced upon the treasures on the hearth, then emptied the stockings with many a shout; the room was vibrant with their joy; they had never known such happiness!

Then Mary happened to glance across the room to an empty bed and a cloud came over her little face. "Where's Papa?"

Winston opened the door, brushed aside the child's anxiety, saying he had come to take them to his home and yes, of course, they could take all their toys along!

Martha was about to arouse the town to search for her missing mate when, looking out the window, she saw him coming up the front walk, flanked by two children, all three heavily encumbered with Christmas accessories. She opened the door, Winston giving her that glance which he had always reserved for times of pith and moment. Seating the children near the base-burner, he led her into the bedroom, concluding his recital with the proclamation that Bill and Mary should have a Christmas, never to be forgotten.

Martha had cooked many famous dinners in her time, but this day she seemed fired with a strange zeal, entering into it with the enthusiasm of a new bride. She piled the table with cakes, pies, jams enough for twenty people, then sat by the oven door, with a big iron spoon, pouring the gravy over the turkey. She heaped their plates again and again, and when finally those children pushed back their chairs, their eyes were popping.

All afternoon those old folks watched the children at their play, and it was early to bed with them, but not for the Winstons, who, with a life-sized emergency on their hands, sat up until eleven o'clock, a high-water mark of dissipation for Wild Cat.

It was agreed the services should be there in their own home, while Martha should tell them everything, a somber task which she performed with the fine technique of a gentle soul who knew the heart of childhood, for she had raised four little ones of her own, now gone out into the world.

The town rocked with excitement when Blake's fate was known, and on the funeral day the Winston home was crowded, chiefly by the curious. Martha sat with her arms around the children, while Winston stood in the doorway, having given his chair to "Aunt Hattie" Frisbee, the oldest inhabitant, who arrived at the last minute to grace the occasion and incidentally preserve a record for never having missed a funeral.

The minister was young and a new arrival in the town, but he had been there long enough to familiarize himself with the intemperance of the deceased. With startling impropriety he proceeded to devote himself not to the tender service of sympathy, but to a vivid portrayal of the evils of strong drink.

John Winston stood with flushed face, his hands slowly opening and closing, and when the parson concluded the tall figure in the doorway stepped forward. "Just a minute—please——"

"John Winston, what are you going to do?" gasped Martha.

"I'm going to give Tom Blake a square deal!"

He turned to the children. "I'm talking to you—Bill and Mary—— Nobody else counts here today—only you—I want you to remember—your father was a real man—always square—never cheated—never stole—worked hard—loved his folks—never lied!—— No, I guess I'll have to take that back—he did, once—but—he did it for Abraham Lincoln—swore he was twenty—when he was only sixteen—did it to get in my company!—— Wish you children could have seen him at Gettysburg—there in the front line—when Pickett charged—there in smoke and fire and blood—and hell!—fighting for his country—— Just a child and I, old enough to be his father—— Well, after the war, he came back here and was the best carpenter Wild Cat ever knew!—— What a useful life—what a splendid life—— Think of the cattle protected by the fences he made; think of the horses, sheltered by the barns he built; think of the families, happy in the houses that stand as monuments to his memory!" Winston paused, looked at the people, leaning forward in their chairs, then at the children gazing at him wistfully, and then he walked over to the coffin and, touching Blake's cold hand, said almost in a whisper: "I'll look after Bill and Mary—just for Gettysburg——"

If Wild Cat had been excited before, it was in a tumult now, but two souls were calm; they were pondering their duty—and their age. They were too old to undertake such a responsibility, but they would find homes for the children, paying liberally for their support, and so they settled it.

They found a place for Bill, then another day they took Mary to her new home, but she was loath to leave them. They drove away very slowly until finally they came to the place where the road joined the pike, going back to Wild Cat, when they glanced at each other in silence.

Mustering all his resolution, Winston leaned over and touched the old bay mare with the whip and then—something happened, as to the meaning of which, if any there be, your opinion is as good as mine.

Instead of increasing her speed, the mare did something very different—she sank in the harness, sank clear down to the snow, and there she stayed.

Winston alighted; the old reliable animal seemed perfectly normal, but she would not move. He shook the bridle; he issued ultimatums; he threatened dire things; he shook his fist in her face, but that old bay mare did not budge one inch!

He looked around, then toward his companion of many years.

"I'm not exactly—superstitious—Martha—but I believe we'd better go back—and get Mary."

The answer from the buggy came quickly: "I think so, too!"

The old mare struggled to her feet and, turning around, they drove back to find Mary, waiting for them at the gate with the glad cry: "I knew you'd come back and get me!"

They bundled her up in the buffalo robe, then the old man started to drive off in a strange direction, and when Martha asked where he was going he flourished the whip and replied with a ring in his voice and a light in his eye: "Why—we're going to do this thing right—we're going over to get Bill!"

The Lord must have smiled upon their endeavor, for He gave them length of days to accomplish it, but it was not altogether a burden, for when those little folks had been in that home two weeks and Bill had followed Winston everywhere, asking a million questions, and Mary had pottered around the house with "Mother," you could not have induced that man and woman to give them up, no—not for all the money in the world!

And this is the story of John Winston, the story they still tell down at the little town of Wild Cat, particularly around Christmas time, for that is when it all happened, many years ago.

Cherished and Shared of Old

SUSAN GLASPELL

Though we know that never a longing mortal
Gains life best—Oh, better it is to pray for
Part in what we cherished and share of old than
Fail to remember.

Attributed to Sappho;
adaptation by George Cram Cook

"THANK goodness for the snow," thought Addie Morrison, as she watched the two children racing round the barn. And she was thinking it was nice there were some things that were everywhere—most everywhere: like sun and rain, like the wind and the snow, so's when you were sent far from your home there were these things—like the stars—to make you feel a little more at home in a distant land.

"Not a soul here they ever knew before," she would think of these two little Dutch children she'd taken into her home. They were warm now at night—not wandering on a road. They weren't hungry now—mercy no, she'd seen to *that*, but what are they *thinking*, she'd wonder, as at times they'd sit there so gravely. She wished they'd do more things they shouldn't, for when you're too good you must be a little afraid.

She hadn't been able to stand the pictures in the papers—so many tired children wanting to get back home. Her daughter Emmey, in the East, was working for little ones who had been

---

Reprinted by permission of Julian Messner, Inc.; copyright date, January 2, 1941, by the author.

turned out into the world. "Mother dear," she wrote, "I can't get home this Christmas—just can't. But I could send you two children for whom you could make a Christmas—the way you used to for me and Jack. You'll be so sorry for Johanna and Piet, and come to love them; perhaps you'll want them to stay on there with you in our old home. There were always children on the Morrison place."

So once more there were children on the old Morrison place, but could she make a happy Christmas for this little girl and boy bereft of their own? She could say "Merry Christmas," but could she make their hearts glad? And what is Christmas if there is not warmth within?

"Maybe *you'll* help," she was saying to the turkey she crammed with savory stuffing. "And what about you?" she thought, regarding with favor the mince pies on the shelf.

She didn't even know what they were used to for Christmas. She wished, for just five minutes, she could talk to their mother. "What would they like?" she'd ask. And their mother would reply—eagerly, so anxious: "Oh, if you would give them——" But this mother couldn't speak up for her children—struck down trying to hurry them to safety.

Germans did that. The Schultzes were Germans—over there in their fine house on the hill. And so her heart hardened anew against Emma Schultz—and that was good, for she found it not so easy to hate Emma at Christmas.

Never a Christmas they hadn't shared—all those years they were growing up. In this very kitchen they'd hung around sniffing and tasting. And when they weren't here they were at the Schultzes'. She had two homes—her own and Schultzes'. And Emma had two—her own and the Morrisons'.

And then they had to act like that! Just to get a piece of land that didn't belong to them at all they'd fought John Morrison, best friend they'd had since they came—greenhorns—into this country. Country where the Morrisons had been since first there were white men in Iowa! Not to her dying day would she forget her father's face that late afternoon he came back from town, and standing by this very table said: "Well, they've won. The court has given them the strip. Don't ask me why. I don't know why. But I do know this! They've won the land—but they've lost the Morrisons. Never again—do you hear me, Addie?—never again can a Morrison be friend to a Schultz."

Oh, she heard him all right, and never forgot. How could she forget, when she saw him change from that day? The land wasn't so very important. But the defeat—bitter words spoken—from that day he began to brood, until soon people were saying: "Why Addie, seems like your father is beginning to fail."

But Emil Schultz—he didn't fail. As the Morrisons began to have less and less, the Schultzes had more and more. Emma Schultz's land-grabbing father lived on till just last year—and many a snow had fallen since they carried John Morrison to the last land he would know.

So a fine daughter she was—letting into her heart memories of those long ago Christmases with Emma Schultz. Memories were tricky things—come Christmas-time. Maybe it was because you went on doing the same things. You made the cranberry sauce, trimmed the tree—doing alone the little things you'd done with someone else—with the dearest friend you'd ever had.

For no one had ever taken Emma's place. Who could take the place of the friend with whom you'd shared all those good years of your life? Emma helped her make all her wedding things. Emma was there when her first baby was born. She'd named that daughter Emma. Later she'd thought of changing it—but not easy to change a name, and anyway she had an aunt named Emma—she got around it that way. And Walter. Emma was to have married Addie's brother Walter. But Walter went away to war—that other time the Germans tried to wreck the world—and he never came back. And they had comforted each other then.

Yes, laughter and sorrow they had shared. And how divided now! That fought-over land connected the Morrison and Schultz farms. Connected only to divide. It wasn't land—it was a gulf, a gulf that had widened with the years. Feeling—that is what lives on. You might even have forgotten what caused it, but it has come to have a life of its own, regardless of what it flamed from long ago. That is why there is hate in the world—(she half knew this, tried not to know)—hate unreasoning, living on because, one way or other, it got there in the first place; and when a thing has existed a long time it gives you the idea you can't change it—even makes you think you don't want to.

The smells of Christmas brought Emma close to her—Christmas smells trying to make her betray the legacy of hate to which she had been so bitterly loyal! "And what if we did *get* many a Christmas dinner together," she thought. Remember the *words*—those very words they spoke!

Yes—the words. How cruel—and again how blessed—were words. They could carry testimony of love, the sympathy that brought heart closer to heart and warmed the world. And they could blast and wound and kill like those contraptions of the devil man used against man in war. And their life was as long as the life of man.

Longer. For the men who had fought for that land were gone now—her father and Emma's. Walter was gone, and Addie's husband. Her children were in homes of their own and she lived on here at the old place—running down now, and she couldn't do anything about that—and over there on the hill, in her fine new house, lived Emma Schultz. She had a frigidaire, they said—a vacuum and everything to make life easy. She wore a sealskin coat and was proud and cold—how she'd laugh if she knew poor old Addie Morrison was thinking of the days they'd made the Christmas candy together—remembering how Emma's stocking hung at the Morrisons', and Addie's at the Schultzes'.

"Come in and get warm!" she called to the children. "Stamp hard! Shake!" she cried gaily. They got in a mix-up getting off Piet's ski pants. "You take one leg and I'll take the other," she said to Johanna. Johanna was the little mother, two years older than Piet, who was four. Addie made a great fuss about this, pretending she couldn't pull so hard, letting on she was going to fall over backward, until Piet laughed out loud and Johanna smiled—her grave little smile that seemed to be feeling its way. "It will take time,"

Addie told herself. Tomorrow they'd have their presents—sleds and skates, toys and new caps and mufflers and mittens. And tomorrow the Allen children were coming over to play with them. Once she heard them break out in laughter that came because it couldn't help itself—how happy she'd be, as if a little of the weight of misery had lifted from the world. Perhaps Christmas could do that. That was what Christmas was for. She wanted them to be happy as she hadn't wanted anything in years. That would be *her* Christmas present—a smile not uncertain, a laugh that was happy clear to the inside. People like Schultzes running little children out of their homes! As for her, she was an *American*. She didn't hold with such things. (And way in her heart Addie Morrison knew Emma Schultz didn't hold with them either—but this she couldn't let herself know.)

Well, if that little fellow wasn't edging up to the cookie-jar. Good! You must think it's *your* house when you go after the cookie-jar.

Johanna said, in her new careful English, "Thank you," for the cookie; little Piet said something she didn't understand, but he smiled and she knew it was "Thank you."

What funny little cookies the Schultzes used to make for Christmas. Cut in all sorts of shapes—a rabbit, a star, a St. Nicholas and something called a grampus, and supposed to be for the bad child, but it had currants and nuts in it just the same, so who cared? Perhaps Johanna and Piet were used to cookies like that. Yes, Emma might know more than she did about what these children were used to. But Emma—warm in a fine sealskin coat—what did *she* care?

"Oh—pret-ty," she heard Johanna murmur, and turned to find her fingering a length of red ribbon that was to be tied on the tree.

Addie stood stock-still watching her, for the little girl's fingers moved over the bright stuff so wistfully, as if—as if she had once loved something like this. "Oh you poor little thing," she thought, in a new wave of sympathy and tenderness—anger too. All the little fineries left behind. Only what you needed—not the pretty things to make life gay.

"Time to dress ourselves up for Christmas," she said, slipping the bright broad ribbon under the collar of Johanna's sweater and making a fine red bow.

And then she began to laugh—Emma running after a pig, trying to catch the pig to tie a red ribbon round his neck. That was one of the crazy things they did together—dressing up the animals for Christmas. Well, Emma caught the pig, but fell down doing it and Emma and pig rolled over and over together—the pig squirming and Emma clutching. Addie could see them now and she went on laughing, until the children, thinking there must be something very funny indeed, politely joined in.

The snow continued to fall softly, knowing it was Christmas and the world should be white, and after the dinner things were cleared away Addie wondered whether they'd like to be bundled up and go out again. That was the trouble—it was still hard to know for sure what they would like, for it wasn't *their* house yet.

But suddenly it was! What in the world were they looking at out that window—dancing up and down, catching hold of each other and squealing and pointing?

Oh—dear. Now what? For there he was—that miserable Schultz dog who came bounding over as if he didn't know a Schultz shouldn't come to the Morrisons'. She started for the door to go chase him away but the children thought she was going to let him in, and they were right upon her, all excited and happy—*natural*—for the first time they really were children. And all because that ugly Schultz dog—for some crazy reason called Doc—was standing there wagging his tail as if waiting for them to come out and play with him.

"Bad dog," she said. "German. Bad German dog"—though she knew she shouldn't be doing this.

But they didn't care. It didn't seem to make any difference to them that Doc was German. And then Addie knew. It wasn't only the ribbons and the toys had been left behind. The dog had been left behind too. . . .

"We'll get a dog," she said. "A nice dog. This is the homeliest dog ever lived."

And Doc *was* a very funny-looking dog. He wasn't *any* kind of dog—just Doc. He had a bulldog face and crooked legs, but he was sort of a dog of all nations, and Addie knew in her heart that the kindness of all nations came together in Doc, and that Doc was a *good* dog. But he was a Schultz.

She tried to interest them in the dog they would have, but they wanted Doc and wanted him right now; and as Addie saw that first flare-up of joy begin to die down into disappointment, of course she couldn't stand it and there began a mad gay scramble to get them into their clothes so they could rush out and play with Doc Schultz.

Then she remembered they were used to having dogs draw things—pictures of Holland always had dogs drawing little carts—so she hurried into the shut-up front room, where the presents waited in secret, to get the Christmas sled—for might as well be killed for a sheep as a lamb, she thought.

Oh they were so delighted! They could scarcely wait to get out—and then they were all in a scramble together, Doc jumping on them and waving his silly tail—and for goodness sakes if the dog didn't seem to be *grinning*—and the children were laughing and screaming and they all went tearing away together.

And Addie Morrison sat there thinking it was strange—so very strange—that their first happy moment on the Morrison place came through Emma Schultz. She sat there alone remembering her dogs and Emma's—new sleds—and other mad scrambles in the Christmas snow.

Emma Schultz was remembering something herself. She was again a little girl not eight—new to America, a greenhorn. And the children at school stared and laughed at her because she talked funny and didn't know their ways. But little Addie Morrison—so pretty then—came up and hooked her arm through Emma's and said: "You and me, lets us be friends."

More than anything else in the world she would like to walk over to Addie Morrison now, open the kitchen door just as she used to, and say—"You and me, lets us be friends."

At Christmas it was so hard not to remember. And this Christmas most of all, because again—after all these years—Addie was befriending the stranger. How good of Addie! How good of America! And she wondered if anyone could love America as did the one who had come here a stranger and been taken in.

She was the one to do something for these children, for who could know better than she what it was to be a child among things not familiar.

She was putting in a big jar the *Lebkuchen,* German Christmas cookies she made every year. She wouldn't have had the heart to make them this year, but her mother hadn't many Christmases left and clung to the things she was used to. Next week Emma's Sunday-school class would come for their party, and they'd have these cookies and their presents. But it was lonely here today.

Ten thousand times she'd wished that land in the bottom of the sea. What is land, compared to the love of friends? How gladly she would have given it back. It had changed things for the Schultzes. Her father grew hard after that and wanted to make money and didn't care about friends. And she herself had to pretend she didn't care, and that made one hard too. The Schultzes didn't like being told they weren't Americans, being shouted at they weren't honest. They'd show them who the Schultzes were! But it had been lonely business, and at Christmas especially she knew there still lived in her heart all she and Addie had loved together, dear things shared. She'd like to cross that strip—and abolish it in crossing—open the kitchen door and see if there wasn't something she could do for these little children against whom a wicked wrong had been worked. But what nonsense. You couldn't change the way things were, and Addie had grown more bitter with the years. She'd *shut* the door—shut it in Emma Schultz's face.

"Emma! I hear Doc barking," her mother called out to her. "He wants to come in."

She opened her own kitchen door, and yes—there stood Doc. But—*what in the world?* He was all decorated for Christmas. Red ribbon was wound round his collar and tied in a big gay bow. Now who could have done *that?*

And suddenly Emma Schultz sat down—so sure there was only

one person in the world could have sent Doc home decorated for Christmas. She and Addie used to do that together. The dogs always had their big red Christmas bows. Addie had not forgotten! Oh, she had sent a message saying she remembered. And Emma Schultz began hurrying fast as she could—getting the cookies—presents for those she had for her Sunday-school class—for couldn't she get others for them?—filling a big basket, hurrying into her boots, her coat, and out into the snow. It was Christmas! She ran across the strip giving it scarcely a thought, so eager to get to the Morrisons'.

But at the kitchen door she paused. So many years . . . Then she knocked, and Addie opened the door.

"Why—why Emma *Schultz,*" she said, as if she didn't know what to say.

"Merry Christmas, Addie," said Emma—timidly, bravely.

"Why—why——" And then all of a sudden Addie cried: "Merry Christmas yourself!"—and swiftly added: "For pity sakes come right in out of the snow!"

A little later they were all sitting round the kitchen stove, nibbling the cookies Emma had brought, Emma and Addie drinking tea and the children their cocoa—so cozy in the Morrison kitchen. Yes, Johanna and Piet knew cookies like these, and great fun they had picking out now a new moon, now a little man—Johanna hugging the doll Emma had brought and Piet dangling the baby panda.

"Emma!" Addie burst out with a laugh—"do you remember the *pig?*"

While they were laughing came a barking and scratching at the door and Johanna and Piet ran to let in their friend Doc.

As the children were busy brushing him off, Emma said, very low: "Oh, Addie—when he came home all fixed up for Christmas—and I knew you had remembered—were telling me you remembered——"

Addie had been sitting with her back to Doc. She turned now, and saw that the bow she had tied on Johanna at this moment adorned Emma's dog Doc.

And Emma thought she had done this! A Schultz thought a Morrison had made the first move.

Ah, there was danger in that moment—danger the world has faced time and again. Old bitter loyalties—resentments of many years—right there, ready to rush in.

But something else came flooding into that moment: It was the children had done this. The children whom hate had driven here—brought love. How strange that this could be. Like a miracle it seemed.

She was afraid she was going to cry, so when Doc came sniffing up to the stove she said, almost crossly: "Why, Emma Schultz—that dog's hungry.

"I'll tell you, children," she went on, "what do you say we give him our beef stew, for tomorrow we'll have turkey."

Doc knew it was to be for him and was dancing all around, his big bow bobbing. "Say Merry Christmas!" cried Addie, holding high the plate. Doc waved a hearty "Merry Christmas"—and they all watched Doc Schultz devour the Morrison stew.

The children clapped their hands at the speed with which he cleaned the plate. Emma and Addie smiled at each other—so much alive and warm between them. Dogs of other years were wearing their Christmas bows and cleaning the plate. In a changing world of many sorrows it can be sad to remember alone. But when friends share dear memories—a fire in the cold, light in the darkness.

And right there the children began a great clatter, running round in circles with Doc. Why, they weren't a *bit* afraid—for all the world as if they knew something had happened there amongst them. Whether they knew it or not, it was true—how blessed and true—that fear flew out through the window when love came in by the door.

The Little Christmas Tree

STELLA GIBBONS

Because she was tired of living in London among clever people, Miss Rhoda Harting, a reserved yet moderately successful novelist in the thirty-third year of her age, retired during one November to a cottage in Buckinghamshire. Nor did she wish to marry.

"I dislike fuss, noise, worry, and all the other accidents, which, so my friends tell me, attend the married state," she said. "I like being alone. I like my work. Why should I marry?"

"You are unnatural, Rhoda," protested her friends.

"Possibly, but at least I am cheerful," retorted Miss Harting. "Which," she added (but this was to herself), "is more than can be said of most of you."

The cottage in Buckinghamshire, which was near Great Missenden, suited her tastes. It had a double holly tree in the garden, and a well in whose dark depths she could see her own silhouette against the wintry blue sky. It stood in a lane, with long fields at the back which sloped up to a hill with a squared beechwood at the summit. Halfway up the hill stood another house, Monkswell, a large, new, red house. Miss Harting used to look at this house and say contentedly, "I feel like the gardener at Monkswell. This used to be his cottage, I am told."

She furnished her cottage fastidiously with English china, Eng-

From *Christmas at Cold Comfort Farm and Other Stories*, by Stella Gibbons, by permission of Longmans, Green & Co., publishers. Reprinted by permission of Pearn, Pollinger & Higham, Ltd., agents for the author.

lish prints, chintz, and a well-equipped kitchen. For the first fortnight she played with it as though it were the dolls' house it so much resembled, but soon she began to work on a new novel, and, as everybody knows, the writing of novels does not allow time for playing at anything.

A quiet, pleasant routine, therefore, replaced her first delighted experiments.

Weeks went past so quickly that she was quite surprised to receive a letter one morning beginning, "Darling Rhoda, you will come to us for Christmas, won't you, unless you have already made other plans"—and headed with an address in Kensington.

She got up from the breakfast table, where the steam from her china tea was wavering peacefully up into the air, and went over to the window and stood looking out.

"No, I shall stay here for Christmas," decided Miss Harting, after a prolonged gaze out of the window. "I shall have a chicken all to myself, and a little tree with candles and those bright, glittery balls we used to buy when we were small." She paused, in her comfortable murmuring to herself, and added contentedly, "It is really shocking. I grow more and more spinsterish every year. Something ought to be done about it. . . ."

Her conscience quieted, Miss Harting went shopping in Great Missenden on Christmas Eve, wandering down the rambling bright-lit High Street with a big basket slung on her arm and her bright eyes dreaming in and out of the shop windows.

The long street was packed with people, and there was a feeling of frost in the air, but no stars, only a dense, muffling bed of cloud almost touching the bare beechwoods on the hidden hills all round the little town. In the butchers' shops the dangling turkeys were tied up with red ribbon, and hares were decorated with spiked bunches of holly and moon-mistletoe, and out of the warm caverns of the two wireless and gramophone shops poured rich, blaring music.

"Seasonable weather, madam," said the poulterer who tied up Miss Harting's small but fat chicken.

"Going to be a regular old-fashioned Christmas, Miss," said the old lady wrapped in a shawl like a thick, blacky-green fishing net, who packed up the silver glass balls and red and green lemons of fairy-glass that Miss Harting had chosen for her Christmas tree.

The old lady looked across at her with something more than professional interest, and enquired civilly:

"Was you wanting them for a Christmas tree of your own, Miss?"

"Yes," murmured Miss Harting.

"Ah! Nephews and nieces coming down from London perhaps?"

"Well—no," confessed her customer.

"Not your own little ones? Excuse me askin', but you can usually tell. I shouldn't have thought . . . Well, there now, I'm sure I beg your pardon. I oughtn't to have said that. Here's the toys, Miss. A happy Christmas to you."

"Er—thank you. The same to you. Good evening."

Miss Harting escaped, aware that the old lady, far from being embarrassed by her mistake, was taking her in from head to feet with lively, curious eyes and thought her a queer one. But Miss Harting was sure that her wildest guesses at the reason why the toys had been bought would come nowhere near the truth. In the circles in which the old lady's tubby person rotated, unmarried females did not buy Christmas trees, decorate them and gloat over them in solitude, however natural such a proceeding might seem in Chelsea.

Perhaps it was this breath of commonsense from the world of unimaginative millions that made Miss Harting feel a little depressed as she got from the Amersham 'bus at the cross roads, and set out along the ringing frosty road to walk the last mile to her cottage. Her basket hung heavily on her arm. She was hungry. She did not feel in the mood for revelling in the bright, miniature prettiness of her Christmas tree. She almost wished she had gone to Kensington, as her friends had proposed. "Good gracious, this will never do," muttered Miss Harting, unlocking her front door. "In the New Year I will go up to London and see people, and invite Lucy or Hans Carter or somebody to come down and stay with me."

When she had eaten her supper, however, she felt better; and began to enjoy bedding the shapely little tree into a flower-pot and fastening the glass bells and lemons on to the tip of its branches. She stood it in the sitting-room window, with the curtains pulled back, when it was ready, and could not resist lighting its tipsy green and white candles, just to see what it would look like.

Oh! the soft light shining round the candles and falling down between the dark green branches! How pretty it was!

She stood for perhaps five minutes dreaming in front of it, in a silence unbroken except by the noise of a car that droned past along the unfrequented lane at the foot of her front garden.

Every year, ever since she could remember, she had had a Christmas tree, either bought for her by her parents, when they were alive, or by herself, with her own money. This year, it was as beautiful and as satisfying as ever.

Yet . . . was it? While she stood looking at it, she remembered the old lady in the little shop. The thought drifted into her mind that hers was a lonely, not to say self-conscious, way of enjoying a Christmas tree. She dismissed the thought impatiently, extinguished the little candles, and spent the rest of the evening profitably at work on her book.

In the night the snow came. She awoke on Christmas morning in that unmistakable light, coming up from the earth and shining between her curtains. All her loneliness and depression had gone. She felt as happy and excited as though she were going to a feast.

But when she had nibbled her breakfast, played Debussy's *Footsteps in the Snow* twice on the gramophone, stuffed her chicken and glanced more than once at her Christmas tree, whose bells glittered darkly against the snow, she found herself trying to feel happy, rather than feeling happy. It was eleven o'clock. The noise of bells was stealing in soft claps of sound on the snow-wind. She suddenly faced the fact that she was both lonely and bored; that eleven more empty hours yawned endlessly in front of her, and that she could do nothing to stop their approach and departure.

It was just at this moment, as she stood staring down at her fingers still greasy with chicken-stuffing, that there came a knock at the front door.

Miss Harting gave a great start.

"Oh!" she thought, with a rush of relief, "perhaps it's some one come down from London to see me!" and she hurried out to the door.

But when she opened the door she saw no gay, familiar face from London. A little girl, wearing a red beret, stood on the doorstep, squarely yet somehow in a pose that suggested she might dash away in a second, looking up with large dark eyes into Miss Harting's surprised face. Two smaller children, in the same tiptoe pose, lurked in the background.

"Good morning," said the red beret loudly and politely. "We are very sorry to trouble you, but please may we take shelter in your house?"

"Shelter?" said Miss Harting, still getting over her silly disappointment that it was not a delightful visitor from London; and perhaps she spoke a little curtly. "Because of the snow, do you mean? But—" she glanced up at the sky—"it isn't snowing. What's the matter? Are your feet wet or something?" (No one but a nieceless spinster would have asked such a question of a little girl on a snowy morning.)

"No, thank you," said the red beret politely. "It isn't that sort of shelter, and our feet are quite dry, thank you very much. But, you see, it is rather necessary that we should take shelter, because—" she looked up candidly into Miss Harting's eyes—"some one is coming after us, and we want to hide."

She glanced round at the two smaller figures, who both nodded violently as though she had pulled a string.

"Who's after you?" asked Miss Harting, startled. "Are you playing a game?"

"Oh, no. *Truly*, it isn't a game. It's rather serious, as a matter of fact. You see, we have a cruel step-mother, and she said we weren't to have a proper Christmas tree this year, and Jane and Harry—these are Jane and Harry" (jerking them forward and muttering, "Say how-do-you-do," which they did, like two polite wool-clad parrots) "cried rather a lot——"

"I didn't, Judy. 'At's a story!" interrupted the other little girl flatly at this point in the narrative. "And if you say I cried like a baby, I shall tell—you-know-what!"

"Oh, well then, perhaps you didn't cry quite as much as Harry," conceded the red beret, darting a lightning grimace at her, laden with menace. "But Harry cried all night. So we got up very early this morning, before it was light, and took some gingerbreads and hid in the woods until it got light, and then we ran down—I mean we walked a long way in the woods, until we saw your house, and as we were rather hung—— I mean, we thought we would ask if we might take shelter here until our step-mother had stopped looking for us. That's what we thought, isn't it?" appealing imperiously to the woolly parrots.

"Yes, we liked your house because it was so *little*," said Jane, accompanying her compliment by a smile of such specious yet goblin charm that Rhoda's heart contracted strangely.

Here Harry, who had been staring at her face, remarked "Absolutely snow," and pointed to the distant fields. He added, after another prolonged stare, "You do look funny," and began to run slowly up and down the path with his hands at his sides, puffing like an engine.

"Harry! That's rude!" cried the red beret, darting down on him. "You mustn't mind him, please. He's only four and doesn't understand things properly yet. Besides, he isn't our brother. He's only a cousin."

A pause followed; an awkward pause. The red beret and the woolly Jane gazed up into Miss Harting's face, too polite to put their request again into words, but with eyes full of pleading and hope.

She did not know quite what to do. She did not, of course, believe a word of the red beret's fantastic story. The red beret, with her overpersuasive eyes and tongue, had betrayed herself with her first sentence as one of those incurable romancers who are doomed never to be believed.

"She will probably earn a large income one day by writing best-sellers," thought Miss Harting, who was now handicapped by having to struggle with the pangs of violent love at first sight. It did not seem at all shocking to her that the red beret should tell lies, but she did wonder very much whether the red beret had a mother, and if so, did she know of the daughter's capacities for inventing? It seemed to Miss Harting that these three needed looking after. In spite of their educated enunciation, their warm clothes and pretty manners, they had a lost look about them.

But, if they felt lost, why in the name of Father Christmas himself should they choose her unromantic doorstep to be lost on? Taking another long look at their anxious faces, she sighed, and gave it up.

She said, cautiously (but a curious warm feeling of happiness began to invade her), "Well, come in by all means, if your stepmother is as bad as all that. You can stay until you're warm, anyway. Jane—that is your name, isn't it?—is beginning to look blue. Er—you can see my Christmas tree, too, if that would amuse you."

The two faces changed with incredible speed. They smiled, but Rhoda felt that was a smile of triumph, of success achieved, rather than one of gratitude. She was sure that only prudence prevented the red beret from saying to Jane, "There you are, clever! I told you so!" and she became more than ever puzzled.

"Oh, thank you *very* much——" gushed the red beret.

"V*ewy* much," came Jane's slower, fatter voice, in dutiful diminuendo.

"I'm afraid there are no presents on it," warned Rhoda, opening the kitchen door. But there was no need for apologies. The three paused on the threshold, staring at the little tree, their faces solemn with pleasure.

"Oh, isn't it *pretty!* It's so *little!* It's like those little ones we saw growing near Barnet," said the red beret. "Daddy told us they were going to be Christmas trees when they got bigger. Oh, what pretty little bell-things. Oh, look Jane, a norange! all made of glass!"

"*Pretty!*" said Jane, intensely. "It's the littlest tree I ever saw. May I touch it? Who is it for?"

"Er—it's for you," said Rhoda, feeling very queer indeed. Yet they were all warmly-clad, all well-fed and healthy. It was ridiculous to feel inclined to cry.

The three faces, incredulous, were lifted to hers.

"For us? Oo! Really? Can we play with it? Can I have the little lemon thing? Can we light those little cangles ourselves?"

"After lunch," said Rhoda, who had suddenly become so full of bustling happiness that she could not keep still, and she began to tie on her white cooking overall with unnecessary energy.

"Is that your lunch cooking?" asked Jane, looking round the kitchen with polite interest. "It smells nice."

"Jane!" warned the red beret. She glanced appealingly at Miss Harting. "Jane's only six. I'm nearly nine. Jane's rather rude sometimes. She's still fairly little, you see."

"I suppose your cruel step-mother hasn't much time to teach Jane manners, either," said Miss Harting drily. She was used, of course, to the type of grown-up person to whom ironical conversation is natural.

But in this case irony would not do. She realized it at once with extreme contrition, as the red beret stared up at her, wounded and rather frightened by her tone. She knelt down in front of her suddenly, and murmured, beginning to unbutton the reefer coat:

"What's your name? Mine's Rhoda Harting. Let me help you off with your coat. Will you please all stay and have lunch?"

"Oo, hooray! I'm so hungry," shouted Harry, who had been poking at the bells on the Christmas tree, and exchanging hoarse whispers with Jane.

"Thank you very much. We should like to. As a matter of fact, we are rather hungry. I'm Juliet Woodhouse, but I'm us'herly called Judy," said the red beret.

Rhoda carefully folded the little coat and put it on her Welsh dresser. "I must cook potatoes," she said.

"Oh, let me help," said Judy eagerly. "May I fill the saucepan? Where is it?"

"We have maids at home to cook our lunch," said Jane, mildly, watching these preparations. She had put her hat and coat on a chair, and now looked more than ever like a gnome. She had the shortest face and nose Rhoda had ever seen, framed in a streaked straw bob. Harry was red and round, and his voice was strident. He said little, but what he said was to the point.

"Is Jane really your sister? You are so fair and she is so dark—like Snow White and Rosy Red. Where do you live?" asked Rhoda, half an hour later, as she and Judy were laying the cloth. Her curiosity refused to lie down and behave politely, even though she was the hostess.

"Yes, she is, really. Oh, we live a long way away from here. I don't expect you would know it," said Judy, vague as the organizer of a charity matinée. "Look! Jane has dropped her apple core on your pretty rug. Do you mind?"

"No," said Rhoda. Nor did she. The kitchen smelled of roast chicken, burnt fir branches (for they had, of course, lit the candles), hot wax, and raspberry jam. Rhoda, putting plates on the table, wondered if it were really only an hour ago that she had felt lonely and bored.

Judy was darting about the kitchen like an elfin actress, fastidiously selecting forks, making her fingers hover undecidedly over spoons and glasses, shaking her dark hair back from her face. Rhoda, watching rather sadly, thought she had seldom seen prettier or more self-conscious actions. She wondered more and more what Judy's mother could be like.

Amid a pleasant scramble Rhoda got the three of them seated at her kitchen table. The white snowlight lit up the two absorbed, innocent faces turned towards the window, and made a background for Judy's dark head. Rhoda looked round at the three of them, blessing the chance that had brought them to her doorstep on Christmas morning, and wondered, as she minced chicken for Harry, whether they would stay the night, who they could possibly be, and—a more serious thought—whether some poor mother was spending a terrible Christmas Day somewhere looking for them.

Yet, beyond her one question to Judy and Judy's casual avoidance of a direct answer, she could not bring herself to ask them bluntly who they were and where they lived. After all, they were her guests, though self-invited. They had thrown themselves on her mercy. She felt she could not take advantage of their childish state and behave to them as a grown-up person. She had to meet them on their own ground. It was delightful to have them at her table, filling her carefully-furnished kitchen with the noise of their merry voices and their polite laughter at her jokes and giggles at their own.

"Is this turkey?" demanded Harry, presently.

"No, darling; it's chicken. Don't you like it?" asked foolish Rhoda, anxiously.

"No. More please," said Harry.

"You are silly, Harry," said Jane. "Saying, 'No, you don't like it,' and then asking if you can have some more. Isn't he silly, Judy?"

"He's only little," from Judy, patronizingly. "Don't worry him."

"If we were at home we *should* be having turkey, but this is much nicer," said Jane. Judy's foot stealthily knocked against hers under the table.

"No, Jane, we shouldn't be having turkey. Our step-mother wouldn't let us, would she?"

"No, I s'pose she wouldn't. She's very crool," said Jane, influenced by the kick and by Judy's meaning nod.

Rhoda had decided that it was not quite fair to show her disbelief in the step-mother legend, so she joined in politely with——

"How disgraceful. Doesn't she even let you have turkey on Christmas Day?"

"No. She's *awful*, isn't she, Jane?"

"Yes, simply *awful*," agreed Jane. "Isn't she awful, Harry?" suddenly giggling into Harry's neck.

"Don't. Old man wiv scissors," said Harry, whose mind was evidently still at work on the pictures in the Nonesuch Blake at which he had been looking.

After Rhoda's little Christmas pudding had been greeted with cries of delight, "Oh, isn't it *little!*" "It's the littlest pudding I ever saw!" and eaten, Rhoda had to confess that she had no crystallized fruits or crackers, so they must light the Christmas tree again and then play games.

The suggestion was welcomed with rapture, and Judy, as the eldest, lit six of the little candles, and Jane and Harry lit the remaining six. Rhoda lifted Harry up, putting her cheek for a moment against his warm head.

Darkness was beginning to fall, and the snow gleamed in its own ghostly light under the deepening blue of the sky.

Now the Christmas tree was all alight, the candles burnt still and pointed against the green branches. Three little faces were turned up to the tree, with the candlelight making aureoles round their hair. They were silent, staring up at the beautiful, half-despoiled little tree.

"Oh," thought Rhoda, looking at them, "that's how it should have been last night! It looks *right* now, somehow. Darlings. . . . How glad I am I had it here, ready for them. . . ."

The entranced pause was broken by a loud knock at the front door.

Judy flew round, her eyes dilated.

"Who's that? That's some one come for us! We won't go! Tell them to go away! I *like* being here! I won't go home!"

"It's Daddy," said Jane, resignedly. "I knew they'd find us, Judy. I told you so."

"I lit free cangles by myself," said Harry, holding up the stump of his match.

Rhoda, smoothing her fingers across her straying hair, with a distressed look on her face, was halfway to the door when Judy came flying down the passage after her, and locked her arms round her waist.

"Don't tell! Don't tell about step-mother," she implored in a frightened whisper, lifting a white, distorted little face in the dusk. "I made it up. I made it all up, and Daddy said I was never to make anything up again—*ever*. We saw your little tree all lit up in the window last night, when Daddy was driving us back from London.

We wanted to see your little tree. We've never had a *little* tree at home. Everything's so *big*. It's horrid. We haven't got any mother—Jane and I haven't. Promise you won't tell about the step-mother? Promise—promise!"

Her grip tightened round Rhoda's waist, her eyes, enormous with terror, stared up imploringly. The knock was repeated, twice, louder, and impatiently.

"No, darling. Of course I won't tell. I promise faithfully, Judy. Now let me go, darling. Take your arm away, there's a dear little girl!"

Judy darted her a look of passionate gratitude and flew back to the kitchen. Rhoda, her heart beating unpleasantly, opened the front door.

The man standing there saw a tall woman, silhouetted against a candle-lit passage, and noticed how white her hand was against the door-handle. He took off his hat.

"Good evening. I'm sorry to disturb you, but I suppose you don't happen to have seen my two daughters and my nephew, do you? My name's Woodhouse. We live up at Monkswell. The three of them have been missing since just after breakfast, and their aunt's nearly frantic. The eldest girl's got on a red tam-o'-shanter, I believe——"

"Yes. They're in here, with me," Rhoda interrupted the uncultured but pleasant voice, and stood aside to let him enter. Over his big shoulder she saw a long saloon car blocking the lane at the foot of her garden. "Won't you come in? I'm so sorry . . . you must have had a terrible day. They've been quite safe, of course, but I couldn't get out of them where they lived or to whom they belonged."

"Ah! Judy romancing again, I suppose."

He came forward into the candlelight. Tall, middle-aged, prosperous; clever eyes, weak mouth, good chin. Not a gentleman. I like him. Rhoda's usually well-ordered thoughts raced confusedly.

"Judy should make her fortune out of writing best-sellers when she is older," she said, stopping just outside the kitchen door, which had been carefully closed by the strategists within; "but I am sure you will not scold her for romancing today. She is very penitent, and they have all been so good and so happy."

"They had a Christmas tree the size of a house at home, and any amount of presents—all the usual things children expect at Christmas," he interrupted, roughly. "Why should they come down here, bothering you? It's intolerable. They get more out of hand every week. Their aunt can't do anything with them, and I'm away all day, and most week-ends. Especially Judy. She's the most shameless little liar—— And yet, you know—" his irritable expression suddenly changed, and his face became cautious, intelligent, as though he were weighing a problem—"it isn't just lying. It's something quite different. She seems to need it, somehow. I haven't the heart to be very hard on her. I'm worried about Judy. She wants some one to look after her."

He paused. "Their mother died when Jane was born. It hasn't been a particularly cheerful household since. I suppose they both need looking after properly."

There was another pause.

In that pause, filled with the soft light of the candles now burning low on the little Christmas tree, and with silence, his unsatisfied, clever eyes took in the fineness of Rhoda's ringless hands, the subtle and tender modelling of her mouth, and the irony which looked out like an armed sentinel from her eyes.

But it seemed to him a sentinel who might be persuaded, one day, to lay aside its weapon.

"Well," said Rhoda, lightly, at last, "shall we go in to the children?"

David's Star of Bethlehem

CHRISTINE WHITING PARMENTER

SCOTT CARSON reached home in a bad humor. Nancy, slipping a telltale bit of red ribbon into her workbasket, realized this as soon as he came in. It was the twenty-first of December, and a white Christmas was promised. Snow had been falling for hours, and in most of the houses wreaths were already in the windows. It was what one calls "a Christmasy-feeling day," yet, save for that red ribbon in Nancy's basket, there was no sign in the Carson home of the approaching festival.

Scott said, kissing her absent-mindedly and slumping into a big chair, "This snow is the very limit. If the wind starts blowing there'll be a fierce time with the traffic. My train was twenty minutes late as it is, and—— There's the bell. Who can it be at this hour? I want my dinner."

"I'll go to the door," said Nancy hurriedly, as he started up. "Selma's putting dinner on the table now."

Relaxing into his chair Scott heard her open the front door, say something about the storm and, after a moment, wish someone a Merry Christmas.

A Merry Christmas! He wondered that she could say it so calmly. Three years ago on Christmas morning, they had lost their boy—swiftly—terribly—without warning. Meningitis, the doctor said. Only a few hours before the child had seemed a healthy,

David's Star of Bethlehem, by Christine Whiting Parmenter; reprinted by permission of Thomas Y. Crowell Company, publishers.

happy youngster, helping them trim the tree; hoping, with a twinkle in the brown eyes so like his mother's, that Santa Claus would remember the fact that he wanted skis! He had gone happily to bed after Nancy had read them "The Night Before Christmas," a custom of early childhood's days that the eleven-year-old lad still clung to. Later his mother remembered, with a pang, that when she kissed him good night he had said his head felt "kind of funny." But she had left him light-heartedly enough and gone down to help Scott fill the stockings. Santa had not forgotten the skis; but Jimmy never saw them.

Three years—and the memory still hurt so much that the very thought of Christmas was agony to Scott Carson. Jimmy had slipped away just as the carolers stopped innocently beneath his window, their voices rising clear and penetrating on the dawn-sweet air:

"Silent night—holy night. . . ."

Scott arose suddenly. He *must* not live over that time again. "Who was it?" he asked gruffly as Nancy joined him, and understanding the gruffness she answered tactfully, "Only the expressman."

"What'd he bring?"

"Just a—a package."

"One naturally supposes that," replied her husband, with a touch of sarcasm. Then, suspicion gripping him, he burst out, "Look here! If you've been getting a Christmas gift for me, I—I won't have it. I told you I wanted to forget Christmas. I——"

"I know, dear," she broke in hastily. "The package was only from Aunt Mary."

"Didn't you tell her we weren't keeping Christmas?" he demanded irritably.

"Yes, Scott; but—but you know Aunt Mary! Come now, dinner's on and I think it's a good one. You'll feel better after you eat."

But Scott found it unaccountably hard to eat; and later, when

Nancy was reading aloud in an effort to soothe him, he could not follow. She had chosen something humorous and diverting; but in the midst of a paragraph he spoke, and she knew that he had not been listening.

"Nancy," he said, "is there any place—any place on God's earth where we can get away from Christmas?"

She looked up, answering with sweet gentleness, "It would be a hard place to find, Scott."

He faced her suddenly: "I feel as if I couldn't stand it—the trees—the carols—the merrymaking, you know. Oh, if I could only sleep this week away! But . . . I've been thinking. . . . Would—would you consider for one moment going up to camp with me for a day or two? I'd go alone, but——"

"Alone!" she echoed. "Up there in the wilderness at Christmas time? Do you think I'd let you?"

"But it would be hard for you, dear, cold and uncomfortable. I'm a brute to ask it, and yet——"

Nancy was thinking rapidly. They could not escape Christmas, of course. No change of locality could make them forget the anniversary of the day that Jimmy went away. But she was worried about Scott, and the change of scene might help him over the difficult hours ahead. The camp, situated on the mountain a mile from any neighbors, would at least be isolated. There was plenty of bedding, and a big fireplace. It was worth trying.

She said, cheerfully, "I'll go with you, dear. Perhaps the change will make things easier for both of us."

This was Tuesday, and on Thursday afternoon they stepped off the northbound train and stood on the platform watching it vanish into the mountains. The day was crisp and cold. "Two above," the station master told them as they went into the box of a station and moved instinctively toward the red-hot "air-tight" which gave forth grateful warmth.

"I sent a telegram yesterday to Clem Hawkins, over on the mountain road," said Scott. "I know you don't deliver a message so far off; but I took a chance. Do you know if he got it?"

"Yep. Clem don't have a 'phone, but the boy come down for

some groceries and I sent it up. If I was you, though, I'd stay to the Central House. Seems as if it would be more cheerful—Christmas time."

"I guess we'll be comfortable enough if Hawkins airs out, and lights a fire," replied Scott, his face hardening at this innocent mention of the holiday. "Is there anyone around here who'll take us up? I'll pay well for it, of course."

"Iry Morse'll go; but you'll have to walk from Hawkinses'. The road ain't dug out beyond. . . . There's Iry now. You wait, an' I'll holler to him. Hey, Iry!" he called, going to the door, "Will you carry these folks up to Hawkinses'? They'll pay for it."

"Iry," a ruddy-faced young farmer, obligingly appeared, his gray work horse hitched to a one-seated sleigh of ancient and uncomfortable design.

"Have to sit three on a seat," he explained cheerfully; "but we'll be all the warmer for it. Tuck the buffalo robe 'round the lady's feet, mister, and you and me'll use the horse blanket. Want to stop to the store for provisions?"

"Yes. I brought some canned stuff, but we'll need other things," said Nancy. "I've made a list."

"Well, you got good courage," grinned the station master. "I hope you don't get froze to death up in the woods. Merry Christmas to yer, anyhow!"

"The same to you!" responded Nancy, smiling; and noted with a stab of pain that her husband's sensitive lips were trembling.

Under Ira's cheerful conversation, however, Scott relaxed. They talked of crops, the neighbors, and local politics—safe subjects all; but as they passed the district school, where a half-dozen sleighs or flivvers were parked, the man explained: "Folks decoratin' the school for the doin's to-morrow afternoon. Christmas tree for the kids, and pieces spoke, and singin'. We got a real live schoolma'am this year, believe *me!*"

They had reached the road that wound up the mountain toward the Hawkins farm, and as they plodded on, a sudden wind arose that cut their faces. Snow creaked under the runners, and as the sun sank behind the mountain Nancy shivered, not so much with cold as with a sense of loneliness and isolation. It was Scott's voice that roused her:

"Should we have brought snowshoes? I didn't realize that we couldn't be carried all the way."

"Guess you'll get there all right," said Ira. "Snow's packed hard as a drumhead, and it ain't likely to thaw yet a while. Here you are," as he drew up before the weatherbeaten, unpainted farmhouse. "You better step inside a minute and warm up."

A shrewish-looking woman was already at the door, opening it but a crack, in order to keep out fresh air and cold.

"I think," said Nancy, with a glance at the deepening shadows, "that we'd better keep right on. I wonder if there's anybody here who'd help carry our bags and provisions."

"There ain't," answered the woman, stepping outside and pulling a faded gray sweater around her shoulders. "Clem's gone to East Conroy with the eggs, and Dave's up to the camp keepin' yer fire goin'. You can take the sled and carry yer stuff on that. There 'tis, by the gate. Dave'll bring it back when he comes. An' tell him to hurry. Like as not, Clem won't get back in time fer milkin'."

"I thought Dave was goin' to help Teacher decorate the school this afternoon," ventured Ira. He was unloading their things as he spoke and roping them to the sled.

"So'd he," responded the woman; "but there wa'n't no one else to light that fire, was they? Guess it won't hurt him none to work for his livin' like other folks. That new schoolma'am, she thinks o' nothin' but——"

"Oh, look here!" said the young man, straightening up, a belligerent light in his blue eyes, "it's Christmas! Can Dave go back with me if I stop and milk for him? They'll be workin' all evenin'—lots of fun for a kid like him, and——"

"No, he can't!" snapped the woman. "His head's enough turned now with speakin' pieces and singin' silly songs. You better be gettin' on, folks. I can't stand here talkin' till mornin'."

She slammed the door, while Ira glared after her retreating figure, kicked the gate post to relieve his feelings, and then grinned sheepishly.

"Some grouch! Why, she didn't even ask you in to get warm! Well, I wouldn't loiter if I was you. And send that kid right back, or he'll get worse'n a tongue-lashin'. Well, good-by to you, folks. Hope you have a merry Christmas."

The tramp up the mountain passed almost entirely in silence, for it took their united energy to drag the sled up that steep grade against the wind. Scott drew a breath of relief when they beheld the camp, a spiral of smoke rising from its big stone chimney like a welcome promise of warmth.

"Looks good, doesn't it? But it'll be dark before that boy gets home. I wonder how old——"

They stopped simultaneously as a clear, sweet voice sounded from within the cabin:

"Silent night . . . holy night . . ."

"My God!"

Scott's face went suddenly dead white. He threw out a hand as if to brush something away, but Nancy caught it in hers, pulling it close against her wildly beating heart.

"All is calm . . . all is bright."

The childish treble came weirdly from within, while Nancy cried, "Scott—dearest, don't let go! It's only the little boy singing the carols he's learned in school. Don't you see? Come! Pull yourself together. We must go in."

Even as she spoke the door swung open, and through blurred vision they beheld the figure of a boy standing on the threshold. He was a slim little boy with an old, oddly wistful face, and big brown eyes under a thatch of yellow hair.

"You the city folks that was comin' up? Here, I'll help carry in yer things."

Before either could protest he was down on his knees in the snow, untying Ira's knots with skillful fingers. He would have lifted the heavy suit case himself, had not Scott, jerked back to the present by the boy's action, interfered.

"I'll carry that in." His voice sounded queer and shaky. "You take the basket. We're late, I'm afraid. You'd better hurry home before it gets too dark. Your mother said——"

"I don't mind the dark," said the boy quietly, as they went within. "I'll coast most o' the way down, anyhow. Guess you heard me singin' when you come along." He smiled, a shy, embarrassed smile as he explained: "It was a good chance to practice the Christmas carols. They won't let me, 'round home. We're goin' to have a show at the school to-morrow. I'm one o' the three kings—you know—'We three kings of Orient are.' I sing the first verse all by myself," he added with childish pride.

There followed a moment's silence. Nancy was fighting a desire to put her arms about the slim boyish figure, while Scott had turned away, unbuckling the straps of his suit case with fumbling hands. Then Nancy said, "I'm afraid we've kept you from helping at the school this afternoon. I'm so sorry."

The boy drew a resigned breath that struck her as strangely unchildlike.

"You needn't to mind, ma'am. Maybe they wouldn't have let me go anyway; and I've got to-morrow to think about. I—I been reading one o' your books. I like to read."

"What book was it? Would you like to take it home with you for a—" she glanced at Scott, still on his knees by the suit case, and finished hurriedly—"a Christmas gift?"

"Gee! Wouldn't I?" His wistful eyes brightened, then clouded. "Is there a place maybe where I could hide it 'round here? They don't like me to read much to home. They" (a hard look crept into his young eyes) "they burned up the book Teacher gave me a while back. It was *David Copperfield,* and I hadn't got it finished."

There came a crash as Scott, rising suddenly, upset a chair. The child jumped, and then laughed at himself for being startled.

"Look here, sonny," said Scott huskily, "you must be getting home. Can you bring us some milk to-morrow? I'll find a place to hide your book and tell you about it then. Haven't you got a warmer coat than this?"

He lifted a shabby jacket from the settle and held it out while the boy slipped into it.

"Thanks, mister," he said. "It's hard gettin' it on because it's tore inside. They's only one button," he added, as Scott groped for them. "She don't get much time to sew 'em on. I'll bring up the milk to-morrow mornin'. I got to hurry now or I'll get fits! Thanks for the book, ma'am. I'd like it better'n anything. Good night."

Standing at the window Nancy watched him start out in the fast descending dusk. It hurt her to think of that lonely walk; but she thrust the thought aside and turned to Scott, who had lighted a fire on the hearth and seemed absorbed in the dancing flames.

"That's good!" she said cheerfully. "I'll get things started for supper, and then make the bed. I'm weary enough to turn in early. You might bring me the canned stuff in your suit case, Scott. A hot soup ought to taste good to-night."

She took an apron from her bag and moved toward the tiny kitchen. Dave evidently knew how to build a fire. The stove lids were almost red, and the kettle was singing. Nancy went about her preparations deftly, tired though she was from the unaccustomed tramp, while Scott opened a can of soup, toasted some bread, and carried their meal on a tray to the settles before the hearthfire. It was all very cozy and "Christmasy," thought Nancy, with the wind blustering outside and the flames leaping up the chimney. But she was strangely quiet. The thought of that lonely little figure trudging off in the gray dusk persisted, despite her efforts to forget. It was Scott who spoke, saying out of a silence, "I wonder how old he is."

"The—the little boy?"

He nodded, and she answered gently, "He seemed no older than—I mean, he seemed very young to be milking cows and doing chores."

Again Scott nodded, and a moment passed before he said, "The work wouldn't hurt him though, if he were strong enough; but—did you notice, Nancy, he didn't look half fed? He is an intelligent little chap, though, and his voice—— Good Lord!" he broke off suddenly, "how can a shrew like that bring such a child into the world? To burn his book! Nancy, I can't understand how things are ordered. Here's that poor boy struggling for development in an unhappy atmosphere—and our Jimmy, who had love, and understanding, and—— Tell me, why is it?"

She stretched out a tender hand; but the question remained unanswered, and the meal was finished in silence.

Dave did not come with the milk next morning. They waited till nearly noon, and then tramped off in the snow-clad, pine-scented woods. It was a glorious day, with diamonds sparkling on every fir tree, and they came back refreshed, and ravenous for their delayed meal. Scott wiped the dishes, whistling as he worked. It struck his wife that he hadn't whistled like that for months. Later, the last kitchen rites accomplished, she went to the window, where he stood gazing down the trail.

"He won't come now, Scott."

"The kid? It's not three yet, Nancy."

"But the party begins at four. I suppose everyone for miles around will be there. I wish——" She was about to add that she wished they could have gone too, but something in Scott's face stopped the words. She said instead, "Do you think we'd better go for the milk ourselves?"

"What's the use? They'll all be at the shindig, even that sour-faced woman, I suppose. But somehow—I feel worried about the boy. If he isn't here bright and early in the morning I'll go down and see what's happened. Looks as if it were clouding up again, doesn't it? Perhaps we'll get snowed in!"

Big, lazy-looking snowflakes were already beginning to drift down. Scott piled more wood on the fire, and stretched out on the settle for a nap. But Nancy was restless. She found herself standing repeatedly at the window looking at the snow. She was there when at last Scott stirred and wakened. He sat up blinking, and asked, noting the twilight, "How long have I been asleep?"

Nancy laughed, relieved to hear his voice after the long stillness. "It's after five."

"Good thunder!" He arose, putting an arm across her shoulders. "Poor girl! I haven't been much company on this trip! But I didn't sleep well last night, couldn't get that boy out of my mind. Why, look!" Scott was staring out of the window into the growing dusk. "Here he is now! I thought you said——"

He was already at the door, flinging it wide in welcome as he went out to lift the box of milk jars from the sled. It seemed to Nancy, as the child stepped inside, that he looked subtly different—discouraged, she would have said of an older person; and when he raised his eyes she saw the unmistakable signs of recent tears.

"Oh, David!" she exclaimed, "why aren't you at the party?"

"I didn't go."

The boy seemed curiously to have withdrawn into himself. His answer was like a gentle "none of your business;" but Nancy was not without a knowledge of boy nature. She thought, "He's hurt—dreadfully. He's afraid to talk for fear he'll cry; but he'll feel better to get it off his mind." She said, drawing him toward the cheerful hearthfire, "But why not, Dave?"

He swallowed, pulling himself together with an heroic effort.

"I had ter milk. The folks have gone to Conroy to Gramma Hawkinses'! I *like* Gramma Hawkins. She told 'em to be sure an' bring me; but there wasn't no one else ter milk, so . . . so . . ."

It was Scott who came to the rescue as David's voice failed suddenly.

"Are you telling us that your people have gone away, for *Christmas,* leaving you home alone?"

The boy nodded, winking back tears as he managed a pathetic smile.

"Oh, I wouldn't ha' minded so much if—if it hadn't been for the doin's at the school. Miss Mary was countin' on me ter sing, and speak a piece. I don't know who they could ha' got to be that wise man." His face hardened in a way not good to see in a little boy, and he burst out angrily, "Oh, I'd have gone—after they got off! *Darn 'em!* But they hung 'round till almost four, and—and when I went for my good suit they—they'd *hid* it—or carried it away! . . . And there was a Christmas tree . . ."

His voice faltered again, while Nancy found herself speechless before what she recognized as a devastating disappointment. She glanced at Scott, and was frightened at the consuming anger in his face; but he came forward calmly, laying a steady hand on the boy's shoulder. He said, and, knowing what the words cost him, Nancy's heart went out to her husband in adoring gratitude, "Buck up, old scout! We'll have a Christmas tree! And we'll have a party too, you and Mother and I—darned if we don't! You can speak your piece and sing your carols for us. And Mother will read us 'The'—" for an appreciable moment Scott's voice faltered, but he went on gamely—" 'The Night Before Christmas.' Did you ever hear it? And I know some stunts that'll make your eyes shine. We'll have our party to-morrow, Christmas Day, sonny; but now" (he was stooping for his overshoes as he spoke), "now we'll go after that tree before it gets too dark! Come on, Mother. We want you, too!"

Mother! Scott hadn't called her that since Jimmy left them! Through tear-blinded eyes Nancy groped for her coat in the diminutive closet. Darkness was coming swiftly as they went into the snowy forest, but they found their tree, and stopped to cut fragrant green branches for decoration. Not till the tree stood proudly in its corner did they remember the lack of tinsel trimmings; but Scott brushed this aside as a mere nothing.

"We've got pop corn, and nothing's prettier. Give us a bite of supper, Nancy, and then I'm going to the village."

"The village! At this hour?"

"You take my sled, mister," cried David, and they saw that his eyes were happy once more, and childlike. "You can coast 'most all the way, like lightning! I'll pop the corn. I'd love to! Gee! it's lucky I milked before I come away!"

The hours that followed passed like magic to Nancy Carson. Veritable wonders were wrought in that small cabin; and oh, it was good to be planning and playing again with a little boy! Not till the child, who had been up since dawn, had dropped asleep on the settle from sheer weariness, did she add the finishing touches to the scene.

"It's like a picture for Christmas," she murmured happily. "The tree, so green and slender with its snowy trimmings—the cone-laden pine at the windows—the bulging stocking at the fireplace, and—and the sleeping boy. I wonder——"

She turned, startled by a step on the creaking snow outside, but it was Scott, of course. He came in quietly, not laden with bundles as she'd expected, but empty-handed. There was, she thought, a strange excitement in his manner as he glanced 'round the fire-lit room, his eyes resting for a moment on David's peaceful face. Then he saw the well-filled stocking at the mantel, and his eyes came back unswervingly to hers.

"Nancy! Is—is it—?"

She drew nearer, and put her arms about him.

"Yes, dear, it's—Jimmy's—just as we filled it on Christmas Eve three years ago. You see, I couldn't quite bear to leave it behind us when we came away, lying there in his drawer so lonely—at Christmas time. Tell me you don't mind, Scott—won't you? We have our memories, but David—he has so little. That dreadful mother, and——"

Scott cleared his throat; swallowed, and said gently, "He has, I think, the loveliest mother in the world!"

"What do you mean?"

He drew her down onto the settle that faced the sleeping boy, and answered, "Listen, Nancy. I went to the schoolhouse. I thought perhaps they'd give me something to trim the tree. The party was over, but the teacher was there with Ira Morse, clearing things away. I told them about David—why he hadn't shown up; and asked some questions. Nancy—what do you think? That Hawkins woman isn't the child's mother! I *knew* it!

"Nobody around here ever saw her. She died when David was a baby, and his father, half crazed, the natives thought, with grief, brought the child here, and lived like a hermit on the mountain. He died when Dave was about six, and as no one claimed the youngster, and there was no orphan asylum within miles, he was sent to the poor farm, and stayed there until last year, when Clem Hawkins wanted a boy to help do chores, and Dave was the cheapest thing in sight. Guess you wonder where I've been all this time?

Well, I've been interviewing the overseer of the poor—destroying red tape by the yard—resorting to bribery and corruption! But—— Hello, old man, did I wake you up?"

David, roused suddenly, rubbed his eyes. Then, spying the stocking, he wakened thoroughly and asked, "Say! Is—is it Christmas?"

Scott laughed and glanced at his watch.

"It will be, in twelve minutes. Come here, sonny."

He drew the boy onto his knee, and went on quietly: "The stores were closed, David, when I reached the village. I couldn't buy you a Christmas gift, you see. But I thought if we gave you a *real mother*, and—and a father——"

"Oh, Scott!"

It was a cry of rapture from Nancy. She had, of course, suspected the ending to his story, but not until that moment had she let herself really believe it. Then, seeing the child's bewilderment, she explained, "He means, dear, that you're our boy now—for always."

David looked up, his brown eyes big with wonder.

"And I needn't go back to Hawkinses'? Not *ever?*"

"Not ever," Scott promised, while his throat tightened at the relief in the boy's voice.

"And I'll have folks, same as the other kids?"

"You've guessed right." The new father spoke lightly in an effort to conceal his feeling. "That is, if you think we'll do!" he added, smiling.

"Oh, you'll——"

Suddenly inarticulate, David turned, throwing his thin arms around Scott's neck in a strangling, boylike hug. Then a bit ashamed because such things were new to him, he slipped away, standing with his back to them at the window, trying, they saw with understanding hearts, to visualize this unbelievable thing that had come, a miracle, into his starved life. When after a silence they joined him, the candle on the table flared up for a protesting moment, and then went out. Only starlight and firelight lit the cabin now; and Nancy, peering into the night, said gently, "How beautifully it has cleared! I think I never saw the stars so bright."

"Christmas stars," Scott reminded her and, knowing the memory that brought the roughness to his voice, she caught and clasped his hand.

It was David who spoke next. He was leaning close to the window, his elbows resting on the sill, his face cupped in his two hands. He seemed to have forgotten them as he said dreamily, "It's Christmas . . . Silent night . . . holy night . . . like the song. I wonder—" he looked up trustfully into the faces above him—"I wonder if—if maybe one of them stars isn't the Star of Bethlehem!"

IV

SOME CHRISTMAS ASPIC

But at the coming of the King of Heaven
  All's set at six and seven:
  We wallow in our sin.
Christ cannot find a chamber in the inn.
We entertain him always like a stranger,
And, as at first, still lodge him in the manger.

ANON: CHRIST CHURCH MS.

Christmas Every Day

W. D. HOWELLS

THE little girl came into her papa's study, as she always did Saturday morning before breakfast, and asked for a story. He tried to beg off that morning, for he was very busy, but she would not let him. So he began:

"Well, once there was a little pig—"

She put her hand over his mouth and stopped him at the word. She said she had heard little pig stories till she was perfectly sick of them.

"Well, what kind of story *shall* I tell, then?"

"About Christmas. It's getting to be the season. It's past Thanksgiving already."

"It seems to me," argued her papa, "that I've told as often about Christmas as I have about little pigs."

"No difference! Christmas is more interesting."

"Well!" Her papa roused himself from his writing by a great effort. "Well, then, I'll tell you about the little girl that wanted it Christmas every day in the year. How would you like that?"

"First-rate!" said the little girl; and she nestled into comfortable shape in his lap, ready for listening.

"Very well, then, this little pig— Oh, what are you pounding me for?"

"Because you said little pig instead of little girl."

"I should like to know what's the difference between a little pig and a little girl that wanted it Christmas every day!"

"Papa," said the little girl, warningly, "if you don't go on, I'll *give* it to you!" And at this her papa darted off like lightning, and began to tell the story as fast as he could.

Well, once there was a little girl who liked Christmas so much that she wanted it to be Christmas every day in the year; and as soon as Thanksgiving was over she began to send postal cards to the old Christmas Fairy to ask if she mightn't have it. But the old Fairy never answered any of the postals; and, after a while, the little girl found out that the Fairy was pretty particular, and wouldn't notice anything but letters, not even correspondence cards in envelopes; but real letters on sheets of paper, and sealed outside with a monogram—or your initial, any way. So, then, she began to send her letters; and in about three weeks—or just the day before Christmas, it was—she got a letter from the Fairy, saying she might have it Christmas every day for a year, and then they would see about having it longer.

The little girl was a good deal excited already, preparing for the old-fashioned, once-a-year Christmas that was coming the next day, and perhaps the Fairy's promise didn't make such an impression on her as it would have made at some other time. She just resolved to keep it to herself, and surprise everybody with it as it kept coming true; and then it slipped out of her mind altogether.

She had a splendid Christmas. She went to bed early, so as to let Santa Claus have a chance at the stockings, and in the morning she was up the first of anybody and went and felt them, and found hers all lumpy with packages of candy, and oranges and grapes, and pocket-books and rubber balls and all kinds of small presents, and her big brother's with nothing but the tongs in them, and her young lady sister's with a new silk umbrella, and her papa's and mamma's with potatoes and pieces of coal wrapped up in tissue paper, just as they always had every Christmas. Then she waited around till the rest of the family were up, and she was the first to burst into the library, when the doors were opened, and look at the large presents laid out on the library-table—books, and portfolios, and boxes of stationery, and breast-pins, and dolls, and little stoves, and dozens of handkerchiefs, and ink-stands, and skates, and snow-shovels, and photograph-frames, and little easels, and boxes of water-colors, and Turkish paste, and nougat, and candied cherries, and dolls' houses, and waterproofs—and the big Christmas-tree, lighted and standing in a waste-basket in the middle.

She had a splendid Christmas all day. She ate so much candy that she did not want any breakfast; and the whole forenoon the presents kept pouring in that the expressman had not had time to deliver the night before; and she went 'round giving the presents she had got for other people, and came home and ate turkey and cranberry for dinner, and plum-pudding and nuts and raisins and oranges and more candy, and then went out and coasted and came in with a stomach-ache, crying; and her papa said he would see if his house was turned into that sort of fool's paradise another year; and they had a light supper, and pretty early everybody went to bed cross.

Here the little girl pounded her papa in the back, again.

"Well, what now? Did I say pigs?"

"You made them *act* like pigs."

"Well, didn't they?"

"No matter; you oughtn't to put it into a story."

"Very well, then, I'll take it all out."

Her father went on:

The little girl slept very heavily, and she slept very late, but she was wakened at last by the other children dancing 'round her bed with their stockings full of presents in their hands.

"What is it?" said the little girl, and she rubbed her eyes and tried to rise up in bed.

"Christmas! Christmas! Christmas!" they all shouted, and waved their stockings.

"Nonsense! It was Christmas yesterday."

Her brothers and sisters just laughed. "We don't know about that. It's Christmas to-day, any way. You come into the library and see."

Then all at once it flashed on the little girl that the Fairy was keeping her promise, and her year of Christmases was beginning. She was dreadfully sleepy, but she sprang up like a lark—a lark that had overeaten itself and gone to bed cross—and darted into the library. There it was again! Books, and portfolios, and boxes of stationery, and breast-pins——

"You needn't go over it all, Papa; I guess I can remember just what was there," said the little girl.

Well, and there was the Christmas-tree blazing away, and the family picking out their presents, but looking pretty sleepy, and her father perfectly puzzled, and her mother ready to cry. "I'm sure I don't see how I'm to dispose of all these things," said her mother, and her father said it seemed to him they had had something just like it the day before, but he supposed he must have dreamed it. This struck the little girl as the best kind of a joke; and so she ate so much candy she didn't want any breakfast, and went 'round carrying presents, and had turkey and cranberry for dinner, and then went out and coasted, and came in with a——

"Papa!"
"Well, what now?"
"What did you promise, you forgetful thing?"
"Oh! oh, yes!"

Well, the next day, it was just the same thing over again, but everybody getting crosser; and at the end of a week's time so many people had lost their tempers that you could pick up lost tempers everywhere; they perfectly strewed the ground. Even when people tried to recover their tempers they usually got somebody else's, and it made the most dreadful mix.

The little girl began to get frightened, keeping the secret all to herself; she wanted to tell her mother, but she didn't dare to; and she was ashamed to ask the Fairy to take back her gift, it seemed ungrateful and ill-bred, and she thought she would try to stand it, but she hardly knew how she could, for a whole year. So it went on and on, and it was Christmas on St. Valentine's Day, and Washington's Birthday just the same as any day, and it didn't skip even the First of April, though everything was counterfeit that day, and that was some *little* relief.

After a while, coal and potatoes began to be awfully scarce, so many had been wrapped up in tissue paper to fool papas and mammas with. Turkeys got to be about a thousand dollars apiece——

"Papa!"

"Well, what?"

"You're beginning to fib."

"Well, *two* thousand, then."

And they got to passing off almost anything for turkeys—half-grown humming-birds, and even rocs out of the "Arabian Nights"—the real turkeys were so scarce. And cranberries—well, they asked a diamond apiece for cranberries. All the woods and orchards were cut down for Christmas-trees, and where the woods and orchards used to be, it looked just like a stubble-field, with the stumps. After a while they had to make Christmas-trees out of rags, and stuff them with bran, like old-fashioned dolls; but there were plenty of rags, because people got so poor, buying presents for one another, that they couldn't get any new clothes, and they just wore their old ones to tatters. They got so poor that everybody had to go to the poor-house, except the confectioners, and the fancy store-keepers, and the picture-booksellers, and the expressmen; and *they* all got so rich and proud that they would hardly wait upon a person when he came to buy; it was perfectly shameful!

Well, after it had gone on about three or four months, the little girl, whenever she came into the room in the morning and saw those great ugly lumpy stockings dangling at the fire-place, and the disgusting presents around everywhere, used to just sit down and burst out crying. In six months she was perfectly exhausted; she couldn't even cry any more; she just lay on the lounge and rolled her eyes and panted. About the beginning of October she took to sitting down on dolls, wherever she found them—French dolls, or any kind—she hated the sight of them so; and by Thanksgiving she was crazy, and just slammed her presents across the room.

By that time people didn't carry presents around nicely any more. They flung them over the fence, or through the window, or anything; and, instead of running their tongues out and taking great pains to write "For dear Papa," or "Mamma," or "Brother," or "Sister," or "Susie," or "Sammie," or "Billie," or "Bobby" or "Jimmie," or "Jennie," or whoever it was, and troubling to get the spelling right, and then signing their names, and " 'Xmas, 188——," they used to write in the gift-books, "Take it, you horrid old thing!" and then go and bang it against the front door. Nearly everybody had built barns to hold their presents, but pretty soon the barns overflowed, and then they used to let them lie out in the rain, or anywhere. Sometimes the police used to come and tell them to shovel their presents off the sidewalk, or they would arrest them.

"I thought you said everybody had gone to the poor-house," interrupted the little girl.

"They did go, at first," said her papa; "but after a while the poor-houses got so full that they had to send the people back to their own houses. They tried to cry, when they got back, but they couldn't make the least sound."

"Why couldn't they?"

"Because they had lost their voices, saying 'Merry Christmas' so much. Did I tell you how it was on the Fourth of July?"

"No; how was it?" And the little girl nestled closer, in expectation of something uncommon.

Well, the night before, the boys stayed up to celebrate, as they always do, and fell asleep before twelve o'clock, as usual, expecting to be wakened by the bells and cannon. But it was nearly eight o'clock before the first boy in the United States woke up, and then he found out what the trouble was. As soon as he could get his clothes on, he ran out of the house and smashed a big cannon-torpedo down on the pavement; but it didn't make any more noise than a damp wad of paper, and, after he tried about twenty or thirty more, he began to pick them up and look at them. Every single torpedo was a big raisin! Then he just streaked it upstairs, and examined his fire-crackers and toy-pistol and two-dollar collection of fireworks, and found that they were nothing but sugar and candy painted up to look like fireworks! Before ten o'clock, every boy in the United States found out that his Fourth of July things had turned into Christmas things; and then they just sat down and cried—they were so mad. There are about twenty million boys in the United States, and so you can imagine what a noise they made. Some men got together before night, with a little powder that hadn't turned into purple sugar yet, and they said they would fire off *one* cannon, any way. But the cannon burst into a thousand pieces, for it was nothing but rock-candy, and some of the men nearly got killed. The Fourth of July orations all turned into Christmas carols, and when anybody tried to read the Declaration, instead of saying, "When in the course of human events it becomes necessary," he was sure to sing, "God rest you, merry gentlemen." It was perfectly awful.

The little girl drew a deep sigh of satisfaction.

"And how was it at Thanksgiving?" she asked.

Her papa hesitated. "Well, I'm almost afraid to tell you. I'm afraid you'll think it's wicked."

"Well, tell, any way," said the little girl.

Well, before it came Thanksgiving, it had leaked out who had caused all these Christmases. The little girl had suffered so much that she had talked about it in her sleep; and after that, hardly anybody would play with her. People just perfectly despised her, because if it had not been for her greediness, it wouldn't have happened; and now, when it came Thanksgiving, and she wanted them to go to church, and have a squash-pie and turkey, and show their gratitude, they said that all the turkeys had been eaten up for her old Christmas dinners, and if she would stop the Christmases, they would see about the gratitude. Wasn't it dreadful? And the very next day the little girl began to send letters to the Christmas Fairy, and then telegrams, to stop it. But it didn't do any good; and then she got to calling at the Fairy's house, but the girl that came to the door always said "Not at home," or "Engaged," or "At dinner," or something like that; and so it went on till it came to the old once-a-year Christmas Eve. The little girl fell asleep, and when she woke up in the morning——

"She found it was all nothing but a dream," suggested the little girl.

"No, indeed!" said her papa. "It was all every bit true!"

"Well, what *did* she find out then?"

"Why, that it wasn't Christmas at last, and wasn't ever going to be, any more. Now it's time for breakfast."

The little girl held her papa fast around the neck.

"You shan't go if you're going to leave it *so!*"

"How do you want it left?"

"Christmas once a year."

"All right," said her papa; and he went on again.

Well, there was the greatest rejoicing all over the country, and it extended clear up into Canada. The people met together everywhere, and kissed and cried for joy. The city carts went around and gathered up all the candy and raisins and nuts, and dumped them into the river; and it made the fish perfectly sick; and the whole United States, as far out as Alaska, was one blaze of bonfires, where the children were burning up their gift-books and presents of all kinds. They had the greatest *time!*

The little girl went to thank the old Fairy because she had stopped its being Christmas, and she said she hoped she would keep her promise, and see that Christmas never, never came again. Then the Fairy frowned, and asked her if she was sure she knew what she meant; and the little girl asked her, why not? and the old Fairy said that now she was behaving just as greedily as ever, and she'd better look out. This made the little girl think it all over carefully again, and she said she would be willing to have it Christmas about once in a thousand years; and then she said a hundred, and then she said ten, and at last she got down to one. Then the Fairy said that was the good old way that had pleased people ever since Christmas began, and she was agreed. Then the little girl said, "What're your shoes made of?" And the Fairy said, "Leather." And the little girl said, "Bargain's done forever," and skipped off, and hippity-hopped the whole way home, she was so glad.

"How will that do?" asked the papa.

"First-rate!" said the little girl; but she hated to have the story stop, and was rather sober. However, her mamma put her head in at the door, and asked her papa:

"Are you never coming to breakfast? What have you been telling that child?"

"Oh, just a moral tale."

The little girl caught him around the neck again.

"*We* know! Don't you tell *what*, Papa! Don't you tell *what!*"

Down Pens

SAKI

"HAVE you written to thank the Froplinsons for what they sent us?" asked Egbert.

"No," said Janetta, with a note of tired defiance in her voice; "I've written eleven letters today expressing surprise and gratitude for sundry unmerited gifts, but I haven't written to the Froplinsons."

"Someone will have to write to them," said Egbert.

"I don't dispute the necessity, but I don't think the someone should be me," said Janetta. "I wouldn't mind writing a letter of angry recrimination or heartless satire to some suitable recipient; in fact, I should rather enjoy it, but I've come to the end of my capacity for expressing servile amiability. Eleven letters today and nine yesterday, all couched in the same strain of ecstatic thankfulness: really, you can't expect me to sit down to another. There is such a thing as writing oneself out."

"I've written nearly as many," said Egbert, "and I've had my usual business correspondence to get through too. Besides, I don't know what it was that the Froplinsons sent us."

"A William the Conqueror calendar," said Janetta, "with a quotation of one of his great thoughts for every day in the year."

"Impossible," said Egbert; "he didn't have three hundred and

---

sixty-five thoughts in the whole of his life, or, if he did, he kept them to himself. He was a man of action, not of introspection."

"Well, it was William Wordsworth, then," said Janetta; "I know William came into it somewhere."

"That sounds more probable," said Egbert; "well, let's collaborate on this letter of thanks and get it done. I'll dictate, and you can scribble it down. 'Dear Mrs. Froplinson—thank you and your husband so much for the very pretty calendar you sent us. It was very good of you to think of us.' "

"You can't possibly say that," said Janetta, laying down her pen.

"It's what I always do say, and what everyone says to me," protested Egbert.

"We sent them something on the twenty-second," said Janetta, "so they simply had to think of us. There was no getting away from it."

"What did we send them?" asked Egbert gloomily.

"Bridge-markers," said Janetta, "in a cardboard case, with some inanity about 'digging for fortune with a royal spade' emblazoned on the cover. The moment I saw it in the shop I said to myself 'Froplinsons' and to the attendant 'How much?' When he said 'Ninepence!' I gave him their address, jabbed our card in, paid tenpence or elevenpence to cover the postage, and thanked heaven. With less sincerity and infinitely more trouble they eventually thanked me."

"The Froplinsons don't play bridge," said Egbert.

"One is not supposed to notice social deformities of that sort," said Janetta; "it wouldn't be polite. Besides, what trouble did they take to find out whether we read Wordsworth with gladness? For all they knew or cared we might be frantically embedded in the belief that all poetry begins and ends with John Masefield, and it might infuriate or depress us to have a daily sample of Wordsworthian products flung at us."

"Well, let's get on with the letter of thanks," said Egbert.

"Proceed," said Janetta.

" 'How clever of you to guess that Wordsworth is our favourite poet,' " dictated Egbert.

Again Janetta laid down her pen.

"Do you realize what that means?" she asked; "a Wordsworth booklet next Christmas, and another calendar the Christmas after, with the same problem of having to write suitable letters of thankfulness. No, the best thing to do is to drop all further allusion to the calendar and switch off on to some other topic."

"But what other topic?"

"Oh, something like this: 'What do you think of the New Year Honours List? A friend of ours made such a clever remark when he read it.' Then you can stick in any remark that comes into your head; it needn't be clever. The Froplinsons won't know whether it is or isn't."

"We don't even know on which side they are in politics," objected Egbert; "and anyhow you can't suddenly dismiss the subject of the calendar. Surely there must be some intelligent remark that can be made about it."

"Well, we can't think of one," said Janetta wearily; "the fact is, we've both written ourselves out. Heavens! I've just remembered Mrs. Stephen Ludberry. I haven't thanked her for what she sent."

"What did she send?"

"I forget; I think it was a calendar."

There was a long silence, the forlorn silence of those who are bereft of hope and have almost ceased to care.

Presently Egbert started from his seat with an air of resolution. The light of battle was in his eyes.

"Let me come to the writing table," he exclaimed.

"Gladly," said Janetta. "Are you going to write to Mrs. Ludberry or the Froplinsons?"

"To neither," said Egbert, drawing a stack of note-paper towards him; "I'm going to write to the editor of every enlightened and influential newspaper in the Kingdom. I'm going to suggest that there should be a sort of epistolary Truce of God during the festivities of Christmas and New Year. From the twenty-fourth of December to the third or fourth of January it shall be considered an offence against good sense and good feeling to write or expect any letter or communication that does not deal with the necessary events of the moment. Answers to invitations, arrangements about trains, renewal of club subscriptions, and, of course, all the ordinary everyday affairs of business, sickness, engaging new cooks, and so forth, these will be dealt with in the usual manner as something inevitable, a legitimate part of our daily life. But all the devastating accretions of correspondence, incident to the festive season, these should be swept away to give the season a chance of being really festive, a time of untroubled, unpunctuated peace and good will."

"But you would have to make some acknowledgment of presents received," objected Janetta; "otherwise people would never know whether they had arrived safely."

"Of course, I have thought of that," said Egbert; "every present that was sent off would be accompanied by a ticket bearing the date of dispatch and the signature of the sender, and some conventional hieroglyphic to show that it was intended to be a Christmas or New Year gift; there would be a counterfoil with space for the recipient's name and the date of arrival, and all you would have to do would be to sign and date the counterfoil, add a conventional hieroglyphic indicating heartfelt thanks and gratified surprise, put the thing into an envelope and post it."

"It sounds delightfully simple," said Janetta wistfully, "but people would consider it too cut-and-dried, too perfunctory."

"It is not a bit more perfunctory than the present system," said Egbert; "I have only the same conventional language of gratitude at my disposal with which to thank dear old Colonel Chuttle for his perfectly delicious Stilton, which we shall devour to the last morsel, and the Froplinsons know that we are bored with their calendar, whatever we may say to the contrary, just as we know that they are bored with the bridge-markers in spite of their written assurance that they thanked us for our charming little gift. What is more, the Colonel knows that even if we had taken a sudden aversion to Stilton or been forbidden it by the doctor, we should still have written a letter of hearty thanks around it. So you see the present system of acknowledgment is just as perfunctory as the counterfoil business would be, only ten times more tiresome and brain-racking."

"Your plan would certainly bring the ideal of a Happy Christmas a step nearer realization," said Janetta.

"There are exceptions, of course," said Egbert, "people who really try to infuse a breath of reality into their letters of acknowledgment. Aunt Susan, for instance, who writes: 'Thank you very much for the ham; not such a good flavor as the one you sent last year, which itself was not a particularly good one. Hams are not what they used to be.' It would be a pity to be deprived of her Christmas comments, but that loss would be swallowed up in the general gain."

"Meanwhile," said Janetta, "what *am* I to say to the Froplinsons?"

Old Folks' Christmas

RING LARDNER

TOM and Grace Carter sat in their living-room on Christmas Eve, sometimes talking, sometimes pretending to read and all the time thinking things they didn't want to think. Their two children, Junior, aged nineteen, and Grace, two years younger, had come home that day from their schools for the Christmas vacation. Junior was in his first year at the university and Grace attending a boarding school that would fit her for college.

I won't call them Grace and Junior any more, though that is the way they had been christened. Junior had changed his name to Ted and Grace was now Caroline, and thus they insisted on being addressed, even by their parents. This was one of the things Tom and Grace the elder were thinking of as they sat in their living-room Christmas Eve.

Other university freshmen who had lived here had returned on the twenty-first, the day when the vacation was supposed to begin. Ted had telegraphed that he would be three days late owing to a special examination which, if he passed it, would lighten the terrific burden of the next term. He had arrived at home looking so pale, heavy-eyed and shaky that his mother doubted the wisdom of the concentrated mental effort, while his father secretly hoped the stuff had been nonpoisonous and would not have lasting effects. Caroline, too, had been behind schedule, explaining that her laundry had gone astray and she had not dared trust others to trace it for her.

Grace and Tom had attempted, with fair success, to conceal their disappointment over this delayed home-coming and had continued with their preparations for a Christmas that would thrill their children and consequently themselves. They had bought an imposing lot of presents, costing twice or three times as much as had been Tom's father's annual income when Tom was Ted's age, or Tom's own income a year ago, before General Motors' acceptance of his new weather-proof paint had enabled him to buy this suburban home and luxuries such as his own parents and Grace's had never dreamed of, and to give Ted and Caroline advantages that he and Grace had perforce gone without.

Behind the closed door of the music-room was the elaborately decked tree. The piano and piano bench and the floor around the tree were covered with beribboned packages of all sizes, shapes and weights, one of them addressed to Tom, another to Grace, a few to the servants and the rest to Ted and Caroline. A huge box contained a sealskin coat for Caroline, a coat that had cost as much as the Carters had formerly paid a year for rent. Even more expensive was a "set" of jewelry consisting of an opal brooch, a bracelet of opals and gold filigree, and an opal ring surrounded by diamonds.

Grace always had preferred opals to any other stone, but now that she could afford them, some inhibition prevented her from buying them for herself; she could enjoy them much more adorning her pretty daughter. There were boxes of silk stockings, lingerie, gloves and handkerchiefs. And for Ted, a three-hundred-dollar watch, a deluxe edition of Balzac, an expensive bag of shiny, new steel-shafted golf-clubs and the last word in portable phonographs.

But the big surprise for the boy was locked in the garage, a black Gorham sedan, a model more up to date and better-looking than Tom's own year-old car that stood beside it. Ted could use it during the vacation if the mild weather continued and could look forward to driving it around home next spring and summer, there being a rule at the university forbidding undergraduates the possession or use of private automobiles.

Every year for sixteen years, since Ted was three and Caroline one, it had been the Christmas Eve custom of the Carters to hang up their children's stockings and fill them with inexpensive toys. Tom and Grace had thought it would be fun to continue the custom this year; the contents of the stockings—a mechanical negro dancing doll, music-boxes, a kitten that meowed when you pressed a spot on her back, et cetera—would make the "kids" laugh. And one of Grace's first pronouncements to her returned offspring was that they must go to bed early so Santa Claus would not be frightened away.

But it seemed they couldn't promise to make it so terribly early. They both had long-standing dates in town. Caroline was going to dinner and a play with Beatrice Murdock and Beatrice's nineteen-year-old brother Paul. The latter would call for her in his car at half past six. Ted had accepted an invitation to see the hockey match with two classmates, Herb Castle and Bernard King. He wanted to take his father's Gorham, but Tom told him untruthfully that the foot-brake was not working; Ted must be kept out of the garage till tomorrow morning.

Ted and Caroline had taken naps in the afternoon and gone off together in Paul Murdock's stylish roadster, giving their word that they would be back by midnight or a little later and that tomorrow night they would stay home.

And now their mother and father were sitting up for them, because the stockings could not be filled and hung till they were safely in bed, and also because trying to go to sleep is a painful and hopeless business when you are kind of jumpy.

"What time is it?" asked Grace, looking up from the third page of a book that she had begun to "read" soon after dinner.

"Half past two," said her husband. (He had answered the same question every fifteen or twenty minutes since midnight.)

"You don't suppose anything could have happened?" said Grace.

"We'd have heard if there had," said Tom.

"It isn't likely, of course," said Grace, "but they might have had an accident some place where nobody was there to report it or telephone or anything. We don't know what kind of a driver the Murdock boy is."

"He's Ted's age. Boys that age may be inclined to drive too fast, but they drive pretty well."

"How do you know?"

"Well, I've watched some of them drive."

"Yes, but not all of them."

"I doubt whether anybody in the world has seen every nineteen-year-old boy drive."

"Boys these days seem so kind of irresponsible."

"Oh, don't worry! They probably met some of their young friends and stopped for a bite to eat or something." Tom got up and walked to the window with studied carelessness. "It's a pretty night," he said. "You can see every star in the sky."

But he wasn't looking at the stars. He was looking down the road for headlights. There were none in sight and after a few moments he returned to his chair.

"What time is it?" asked Grace.

"Twenty-two of," he said.

"Of what?"

"Of three."

"Your watch must have stopped. Nearly an hour ago you told me it was half past two."

"My watch is all right. You probably dozed off."

"I haven't closed my eyes."

"Well, it's time you did. Why don't you go to bed?"

"Why don't you?"

"I'm not sleepy."

"Neither am I. But honestly, Tom, it's silly for you to stay up. I'm just doing it so I can fix the stockings, and because I feel so wakeful. But there's no use of your losing your sleep."

"I couldn't sleep a wink till they're home."

"That's foolishness! There's nothing to worry about. They're just having a good time. You were young once yourself."

"That's just it! When I was young, I was young." He picked up his paper and tried to get interested in the shipping news.

"What time is it?" asked Grace.

"Five minutes of three."

"Maybe they're staying at the Murdocks' all night."

"They'd have let us know."

"They were afraid to wake us up, telephoning."

At three-twenty a car stopped at the front gate.

"There they are!"

"I told you there was nothing to worry about."

Tom went to the window. He could just discern the outlines of the Murdock boy's roadster, whose lighting system seemed to have broken down.

"He hasn't any lights," said Tom. "Maybe I'd better go out and see if I can fix them."

"No, don't!" said Grace sharply. "He can fix them himself. He's just saving them while he stands still."

"Why don't they come in?"

"They're probably making plans."

"They can make them in here. I'll go out and tell them we're still up."

"No, don't!" said Grace as before, and Tom obediently remained at the window.

It was nearly four when the car lights flashed on and the car drove away. Caroline walked into the house and stared dazedly at her parents.

"Heavens! What are you doing up?"

Tom was about to say something, but Grace forestalled him.

"We were talking over old Christmases," she said. "Is it very late?"

"I haven't any idea," said Caroline.

"Where is Ted?"

"Isn't he home? I haven't seen him since we dropped him at the hockey place."

"Well, you go right to bed," said her mother. "You must be worn out."

"I am, kind of. We danced after the play. What time is breakfast?"

"Eight o'clock."

"Oh, Mother, can't you make it nine?"

"I guess so. You used to want to get up early on Christmas."

"I know, but——"

"Who brought you home?" asked Tom.

"Why, Paul Murdock—and Beatrice."

"You looked rumpled."

"They made me sit in the 'rumple' seat."

She laughed at her joke, said good night and went upstairs. She had not come even within hand-shaking distance of her father and mother.

"The Murdocks," said Tom, "must have great manners, making their guest ride in that uncomfortable seat."

Grace was silent.

"You go to bed, too," said Tom. "I'll wait for Ted."

"You couldn't fix the stockings."

"I won't try. We'll have time for that in the morning; I mean, later in the morning."

"I'm not going to bed till you do," said Grace.

"All right, we'll both go. Ted ought not to be long now. I suppose his friends will bring him home. We'll hear him when he comes in."

There was no chance not to hear him when, at ten minutes before six, he came in. He had done his Christmas shopping late and brought home a package.

Grace went downstairs again at half past seven, telling the servants breakfast would be postponed till nine. She nailed the stockings beside the fireplace, went into the music-room to see that nothing had been disturbed and removed Ted's hat and overcoat from where he had carefully hung them on the hall floor.

Tom appeared a little before nine and suggested that the children ought to be awakened.

"I'll wake them," said Grace, and went upstairs. She opened Ted's door, looked and softly closed it again. She entered her daughter's room and found Caroline semiconscious.

"Do I have to get up now? Honestly I can't eat anything. If you could just have Molla bring me some coffee. Ted and I are both invited to the Murdocks' for breakfast at half past twelve, and I could sleep for another hour or two."

"But dearie, don't you know we have Christmas dinner at one?"

"It's a shame, Mother, but I thought of course our dinner would be at night."

"Don't you want to see your presents?"

"Certainly I do, but can't they wait?"

Grace was about to go to the kitchen to tell the cook that dinner would be at seven instead of one, but she remembered having promised Signe the afternoon and evening off, as a cold, light supper would be all anyone wanted after the heavy midday meal.

Tom and Grace breakfasted alone and once more sat in the living-room, talking, thinking and pretending to read.

"You ought to speak to Caroline," said Tom.

"I will, but not today. It's Christmas."

"And I intend to say a few words to Ted."

"Yes, dear, you must. But not today."

"I suppose they'll be out again tonight."

"No, they promised to stay home. We'll have a nice cozy evening."

"Don't bet too much on that," said Tom.

At noon the "children" made their entrance and responded to their parents' salutations with almost the proper warmth. Ted declined a cup of coffee and he and Caroline apologized for making a "breakfast" date at the Murdocks'.

"Sis and I both thought you'd be having dinner at seven, as usual."

"We've always had it at one o'clock on Christmas," said Tom.

"I'd forgotten it was Christmas," said Ted.

"Well, those stockings ought to remind you."

Ted and Caroline looked at the bulging stockings.

"Isn't there a tree?" asked Caroline.

"Of course," said her mother. "But the stockings come first."

"We've only a little time," said Caroline. "We'll be terribly late as it is. So can't we see the tree now?"

"I guess so," said Grace, and led the way into the music-room.

The servants were summoned and the tree stared at and admired.

"You must open your presents," said Grace to her daughter.

"I can't open them all now," said Caroline. "Tell me which is special."

The cover was removed from the huge box and Grace held up the coat.

"Oh, Mother!" said Caroline. "A sealskin coat!"

"Put it on," said her father.

"Not now. We haven't time."

"Then look at this!" said Grace, and opened the case of jewels.

"Oh, Mother! Opals!" said Caroline.

"They're my favorite stone," said Grace quietly.

"If nobody minds," said Ted, "I'll postpone my personal investigation till we get back. I know I'll like everything you've given me. But if we have no car in working order, I've got to call a taxi and catch a train."

"You can drive in," said his father.

"Did you fix the brake?"

"I think it's all right. Come up to the garage and we'll see."

Ted got his hat and coat and kissed his mother good-by.

"Mother," he said, "I know you'll forgive me for not having any presents for you and Dad. I was so rushed the last three days at school. And I thought I'd have time to shop a little when we got in yesterday, but I was in too much of a hurry to be home. Last night, everything was closed."

"Don't worry," said Grace. "Christmas is for young people. Dad and I have everything we want."

The servants had found their gifts and disappeared, expressing effusive Scandinavian thanks.

Caroline and her mother were left alone.

"Mother, where did the coat come from?"

"Lloyd and Henry's."

"They keep all kinds of furs, don't they?"

"Yes."

"Would you mind horribly if I exchanged this?"

"Certainly not, dear. You pick out anything you like, and if it's a little more expensive, it won't make any difference. We can go in town tomorrow or next day. But don't you want to wear your opals to the Murdocks'?"

"I don't believe so. They might get lost or something. And I'm not—well, I'm not so crazy about——"

"I think they can be exchanged, too," said Grace. "You run along now and get ready to start."

Caroline obeyed with alacrity, and Grace spent a welcome moment by herself.

Tom opened the garage door.

"Why, you've got two cars!" said Ted.

"The new one isn't mine," said Tom.

"Whose is it?"

"Yours. It's the new model."

"Dad, that's wonderful! But it looks just like the old one."

"Well, the old one's pretty good. Just the same, yours is better. You'll find that out when you drive it. Hop in and get started. I had her filled with gas."

"I think I'd rather drive the old one."

"Why?"

"Well, what I really wanted, Dad, was a Barnes sport roadster, something like Paul Murdock's, only a different color scheme. And if I don't drive this Gorham at all, maybe you could get them to take it back or make some kind of a deal with the Barnes people."

Tom didn't speak till he was sure of his voice. Then: "All right, son. Take my car and I'll see what can be done about yours."

Caroline, waiting for Ted, remembered something and called to her mother. "Here's what I got for you and Dad," she said. "It's two tickets to 'Jolly Jane,' the play I saw last night. You'll love it!"

"When are they for?" asked Grace.

"Tonight," said Caroline.

"But dearie," said her mother, "we don't want to go out tonight, when you promised to stay home."

"We'll keep our promise," said Caroline, "but the Murdocks may drop in and bring some friends and we'll dance and there'll be music. And Ted and I thought you'd rather be away somewhere so our noise wouldn't disturb you."

"It was sweet of you to do this," said her mother, "but your father and I don't mind noise as long as you're enjoying yourselves."

"It's time anyway that you and Dad had a treat."

"The real treat," said Grace, "would be to spend a quiet evening here with just you two."

"The Murdocks practically invited themselves and I couldn't say no after they'd been so nice to me. And honestly, Mother, you'll love this play!"

"Will you be home for supper?"

"I'm pretty sure we will, but if we're a little late, don't you and Dad wait for us. Take the seven-twenty so you won't miss anything. The first act is really the best. We probably won't be hungry, but have Signe leave something out for us in case we are."

Tom and Grace sat down to the elaborate Christmas dinner and didn't make much impression on it. Even if they had had any appetite, the sixteen-pound turkey would have looked almost like new when they had eaten their fill. Conversation was intermittent and related chiefly to Signe's excellence as a cook and the mildness of the weather. Children and Christmas were barely touched on.

Tom merely suggested that on account of its being a holiday and their having theatre tickets, they ought to take the six-ten and eat supper at the Metropole. His wife said no; Ted and Caroline might come home and be disappointed at not finding them. Tom seemed about to make some remark, but changed his mind.

The afternoon was the longest Grace had ever known. The children were still absent at seven and she and Tom taxied to the train. Neither talked much on the way to town. As for the play, which Grace was sure to love, it turned out to be a rehash of "Cradle Snatchers" and "Sex," retaining the worst features of each.

When it was over Tom said: "Now I'm inviting you to the Cove Club. You didn't eat any breakfast or dinner or supper and I can't have you starving to death on a feast-day. Besides, I'm thirsty as well as hungry."

They ordered the special *table d'hôte* and struggled hard to get away with it. Tom drank six high-balls, but they failed to produce the usual effect of making him jovial. Grace had one high-ball and some kind of cordial that gave her a warm, contented feeling for a moment. But the warmth and contentment left her before the train was half way home.

The living-room looked as if von Kluck's army had just passed through. Ted and Caroline had kept their promise up to a certain point. They had spent part of the evening at home, and the Murdocks must have brought all their own friends and everybody else's, judging from the results. The table and floors were strewn with empty glasses, ashes and cigaret stubs.

The stockings had been torn off their nails and the wrecked contents were all over the place. Two sizable holes had been burnt in Grace's favorite rug.

Tom took his wife by the arm and led her into the music-room.

"You never took the trouble to open your own present," he said.

"And I think there's one for you, too," said Grace. "They didn't come in here," she added, "so I guess there wasn't much dancing or music."

Tom found his gift from Grace, a set of diamond studs and cuff buttons for festive wear. Grace's present from him was an opal ring.

"Oh, Tom!" she said.

"We'll have to go out somewhere tomorrow night, so I can break these in," said Tom.

"Well, if we do that, we'd better get a good night's rest."

"I'll beat you upstairs," said Tom.

The Christmas Card

JAMES BRIDIE

Once upon a time there was a stout little knight who lived in Alpaca Square—a round peg in a Square hole, he used laughingly to say to his guests at dinner. As he grew wealthier and wealthier he moved into Eaton Square. He didn't like Eaton Square at all (who would?), but he was a man who liked to keep his guests amused. It had to be some sort of Square.

It would be unfair and perhaps dangerous to print his name, so I shall call him Sir James Watson, and his wife, Lady Watson. Lady Watson's hair was, at the time the story opens, of bright copper colour brindled with, perhaps, slightly less artificial bands of pure white. She was many years younger than her husband in fact and in spirit, a lover of balls, routs, and assemblies, and a laugher of gay laughter. As she went from room to room of her large house, one would have thought that an Italian soprano was practising. She had another note in her voice that sounded like a file, but she seldom employed that note except in the privacy of her own bedroom when Sir James came in to kiss her good morning before going out to make money at his office.

They had married latish in life. Sir James (as I prefer to call him) had wooed and won her as a corollary of a situation few ladies can resist. In the knightliest possible fashion, he had rescued her from a caitiff of the same degree whose name was Sir Isadore Waldteufel. Like some Old Lochinvar he had seized his bride from the very steps of the altar, or worse. I should give you more in the way of detail, but I am afraid that you would recognize that celebrated cause or seek the files of the newspapers for it. It was in all the papers.

This was all very well; but, when a romance begins so auspiciously as that I wish I were in a position to describe to you, to provide a series of mounting climaxes is a very difficult job. Without them the dread anticlimax is sure to set in, sooner or later. To a spirit like that of Lady Watson, an anticlimax is as abhorrent as a vacuum is to her Mother Nature.

She was a true child of Nature and, in a sense, of Bohemia. She liked happy faces around her in large numbers and loud noises and continuous enrapturing movement. It was otherwise with her chubby husband. He also, it is true, liked happy faces; but he preferred them in small doses. He liked his noises quiet and select. The gentle rhythmic movements made by a fat man with a cat on his lap sleeping in an armchair before a large fire were movement enough for him. He was looking forward with a certain warmth of pride to his seventieth birthday.

Lady Watson was passionately fond of dancing, but so was not he. Lady Watson was fond of gin mixed with Bacardi and Cointreau. He preferred whisky for most occasions or, after dinner, a rather heavy and sticky opaque kind of port wine of which he was very proud. Lady Watson liked young men with curly hair, loud laughs, and prominent front teeth. Sir James didn't. Lady Watson liked her motor cars to be shaped like torpedoes or sharks. Sir James liked them like hearses. Sir James liked jokes that took a long time to tell. Lady Watson liked short jokes. Sir James liked Mendelssohn's *Songs without Words,* the Barcarolle from *Tales of Hoffmann,* and one or two pieces by Grieg. These tunes made Lady Watson scream and turn off the gramophone. Lady Watson liked dressing up. Hard collars cut Sir James's neck and stiff shirt fronts pressed into his abdomen and gave him indigestion. Lady Watson liked playing contract bridge and making a great song about it, though, indeed, she played abominably. Sir James had not been averse to a rubber of whist in his day, but he was not heart-broken to find that nobody played that game in the year in which this story is taking such an unconscionable time in opening.

On November the twenty-first, in nineteen hundred and thirty-four, Lady Watson had gone out to the play. Her escort was a young fellow whose deep, abiding, and hereditary sense of honour was attested by the designation "The Honourable," whenever his name appeared in print, which it did many times, often with the word Goofy in brackets and inverted commas between his Christian name and his surname. The play they went to see had been written by James Bridie and they talked all through it, for they had much in common, this ripe and handsome matron and that innocent and lively young man. After the play they went behind the scenes and Lady Watson kissed the leading lady and told her she was marvellous, which was perfectly true. They then went to a dancing club and ate a hearty meal, during and after which they walked about in each other's embrace, threading their way with much grace and skill through a mob behaving in a like fashion. They got to their respective homes at about three in the morning.

While all this was going on, the cat, Riza Khan, sat on the lap of its master, Sir James Watson, or on what was left of that lap, which was not a great deal. Riza Khan's golden eyes were closed, but the blue eyes of Sir James were open and staring into the fire. He was thinking that it would soon be Christmas and that he would like to send Lady Watson a Christmas card.

The word "send" might imply that he hoped or intended to be at some distance from Lady Watson when Christmastide came round, but this was not the chain of thought that had led him to this curious idea. While he was stroking the silvery back of Riza Khan a difference between ladies and cats occurred to him. Cats, he thought, are prepared to put up a show of affection where their affections are not engaged. This, he imagined, was seldom true of ladies. At least, he corrected himself, for any extended period; for Lady Watson *had,* over a period of several weeks, shown some sort of interest in him and even laughed at his little jokes. That was some time ago—ten or fifteen years—shortly after they first met. It was a long time since he had so much as made her laugh. Lately she had not laughed *at* him. She seemed to find him tiresome. He was sorry. His strong card was making people laugh. He was a funny-looking little ticket.

Sir James Watson thought: "Why, bless my heart, I can do most things I set out to do in a determined way. And surely it is a little thing to make her ladyship laugh. She has a very strong sense of humour and laughs quite frighteningly at a great many things. I am determined to make her laugh. I shall give myself till Christmas time. That is nearly a month. More than a month."

The trouble was that, in his sad mood, he could not think of anything funny; and when an idea did come to him he could not disguise from himself the fact that it was not so much funny as *outré*. Yet many a time and oft Lady Watson had laughed at things which were not so much funny as *outré*. One afternoon at a sherry party a lord had persuaded Goofy that if he held a glass full of sherry hard against the roof with a curtain pole the molecular attraction and the contraction of the surface air would cause the glass to stick to the roof. Goofy had stood for half an hour holding his end of the curtain pole and Lady Watson had laughed herself quite sick; for, of course, everybody knows that a glass will not stick to the roof in these circumstances. The only feelings aroused in Sir James Watson's bosom were feelings of pity for Goofy; but then he did not laugh at things that were *outré*, only at things that were funny.

The idea that came to him was that, instead of giving Lady Watson a costly present this Christmas, he would send her a Christmas card. If this didn't succeed of its purpose, he would at least save money, for he always gave Lady Watson very costly presents indeed. He thought he would get someone to design a very comical Christmas card for him and then he thought that wouldn't be fair. If the card amused Lady Watson it would be the work of the artist that would get the credit. He decided to design the Christmas card himself.

He put Riza Khan gently on to the rug and began to wander round the house looking for material on which to jot down his preliminary sketch. He wandered from room to room. He could not help feeling that the rooms, which had been decorated (or, if you prefer it, undecorated) by a famous and costly firm, were perhaps more notable as works of art than as places in which a person could live. Except for one room they looked like brand-new railway station lavatories. The one room was furnished and decorated as the subjects of Good Queen Victoria were supposed to furnish their rooms. Lady Watson used to take her guests into it and they would all laugh merrily and say it was sweet. Well, Sir James Watson had been a subject of Good Queen Victoria himself and could not remember ever having lived in a room like that. . . . Still, it was full of a number of things and it had made Lady Watson laugh, which was more than he could do.

At the far end of the Victorian Room there was an oblong object covered with a rusty bed-sheet. Sir James Watson recognized it as the portrait of Lady Watson which was being made by an artist in Lady Watson's spare time. Sir James Watson had painted in water-colours several very nice pictures of the Lake District when he was a young man, but he had never painted in oils and sometimes thought he would like to try. He went up to the artist's picture and turned aside the bed-sheet wrapping. He remembered the artist saying to Lady Watson that he definitely must paint her in the Victorian Room; and, though Lady Watson, like a true child of Bohemia, much preferred to have her portrait taken in a real artist's studio, she consented. She had been afraid during the evening, from his reactions to her skilful hintings, that the artist might not paint her at all. That would have been terrible; because this particular artist was the only artist nobody sneered at who did portraits that did not look like mad prize potatoes in a snowstorm. Lady Watson liked her pictures like that, but there is a point at which every one must draw the line, and she drew it at having her figure distorted and her features put out of drawing and her neck stretched, and her very careful complexion rendered like tinned salmon that has been cooled a long time in the deep-delved earth.

Sir James Watson thought that the portrait, in its unfinished state, was not unlike what he thought she had been like when he first rescued her from Sir Isadore Waldteufel's clammy clutch. He also peered into the portrait very carefully to see how it was done. He thought that he could paint in oils too, that there was nothing really in it. He thought that he would paint his Christmas card in oils. He thought that he would make it of enormous size and put into it not robins and church-steeples merely, but anything that came into his head. He thought that he would at least manage to compose something *outré*. He went to bed feeling happier than he had felt for many a day.

By the following afternoon he had begun his Christmas card. He found a large attic above the servants' bedrooms. It was full of a great deal of rubbish and of that delightful dust that lies in attics and is the softest of all created or collected things. Sir James Watson and some of the pleasantest of his servants cleared the attic. Sir James Watson himself worked the vacuum cleaner. This gave him great pleasure, as to whom would it not? At intervals he ran downstairs to the telephone and gave orders and yet further orders to a firm of purveyors of artists' materials. By the afternoon he had set up his easel and was preparing his canvas with the help of the artists' material man who had brought the stuff round. They both consulted a very good book on the subject and by the time the north light which illumined the attic was fading, they had covered the canvas very evenly with the particular kind of white paint recommended by the book. At that point Sir James Watson recollected with a start that he had not seen Lady Watson all day. He cleaned himself with turpentine, put on a black jacket, a grey necktie, and merino trousers, and went downstairs to his wife's boodwar with a cunning look on his round face.

Lady Watson happened to be in. She was busy polishing her finger-nails with a thing for polishing finger-nails, for she was very careful about her personal appearance. She was none of your careless sluts or trollops, was Lady Watson.

She gave Sir James Watson a suspicious look as he came in, though what she had to be suspicious about, the Lord knows. The look of innocent cunning on Sir James Watson's face was no more sinister than a beam of sunlight filtered through a cupboard keyhole lighting up a Danish cheese. Yet the subtle alteration caused by the appearance of any sort of expression at all on that countenance which had once beamed upon her with love divine, woke a faint misgiving in Lady Watson's bosom.

She said: "What have you been doing?"

He said: "Nothing."

She said: "I wish you would get some sort of hobby. You are getting on in life and people like that go mad when they have nothing to do."

He said: "Yes. I suppose they do. But there is always the office."

She said: "I am sick to death of you being Something in the City. It used to be quite a respectable thing to be; but now the very phrase connotes an outrageous blend of imbecility and knavery. Why don't you go into politics, or buy Leeds University, or write your autobiography or something?"

He said: "Because I don't want to do any of these things, my dear."

She said: "You think of nobody but yourself. Does it never occur to you that I might like to be a viscountess?"

He said: "Would you?"

She said: "Not particularly, but one likes to provide for one's old age. Now run along. Perhaps you don't realize it, but I require some rest. I am going to lie down for an hour."

He said: "Are you dining at home to-night?"

She said: "No."

He went away thinking that it was rather clever of her to spot that he wanted a hobby. Perhaps that was what he had needed all these years. He certainly felt happier now that he had got one.

He changed into an old flannel suit and a Harris tweed jacket and joined Riza Khan by the fireside.

Next day he got to work on his Christmas card in earnest. He had not slept much because he could not hit on a design. But, in the morning in his bath, he thought: "Why have a design at all?" The canvas was large. It measured fifteen feet by twelve feet. It was as big as the screen in Sir James Watson's nursery before he had become Sir James and received his monarch's accolade on that sovereign's birthday. That screen was the most beautiful work of art young James Watson (as he then was) had ever seen. It was made of papier mâché on a wooden frame. Loving hands had stuck all over it figures cut from illustrated papers and scraps. The scraps were mostly in low relief and painted in bright colours. They represented humming-birds, cockatoos, bunches of flowers, gipsies, soldiers in uniform, plates of fruit, tambourines, clowns, the heads of cherubim, and true lovers' knots in scarlet, blue, and orange coloured ribbons. When the surface of the screen had been filled with these things and portraits of Queen Victoria and Mr. Gladstone affixed to the middle of each section, the whole was spread with thick and shiny varnish and the effect was superb. Sir James Watson decided to paint his Christmas card in a thousand little bits just as they came into his head. In the issue it would look like a carnival or his nursery screen and nothing could be more delightful.

There was this in it, that the work would take some time and there was very little time to lose. It was now the twenty-third of November, only thirty-two days till Christmas, if he worked on the Sabbath. He reflected, however, that he had really nothing else to do. True, there was the City; but the City had got on without him before he was born and would get on without him after he was dead. Besides, the peculiar thing about money is that after you have made a certain amount it goes on making itself in quite sufficient quantities to meet the simple needs of such people as Sir James and Lady Watson, with a little over to invest in organizations that were only too delighted to make more still without any call upon the exertions of Sir James and his lady. Sir James paid handsomely a number of men and women who were prepared to take even this simple matter of investment off his shoulders, and his visits to the City were, perhaps, less the formidable forays of a merchant prince than an old josser seeking a palliative for his loneliness.

His club in St. James's would not miss him for a month or so. The members seldom spoke to one another and one bald man more or less asleep in a saddle-backed chair made little difference to a club of its distinction. As for Lady Watson, she did, indeed, from time to time, ask him where he had been and what he had been doing with himself; but, like Jesting Pilate, she seldom waited for a reply.

He took off his coat, rolled up his sleeves, fastened a bath-towel round his neck, and began to prepare his palette. He squeezed out of his tubes serpent after serpent, gaudy and fresh in colour, intoxicating in smell. He could have gone on doing that all day, but he thought of the briefness of time that was his portion, heaved a sigh, and mounted a small library ladder to begin, methodically enough, on the top left-hand corner.

With a brush loaded with prussian blue he made a curving gesture at his canvas and a start was made. The record of his gesture was like a beak of a toucan, so he painted a toucan, an interesting and not too difficult fowl. He perched it upon what he intended for a branch, but it turned out to be the Forth Bridge in burnt sienna. He placed a vermilion wart on the toucan's forehead and began a new piece while the toucan dried sufficiently to put in a background of lemon yellow. This time he began with the background and made a sky by mixing chinese white with ultramarine, and a royal blue sea. Beyond this he painted a chrome yellow land with a magenta and purple jungle growing out of it and then he went back and finished the toucan's sky, joining it to the ocean sky with a rather bulbous drawing of Wren's masterpiece (St. Paul's Cathedral) in crimson lake. When the sea was dry he put a schooner and some waves on it, and when the jungle was dry he filled it with flying birds of many colours. To use up these colours, he painted Joseph in his grand coat on the steps of the cathedral being welcomed by the sub-dean in lamp-black. He painted a train of Joseph's camels moving along a chrome desert in front of the sea. Behind them a line of pilgrims taking the Golden Road to Samarkand, clothed to their feet and easy to draw. Farther along he put the gilt minarets of Bagdad which they had just left. A chimney-stack divided the olive Mesopotamian sky from that he had set above the ocean. A grove of palm-trees surmounted by flying kites took him to the top right-hand corner, and darkness fell on Eaton Square. There was now a frieze above the virgin stretch of canvas

"The moment I saw it in the shop I said to myself 'Froplinsons' "

DOWN PENS

Story on page 242

and it looked awful. Sir James Watson did not, however, despair. He climbed down his ladder and down the attic stairs and had a bath and a glass of sherry. He was ahead of schedule.

In bed at night he had only to close his eyes to see the wonderful things. He saw whorls of vivid peacock blue shot with silver stars. He saw dark velvet green poplar-trees under innumerable scarlet moons. He saw glittering fish and stately dragons and bright-eyed birds. He saw spray and beech hedges and rose petals on the snow. He tried to remember all these things to put on his Christmas card, but he fell asleep and forgot them. He remembered, however, a flight of flamingoes and it went into the picture.

So the days went by. Sir James Watson became more inventive and speculative in the things he put into his picture. The wart on the toucan's forehead made him think of Oliver Cromwell, "under whose warts beat a heart primed with true religious sentiment"; and he drew the Lord Protector and his primed heart. This led to "Where is your father, boy?" and Japhet in search of a father. He had very vague recollections of that book, but he painted Japhet and many of the imagined incidents of his search. This led on to Shem and Ham and the final discovery of Noah twined in his vine and surrounded by wondering (if destructive) Little Foxes. The Little Foxes (who spoil our vines) made a charming excuse for a hunt in full cry and many of the beauties of the Handley Cross countryside. He painted then a picture of the first hunt he had seen when he had fallen in love afar off with a girl of five on a Shetland pony. Since that day she had had four husbands, including a member of the Russian imperial family, and she was now a wizened harridan and a tormentor of the poor. He drew her four husbands. The Russian he drew performing a Caucasian dance, surrounded by wild Cossacks in furry hats.

Odd, forgotten incidents and sights began to appear in his picture. His enormous nurse with an apron over her crinoline loomed through the steam of his bath before the fire. A long-dead dog barked at an impudent rabbit. A bearded gardener dug in a kitchen garden. A sailor unfastened his wooden leg and made it dance by itself. A canary drank out of a dribbling tap. The sea washed right up on to the floor of a summer-house. An errand-boy stole a packet of gelatine sweeties shaped like lions, elephants, tigers, and babies. A snowball struck a clergyman in the eye. A bus-driver coughed over his horses going down High Holborn. A hansom cab drove Sir James Watson to the dentist's and the dentist gave him a shilling for being brave. A missel thrush looked out of its nest with an angry eye. The glories of Edgbaston, Birmingham, where Aunt Alicia lived, were suitably suggested, as was the top of a haystack in the hot sunshine and a water wheel and a fast mill lode where a man had once been drowned. There was a curious bit showing a boy relieving the tedium of a sermon by doing acrobats along the nave and swinging on the chandelier.

From this point, architecture and landscape began to take up the rest of the Christmas card. Fields with giraffes and leopards as well as cows began to appear with woods, mountains, and caverns measureless to man. Cataracts roared down gullies past castles and huts, cathedrals, public houses, and shops. More fantastic buildings with ladies looking out of the windows at soldiers marching past to the tap of the drum found their way into the picture. There was an exciting mixture of perspectives, but in odd places a sort of distance grew.

Sir James Watson, as time hurried on, began to work at night, by the light of an oil lamp. He found that the parts he painted thus looked different in daylight, but this was all to the good. His sleeping time dwindled to four hours every night, and twice, in the week before Christmas, he did not go to bed at all.

By the twenty-second of December the canvas was full.

Sir James Watson sat looking at it for a whole day before he began to varnish it. He felt very much astonished at himself, as well he might. It was a great feat for a man who had painted nothing for fifty years and then only in water-colour, to complete a picture a hundred and eighty square feet in size. Nay, more, it was a very satisfying picture. A stranger, seeing it for the first time, might well have been puzzled as to what it was all about. But to know at a glance what a picture is all about is not essential to the enjoyment of it. The totality of Sir James Watson's picture was satisfying as a crazy quilt is satisfying. There was warmth and movement in it. There were startling associations of discordant colour. There was a strange sense of life in it, as there is in a jam-pot containing worms for bait.

To one person at least, Sir James Watson himself, every square inch was packed with significance.

There was no beginning and end about the picture. There was no orderly pattern. But it had its key-point where a road suddenly began to go beside a river, through a mountain pass and up to a far-away town in a blue mist high up the mountain side. It was in this part of the picture that Sir James Watson had been most successful in conveying distance, and he could not keep his eyes off it.

When the varnish was dry, Sir James Watson took the canvas off the frame and rolled it up, for he could not get such a large picture otherwise through the exiguous trap-door of the attic. He took it down to a room on the second floor which was seldom visited by any member of his household and never by Lady Watson. There he had it remounted and framed in a gilt frame. To the foot of the frame he had attached a gilt label on which was written in Gothic letters:

A MERRY CHRISTMAS TO LADY WATSON FROM
SIR JAMES WATSON

He then covered the picture with a brown cloth and awaited the day. He hardly knew what to hope from Lady Watson. He felt pretty certain that she would be surprised and that would be, at least, something.

On Christmas Eve he was neither, as the Scots say, to hold nor to bind. Lady Watson was spending this phase of the great religious festival in the "Hell Hole," quietly, with a few friends. The "Hell Hole" is, I think, off Oxford Street and specializes in bottle parties and a Malayan orchestra.

Sir James Watson was too restless to sit at home by the fireside, so he went to his club and talked to one of the waiters whose name was Hogge. Hogge's wife was ill and Sir James was sorry to hear it, for Hogge was a dismal enough person by nature without having illness in the house on top of it all. Hogge had been a soldier in the Great War and had been buried by a shell-burst at Ypres. This had left him with a peculiar twitching of the left side of his face.

He told Sir James Watson about his wife's eight operations. He was not usually so communicative, but Sir James Watson was the only member in the club on that night and Hogge felt that it was his bounden duty to entertain him by all the means in his power. So he came and went, telling a fresh instalment of his wife's sad history at each visit to Sir James Watson's table and, later, to his chair in the library. In addition to the pleasures of conversation with Hogge, Sir James Watson had treated himself to two Coronas and three glasses of port after dinner. He went home by taxi at half-past eleven and went to bed. Sir James Watson slept.

When I tell you what happened on Christmas Day you can believe me or not as you like. Before you dismiss it all as a fiction, think for a little. When a man, for the first time for many a year, suddenly does a piece of creative work, phenomenal things happen to him and to it. His work is apt to possess him, to master him, to dissolve his identity in its own. Any amount of experience of material facts will not help us to explain this mastery and this solution.

Sir James Watson's creation was something new. What happened to Sir James Watson must be judged as something new. Old standards do not apply to it.

He hung holly and mistletoe on his veiled Christmas card and, calling up all his rusty determination, induced Lady Watson to come to the room to see it. He unveiled the picture with a tremulous flourish. Lady Watson screwed in an eye-glass to look at it and this dialogue followed:

"Whose is it?"

"It is yours, my dear. It is a sort of a Christmas card."

"No, no. I mean who did it?"

"I did."

"*You* did? You painted that thing?"

"Yes."

"That's what comes of having no hobbies. You must see a

psychotherapist at once. I'll tell Miss Smith to ring up Dr. Liebestraum."

That was all. She did not laugh. It was something, however, that she took it seriously. She went into the Victorian Room and rang for Miss Smith, the secretary. Although her car was waiting in the Christmas rain, she took time to give Miss Smith certain instructions.

Upstairs Sir James Watson was still looking at his picture. In that moment he loved it more than he loved Lady Watson. His eyes were fixed on the part in which he had most successfully conveyed distance. Without any real intention of doing anything at all, he slowly stepped over the gilt border and into his picture. His eyes still sought his cunningly conveyed distance as he walked slowly up the road that led to the mountain pass.

When Dr. Liebestraum arrived he was nowhere to be found. Lady Watson caused Miss Smith to call WHItehall 1212 in vain. The picture was dismantled, rolled, and returned to the attic where it was born. Nobody ever saw Sir James Watson again.

The Christmas Carp

VICKI BAUM

For the Lanner children Christmas began on the sixth of December, for that was the day when Santa Claus would come. Of course, in Vienna he wasn't called Santa Claus but by his Italian name: The Nikolo. The Nikolo was a kindly looking old gentleman with a benignant smile hidden under a long white beard, and he was dressed in a bishop's solemn garments and carried a bishop's staff in his hand. The exciting thing for all Austrian children was the fact that along with Saint Nicholas—and as his evil counterpart—there went a hairy black fellow called The Crampus. The Crampus was a devil with horns; he had a long fiery tongue hanging down his black front and a hellish looking trident in his hand with which to fork up bad children. You could see The Nikolo and The Crampus in all shop windows long before the beginning of December, but the night of the sixth was when they really arrived in town. That evening the Lanner children would put their shoes into the window, their little hands trembling, their hearts palpitating, fearing the worst but hoping for the best. For if you had been good you would find your shoe filled with candied fruit and dates and figs and nuts in the morning; but had you been bad Nikolo would leave your shoe empty, and The Crampus would stick a birch broom into it, indicating that your parents had better use it on your backside.

There were three children in the Lanner home; Friedel, the

oldest one, a wild little fellow with blue eyes, black hair, and blazing cheeks, and then the twins, Annie and Hans. Annie was a cheerful, busy, preoccupied little woman and Hans was her timid and obedient shadow. For all three of them the sixth of December meant not only Nikolo and The Crampus, sweets or broom, but more important yet, it meant the day when Aunt Mali would arrive from the country. In fact for a long time the Lanner children were inclined to look upon Aunt Mali as the third figure in this trinity, and they never were quite clear if Aunt Mali was sent to them from Heaven or from Hell.

Aunt Mali was quite a character. She was tall and thin and as full of speed and energy as if she hadn't arrived in Vienna by train but had been shot into town on a rocket. As far back as the children could remember she had always been gray and old; but while they themselves grew up, passing through various stages of school troubles, pimpled complexions, daydreaming adolescence, and first puppy love, Aunt Mali never seemed to get a day older than she had always been.

Aunt Mali came from the country; she was deeply religious and very strict; she would not stand for being contradicted, not even by Dr. Lanner, who was one of the best surgeons in Vienna and a great authority and didn't like being contradicted himself. Aunt Mali's tempers were feared by the whole family, and everything was done to appease her wrath. In short, Aunt Mali was a dictator long before the world had become aware of dictatorship.

Only after Aunt Mali had arrived, had tied on her big apron and taken over the reins of the kitchen, could Vienna turn in earnest to the business of getting ready for Christmas—or so at least it appeared to the children. It could not be just an accident that every year on the day of Aunt Mali's arrival the Christmas markets began to mushroom on the allotted square of the town; a glittering, tinkling, fragrant jumble of stalls and booths filled with all the paraphernalia of the holiday time and full of candies, candles, ornaments, promise, and excitement.

Aunt Mali settled down in the kitchen, opened her magic black bag, and conjured from it a wealth of spices and condiments, a cloud of Christmas smells, and, most fascinating of all, the Book. The Book was very old and some of its pages had been thumbed and fingered to shreds by generations of ambitious women in the Lanner family. The Book had been started on December 25, 1798, by one Anna Maria Amalia Lanner, the great-grandmother of Aunt Mali. The date could still be seen on the first page, written in Anna Maria Amalia's lacelike handwriting and followed by a nicely calligraphed: "!!!God be with us!!!"

The first cooking recipe she had entered in her book was for some sort of cake called Gupelhupf, indispensable at any festive occasion in Vienna, and it asked for so many eggs and so much butter that it made Mother dizzy, or so Frau Lanner claimed at least. (Mother, Dr. Lanner's wife, was the one from whom little Hans had inherited his nice and timid manners and his pliable little soul.) Following that first recipe were others, written down by Anna Maria Amalia's daughters and daughters-in-law, by nieces, granddaughters, and great-granddaughters, by chains of female descendants, good cooks all of them, as most Austrian women are.

In a way the Book mirrored the ups and downs of the family as well as of the times, and some young sociologist could well have used it as a basis for his master's thesis. For the children it was endless fun to have their mother read to them the scribbled pages. They could laugh as much about the twelve eggs and five pounds of butter that went into Anna Maria Amalia's simple little Gupelhupf as over the recipes Aunt Mali in person had entered during the World War, when there was no food in Austria and people made cakes from carrots and black beans.

Aunt Mali grimly went to work, with the clattering of pots and pans, in clouds of flour. Flour covered her eyelashes, chocolate was spattered over her starched white apron, the scent of cinnamon was all around her, and her bare arms were soon spotted with burns as the arms of an old warrior are marked by honorable scars. Frau Lanner didn't dare enter the kitchen where Aunt Mali worked with the devastating vigor of a hurricane; and Kati, the hired maid, who at other times did the cooking, went into her room in fits of crying and rage and having her feelings hurt. The weeks between December 6 and December 24 were a period of suspense, fear, terror, and hope for all of them.

Aunt Mali was baking Christmas cookies.

She baked cinnamon stars and chocolate rings and Anna Maria Amalia's Husaren Krapferl, which melted in your mouth and tasted better and better the longer you kept them in the big earthenware jar. She baked crisp brown letters—a whole alphabet of them—called Patience, and little blobs of weightless white foam called Spanish Wind; she made marzipan and quince jelly and rum truffles. She baked breads and cakes of all shapes and tastes and in varying shades of sweetness, and the good warm scent of yeast drifted into every nook and corner, keeping the Lanner children in a constant state of yearning and hungry anticipation. Little Annie was occasionally admitted to the kitchen and allowed to stir dough or paint eggwhites on the cookies—because you couldn't begin early enough if you wanted to become a good cook. The two boys were kept strictly away from the sacred realms, but every evening Aunt Mali would serve them some tiny samples of the joys to come. Their great day arrived when they accompanied her to the market to buy the Carp; because all this tempest of cooking and baking and preparing rose and rose and finally reached a climax in what in Vienna was called *fasting*. And the fasting again had its own peak on Christmas Eve, when the Christmas Carp was served.

The buying of this carp was a feverishly anticipated ceremony. On the morning of December 24 and not a day sooner the children would go to the market with Aunt Mali; Kati formed the rear guard as an advisory and supporting force in the important battle for the best carp to be had. As every family in Vienna wanted the best carp for their Christmas Eve dinner, and each family dispatched some expert buying squad to the market, the pushing, yelling, and grabbing were fierce and embittered. And there they were, thousands of carps, squirming, splashing, and wriggling in their tubs and vats, a fat, lively, rich, plentiful abundance of silvery fish. Aunt Mali had hard, tough elbows, and she pushed her way from tub to tub, searching for the one, the best, the perfect, the Super Christmas Carp.

It had to be a mirror carp, nude except for four rows of silvery scales down his flanks. He should be big but not too old or he would taste brackish. He should be a male by all means, because the spawn inside a full-grown male carp was a delicacy in itself. His gills had to be red and his eyes were to protrude and look lively. The whole fish had to quiver with life and strength; and when Aunt Mali at last found the right one and he slapped her hand with his tail and leaped back into the tub with the spring and grace of a trapeze artist in the circus she laughed out loud and paid whatever price Jakob Fisch asked for him. It so happened that Aunt Mali always ended up by buying from Jakob Fisch, because no doubt he had the best carps on the market. "I know fish because I'm a Fisch myself," he said every year, savoring his eternal joke. He certainly knew fish; he traveled all the way to Hungary and Czechoslovakia when the waters in the big carp ponds were let off, to pick himself the best of the crop. He was the best fishmonger in the market, and never mind that he was a Jew. In Austria no one celebrated Christmas with more ardor and zest than the Jews did. They even went to church on Christmas morning, because the service was so lovely and the music so beautiful.

Came the moment when the carp had to be killed—the moment the twins dreaded and Friedel loved. With a wooden mallet Jakob Fisch skillfully knocked the fish unconscious, slit him open, and dug into him for the spawn and the liver. "Careful, careful, the gall——" Aunt Mali and Kati would cry every time, and every time Jakob Fisch would answer condescendingly: "Ladies, I killed and dressed carps while you were still in your diapers." At that Kati would giggle and Aunt Mali would laugh, and this was the signal for Annie to take her hands from her eyes, because then she was sure that the carp was dead. The terrible thing was that he kept on squirming and quivering in the basket in which Kati carried him home, stuffed with parsley and stone-dead as he was.

"Don't act so silly," Friedel would tell his sister. "These are only reflections." He didn't mind killing frogs or dissecting animals, because his father was a surgeon and he wanted to become a surgeon too someday.

The house smelled of Christmas tree and surprises when they came home. That afternoon seemed endless for the children, locked up in the nursery as they were. Even Friedel condescended to play dominoes with them to pass the time. At last it got dark. At last they got washed and dressed. At last their mother poked her head into the room and whispered that she believed she had seen the Christkindl bring some parcels, and would they, please, not make so much noise. At last there tinkled the Christmas bell, and they stormed into the living room and stopped in the door, overcome with the loveliness of it all.

There was the Christmas tree, a really big one, reaching from the floor almost to the ceiling. A little angel glittered from its top, and under its lowest branches there was the stable with the Christkindl—the little child in the manger—Maria kneeling at its side and Joseph standing behind it. There were the Three Wise Men and the shepherds and the ox and the little ass and some more angels, all looking at the Christkindl. The branches of the tree were loaded with apples and gilded nuts and with Aunt Mali's masterpieces, the Patience, the Spanish Wind, the chocolate rings, the cinnamon stars. There were moreover what looked a thousand burning wax candles, and it was this sweet scent of wax that made Christmas Eve perfect and complete to the Lanner children. Kati, stiff as a sentinel and with a wet rag in her big red hands, stood by, watchful for any branch that might catch fire. Aunt Mali, dressed in black silk and crowned with an overwhelming set of false brown curls on her gray head, commanded the children in a strict whisper to sing. They grabbed one another's hands and with their trebling voices they began to sing, while the reflection of the thousand wax candles glittered in their eyes and their feet grew cold with excitement, because along the wall there were three little tables, each one covered with a white damask cloth under which their presents were hiding. But only after Annie, who by general consent was declared the younger of the twins, had recited St. Luke's Gospel were they allowed to uncover their tables. Dr. Lanner usually cut short their suspense by getting up from the piano right after: "Glory to God in the highest, and on earth peace, good will toward men," and calling: "Get to it, brats!" And with this signal the solemn part of the evening was over and the rest was pure fun. The children had sweet wine with their Christmas dinner, and the doctor gave a humorous toast. Aunt Mali became sentimental over the soup, and remembered her deceased husband, but caught hold of herself and marched off to the kitchen, because it was a tradition that she herself would carry in the carp. She came in with it: a mountain of golden, fried carp, piled high on the old Vienna porcelain platter with the hand-painted rose pattern. The children banged their knives against their wineglasses, they tramped with their feet, and made every conceivable noise. The doctor put a few of the scales into his purse so that he would have money all year long, and Frau Lanner said: "Now eat and don't talk, children, and be careful with the fishbones." And Aunt Mali, in a glow that came partly from the stove and partly from her success with the carp, relaxed and began to tell them once more how it was on Christmas night in the country, where you went to High Mass at midnight and all the farmers came across the snowed-in hills with their little lanterns and everyone brought some peculiar Christmas felt slippers along so that their feet wouldn't get too cold in church.

The children never grew tired listening to this, and it melted together with the good rich taste of the carp and the warmth of the sweet wine and the scent of the wax candles and the presents on the tables in the living room and the funny feeling of having eaten more than was good for you and the whole boundless joy and loveliness of Christmas Eve.

That's at last how the Lanner children remembered it when they were not children any longer and everything had changed.

First came this and that. Then there came the Anschluss. Then there came the war. Dr. Lanner had become very quiet, and Frau Lanner, who had always been quiet, had acquired a nervous little flutter of her hands and a nervous little twitch in her eyelids. Friedel had become a flier, and she thought that he was a little funny since that crack-up, or maybe the strain of all those bombing attacks was too much for the boy. Annie was engaged to a lieutenant who was stationed in occupied France, and Hans, who was to become a chemist, worked in some ammunition plant. He was a bit too lean and too lanky, and his father seemed to think that his lungs were not quite in order.

Yes, everything had changed, except Aunt Mali. Punctually on December 6 she blew into town, complete with black bag and the Book, ready to go to work in the kitchen.

"You might as well have left the Book at home," Frau Lanner said resignedly. And the doctor added an old Austrian proverb: "You know that one can't make apple pie from horse apples."

"I have my good old war recipe for carrot tartlets in the book," Aunt Mali said, undaunted. "And the bean pie. It tastes almost like Sacher Torte."

"I like my beans to taste like beans; but they don't," said the doctor.

"And I brought some butterfat along too," Aunt Mali said. "At least we can have fried carp on Christmas Eve, and that's the main thing."

"Fried carp! The very idea!" Frau Lanner said. "There won't be a single carp to be had on the market. There won't be a single carp to be had in the whole of Vienna this Christmas."

"Yes, I know," Aunt Mali said. "That's why I brought one along."

"You did what?"

"I brought a carp along. I left him in the kitchen in his pail."

"Where did you get it?" Frau Lanner asked feebly, overwhelmed by respect and admiration.

"From our old friend. From whom else? From Jakob Fisch. Of course he has no stall on the market any longer, because he is a Jew. But he got me a carp nevertheless, privately, you know. He got him from some relative who lives across the Hungarian border. He's not a very good carp, but then there is war, and there won't be a carp to be had on Christmas. All we have to do is keep him alive until then."

"Sure. That's simple, isn't it?" Frau Lanner said bitterly. "Keep a carp alive for three weeks in a four-room apartment. Where will we put him?"

"In the bathtub," said Aunt Mali, every inch a victorious kitchen-Napoleon.

It was a weakly sort of carp in any case; he was young and thin and had pale, anemic gills. His belly was flat, void of either roe or spawn, and he gave only a feeble flip with his tail when Aunt Mali placed him in the bathtub. But it was a carp, and against all expectations he stayed alive. He even seemed to like his new abode, and Aunt Mali, who fed him eagerly with goldfish food, claimed that he put on weight. She also claimed that he knew the family and came when you called his name. Dr. Lanner had named him Adalbert, and the relation between the doctor and the carp was one of mutual attachment. The doctor would get into the tub every morning and turn on the cold shower. "Excuse me, Adalbert," he would say. "I hope you don't mind." Adalbert did not mind. On the contrary he seemed to love the cold water that came splashing down into the old-fashioned tub. He swam in vigorous, quick circles, round and round the tub, his protruding eyes affectionately focused on the doctor's legs in the water. After breakfast Aunt Mali would feed him, and an hour later Annie would come and change the water in the tub for him. Adalbert would stand very still during this process, only flipping his fins and permitting Annie to tickle his belly. Hans even claimed that Adalbert had smiled at him while he was shaving. Although it took Frau Lanner almost a week to become reconciled to the presence of a live carp in her fine clean bathtub she too got used to Adalbert in the end and was even heard to talk to him in the sort of baby talk she had not used since the twins had been three years old. She spent longer and longer minutes alone with Adalbert, and once she confided to her husband that the company of the carp was rather soothing for her frayed nerves. Of course no one could take a hot bath during the weeks of Adalbert's presence, but then, according to the new regulations, you could get hot water only on Saturday evenings anyway, and then only for two hours, and thus Adalbert did not disturb the Lanner family much.

As Christmas drew closer and closer they grew fonder and fonder of Adalbert. He was something unique after all, their secret joy, their hidden treasure, their great pride. There were very few people in strictly rationed Vienna who would be able to eat fried carp on Christmas Eve. But then it grew harder and harder to think of Adalbert as a pile of crisply fried, golden delicacy on the old rose-pattern platter. It was also doubtful if there would be enough of Adalbert to get around the whole family, because Friedel as well as Paul, Annie's fiancé, came home on a holiday furlough. Both were formally presented to Adalbert, who scrutinized them with a wicked expression. Friedel took an immediate liking to him, while Paul muttered that he would have preferred not to have seen him uncooked. However, he too watched Adalbert doing his modest little tricks. He leaped and swam in circles when the doctor turned on the shower; he seemed to listen when Aunt Mali called his name, and he permitted Annie to tickle his belly. When the family left the bathroom they all told one another how marvelous it was that they would get fried carp on Christmas Eve and how good it would taste, but there hung a little pall over their forced cheerfulness.

The trouble started on the morning of December 24. "Who's going to kill the carp for me?" Aunt Mali asked during breakfast. She did not call him by his name, almost as if to cut off all personal relations with Adalbert.

"Please, Auntie, please——" Annie cried, getting a bit pale, because she could not see blood, nor even think of it without feeling funny in the stomach.

"Please, what? If we want to eat him we have to kill him," Aunt Mali said, unmoved. "How about you?" she turned to the doctor. "You're a surgeon; you would know exactly how."

"I'm sorry—er—I have no time——" Dr. Lanner muttered and left in a hurry. Annie had gone from the room before him.

"You Hans?"

"I couldn't even think of it. We are friends, Adalbert and I. You must excuse me, Auntie."

"Paul? Friedel?"

Both young men, trim in their uniforms, refused. They said they couldn't do it. You can't just go and kill a pet, they said. At that

Aunt Mali grew angry. "Do you mean to tell me that you can bomb cities and burn houses but that you're softies who wouldn't kill a fish?" she yelled at them. The two officers shrugged their shoulders. "That's something different, Aunt Mali——" Friedel said at last with an uncomfortable smile. "We have no war with the carps."

In the end Aunt Mali ordered Kati to do the job, and Kati, grumbling and remonstrating, disappeared into the bathroom. There was a brief, ominous silence, and then there came a shriek, a splash, a bump, followed by a funny padding noise. When Aunt Mali rushed to Kati's aid she found the maid in the bathtub, drenched and cursing, and Adalbert wriggling and hopping on the linoleum floor. Aunt Mali said several unfriendly things, dragged Kati from her cold bath, and restored the carp in the tub. Then she set her teeth, went for a hammer and a knife, returned to the bathroom, and locked the door behind herself.

No one dared to ask her what had happened to Adalbert.

That evening there were no wax candles on the tree, no cookies, no Patience, no Spanish Wind. The gifts on the little tables were scanty, and the white damask to cover them so threadbare Frau Lanner had to apologize. Annie asked her father if he would like her to recite the Gospel, but the doctor answered only with a slack resigned movement of his hand, and they all went into the dining room and sat down. There was the holiday smell of frying butter, and the doctor perked up and took a deep whiff of it. "Smells good, doesn't it?" he said, rubbing his hands.

"Almost like old times——" his wife said but stopped at once as if she had made an embarrassing remark.

"Here comes Adalbert now——" Hans said into the silence that followed her gauche little remark. He shouldn't have said it. The door opened, and Aunt Mali entered, carrying high the old platter with the rose pattern on which rested in a small heap the mortal parts of Adalbert, brown crisp and perfect. They all cast down their eyes, and Annie turned pale once more and grabbed under the table for the hand of her fiancé. Friedel made a small effort at banging on his glass and applauding as he had done when a little boy, but the little tinkle died down at once.

"Take a piece, there is plenty," Aunt Mali urged. "Here, this is from the middle. Take it, eat it, it's a delicacy, I fried him in pure butterfat—here, Paul, Friedel, Annie—eat. There aren't many people in Vienna tonight who can eat a Christmas carp."

They all tried to eat and they all gave up. "I can't——" said the surgeon. "So help me God, I can't. He knew me, he liked me. Only this morning—you should have seen him jump and leap when I turned on the cold shower——"

"And you are a surgeon!" Aunt Mali said grimly. "Hans!—how about you?"

"Thanks, Auntie—I'm not hungry."

"Friedel? Annie?"

"I couldn't—really, I couldn't, Aunt Mali."

"You, Paul?"

"Thanks, I never cared for carp——"

The young flier, the young lieutenant, the young chemist—they all pushed back their plates and put down their forks. Then something totally unexpected happened.

Aunt Mali began to cry.

Aunt Mali, the rock, the woman of iron, the kitchen dictator, flung her arms upon the table, rested her face on them, and sobbed loudly. The Lanner children stared at her as one stares at some elementary catastrophe, a landslide, a breaking dam, a hurricane. They patted her shoulders and stroked her false brown curls and tried to console her. At last they could understand the words she was sobbing.

"What's the use of killing him? Can you tell me? What's the use of killing him?" sobbed Aunt Mali.

They looked at one another, dumbfounded, and then at the doctor. He sat straight in his chair and looked across the platter, across the table, across the room, he looked across a great, wide wasteness they could not see and he said slowly: "Yes—what's the use of killing? What's the use? What's the use?"

And they were not sure if he was talking about the Christmas carp.

Christmas Formula

STELLA BENSON

I MUST have got into the wrong ship at Shanghai, I suppose. I remember thinking vaguely at the time that she looked an odd vessel—quite unlike what I had expected s.s. *Homebound* to look like. She looked blind, somehow—windowless and steely and cold-hearted—much more like a huge submarine than a liner. However, I had a great many things on my mind and my abstraction made me an easy victim to a coolie—a fat funny-looking fellow almost like a Tibetan, I thought—who appeared from nowhere on the wharf, as coolies do, carried my traps on board and into my cabin, and left me. It was certainly his fault if I was on board the wrong ship. She sailed almost at once, and so engrossed was I throughout the voyage in the solving of a book full of crossword puzzles—(a substitute for mental exercise that had only just reached Tibet, where I lived)—that I only vaguely noticed the oddity of my ship's gait, so to speak. I remember saying to myself that she advanced with a spinning glide rather than with the usual drumming limp of a steamer. When the steward told me we were within sight of Tilbury, it seemed to me that the time of the voyage had been a *hole* in time—a space of such rapt oblivion that it might have been a minute or it might have been a hundred years since we left Shanghai.

"We're practically home now," said the steward, in such an American voice that it seemed surprising to hear him say *home* in this English drizzle. "Skipper was determined to get into port by Christmas morning—listen, you can hear the Christmas bells on our loud-speaker. . . ."

So I could. I listened sentimentally for a moment, shutting my eyes to imprison behind the lids a Christmas fancy of robins, and winking lights over the snow from the jewelled windows of a village church on a dark winter morning. "Christmas bells . . ." I murmured. "How they bring childhood back to me. . . . What church, I wonder, are we hearing?" . . . But it didn't matter, because of course to me it was the voice of the stumpy little Shropshire church of my youth.

"What church?" echoed the steward—a rather unpleasant man. "How d'you mean—what church? That's not a church—that's the wireless."

"Of course it is," I said irritably. "But the wireless is only an artificial medium, isn't it?—a formula for some fact or other. That's certainly a church peal we hear—though we hear it artificially."

"I dunno what you mean," said the steward. "Nothing artificial about a wireless, is there? And what's a church to do with Christmas anyway?"

I looked at the man haughtily. "Don't you know what Christmas means?" I asked. "Any Tibetan knows that."

" 'Course I know," he replied rudely, and gabbled, "Christmas-the-season-a-peason-good*will*. . . . Nothing about churches there, is there?"

I looked at him haughtily, and changed the subject. "Well, what do I do about my passport? I want to get ashore quickly and enjoy Christmas."

"Passports nothing," said the steward. "You're talking like a history formula. You don't want no passport. You only have to Kiss Mother as usual and then you can go ashore."

"Kiss Mother?" I exclaimed, but the man was gone. I stood in the passage looking after him and saw a distant sight that made my heart yearn for quiet China. The old fat flabby coolie I had seen as I left Shanghai now squatted on the floor, doing nothing except pick his teeth. I approached him, attracted by his serenity.

"Wantchee go look-see-England-side?" I asked him idiotically, relieved to be near such a slow irrational contrast to my iron-mannered steward.

The man made no answer.

"What for you come this side?" I persisted. He indicated a pile of empty shoe-polish tins near him, but spoke no word. He just sat still, picking his teeth, spitting occasionally, his lids heavy with indolence. I saw that he was the ship's Boots, and smiled at myself because, for a moment, he had seemed to me a desirable friend.

I went on deck, rather refreshed—I didn't know why—— The first sight of England, from which I had long been an exile, completely jolted me out of the rut of abstraction to which my mind had been confined during the strange drowsy voyage. For what had happened to my England?

"But this is New York, isn't it?" I said to a man standing next to me on deck.

"Technically, yes," said the man. "New York, S.E. 416. But we still keep up the old customs—we like to call it London. But, good heavens, sir, where do you come from, that you don't know where you are? From Tibet, I suppose."

"As a matter of fact, I *have* lived for more years than I can count on the borders of Yunnan and Tibet. How did you know?"

"Well, I've heard, of course, that Tibet is the only independent state left outside the jurisdiction of the United World Government. I've even heard that they have no Board of Salesmen there, and don't use any of the recognized formulae. So as soon as you spoke, I guessed. . . . I say, this is very interesting—I suppose all this is entirely strange to you. I say, I wish you'd let me come ashore with you and watch your reactions. You probably aren't ashamed of reacting emotionally to surprise—I dare say you have no formula or substitute for natural surprise. I'm rather a barbarian too, in my way—I'm always getting into trouble for *feeling* as well as *speaking*—quite contrary to the Board of Salesmen's regulations. So I don't mind admitting—confidentially—a spontaneous old-world interest in your reactions."

"I don't understand you," I gaped. "Why should you mind admitting? Why should I mind reacting? And why *old-world?*"

"Oh, I can't explain—you'll understand soon. . . . Gosh—I feel like a boy again, reacting emotionally to what you say, like this. Your spontaneity is infectious. Did you notice, I haven't even uttered the correct *Oh* in the fourth tone—the prescribed Surprise-and-Interest Formula? If I uttered an *Oh* at all, it was a *felt* one and quite unorthodox. Get ready for Mother's Kiss—" he removed his hat for a second—"and we'll go and have a Merry Christmas together."

Mother's Kiss again! But I had no time to ask questions, for the crowd of passengers began to surge from the deck to the shore along three or four gangways. At the shore end of each gangway stood a white-haired woman, dressed in a rather Pickwickian style—lace cape—check shawl—hair brooch—wearing an armlet labelling her as *Mother*. As I stumbled in the packed crowd down the slope, I had only time to notice that these Mothers were all practically identical, before I arrived at the Mother who corked up the end of my own gangway. She threw a pair of stout arms round me and kissed me abruptly on each cheek, saying in a cross hurried voice, "Welcome-'Ome-my-dear-dear-boy." Then, deftly unwinding her arms from my neck, she dipped a rubber squirt into a bottle slung from her belt, labelled, "Mother's Tear of Joy Certified 100 per cent. Pure," and squirted one drop onto my forehead. "Pass on, please, pass on," she added instantly. My new friend followed me, wiping the Tear of Joy from his eyebrow.

"You'll notice we've reduced the formalities of homecoming to something quite negligible. I see, as it's Merry Christmas, we have to pass the Present-Giving Turnstile today, but as a rule, Mother's Kiss is the only formality, nowadays."

"Mother's Kiss indeed," I snapped, for I had felt a fool in the old woman's perfunctory embrace. "What's the good of Mother's Kiss? It means nothing."

"Means nothing?" said my friend. "(By the way, I wish you'd remove your hat when using the word Mother. They probably didn't teach you the correct Filial Formula in Tibet, but that's Number Five—a very important one—and the police are very strict about it.) What do you mean when you ask what does it mean? Don't you know that a Mother's Kiss and Mother's Tears are sacred?"

"Not unless they're genuine, surely," I argued feebly.

"I don't know what you mean by *genuine*. I can see the Tear still on your eyelash. You couldn't want a more genuine Tear than that—brine percentage absolutely correct, you may be sure. But never mind. . . . It's all very interesting. I ought to introduce myself, by the way. Tom 170009 is my name, from Incubator AZR-14. . . ."

At the next barrier we were obliged to pay a Merry-Christmas-Present Levy of fifty dollars—quite a large sum, I thought. However, I gave it with a good grace. "For the poor, I suppose—a good idea," I said, trying to look nonchalant.

"The poor? Poor what? Why should Merry-Christmas-presents be given to poor anythings? The money goes to the Business Houses and the Board of Salesmen of course. I should have thought you'd be familiar with that Merry-Christmas custom—it's a very old one."

"Well . . . perhaps . . . in a way. . . . But we used to get something in return for our money."

"You have your receipt, haven't you? signed by the Board of Salesmen. That's the Merry-Christmas-Present Formula. Now, here we are, ready for all the enjoyment formulae that London can produce. We'll have a Merry-Christmas Dinner and then go to Peter Pan."

I was just beginning to smile delightedly at the dear sentimental memories evoked by these words when a policeman stopped me. "Why-'aven't-you-got-ya-mistletoe-in-ya-button'ole?" he gabbled roughly.

"My mistletoe?" I echoed, smiling archly at him; this was a thorough Christmas indeed if even the police entered so wholeheartedly into the spirit of the fun. "I'll remember to get some, officer—thanks for reminding me."

"I'll have to endorse your Licence-to-Enjoy-Merry-Christmas," said the policeman. " 'And it out!"

But Tom 170009 came to my rescue. "Officer-please-overlook-an-unintentional-and-deeply-regretted-breach-of-the-law," he whined mechanically, evidently uttering some compulsory formula. "This man had only just arrived from Tibet so he knows no formulae. We're on our way to the Town Hall now, to Enjoy-Merry-Christmas, we'll get the mistletoe and the Licence there."

Crowds of men and women, some dragging reluctant children, were pressing up the steps of the Town Hall as glumly as though on their way to a dentist. We fitted ourselves to the tail of a queue—a tail-between-the-legs sort of queue. "We'll be through with all these Enjoyment Formulae soon, and then we can have a good time," said Tom, seeing my apprehensive face. At the top of the steps, my licence was given me by a sullen official wearing the rudiments of a Father Christmas disguise—red coat and a cotton-wool stock under his chin—(the debased remnant, I guessed, of dear Santa Claus's woolly beard). My licence had a smudged robin stamped in one corner, and the words, "Board of Salesmen's Licence to Enjoy M^{y} X^{s} & H^{y} N^{w} Y^{r} No. 928593."

Officials herded us impatiently in single file past a big table decorated lamentably with moth-eaten paper rosettes. At one end of it a large effigy of a roast turkey was nailed upon a platter. It was really a registering machine, and every man, woman, or child that passed it was required to press down one of the wooden drumsticks—actually a lever. As one pressed it, a ticket shot out of a slot in a round metal representation of a plum-pudding a few yards further on. "This is to Certify," said my ticket, "that the holder has Attended One Merry-Christmas Festive Board."

"Now to Peter Pan, and then we're finished," said Tom. "It's an old official custom so it'll probably appeal to you."

"It will indeed," I said happily, but I was puzzled by the unexpectant expressions of the tired children being dragged towards a door opening out of a corridor into a vast auditorium.

"Nobody quite knows the origin of the Merry-Christmas custom of Peeting Up Ann," said Tom. "I've heard it was a religious rite. You had to do it too in your day, didn't you?"

"Peter Pan?" I echoed, a little puzzled. "Well, we didn't have to. . . . At first it was optional, though I admit it became less and less so. . . ."

"Here we are. Reminds you of old times, doesn't it?"

"More or less," I said doubtfully, as we sat down on plush seats in the great hall among thousands of our fellow-men. There was certainly something that looked like a stage and a curtain, topped by a great scroll with the words in large gold letters, PEET UP ANN. On to the screen of the curtain a cinematograph apparatus threw a dazzling series of talking pictures. "No More Corns—Get Alf Burman to Remove Your Feet Painlessly—Artificial Aluminum Feet at Cost Price—Absolutely Undetectable—Why Not Give The Neighborhood Incubator an Electro-Plated Phosphorescent Old-Fashioned Dumb Nanny For the New Year—This Month's Fashions in Houses—Roofs Must be Worn Lopsided by Order of the Board of Salesmen—Sufferers From Superfluous Hair, Remember, Kollision of Whiskers Kills——"

"Oh, Lord!" I said. "When does Peter Pan begin?"

"What do you mean? We are Peeting Up Ann, aren't we?"

I rose in panic. "Oh—what has happened? Has everything in this world a name and nothing else?" The silly heartless words of the machine still dinned upon the sad tawdry air as I pressed towards the door. As we passed out, a woman barred our way, dressed rather like the Mother, but labelled Auntie. She presided over a booth labelled "A Merry-Christmas-Present—With Auntie's Love—To YOU." I hesitated. "Do we get one?" I asked, for I was hungry for something personal.

"Of course. It's the custom."

We were each given a large camera, with an official kiss such as I had already experienced. "Well, really," I said, pleased. "This is certainly——" but as I spoke, my camera, which was only made of paper, collapsed in my hasty hand. "What—it doesn't work?"

"How d'you mean—work?" said Tom. "It's called a camera."

"Well, but cameras ought to take photographs."

"There is a photograph inside each one," said Tom triumphantly.

I looked inside the ruins of my poor present. There was a photograph—of a human skull—labeled *You*. Panic rushed upon me. I stumbled down the steps into the bleak streets, quickly outdistancing the protesting Tom. Instinctively I ran towards the dock . . . towards Tibet. . . . My bewildered mind registered very little, consciously, but now, looking back, I remember numbly noticing severe policemen walking from dark door to door, turning their flashlights on something limp hanging from each front door-handle. What? A stocking. . . . "Empty—empty—empty—incurably empty. . . ."

I found myself running up the gangway to the ship I had left that morning. As soon as I reached her deck, she cast loose and sailed. There were no other passengers. No one wanted to go back to the old world. Only, at the end of the passage outside my cabin, squatted the old Tibetan bootcleaner, fat and flaccid, picking his teeth. When he saw me, he pointed at my shoes. They were very dusty and I advanced first one foot and then the other, that he might brush the dust away.

stumbled down the steps into the black street, quickly outside [illegible] the protesting Tom. Instinctively I ran towards the dock. "Towards Eire!" ... My bewildered mind registered very little consciously but now, looking back, I remember numbly [illegible] [illegible] a sulking from dark door to door, [illegible] their [illegible] something [illegible] a [illegible] door handle. What? A stocking ... an empty—empty—empty—empty ... empty ...

I found myself running up the gangway of the ship I had left that morning. As soon as I reached her deck she cast off and sailed. There were no other passengers. No one wanted to go back to the old world. Only at the end of the passage outside my cabin [illegible] the old [illegible] bootblack, fat and placid, picking his teeth. When he saw me he pointed at my shoes. They were very dusty, and I advanced first one foot and then the other, that he might brush the dust away.

V

CHRISTMAS AT HOME AND ABROAD

In the bleak mid-winter
  Frosty wind made moan,
Earth stood hard as iron,
  Water like a stone;
Snow had fallen, snow on snow,
  Snow on snow,
In the bleak mid-winter
  Long ago.

Our God, Heaven cannot hold Him,
  Nor earth sustain;
Heaven and earth shall flee away
  When He comes to reign:
In the bleak mid-winter
  A stable-place sufficed
The Lord God Almighty
  Jesus Christ.

CHRISTINA ROSSETTI

Christmas in Maine

ROBERT P. TRISTRAM COFFIN

If you want to have a Christmas like the one we had on Paradise Farm when I was a boy, you will have to hunt up a salt-water farm on the Maine coast, with bays on both sides of it, and a road that goes around all sorts of bays, up over Misery Hill and down, and through the fir trees so close together that they brush you and your horse on both cheeks. That is the only kind of place a Christmas like that grows. You must have a clear December night, with blue Maine stars snapping like sapphires with the cold, and the big moon flooding full over Misery, and lighting up the snowy spruce boughs like crushed diamonds. You ought to be wrapped in a buffalo robe to your nose, and be sitting in a family pung, and have your breath trailing along with you as you slide over the dry, whistling snow. You will have to sing the songs we sang, "God Rest You Merry, Gentlemen" and "Joy to the World," and you will be able to see your songs around you in the air like blue smoke. That's the only way to come to a Paradise Christmas.

And you really should cross over at least one broad bay on the ice, and feel the tide rifts bounce you as the runners slide over them. And if the whole bay booms out, every now and then, and the sound echoes around the wooded islands for miles, you will be having the sort of ride we loved to take from town, the night before Christmas.

I won't insist on your having a father like ours to drive you home to your Christmas. One with a wide moustache full of icicles, and eyes like the stars of the morning. That would be impossible, anyway, for there has been only one of him in the world. But it is too bad, just the same. For you won't have the stories we had by the fireplace. You won't hear about Kitty Wells who died beautifully in song just as the sun came over the tops of the eastern mountains and just after her lover had named the wedding day, and you will not hear how Kitty's departure put an end to his mastering the banjo:

"But death came in my cabin door
And took from me my joy, my pride,
And when they said she was no more,
I laid my banjo down and cried."

But you will be able to have the rooms of the farmhouse banked with emerald jewels clustered on bayberry boughs, clumps of everlasting roses with gold spots in the middle of them, tree evergreens, and the evergreen that runs all over the Maine woods and every so often puts up a bunch of palm leaves. And there will be rose-hips stuck in pine boughs. And caraway seeds in every crust and cookie in the place.

An aunt should be on hand, an aunt who believes in yarrow tea and the Bible as the two things needed to keep children well. She will read the Nativity story aloud to the family, hurrying over the really exciting parts that happened at the stable, and bearing down hard on what the angels had to say and the more edifying points that might be supposed to improve small boys who like to lie too long abed in the mornings. She will put a moral even into Christmas greens, and she will serve well as a counterirritant to the overeating of mince pies. She will insist on all boys washing behind their ears, and that will keep her days full to the brim.

The Christmas tree will be there, and it will have a top so high that it will have to be bent over and run along the ceiling of the sitting room. It will be the best fir tree of the Paradise forests, picked from ten thousand almost perfect ones, and every bough on it will be like old-fashioned fans wide open. You will have brought it home that very morning, on the sled, from Dragonfly Spring.

Dragonfly Spring was frozen solid to the bottom, and you could look down into it and see the rainbows where you dented it with your copper-toed boots, see whole ferns caught motionless in the crystal deeps, and a frog, too, down there, with hands just like a baby's on him. Your small sister—the one with hair like new honey laid open—in the middle of a honeycomb—had cried out, "Let's dig him up and take him home and warm his feet!" (She is the same sister who ate up all your more vivid pastel crayons when you were away at school, and then ate up all the things you had been pretty sure were toadstools in Bluejay Woods, when you were supposed to be keeping an eye on her, but were buried so deep in "Mosses from an Old Manse" that you couldn't have been dug up with horses and oxen.)

Your dog, Snoozer, who is a curious and intricate combination of many merry pugs and many mournful hound-dogs, was snuffling all the time, hot on the feather-stitching the mice had made from bush to bush while you were felling the Christmas tree. A red squirrel was taking a white-pine cone apart on a hemlock bough, and telling Snoozer what he thought of him and all other dogs, the hour or so you were there.

There will be a lot of aunts in the house besides the Biblical one. Aunts of every complexion and cut. Christmas is the one time that even the most dubious of aunts take on value. One of them can make up wreaths, another can make rock candy that puts a tremble on the heart, and still another can steer your twelve-seater bob-sled—and turn it over, bottom up, with you all in just the right place for a fine spill.

There will be uncles, too, to hold one end of the molasses taffy you will pull sooner or later, yanking it out till it flashes and turns into cornsilk that almost floats in the air, tossing your end of it back and probably lassoing your uncle around his neck as you do it, and pulling out a new rope of solid honey.

The uncles will smoke, too, and that will be a help to all the younger brothers who have been smoking their acorn-pipes out in the woodshed, and who don't want their breaths to give them away. The uncles will make themselves useful in other ways. They will rig up schooners no bigger than your thumb, with shrouds like cobwebs; they will mend the bob-sled, tie up cut fingers, and sew on buttons after you shin up to the cupola in the barn; and—if you get on the good side of them—they will saw you up so much birch wood that you won't have to lay hand to a bucksaw till after New Year's.

There will be cousins by the cart load. He-ones and she-ones. The size you can sit on, and the size that can sit on you. Enough for two armies, on Little Round Top and on Big, up in the haymow. You will play Gettysburg there till your heads are full of hay chaff that will keep six aunts busy cleaning it out. And then you will come in to the house and down a whole crock of molasses cookies—the kind that go up in peaks in the middle—which somebody was foolish enough to leave the cover off.

Every holiday that came along, in my father's house, was the gathering of an Anglo-Saxon clan. My father was built for lots of people 'round him. But Christmas was a whole assembly of the West Saxons! My father wanted people in squads. There were men with wide moustaches and men with smooth places on top of their heads, women wide and narrow. Cousins of the second and third water, even, were there. Hired men, too. They were special guests and had to be handled with kid gloves, as New England hired men must. They had to have the best of everything, and you could not find fault with them, as you could with uncles, if they smacked you for upsetting their coffee into their laps. Babies were underfoot in full cry. The older children hunted in packs. The table had to be pieced out with flour barrels and bread boards and ironing boards. It was a house's length from the head of the table, where your father sat and manufactured the roast up into slivers, to your mother dishing out the pork gravy. Whole geese disappeared on the way down. The Christmas cake, which had been left sweetly to itself for a month to age into a miracle, was a narrow isthmus when it got to Mother. But Mother always said that Christmas, to her, was watching other people eat. She was the kind of mother who

"You will all bundle up together for a ride in the afternoon."

CHRISTMAS IN MAINE

Story on page 295

claimed that the neck and the back of the chicken were the tastiest parts.

The prize goose, whom you had brought up by hand and called Oliver Cromwell, Old Ironsides, or some such distinguished title, was duly carved. And Father found his wishbone snow-white and you all applauded, for that meant lots of snow and two more months of coasting on your sleds. There were mince pies by the legion. And if Uncle Tom were there, a whole raccoon baked just for him and girt around with browned sweet potatoes. Mother's wild strawberry jam was there on deck, winking at you like rubies from the holes in tarts that melted away like bubbles in the mouth. That dinner was three hours in Beulah Land!

Of course, there will be an apple pudding at such a season. Steamed in a lard bucket, and cut open with a string. A sauce of oranges and lemons to make an ocean around each steaming volcano of suet and russet apples as it falls crumbling from the loop of twine. It will have to be steamed in the boiler, if your Christmas is to be the size of ours, and cooked in a ten-pound lard pail. Better use a cod line instead of the twine of other holidays, to parcel it out to the members of the clan.

The whole nation of you in the house will go from one thing to another. The secret of the best Christmases is everybody doing the same things all at the same time. You will all fall to and string cranberries and popcorn for the tree, and the bright lines each of you has a hold on will radiate from the tree like ribbons on a maypole. Everybody will have needles and thread in the mouth, you will all get in each other's way, but that is the art of doing Christmas right. You will all bundle up together for a ride in the afternoon. You had better take the horse-sled, as the pung will not begin to hold you. And even then a dozen or so of assorted uncles and aunts and cousins will have to come trooping after through the deep snow, and wait for their turn on the straw in the sled. Smaller cousins will fall off over the sides in great knots and never be missed, and the hullabaloo will roar on and send the rabbits flying away through the woods, showing their bobbing scuts.

Everybody will hang presents on the tree at once, when the sun has dipped down into the spruces in the west and you are back home in the sitting-room. There will be no nonsense of tiptoeing up and edging a package on when nobody is looking. Everybody knows who is giving him what. There is no mystery about it. Aunt Ella has made rag dinahs for all hands and the cook—for all under fourteen years of age—and she does not care who knows it. The dinahs are all alike, except that those for the children whose lower garments are forked have forked red-flannel pants instead of red-flannel petticoats. They all have pearl button eyes and stocking toes for faces. There will be so many hands at work on the tree at once that the whole thing will probably go over two or three times, and it will be well to make it fast with a hawser or so.

And then you will turn right around and take the presents off again, the minute you have got them all on and have lighted the candles up. There will be no waiting, with small children sitting around with aching hearts. The real candles will be a problem, in all that mass of spills. Boughs will take fire here and there. But there will be plenty of uncles around to crush out the small bonfires in their big brown hands. All the same, it would be well to have an Uncle Thomas who can take up a live coal in his thumb and finger, and light his pipe from it, cool as a cucumber. Better turn the extinguishing of the tree over to him.

There will be boughten presents, to be sure—a turtle of cardboard in a glassed, dainty box, hung on springs and swimming for dear life with all four feet, and popguns with their barrels ringed and streaked with red and yellow lines. Why popguns should be painted like broomsticks is one of the mysteries, along with the blue paint you always find on Maine cartwheels. Somebody will probably get one of those Swiss music-boxes that will eke out a ghostly "Last Rose of Summer," if tenderly cranked. There should be those little bottles of transparent candies, with real syrup in them, which I used to live for through the years. And there must be a German doll for every last girl, with mountains of yellow hair and cheeks looking as if life were a continuous blowing of bubbles. Boughten things are all right.

But if it is going to be our kind of Christmas, most of the presents will be home-made. Socks knit by the aunt who swears only by useful gifts. You have seen those socks growing up from their white toes for the last two weeks. Wristers, always red. A box of Aunt Louise's candied orange peel that she will never let on to anybody how she makes. Your father will have made a sled for every mother's son and daughter of you, with a bluebird, or robin redbreast, more real than life, painted on each one and your name underneath. You will never have another present to match that, though you grow up and become Midases. Popcorn balls, big as muskmelons, will be common ware. They will be dripping with molasses, and will stick your wristers and socks and other treasures together.

But the pith of the party is not reached until the whole nation of you sits down in rocking chairs, or lies down on their bellies in front of the six-foot gulf of the fireplace. The presents are all stowed, heaped and tucked away, stuck fast with cornballs. The last lamps are out. The firelight dances on the ceiling. It lights up the steel engraving of Major McCullock leaping from Kentucky to Ohio, with ten thousand mounted redskins yelling and reining in their steeds behind him. It lights up Daniel Boone's daughters as they lean away towards their boat's end and scream their silent screams and drop their water lilies, while Indian head after Indian head grins up at them from the river of the Dark and Bloody Ground.

All the babies will be hushed and put away. All the younger fry will be more than half asleep. The toasted cheese and red herring will go 'round. The herring, by the way—if you are worthy to wear my shoes after me—which you yourself have smoked with green oak, and have gotten your own two eyes so that they looked like two burnt holes in a blanket while doing it, and have hugely enjoyed every hour of it all.

Then you had best find a fair substitute for my father. Give him the best chair in the house—and the way to find *that* is to push the cat out of it—and let him tear! He will begin by telling you about such people as the brilliant young ladies of Philadelphia who had a piano too big to fit their house, so they put it on the porch and played on it through the open window. Then he will sit back and work his way to the Caliph of Bagdad, who had a daughter so homely that she had to wear a sack on her head when her suitors came awooing, and how she fell down a well and made herself a great fortune, and won the handsomest husband that ever wore a turban. That story, by the way, you will not find in the "Arabian Nights" even though you look for it, as I have done, till you have gray hairs in your head.

The firelight will get into your father's eyes and on his hair. He will move on from Bagdad to Big Bethel, and tell you all how the Yankee campfires looked like the high Milky Way itself, all night long before the battle; how the dew silvered every sleeping soldier's face and the stacked rifles, as the dawn came up with the new day and death. And you will hug your knees and hear the wind outside going its rounds among the snowy pines, and you will listen on till the story you are hearing becomes a part of the old winds of the world and the motion of the bright stars. And probably it will take two uncles at least to carry you to bed.

What Amelia Wanted

ELSIE SINGMASTER

"THIS shall go here and that there."

The widow Herr stood in the middle of the kitchen, her arms akimbo, her keen eyes surveying the collection of foodstuffs assembled on chairs and table and sink. She was large and stout: her dress was a beautiful oft-washed gray gingham, draped across the shoulders with a little shawl of the same material. Though it was past the middle of the night, when full garb could scarcely be required of even the straitest of sects, she wore on her smooth hair the thin white cap which signified her full membership in the Church of the Brethren, called Dunkers by the world. At this moment she frowned. She was not disturbed by finding herself thus surrounded at three o'clock in the morning, nor was she bewildered by the quantity of merchandise; she was merely directing her daughter, Amelia, how to pack the baskets and hampers which stood ready on the floor.

Amelia too wore a dress of oft-washed gingham, but the color was pale blue, and cap and shawl were lacking. She was still worldly, she had not yet been immersed or received into the church. Conscientious as Mrs. Herr was about religious matters, she had never insisted that Amelia become 'plain'; eventually, she was certain, Amelia would don the quiet garb. Amelia had a delicate complexion, but she was always well; she shuddered when her mother said that she herself had once been slender. She did not wish to grow broad and wear a Dunker cap. She was in love, and the object of her affection was of the world.

The vegetables and preserves and fowls and baked stuff were not the accumulation of months, but merely the merchandise carried by Mrs. Herr each Wednesday morning and Saturday afternoon to market at Harrisburg. On the table were a dozen round loaves of rye bread; there were pies and Schwenkfelder cakes and iced cakes and potato rolls and a huge platter of doughnuts. A turkey, a half-dozen chickens, and as many squabs lay side by side, their legs neatly crossed. In a row stood bowls of endive and celery, a crock of sauerkraut and a crock of baked beans. The mantel was laden with jellies and preserves, flanked by glasses of walnut and hickory kernels and grated horseradish.

Mrs. Herr thought that Amelia did not seem interested, but that did not prevent her from going on with her planning. She indicated the endive and celery with a sweep of her arm.

"These here, they go in the little basket. The baked stuff, except the Fastnacht cakes and the Schwenkfelders, shall go in one flat, the pies and layer cakes in the other. The buttermilk and cider you can carry at once to the wagon. I never held with those that pack overnight—things catch so smells. Mary Jonathan Herr, she has no sense; she once packed her onions with her other things overnight. It spoiled her trade. The smearcase can go as it is, in the pitcher. The cup cheese you wrap nice up. Don't you feel good, Amelia?"

Amelia said absently, "Of course I feel good!" She took her shawl from the peg behind the door and wrapped it round her. Outside, the deaf and dumb hired man grunted to the white mare which never set one foot before the other unless she was urged. He flung the door open and he and Amelia began to carry out the commodities and place them in the small covered wagon.

Amelia moved as though treading on air. Already in her imagination she was seated beside the deaf and dumb man, her folded arms hugging her pleasant thoughts. She would see the dim glow of the city lights in the distance, then the broad gray ribbon of the Susquehanna; she would watch the lights pale, and the east turn from gray to pink and blue and green and gold as the sun rose. It was only lately that she had been thrilled by the glories of the sunrise.

The drive to market was the happiest time of her life. Even the few minutes which the strange young man spent before her stall were not so blissful, because in his presence she scarcely dared look up. He was not so tall as to be alarming and he had curly hair and bright brown eyes. When he left, her eyes followed him down the aisle to the corner of the market house where a young city woman sold goods from a bakery. She was tall and self-possessed and she dressed with shocking bareness of neck and arm. Amelia did not like to look at her, but she could not keep her eyes away. She laughed loudly at what the young man said, and once, leaning over the counter, she gave him a playful push. Amelia hated her.

The sky was bright with stars; otherwise the world was dark, except for the light which shone from the kitchen door and the reflection in the little stream flowing a few yards from the house. The whitewashed fence showed straight and ghostly, the ovals of clam shells surrounding flower-beds whose plants now flourished in windows were vaguely discernible. Amelia sniffed a leafy odor from the woods near by. It was almost the middle of December, but there had been little frost and a good deal of rain and the woods smelled like summer.

Mrs. Herr continued to supervise the carrying out of baskets. She directed the hired man with signs and her daughter with words. "The pies shall be fifteen cents, Amelia, unless they don't go so quick, then ten." She paused for a response, but received none. "If you can't sell the last chicken quick, then bring it home. It might be someone would come tomorrow account of Deardorf's funeral. Do you hear, Amelia?"

"Yes, mom."

"And bring thread home, white thread, two dozen spools, so I can get at quilting. And buy you a pair of shoes. Are you tired, Amelia?" Without answering Amelia climbed into the wagon. "One of these days I go once more to market. It's hard for you. I'm stronger. I——"

If Mrs. Herr finished her sentence, her daughter did not hear.

The deaf and dumb man lifted the reins, the wagon moved. Amelia clasped her hands.

"I *must* go to market," she said, aloud. "Whatever happens, I *must* go."

Until the wagon turned from the muddy lane into Route Fifteen, which crossed the many states, they had no companions. Then they met rumbling trucks piled with bootlegged coal and were overtaken by huge oil tanks whose drivers wished the little wagon off the face of the earth. The river showed gray between its lighted banks, the dome of the Capitol gleamed like a stupendous pearl. They descended a hill and were on a long bridge, cars accumulating behind them. Amelia began to grow nervous, though the young man never came to the stall before eight, when he stopped on his way to work, and it was not yet six. She nudged the hired man and leaned forward, imitating a hand lashing the mare's back. The hired man grunted, but he did not hurry the mare.

The Herr stall in the market house on the hill was small and obscure, but the Herr baskets always returned empty. Mrs. Herr's customers would have no other butter, no other eggs, no other dressed fowls. As Amelia was one of the first to arrive, she had hitherto been almost the first to leave, but lately she had lingered, keeping a few articles under the counter. When the young man did not come at eight, he came at twelve. He bought no staple food such as a householder would buy, but cakes and pies for a bachelor's lunch. He walked swiftly; Amelia could see him far up the long aisle. She caught her breath and closed her eyes and lo! there he was, laughing at her.

"Well!" he would say. "How's the pie crop this morning?" Or, "How about the cruller tree?"

Occasionally he ate a small pie or a doughnut or cruller as he stood before the stall. He always stopped to talk to the hateful girl at the corner before he passed out the main door. Amelia believed the girl hailed him in a free way and asked him to stop. Amelia did not know his name or where he lived or what his work was; she blushed at a wish that the hired man were not deaf and dumb, so that she might ask him to follow the young man.

The arched market house had never appeared so beautiful. Christmas wreaths hung before many stalls as samples from which the country people would take orders. A florist had rented a stall and Amelia looked past masses of feathery fern fronds. Finding a fern on the sawdust-covered floor, she brushed it off and pinned it to her dress. She sniffed the odor of roses and carnations and her cheeks glowed.

The eggs were gone in fifteen minutes, all the vegetables in a half-hour. It was six o'clock, then seven, then half-past; it was eight and eight-fifteen, and still the young man had not come. Amelia sighed, then she smiled, then she frowned. It was pleasanter to have the young man's visit in the future than in the past. But her counter was almost empty—her neighbors would wonder why she lingered.

When only one Schwenkfelder cake remained, she told what was almost a lie.

"I'll take that," said a customer, opening the lid of her basket.

"*Ach*, it's already taken!" said Amelia, quick as a flash. She flushed crimson. It was not quite a lie—the cake belonged to the young man, who always bought something. The young man did not come; instead, the deaf and dumb man inquired with uncouth gestures why she did not leave. He hung the baskets and pails on his arm and stacked the crocks.

The girl at the baker's stall had given her baskets to the baker's man and she was now patting into place the curls which hung on her neck. Unconsciously Amelia patted her own hair which waved from the root and not merely at the tips. If only the baker's clerk would go quickly! Perhaps the young man might still come. Tears filled Amelia's eyes—she could postpone departure no longer. Her hand shook when she lifted the Schwenkfelder cake.

As she put her foot on the step of the wagon, she glanced across the street. The baker's clerk stood at the corner waiting for a bus. No, she was not waiting for a bus, she was waiting for the young man who came hurrying up the street. Amelia's foot, with the weight of her body already upon it, slipped, and she struck her knee against the sharp edge of the iron step. With guttural expressions of sympathy and alarm, the deaf and dumb man lifted her to the seat. She forgot the Schwenkfelder cake rolling on the ground, she forgot the thread for her mother's quilting, she forgot her new shoes, she hid her face and wept.

When she reached the farm her mother helped her into the house. Mrs. Herr made signs to the hired man and he drove the wagon rapidly toward Route Fifteen and the doctor's. He was afraid that Amelia might die.

Amelia's injury proved to be a bruised and torn ligament; the doctor forbade her to take a step till he came again.

"But I'll have to go Saturday afternoon to market!"

"What foolish talk!" cried Mrs. Herr. "I go Saturdays. Why would you limp to market, Amelia? You have a mother." Mrs. Herr had a militant air, as though she meant to do battle for Amelia. Amelia wanted something, and so far she had always got for Amelia what she wanted.

On Saturday afternoon Amelia laid her cheek against the back of the rocking-chair. Her leg was elevated on another chair; beside her on the table was sewing and an abundant supper covered by lids and napkins. She said to herself that whatever happened she would go to market on Wednesday. She saw the bright-eyed young man stepping down the aisle, his eyes seeking her, then finding her mother. Her mother would be laughing and talking with the men and women in the stalls on either side, she would pay no attention to the young man. Worse still, the young man would pay no attention to her, except, perhaps, to be a little amused. He would turn at once to the baker's clerk.

On Wednesday Amelia could not stir. Her mother helped her dress and Amelia watched her pack the baskets and drive away with the hired man into the darkness. She begged her to wear her black dress, instead of the stiffly starched gray gingham, and her mother stared at her amazed.

"Shall I drag my Sunday dress in the sawdust, or get grease on it, or something sticky, say?"

Early in the afternoon, Mrs. Herr was at home.

"I sold by ten o'clock out," she boasted. "I can sell faster than you, Amelia. Then I went in the store. I got the thread and the new shoes and a dress yet for you. See!"

Amelia's heart could not repress a throb of joy. The dress was Alice-blue wool, the color of her eyes, her color. But for whom should she wear it?

"All bought wreaths and bunches of holly. It's a waste to make so much of Christmas. We don't make so much in our religion. Pretty near everything people buy gets afterwards thrown out. A chicken I like to have always, or a guinea, but that's not wasteful—you have to eat, if it is Christmas."

"Did you have many—many new customers?"

"No, not to say many. My old customers snapped everything too quick up. They were glad to see me. Next week, while you're still sitting, you can sew your dress."

Amelia's sad thoughts traveled to Saturday. By that time the young man would hardly cast a glance toward her corner. Doubtless, if he came to market, he would escort the baker's clerk to her home. Perhaps he would go with her to church on Sunday. Amelia saw herself sitting in Dunker meeting with the wonderful stranger across the aisle on the men's side. People had odd ways in worldly churches—it was said men and women sat together.

"Don't you like your new dress?" asked Mrs. Herr.

"*Ach*, to be sure!"

On Saturday Amelia was still unable to walk. Her cheeks were pale, her eyes dull, her dress only begun. The doctor came to call, pronounced the knee better, forbade her to walk for another week, ate two doughnuts and drank a glass of cider, and went away.

On Wednesday Mrs. Herr spent only a few hours at market. Together with her empty baskets she brought news—at which Amelia's cheeks paled.

"That one at the corner, Amelia, did you see her?"

"Yes, I did."

"Well, I don't like that one. She's too—too bare, and too English for me. It's a nice young man talks to her. He's too good for that one."

"He is, oh, he is!" echoed Amelia's soul.

By Saturday the color had still not returned to Amelia's cheeks. She could not sleep till late at night and she woke each morning with a spring which made her whole body ache. She determined not to think of the young man, but her resolutions were vain. At noon she was still in bed. She could hobble without help from the sitting-room, where she slept, into the kitchen. There was no place for her in the kitchen until the enormous assemblage of Christmas cakes and pies was removed.

"I don't like to go, and you alone," said Mrs. Herr, uneasily.

"Of course go!" Amelia thought she had never seen her mother look so large and so plain. She cried when the wagon drove away. The ground was frozen hard now and the wheels creaked. She followed it in her thoughts along the road, to the concrete highway, across the bridge. She saw the bright market house. People would shout "Merry Christmas!"—it was lovely to hear them. There would be wreaths and festoons everywhere and every single article would be swept from the counters by excited buyers. She rose and dressed and hobbled into the kitchen.

Mrs. Herr did not return till late in the evening and Amelia was still up. Her cheeks burned feverishly; she expected news of the hateful young woman. All afternoon she sat with her sewing in her lap, but she did not even complete the hem already half done.

"Something might happen," she said to herself. "No, nothing will happen. What could happen?"

Mrs. Herr bustled into the kitchen; the deaf and dumb man came grunting behind. He clapped his hands as a sign of satisfaction with Amelia's improvement. Mrs. Herr sat down and took off her bonnet and let her shawl drop from her shoulders.

"You look right good, Amelia."

Amelia tried to smile.

"I sold soon everything, but again I was talking."

Amelia had suddenly a recurrence of a sickening fear. Her mother's cheeks were red, her eyes danced; more than one Dunker widower had courted her.

"Why, your dress is finished!" cried Mrs. Herr.

"At last."

Mrs. Herr held up the dress and gazed at it admiringly. The disapproval of the elders would have been strong indeed—Amelia had cut the neck in a V.

"Are you very tired, Amelia?"

"Not so very." Amelia leaned back her head.

"I talked to a young man from Ohio," said Mrs. Herr.

"From Ohio?" There was a close connection between the Dunkers in Pennsylvania and those in Ohio—perhaps her mother had taken a fancy to a young Dunker. "Does he visit the meeting?"

"No," answered Mrs. Herr. "This is the way. A week ago, he came to buy a Schwenkfelder or other baked things, and my baked things were all. It spited me, he was such a nice young man. Then he went and bought such baker's crullers from that girl—I told you about her. Baker's crullers are poison. So is she poison. He was such a nice young man, I walked in one piece after him to the door. I said to him, 'Do you come always to market?' Yes, he said, he did. 'Well,' I said, 'you come Wednesdays and I save a Schwenkfelder for you.' Well, Wednesdays he was there." The eyes of Mrs. Herr sparkled, it was possible to understand how she had once looked like Amelia.

"He was!" breathed Amelia, not knowing that she had spoken.

"He was. He said it was queer, I was a new one at the stall, but the Schwenkfelder was the same. I said I was your mother, and he asked me three times in five minutes about you. I had to tell him everything. I got everything out of him—what his name is and where he works—he gets more than a hundred dollars a month—and where he boards. He has a poor place to eat, it's a wonder he lives."

"Did he talk again to her?" breathed Amelia.

"I kept him till she was long gone," said Mrs. Herr. "She looked in his direction, but I kept his back all the time turned. He helped the deaf and dumb one carry the baskets and he stood long at the wagon and talked."

"Did he come this evening?"

"He did. His people are plain people like us, Amelia. He said he pretty near jumped for joy when he seen my cap. I said he should come out to dinner tomorrow. I said we didn't make so much of Christmas, but we would of course eat. I kept back a chicken and I have ham of course and all vegetables, green and canned, and the mince pies are quick made. I make apple pie too, and a custard. It won't be like sometimes, but it will do. He said——" Mrs. Herr clapped her hands across her mouth to stifle her words.

"You mean he comes here to dinner?"

"He does. He comes in the bus to the corner; from there he walks."

"Tomorrow?"

"Tomorrow. December twenty-five. Twelve o'clock."

"What else did he say?"

"He said——" Mrs. Herr hung the blue dress carefully over the back of a chair. She began to laugh and her laughter filled the kitchen and the house. "He said I looked beautiful to him."

"He did?" Amelia looked at her mother and again tears came into her eyes. "You look beautiful to me, Mom," she said.

Mr. Kaplan and the Magi

LEONARD Q. ROSS

WHEN Mr. Parkhill saw that Miss Mitnick, Mr. Bloom, and Mr. Hyman Kaplan were absent, and that a strange excitement pervaded the beginners' grade, he realized that it was indeed the last night before the holidays and that Christmas was only a few days off. Each Christmas the classes in the American Night Preparatory School for Adults gave presents to their respective teachers. Mr. Parkhill, a veteran of many sentimental Yuletides, had come to know the procedure. That night, before the class session had begun, there must have been a hurried collection; a Gift Committee of three had been chosen; at this moment the Committee was probably in Mickey Goldstein's Arcade, bargaining feverishly, arguing about the appropriateness of a pair of pajamas or the color of a dozen linen handkerchiefs, debating whether Mr. Parkhill would prefer a pair of fleece-lined slippers to a set of mother-of-pearl cuff links.

"We shall concentrate on—er—spelling drill tonight," Mr. Parkhill announced.

The students smiled wisely, glanced at the three empty seats, exchanged knowing nods, and prepared for spelling drill. Miss Rochelle Goldberg giggled, then looked ashamed as Mrs. Rodriguez shot her a glare of reproval.

Mr. Parkhill always chose a spelling drill for the night before the

Christmas vacation: it kept all the students busy simultaneously; it dampened the excitement of the occasion; above all, it kept him from the necessity of resorting to elaborate pedagogical efforts in order to hide his own embarrassment.

Mr. Parkhill called off the first words. Pens and pencils scratched, smiles died away, eyes grew serious, preoccupied, as the beginners' grade assaulted the spelling of "Banana . . . Romance . . . Groaning." Mr. Parkhill sighed. The class seemed incomplete without its star student, Miss Mitnick, and barren without its most remarkable one, Mr. Hyman Kaplan. Mr. Kaplan's most recent linguistic triumph had been a fervent speech extolling the D'Oyly Carte Company's performance of an operetta by two English gentlemen referred to as "Goldberg and Solomon."

"Charming . . . Horses . . . Float," Mr. Parkhill called off.

Mr. Parkhill's mind was not really on "Charming . . . Horses . . . Float." He could not help thinking of the momentous event which would take place that night. After the recess the students would come in with flushed faces and shining eyes. The Committee would be with them, and one member of the Committee, carrying an elaborately bound Christmas package, would be surrounded by several of the largest students in the class, who would try to hide the parcel from Mr. Parkhill's eyes. The class would come to order with uncommon rapidity. Then, just as Mr. Parkhill resumed the lesson, one member of the Committee would rise, apologize nervously for interrupting, place the package on Mr. Parkhill's desk, utter a few half-swallowed words, and rush back to his or her seat. Mr. Parkhill would say a few halting phrases of gratitude and surprise, everyone would smile and fidget uneasily, and the lesson would drag on, somehow, to the final and distant bell.

"Accept . . . *Ex*cept . . . Cucumber."

And as the students filed out after the final bell, they would cry "Merry Christmas, Happy New Year!" in joyous voices. The Committee would crowd around Mr. Parkhill with tremendous smiles to say that if the present wasn't *just right* in size or color (if it was something to wear) or in design (if it was something to use), Mr. Parkhill could exchange it. He didn't *have* to abide by the Committee's choice. He could exchange the present for *any*thing. They would have arranged all that carefully with Mr. Mickey Goldstein himself.

That was the ritual, fixed and unchanging, of the last night of school before Christmas.

"Nervous . . . Goose . . . Violets."

The hand on the clock crawled around to eight. Mr. Parkhill could not keep his eyes off the three seats, so eloquent in their vacancy, which Miss Mitnick, Mr. Bloom, and Mr. Kaplan ordinarily graced with their presences. He could almost see these three in the last throes of decision in Mickey Goldstein's Arcade, harassed by the competitive attractions of gloves, neckties, an electric clock, a cane, spats, a "lifetime" fountain pen. Mr. Parkhill grew cold as he thought of a fountain pen. Three times already he had been presented with "lifetime" fountain pens, twice with "lifetime" pencils to match. Mr. Parkhill had exchanged these gifts: he had a fountain pen. Once he had chosen a woolen vest instead; once a pair of mittens and a watch chain. Mr. Parkhill hoped it wouldn't be a fountain pen. Or a smoking jacket. He had never been able to understand how the Committee in '32 had decided upon a smoking jacket. Mr. Parkhill did not smoke. He had exchanged it for fur-lined gloves.

Just as Mr. Parkhill called off "Sardine . . . *Ex*quisite . . . Palace" the recess bell rang. The heads of the students bobbed up as if propelled by a single spring. There was a rush to the door, Mr. Sam Pinsky well in the lead. Then, from the corridor, their voices rose. Mr. Parkhill began to print "Banana" on the blackboard, so that the students could correct their own papers after recess. He tried not to listen, but the voices in the corridor were like the chatter of a flock of sparrows.

"Hollo, Mitnick!"

"Bloom, Bloom, vat is it?"

"So vat did you gat, Keplen? Tell!"

Mr. Parkhill could hear Miss Mitnick's shy "We bought——" interrupted by Mr. Kaplan's stern cry, "Mitnick! Don' say! Plizz, faller-students! Come *don* mit de voices! Titcher vill awreddy hearink, you hollerink so lod! Still! Order! Plizz!" There was no question about it: Mr. Kaplan was born to command.

"Did you bought a Tsheaffer's Fontain Pan Sat, guarantee for de whole life, like *I* said?" one voice came through the door. A Sheaffer Fountain Pen Set, Guaranteed. That was Mrs. Moskowitz. Poor Mrs. Moskowitz, she showed so little imagination, even in her homework. "Moskovitz! Mein Gott!" the stentorian whisper of Mr. Kaplan soared through the air. "Vy you don' open op de door Titcher should *positivel* hear? Ha! Let's goink to odder and fromm de hall!"

The voices of the beginners' grade died away as they moved to the "odder and" of the corridor, like the chorus of *Aïda* vanishing into Egyptian wings.

Mr. Parkhill printed "Charming" and "Horses" on the board. For a moment he thought he heard Mrs. Moskowitz's voice repeating stubbornly, "Did—you—bought—a—Tsheaffer—Fontain—Pan—Sat—*Guarantee?*"

Mr. Parkhill began to say to himself, "Thank you, all of you. It's *just* what I wanted," again and again. One Christmas he hadn't said "It's just what I wanted" and poor Mrs. Oppenheimer, chairman of the Committee that year, had been hounded by the students' recriminations for a month.

It seemed an eternity before the recess bell rang again. The class came in *en masse*, and hastened to the seats from which they would view the impending spectacle. The air hummed with silence.

Mr. Parkhill was printing "Cucumber." He did not turn his face from the board as he said, "Er—please begin correcting your own spelling. I have printed most of the words on the board."

There was a low and heated whispering. "Stend op, Mitnick!" he heard Mr. Kaplan hiss. "You should stend op *too!*"

"The *whole* Committee," Mr. Bloom whispered. "Stand op!"

Apparently Miss Mitnick, a gazelle choked with embarrassment, did not have the fortitude to "stend op" with her colleagues.

"A fine raprezantitif *you'll* gonna make!" Mr. Kaplan hissed scornfully. "Isn't for *mine* sek I'm eskink, Mitnick. Plizz *stend op!*"

There was a confused, half-muted murmur, and the anguished

voice of Miss Mitnick saying, "I *can't.*" Mr. Parkhill printed "Violets" on the board. Then there was a tense silence. And then the voice of Mr. Kaplan rose, firmly, clearly, with a decision and dignity which left no doubt as to its purpose.

"Podden me, Mr. Pockheel!"

It had come.

"Er—yes?" Mr. Parkhill turned to face the class.

Messrs. Bloom and Kaplan were standing side by side in front of Miss Mitnick's chair, holding between them a large, long package, wrapped in cellophane and tied with huge red ribbons. A pair of small hands touched the bottom of the box, listlessly. The owner of the hands, seated in the front row, was hidden by the box.

"De hends is Mitnick," Mr. Kaplan said apologetically.

Mr. Parkhill gazed at the tableau. It was touching.

"Er—yes?" he said again feebly, as if he had forgotten his lines and was repeating his cue.

"Hau Kay!" Mr. Kaplan whispered to his confreres. The hands disappeared behind the package. Mr. Kaplan and Mr. Bloom strode to the platform with the box. Mr. Kaplan was beaming, his smile rapturous, exalted. They placed the package on Mr. Parkhill's desk, Mr. Bloom dropped back a few paces, and Mr. Kaplan said, "Mr. Pockheel! Is mine beeg honor, becawss I'm Chairman fromm de Buyink an' Deliverink to You a Prazent Committee, to givink to you dis fine peckitch."

Mr. Parkhill was about to stammer, "Oh, thank you," when Mr. Kaplan added hastily, "Also I'll sayink a few voids."

Mr. Kaplan took an envelope out of his pocket. He whispered loudly, "Mitnick, *you still got time to comm op mit de Committee,*" but Miss Mitnick only blushed furiously and lowered her eyes. Mr. Kaplan sighed, straightened the envelope, smiled proudly at Mr. Parkhill, and read.

"Dear Titcher—dat's de beginnink. Ve stendink on de adge fromm a beeg holiday." He cleared his throat. "Ufcawss is all kinds holidays in U.S.A. Holidays for politic, for religious, an' *plain* holidays. In Fabrary, ve got Judge Vashington's boitday, a *fine* holiday. Also Abram Lincohen's. In May ve got Memorable Day, for dad soldiers. In July comms, netcheral, Fort July. Also ve have Labor Day, Denksgivink, for de Peelgrims, an' for de feenish fromm de Voild Var, Armistress Day."

Mr. Parkhill played with a piece of chalk nervously.

"But arond dis time year ve have a *difference* kind holiday, a spacial, movvellous time. Dat's called—Chrissmas."

Mr. Parkhill put the chalk down.

"All hover de voild," Mr. Kaplan mused, "is pipple celebraking dis vunderful time. Becawss of som pipple is Chrissmas like for *odder* pipple is Passover. Or Chanukah, batter. De most fine, de most beauriful, de most *secret* holiday fromm de whole bunch!"

(" 'Sacred,' Mr. Kaplan, 'sacred,' " Mr. Parkhill thought, ever the pedagogue.)

"Ven ve valkink don de stritt an' is snow on de floor an' all kinds tarrible cold!" Mr. Kaplan's hand leaped up dramatically, like a flame. "Ven ve see in de vindows trees mit rad an' grin laktric lights boinink! Ven is de time for tellink de fancy-tales about Sandy Claws commink fromm Naut Pole on rain-enimals, an' climbink don de jiminies mit *stockings* for all de leetle kits! Ven ve hearink abot de beauriful toughts of de Tree Vise Guys who vere follerink a star fromm de dasert! Ven pipple sayink, 'Oh, Mary Chrissmas! Oh, Heppy Noo Yiss! Oh, bast regotts!' Den ve *all* got a varm fillink in de heart for all humanity vhich should be brodders!"

Mr. Feigenbaum nodded philosophically at this profound thought; Mr. Kaplan, pleased, nodded back.

"*You* got de fillink, Mr. Pockheel. *I* got de fillink, dat's no qvastion abot! Bloom, Pinsky, Caravello, Schneiderman, even Mitnick—" Mr. Kaplan was punishing Miss Mitnick tenfold for her perfidy—"got de fillink! An' vat is it?" There was a momentous pause. "De Chrissmas Spirits!"

(" 'Spir*it*,' Mr. Kaplan, 'spir*it*,' " the voice of Mr. Parkhill's conscience said.)

"Now I'll givink de prazent," Mr. Kaplan announced subtly. Mr. Bloom shifted his weight. "Becawss you a foist-class titcher, Mr. Pockheel, an' learn abot gremmer an' spallink an' de hoddest pots pernonciation—ve know is a planty hod job mit soch students—so ve fill you should havink a sample fromm our—fromm our—" Mr. Kaplan turned the envelope over hastily—"aha! Fromm our santimental!"

Mr. Parkhill stared at the long package and the huge red ribbons. "Fromm de cless, to our lovely Mr. Pockheel!"

Mr. Parkhill started. "Er—?" he asked involuntarily.

"Fromm de cless, to our lovely Mr. Pockheel!" Mr. Kaplan repeated with pride.

(" '*Beloved*,' Mr. Kaplan, '*beloved*.' ")

A hush had fallen over the room. Mr. Kaplan, his eyes bright with joy, waited for Mr. Parkhill to take up the ritual. Mr. Parkhill tried to say, "Thank you, Mr. Kaplan," but the phrase seemed meaningless, so big, so ungainly, that it could not get through his throat. Without a word Mr. Parkhill began to open the package. He slid the big red ribbons off. He broke the tissue paper inside. For some reason his vision was blurred and it took him a moment to identify the present. It was a smoking jacket. It was black and gold, and a dragon with a green tongue was embroidered on the breast pocket.

"Horyantal style," Mr. Kaplan whispered delicately.

Mr. Parkhill nodded. The air trembled with the tension. Miss Mitnick looked as if she were ready to cry. Mr. Bloom peered intently over Mr. Kaplan's shoulder. Mrs. Moskowitz sat entranced, sighing with behemothian gasps. She looked as if she were at her daughter's wedding.

"Thank you," Mr. Parkhill stammered at last. "Thank you, all of you."

Mr. Bloom said, "Hold it op everyone should see."

Mr. Kaplan turned on Mr. Bloom with an icy look. "***I'm*** de chairman!" he hissed.

"I—er—I can't tell you how much I appreciate your kindness," Mr. Parkhill said without lifting his eyes.

Mr. Kaplan smiled. "So now you'll plizz hold op de prazent. Plizz."

Mr. Parkhill took the smoking jacket out of the box and held it up for all to see. There were gasps—"Oh!s" and "Ah!s" and Mr.

Kaplan's own ecstatic "My! Is beauriful!" The green tongue on the dragon seemed alive.

"Maybe ve made a mistake," Mr. Kaplan said hastily. "Maybe you don' smoke—dat's how *Mitnick* tought." The scorn dripped. "But I said, 'Ufcwass is Titcher smokink! Not in de cless, netcheral. At home! At least a *pipe!*' "

"No, no, you didn't make a mistake. It's—it's *just* what I wanted!"

The great smile on Mr. Kaplan's face became dazzling. "Hooray! Vear in de bast from helt!" he cried impetuously. "Mary Chrissmas! Heppy Noo Yiss! You should have a *hondert* more!"

This was the signal for a chorus of acclaim. "Mary Chrissmas!" "Wear in best of health!" "Happy New Year!" Miss Schneiderman burst into applause, followed by Mr. Scymzak and Mr. Weinstein. Miss Caravello, carried away by all the excitement, uttered some felicitations in rapid Italian. Mrs. Moskowitz sighed once more and said, "Soch a *sveet* ceremonia." Miss Mitnick smiled feebly, blushing, and twisted her handkerchief.

The ceremony was over. Mr. Parkhill began to put the smoking jacket back into the box with fumbling hands. Mr. Bloom marched back to his seat. But Mr. Kaplan stepped a little closer to the desk. The smile had congealed on Mr. Kaplan's face. It was poignant and profoundly earnest.

"Er—thank you, Mr. Kaplan," Mr. Parkhill said gently.

Mr. Kaplan shuffled his feet, looking at the floor. For the first time since Mr. Parkhill had known him, Mr. Kaplan seemed to be embarrassed. Then, just as he turned to rush back to his seat, Mr. Kaplan whispered, so softly that no ears but Mr. Parkhill's heard it, "Maybe de spitch I rad vas too *formmal.* But avery void I said—it came fromm *below mine heart!*"

Mr. Parkhill felt that, for all his weird, unorthodox English, Mr. Kaplan had spoken with the tongues of the Magi.

A Little Rain

BRENDAN GILL

FATHER CARROLL opened the window of the parish house. He blew drifts of coal dust from the sill, then set his palms against it and leaned into the night. The air was hot. Rain was falling noisily on the tin roof, silently on the nearly invisible statue of Mary crowning the chapel. Between the house and the chapel, a bank of red Carolina clay had been cut to frothing gullies. The first day of the downpour, Father Carroll had said to Buck, his colored altar boy, "Now the heat is bound to break. Now winter's coming at last." But Buck had said, "Hit don't make no difference about the rain, sir. Rain'll just gobble up the air."

That was what the rain had done. Father Carroll felt as if he had been drowning minute after minute for five days. He could hardly breathe. From his narrow window, he looked across the town. Hundreds of dancing oblongs of light fell from the windows on the opposite hillside, where the white people lived. Here, about the new Franciscan chapel and the school for colored children, a handful of yellow lamps swam in the dark. Father Carroll shivered. How was he to learn what lay beyond the lamps? With the roads growing impassable, school had been dismissed. One by one, the children had been drawn back into their crowded, unpainted, inscrutable shacks. Buck, Father Carroll's first convert, had missed Mass this morning. Unless the rain stopped soon, it was plain to Father Carroll that his year's work down here might go for nothing.

Buck was sixteen, two years beyond the age limit of the school, so Father Carroll had trained him as an altar boy. That had turned out to be such excellent strategy that Father Carroll suffered occasional twinges of conscience. The younger boys were eager to worship what Buck worshipped. Buck would whisper to them after Mass, "Look at 'em candles, boy! Look at 'em shine! And do you smell what I smell? Do you smell that ol' incense burnin'? Ain't that some smell?"

The younger boys would roll their eyes. "And you can light 'em candles, Buck?" one of them would say. "And swing that goldy-lookin' thing?"

"Sure I can. Anybody can that gets this here rollin' Catholicism," Buck would answer.

"What's 'em words, Buck?"

"Why, if you want to know—why, I reckon Father Carroll's the man you want to see. I just reckon he's the one."

In less than a year, Father Carroll had raised the school's enrollment from twenty-five to over seventy colored boys and girls. Three extra nuns had been sent down from the mother house in Alleghany, New York, to take charge of the overflow. Plans had been drawn for an addition to the chapel. But lately, after summer passed and the burning sun held on through autumn, Father Carroll felt less certain of himself. Perhaps the job had seemed too simple. Perhaps these grinning, unfathomable kids would slip away from him as easily as they had come. Watching the rain, trying to draw a breath in the still night air, Father Carroll saw that he held no proof of his success. He stood alone in an empty house, beside an empty chapel, on Christmas Eve. The world that lay about him was not his world.

He tightened his grip on the sill. In the North tonight the snow would be lying deep in the yards or piled high beside the roads by the big ploughs. The air would be cold and sharp, the sky crammed with stars. Candles would be lighted in the windows of houses. Through the windows you would see—as last year, walking about the city where he had been living, Father Carroll had seen—trees covered with tinsel and ornaments, trees glittering with tiny bulbs. In one yard he had caught sight of a spruce, taller than the house behind it, glowing with blue lights. In another yard someone had fashioned out of snow Mary and the Child, the moonlight falling ice-blue, like satin, on Mary's head and cradled arms.

Up there, Father Carroll had seen Christmas in the faces passing him on the street. He had heard it in voices speaking while doors were opened and closed against the cold: "Come in. How good of you to come!" "I can't stay. But I had to tell you merry Christmas." He had been shaken by it, standing under the brassy amplifiers in the city park: "Oh, little town of Bethlehem, how still we see thee lie!" And later, in his room in that other parish house, Father Carroll had arranged last year his private Christmas. He had set a shoe box on its side on the table beyond his cot. He had covered it with pine twigs broken from shrubs around the house. He had placed inside the shoe box a plaster Jesus and Mary from the five-and-ten, a prayerful Joseph, and two placid cows. When he went shopping that morning, he had had money enough to buy either a set of shepherds or a set of Wise Men. He had weighed the decision carefully, while the girl behind the counter tapped with her painted nails on a hill of sparkling snow. Father Carroll had chosen the shepherds. They had seemed closer to him than the Wise Men, with their proud names and gorgeous clothes. That night he had propped the shepherds upright by the infant Jesus. Then he had knelt in front of the shoe box to say his rosary.

For a moment now the rain seemed to slacken. Father Carroll heard water foaming in the gullies and circling the open foundations of the house. He heard a report that might have been a shot fired at a rat in a nearby shanty or a car backfiring. Somewhere down the slope a tethered donkey began to bray. Then the rain came down once more through its sieve of heat, on the slick banks and the sodden road. Father Carroll turned from the window to study the room behind him. No crèche stood on the flat pine table. Somehow, hundreds of miles from home, Father Carroll had lacked the will to make one. Coming among these people, he had promised himself to follow their customs. Apparently they had no customs. The room was bare.

He heard a second report, followed by a sound of voices. Beyond the roofs of the house and chapel, a faint glow colored the sky. It looked to Father Carroll like a fire. Nearly every week a faulty stove set ablaze one of the shanties surrounding the chapel. Father Carroll leaned out of the window but saw nothing. The glow faded and returned, closer to the chapel. Father Carroll heard a series of reports behind the curtain of rain. A bright-yellow explosion lighted the road in front of the house. He saw that the road was filled with boys and he shouted, "What's happened? What's the matter? Do you need help?"

The crowd surged under his window, ankle-deep in mud. Father Carroll saw that Buck was leading them, his kinky hair glittering with raindrops, a pine torch in his right hand. The crowd shouted, "Merry Christmas, Father!" A dozen firecrackers exploded over his head. He said sharply, "Buck, what's the meaning of this? Firecrackers on Christmas Eve!"

Buck's eyes gleamed. He lighted a fuse with his torch, then he sent his firecracker looping beyond the crowd. In cheerful contempt he said, "Don't you celebrate Christmas up North?"

"Of course we celebrate Christmas," Father Carroll said, "but we celebrate it as it ought to be——" He bit his lip. After a moment he said, "Can I light one, too?"

The crowd grinned up at him. Buck pulled a six-inch salute from his pocket and said, "We bought this little old baby just for you." He handed the salute to Father Carroll, then he lifted his pine torch to the sill. Father Carroll held the fuse against the torch's flame. "Watch this little old baby fly!" he shouted, and with all his strength he hurled the salute toward the chapel roof. It climbed through the streaming dark, its fuse faintly spiralling; then it burst in a white flame over Mary's head.

To the bare room, Father Carroll whispered, "Now, that's what I call a regular Christmas firecracker." He crossed himself. It would take him only a minute to put on his hat and rubbers and join the boys. A little rain never hurt anybody.

The Christmas Tree Ship

HARRY HANSEN

CHRISTMAS in Chicago, fifty years ago, was a happy, home festival in a city not yet too rich, too pretentious, to be neighborly. There was usually snow at Christmas; it lay in large heaps in the gutters and was packed solid on the streets. When snow fell it was heavy with moisture; it blocked trains and held up streetcars. The average citizen shoveled his own sidewalks clean and looked after his own fires. A few blocks beyond the Loop, where the gray wooden cottages with their scrollwork porches stretched for miles, householders would be out early in the mornings wielding their shovels, amid shouts to their neighbors, for in those days families lived long enough in one locality to become known to one another.

In the houses on the near North Side, where brick buildings abounded, the windows had little wooden blinds inside through which came the yellow rays of light from gas jets. The air in the streets outside had the close feeling of a low-ceilinged room and shouts rebounded from wall to wall. In that air bells on sleighs jingled in time a long way off and hoofbeats made a dull patter on the packed snow. As the sleigh passed under the light of the gas lamp at the corner you could see the prancing horse, the curved dashboard, the gleam of the nickeled bars across the front, the flash of the runners. The driver would be wearing a wide fur collar and a fur cap; the woman beside him would be tucked under fur robes and look very comfortable in a brown fur neckpiece and toque.

Inside, the house was warm and a bit stuffy with dry air. The carpets had a firm surface and gay curlicues of vine leaves all over them. The hall might be dark; its walls were covered with embossed paper, stained to the color of leather, and the gaslight flickered behind a globe of pink glass ornamented with a trailing vine. You walked quickly past the parlor, which had a mantelpiece of black slate and a mirror over the fireplace and heavy chairs and settees with curved walnut legs, to the back room where all the family gathered. Here the walls were hung with photographs of young and old and there were music racks and bookshelves. If the house was heated by a furnace, the hot air flooded up through a register in the floor, but more likely a big-bellied stove, consuming anthracite coal, gleamed red through mica windows in a corner. And in the bay stood the Christmas tree.

Most likely the father of the family had picked it out and carried it home. Men and women carried their own bundles in those days. Perhaps he walked down to the Clark Street bridge, a week or two before Christmas, to see if the Schuenemanns had come down from Wisconsin with a load of spruce trees. Invariably the two big, brawny lads would be there with a fishing schooner loaded with trees that they themselves had cut in the Michigan woods. They were fine, well-shaped trees and cost so little—for 75 cents you bought a fullsized tree; for $1 you had your choice of the best. Even saplings provided bright decorations for a city where people were making money, but not too much money, and where the average citizen was always fearful of hard times.

As long ago as 1887 the two Schuenemanns, Herman and August, had sailed down in a schooner from Manistique, Michigan, with a load of spruce and tied up beside the dock behind the old red-brick commission houses at the Clark Street bridge. There Chicago found them and bought their stock, and called Herman captain and remembered to look for him the following year. When snow fell on Chicago's streets in December days the father of the family would say, "Guess I'll have to go down to the Clark Street bridge to see if the captain is in and get us a tree."

Fifty years ago the work of providing trees for Christmas was not yet the mass-production business it has become in recent times. No dealer contracted for thousands of trees as a speculation and destroyed great numbers if he had guessed wrong on the demand. No man cut down whole hillsides to satisfy the whims of people who followed a custom but didn't know how to pray. There were plenty of trees for all. The Schuenemanns went into the woods behind Manistique and Thompson, Michigan, where young trees grew on land that had been cut over to make the lumber that went into midwestern houses a generation before. They chose the trees carefully, including some tall ones for which they had orders from churches and hotels. Sometimes they had to work in the snow and when the trees reached Chicago there was still snow on the branches. The brothers thought they had done well when they made a modest profit on a trip that occupied about six weeks of the wintry season, when it was hard to haul other cargoes.

The work was not easy, neither the cutting nor the sailing, for they always came when Lake Michigan kicked up a lot of rough sea. In 1898 August had just set sail with a load of trees when a storm arose and he and his ship were lost. Thereupon Herman determined to carry on alone. In 1899 he was back at the Clark Street dock with his boat, the *Rouse Simmons,* loaded with Christmas trees. He was a jovial man, with a very ruddy complexion and laughing wrinkles around his blue eyes, and everybody liked him.

For eleven years Herman arrived with his cargo and many people depended on him for a tree year after year. Then came the hard season of 1912, with storms and heavy seas on Lake Michigan. Late in November Herman cut his trees in the woods behind Manistique and started for Chicago in the *Rouse Simmons,* with a crew of seventeen men. There were head winds and heavy seas from the start and soon the schooner was struggling in a raging snowstorm. What took place on board we can only guess. The *Rouse Simmons* sailed into the silence that covers all the fine ships that have fallen victim to the gales of Lake Michigan, which have taken the lives of so many, from the days of La Salle's *Griffon* until now.

Long before Chicago missed the *Rouse Simmons* at its dock

reports began to come of the ship's distress. A schooner resembling it was said to have been sighted off Kewaunee, Wisconsin, flying distress signals. The steamer *George W. Orr* reported to the revenue cutter *Tuscarora* that she had seen the *Rouse Simmons* three miles offshore, but the captain later admitted that he might have been mistaken. But on December 5, 1912, fishermen off Two Rivers Point, seven miles north of Manitowoc, Wisconsin, found the tops of spruce trees entangled in their nets. Trees had been roped together on the deck of the *Rouse Simmons,* and how could they get into the lake at that point if not off a ship?

On December 13th a watcher on the beach at Sheboygan, Wisconsin, reported that he had picked up a bottle containing a message that came from the captain. It had been written on a page of the ship's log and read:

> Friday—Everybody goodbye. I guess we are all through. Sea washed over our deckload Thursday. During the night the small boat was washed over. Leaking bad. Ingvald and Steve fell overboard Thursday. God help us.
>
> Herman Schuenemann

The men referred to were believed to have been Steve E. Nelson, mate, and Ingvald Nylons, seaman. But if there was such a message, it never reached the captain's wife, who was eagerly waiting for scraps of news in her Manistique home. She was a valiant little woman, with a great deal of stamina. When she realized that her three little girls, Elsie and the twins, Pearl and Hazel, were now dependent wholly on her efforts, she resolved to take up her husband's task.

There was no Christmas ship at the Clark Street dock in 1912. But when 1913 came, Chicago residents who looked over the railings of the bridge beheld another schooner, loaded with trees, as in the days when Captain Herman held forth there. On board was the plucky little wife of the captain. She had gone into the woods with the woodcutters and supervised the felling of the trees. With her, too, were her girls, as well as women to weave wreaths and garlands. Chicago was to become well acquainted with the Schuenemanns.

They were to come season after season for twenty-two years after the *Rouse Simmons* went down.

For years Chicago friends would ask the captain's wife whether there had been any definite report on the *Rouse Simmons*, and she could only shake her head sorrowfully. Yet the sea, which guards its secrets well, reluctantly gave up tangible evidence fourteen years after the disaster. On April 23, 1924, the wallet of Captain Schuenemann was found at Two Rivers Point, where the spruce trees had been tangled in the fishermen's nets. It still had the original rubber band around it and the cards and clippings inside seemed to be made of plaster. Some of the clippings related to earlier voyages of the Christmas tree ship. Three years after this find a bottle with a note signed by Charles Nelson was picked up. It read:

These lines were written at 10:30 P.M. Schooner R. S. ready to go down about 20 miles southeast Two Rivers Point between fifteen or twenty miles off shore. All hands lashed to one line. Goodbye.

Eventually the family made its last voyage to the Chicago market with Christmas trees. The mother had grown gray; the girls were handsome young women. Forty-seven years had elapsed since Herman, as an 18-year-old lad, had steered his first cargo into the Chicago. The ship had become an institution.

Its fame grew. Today when the winds blow hard on the lake and the heavy surf pounds the frozen shore line watchers in the lighthouse recall the *Rouse Simmons*. Long ago it inspired a ballad. When word of its loss reached Chicago newspapers Vincent Starrett, bibliophile and author of many books of fiction and belles-lettres, was a reporter on the *Daily News*. His editor was Henry Justin Smith. "It would make a fine ballad," said Starrett. "Why don't you write it?" replied Smith. So Starrett composed "The Ballad of the Christmas Ship," a poem of many, many quatrains, and Smith found room for it among the crowded columns of the day's news. It may never challenge the efforts of youthful orators as often as "The Wreck of the Hesperus," but the legend is just as moving and thc intentions of the poet were as good as Longfellow's.

Star in the East

FRED WARD

THE Christmas story that I remember best is not one that I read. It is one that I saw, and it happened down in the "breaks" of eastern Montana over thirty years ago.

They were putting on a program in the Lame Jones School beyond the "breaks" of Upper Sandstone. I had visited this unit frequently, for it was in the district where I was superintendent; and one afternoon I listened to the children practice. I promised them that I would come again the night they gave it.

It was snowing when I left home but when I got to Lame Jones I found that the whole community had turned out. They had a tree that someone had brought in from the pine hills of Pennel Creek and they had lighted it with candles.

There were fourteen children in the school and every one had some part in the program. There was one dialog with five of the smaller children in it. I remember this much of it; it started out with a boy named Ralph Sandaas coming out dressed like Santa Claus. He said: "I brekt the chimney off because 'twas much too small for Santa Claus."

But the big event of the evening was the final number. In this a little girl named Heisley Stockfisch was the mother of a brood of children; someone knocked at her door and she came out and she said: "My day, who can this be, knocking at my door so early on Christmas morning?"

Reprinted from the *Meagher County News,* White Sulphur Springs, Montana, December 26, 1945, by permission of Mr. Ward, author and publisher.

They had an intermission while they hung sheets in front for a curtain and the crowd had got to talking about themselves. Thinking to help the teacher, I pounded on the desk for silence.

This was a mistake, for when I pounded, Heisley came out and exclaimed: "My day, who can this be, knocking at my door so early on Christmas morning?"

The teacher, who had been behind the curtain helping the other children make up for their parts, rushed out and led Heisley back.

The crowd was still talking, so I pounded on the desk again. And again Heisley rushed out and she said: "My day, who can this be, knocking at my door so early on Christmas morning?"

Again the teacher rushed out and retrieved this little girl. I knew better than to hammer on the desk again, so I bellered, "Quiet!" A woman standing within a foot of me almost jumped out of her skin.

Order was finally restored. The mailman knocked at the door, but this time Heisley was not to be fooled. The teacher had to lead her out on the stage, and she said, with a sigh of deep resignation: "My day, who can this be, knocking at my door so early on Christmas morning?"

Two of the Diesterhaft girls that evening sang a song in the tongue of their ancestors:

O Tannenbaum, O Tannenbaum,
Wie treu sind deine Blätter!

It had been snowing, and I had to go as soon as the presents were given away. I had left my car at the Stockfisch homestead, for there was no road down through the "breaks." I had found deep drifts walking to the schoolhouse, but they explained that there was a shorter path by the coal mine. Heisley volunteered to show me the way.

When we walked out into the night, the sky was clear. A slim moon hung over the rim of the prairie. Heisley clutched at her Christmas gifts as we waded through the heavy snow. She pointed to a big yellow star that was rising in the east.

"Lookit," she said. "Just like the story in the book. The star in the east."

I might have told her that the light of the star and of the Prince of Peace was not something which existed only in the ages of long ago, but like the brightness I had seen that night in the eyes of little children who were glad, it was something eternal and unchanging. But that thought did not strike me for thirty years. It had to await the coming of war and the uneasy peace after the war; then war again and another peace ushered into the world.

The homesteaders on Lame Jones Creek were mainly Ukranian Russians. They spoke German and English with equal fluency. When finally I got the cold car started, I leaned from the driver's seat: "Guten Abend, Heisley."

And the little girl called back: "Gute Nacht, Herr Professor. Lustige Weinacht."

St. Anthony's First Christmas

WILFRED THOMASON GRENFELL

A UNIVERSAL robe of white had long covered our countryside, hiding the last vestige of the rocky soil, and every trace of the great summer fishery. The mail steamer had paid its final visit for six months to come. The last link with civilization was broken. Even the loitering sea ducks and lesser auks had left us. The iron grip of winter lay on sea and shore.

At its best, the land here scarcely suggests the word "country" to a Southerner. The rock is everywhere close to the surface, and mosses and lichens are its chief coverings. The larger part of the country we call "barrens."

Few of the houses deserve even the name of cottages, for all are of light, rough wood. Most consist of only one story, and contain but two rooms. To the exacting taste of civilization, the word "huts" would convey a more accurate idea of these humble abodes. The settlements themselves are small and scattered and at this season of the year the empty tilts of the summer fishermen give a still more desolate aspect to these lonely habitations.

Early in December we had been dumped from the little mail steamer on the ice of St. Anthony Harbor about half a mile from shore, and hauled "on dogs" to the little hospital, where we were to make our headquarters for the winter. Christmas was close upon us. Not unnaturally, our thoughts went over the sea to the family

From *Northern Neighbors, Stories of the Labrador People,* by Wilfred Thomason Grenfell; copyright, 1923, by Wilfred Thomason Grenfell; by permission of Houghton Mifflin Company, publishers.

gathering at home, at which our places would be vacant. We should miss the holly and mistletoe, the roast beef and plum pudding, the inevitable crackers, and the giving and receiving of presents, which had always seemed essential to a full enjoyment of the Christmas season.

Few of the children of our harbor had ever possessed a toy; there was scarcely a "little maid" who owned a doll. Now and again one would see, nailed high up on the wall, well out of reach of the children, a flimsy, cheaply painted doll; and the mother would explain that her "Pa got un from a trader, sir, for thirty cents. No, us don't 'low Nellie to have it, 'feared lest she might spoil un"—a fear I found to be only too well grounded when I came to examine its anatomy more closely.

Christmas-trees in plenty grew near the hospital. "Father Christmas" could easily be persuaded to attend a "Tree." The only question was whether our stock of toys would justify us in inviting so many children as would want to come. It is easy to satisfy children like these, however, and so we announced that we expected Santa Claus on a certain day. Forthwith, whispers reached us that Aunt Mary thought her Joe weren't too big to come; sure, "he'd be only sixteen." May White was "going eighteen," but she would love to come. Old Daddy Gilliam would like to sit in a corner. He'd never seen a Christmas-tree, and he was "nigh on eighty." We were obliged to yield, and with guilty consciences consented to twice as many as the room would hold. All through the day before the event, the Sister was busy making buns; and it was even noised abroad that a barrel of apples had been carried over to the "Room."

In the evening of the day previous, a sick-call carried me north to a tiny place on the Straits of Belle Isle, where a woman lay in great pain, and by all accounts dying. The dogs were in their best form and traveling was fair enough till we came to a huge arm of the sea, which lay right in our path and was only recently "caught over" with young ice. To reach the other shore we had to make a wide detour, bumping our way along the rough ballicaters of the old standing ice. Even here the salt water came up through the snow, and the dogs sank to their shoulders in a cold mush that turned each mile into half a dozen. We began to think that our chance of getting back in time on the morrow was small indeed.

One thing went a long way toward reconciling us to the disappointment. The case we had come to see proved to be one in which skilled help was of real service. So we were a contented company round the log fire in the little cottage, as we sat listening to stories from one and another of the neighbors, who, according to custom, had dropped in to see "t' Doctor." Before long my sleeping-bag was loudly calling to me after the exercise of the day. "We must be off by dawn, Uncle Phil, for there's no counting on these short days, and we have promised to see that Santa Claus is in time for the Christmas-tree tomorrow night at St. Anthony," I told my driver.

Only a few minutes seemed to have passed when, " 'Twill be dawning shortly, Doctor," the familiar tones of my driver's voice came filtering into my sleeping-bag. "Right you are, Phil; put the kettle on and call the dogs; I will be ready in a couple of shakes."

Oh, what a glorious morning! An absolute stillness, and the air as sweet as sugar! Everywhere there was a mantle of perfect white below, a fathomless depth of cloudless blue overhead—and the first radiances of the coming day blending one into the other with rich, transparent reds. We found it a hard job to tackle up the dogs, they were so mad to be off. As we topped the first hill and the great bay that had caused us so much trouble lay below us, my driver gave a joyous shout. "Hurrah, Doctor! there's a lead for us." Far out on the ice he had spied a black speck moving toward the opposite shore. A komatik had ventured over the young ice, and to follow it would mean a saving of five miles to us.

We made a good landing and scaled the opposite hill, and were galloping over the high barrens, when the dogs began to give tongue, loudly announcing that a team was coming from the opposite direction. As we drew near a muffled figure jumped off, and, hauling his dogs to one side, shouted the customary "What cheer?"

Then a surprised "The Doctor, as I live! Why, there's komatiks gone all over the country after you. A lad has shot hisself down at St. Ronald's, and he's bleeding shocking."

"All right, Jake. The turn for the path is off the big pond, is it not?"

"That's it, Doctor, but I'm coming along anyhow, 'feared I *might* be wanted."

My little leader must have overheard this conversation, for she simply flew over the hills. Yet the early winter dusk was already falling when at length we shot down the semi-precipice on the side of which my patient's house clung like a barnacle. The anxious crowd, gathered to await our arrival, disappeared like morning mist at sunrise. The tiny, naked room was already choked with well-meaning visitors, though they were able to do nothing but look on and defile what little air made its way in through the fixed windows. Fortunately, for want of putty, a little air leaked in around the panes.

Stretched on the floor behind the stove lay a pale-faced boy of about ten years. His clothes had been taken off, and an old patchwork quilt covered his shivering body. His right thigh was bound with a heterogeneous mass of bloody rags. Sitting by him was his mother, her forehead resting on her clenched hands. She rose as I entered, and without waiting for questions, broke out: " 'Tis Clem, Doctor. He got Dick here to give him the gun to try and shoot a gull, and there were a high ballicater of ice in the way, and he were trying to climb up over it, and he pushed the gun before him with the bar'l turned t'wards hisself, and she went off and shot him, and us doesn't know what to do next—next, and——"

While she ran on with her lament, I cleared the room of visitors, and kneeling down by the boy, removed the dirty mass of rags that had been used to staunch the blood. The charge had entered the thigh at close quarters above the knee, and passed downwards, blowing the kneecap to pieces. Most of it had passed out again. The loose fragments of bone still adhering to the ragged flesh, the bits of clothing blown into it, and the foul smell and discoloration added by the gunpowder made the outlook a very ugly one. Moreover, there rose to my mind the memory of a similar case in which we had come too late, as blood poisoning had set in, and the child died after much suffering.

The mother had by this time quieted down, and simply kept on repeating, "What shall us do?"

"There's only one thing to be done. We must pack Clem up and carry him to the hospital right away."

"Iss, Doctor. 'Tis the only way, I'm thinking," she replied. "An' I suppose you'll cut off his leg, and he'll never walk no more, and oh, dear! what——"

"Come, tear up this calico into strips and bring me some boiling water—mind, it must be well boiled; and get me that board over there—it will serve to make a splint; and then go and tell Dick to get the dogs ready at once; for we've a Christmas-tree at St. Anthony tonight, and I must be back at all costs."

In this way we kept her too busy to worry or hesitate about letting the child go; for we well knew it was his only chance, and as she had never seen a hospital, the idea of one was as terrifying as a morgue.

"Home, home, home!" to the dogs—and once again our steel runners were humming over the crisp snow. Now in the darkness we were clinging to our hand-ropes as we shot over the hills. Soon the hospital lights were coming up, and then the lights in the windows of the "Room." As we drew near they looked so numerous and so cheerful that we could almost imagine we were approaching a town. Then we could hear the merry ring of the children's voices, and make out a crowd of figures gathered around the half-open doorway. They were anxiously awaiting the tardy arrival of "Sandy Claws." Of course, we were at once recognized, and there was a general hush of disappointment. They had thought that at last "Sandy" himself was come.

"He is only a bit behind us," we shouted. "He is coming like a whirlwind. Look out, everybody, when he gets here. Don't get too close to his dogs."

Only a little while later, and the barking of our team announced the approach of the other komatik. Some one was calling from the darkness, and a long sleigh with a double-banked team of dogs had drawn up opposite the doorway. Two fur-clad figures standing by it steadied a huge box which was lashed upon it. The light shining on the men revealed only sparkling eyes and large icicles hanging from their heavy mustaches and whiskers, over their mufflers, like the ivory tusks of some old bull walrus. Both men were panting with exertion, and blowing out great clouds of steam like galloping horses on a frosty morning. There could be no doubt about it this time. Here was the real "Sandy Claws" at last, come mysteriously over the snows from the polar sea with his dogs and komatik and big box and all!

The excitement of the crowd, already tense from anxiety over our own delay, now knew no bounds. Where had they come from? What could be in that huge box? How large it loomed in the darkness! Could it have really been dragged all the way from the North Pole? Luckily, no one had the courage left to go near enough to discover the truth.

The hospital door was swung open, and a loud voice cried out: "Welcome, welcome, Sandy Claws! We're all so glad you've come; we thought you'd forgotten us. Come right in. Oh, no! don't think of undoing the box outside; why, you'd freeze all those toys! Just unlash it and bring it right in as it is. There's a cup of tea waiting for you before you go over to start your tree."

There had been rumors all the week that "Sandy Claws" would bring his wife this year. So we could explain the second man; for the Eskimo men and women all dress alike in North Labrador, which would account for Mrs. Claws' strange taste in clothes. A discreet silence was observed about her frozen whiskers.

A few minutes later another large box was carried over to the "Room." It was full of emptiness, for the toys were on the tree long before. However, two strange masked and bewigged figures stumbled over the snow with it, to carry out the little drama to its close. So complete was the faith in the unearthly origin of these our guests, that when the curtain went up more than one voice was heard to be calling out fearfully for "Ma" and "Dad," while a lad of several summers was found hidden under the seat, when it came his turn to go up and get his "prize."

Christmas has gone long ago. Already we have heard the ominous groaning of the heavy ice along the land-wash, warning us that the season of open water is getting nearer, and that soon our icy fetters will be broken. "Clem" has gone to his home again. He is able to run and walk like the merry lad he is, for not only his life, but his limb also, has been saved to him. Thus Santa Claus came to St. Anthony and brought a gift for us as well as presents for the children. Indeed, he kept the best for us, for our Christmas gift was the chance to save Clem's life and we would not have exchanged it for any we had ever heard of.

A Somerset Christmas

LLEWELYN POWYS

It would be a mistake to imagine that old people cannot enjoy the feast of Christmas. Many a grandfather and many a grandmother, seated close and quiet by the fire amid the revelries of children and young people, enter with their long, long memories more deeply into the true spirit of the night than do their light-hearted descendants for all their shining eyes, tossing curls, and merry mistletoe-laughing voices.

Yet Christmas remains, in its essence, the especial festival of the young. It is they who possess imaginations sensitive enough to respond with unspoilt eagerness to the glamour of the day. In my own case it has been most certainly so, and with the remembrance of half a century of Christmases held in my mind, it is to the first twenty that I look back with the most joy. My brother Bertie and I would begin to be aware of the approach of Christmas even before the end of the autumn term at Sherborne. We used, I remember, to walk to a certain holly tree growing in the field to the right of Babylon Hill from which we could look across the town of Yeovil to the leafless outlines of Odcombe, Montacute Hill, Hedgecock, and Ham Hill fretted in a miniature landscape on the wintry western horizon. This last-Sunday-of-the-term ritual we performed in a mood of exultant anticipation of the Christmas holidays.

No Christmas Day could have been passed more simply and in-

From *A Baker's Dozen*, by Llewelyn Powys; copyright, 1939, by Trovillion Private Press, At the Sign of the Silver Horse, Herrin, Illinois; by permission of the publishers.

nocently than ours was at Montacute Vicarage, and yet in retrospect every moment of it seems to have been full of an indescribable golden happiness. The celebrations had their beginning on Christmas Eve with the decorating of the horns in the hall and the pictures in the dining-room. All the day long my brother and I would have been busy collecting, in two large baker's baskets, moss and fir branches for the church, and holly and mistletoe for our own home. The best branches of mistletoe in the glebe orchard we had marked down at the end of the summer holidays when the ground was still thick-strewn with over-ripe, wasp-eaten apples, but these we kept for our requirements at home, and in truth I do not think the pious ladies who were so busy with the pulpit and lectern and windows and pews of St. Catharine's, would have welcomed the strange white-berried plant, the very look of whose horned Pagan leaves is remote from ecclesiastical sentiment.

At midnight, with the appearance of the carol singers, the real Christmas celebrations would begin. The men—masons, farm labourers, quarrymen, and gardeners—would stand with their lanterns outside the front door to sing "Joy to the World," a Christmas carol, the words and music of which had been composed by the delicate genius of Thomas Shoel. At the first note of the concertina, flute, and harmonium sounding along the dark rambling passage of the silent house, we children would hasten to the dining-room, and, collecting on the sofa, wrapped in dressing-gowns and blankets, would peer out into the darkness to see what we might see of the dim dignified figures of old Geard, of Mr. William Johnston, of Charley Blake, of Russ, and of a score of other notable personalities familiar enough in the streets of Montacute forty years ago. How strange it was to look out upon the drive, with the tennis lawn obscurely visible beyond the wicker-work fence, and to hear the ancient strains redolent of man's desperate hopes, rise up from the secure Victorian garden into the sky, into eternity! The nativity music would be brought to an end at last with the words "A merry Christmas and a happy New Year," and afterwards we would hear the opening of the window upstairs, followed by the sound of our father's voice giving the men his thanks and good wishes for the season as he stood in his nightgown by the old broad family bed.

Only a few hours would be allowed to go by in a dreamless sleep and then my brother and I would light candles at our bedside and would begin to examine our stockings—stockings that still contained scraps of lichen from the trunks of the apple trees up which we had swarmed the day before. With our cheeks crammed, like the cheeks of monkeys, with sugar biscuits and sweetmeats, we would occupy ourselves with our presents until the moment came to hurry down to prayers in the dining-room, into which the winter sun, half-way through breakfast, would suddenly penetrate, shining between the naked beech trees that surrounded John Scott's house, from a round ball red as a ruby. John Scott acted as huntsman for one of the Squires for many years. He is buried in the Montacute Churchyard. An epitaph on his stone reads:

Here lies John Scott;
It was his lot
A huntsman bold to be.
He loved his can
Like any man,
And drank like a fish in the sea.

At the foot of this ribald drinking doggerel may be read these two curt lines, said to have been carved on the disreputable stone at the order of one of the Bishops of Bath and Wells:

And now, God wot,
He has got his lot.

The old house in Dunster's Orchard has recently, I understand, been demolished. The late Mr. Wyndham Goodden could remember when it was inhabited, but it was in ruins when I knew it.

It was typical of those spacious, old-fashioned, genial decades that the first happy meal of the day should each year have been regularly interrupted by a card sent up to the Vicarage by the famous old liberal Baptist minister, the Rev. Henry Hardin, with greetings to my father. After breakfast we were free till the morning service, but on such a day, with the familiar chapter from Isaiah, "Unto us a Child is born," and with the singing of "While shepherds watched their flocks by night," even being in church was not irksome, especially if my brother Bertie and I, owing to the largeness of our family gathering, were allowed to enjoy the novel experience of sitting on the row of chairs by the Phelips' monuments, where we could whisper to each other and meditate upon Mrs. Hodder's turkey that had been hanging "in the pride of its grease" head downwards in the larder for the last week. After we were home again and the turkey, surrounded by sausages—Maynard's sausages, thin, crisp, bursted, and sizzling, such as I have never tasted since—had been devoured, with the mince-pies and a plum-pudding decorated with a spray of holly, red as a cock's comb, we would gather to have the contents of the Christmas hamper, sent by our Norwich aunts, distributed amongst us by our father, each of us holding out our hands with eager self-interest. Then in the late evening, after our turkey thirst had been thoroughly quenched at the family tea-table, where we all sat snug around the tall oil-lamp, warm behind heavy winter curtains, the hall bell would ring to announce that the Christmas-tree was ready in the school-room.

This was the most valued part of the whole day. It was on the Christmas-tree that we hung the presents that we gave to each other. The tree was dug up every Christmas and replanted the next morning, and seemed little the worse for its annual visit to the house. And how resplendent the spruce sapling would look, upright in its box in the centre of the school-room, in the centre of what in Mr. Goodden's days was called "the servants' hall." It is odd to remember that the Christmas-tree was practically unknown in England until, by the marriage of Queen Victoria to the Prince Consort, the custom was introduced from Germany, its kinship perhaps with unrecorded fire-worshipping practises rendering this primitive ritual easily acceptable, even in so conservative an island as England, used for time out of mind to the burning of a yule log.

In an hour the floor would be littered with tinsel paper and the coloured candles would be flaring low in their sockets, till, one after another, a feathered fir twig would fill the room with the incense of the wild forest. Then the moment would come when, with crossed arms, we would dance in a ring about the innocent tree, singing "Auld Lang Syne." I can even now, in my mind's eye, see the tall figure of my father, with child-like benedictions emanating from his good face, as our voices rose and fell loud enough to be heard out on the cold deserted allotment plots where parcels of roughed-up wintry ground were waiting to be re-dug for the planting on Good Friday of well-sprouted potato seedlings. As we swayed backwards and forwards about the tree with laughing voices, not one of us, I suppose, was cognizant of the calm processes of nature which were taking place around the house—the grasses on the lawn sparkling as brightly as the stars in the heaven, while beneath the comfortable slate roof of Montacute Vicarage the lives of old and young were passing away under the shadow of God's irreversible ordinance.

Christmas Day at Kirkby Cottage

ANTHONY TROLLOPE

I

What Maurice Archer Said About Christmas

"AFTER all, Christmas is a bore!"

"Even though you should think so, Mr. Archer, pray do not say so here."

"But it is."

"I am very sorry that you should feel like that; but pray do not say anything so very horrible."

"Why not? and why is it horrible? You know very well what I mean."

"I do not want to know what you mean; and it would make papa very unhappy if he were to hear you."

"A great deal of beef is roasted, and a great deal of pudding is boiled, and then people try to be jolly by eating more than usual. The consequence is, they get very sleepy, and want to go to bed an hour before the proper time. That's Christmas."

He who made this speech was a young man about twenty-three years old, and the other personage in the dialogue was a young lady, who might be, perhaps, three years his junior. The "papa" to whom the lady had alluded was the Reverend John Lownd, parson of Kirkby Cliffe, in Craven, and the scene was the parsonage library, as pleasant a little room as you would wish to see, in which the young man who thought Christmas to be a bore was at present sitting over the fire, in the parson's arm-chair, with a novel in his hand, which he had been reading till he was interrupted by the parson's daughter. It was nearly time for him to dress for dinner, and the young lady was already dressed. She had entered the room on the pretext of looking for some book or paper, but perhaps her main object may have been to ask for some assistance from Maurice Archer in the work of decorating the parish church. The necessary ivy and holly branches had been collected, and the work was to be performed on the morrow. The day following would be Christmas Day. It must be acknowledged that Mr. Archer had not accepted the proposition made to him very graciously.

Maurice Archer was a young man as to whose future career in life many of his elder friends shook their heads and expressed much fear. It was not that his conduct was dangerously bad, or that he spent his money too fast, but that he was abominably conceited, so said these elder friends; and then there was the unfortunate fact of his being altogether beyond control. He had neither father, nor mother, nor uncle, nor guardian. He was the owner of a small property not far from Kirkby Cliffe, which gave him an income of some six or seven hundred a year, and he had altogether declined any of the professions which had been suggested to him. He had, in the course of the year now coming to a close, taken his degree at Oxford, with some academical honours, which were not high enough to confer distinction, and had already positively refused to be ordained, although, would he do so, a small living would be at his disposal on the death of a septuagenarian cousin. He intended, he said, to farm a portion of his own land, and had already begun to make amicable arrangements for buying up the interest of one of his two tenants. The rector of Kirkby Cliffe, the Reverend John Lownd, had been among his father's dearest friends, and he was now the parson's guest for the Christmas.

There had been many doubts in the parsonage before the young man had been invited. Mrs. Lownd had considered that the visit would be dangerous. Their family consisted of two daughters, the youngest of whom was still a child; but Isabel was turned twenty, and if a young man were brought into the house, would it not follow, as a matter of course, that she should fall in love with him? That was the mother's first argument. "Young people don't always fall in love," said the father. "But people will say that he is brought here on purpose," said the mother, using her second argument. The parson, who in family matters generally had his own way, expressed an opinion that if they were to be governed by what other people might choose to say, their course of action would be very limited indeed. As for his girl, he did not think she would ever give her heart to any man before it had been asked; and as for the young man—whose father had been for over thirty years his dearest friend—if he chose to fall in love, he must run his chance, like other young men. Mr. Lownd declared he knew nothing against him, except that he was, perhaps, a little self-willed; and so Maurice Archer came to Kirkby Cliffe, intending to spend two months in the same house with Isabel Lownd.

Hitherto, as far as the parents or the neighbours saw—and in their endeavours to see, the neighbours were very diligent—there had been no love-making. Between Mabel, the young daughter, and Maurice, there had grown up a violent friendship—so much so, that Mabel, who was fourteen, declared that Maurice Archer was "the jolliest person" in the world. She called him Maurice, as did Mr. and Mrs. Lownd; and to Maurice, of course, she was Mabel. But between Isabel and Maurice it was always Miss Lownd and Mr. Archer, as was proper. It was so, at least, with this difference, that each of them had got into a way of dropping, when possible, the other's name.

It was acknowledged throughout Craven—which my readers of course know to be a district in the northern portion of the West Riding of Yorkshire, of which Skipton is the capital—that Isabel Lownd was a very pretty girl. There were those who thought that Mary Manniwick, of Barden, excelled her; and others, again, expressed a preference for Fanny Grange, the pink-cheeked daughter of the surgeon at Giggleswick. No attempt shall here be made to award the palm of superior merit; but it shall be asserted boldly, that no man need desire a prettier girl with whom to fall in love than was Isabel Lownd. She was tall, active, fair, the very picture of feminine health, with bright gray eyes, a perfectly beautiful nose—as is common to almost all girls belonging to Craven—a mouth by no means delicately small, but eager, eloquent and full of spirit, a well-formed short chin, with a dimple, and light brown hair, which was worn plainly smoothed over her brows, and fell in short curls behind her head. Of Maurice Archer it cannot be said that he was handsome. He had a snub nose; and a man so visaged can hardly be good-looking, though a girl with a snub nose may be very pretty. But he was a well-made young fellow, having a look of power about him, with dark-brown hair, cut very short, close shorn, with clear but rather small blue eyes, and an expression of countenance which allowed no one for a moment to think that he was weak in character, or a fool. His own place, called Hundlewick Hall, was about five miles from the parsonage. He had been there four or five times a week since his arrival at Kirkby Cliffe, and had already made arrangements for his own entrance upon the land in the following September. If a marriage were to come of it, the arrangement would be one very comfortable for the father and mother at Kirkby Cliffe. Mrs. Lownd had already admitted as much as that to herself, though she still trembled for her girl. Girls are so prone to lose their hearts, whereas the young men of these days are so very cautious and hard! That, at least, was Mrs. Lownd's idea of girls and young men; and even at this present moment she was hardly happy about her child. Maurice, she was sure, had spoken never a word that might not have been proclaimed from the church tower; but her girl, she thought, was not quite the same as she had been before the young man had come among them. She was somewhat less easy in her manner, more preoccupied, and seemed to labour under a conviction that the presence in the house of Maurice Archer must alter the nature of her life. Of course it had altered the nature of her life, and of course she thought a great deal of Maurice Archer.

It had been chiefly at Mabel's instigation that Isabel had invited the co-operation of her father's visitor in the adornment of the church for Christmas Day. Isabel had expressed her opinion that Mr. Archer didn't care a bit about such things, but Mabel declared that she had already extracted a promise from him. "He'll do anything I ask him," said Mabel, proudly. Isabel, however, had not cared to undertake the work in such company, simply under her sister's management, and had proffered the request herself. Maurice had not declined the task—had indeed promised his assistance in some indifferent fashion—but had accompanied his promise by a suggestion that Christmas was a bore! Isabel had rebuked him, and then he had explained. But his explanation, in Isabel's view of the case, only made the matter worse. Christmas to her was a very great affair indeed—a festival to which the roast beef and the plum pudding were, no doubt, very necessary; but not by any means the essence, as he had chosen to consider them. Christmas a bore! No; a man who thought Christmas to be a bore should never be more to her than a mere acquaintance. She listened to his explanation, and then left the room, almost indignantly. Maurice, when she had gone, looked after her, and then read a page of his novel; but he was thinking of Isabel, and not of the book. It was quite true that he had never said a word to her that might not have been declared from the church tower; but, nevertheless, he had thought about her a good deal. Those were days on which he was sure that he was in love with her, and would make her his wife. Then there came days on which he ridiculed himself for the idea. And now and then there was a day on which he asked himself whether he was sure that she would take him were he to ask her. There was sometimes an air with her, some little trick of the body, a manner of carrying her head when in his presence, which he was not physiognomist enough to investigate, but which in some way suggested doubts to him. It was on such occasions as this that he was most in love with her; and now she had left the room with that particular motion of her head which seemed almost to betoken contempt.

"If you mean to do anything before dinner you'd better do it at once," said the parson, opening the door. Maurice jumped up, and in ten minutes was dressed and down in the dining-room. Isabel was there, but did not greet him. "You'll come and help us to-morrow," said Mabel, taking him by the arm and whispering to him.

"Of course I will," said Maurice.

"And you won't go to Hundlewick again till after Christmas?"

"It won't take up the whole day to put up the holly."

"Yes it will—to do it nicely—and nobody ever does any work the day before Christmas."

"Except the cook," suggested Maurice. Isabel, who heard the words, assumed that look of which he was already afraid, but said not a word. The dinner was announced, and he gave his arm to the parson's wife.

Not a word was said about Christmas that evening. Isabel had threatened the young man with her father's displeasure on account of his expressed opinion as to the festival being a bore, but Mr. Lownd was not himself one who talked a great deal about any Church festival. Indeed, it may be doubted whether his more enthusiastic daughter did not in her heart think him almost too indifferent on the subject. In the decorations of the church he, being an elderly man, and one with other duties to perform, would of course take no part. When the day came he would preach, no doubt, an appropriate sermon, would then eat his own roast beef and pudding with his ordinary appetite, would afterwards, if allowed to do so, sink into his arm-chair behind his book—and then, for him, Christmas would be over. In all this there was no disrespect for the day, but it was hardly an enthusiastic observance. Isabel desired to greet the morning of her Saviour's birth with some special demonstration of joy. Perhaps from year to year she was somewhat disappointed—but never before had it been hinted to her that Christmas was a bore.

On the following morning the work was to be commenced immediately after breakfast. The same thing had been done so often at Kirkby Cliffe, that the rector was quite used to it. David Drum, the clerk, who was also schoolmaster, and Barty Crossgrain, the parsonage gardener, would devote their services to the work in hand throughout the whole day, under the direction of Isabel. Mabel would of course be there assisting, as would also two daughters of a neighbouring farmer. Mrs. Lownd would go down to the church about eleven, and stay till one, when the whole party would come up to the parsonage for refreshment. Mrs. Lownd would not return to the work, but the others would remain there till it was finished, which finishing was never accomplished till candles had been burned in the church for a couple of hours. Then there would be more refreshments; but on this special day the parsonage dinner was never comfortable and orderly. The rector bore it all with good humour, but no one could say that he was enthusiastic in the matter. Mabel, who delighted in going up ladders, and leaning over the pulpit, and finding herself in all those odd parts of the church to which her imagination would stray during her father's sermons, but which were ordinarily inaccessible to her, took great delight in the work. And perhaps Isabel's delight had commenced with similar feelings. Immediately after breakfast, which was much hurried on the occasion, she put on her hat and hurried down to the church, without a word to Maurice on the subject. There was another whisper from Mabel, which was answered also with a whisper, and then Mabel also went. Maurice took up his novel, and seated himself comfortably by the parlour fire.

But again he did not read a word. Why had Isabel made herself so disagreeable, and why had she perked up her head as she left the room in that self-sufficient way, as though she was determined to show him that she did not want his assistance? Of course, she had understood well enough that he had not intended to say that the ceremonial observance of the day was a bore. He had spoken of the beef and the pudding, and she had chosen to pretend to misunderstand him. He would not go near the church. And as for his love, and his half-formed resolution to make her his wife, he would get over it altogether. If there were one thing more fixed with him than another, it was that on no consideration would he marry a girl who should give herself airs. Among them they might decorate the church as they pleased, and when he should see their handiwork—as he would do, of course, during the service of Christmas Day—he would pass it by without a remark. So resolving, he again turned over a page or two of his novel, and then remembered that he was bound, at any rate, to keep his promise to his friend Mabel. Assuring himself that it was on that plea that he went, and on no other, he sauntered down to the church.

II

Kirkby Cliffe Church

Kirkby Cliffe Church stands close upon the River Wharfe, about a quarter of a mile from the parsonage, which is on a steep hill-side running down from the moors to the stream. A prettier little church or graveyard you shall hardly find in England. Here, no large influx of population has necessitated the removal of the last home of the parishioners from beneath the shelter of the parish church. Every inhabitant of Kirkby Cliffe has, when dead, the privilege of rest among those green hillocks. Within the building is still room for tablets commemorative of the rectors and their wives and families, for there are none others in the parish to whom such honour is accorded. Without the walls, here and there, stand the tombstones of the farmers; while the undistinguished graves of the peasants lie about in clusters which, solemn though they be, are still picturesque. The church itself is old, and may probably be doomed before long to that kind of destruction which is called restoration; but hitherto it has been allowed to stand beneath all its weight of ivy, and has known but little change during the last two hundred years. Its old oak pews, and ancient exalted reading-desk and pulpit are offensive to many who come to see the spot; but Isabel Lownd is of opinion that neither the one nor the other could be touched, in the way of change, without profanation.

In the very porch Maurice Archer met Mabel, with her arms full of ivy branches, attended by David Drum. "So you have come at last, Master Maurice?" she said.

"Come at last! Is that all the thanks I get? Now let me see what it is you're going to do. Is your sister here?"

"Of course she is. Barty is up in the pulpit, sticking holly branches round the sounding-board, and she is with him."

"T'boorde's that rotten an' maaky, it'll be doon on Miss Is'bel's heede, an' Barty Crossgrain ain't more than or'nary saft-handed," said the clerk.

They entered the church, and there it was, just as Mabel had said. The old gardener was standing on the rail of the pulpit, and Isabel was beneath, handing up to him nails and boughs, and giving him directions as to their disposal. "Naa, miss naa; it wonot do that a-way," said Barty. "Thou'll ha' me o'er on to t'stanes—thou wilt, that a-gait. Lard-a-mussy, miss, thou munnot clim' up, or thou'lt be doon, and brek thee banes, thee ull!" So saying, Barty Crossgrain, who had contented himself with remonstrating when called upon by his young mistress to imperil his own neck, jumped on to the floor of the pulpit and took hold of the young lady by both her ankles. As he did so, he looked up at her with anxious eyes, and steadied himself on his own feet, as though it might become necessary for him to perform some great feat of activity. All this Maurice Archer saw, and Isabel saw that he saw it. She was not well pleased at knowing that he should see her in that position, held by the legs by the old gardener, and from which she could only extricate herself by putting her hand on the old man's neck as she jumped down from her perch. But she did jump down, and then began to scold Crossgrain, as though awkwardness had come from fault of his.

"I've come to help, in spite of the hard words you said to me yesterday, Miss Lownd," said Maurice, standing on the lower steps of the pulpit. "Couldn't I get up and do the things at the top?" But Isabel thought that Mr. Archer could not get up and "do the things at the top." The wood was so far decayed that they must abandon the idea of ornamenting the sounding-board, and so both Crossgrain and Isabel descended into the body of the church.

Things did not go comfortably with them for the next hour. Isabel had certainly invited his co-operation, and therefore could not tell him to go away; and yet, such was her present feeling towards him, she could not employ him profitably, and with ease to herself. She was somewhat angry with him, and more angry with herself. It was not only that she had spoken hard words to him, as he had accused her of doing, but that, after the speaking of the hard words, she had been distant and cold in her manner to him. And yet he was so much to her! she liked him so well!—and though she had never dreamed of admitting to herself that she was in love with him, yet—yet it would be so pleasant to have the opportunity of asking herself whether she could not love him, should he ever give her a fair and open opportunity of searching her own heart on the matter. There had now sprung up some half-quarrel between them, and it was impossible that it could be set aside by any action on her part. She could not be otherwise than cold and haughty in her demeanour to him. Any attempt at reconciliation must come from him, and the longer that she continued to be cold and haughty, the less chance there was that it would come. And yet she knew that she had been right to rebuke him for what he had said. "Christmas a bore!" She would rather lose his friendship for ever than hear such words from his mouth, without letting him know what she thought of them. Now he was there with her, and his coming could not but be taken as a sign of repentance. Yet she could not soften her manners to him, and become intimate with him, and playful, as had been her wont. He was allowed to pull about the masses of ivy, and to stick up branches of holly here and there at discretion; but what he did was done under Mabel's direction, and not under hers—with the aid of one of the farmer's daughters, and not with her aid. In silence she continued to work round the chancel and communion-table, with Crossgrain, while Archer, Mabel, and David Drum used their taste and diligence in the nave and aisles of the little church. Then Mrs. Lownd came among them, and things went more easily; but hardly a word had been spoken between Isabel and Maurice when, after sundry hints from David Drum as to the lateness of the hour, they left the church and went up to the parsonage for their luncheon.

Isabel stoutly walked on first, as though determined to show that she had no other idea in her head but that of reaching the parsonage as quickly as possible. Perhaps Maurice Archer had the same idea, for he followed her. Then he soon found that he was so far in advance of Mrs. Lownd and the old gardener as to be sure of three minutes' uninterrupted conversation; for Mabel remained with her mother, making earnest supplication as to the expenditure of certain yards of green silk tape, which she declared to be necessary for the due performance of the work which they had in hand. "Miss Lownd," said Maurice, "I think you are a little hard upon me."

"In what way, Mr. Archer?"

"You asked me to come down to the church, and you haven't spoken to me all the time I was there."

"I asked you to come and work, not to talk," she said.

"You asked me to come and work with you."

"I don't think that I said any such thing; and you came at Mabel's request, and not at mine. When I asked you, you told me it was all—a bore. Indeed you said much worse than that. I certainly did not mean to ask you again. Mabel asked you, and you came to oblige her. She talked to you, for I heard her; and I was half disposed to tell her not to laugh so much, and to remember that she was in church."

"I did not laugh, Miss Lownd."

"I was not listening especially to you."

"Confess, now," he said, after a pause; "don't you know that you misinterpreted me yesterday, and that you took what I said in a different spirit from my own."

"No; I do not know it."

"But you did. I was speaking of the holiday part of Christmas, which consists of pudding and beef, and is surely subject to ridicule, if one chooses to ridicule pudding and beef. You answered me as though I had spoken slightingly of the religious feeling which belongs to the day."

"You said that the whole thing was—I won't repeat the word. Why should pudding and beef be a bore to you, when it is prepared as a sign that there shall be plenty on that day for people who perhaps don't have plenty on any other day of the year? The meaning of it is, that you don't like it all, because that which gives unusual enjoyment to poor people, who very seldom have any pleasure, is tedious to you. I don't like you for feeling it to be tedious. There! that's the truth. I don't mean to be uncivil, but——"

"You are very uncivil."

"What am I to say, when you come and ask me?"

"I do not well know how you could be more uncivil, Miss Lownd. Of course it is the commonest thing in the world, that one person should dislike another. It occurs every day, and people know it of each other. I can perceive very well that you dislike me, and I have no reason to be angry with you for disliking me. You have a right to dislike me, if your mind runs that way. But it is very unusual for one person to tell another so to his face—and more unusual to say so to a guest." Maurice Archer, as he said this, spoke with a degree of solemnity to which she was not at all accustomed, so that she became frightened at what she had said. And not only was she frightened, but very unhappy also. She did not quite know whether she had or had not told him plainly that she disliked him, but she was quite sure that she had not intended to do so. She had been determined to scold him—to let him see that, however much of real friendship there might be between them, she would speak her mind plainly, if he offended her; but she certainly had not desired to give him cause for lasting wrath against her. "However," continued Maurice, "perhaps the truth is best after all, though it is so very unusual to hear such truths spoken."

"I didn't mean to be uncivil," stammered Isabel.

"But you meant to be true?"

"I meant to say what I felt about Christmas Day." Then she paused a moment. "If I have offended you, I beg your pardon."

He looked at her and saw that her eyes were full of tears, and his heart was at once softened towards her. Should he say a word to her, to let her know that there was—or, at any rate, that henceforth there should be no offence? But it occurred to him that if he did so, that word would mean so much, and would lead perhaps to the saying of other words, which ought not to be shown without forethought. And now, too, they were within the parsonage gate, and there was no time for speaking. "You will go down again after lunch?" he asked.

"I don't know; not if I can help it. Here's papa." She had begged his pardon, had humbled herself before him. And he had not said a word in acknowledgment of the grace she had done him. She almost thought that she did dislike him—really dislike him. Of course he had known what she meant, and he had chosen to misunderstand her and to take her, as it were, at an advantage. In her difficulty she had abjectly apologized to him, and he had not even deigned to express himself as satisfied with what she had done. She had known him to be conceited and masterful; but that, she had thought, she could forgive, believing it to be the common way with men—imagining, perhaps, that a man was only the more worthy of love on account of such fault; but now she found that he was ungenerous also, and deficient in that chivalry without which a man can hardly appear at advantage in a woman's eyes. She went on into the house, merely touching her father's arm, as she passed him, and hurried up to her own room. "Is there anything wrong with Isabel?" asked Mr. Lownd.

"She has worked too hard, I think, and is tired," said Maurice.

Within ten minutes they were all assembled in the dining-room, and Mabel was loud in her narrative of the doings of the morning.

Barty Crossgrain and David Drum had both declared the sounding-board to be so old that it mustn't even be touched, and she was greatly afraid that it would tumble down some day and "squash papa" in the pulpit. The rector ridiculed the idea of any such disaster; and then there came a full description of the morning's scene, and of Barty's fears lest Isabel should "brek her banes." "His own wig was almost off," said Mabel, "and he gave Isabel such a lug by the leg that she very nearly had to jump into his arms." "I didn't do anything of the kind," said Isabel. "You had better leave the sounding-board alone," said the parson.

"We have left it alone, papa," said Isabel, with great dignity. "There are some other things that can't be done this year." For Isabel was becoming tired of her task, and would not have returned to the church at all could she have avoided it.

"What other things?" demanded Mabel, who was as enthusiastic as ever. "We can finish all the rest. Why shouldn't we finish it?

We are ever so much more forward than we were last year, when David and Barty went to dinner. We've finished the Granby-Moor pew, and we never used to get to that till after luncheon." But Mabel on this occasion had all the enthusiasm to herself. The two farmer's daughters, who had been brought up to the parsonage as usual, never on such occasions uttered a word. Mrs. Lownd had completed her part of the work; Maurice could not trust himself to speak on the subject; and Isabel was dumb. Luncheon, however, was soon over, and something must be done. The four girls of course returned to their labours, but Maurice did not go with them, nor did he make any excuse for not doing so.

"I shall walk over to Hundlewick before dinner," he said, as soon as they were all moving. The rector suggested that he would hardly be back in time. "Oh, yes; ten miles—two hours and a half; and I shall have two hours there besides. I must see what they are doing with our own church, and how they mean to keep Christmas there. I'm not quite sure that I shan't go over there again to-morrow." Even Mabel felt that there was something wrong, and said not a word in opposition to this wicked desertion.

He did walk to Hundlewick and back again, and when at Hundlewick he visited the church, though the church was a mile beyond his own farm. And he added something to the store provided for the beef and pudding of those who lived upon his own land; but of this he said nothing on his return to Kirkby Cliffe. He walked his dozen miles, and saw what was being done about the place, and visited the cottages of some who knew him, and yet was back at the parsonage in time for dinner. And during his walk he turned many things over in his thoughts, and endeavoured to make up his mind on one or two points. Isabel had never looked so pretty as when she jumped down into the pulpit, unless it was when she was begging his pardon for her want of courtesy to him. And though she had been, as he described it to himself, "rather down upon him," in regard to what he had said of Christmas, did he not like her better for having an opinion of her own? And then, as he had stood for a few minutes leaning on his own gate, and looking at his own house at Hundlewick, it had occurred to him that he could hardly live there without a companion. After that he had walked back again, and was dressed for dinner, and in the drawing-room before any one of the family.

With poor Isabel the afternoon had gone much less satisfactorily. She found that she almost hated her work, that she really had a headache, and that she could put no heart into what she was doing. She was cross to Mabel, and almost surly to David Drum and Barty Crossgrain. The two farmer's daughters were allowed to do almost what they pleased with the holly branches—a state of things which was most unusual—and then Isabel, on her return to the parsonage, declared her intention of going to bed! Mrs. Lownd, who had never before known her to do such a thing, was perfectly shocked. Go to bed, and not come down the whole of Christmas Eve! But Isabel was resolute. With a bad headache she would be better in bed than up. Were she to attempt to shake it off, she would be ill the next day. She did not want anything to eat, and would not take anything. No; she would not have any tea, but would go to bed at once. And to bed she went.

She was thoroughly discontented with herself, and felt that Maurice had, as it were, made up his mind against her forever. She hardly knew whether to be angry with herself or with him; but she did know very well that she had not intended really to quarrel with him. Of course she had been in earnest in what she had said; but he had taken her words as signifying so much more than she had intended! If he chose to quarrel with her, of course he must; but a friend could not, she was sure, care for her a great deal who would really be angry with her for such a trifle. Of course this friend did not care for her at all—not the least, or he would not treat her so savagely. He had been quite savage to her, and she hated him for it. And yet she hated herself almost more. What right could she have had first to scold him, and then to tell him to his face that she disliked him? Of course he had gone away to Hundlewick. She would not have been a bit surprised if he had stayed there and never come back again. But he did come back, and she hated herself as she heard their voices as they all went in to dinner without her. It seemed to her that his voice was more cheery than ever.

Last night and all the morning he had been silent and almost sullen, but now, the moment that she was away, he could talk and be full of spirits. She heard Mabel's ringing laughter downstairs, and she almost hated Mabel. It seemed to her that everybody was gay and happy because she was upstairs in her bed, and ill. Then there came a peal of laughter. She was glad that she was upstairs in bed, and ill. Nobody would have laughed, nobody would have been gay, had she been there. Maurice Archer liked them all, except her—she was sure of that. And what could be more natural after her conduct to him? She had taken upon herself to lecture him, and of course he had not chosen to endure it. But of one thing she was quite sure, as she lay there, wretched in her solitude—that now she would never alter her demeanour to him. He had chosen to be cold to her, and she would be like frozen ice to him. Again and again she heard their voices, and then, sobbing on her pillow, she fell asleep.

III

Showing How Isabel Lownd Told a Lie

On the following morning—Christmas morning—when she woke, her headache was gone, and she was able, as she dressed, to make some stern resolutions. The ecstasy of her sorrow was over, and she could see how foolish she had been to grieve as she had grieved. After all, what had she lost, or what harm had she done? She had never fancied that the young man was her lover, and she had never wished—so she now told herself—that he should become her lover. If one thing was plainer to her than another, it was this—that they two were not fitted for each other. She had sometimes whispered to herself, that if she were to marry at all, she would fain marry a clergyman. Now, no man could be more unlike a clergyman than Maurice Archer. He was, she thought, irreverent, and at no pains to keep his want of reverence out of sight, even in that house. He had said that Christmas was a bore, which, to her thinking, was abominable. Was she so poor a creature as to go to bed and cry for a man who had given her no sign that he even liked her, and of whose ways she disapproved so greatly, that even were he to offer her his hand she would certainly refuse it? She consoled herself for the folly of the preceding evening by assuring herself that she had really worked in the church till she was ill, and that she would have gone to bed, and must have gone to bed, had Maurice Archer never been seen or heard of at the parsonage. Other people went to bed when they had headaches, and why should not she? Then she resolved, as she dressed, that there should be no sign of illness, nor bit of ill-humour on her, on this sacred day. She would appear among them all full of mirth and happiness, and would laugh at the attack brought upon her by Barty Crossgrain's sudden fear in the pulpit; and she would greet Maurice Archer with all possible cordiality, wishing him a merry Christmas as she gave him her hand, and would make him understand in a moment that she had altogether forgotten their mutual bickerings. He should understand that, or should, at least, understand that she willed that it should all be regarded as forgotten. What was he to her, that any thought of him should be allowed to perplex her mind on such a day as this?

She went down stairs, knowing that she was the first up in the house—the first, excepting the servants. She went into Mabel's room, and kissing her sister, who was only half awake, wished her many, many, many happy Christmases.

"Oh, Bell," said Mabel, "I do so hope you are better!"

"Of course I am better. Of course I am well. There is nothing for a headache like having twelve hours round of sleep. I don't know what made me so tired and so bad."

"I thought it was something Maurice said," suggested Mabel.

"Oh, dear, no. I think Barty had more to do with it than Mr. Archer. The old fellow frightened me so when he made me think I was falling down. But get up, dear. Papa is in his room, and he'll be ready for prayers before you."

Then she descended to the kitchen, and offered her good wishes to all the servants. To Barty, who always breakfasted there on Christmas mornings, she was especially kind, and said something civil about his work in the church.

"She'll 'bout brek her little heart for t' young mon there, an' he's naa true t' her," said Barty, as soon as Miss Lownd had closed the kitchen door; showing, perhaps, that he knew more of the matter concerning herself than she did.

She then went into the parlour to prepare the breakfast, and to put a little present, which she had made for her father, on his plate, when, whom should she see but Maurice Archer!

It was a fact known to all the household, and a fact that had not recommended him at all to Isabel, that Maurice never did come down stairs in time for morning prayers. He was always the last; and, though in most respects a very active man, seemed to be almost a sluggard in regard to lying in bed late. As far as she could remember at the moment, he had never been present at prayers a single morning since the first after his arrival at the parsonage, when shame, and a natural feeling of strangeness in the house, had brought him out of his bed. Now he was there half an hour before the appointed time, and during that half-hour she was doomed to be alone with him. But her courage did not for a moment desert her.

"This is a wonder!" she said, as she took his hand. "You will have a long Christmas Day, but I sincerely hope that it may be a happy one."

"That depends on you," said he.

"I'll do everything I can," she answered. "You shall only have a very little bit of roast beef, and the unfortunate pudding shan't be brought near you." Then she looked in his face, and saw that his manner was very serious—almost solemn—and quite unlike his usual ways. "Is anything wrong?" she asked.

"I don't know; I hope not. There are things which one has to say which seem to be so very difficult when the time comes. Miss Lownd, I want you to love me."

"What!" She started back as she made the exclamation, as though some terrible proposition had wounded her ears. If she had ever dreamed of his asking for her love, she had dreamed of it as a thing that future days might possibly produce—when he should be altogether settled at Hundlewick, and when they should have got to know each other intimately by the association of years.

"Yes, I want you to love me, and to be my wife. I don't know how to tell you; but I love you better than anything and everything in the world—better than all the world put together. I have done so from the first moment that I saw you; I have. I knew how it would be from the first moment that I saw your dear face, and every word you have spoken, and every look out of your eyes, has made me love you more and more. If I offended you yesterday, I will beg your pardon."

"Oh, no," she said.

"I wish I had bitten my tongue out before I had said what I did about Christmas Day. I do, indeed. I only meant, in a half-joking way, to—to—to—— But I ought to have known you wouldn't like it, and I beg your pardon. Tell me, Isabel, do you think that you can love me?"

Not half an hour since she had made up her mind that, even were he to propose to her—which she then knew to be absolutely impossible—she would certainly refuse him. He was not the sort of man for whom she would be a fitting wife; and she had made up her mind also, at the same time, that she did not at all care for him, and that he certainly did not in the least care for her. And now the offer had absolutely been made to her! Then came across her mind an idea that he ought in the first place to have gone to her father; but as to that she was not quite sure. Be that as it might, there he was, and she must give him some answer. As for thinking about it, that was altogether beyond her. The shock to her was too great to allow of her thinking. After some fashion, which afterwards was quite unintelligible to herself, it seemed to her, at that moment, that duty, and maidenly reserve, and filial obedience, all required her to reject him instantly. Indeed, to have accepted him would have been quite beyond her power. "Dear Isabel," said he, "may I hope that some day you will love me?"

"Oh! Mr. Archer, don't," she said. "Do not ask me."

"Why should I not ask you?"

"It can never be." This she said quite plainly, and in a voice that seemed to him to settle his fate for ever; and yet at the moment her heart was full of love towards him. Though she could not think, she could feel. Of course she loved him. At the very moment in which she was telling him that it could never be, she was elated by an almost ecstatic triumph, as she remembered all her fears, and now knew that the man was at her feet.

When a girl first receives the homage of a man's love, and receives it from one whom, whether she loves him or not, she thoroughly respects, her earliest feeling is one of victory—such a feeling as warmed the heart of a conqueror in the Olympian games. He is the spoil of her spear, the fruit of her prowess, the quarry brought down by her own bow and arrow. She, too, by some power of her own which she is hitherto quite unable to analyze, has stricken a man to the very heart, so as to compel him for the moment to follow wherever she may lead him. So it was with Isabel Lownd as she stood there, conscious of the eager gaze which was fixed upon her face, and fully alive to the anxious tones of her lover's voice. And yet she could only deny him. Afterwards, when she thought of it, she could not imagine why it had been so with her; but, in spite of her great love, she continued to tell herself that there was some obstacle which could never be overcome—or was it that a certain maidenly reserve sat so strong within her bosom that she could not bring herself to own to him that he was dear to her?

"Never!" exclaimed Maurice, despondently.

"Oh, no!"

"But why not? I will be very frank with you, dear. I did think you liked me a little before that affair in the study." Like him a little! Oh, how she had loved him! She knew it now, and yet not for worlds could she tell him so. "You are not still angry with me, Isabel?"

"No; not angry."

"Why should you say never? Dear Isabel, cannot you try to love me?" Then he attempted to take her hand, but she recoiled at once from his touch, and did feel something of anger against him in that he should thus refuse to take her word. She knew not what it was that she desired of him, but certainly he should not attempt to take her hand, when she told him plainly that she could not love him. A red spot rose to each of her cheeks as again he pressed her. "Do you really mean that you can never, never love me?" She muttered some answer, she knew not what, and then he turned from her, and stood looking out upon the snow which had fallen during the night. She kept her ground for a few seconds, and then escaped through the door, and up to her own bedroom. When once there, she burst out into tears. Could it be possible that she had thrown away for ever her own happiness, because she had been too silly to give a true answer to an honest question? And was this the enjoyment and content which she had promised herself for Christmas Day? But surely, surely he would come to her again. If he really loved her as he had declared, if it was true that ever since his arrival at Kirkby Cliffe he had thought of her as his wife, he would not abandon her because in the first tumult of her surprise she had lacked courage to own to him the truth; and then in the midst of her tears there came upon her that delicious recognition of a triumph which, whatever be the victory won, causes such elation to the heart! Nothing, at any rate, could rob her of this—that he had loved her. Then, as a thought suddenly struck her, she ran quickly across the passage, and in a moment was upstairs, telling her tale with her mother's arm close folded round her waist.

In the meantime Mr. Lownd had gone down to the parlour, and had found Maurice still looking out upon the snow. He, too, with some gentle sarcasm, had congratulated the young man on his early rising, as he expressed the ordinary wish of the day. "Yes," said Maurice, "I had something special to do. Many happy Christmases, sir! I don't know much about its being happy to me."

"Why, what ails you?"

"It's a nasty sort of day, isn't it?" said Maurice.

"Does that trouble you? I rather like a little snow on Christmas Day. It has a pleasant, old-fashioned look. And there isn't enough to keep even an old woman at home."

"I dare say not," said Maurice, who was still beating about the bush, having something to tell, but not knowing how to tell it. "Mr. Lownd, I should have come to you first, if it hadn't been for an accident."

"Come to me first! What accident?"

"Yes; only I found Miss Lownd down here this morning, and I asked her to be my wife. You needn't be unhappy about it, sir. She refused me point blank."

"You must have startled her, Maurice. You have startled me, at any rate."

"There was nothing of that sort, Mr. Lownd. She took it all very easily. I think she does take things easily." Poor Isabel! "She just told me plainly that it never could be so, and then she walked out of the room."

"I don't think she expected it, Maurice."

"Oh, dear no! I'm quite sure she didn't. She hadn't thought about me any more than if I were an old dog. I suppose men do make fools of themselves sometimes. I shall get over it, sir."

"Oh, I hope so."

"I shall give up the idea of living here. I couldn't do that. I shall probably sell the property, and go to Africa."

"Go to Africa!"

"Well, yes. It's as good a place as any other, I suppose. It's wild, and a long way off, and all that kind of thing. As this is Christmas, I had better stay here to-day, I suppose."

"Of course you will."

"If you don't mind, I'll be off early to-morrow, sir. It's a kind of thing, you know, that does flurry a man. And then my being here may be disagreeable to her—not that I suppose she thinks about me any more than if I were an old cow."

It need hardly be remarked that the rector was a much older man than Maurice Archer, and that he therefore knew the world much better. Nor was he in love. And he had, moreover, the advantage of a much closer knowledge of the young lady's character than could be possessed by the lover. And, as it happened, during the last week, he had been fretted by fears expressed by his wife—fears which were altogether opposed to Archer's present despondency and African resolutions. Mrs. Lownd had been uneasy—almost more than uneasy—lest poor dear Isabel should be stricken at her heart; whereas, in regard to that young man, she didn't believe that he cared a bit for her girl. He ought not to have been brought into the house. But he was there, and what could they do? The rector was of opinion that things would come straight—that they would be straightened not by any lover's propensities on the part of his guest, as to which he protested himself to be altogether indifferent, but by his girl's good sense. His Isabel would never allow herself to be seriously affected by a regard for a young man who had made no overtures to her. That was the rector's argument; and perhaps, within his own mind, it was backed by a feeling that, were she so weak, she must stand the consequence. To him it seemed to be an absurd degree of caution that two young people should not be brought together in the same house lest one should fall in love with the other. And he had seen no symptoms of such love. Nevertheless his wife had fretted him, and he had been uneasy. Now the shoe was altogether on the other foot. The young man was the despondent lover, and was asserting that he must go instantly to Africa, because the young lady treated him like an old dog, and thought no more about him than of an old cow.

A father in such a position can hardly venture to hold out hopes to a lover, even though he may approve of the man as a suitor for his daughter's hand. He cannot answer for his girl, nor can he very well urge upon a lover the expediency of renewing his suit. In this case Mr. Lownd did think, that in spite of the cruel, determined obduracy which his daughter was said to have displayed, she might probably be softened by constancy and perseverance. But he knew nothing of the circumstances, and could only suggest that Maurice should not take his place for the first stage on his way to Africa quite at once. "I do not think you need hurry away because of Isabel," he said, with a gentle smile.

"I couldn't stand it—I couldn't indeed," said Maurice, impetuously. "I hope I didn't do wrong in speaking to her when I found her here this morning. If you had come first I should have told you."

"I could only have referred you to her, my dear boy. Come—here they are; and now we will have prayers." As he spoke, Mrs. Lownd entered the room, followed closely by Mabel, and then at a little distance by Isabel. The three maid-servants were standing behind in a line, ready to come in for prayers. Maurice could not but feel that Mrs. Lownd's manner to him was especially affectionate; for, in truth, hitherto she had kept somewhat aloof from him, as though he had been a ravening wolf. Now she held him by the hand, and had a spark of motherly affection in her eyes, as she, too, repeated her Christmas greeting. It might well be so, thought Maurice. Of course she would be more kind to him than ordinary, if she knew that he was a poor blighted individual. It was a thing of course that Isabel should have told her mother; equally a thing of course that he should be pitied and treated tenderly. But on the next day he would be off. Such tenderness as that would kill him.

As they sat at breakfast, they all tried to be very gracious to each other. Mabel was sharp enough to know that something special had happened, but could not quite be sure what it was. Isabel struggled very hard to make little speeches about the day, but cannot be said to have succeeded well. Her mother, who had known at once how it was with her child, and had required no positive answers to direct questions to enable her to assume that Isabel was now devoted to her lover, had told her girl that if the man's love were worth having, he would surely ask her again. "I don't think he will, mamma," Isabel had whispered, with her face half-hidden on her mother's arm. "He must be very unlike other men if he does not," Mrs. Lownd had said, resolving that the opportunity should not be wanting. Now she was very gracious to Maurice, speaking before him as though he were quite one of the family. Her trembling maternal heart had feared him, while she thought that he might be a ravening wolf, who would steal away her daughter's heart, leaving nothing in return; but now that he had proved himself willing to enter the fold as a useful domestic sheep, nothing could be too good for him. The parson himself, seeing all this, understanding every turn in his wife's mind, and painfully anxious that no word might be spoken which should seem to entrap his guest, strove diligently to talk as though nothing was amiss. He spoke of his sermon, and of David Drum, and of the allowance of pudding that was to be given to the inmates of the neighbouring poor-house. There had been a subscription, so as to relieve the rates from the burden of the plum-pudding, and Mr. Lownd thought that the farmers had not been sufficiently liberal. "There's Furness, at Loversloup, gave us a half-a-crown. I told him he ought to be ashamed of himself. He declared to me to my face that if he could find puddings for his own bairns, that was enough for him."

"The richest farmer in these parts, Maurice," said Mrs. Lownd.

"He holds above three hundred acres of land, and could stock double as many, if he had them," said the would-be indignant rector, who was thinking a great deal more of his daughter than of the poor-house festival. Maurice answered him with a word or two, but found it very hard to assume any interest in the question of the pudding. Isabel was more hard-hearted, he thought, than even Farmer Furness, of Loversloup. And why should he trouble himself about these people—he, who intended to sell his acres, and go away to Africa? But he smiled and made some reply, and buttered his toast, and struggled hard to seem as though nothing ailed him.

The parson went down to church before his wife, and Mabel went with him. "Is anything wrong with Maurice Archer?" she asked her father.

"Nothing, I hope," said he.

"Because he doesn't seem to be able to talk this morning."

"Everybody isn't a chatter-box like you, Mab."

"I don't think I chatter more than mamma, or Bell. Do you know, papa, I think Bell has quarrelled with Maurice Archer."

"I hope not. I should be very sorry that there should be any quarrelling at all—particularly on this day. Well, I think you've done it very nicely; and it is none the worse because you've left the sounding-board alone." Then Mabel went over to David Drum's cottage, and asked after the condition of Mrs. Drum's plum-pudding.

No one had ventured to ask Maurice Archer whether he would stay in church for the sacrament, but he did. Let us hope that no undue motive of pleasing Isabel Lownd had any effect upon him at such a time. But it did please her. Let us hope also that, as she knelt beside her lover at the low railing, her young heart was not too full of her love. That she had been thinking of him throughout her father's sermon—thinking of him, then resolving that she would think of him no more, and then thinking of him more than ever—must be admitted. When her mother had told her that he would come again to her, she had not attempted to assert that, were he to do so, she would again reject him. Her mother knew all her secret, and, should he not come again, her mother would know that she was heart-broken. She had told him positively that she would never love him. She had so told him, knowing well that at the very moment he was dearer to her than all the world beside. Why had she been so wicked as to lie to him? And if now she were punished for her lie by his silence, would she not be served properly? Her mind ran much more on the subject of this great sin which she had committed on that very morning—that sin against one who loved her so well, and who desired to do good to her—than on those general arguments in favour of Christian kindness and forbearance which the preacher drew from the texts applicable to Christmas Day. All her father's eloquence was nothing to her. On ordinary occasions he had no more devoted listener; but, on this morning, she could only exercise her spirit by repenting her own unchristian conduct. And then he came and knelt beside her at that sacred moment! It was impossible that he should forgive her, because he could not know that she had sinned against him.

There were certain visits to her poorer friends in the immediate village which, according to custom, she would make after church. When Maurice and Mrs. Lownd went up to the parsonage, she and Mabel made their usual round. They all welcomed her, but they felt that she was not quite herself with them, and even Mabel asked her what ailed her.

"Why should anything ail me?—only I don't like walking in the snow."

Then Mabel took courage. "If there is a secret, Bell, pray tell me. I would tell you any secret."

"I don't know what you mean," said Isabel, almost crossly.

"Is there a secret, Bell? I'm sure there is a secret about Maurice."

"Don't—don't," said Isabel.

"I do like Maurice so much. Don't you like him?"

"Pray do not talk about him, Mabel."

"I believe he is in love with you, Bell; and, if he is, I think you ought to be in love with him. I don't know how you could have anybody nicer. And he is going to live at Hundlewick, which would be such great fun. Would not papa like it?"

"I don't know. Oh, dear!—oh, dear!" Then she burst out into tears, and, walking out of the village, told Mabel the whole truth. Mabel heard it with consternation, and expressed her opinion that, in these circumstances, Maurice would never ask again to make her his wife.

"Then I shall die," said Isabel, frankly.

IV

Showing How Isabel Lownd Repented Her Fault

In spite of her piteous condition and near prospect of death, Isabel Lownd completed her round of visits among her old friends. That Christmas should be kept in some way by every inhabitant of Kirkby Cliffe, was a thing of course. The district is not poor, and plenty on that day was rarely wanting. But Parson Lownd was not what we call a rich man; and there was no resident squire in the parish. The farmers, comprehending well their own privileges, and aware that the obligation of gentle living did not lie on them, were inclined to be close-fisted; and thus there was sometimes a difficulty in providing for the old and the infirm. There was a certain ancient widow in the village, of the name of Mucklewort, who was troubled with three orphan grandchildren and a lame daughter; and Isabel had, some days since, expressed a fear up at the parsonage that the good things of this world might be scarce in the old widow's cottage. Something had, of course, been done for the old woman, but not enough, as Isabel had thought. "My dear," her mother had said, "it is no use trying to make very poor people think that they are not poor."

"It is only one day in the year," Isabel had pleaded.

"What you give in excess to one, you take from another," replied Mrs. Lownd, with the stern wisdom which experience teaches. Poor Isabel could say nothing further, but had feared greatly that the rations in Mrs. Mucklewort's abode would be deficient. She now entered the cottage, and found the whole family at that moment preparing themselves for the consumption of a great Christmas banquet. Mrs. Mucklewort, whose temper was not always the best in the world, was radiant. The children were silent, open-eyed, expectant, and solemn. The lame aunt was in the act of transferring a large lump of beef, which seemed to be commingled in a most inartistic way with potatoes and cabbage, out of a pot on to the family dish. At any rate there was plenty; for no five appetites—had the five all been masculine, adult, and yet youthful—could, by any feats of strength, have emptied that dish at a sitting. And Isabel knew well that there had been pudding. She herself had sent the pudding; but that, as she was well aware, had not been allowed to abide its fate till this late hour of the day. "I'm glad you're all so well employed," said Isabel. "I thought you had done dinner long ago. I won't stop a minute now."

The old woman got up from her chair, and nodded her head, and held out her withered old hand to be shaken. The children opened their mouths wider than ever, and hoped there might be no great delay. The lame aunt curtseyed and explained the circumstances. "Beef, Miss Isabel, do take a mortal time t' boil; and it ain't no wise good for t' bairns to have it any ways raw." To this opinion Isabel gave her full assent, and expressed her gratification that the amount of the beef should be sufficient to require so much cooking. Then the truth came out. "Muster Archer just sent us over from Rowdy's a meal's meat with a vengeance; God bless him!" "God bless him!" crooned out the old woman, and the children muttered some unintelligible sound, as though aware that duty required them to express some Amen to the prayer of their elders. Now Rowdy was the butcher living at Grassington, some six miles away—for at Kirkby Cliffe there was no butcher. Isabel smiled all round upon them sweetly with her eyes full of tears, and then left the cottage without a word.

He had done this because she had expressed a wish that these people should be kindly treated—had done it without a syllable spoken to her or to any one—had taken trouble, sending all the way to Grassington for Mrs. Mucklewort's beef! No doubt he had given other people beef, and had whispered no word of his kindness to any one at the rectory. And yet she had taken upon herself to rebuke him, because he had not cared for Christmas Day! As she walked along, silent, holding Mabel's hand, it seemed to her that of all men he was the most perfect. She had rebuked him, and had then told him—with incredible falseness—that she did not like him; and after that, when he had proposed to her in the kindest, noblest manner, she had rejected him—almost as though he had not been good enough for her! She felt now as though she would like to bite the tongue out of her head for such misbehaviour.

"Was not that nice of him?" said Mabel. But Isabel could not answer the question. "I always thought he was like that," continued the younger sister. "If he were my lover, I'd do anything he asked me, because he is so good-natured."

"Don't talk to me," said Isabel. And Mabel, who comprehended something of the condition of her sister's mind, did not say another word on their way back to the parsonage.

It was the rule of the house that on Christmas Day they should dine at four o'clock—a rule which almost justified the very strong expression with which Maurice first offended the young lady whom he loved. To dine at one or two o'clock is a practice which has its recommendations. It suits the appetite, is healthy, and divides the day into two equal halves, so that no man so dining fancies that his dinner should bring to him an end of his usual occupations. And to dine at six, seven, or eight is well adapted to serve several purposes of life. It is convenient, as inducing that gentle lethargy which will sometimes follow the pleasant act of eating at a time when the work of the day is done; and it is both fashionable and comfortable. But to dine at four is almost worse than not to dine at all. The rule, however, existed at Kirkby Cliffe parsonage in regard to this one special day in the year, and was always obeyed.

On this occasion Isabel did not see her lover from the moment in which he left her at the church door till they met at table. She had been with her mother, but her mother had said not a word to her about Maurice. Isabel knew very well that they two had walked home together from the church, and she had thought that her best chance lay in the possibility that he would have spoken of what had occurred during the walk. Had this been so, surely her mother would have told her; but not a word had been said; and even with her mother Isabel had been too shamefaced to ask a question. In truth, Isabel's name had not been mentioned between them, nor had any allusion been made to what had taken place during the morning. Mrs. Lownd had been too wise and too wary—too well aware of what was really due to her daughter—to bring up the subject herself; and he had been silent, subdued, and almost sullen. If he could not get an acknowledgment of affection from the girl herself, he certainly would not endeavour to extract a cold compliance by the mother's aid. Africa, and a disruption of all the plans of his life, would be better to him than that. But Mrs. Lownd knew very well how it was with him; knew how it was with them both; and was aware that in such a condition things should be allowed to arrange themselves. At dinner, both she and the rector were full of mirth and good humour, and Mabel, with great glee, told the story of Mrs. Mucklewort's dinner. "I don't want to destroy your pleasure," she said, bobbing her head at Maurice; "but it did look so nasty! Beef should always be roast beef on Christmas Day."

"I told the butcher it was to be roast beef," said Maurice sadly.

"I dare say the little Muckleworts would just as soon have it boiled," said Mrs. Lownd. "Beef is beef to them, and a pot for boiling is an easy apparatus."

"If you had beef, Miss Mab, only once or twice a year," said her father, "you would not care whether it were roast or boiled." But Isabel spoke not a word. She was most anxious to join the conversation about Mrs. Mucklewort, and would have liked much to give testimony to the generosity displayed in regard to quantity; but she found that she could not do it. She was absolutely dumb. Maurice Archer did speak, making, every now and then, a terrible effort to be jocose; but Isabel from first to last was silent. Only by silence could she refrain from a renewed deluge of tears.

In the evening two or three girls came in with their younger brothers, the children of farmers of the better class in the neighbourhood, and the usual attempts were made at jollity. Games were set on foot, in which even the rector joined, instead of going to sleep behind his book, and Mabel, still conscious of her sister's wounds, did her very best to promote the sports. There was blindman's-buff, and hide and seek, and snapdragon, and forfeits, and a certain game with music and chairs—very prejudicial to the chairs—in which it was everybody's object to sit down as quickly as possible when the music stopped. In the game Isabel insisted on playing, because she could do that alone. But even to do this was too much for her. The sudden pause could hardly be made without a certain hilarity of spirit, and her spirits were unequal to any exertion. Maurice went through his work like a man, was blinded, did his forfeits, and jostled for the chairs with the greatest diligence; but in the midst of it all he, too, was as solemn as a judge and never once spoke a single word to Isabel. Mrs. Lownd, who usually was not herself much given to the playing of games, did on this occasion make an effort, and absolutely consented to cry the forfeits; but Mabel was wonderfully quiet, so that the farmers' daughters hardly perceived that there was anything amiss.

It came to pass, after a while, that Isabel had retreated to her room—not for the night, as it was as yet hardly eight o'clock—and she certainly would not disappear till the visitors had taken their departure—a ceremony which was sure to take place with the greatest punctuality at ten, after an early supper. But she had escaped for awhile, and in the meantime some frolic was going on which demanded the absence of one of the party from the room, in order that mysteries might be arranged of which the absent one should remain in ignorance. Maurice was thus banished, and desired to remain in desolation for the space of five minutes; but, just as he had taken up his position, Isabel descended with slow, solemn steps and found him standing at her father's study door. She was passing on, and had almost entered the drawing-room, when he called her.

"Miss Lownd," he said. Isabel stopped, but did not speak; she was absolutely beyond speaking. The excitement of the day had been so great, that she was all but overcome by it, and doubted, herself, whether she would be able to keep up appearances till the supper should be over, and she should be relieved for the night. "Would you let me say one word to you?" said Maurice. She bowed her head and went with him into the study.

Five minutes had been allowed for the arrangement of the mysteries, and at the end of five minutes Maurice was authorized, by the rules of the game, to return to the room. But he did not come, and upon Mabel's suggesting that possibly he might not be able to see his watch in the dark, she was sent to fetch him. She burst into the study, and there she found the truant and her sister, very close, standing together on the hearthrug. "I didn't know you were here, Bell," she exclaimed. Whereupon Maurice, as she declared afterwards, jumped round the table after her, and took her in his arms and kissed her. "But you must come," said Mabel, who accepted the embrace with perfect good-will.

"Of course you must. Do go, pray, and I'll follow—almost immediately." Mabel perceived at once that her sister had altogether recovered her voice.

"I'll tell 'em you're coming," said Mabel, vanishing.

"You must go now," said Isabel. "They'll all be away soon, and then you can talk about it." As she spoke, he was standing with his arm round her waist, and Isabel Lownd was the happiest girl in all Craven.

Mrs. Lownd knew all about it from the moment in which Maurice Archer's prolonged absence had become cause of complaint among the players. Her mind had been intent upon the matter, and she had become well aware that it was only necessary that the two young people should be alone together for a few moments. Mabel had entertained great hopes, thinking, however, that perhaps three or four years must be passed in melancholy gloomy doubts before the path of true love could be made to run smooth; but the light had shone upon her as soon as she saw them standing together. The parson knew nothing about it till the supper was over. Then, when the front door was open, and the farmers' daughters had been cautioned not to get themselves more wet than they could help in the falling snow, Maurice said a word to his future father-in-law. "She has consented at last, sir. I hope you have nothing to say against it."

"Not a word," said the parson, grasping the young man's hand, and remembering, as he did so, the extension of the time over which that phrase "at last" was supposed to spread itself.

Maurice had been promised some further opportunity of "talking about it," and of course claimed a fulfilment of the promise. There was a difficulty about it, as Isabel, having now been assured of her happiness, was anxious to talk about it all to her mother rather than to him; but he was imperative, and there came at last for him a quarter of an hour of delicious triumph in that very spot on which he had been so scolded for saying that Christmas was a bore. "You were so very sudden," said Isabel, excusing herself for her conduct in the morning."

"But you did love me?"

"If I do now, that ought to be enough for you. But I did, and I've been so unhappy since; and I thought that, perhaps, you would never speak to me again. But it was all your fault; you were so sudden. And then you ought to have asked papa first—you know you ought. But, Maurice, you will promise me one thing. You won't ever again say that Christmas Day is a bore!"

The Magic Tree

ELISABETH NEILSON

CHRISTMAS was the core of winter. It lay like an island of pine branches perfumed by resin and wax candles in the white frozen landscape. It began when ice-flowers froze on the windows and the days were short, for its messenger, *der Nicolaus,* that rough saint, might now appear any night. In the evening the corners of the room looked darker, and we gathered closer around our parents, nearer to the circle of light. Again and again we rehearsed our little verses or the song we had learned; and when at last I heard the heavy stamping steps in the hall, my heart began to beat so fast that my breath was short. Then came the expected hard knock at the door. My father and mother would rise deferentially to receive this venerable guest from another world. Nicolaus's fur coat showed that he had tramped a long time through wood and snow. I remember seeing a pine cone which had been caught in his beard. His fur cap came down low over two bushy eyebrows, under which he would look at us seriously, but not unkindly. And then came the dreaded question, "How are you satisfied with the children?" My mother might truthfully answer with some complaint about lack of quick obedience, about bad manners toward the servants. But my father would at once come to our help, saying, "Yes, but on the whole they have been good." The switch of birch branches which he carried was never used; we were not even threatened with it.

Our fear, though extreme, was really in great part due to the awe in which we held this saint, who, we imagined, lived roughly in the woods yet was in constant communication with heaven. We looked at him with love, for was he not the kind old man who did all the hard work to save the *Christkindchen* the trouble of carrying parcels, or getting the Christmas trees from the woods? After we had sung our song, or said our poem, he would disappear as suddenly as he had come, but not before he had emptied his big bag on the floor so that nuts and apples rolled around.

All this was only a preliminary. If it hadn't yet begun to snow, we ardently hoped for it. I remember one time standing at the window of the dining-room and looking at the gray sky, watching one white flake and then another one and still another drifting slowly past; and my mother, looking up smilingly, said to me what she always said at the first snow:

> *Es schneit, es schneit, dass Flocke geit,*
> *Christkindlein ist nimmer weit.**

Now I knew it really had begun. And very soon my mother asked me to let her write to the *Christkind* about my Christmas wishes. The letter was put outside the window and in the morning I felt assured that it had been taken, for I found one or two silver threads that had been lost during the heavenly visit. How the suffering Christ, how the infant of the Bethlehem stable, had become changed into this angel, more a girl angel than a man angel, nobody seemed to know; but that it lived for the children there is no doubt, for its form, supernatural and also human, magical and at the same time embodying love and goodness, was near enough to be childishly embraced and distant enough to be longingly adored.

Now the house would take on an atmosphere of its own, in which we lived all together. We liked to feel more shut in, more intensely a part of the family. After supper my mother tied on an apron, while we children and any visitor who might chance to be present

---

* *It snows, it snows, the flakes fall,*
Christ child is not far away.

began to shred almonds, each with a little board before him, or to chop nuts. Our fingers soon became sticky with orange and lemon peel, with citron and raisins. The maid put an earthenware bowl, a big wooden baking board, and spoons and knives on the dining-room table, and Christmas baking would be started with the making of a special kind of cookie, called *Springerle*, for it needed four weeks to soften them enough to be chewed. The dough had to be stirred for one hour, then kneaded vigorously and rolled out thick enough to stand the pressure of the wooden molds which printed pictures in relief. It had to be cut out with the greatest accuracy and with a very sharp knife in even little squares. We helped to dust the molds with flour, which was lightly moved across them in muslin bags. Not only did we help, but we manufactured on a tiny scale our own cookies, also stamped with little molds and destined for the dolls' Christmas. All day long the house was filled with sweet odors; the dining-room as well as the kitchen was full of trays holding sugar-frosted cinnamon stars, butter circles, almond pretzels, honey hearts, and a variety of more or less recognizable animals cut out with tin shapes. It was all done with loving care and with a feeling that we came nearer and nearer a center which shed a magic light on every single one of our preparations. We never saw the cakes again till the evening before Christmas, and then only after we had reached the age to help with the trimming of the tree, when we were at least eleven or twelve years old.

Then one day my mother announced that we must not enter the Christmas room, a room set apart for the celebration. This marked a definite step in advance, as from now on the whole household shared more consciously in the different tenor of our life. My mother disappeared for long hours; and on her homecoming she would with a quick gesture hide something rustling with tissue paper in a corner when I entered unexpectedly.

We sang our Christmas songs running upstairs and downstairs, baking and sewing, getting up and going to bed. During those dark winter evenings when the snow fell silently and incessantly, we liked to go to town to look at the few shop windows which displayed toys and presents for the grown-ups. People looked at you as if they knew you, and a stranger might greet you with a warm smile; but my parents did not favor these excursions. They naturally feared that seeing Christmas trees piled in street corners and ornaments behind glass panes, I would lose my belief that it was the *Christkind* who brought me everything for Christmas.

I stood often at the window watching the snow as it blew delicate swirls in the air, which was full of a white soundless confusion. But it all sank into calm as it fell on the Earth, who drew it incessantly to her till it became part of her profound sleep. There were even stiller days when it fell in long lines and much more slowly, more like a dream which has its own muffled reality. For me it belonged to the season that there was no line dividing heaven and earth, and that the white eternity over the landscape outside was all part of what was happening inside the house. Landmarks were wiped out and even the tree and the lamp-post, the pump and the fence, were taken out of their former familiar world into this dream, with the snow piling on at a tipsy angle and distorting them softly into round-capped shapes.

As I pressed my nose against the pane, watching the fall of the big watery flakes, I hoped for a glimpse of the *Christkind*, of his white wing behind the feathery snow. In the evenings when the sun had set in a clear cold sky, and when I had looked into the red glow till I saw black spots, I was sure I had really seen it, and at night I felt it flying softly round the windows, especially round the window of my bedroom. Those white wings seemed almost to touch my childish heart and warm it with the desire to be good; but, put to the test, it rarely seemed to work.

Two days before the twenty-fourth, my aunts and my cousin arrived, for they always spent Christmas with us. And every year I went through the same disappointment. I had looked forward with such intensity to their coming that when they really arrived I could feel nothing, for I had exhausted myself in anticipation. One of my aunts soon took me into a corner to look into the state of my needlework, which was planned as a surprise for my mother; and there, screened from sight by chairs and cushions, she would help me to finish it. I was always behind with my work for everybody, for I was awkward and constantly miscounted the stitches of the simple embroidery I was trying to do. Though the wool lost its original color and smoothness from having to be constantly pulled apart, even the feeling of failure which followed belonged somehow to the season.

On the morning of the twenty-fourth, we would beg a pine branch to trim a Christmas tree for our dolls, who had disappeared, only to reappear in carefully washed and ironed clothes or even fitted with new garments. No button was missing; even their underwear was mended and pressed. We never had anything to trim our tree with, but thought it a favor if somebody gave us a few half-burned candles, which we cut into pieces and laboriously tried to fasten to the branch without any holders. Two or three small apples begged from the kitchen, and—oh, heavenly treasure!—the few bits of tinsel the *Christkind* had left us on his visit the previous night completed our work. All morning long my mother would be busy making packages and sending them, trimmed with little pine branches, to the needy families of the town. Otherwise we did not give nor did we receive presents outside the family.

I shall never forget how slowly dusk came on that day. At teatime mother joined us for a moment, looking tired and preoccupied, and father would pretend to shock Aunt Franziska with the same old jokes to raise the atmosphere to a gayer, more festive pitch. Christmas was like that—the familiar and everyday happenings remaining the same, but warmed by the glow which lay over people and their words.

After tea we changed our clothes, and it was only then that my father in a panic, which was the same every year, left us to buy some more presents. He was always sure that there was not enough, and very often he brought home, to my mother's grief, costly and most unsuitable things, bought in that mood and at the last moment. Of course we knew nothing of all this, for by now we sat singing and shivering with happiness in the corner of a room downstairs, where at the same time the maids were trying to re-establish order.

By and by, we were asked to go upstairs to the living-room. At the last moment my mother, with the signs of hurry still evident, entered, bringing in her smile, more distant than usual, all her love for us, but also an awareness of that other love which at this hour we felt around us.

"You might begin with the singing," she said. We all stood at the piano and began with *"Stille Nacht, heilige Nacht."* My father and one aunt often sang the second voice, but even this solemn occasion did not hinder my mother from looking reproachfully at him if he allowed himself any musical extravagances. Especially would she dislike it if he carried the second voice above the first, and her happy expression might change in a moment into a frown while she quietly but intensely whispered to him, "Stay down!"

We kept on singing slowly and as well as we knew how till we heard a little bell, never heard at any other time. It was the *Christkind's* bell, and its thin glassy tone struck the innermost spot of my heart and set it trembling; for now the big double doors opened as if by themselves, and we at last entered into the very center of wonder as we approached the tree, which stood glowing softly in the light of many candles. Its branches stretched wide and shimmering with magic silver, but here, as in everything which touched Christmas, the familiar, the homely were inextricably mixed with the distant and the awe-inspiring; and the tree, felt as a definite symbol of the marvelous and mysterious, yet belonged to us also in another sense, as we recognized year after year the little baskets delicately fashioned of white and blue beads, the tiny trumpets which you could blow, the quince sausages hanging in pairs from the ends of little branches, the birds, and above all the star which always glittered from the top.

But it was not long that the tree held us. We knew that it would be there to play with a long time. It was the *Bescheerung* we wanted, our presents, beautifully arranged on white cloths which covered couches and tables. The maids were called in; for once there disappeared the difference between servant and master.

Not all Christmas celebrations are equally vividly remembered. Unforgettable is the year when I found at my place a white cap and a muff of sea-gull feathers. Another year it was the shop which had everything a drygoods store could have, down to the counter with the glass cases, the shelves filled with silk and woollen dress goods, the spools of thread, the laces, the colored yarns. But the deepest impression of all was made by the baby doll, who had a complete outfit, starting with diapers and tiny safety pins, nursing-bottles and nipples, hot-water bottles and belly-bands, and ending with knitted jackets and long and short dresses. It had its cradle to sleep in and its high chair to sit in later. I was for some time constantly occupied with this doll, carrying it out on its cushion into the sun, attending to its food, its washing, and holding it tenderly and longingly in my arms. But it did not last. Unfortunately I saw my mother, amused and delighted with my motherly ways, exchange a glance with my aunt. Since my feeling had been very real, my shame was extreme, and I never played again with dolls.

During the Christmas vacation my father looked in more often, hurriedly always, yet not too hurriedly to joke with us, to repeat his standing phrase, "One eats decidedly too much," to open the windows; for he was always wanting fresh air. Aunt Franziska was constantly putting on her big red shawl, because she suffered from so much cold. Every noon meal her present, the goose-liver pie, was fetched from its place between the window and the storm window of the dining-room. We all got a tiny slice which we ate in silence so as to lose nothing of the flavor. At the end of every meal, the big cardboard boxes with the cookies baked by the aunts, as well as the box with our own cookies, were put on the table. The rule that one must take what is nearest to you did not hold during these days. Like birds of prey, we hovered over those cakes till we knew just where to dive to extricate the desired dainty from the heap. Father might well sigh and repeat, "One eats decidedly too much."

The life of the family was on the whole lived in its own closed group, and few visitors were really welcome. I still see the flight of everybody when the doorbell rang—especially Aunt Franziska in her red shawl was up and gone in a moment. But it was our custom to go and see the tree of the family of my mother's most intimate friend. I always knew beforehand how it would be, and tried to shelter myself from disappointment by admitting that it was going to be a failure, but I never succeeded. As soon as we entered the salon, where a meager tree in a corner could not dominate the heavy dark red plush furniture on which a few presents lay around as if by accident, I felt a general grayness over everything. Much smaller than ours, thinly branched, often poorly grown, and trimmed with many red and green balls, the tree stood in a corner as if ashamed. But what concentrated my discomfort till it became real unhappiness was that it possessed only a front, that the part toward the wall had remained unadorned. Our tree was carefully trimmed all round. It was tall and proud in the center of the room, and I was little enough to creep under it and look up through that green world and hear its silver stir at the slightest current of air. I lay there often after luncheon when the sun trembled on the narrow bands of tinsel. I lay very still, close to it all, watching for the shafts of light reflected from the silver balls, and hidden from everyone, even from myself, in the life of the tree. It was the time when the rest of the family took their afternoon nap all together in the living-room; for it never occurred to anyone to retire to his own room. As there were not enough couches, my cousin and my sister and I constructed something to lie on with chairs, and we had a special technique for getting off and on these most uncomfortable couches without stepping on any creaking boards. The center of the house during the whole season was the Christmas room, where we left our gifts for at least ten days, and whither we rushed in the morning in our nightgowns eager to see our presents again and again, and to smell the mixture of pine and cookies.

The Christmas vacation stopped only at New Year's Day, when the big pretzel stood on the table, and when right after breakfast we ran away to be the first to shout "*Prosit Neu Jahr*" to our friends, an important performance which meant sly, roundabout approaches to their dwellings so as to take them by surprise. After we were a little older, New Year's Eve took on its own special color. The first hours after supper, the grown-ups played cards or dice games with us, all sitting round the dining-room table. Our cheeks were very hot, even before we started to drink the punch which my father prepared himself. Charades, or some dramatic performance, most often a fairy tale like the Devil with the three golden hairs, with Tante Franziska in the part of the Prince of Darkness crouching before a hell made of shawls over chairs, filled the time till shortly before twelve o'clock.

When it came close to midnight, my father held his watch in his hand, and we all gathered in the adjoining room, which was dark. Father flung the window open and the clanging of all the church bells came streaming into the room with the cold air, filling it completely and enveloping us as we stood silent in its tremendous swinging rhythm. Somebody broke it with "*Prosit Neu Jahr*." Our parents would kiss us, and I remember my father's voice as slightly hoarse, whilst my mother's was guarded with a peculiar dry friendliness. Aunt Franziska always stood alone, for once not shivering, near the window, and I saw to my discomfort that she wiped her eyes.

One day, without leaving any trace, the tree had disappeared into the unknown as it had come from the unknown, and life moved back into its old grooves. Right after Epiphany, the maids began to talk about meeting masques, chiefly dominoes, when they mailed letters for us late in the evening. My mother looked annoyed, for she did not approve of a prolonged period of foolery before the real beginning of Shrovetide, as it often led to more or less scandalous conduct. But we, the children, were not touched by these noisy outbursts of a people who knew that Lent was not far off.

We were safely tucked away in bed. Father pulled up my little feather bed and felt to see whether I was warm enough.

"Ah!" he would say, "outside there is a cold man, but you are warm and cozy. It is a fine night for sleep."

Mother would bend over my bed to hear my prayers.

Ich bin noch klein.
Mein Herz ist rein.
Soll Niemand drin wohnen
*Als Jesus allein**

mother had taught me.

But Aunt Luise, when she listened to me, corrected one line: "*Mein Herz mach' rein* (make pure)," she insisted.

"*Mein Herz ist rein,*" I prayed, never giving it a thought.

By the beginning of February the nights began to feel milder. The icicles all melted, and I listened to the dripping and the sucking noises of the melting snow. The wind changed, and in the garden there would soon appear the sharp green blades of the snowdrop, folding around its half-frozen green-white flower closely and tightly. I lay in bed listening and thinking of the wet dripping garden, which to me was the world outside. I lay there on my horsehair pillow under my feather bed, warm and incredibly sheltered, with the house around me and my parents close by, watching over every hour of my life. And God was in heaven and was always ready to settle any difficulty carefully and justly.

---

* *I am yet little.*
My heart is pure.
No one shall dwell in it
But Jesus alone.

The Hallelujah Chorus

PIERRE VAN PAASSEN

THE feast of Saint Nicholas on December 6, with its brightly decorated shops and the children's processions through the streets, provided a brief respite from the monotony of the long winter months. But Christmas Day did not. With us the commemoration of the Saviour's birth was by no means a joyous celebration, or the occasion for mirth, conviviality, good cheer, and pleasant social gatherings, as it is in all other countries of Christendom, and in latter years, I understand, in many places in Holland too. In my youth we clung to the old Calvinist interpretation of Christmas as handed down, I presume, from that gloomiest of men, John Calvin himself. Christmas was a purely ecclesiastical function, a solemn observance of the most awesome mystery of the ages; the Incarnation of God Himself.

Others may look upon the birth in Bethlehem as a turning-point in human history, as the dawn of a new era of grace and freedom, and thus make it the occasion of rejoicing. Not so our spiritual leaders. There are some out-of-the-way places in the highlands of Scotland and in the Cévennes in France, among kirkmen and Huguenots of the old stamp, where the same mournful and funereal atmosphere prevails around Christmas. But I think we were unique in this respect, that even the singing of carols was considered tantamount to blasphemy, that festive candles and gaily decorated fir trees were deemed pagan abominations, while light talk or a specially elaborate meal on that day was a snare of Satan.

I do not recall the year—it may have been 1911, but it may also have been a year earlier or a year later—when an incident occurred that makes the memory of an old-fashioned Calvinist Christmas linger in my mind with dread and amusement. It was bitter cold in the Great Church that morning. Worshipers pulled the collars of their overcoats up around their chins and sat with their hands in their pockets. Women wrapped their shawls tightly around their shoulders, for the vast nave and transept were unheated, except for little wooden boxes open on one side to hold a small earthen pot with charcoal. The heat escaping through five holes in the top of the box, or *stoof*, as it was called, was supposed to keep your feet warm.

These boxes were carried around in huge stacks by the ushers before the service. You could get one for the price of ten cents. Many men covered their heads with skullcaps such as the Jews wear in their synagogues, or they simply kept their hats on. That morning I had a muffler wrapped around my face and still my teeth chattered with the cold. When the congregation sang, their breath steamed up in faint white clouds toward the golden chandeliers.

The preacher that morning was a certain Dr. van Hoorn, a man of small stature with dark eyes and a coal-black beard. He was a representative of the ultraorthodox or confessional faction. Nobody in our family ever went to hear him. But that Christmas morning we made an exception.

For it so happened that on Christmas Eve, the organist Frans Pommard, alias Orpheus, had sent word to my Uncle Kees that he was too ill to fulfill his duties at the service on the morrow. Kees, happy over the opportunity to play the great organ, now sat in the loft peering down through the green-baize curtains on the congregation of about two thousand souls and on the pulpit, which stood fifteen feet high, a sculptured wooden tower, with its back to one of the pillars in the middle of the nave.

The organ, a towering structure, rested on two marble columns and stood in a niche on the west side of the church on the site where in pre-Reformation days had been the high altar. It reached upward a full hundred and twenty-five feet. Although quite old, it still had a superb tone. Its viola da gamba and its vox humana especially were renowned throughout the land and indeed in all Europe, having been deemed worthy of praise by four master organists as far apart in time as Constantine Huygens, Pieter Sweelinck, Widor, and Albert Schweitzer. All four had played on it.

It had three keyboards, one free pedal, thirty-eight so-called "speaking voices," and forty-eight stops. The wind was provided by a man treading over a huge pedal consisting of twelve parallel beams. By stepping on those beams air was blown into the bellows. These beam pedals were located in a large inner room above the Consistory Chambers, that is, outside the church proper. A narrow passage between the pipes led from the organist's seat to the pedal room.

Uncle Kees took my brother and myself with him into the loft that morning. He chuckled softly as the minister in his opening prayer blessed the Almighty for having called "but one from a house and two from a city" to form with the other elect of all the ages "Thine own Israel in all eternity." But that was only the beginning. In his sermon Dr. van Hoorn soon struck an even more pessimistic note. Christmas, he said, signified the descent of God into the tomb of human flesh, "that charnel house of corruption and dead bones." He called it an inconceivable humiliation for the Divine Majesty to have left His glory in Heaven behind and to have entered the vile cesspool of time by clothing Himself with the mantle of our sordid humanity. He dwelt almost sadistically on our depravity, our utter worthlessness, the blackness of our hearts, tainted as we were from birth with original sin. We were worms, we were gall, we were abject, contemptible, and black as the night with sin.

Kees listened spellbound as the minister grew more dismal every minute. Christmas was God's descent into Hell, into torture unimaginable, eternity voluntarily submitting to the limitation of time. The assumption of the human estate was so at variance with the divine essence that it amounted to God's self-immolation. The dominie groaned and the men and women of the congregation bowed their heads in awful awareness of guilt for God's distress.

As the sermon progressed—sermons usually lasted a full two hours—Kees grew more and more restless. He scratched his head, pulled his hair back and forth onto his face, giving himself alternately a ludicrous and a sinister appearance. Then again he tugged at his mustache and goatee in a manner betraying extreme nervous tension and mental agitation. He could scarcely sit still for a minute. Now he rose from his seat to take a few steps in the narrow space in front of the organ bench only to sit down again and, with a rapid gesture, spreading apart the short curtains above the balustrade and cupping his head in his hands, to resume his fixed staring at the pulpit.

"Man, man," he muttered, shaking his head, "are these the good tidings, the simple glad message, that?" And turning to my brother and myself, he whispered fiercely: "That man smothers the hope of the world in the dustbin of theology!"

We sang a doleful psalm by way of interlude and the sermon, which had already lasted an hour and forty minutes, now moved toward its climax. It ended in so deep a note of despair that across the span of years I still feel a recurrence of the anguish I then experienced. It was quite well possible, nay, it was more than likely, the Doctor threw out by way of a parting shot that of his entire congregation not a single soul would enter the Kingdom of Heaven. Many were called, but few were chosen. The number and the identity of the elect was God's own secret, guarded from before the beginning of time, which we should not even try to unravel, for that would be pride and presumption. Man's eternal fate was settled, he said, and nothing, not good works or contrition, not piety or merit, not the most ardent prayers, could change by as much as one iota the immutability of the divine decree.

Kees shook with indignation as the minister concluded. He seated himself on the organ bench and began leafing through a volume of Bach's postludes. But after one glance he slammed the book shut.

For a moment I feared that he would not play any postlude at all and would walk off in a huff. I had known him to do rash things before in a fit of exasperation or impatience. Down below in the church Dr. van Hoorn could be seen lifting his hands for the benediction. Kees looked away from the scene and suddenly threw off his jacket, kicked off his shoes and pulled out all the stops in the organ. From the nave, reverberating against the vaulted ceiling, came the unctuous voice of the Doctor. When he had finished speaking there followed a moment of intense silence.

Presently the minister put on his velvet cap and, holding up the skirts of his Geneva gown, began the descent of the spiral pulpit stair. Six of the Elders, dressed in frock coats, stood waiting for him at the foot of the steps. They formed a small procession, the Elders walking in pairs and the Pastor bringing up the rear. They went in the direction of the Consistory Chambers, the entrance to which lay through a door situated directly beneath the organ.

"Is he down?" asked Kees, who had just pulled the bell cord to give the signal to the organ attendant to begin working the bellows. He sat facing the keyboard with his back to the nave and could therefore not see what went on below.

"Yes," I said, "they are walking this way."

Kees waited one instant longer while we heard the air pour into the old instrument. His face was set and grim and he looked extremely pale. He was biting his mustache and I noticed that his chin trembled as my mother's chin trembled when she was overcome with emotion. Then, throwing his head back and opening his mouth as if he were going to shout, he brought his fingers down on the keyboard.

Hallelujah! Hallelujah! Hallelujah! Hallelujah!

The organ roared the tremendous finale of Händel's chorus from *The Messiah*. And again with an abrupt crashing effect, as if a million voices burst into song: Hallelujah! Hallelujah! Hallelujah! The music swelled and rolled with the boom of thunder against the vaulted dome, returning again and again with the hallelujah blast of praise like breakers bursting on the seashore.

It was a storm of music that Kees unleashed, a tornado of melody.

Heaven and earth, the voices of men and angels, seemed joined in a hymn of praise to a God who did not doom and damn, but who so loved, loved, loved the world . . . Kees played on. Mountains leaped with joy. Icebergs melted. The hills and the seas clapped their hands in gladness.

The perspiration was rolling in big drops off his fine face. His eyes were blurred with tears. But his hands moved over the keyboard with speed and force. His stockinged feet flew over the pedals as if their owner were dashing in haste on a desperate errand. . . .

Now the vox humana softly intoned the tender, plaintive recital that comes just before the end. It was like the still small voice that followed the whirlwind of Elijah's vision in the wilderness. Kees beckoned to me with his head. I stepped nearer. "More air!" he called out. "Tell Leendert to give me more air!"

I ran back quickly behind the pipe cases into the bellows chamber, where the attendant, Leendert Bols, was stamping down the beams like a madman, transported by the music, waving his arms in the air.

"More air!" I shouted. "He wants more air!"

"Hallelujah!" Leendert shouted back. "Hallelujah!" The man grabbed me by the arm and together we fairly broke into a trot on the pedal beams.

Once more the organ's notes were swelling into that crescendo of hallelujahs which seems to reach forth to the end of time. Then the anthem came to a close.

But Kees was not through yet. He pushed in a few stops, and now the organ sang out sweetly what is the Dutch people's most-beloved evangelical song: "The Name above every Name, the Name of Jesus!" which is sung in Holland to a tune very similar to "Home, Sweet Home."

We sang it with all our hearts, Leendert, my brother, and I, and below in the church the congregation, on its way out, could be heard joining the chorus. Kees had triumphed.

His face was bathed in sweat. He wiped his forehead. I noticed that his handkerchief was wringing wet. In the subzero temperature the steam rose from his body. Leendert Bols came out of the bellows chamber and stood gazing at my uncle as if he beheld a phantom.

Kees had finished putting on his shoes and now he threw his Sunday cloak over his shoulders. He did not say a word as we clattered down the stone steps of the narrow staircase that ran from the organ loft into the nave. But as he flung open the iron door at the foot of the stairs we stood face to face with Dr. van Hoorn and the Elders. Crowding behind them were hundreds of members of the congregation, curiously craning their necks to witness the encounter between the Doctor and the organist.

"You?" exclaimed the Pastor even before we had closed the door behind us. "You? How did you get up there? Since when are you the organist? If I had known . . ." He did not finish the sentence, for Kees interrupted him by explaining the circumstance of Frans Pommard's illness.

"But why did you do that, play that?" Dr. van Hoorn in turn interrupted angrily.

"That," said Kees, "that was a protest against your sermon!"

"You have no right to protest!" fairly shouted the minister.

"I did protest, nevertheless," said Kees, "I protested because you dishonored man. You . . ." He got no further.

"*Ketter!*" screamed the minister, and his fanatical black eyes darted flames of wrath. "Heretic, madman, anarchist, that you are! Go away from God's house! Never," he yelled, "never, do you hear, will you play that tune again! Never will you . . ."

Kees threw his head back and burst into laughter. And then, bending forward, for he towered over the raging Pastor, my uncle said quietly: "You are wrong again, Doctor! I shall be playing that hymn, only much better, I trust, up there in Heaven on the day when you and millions and millions of the elect come marching in!"

With that he swept his hand from his cloak in a gesture that embraced the whole world.

VI

CHRISTMAS ADVENTURES

Was this His coming! I had hoped to see
A scene of wondrous glory, as was told
Of some great God who in a rain of gold
Broke open bars and fell on Danaë:
Or a dread vision as when Semele
Sickening for love and unappeased desire
Prayed to see God's clear body, and the fire
Caught her brown limbs and slew her utterly:
With such glad dreams I sought this holy place,
And now with wondering eyes and heart I stand
Before this supreme mystery of Love:
Some kneeling girl with passionless pale face,
An angel with a lily in his hand,
And over both the white wings of a Dove.

OSCAR WILDE

Merry Christmas

HERMAN MELVILLE

At length, towards noon, upon the final dismissal of the ship's riggers, and after the *Pequod* had been hauled out from the wharf, and after the ever-thoughtful Charity had come off in a whale-boat, with her last gift—a night-cap for Stubb, the second mate, her brother-in-law, and a spare Bible for the steward—after all this, the two Captains, Peleg and Bildad, issued from the cabin, and turning to the chief mate, Peleg said:

"Now, Mr. Starbuck, are you sure everything is right? Captain Ahab is all ready—just spoke to him—nothing more to be got from shore, eh? Well, call all hands, then. Muster 'em aft here—blast 'em!"

"No need of profane words, however great the hurry, Peleg," said Bildad, "but away with thee, friend Starbuck, and do our bidding."

How now! Here upon the very point of starting for the voyage, Captain Peleg and Captain Bildad were going it with a high hand on the quarter-deck, just as if they were to be joint-commanders at sea, as well as to all appearances in port. And, as for Captain Ahab, no sign of him was yet to be seen; only, they said he was in the cabin. But then, the idea was, that his presence was by no means necessary in getting the ship under weigh, and steering her well out to sea. Indeed, as that was not at all his proper business, but the pilot's; and as he was not yet completely recovered—so they said—therefore, Captain Ahab stayed below. And all this seemed natural enough; especially as in the merchant service many captains never show themselves on deck for a considerable time after heaving up the anchor, but remain over the cabin table, having a farewell merry-making with their shore friends, before they quit the ship for good with the pilot.

But there was not much chance to think over the matter, for Captain Peleg was now all alive. He seemed to do most of the talking and commanding, and not Bildad.

"Aft here, ye sons of bachelors," he cried, as the sailors lingered at the main-mast. "Mr. Starbuck, drive 'em aft."

"Strike the tent there!"—was the next order. As I hinted before, this whalebone marquee was never pitched except in port; and on board the *Pequod*, for thirty years, the order to strike the tent was well known to be the next thing to heaving up the anchor.

"Man the capstan! Blood and thunder!—jump!"—was the next command, and the crew sprang for the handspikes.

Now in getting under weigh, the station generally occupied by the pilot is the forward part of the ship. And here Bildad, who, with Peleg, be it known, in addition to his other officers, was one of the licensed pilots of the port—he being suspected to have got himself made a pilot in order to save the Nantucket pilot-fee to all the ships he was concerned in, for he never piloted any other craft—Bildad, I say, might now be seen actively engaged in looking over the bows for the approaching anchor, and at intervals singing what seemed a dismal stave of psalmody, to cheer the hands at the windlass, who roared forth some sort of chorus about the girls in Booble Alley, with hearty good will. Nevertheless, not three days previous, Bildad had told them that no profane songs would be allowed on board the *Pequod*, particularly in getting under weigh; and Charity, his sister, had placed a small choice copy of Watts in each seaman's berth.

Meantime, overseeing the other part of the ship, Captain Peleg ripped and swore astern in the most frightful manner. I almost thought he would sink the ship before the anchor could be got up; involuntarily I paused on my handspike, and told Queequeg to do the same, thinking of the perils we both ran, in starting on the voyage with such a devil for a pilot. I was comforting myself, however, with the thought that in pious Bildad might be found some salvation, spite of his seven hundred and seventy-seventh lay; when I felt a sudden sharp poke in my rear, and turning round, was horrified at the apparition of Captain Peleg in the act of withdrawing his leg from my immediate vicinity. That was my first kick.

"Is that the way they heave in the marchant service?" he roared. "Spring, thou sheep-head; spring, and break thy backbone! Why don't ye spring, I say, all of ye—spring! Quohog! spring, thou chap with the red whiskers; spring there, Scotch-cap; spring, thou green pants. Spring, I say, all of ye, and spring your eyes out!" And so saying, he moved along the windlass, here and there using his leg very freely, while imperturbable Bildad kept leading off with his psalmody. Thinks I, Captain Peleg must have been drinking something to-day.

At last the anchor was up, the sails were set, and off we glided. It was a short, cold Christmas; and as the short northern day merged into night, we found ourselves almost broad upon the wintry ocean, whose freezing spray cased us in ice, as in polished armor. The long rows of teeth on the bulwarks glistened in the moonlight; and like the white ivory tusks of some huge elephant, vast curving icicles depended from the bows.

Lank Bildad, as pilot, headed the first watch, and ever and anon, as the old craft deep dived into the green seas, and sent the shivering frost all over her, and the winds howled, and the cordage rang, his steady notes were heard—

"Sweet fields beyond the swelling flood,
Stand dressed in living green.
So to the Jews old Canaan stood,
While Jordan rolled between."

Never did those sweet words sound more sweetly to me than then. They were full of hope and fruition. Spite of this frigid winter night in the boisterous Atlantic, spite of my wet feet and wetter jacket, there was yet, it then seemed to me, many a pleasant haven in store; and meads and glades so eternally vernal, that the grass shot up by the spring, untrodden, unwilted, remains at midsummer.

At last we gained such an offing, that the two pilots were needed no longer. The stout sail-boat that had accompanied us began ranging alongside.

It was curious and not unpleasing, how Peleg and Bildad were affected at this juncture, especially Captain Bildad. For loath to depart, yet; very loath to leave, for good, a ship bound on so long and perilous a voyage—beyond both stormy Capes; a ship in which some thousands of his hard earned dollars were invested; a ship, in which an old shipmate sailed as captain; a man almost as old as he, once more starting to encounter all the terrors of the pitiless jaw; loath to say good-bye to a thing so every way brimful of every interest to him—poor old Bildad lingered long; paced the deck with anxious strides; ran down into the cabin to speak another farewell word there; again came on deck, and looked to windward; looked towards the wide and endless waters, only bounded by the far-off unseen Eastern Continents; looked towards the land; looked aloft; looked right and left; looked everywhere and nowhere; and at last, mechanically coiling a rope upon its pin, convulsively grasped stout Peleg by the hand, and holding up a lantern, for a moment stood gazing heroically in his face, as much as to say, "Nevertheless, friend Peleg, I can stand it; yes, I can."

As for Peleg himself, he took it more like a philosopher; but for all his philosophy, there was a tear twinkling in his eye, when the lantern came too near. And he, too, did not a little run from the cabin to deck—now a word below, and now a word with Starbuck, the chief mate.

But, at last, he turned to his comrade, with a final sort of look about him—"Captain Bildad—come, old shipmate, we must go. Back the mainyard there! Boat ahoy! Stand by to come close alongside, now! Careful, careful!—come, Bildad, boy—say your last. Luck to ye, Starbuck—luck to ye, Mr. Stubb—luck to ye, Mr. Flask—good-bye and good luck to ye all—and this day three years I'll have a hot supper smoking for ye in old Nantucket. Hurrah and away!"

"God bless ye, and have ye in His holy keeping, men," murmured old Bildad, almost incoherently. "I hope ye'll have fine weather now, so that Captain Ahab may soon be moving among ye—a pleasant sun is all he needs, and ye'll have plenty of them in the tropic voyage ye go. Be careful in the hunt, ye mates. Don't stave the boats needlessly, ye harpooneers; good white cedar plank is raised full three per cent. within the year. Don't forget your prayers, either. Mr. Starbuck, mind that cooper don't waste the spare staves. Oh! the sail-needles are in the green locker! Don't whale it too much a' Lord's day, men; but don't miss a fair chance either, that's rejecting Heaven's good gifts. Have an eye to the molasses tierce, Mr. Stubb; it was a little leaky, I thought. If ye touch at the islands, Mr. Flask, beware of fornication. Good-bye, good-bye! Don't keep that cheese too long down in the hold, Mr. Starbuck; it'll spoil. Be careful with the butter—twenty cents the pound it was, and mind ye, if——"

"Come, come, Captain Bildad; stop palavering—away!" and with that, Peleg hurried him over the side, and both dropt into the boat.

Ship and boat diverged; the cold, damp night breeze blew between; a screaming gull flew overhead; the two hulls wildly rolled; we gave three heavy-hearted cheers, and blindly plunged like fate into the lone Atlantic.

The Seven Poor Travellers

CHARLES DICKENS

I

In the Old City of Rochester

STRICTLY speaking, there were only six Poor Travellers; but, being a Traveller myself, though an idle one, and being withal as poor as I hope to be, I brought the number up to seven. This word of explanation is due at once, for what says the inscription over the quaint old door?

RICHARD WATTS, *Esq.*
by his Will, dated 22 Aug. 1579,
founded this Charity
for Six poor Travellers,
who not being ROGUES, or PROCTORS,
May receive gratis for one Night,
Lodging, Entertainment,
and Fourpence each.

It was in the ancient little city of Rochester in Kent, of all the good days in the year upon a Christmas-eve, that I stood reading this inscription over the quaint old door in question. I had been wandering about the neighbouring Cathedral, and had seen the tomb of Richard Watts, with the effigy of worthy Master Richard starting out of it like a ship's figure-head; and I had felt that I could do no less, as I gave the Verger his fee, than inquire the way to Watts's Charity. The way being very short and very plain, I had come prosperously to the inscription and the quaint old door.

"Now," said I to myself, as I looked at the knocker, "I know I am not a Proctor; I wonder whether I am a Rogue!"

Upon the whole, though Conscience reproduced two or three pretty faces which might have had smaller attraction for a moral Goliath than they had had for me, who am but a Tom Thumb in that way, I came to the conclusion that I was not a Rogue. So, beginning to regard the establishment as in some sort my property, bequeathed to me and divers co-legatees, share and share alike, by the Worshipful Master Richard Watts, I stepped backward into the road to survey my inheritance.

I found it to be a clean white house, of a staid and venerable air, with the quaint old door already three times mentioned (an arched door), choice little long low lattice-windows, and a roof of three gables. The silent High-street of Rochester is full of gables, with old beams and timbers carved into strange faces. It is oddly garnished with a queer old clock that projects over the pavement out of a grave red-brick building, as if Time carried on business there, and hung out his sign. Sooth to say, he did an active stroke of work in Rochester, in the old days of the Romans, and the Saxons, and the Normans; and down to the times of King John, when the rugged castle—I will not undertake to say how many hundreds of years old then—was abandoned to the centuries of weather which have so defaced the dark apertures in its walls, that the ruin looks as if the rooks and daws had pecked its eyes out.

I was very well pleased, both with my property and its situation. While I was yet surveying it with growing content, I espied, at one of the upper lattices which stood open, a decent body, of a wholesome matronly appearance, whose eyes I caught inquiringly addressed to mine. They said so plainly, "Do you wish to see the house?" that I answered aloud, "Yes, if you please." And within a minute the old door opened, and I bent my head, and went down two steps into the entry.

"This," said the matronly presence, ushering me into a low room on the right, "is where the Travellers sit by the fire, and cook what bits of suppers they buy with their fourpences."

"O! Then they have no Entertainment?" said I. For the inscription over the outer door was still running in my head, and I was mentally repeating, in a kind of tune, "Lodging, entertainment, and fourpence each."

"They have a fire provided for 'em," returned the matron—a mighty civil person, not, as I could make out, overpaid; "and these cooking utensils. And this what's painted on a board is the rules for their behaviour. They have their fourpences when they get their tickets from the steward over the way—for I don't admit 'em myself, they must get their tickets first—and sometimes one buys a rasher of bacon, and another a herring, and another a pound of potatoes, or what not. Sometimes two or three of 'em will club their fourpences together, and make a supper that way. But not much of anything is to be got for fourpence, at present, when provisions is so dear."

"True indeed," I remarked. I had been looking about the room, admiring its snug fireside at the upper end, its glimpse of the street through the low mullioned window, and its beams overhead. "It is very comfortable," said I.

"Ill-conwenient," observed the matronly presence.

I liked to hear her say so; for it showed a commendable anxiety to execute in no niggardly spirit the intentions of Master Richard Watts. But the room was really so well adapted to its purpose that I protested, quite enthusiastically, against her disparagement.

"Nay, ma'am," said I, "I am sure it is warm in winter and cool in summer. It has a look of homely welcome and soothing rest. It has a remarkably cosy fireside, the very blink of which, gleaming out into the street upon a winter night, is enough to warm all Rochester's heart. And as to the convenience of the six Poor Travellers——"

"I don't mean them," returned the presence. "I speak of its being an ill-conwenience to myself and my daughter, having no other room to sit in of a night."

This was true enough, but there was another quaint room of

corresponding dimensions on the opposite side of the entry: so I stepped across to it, through the open doors of both rooms, and asked what this chamber was for.

"This," returned the presence, "is the Board Room. Where the gentlemen meet when they come here."

Let me see. I had counted from the street six upper windows besides these on the ground-story. Making a perplexed calculation in my mind, I rejoined, "Then the six Poor Travellers sleep upstairs?"

My new friend shook her head. "They sleep," she answered, "in two little outer galleries at the back, where their beds has always been, ever since the Charity was founded. It being so very ill-conwenient to me as things is at present, the gentlemen are going to take off a bit of the back yard, and make a slip of a room for 'em there, to sit in before they go to bed."

"And then the six Poor Travellers," said I, "will be entirely out of the house?"

"Entirely out of the house," assented the presence, comfortably smoothing her hands. "Which is considered much better for all parties, and much more conwenient."

I had been a little startled, in the Cathedral, by the emphasis with which the effigy of Master Richard Watts was bursting out of his tomb; but I began to think, now, that it might be expected to come across the High-street some stormy night, and make a disturbance here.

Howbeit, I kept my thoughts to myself, and accompanied the presence to the little galleries at the back. I found them on a tiny scale, like the galleries in old inn-yards; and they were very clean. While I was looking at them, the matron gave me to understand that the prescribed number of Poor Travellers were forthcoming every night from year's end to year's end; and that the beds were always occupied. My questions upon this, and her replies, brought us back to the Board Room so essential to the dignity of "the gentlemen," where she showed me the printed accounts of the Charity hanging up by the window. From them I gathered that the greater part of the property bequeathed by the Worshipful Master

Richard Watts for the maintenance of this foundation was, at the period of his death, mere marshland; but that, in course of time, it had been reclaimed and built upon, and was very considerably increased in value. I found, too, that about a thirtieth part of the annual revenue was now expended on the purposes commemorated in the inscription over the door; the rest being handsomely laid out in Chancery, law expenses, collectorship, receivership, poundage, and other appendages of management, highly complimentary to the importance of the six Poor Travellers. In short, I made the not entirely new discovery that it may be said of an establishment like this, in dear old England, as of the fat oyster in the American story, that it takes a good many men to swallow it whole.

"And pray, ma'am," said I, sensible that the blankness of my face began to brighten as the thought occurred to me, "could one see these Travellers?"

"Well!" she returned dubiously, "no!"

"Not to-night, for instance!" said I.

"Well!" she returned more positively, "no. Nobody ever asked to see them, and nobody ever did see them."

As I am not easily baulked in a design when I am set upon it, I urged to the good lady that this was Christmas-eve; that Christmas comes but once a year—which is unhappily too true, for when it begins to stay with us the whole year round we shall make this earth a very different place; that I was possessed by the desire to treat the Travellers to a supper and a temperate glass of hot Wassail; that the voice of Fame had been heard in that land, declaring my ability to make hot Wassail; that if I were permitted to hold the feast, I should be found conformable to reason, sobriety, and good hours; in a word, that I could be merry and wise myself, and had been even known at a pinch to keep others so, although I was decorated with no badge or medal, and was not a Brother, Orator, Apostle, Saint, or Prophet of any denomination whatever. In the end I prevailed, to my great joy. It was settled that at nine o'clock that night a Turkey and a piece of Roast Beef should smoke upon the board; and that I, faint and unworthy minister for once of

Master Richard Watts, should preside as the Christmas-supper host of the six Poor Travellers.

I went back to my inn to give the necessary directions for the Turkey and Roast Beef, and, during the remainder of the day, could settle to nothing for thinking of the Poor Travellers. When the wind blew hard against the windows—it was a cold day, with dark gusts of sleet alternating with periods of wild brightness, as if the year were dying fitfully—I pictured them advancing towards their resting-place along various cold roads, and felt delighted to think how little they foresaw the supper that awaited them. I painted their portraits in my mind, and indulged in little heightening touches. I made them footsore; I made them weary; I made them carry packs and bundles; I made them stop by finger-posts and milestones, leaning on their bent sticks, and looking wistfully at what was written there; I made them lose their way; and filled their five wits with apprehensions of lying out all night, and being frozen to death. I took up my hat, and went out, climbed to the top of the Old Castle, and looked over the windy hills that slope down to the Medway, almost believing that I could descry some of my Travellers in the distance. After it fell dark, and the Cathedral bell was heard in the invisible steeple—quite a bower of frosty rime when I had last seen it—striking five, six, seven, I became so full of my Travellers that I could eat no dinner, and felt constrained to watch them still in the red coals of my fire. They were all arrived by this time, I thought, had got their tickets, and were gone in. . . . There my pleasure was dashed by the reflection that probably some Travellers had come too late and were shut out.

After the Cathedral bell had struck eight, I could smell a delicious savour of Turkey and Roast Beef rising to the window of my adjoining bedroom, which looked down into the inn-yard just where the lights of the kitchen reddened a massive fragment of the Castle Wall. It was high time to make the Wassail now; therefore I had up the materials (which, together with their proportions and combinations, I must decline to impart, as the only secret of my own I was ever known to keep), and made a glorious jorum. Not in a bowl; for a bowl anywhere but on a shelf is a low superstition, fraught with cooling and slopping; but in a brown earthenware pitcher, tenderly suffocated, when full, with a coarse cloth. It being now upon the stroke of nine, I set out for Watts's Charity, carrying my brown beauty in my arms. I would trust Ben, the waiter, with untold gold; but there are strings in the human heart which must never be sounded by another, and drinks that I make myself are those strings in mine.

The Travellers were all assembled, the cloth was laid, and Ben had brought a great billet of wood, and had laid it artfully on the top of the fire, so that a touch or two of the poker after supper should make a roaring blaze. Having deposited my brown beauty in a red nook of the hearth, inside the fender, where she soon began to sing like an ethereal cricket, diffusing at the same time odours as of ripe vineyards, spice forests, and orange groves—I say, having stationed my beauty in a place of security and improvement, I introduced myself to my guests by shaking hands all round, and giving them a hearty welcome.

I found the party to be thus composed. Firstly, myself. Secondly, a very decent man indeed, with his right arm in a sling, who had a certain clean agreeable smell of wood about him, from which I judged him to have something to do with shipbuilding. Thirdly, a little sailor-boy, a mere child, with a profusion of rich dark brown hair, and deep womanly-looking eyes. Fourthly, a shabby-genteel personage in a threadbare black suit, and apparently in very bad circumstances, with a dry suspicious look; the absent buttons on his waistcoat eked out with red tape; and a bundle of extraordinarily tattered papers sticking out of an inner breast-pocket. Fifthly, a foreigner by birth, but an Englishman in speech, who carried his pipe in the band of his hat, and lost no time in telling me, in an easy, simple, engaging way, that he was a watchmaker from Geneva, and travelled all about the Continent, mostly on foot, working as a journeyman, and seeing new countries—possibly (I thought) also smuggling a watch or so, now and then. Sixthly, a little widow, who had been very pretty and was still very young, but whose beauty had been wrecked in some great misfortune, and whose manner was remarkably timid, scared, and solitary. Seventhly and lastly, a

Traveller of a kind familiar to my boyhood, but now almost obsolete—a Book-Pedlar, who had a quantity of Pamphlets and Numbers with him, and who presently boasted that he could repeat more verses in an evening than he could sell in a twelvemonth.

All these I have mentioned in the order in which they sat at table. I presided, and the matronly presence faced me. We were not long in taking our places, for the supper had arrived with me, in the following procession:

Myself with the pitcher.
Ben with Beer.
Inattentive Boy with hot plates. Inattentive Boy with hot plates.
THE TURKEY
Female carrying sauces to be heated on the spot.
THE BEEF
Man with Tray on his head, containing Vegetables and Sundries.
Volunteer Hostler from Hotel, grinning,
And rendering no assistance.

As we passed along the High-street, comet-like, we left a long tail of fragrance behind us which caused the public to stop, sniffing in wonder. We had previously left at the corner of the inn-yard a wall-eyed young man connected with the Fly department, and well accustomed to the sound of a railway whistle which Ben always carries in his pocket, whose instructions were, so soon as he should hear the whistle blown, to dash into the kitchen, seize the hot plum-pudding and mince-pies, and speed with them to Watts's Charity, where they would be received (he was further instructed) by the sauce-female, who would be provided with brandy in a blue state of combustion.

All these arrangements were executed in the most exact and punctual manner. I never saw a finer turkey, finer beef, or greater prodigality of sauce and gravy; and my Travellers did wonderful justice to everything set before them. It made my heart rejoice to observe how their wind and frost-hardened faces softened in the clatter of plates and knives and forks, and mellowed in the fire and supper heat. While their hats and caps and wrappers, hanging up, a few small bundles on the ground in a corner, and in another corner three or four old walking-sticks, worn down at the end to mere fringe, linked this snug interior with the bleak outside in a golden chain.

When supper was done, and my brown beauty had been elevated on the table, there was a general requisition to me to "take the corner"; which suggested to me comfortably enough how much my friends here made of a fire—for when had *I* ever thought so highly of the corner, since the days when I connected it with Jack Horner? However, as I declined, Ben, whose touch on all convivial instruments is perfect, drew the table apart, and instructing my Travellers to open right and left on either side of me, and form round the fire, closed up the centre with myself and my chair, and preserved the order we had kept at table. He had already, in a tranquil manner, boxed the ears of the inattentive boys until they had been by imperceptible degrees boxed out of the room; and he now rapidly skirmished the sauce-female into the High-street, disappeared, and softly closed the door.

This was the time for bringing the poker to bear on the billet of wood. I tapped it three times, like an enchanted talisman, and a brilliant host of merry-makers burst out of it, and sported off by the chimney—rushing up the middle in a fiery country dance, and never coming down again. Meanwhile, by their sparkling light, which threw our lamp into the shade, I filled the glasses, and gave my Travellers, CHRISTMAS!—CHRISTMAS-EVE, my friends, when the shepherds, who were Poor Travellers, too, in their way, heard the Angels sing, "On earth, peace. Good-will towards men!"

I don't know who was the first among us to think that we ought to take hands as we sat, in deference to the toast, or whether any one of us anticipated the others, but at any rate we all did it. We then drank to the memory of the good Master Richard Watts. And I wish his Ghost may never have had worse usage under that roof than it had from us.

It was the witching time for Story-telling. "Our whole life, Travellers," said I, "is a story more or less intelligible—generally less; but we shall read it by a clearer light when it is ended. I, for one, am so divided this night between fact and fiction, that I scarce know which is which. Shall I beguile the time by telling you a story as we sit here?"

They all answered, yes. I had little to tell them, but I was bound by my own proposal. Therefore, after looking for awhile at the spiral column of smoke wreathing up from my brown beauty, through which I could have almost sworn I saw the effigy of Master Richard Watts less startled than usual, I fired away.

II

The Story of Richard Doubledick

In the year one thousand seven hundred and ninety-nine, a relative of mine came limping down, on foot, to this town of Chatham. I call it this town, because if anybody present knows to a nicety where Rochester ends and Chatham begins, it is more than I do. He was a poor traveller, with not a farthing in his pocket. He sat by the fire in this very room, and he slept one night in a bed that will be occupied to-night by some one here.

My relative came down to Chatham to enlist in a cavalry regiment, if a cavalry regiment would have him; if not, to take King George's shilling from any corporal or sergeant who would put a bunch of ribbons in his hat. His object was to get shot; but he thought he might as well ride to death as be at the trouble of walking.

My relative's Christian name was Richard, but he was better known as Dick. He dropped his own surname on the road down, and took up that of Doubledick. He was passed as Richard Doubledick; age, twenty-two; height, five foot ten; native place, Exmouth, which he had never been near in his life. There was no cavalry in Chatham when he limped over the bridge here with half a shoe to his dusty feet, so he enlisted into a regiment of the line, and was glad to get drunk and forget all about it.

You are to know that this relative of mine had gone wrong, and run wild. His heart was in the right place, but it was sealed up. He had been betrothed to a good and beautiful girl, whom he had loved better than she—or perhaps even he—believed; but in an evil hour he had given her cause to say to him solemnly, "Richard, I will never marry another man. I will live single for your sake, but Mary Marshall's lips—" her name was Mary Marshall—"never address another word to you on earth. Go, Richard! Heaven forgive you!" This finished him. This brought him down to Chatham. This made him Private Richard Doubledick, with a determination to be shot.

There was not a more dissipated and reckless soldier in Chatham barracks, in the year one thousand seven hundred and ninety-nine, than Private Richard Doubledick. He associated with the dregs of every regiment; he was as seldom sober as he could be, and was constantly under punishment. It became clear to the whole barracks that Private Richard Doubledick would very soon be flogged.

Now the Captain of Richard Doubledick's company was a young gentleman not above five years his senior, whose eyes had an expression in them which affected Private Richard Doubledick in a very remarkable way. They were bright, handsome, dark eyes—what are called laughing eyes generally, and, when serious, rather steady than severe—but they were the only eyes now left in his narrowed world that Private Richard Doubledick could not stand. Unabashed by evil report and punishment, defiant of everything else and everybody else, he had but to know that those eyes looked at him for a moment, and he felt ashamed. He could not so much as salute Captain Taunton in the street like any other officer. He was reproached and confused—troubled by the mere possibility of the Captain's looking at him. In his worst moments, he would rather turn back, and go any distance out of his way, than encounter those two handsome, dark, bright eyes.

One day, when Private Richard Doubledick came out of the Black hole, where he had been passing the last eight-and-forty hours, and in which retreat he spent a good deal of his time, he was ordered to betake himself to Captain Taunton's quarters. In the stale and squalid state of a man just out of the Black hole, he had less fancy than ever for being seen by the Captain; but he was not so mad yet as to disobey orders, and consequently went up to the terrace overlooking the parade-ground, where the officers' quarters were; twisting and breaking in his hands, as he went along, a bit of the straw that had formed the decorative furniture of the Black hole.

"Come in!" cried the Captain, when he knocked with his knuckles at the door. Private Richard Doubledick pulled off his cap, took a stride forward, and felt very conscious that he stood in the light of the dark, bright eyes.

There was a silent pause. Private Richard Doubledick had put the straw in his mouth, and was gradually doubling it up into his windpipe and choking himself.

"Doubledick," said the Captain, "do you know where you are going to?"

"To the Devil, Sir?" faltered Doubledick.

"Yes," returned the Captain. "And very fast."

Private Richard Doubledick turned the straw of the Black hole in his mouth, and made a miserable salute of acquiescence.

"Doubledick," said the Captain, "since I entered his Majesty's service, a boy of seventeen, I have been pained to see many men of promise going that road; but I have never been so pained to see a man determined to make the shameful journey as I have been, ever since you joined the regiment, to see you."

Private Richard Doubledick began to find a film stealing over the floor at which he looked; also to find the legs of the Captain's breakfast-table turning crooked, as if he saw them through water.

"I am only a common soldier, Sir," said he. "It signifies very little what such a poor brute comes to."

"You are a man," returned the Captain, with grave indignation, "of education and superior advantages; and if you say that, meaning what you say, you have sunk lower than I had believed. How low that must be, I leave you to consider, knowing what I know of your disgrace, and seeing what I see."

"I hope to get shot soon, Sir," said Private Richard Doubledick;

"and then the regiment and the world together will be rid of me."

The legs of the table were becoming very crooked. Doubledick, looking up to steady his vision, met the eyes that had so strong an influence over him. He put his hand before his own eyes, and the breast of his disgrace-jacket swelled as if it would fly asunder.

"I would rather," said the young Captain, "see this in you, Doubledick, than I would see five thousand guineas counted out upon this table for a gift to my good mother. Have you a mother?"

"I am thankful to say she is dead, Sir."

"If your praises," returned the Captain, "were sounded from mouth to mouth through the whole regiment, through the whole army, through the whole country, you would wish she had lived to say, with pride and joy, 'He is my son!' "

"Spare me, Sir," said Doubledick. "She would never have heard any good of me. She would never have had any pride and joy in owning herself my mother. Love and compassion she might have had, and would have always had, I know; but not—— Spare me, Sir! I am a broken wretch, quite at your mercy!" And he turned his face to the wall, and stretched out his imploring hand.

"My friend——" began the Captain.

"God bless you, Sir!" sobbed Private Richard Doubledick.

"You are at the crisis of your fate. Hold your course unchanged a little longer, and you know what must happen. *I* know even better than you can imagine, that, after that has happened, you are lost. No man who could shed those tears could bear those marks."

"I fully believe it, Sir," in a low, shivering voice said Private Richard Doubledick.

"But a man in any station can do his duty," said the young Captain, "and, in doing it, can earn his own respect, even if his case should be so very unfortunate and so very rare that he can earn no other man's. A common soldier, poor brute though you called him just now, has this advantage in the stormy times we live in, that he always does his duty before a host of sympathising witnesses. Do you doubt that he may so do it as to be extolled through a whole regiment, through a whole army, through a whole country? Turn while you may yet retrieve the past, and try."

"I will! I ask for only one witness, Sir," cried Richard, with a bursting heart.

"I understand you. I will be a watchful and a faithful one."

I have heard from Private Richard Doubledick's own lips, that he dropped down upon his knee, kissed that officer's hand, arose, and went out of the light of the dark, bright eyes, an altered man.

In that year, one thousand seven hundred and ninety-nine, the French were in Egypt, in Italy, in Germany, where not? Napoleon Bonaparte had likewise begun to stir against us in India, and most men could read the signs of the great troubles that were coming on. In the very next year, when we formed an alliance with Austria against him, Captain Taunton's regiment was on service in India. And there was not a finer non-commissioned officer in it—no, nor in the whole line—than Corporal Richard Doubledick.

In eighteen hundred and one, the Indian army were on the coast of Egypt. Next year was the year of the proclamation of the short peace, and they were recalled. It had then become well known to thousands of men, that wherever Captain Taunton, with the dark, bright eyes, led, there, close to him, ever at his side, firm as a rock, true as the sun, and brave as Mars, would be certain to be found, while life beat in their hearts, that famous soldier, Sergeant Richard Doubledick.

Eighteen hundred and five, besides being the great year of Trafalgar, was a year of hard fighting in India. That year saw such wonders done by a Sergeant-Major, who cut his way single-handed through a solid mass of men, recovered the colours of his regiment, which had been seized from the hand of a poor boy shot through the heart, and rescued his wounded Captain, who was down, and in a very jungle of horses' hoofs and sabres—saw such wonders done, I say, by this brave Sergeant-Major, that he was specially made the bearer of the colours he had won; and Ensign Richard Doubledick had risen from the ranks.

Sorely cut up in every battle, but always reinforced by the bravest of men—for the fame of following the old colours, shot through and through, which Ensign Richard Doubledick had saved, inspired all breasts—this regiment fought its way through the Peninsular war, up to the investment of Badajos in eighteen hundred and twelve. Again and again it had been cheered through the British ranks until the tears had sprung into men's eyes at the mere hearing of the mighty British voice, so exultant in their valour; and there was not a drummer-boy but knew the legend, that wherever the two friends, Major Taunton, with the dark, bright eyes, and Ensign Richard Doubledick, who was devoted to him, were seen to go, there the boldest spirits in the English army became wild to follow.

One day, at Badajos—not in the great storming, but in repelling a hot sally of the besieged upon our men at work in the trenches, who had given way—the two officers found themselves hurrying forward, face to face, against a party of French infantry, who made a stand. There was an officer at their head, encouraging his men—a courageous, handsome, gallant officer of five-and-thirty, whom Doubledick saw hurriedly, almost momentarily, but saw well. He particularly noticed this officer waving his sword, and rallying his men with an eager and excited cry, when they fired in obedience to his gesture, and Major Taunton dropped.

It was over in ten minutes more, and Doubledick returned to the spot where he had laid the best friend man ever had on a coat spread upon the wet clay. Major Taunton's uniform was opened at the breast, and on his shirt were three little spots of blood.

"Dear Doubledick," said he, "I am dying."

"For the love of Heaven, no!" exclaimed the other, kneeling down beside him, and passing his arm round his neck to raise his head. "Taunton! My preserver, my guardian angel, my witness! Dearest, truest, kindest of human beings! Taunton! For God's sake!"

The bright, dark eyes—so very, very dark now, in the pale face—smiled upon him; and the hand he had kissed thirteen years ago laid itself fondly on his breast.

"Write to my mother. You will see Home again. Tell her how we became friends. It will comfort her, as it comforts me."

He spoke no more, but faintly signed for a moment towards his hair as it fluttered in the wind. The Ensign understood him. He smiled again when he saw that, and, gently turning his face over on the supporting arm as if for rest, died, with his hand upon the breast in which he had revived a soul.

No dry eye looked on Ensign Richard Doubledick that melancholy day. He buried his friend on the field, and became a lone, bereaved man. Beyond his duty he appeared to have but two remaining cares in life—one, to preserve the little packet of hair he was to give to Taunton's mother; the other, to encounter that French officer who had rallied the men under whose fire Taunton fell. A new legend now began to circulate among our troops; and it was, that when he and the French officer came face to face once more, there would be weeping in France.

The war went on—and through it went the exact picture of the French officer on the one side, and the bodily reality upon the other—until the Battle of Toulouse was fought. In the returns sent home appeared these words: "Severely wounded, but not dangerously, Lieutenant Richard Doubledick."

At Midsummer-time, in the year eighteen hundred and fourteen, Lieutenant Richard Doubledick, now a browned soldier, seven-and-thirty years of age, came home to England invalided. He brought the hair with him, near his heart. Many a French officer had he seen since that day; many a dreadful night, in searching with men and lanterns for his wounded, had he relieved French officers lying disabled; but the mental picture and the reality had never come together.

Though he was weak and suffered pain, he lost not an hour in getting down to Frome in Somersetshire, where Taunton's mother lived. In the sweet, compassionate words that naturally present themselves to the mind to-night, "he was the only son of his mother, and she was a widow."

It was a Sunday evening, and the lady sat at her quiet garden-window, reading the Bible; reading to herself, in a trembling voice, that very passage in it, as I have heard him tell. He heard the words: "Young man, I say unto thee, arise!"

He had to pass the window; and the bright, dark eyes of his debased time seemed to look at him. Her heart told her who he was; she came to the door quickly, and fell upon his neck.

"He saved me from ruin, made me a human creature, won me from infamy and shame. O, God for ever bless him! As He will, He will!"

"He will!" the lady answered. "I know he is in Heaven!" Then she piteously cried, "But, O, my darling boy, my darling boy!"

Never from the hour when Private Richard Doubledick enlisted at Chatham had the Private, Corporal, Sergeant, Sergeant-Major, Ensign, or Lieutenant breathed his right name, or the name of Mary Marshall, or a word of the story of his life, into any ear except his reclaimer's. That previous scene in his existence was closed. He had firmly resolved that his expiation should be to live unknown; to disturb no more the peace that had long grown over his old offences; to let it be revealed, when he was dead, that he had striven and suffered, and had never forgotten; and then, if they could forgive him and believe him—well, it would be time enough—time enough!

But that night, remembering the words he had cherished for two years, "Tell her how we became friends. It will comfort her, as it comforts me," he related everything. It gradually seemed to him as if in his maturity he had recovered a mother; it gradually seemed to her as if in her bereavement she had found a son. During his stay in England, the quiet garden into which he had slowly and painfully crept, a stranger, became the boundary of his home; when he was able to rejoin his regiment in the spring, he left the garden, thinking was this indeed the first time he had ever turned his face towards the old colours with a woman's blessings!

He followed them—so ragged, so scarred and pierced now, that they would scarcely hold together—to Quatre Bras and Ligny. He stood beside them, in an awful stillness of many men, shadowy through the mist and drizzle of a wet June forenoon, on the field of Waterloo. And down to that hour the picture in his mind of the French officer had never been compared with the reality.

The famous regiment was in action early in the battle, and received its first check in many an eventful year, when he was seen to fall. But it swept on to avenge him, and left behind it no such creature in the world of consciousness as Lieutenant Richard Doubledick.

Through pits of mire, and pools of rain; along deep ditches, once roads, that were pounded and ploughed to pieces by artillery, heavy waggons, tramp of men and horses, and the struggle of every wheeled thing that could carry wounded soldiers; jolted among the dying and the dead, so disfigured by blood and mud as to be hardly recognisable for humanity; undisturbed by the moaning of men and the shrieking of horses, which, newly taken from the peaceful pursuits of life, could not endure the sight of the stragglers lying by the wayside, never to resume their toilsome journey; dead, as to any sentient life that was in it, and yet alive—the form that had been Lieutenant Richard Doubledick, with whose praises England rang, was conveyed to Brussels. There it was tenderly laid down in hospital; and there it lay, week after week, through the long bright summer days, until the harvest, spared by war, had ripened and was gathered in.

Over and over again the sun rose and set upon the crowded city; over and over again the moonlight nights were quiet on the plains of Waterloo: and all the time was a blank to what had been Lieutenant Richard Doubledick. Rejoicing troops marched into Brussels, and marched out; brothers and fathers, sisters, mothers, and wives, came thronging thither, drew their lots of joy or agony, and departed; so many times a day the bells rang; so many times the shadows of the great buildings changed; so many lights sprang up at dusk; so many feet passed here and there upon the pavements; so many hours of sleep and cooler air of night succeeded: indifferent to all, a marble face lay on a bed, like the face of a recumbent statue on the tomb of Lieutenant Richard Doubledick.

Slowly labouring, at last, through a long heavy dream of confused time and place, presenting faint glimpses of army surgeons whom he knew, and of faces that had been familiar to his youth—dearest and kindest among them, Mary Marshall's, with a solicitude upon it more like reality than anything he could discern—Lieutenant Richard Doubledick came back to life. To the beautiful life of a fresh quiet room with a large window standing open; a balcony beyond, in which were moving leaves and sweet-smelling flowers; beyond, again, the clear sky, with the sun full in his sight, pouring its golden radiance on his bed.

It was so tranquil and so lovely that he thought he had passed into another world. And he said in a faint voice. "Taunton, are you near me?"

A face bent over him. Not his, his mother's.

"I came to nurse you. We have nursed you many weeks. You were moved here long ago. Do you remember nothing?"

"Nothing."

The lady kissed his cheek, and held his hand, soothing him.

"Where is the regiment? What has happened? Let me call you mother. What has happened, mother?"

"A great victory, dear. The war is over, and the regiment was the bravest in the field."

His eyes kindled, his lips trembled, he sobbed, and the tears ran down his face. He was very weak, too weak to move his hand.

"Was it dark just now?" he asked presently.

"No."

"It was only dark to me? Something passed away, like a black shadow. But as it went, and the sun—O the blessed sun, how beautiful it is!—touched my face, I thought I saw a light white cloud pass out at the door. Was there nothing that went out?"

She shook her head, and in a little while he fell asleep, she still holding his hand and soothing him.

From that time, he recovered. Slowly, for he had been desperately wounded in the head, and had been shot in the body, but making some little advance every day. When he had gained sufficient strength to converse as he lay in bed, he soon began to remark that Mrs. Taunton always brought him back to his own history. Then he recalled his preserver's dying words, and thought, "It comforts her."

One day he awoke out of a sleep, refreshed, and asked her to read to him. But the curtain of the bed, softening the light, which she always drew back when he awoke, that she might see him from her table at the bedside where she sat at work, was held undrawn; and a woman's voice spoke, which was not hers.

"Can you bear to see a stranger?" it said softly. "Will you like to see a stranger?"

"Stranger!" he repeated. The voice awoke old memories, before the days of Private Richard Doubledick.

"A stranger now, but not a stranger once," it said in tones that thrilled him. "Richard, dear Richard, lost through so many years, my name——"

He cried out her name, "Mary," and she held him in her arms, and his head lay on her bosom.

"I am not breaking a rash vow, Richard. These are not Mary Marshall's lips that speak. I have another name."

She was married.

"I have another name, Richard. Did you ever hear it?"

"Never!"

He looked into her face, so pensively beautiful, and wondered at the smile upon it through her tears.

"Think again, Richard. Are you sure you never heard my altered name?"

"Never!"

"Don't move your head to look at me, dear Richard. Let it lie here, while I tell my story. I loved a generous, noble man; loved him with my whole heart; loved him for years and years; loved him faithfully, devotedly; loved him with no hope of return; loved him, knowing nothing of his highest qualities—not even knowing that he was alive. He was a brave soldier. He was honoured and beloved by thousands of thousands, when the mother of his dear friend found me, and showed me that in all his triumphs he had never forgotten me. He was wounded in a great battle. He was brought, dying, here, into Brussels. I came to watch and tend him, as I would have joyfully gone, with such a purpose, to the dreariest ends of the earth. When he knew no one else, he knew me. When he suffered most, he bore his sufferings barely murmuring, content to rest his head where yours rests now. When he lay at the point of death, he married me, that he might call me Wife before he died. And the name, my dear love, that I took on that forgotten night——"

"I know it now!" he sobbed. "The shadowy remembrance strengthens. It is come back. I thank Heaven that my mind is quite restored! My Mary, kiss me; lull this weary head to rest, or I shall die of gratitude. His parting words were fulfilled. I see Home again!"

Well! They were happy. It was a long recovery, but they were happy through it all. The snow had melted on the ground, and the birds were singing in the leafless thickets of the early spring, when those three were first able to ride out together, and when people flocked about the open carriage to cheer and congratulate Captain Richard Doubledick.

But even then it became necessary for the Captain, instead of returning to England, to complete his recovery in the climate of Southern France. They found a spot upon the Rhone, within a ride of the old town of Avignon, and within view of its broken bridge, which was all they could desire; they lived there, together, six months; then returned to England. Mrs. Taunton, growing old after three years—though not so old as that her bright, dark eyes were dimmed—and remembering that her strength had been benefited by the change, resolved to go back for a year to those parts. So she went with a faithful servant, who had often carried her son in his arms; and she was to be rejoined and escorted home, at the year's end, by Captain Richard Doubledick.

She wrote regularly to her children (as she called them now,) and they to her. She went to the neighbourhood of Aix; and there, in her own chateau near the farmer's house she rented, she grew into intimacy with a family belonging to that part of France. The intimacy began in her often meeting among the vineyards a pretty child, a girl with a most compassionate heart, who was never tired of listening to the solitary English lady's stories of her poor son and the cruel wars. The family were as gentle as the child, and at length she came to know them so well that she accepted their invitation to pass the last month of her residence abroad under their roof. All this intelligence she wrote home, piecemeal as it came about, from time to time; and at last enclosed a polite note, from the head of the chateau, soliciting, on the occasion of his approaching mission to the neighbourhood, the honour of the company of cet homme si justement célèbre, Monsieur le Capitaine Richard Doubledick.

Captain Doubledick, now a hardy, handsome man in the full vigour of life, broader across the chest and shoulders than he had ever been before, dispatched a courteous reply, and followed it in person. Travelling through all that extent of country after three years of Peace, he blessed the better days on which the world had fallen. The corn was golden, not drenched in unnatural red; was bound in sheaves for food, not trodden underfoot by men in mortal fight. The smoke rose up from peaceful hearths, not blazing ruins. The carts were laden with the fair fruits of the earth, not with wounds and death. To him who had so often seen the terrible reverse, these things were beautiful indeed; and they brought him in a softened spirit to the old chateau near Aix upon a deep blue evening.

It was a large chateau of the genuine old ghostly kind, and round towers, and extinguishers, and a high leaden roof, and more windows than Aladdin's Palace. The lattice blinds were all thrown open after the heat of the day, and there were glimpses of rambling walls and corridors within. Then there were immense out-buildings fallen into partial decay, masses of dark trees, terrace-gardens, balustrades; tanks of water, too weak to play and too dirty to work; statues, weeds, and thickets of iron railing that seemed to have overgrown themselves like the shrubberies, and to have branched out in all manner of wild shapes. The entrance doors stood open, as doors often do in that country when the heat of the day is past; and the Captain saw no bell or knocker, and walked in.

He walked into a lofty stone hall, refreshingly cool and gloomy after the glare of a Southern day's travel. Extending along the four sides of this hall was a gallery, leading to suites of rooms; and it was lighted from the top. Still no bell was to be seen.

"Faith," said the Captain halting, ashamed of the clanking of his boots, "this is a ghostly beginning!"

He started back, and felt his face turn white. In the gallery, looking down at him, stood the French officer—the officer whose picture he had carried in his mind so long and so far. Compared with the original, at last—in every lineament how like it was!

He moved, and disappeared, and Captain Richard Doubledick heard his steps coming quickly down into the hall. He entered through an archway. There was a bright, sudden look upon his face, much such a look as it had worn in that fatal moment.

Monsieur le Capitaine Richard Doubledick? Enchanted to receive him! A thousand apologies! The servants were all out in the air. There was a little fête among them in the garden. In effect, it was the fête day of my daughter, the little cherished and protected of Madame Taunton.

He was so gracious and so frank that Monsieur le Capitaine Richard Doubledick could not withhold his hand. "It is the hand of a brave Englishman," said the French officer, retaining it while he spoke. "I could respect a brave Englishman, even as my foe, how much more as my friend! I also am a soldier."

"He has not remembered me, as I have remembered him; he did not take such note of my face, that day, as I took of his," thought Captain Richard Doubledick. "How shall I tell him?"

The French officer conducted his guest into a garden and presented him to his wife, an engaging and beautiful woman, sitting with Mrs. Taunton in a whimsical old-fashioned pavilion. His daughter, her fair young face beaming with joy, came running to embrace him; and there was a boy-baby to tumble down among the orange trees on the broad steps, in making for his father's legs. A multitude of children visitors were dancing to sprightly music; and all the servants and peasants about the chateau were dancing too. It was a scene of innocent happiness that might have been invented for the climax of the scenes of peace which had soothed the Captain's journey.

He looked on, greatly troubled in his mind, until a resounding bell rang, and the French officer begged to show him his rooms. They went upstairs into the gallery from which the officer had looked down; and Monsieur le Capitaine Richard Doubledick was cordially welcomed to a grand outer chamber, and a smaller one within, all clocks and draperies, and hearths, and brazen dogs, and tiles, and cool devices, and elegance, and vastness.

"You were at Waterloo," said the French officer.

"I was," said Captain Richard Doubledick. "And at Badajos."

Left alone with the sound of his own stern voice in his ears, he sat down to consider, What shall I do, and how shall I tell him? At that time, unhappily, many deplorable duels had been fought between English and French officers, arising out of the recent war; and these duels, and how to avoid this officer's hospitality, were the uppermost thoughts in Captain Richard Doubledick's mind.

He was thinking, and letting the time run out in which he should have dressed for dinner, when Mrs. Taunton spoke to him outside the door, asking if he could give her the letter he had brought from Mary. "His mother, above all," the Captain thought. "How shall I tell *her*?"

"You will form a friendship with your host, I hope," said Mrs. Taunton, whom he hurriedly admitted, "that will last for life. He is so true-hearted and so generous, Richard, that you can hardly fail to esteem one another. If He had been spared—" she kissed (not without tears) the locket in which she wore his hair—"he would have appreciated him with his own magnanimity, and would have been truly happy that the evil days were past which made such a man his enemy."

She left the room; and the Captain walked, first to one window, whence he could see the dancing in the garden, then to another window, whence he could see the smiling prospect and the peaceful vineyards.

"Spirit of my departed friend," said he, "is it through thee these better thoughts are rising in my mind? Is it thou who hast shown me, all the way I have been drawn to meet this man, the blessings of the altered time? Is it thou who hast sent thy stricken mother to me, to stay my angry hand? Is it from thee the whisper comes, that this man did his duty as thou didst—and as I did, through thy guidance, which has wholly saved me here on earth—and that he did no more?"

He sat down, with his head buried in his hands, and, when he rose up, made the second strong resolution of his life—that neither to the French officer, nor to the mother of his departed friend, nor to any soul, while either of the two was living, would he breathe what only he knew. And when he touched that French officer's glass with his own, that day at dinner, he secretly forgave him in the name of the Divine Forgiver of injuries.

Here I ended my story as the first Poor Traveller. But, if I had told it now, I could have added that the time has since come when the son of Major Richard Doubledick, and the son of that French officer, friends as their fathers were before them, fought side by side in one cause, with their respective nations, like long-divided brothers whom the better times have brought together, fast united.

III

The Road

My story being finished, and the Wassail too, we broke up as the Cathedral bell struck Twelve. I did not take leave of my travellers that night; for it had come into my head to reappear, in conjunction with some hot coffee, at seven in the morning.

As I passed along the High-street, I heard the Waits at a distance, and struck off to find them. They were playing near one of the old gates of the City, at the corner of a wonderfully quaint row of red-brick tenements, which the clarionet obligingly informed me were inhabited by the Minor-Canons. They had odd little porches over the doors, like sounding-boards over old pulpits; and I thought I should like to see one of the Minor-Canons come out upon his top step, and favour us with a little Christmas discourse about the poor scholars of Rochester; taking for his text the words of his Master relative to the devouring of Widows' houses.

The clarionet was so communicative, and my inclinations were (as they generally are) of so vagabond a tendency, that I accompanied the Waits across an open green called the Vines, and as-

"And holding up a lantern, for a moment stood gazing heroically in his face"

MERRY CHRISTMAS

Story on page 397

sisted—in the French sense—at the performance of two waltzes, two polkas, and three Irish melodies, before I thought of my inn any more. However, I returned to it then, and found a fiddle in the kitchen, and Ben, the wall-eyed young man, and two chambermaids, circling round the great deal table with the utmost animation.

I had a very bad night. It cannot have been owing to the turkey or the beef—and the Wassail is out of the question—but in every endeavour that I made to get to sleep I failed most dismally. I was never asleep; and in whatsoever unreasonable direction my mind rambled, the effigy of Master Richard Watts perpetually embarrassed it.

In a word, I only got out of the Worshipful Master Richard Watts's way by getting out of bed in the dark at six o'clock, and tumbling, as my custom is, into all the cold water that could be accumulated for the purpose. The outer air was dull and cold enough in the street, when I came down there; and the one candle in our supper-room at Watts's Charity looked as pale in the burning as if it had had a bad night too. But my Travellers had all slept soundly, and they took to the hot coffee, and the piles of bread-and-butter, which Ben had arranged like deals in a timber-yard, as kindly as I could desire.

While it was yet scarcely daylight, we all came out into the street together, and there shook hands. The widow took the little sailor towards Chatham, where he was to find a steamboat for Sheerness; the lawyer, with an extremely knowing look, went his own way, without committing himself by announcing his intentions; two more struck off by the cathedral and old castle for Maidstone; and the book-pedlar accompanied me over the bridge. As for me, I was going to walk by Cobham Woods, as far upon my way to London as I fancied.

When I came to the stile and footpath by which I was to diverge from the main road, I bade farewell to my last remaining Poor Traveller, and pursued my way alone. And now the mists began to rise in the most beautiful manner, and the sun to shine; and as I went on through the bracing air, seeing the hoar-frost sparkle everywhere, I felt as if all Nature shared in the joy of the great Birthday.

Going through the woods, the softness of my tread upon the mossy ground and among the brown leaves enhanced the Christmas sacredness by which I felt surrounded. As the whitened stems environed me, I thought how the Founder of the time had never raised his benignant hand, save to bless and heal, except in the case of one unconscious tree. By Cobham Hall, I came to the village, and the churchyard where the dead had been quietly buried, "in the sure and certain hope" which Christmas-time inspired. What children could I see at play, and not be loving of, recalling who had loved them! No garden that I passed was out of unison with the day, for I remembered that the tomb was in a garden, and that "she, supposing him to be the gardener," had said, "Sir, if thou have borne him hence, tell me where thou hast laid him, and I will take him away." In time, the distant river with the ships came full in view, and with it pictures of the poor fishermen, mending their nets, who arose and followed him—of the teaching of the people from a ship pushed off a little way from shore, by reason of the multitude—of a majestic figure walking on the water, in the loneliness of night. My very shadow on the ground was eloquent of Christmas; for did not the people lay their sick where the mere shadows of the men who had heard and seen him might fall as they passed along?

Thus Christmas begirt me, far and near, until I had come to Blackheath, and had walked down the long vista of gnarled old trees in Greenwich Park, and was being steam-rattled through the mists now closing in once more, towards the lights of London. Brightly they shone, but not so brightly as my own fire, and the brighter faces around it, when we came together to celebrate the day. And there I told of worthy Master Richard Watts, and of my supper with the Six Poor Travellers who were neither Rogues nor Proctors, and from that hour to this I have never seen one of them again.

A Stranger Knocked

JOSEPH SHEARING

NO ONE knew who had admitted the old man. He was suddenly there, in the chimney corner, warming his hands before the glow of the Yule log. The guests were a little weary with singing and laughing. They had fallen on a silence disturbed only by the chatter of the children who sat on the floor playing with tinsel ornaments.

The Yule wreath hung overhead, stuck with apples, holly and candles. Everyone dreamed differently as they looked at it; some were too drowsy to dream at all.

One asked his neighbour: "Who is the old man?"

Another was curious enough to ask this question of the master of the house. He sent for the porter, who knew nothing. But then, the gates had stood wide all day; who could be refused admission during the Christmas Festival? The master of the house agreed, adding, "Perhaps he has come with one of the children, there are so many, one invites another——"

It was a large house, justly famous for its hospitality. For weeks the cooks had been baking biscuits, cakes and sweetmeats. The air was rich with the scent of spices, from open fires, symbolic of the offerings of the Magi.

The musicians had just left the upper gallery. There were no lights save the candles on the Yule wreath, whose flames tapered upwards into the darkness of the large room. The brocade curtains had not been drawn across the long oriel windows. Without could be seen the unceasing snow flakes.

The old man was handsome, upright and stately. Yet he continued to warm his hands as if he had come a long way, on a far cold journey.

The master of the house approached him, offering him a cup of wine, as if, now he had perceived him, he welcomed him.

The old man declined, with a courteous inclination of his massive head.

Everyone was now looking at him, even the children who played on the floor.

"I like to spend Christmas in company," he said in a voice touched with a strange, perhaps a foreign, accent. He glanced round the circle of faces. "Do you think of Christmas as merely a festival?" he asked.

No one answered the direct question.

"The twelve days of Christmas," murmured a young girl, "it is a merry holiday."

"Ah," exclaimed the old man looking at her sharply. "Those pretty flowers you wear; it was I who brought them to England."

The girl put her hands to her wreath as if she feared it would dissolve, like fairy blooms, and the company, smiling, conceded the old man's whim, to describe himself as a magician.

But he continued quietly: "I am a botanist. Years ago, before you were born, my dear young lady, I brought some roots of that little blossom from Asia, and now it grows at Christmas in your stone houses."

"You have earned your place at the fireside for that alone," said the master of the house, smiling.

"No," replied the old man. "I have my place out of charity."

They all protested, languidly. He was harmless, perhaps distinguished. The master of the house thought: "Perhaps it was a stupid indiscretion not to have invited him."

"I must explain myself. I am a professor of natural history. I have outlived all my friends, and I never married. Until last

Christmas I found, however, company. This year I was obliged to come among strangers."

"You are truly welcome," cried the master of the house, glancing at his wife. And she half rose from her sofa and repeated, "You are truly welcome, but excuse me, sir, I do not remember seeing you in these parts."

"I live the other side of the forest," said the professor, "and I seldom go abroad. I amuse myself with writing, or with going over my collections. I have travelled, of course, over the whole world."

"Some old fellow," whispered a youth, "in his second childhood, and already forgotten by everyone."

Yet the company seemed to circle round him, as if he were the person everyone had come to see. The snowflakes fell softly on the diamond panes of the window; the night showed purple beyond the warm lit room.

The small children fell asleep on their mother's laps, and the older children stared at the professor of natural history.

His clothes were very old-fashioned, but neat and fresh. The Yule log was sinking into fiery particles; it had burnt for three days. The room was so hot that the master of the house did not order any more wood to be piled on the hearth. The steady glow filled the room, making warm shadows behind the group of people, glinting in glasses and decanters, shining in brown and gold locks and on the folds of silk and satin gowns.

They all wished that the old naturalist would go; he made them and their merrymaking seem foolish.

"Yesterday," he said, "I was out alone, walking beyond the forest; all seemed dark, dead, sombre, with the snow coming on, and one solitary jay screaming, when I found some goldilocks moss, just at my feet. And it reminded me——"

"Ay, tell us a tale!" cried a boy looking up from a castle he was building of toy bricks.

"—how I nearly became a murderer on Christmas Day," added the old man.

Everyone was now silent. The mimic tower fell over. Time

seemed to glide away swiftly as if all Christmas sports were now over. The mistress of the house rose quietly and drew the curtains over the storm. The wind had risen and a certain shudder was felt even in this serene room. The garlands of mistletoe, ivy and holly shivered in their places.

"The weather was like this," said the old man. "A blustering storm rising, everything frozen, and, as I recall, a giant yew cast down in the churchyard. You know a fruit tree can be overthrown and then propped up, but a yew tree—never. It dies at once."

"Where was the place and when was the time?" asked the master of the house.

"Far, far from here" was the reply, "on the wild coast of Wales. And in time, I do not know how long; I have ceased to count the years."

He settled himself to his tale, that he gave as a gift or offering, and as such they took it, while the gale increased and scattered the sparks on the hearth and struggled at the firmly bolted door.

The house was believed to be haunted, though no one spoke of that. But there were those in the group gathered round the fire who thought of this now, of invisible beings who might be peering over their shoulders or floating in the dark air above the circle of candles.

"I was coming home," said the professor of natural history, "after several years of wandering. I had been in China and Tibet. There were some curiosities I was resolved to have."

"You must," said the master of the house, "have met with many adventures."

"By land and sea. One can become obsessed, of course, by such a quest. I fell ill. I lost my basket of specimens. I was robbed."

"All for a few flowers!" murmured the girl with the wreath. "And we have enough at home——"

"Who is ever content with what he has at home? Besides, I was not searching for new ornaments, but for medicinal plants—some gallant and universal balm." He changed his tone abruptly, and added in a firm voice that seemed that of a much younger man, "But I always corresponded with Isabelle Blount."

"A love story," said the mistress of the house with a little sigh. Her own had been a very happy one but she was conscious of the passing of the years.

"We were betrothed." The old man used the formal word with a flourish. "I had money and a fine house, and so had her brother; as children we played together. It was early understood between us that we were to be married as soon as my wanderings were over——"

"Ah, you were the tyrant and set the choice," said one of the ladies thoughtfully.

"Not at all—she was willing to wait. Even wishful to prolong her childhood. At first there were her parents to be considered, then her brother. It was something we looked forward to—our marriage—as a golden certainty."

"You must have been a sober pair," said the master of the house.

"No," said the old man distinctly, "we were full of zest and enthusiasm. I wished to fulfil my destiny as I was pleased to name it. Isabelle learned every accomplishment. Ours was to be a planned, a leisured happiness. She shared my interests. The stone house built for her was filled by the treasures I had brought home. Every month she wrote me accounts of our native flowers—even from the first of the year, the dark red nettle, the grass groundsell, the daisy—all manner of little conceits and fancies we shared. She would write to me of the prickly furze, glazed with the hoar frost, and I of a valley filled with azaleas the colours of corals and shells."

"And did you write of nothing else?" asked one of the listeners.

"We wrote of everything else," replied the old man with dignity. "Whatever peril or discomfort I might be in, I kept calm by the remembrance of Isabelle Blount. We intended to settle in our Welsh home and to live——"

"Happily ever after," put in the boy with the bricks that he had now piled into the semblance of a palace.

"Why not?" asked the old man patiently. "There was no flaw in our scheme. I encountered much weariness. I have rested, exhausted, by an abandoned gilt pagoda in the jungle to think of

Isabelle wandering among my native rocks to pick the sea mallow."

"Very poetic, sir, but I think the lady was left too much alone."

The old man looked coolly at the speaker, a brisk youth helping himself to wine.

"Isabelle was never alone. She had her family, her duties. I was successful and not without honour. I received awards, gold and silver medals. I lectured to distinguished audiences. She had reason to be proud of me, as my reputation settled into a steady brilliance."

"Come, sir!" cried the young man finishing his wine. "This was to be a murderer's story."

The old man ignored this. He took a pair of spectacles from his forehead, polished them and set them on his nose.

"It was a settled frost when I said good-bye to her. We walked along the stream; the sedges sparkled with ice; the night before had been clear blue weather, with a missel thrush singing. Now the wind parted her hair as she laid her hand in mine; mosses, such as I saw today, glowed on the twisted trunks of the oak trees. We renewed our vows. One year more—and I should be free."

"It was a pretty picture," said the mistress of the house.

And in truth the old man had that much art, that he could make them all, idle as they were, see the young lovers by the wintry stream.

"She went with me over my home, suggesting changes here and there, and said that if she were not mistress there by next Christmas, she would be by the Christmas after. She chose the room that should be hers, and I at once planned how I would see that it was always filled by the choicest plants I brought from the East. A kingfisher was startled from our path as we parted by the stream, halfway between her house and mine. I took that blue-winged flash to be an augury.

"I went to China and I found the plant for which I was searching."

"Tell us what it was," asked several idle voices.

"It has remained nameless and useless," the old man replied.

"Because—cannot you have guessed? The name it should have had was *her* name, and the benefits it should have conferred on mankind should have seemed to come from her——"

"Do you want to tell this story?" asked the mistress of the house gently. "Shall we not rather sing a hymn or a carol before we go in to dinner?"

"It is a tale that must be told," insisted the old man. He folded his hands in the bosom of his coat, as if they were sufficiently warmed, or perhaps chilled beyond any hope of warmth.

The company was lulled; a servant appeared in the doorway with candles but was waved aside by the master of the house.

The glow of the Yule log was sufficient for the telling of this tale.

"I was captured by some imperious mandarins who supposed I had gazed too long at some rarities in their gardens. They enclosed me in a tower. From my window I could see some misty peaks, broken by dark hollows that made me long to set out on my explorations again.

"I was well fed, and, I suppose, discovered to be harmless, for after some months I was released. And not without some words of wisdom as to limiting my curiosity. And not without some reward for my patience under punishment. The mandarins had been through my specimens and declared that I had loaded myself up with trim weeds of no consequence. The package that they put into my hand as they set me on my way contained the exquisite plant of almost magical properties that I intended to name after my Isabelle."

Each of the company sought to remember what this flower might be, but their thoughts were sluggish.

The candles flickered out on the Yule wreath where the red apples bobbed, and only the vast glow from the hearth lit the room.

The master of the house begged the old man to take a more comfortable chair, but he had settled in his chimney corner and continued his tale.

"My precious plants, like so many dried anatomies, were placed in a sandalwood box, wrapped in mosses, and I set out for England.

"There were several delays in my journey. I cannot even call them to mind. Indeed, from the moment I left the hands of my considerate captors, my adventures took on a dream-like quality. I seemed to meet with some very queer companions and to put up at some very odd places——"

"Do tell us!" cried one of the children, suddenly awaking.

The old man frowned.

"It was a long way and I lost count of time; there was winter, but no snow fell. I lost my servant; he was bribed away, I think, by a wealthy nabob, but of that I cannot be sure. Somehow there was always money in my pocket. I found myself in London the day before Christmas Eve.

"I had my treasured plants with me safely and as I looked on the magnificent array of jewels, laces, flowers and other costly gifts in the merchants' displays, I was proud because I had something much rarer than those to offer my Isabelle.

"Owing to my rapid moving about I had not heard from her for several weeks. The greater surprise and delight should therefore mark our meeting. This time it would be never to part again.

"I stayed at a hotel in a street of the Strand where I was not known, and reposed myself after my fatigues and troubles. Snow fell in the evening, but the morning shone clearly over the Thames, and the people hurried up and down with their parcels, wreaths of holly and clusters of mistletoe.

"Imagination made my dried plants bloom. My musty chamber was filled with the scent of a thousand silver stars. This peculiar flower was said by the Chinese to be the flower of the dead that ghosts came to smell at. For the living it has no perfume. Think of me then, as alone in London, secure in this obscure hotel, with the great treasure in my possession, the wonderful plant that should bear the name of my beloved and bring me the final glory of my already honoured career."

As he spoke these words the old man held up his head with an almost infernal pride and his frame, still powerful in outline, trembled with fatigue and passion. He seemed to observe the impression he made on his listeners and that they shrank a little from him.

"What is man," he demanded, "but a ruined archangel? I certainly felt that I was possessed of supernatural powers, having in that humble box I kept under lock and key, the powers of life and death." Lowering his voice he added in a confidential tone that yet carried to every corner of the room, "But when I came to consult my calendar, I found I was out of my calculations. Most abominably deceived! Where had I lost the time?"

"Can one lose time?" asked the master of the house thoughtfully.

"I had lost two years. In prison, in travel, in hallucinations. I was that much out of my reckoning."

"We never have as much time as we hope," said the master of the house.

"But who realises that?" asked his wife with a sad tenderness.

"None of us," put in the old man. "We play with delusions all the time."

One of his listeners, secure in youth and happiness, protested with a smile. He was sure of himself, and the girl beside him and their future.

Ignoring this, the old man continued, with an increasing eagerness:

"Very few people make the miscalculations I did—I had lost two years——"

"Still, in so long a life——" murmured one of the youths pertly.

The professor of natural history took up the challenge.

"I should not miss them you think? But they were those particular years, you see, just those during which Isabelle was waiting for me."

"Her letters?" asked the master of the house. "There must have been some confusion there."

They all felt a kindness for this Isabelle, as if they would have liked to have asked her to join the circle, to draw up to the fire, and tell her side of the tale of all the years when she was waiting in a lonely home for a man greedy for wealth and honour.

"Yes, her letters," agreed the old man slowly. "I told you there was a gap when I did not receive any at all. Then she had a habit of not putting dates—only Monday or Tuesday. Some must have been very much delayed; some I never got at all."

He put aside this subject with impatience.

"I was talking of my stay in London. No one thought of anything but Christmas. The manager of the hotel put a ticket into my hand and told me a ball was being held in the house at the end of the street. I had a whim to go to this. Of course there were many people in London who would have been glad to receive me. But I felt shy. Perhaps I was changed. I did not know how to adjust myself to those lost years. I sent a letter to Isabelle, saying I would be with her on Christmas Day——"

"Did it not occur to you that *she* might be surprised, perhaps dismayed by your long disappearances?" asked the master of the house.

"Sir, it did not. I thought I had explained that we loved one another."

"Oh," cried a lady who had been half asleep, "if you think that covers everything!"

"I thought so then." He gave a stiff bow. "I hope you think so now." With a brusque glance at his host he added, "Perhaps you find my tale tedious?"

But no, everyone wanted him to continue. The story was like a spell to hold them together, an excuse rather for not moving, for not having the candles in, for not calling for wraps and going home. The horses were warm in the stables, the coachmen in the servants' hall; it seemed a pity to break up the party.

So thought the visitors, while the host and his wife, who were childless, had no wish to be left alone in the house that was supposed to be haunted. If need be, everyone could be accommodated for the night. So the old man was encouraged to tell them of the ball he had attended, during the festival, so many years before.

"You can," he said, "imagine my feeling, filled for so many years with Isabelle, rare plants, and the various incidents of my curious journeys. Who, I asked myself, were all these people? The women had hot-house flowers, quite dead, pinned with diamonds to their rich falls of laces; some of their little slippers were quite worn out; as they rested, I saw the fine satin rubbed through at the toes. The room had become overheated and someone had pulled back the curtains to let in the icy light of the dawn. The sheen from the river was reflected in the mirrors, and in the drops from the candelabra, where the last candles were guttering. The musicians drooped in their places, but continued to scrape out waltzes, when they began on carols as a reminder that the dance was at an end. I made my escape. No one had noticed me. What humbug this festival is! I reflected. Of course I was soon proved wrong, and that is why I am telling you this story.

"I secretly confounded all such gaiety where I had not been made welcome, and dwelt with pleasure on the self-contained lives that I and Isabelle would lead with our exclusive interests.

"It was late on Christmas Eve when I arrived at my house. I had not remembered that it was in such a lonely situation. It had taken the contents of my wallet to induce a coachman to take me from the railway station.

"There was no sign of welcome, but that was my own fault; I had sent no letters in advance. Still I had always pictured the house as ready and waiting for my return. Surely they could have, at least, kept a light in the hall. The hackney soon departed, leaving me and my simple baggage on the doorstep. I had to ring several times before a person unknown to me, with a tallow dip in his hand, cautiously responded to my bell ringing. He explained that he was the caretaker, I, that I was the master of the house.

"Dubiously, he at length admitted me. What he had to say was trivial, but exasperating. My heirs-at-law, distant cousins whom I disliked, were claiming my property. My lawyers were playing a delaying game and had searched for me all over the world.

"When it came to it, I had no recollection of having written to them for years. There was that unpleasant lapse of time, you see. My excellent steward, my good servants had all left. My lawyers would not be at their expense. As I passed from one room to another, partly dismantled, partly neglected, followed by my grim unwilling guide, I became angry, mainly with myself. Why had I not made a will, leaving everything to Isabelle? For the first time in my life, I admitted that I was an eccentric fellow and managed my affairs in a peculiar way.

"Still, that was all over now. The house and the estate would soon be set to rights, and I should become a very decent member of the county.

"My familiarity with the house had convinced the caretaker that I knew the place; the sight of my name on some foreign passports and letters satisfied him that I was indeed the owner. Or so he pretended, for I soon discovered that he had a reason for this complacence. Some plan had fallen through at the last moment whereby he had this charge alone, on Christmas Eve; high wage and some sense of duty had obliged him to keep trust. Now he saw his chance. He lived near—near to him who knew all the woodland paths—and as I had returned to claim my property, could I not excuse his service?

"I at once granted this favour; before the man had spoken, I had resolved to exchange my forlorn dwelling for that of Isabelle and her brother. There, there would be warmth and light and probably merriment, for they must have had my letter.

"So I gladly let the man go, and as he was eagerly lighting his storm lantern, I mentioned, for the pleasure of hearing it, the name of my beloved. The nature of our attachment had been kept secret, but I suppose there might have been some talk. My caretaker looked at me a little oddly, and told me that Isabelle had been married, for two years or more.

"I detained him, grasping his greatcoat with a strength that seemed other than my own.

"But, though utterly alarmed by my demeanour, he had little more to tell me. The brother was dead, the man she had married of a station below her own. They were living in her old home.

"On hearing this, I at once knew what to do. Disguising my fury, I sent the caretaker off with a gold piece and good wishes.

"The night was too wild for me to remain at the open door, but drawing aside the slightly tattered curtains of an upper window, I watched the light of the storm lantern disappear into the bare woods.

"Thus it came that I was alone in my deserted home on Christmas Eve, determined on murder, and lit only by a rush light.

"I had at once decided to kill Isabelle's husband."

"Being forsaken of God and man," said the mistress of the house, glancing about to see if the children were all asleep. And so they were, save those who had crept away, and whose distant laughter could be faintly heard.

"Yes," responded the old man vigorously. "I believe I was thus forsaken. Consider how many curious circumstances had led to my being there, alone, at that precise hour, with that precise news. I was beyond reason. I merely recalled to mind several incidents of my travels that would be considered barbarous in England. I found I had become hardened to ideas of cruelty and violence. I was no longer the civilised creature I had been when I left Cambridge University. It seemed obvious that my supplanter was not fit to live, and that it was I who must remove him from the earth. I went into one of the kitchens, the place most likely to be furnished with what I needed. And there, indeed, I found food and wine and a long, thin knife, such as cooks use for the slicing of meat.

"It had recently been in use and was well sharpened. I regarded it as put directly into my hand. My plan was simple. I would call on this faithless couple, and keep this weapon hidden in my cloak. Then I would kill him, in front of her. I had learned how such deeds were done. Indeed, although I had always acted in self-defence, I was no novice in the use of steel.

"There was an oil lamp in the kitchen. I lit that, as the tallow candle was sputtering out and took it up to the great library I knew so well, and where some of my happiest hours had been passed.

"I was disgusted to see that the caretaker had used this noble apartment as a sleeping place, for, in an alcove where I had kept an elegant Etruscan vase, a rude bed, with heavy blankets, had been rigged up.

"I dropped the green moiré curtain, still in place though frayed, across the unsightly couch, and sat down at my familiar desk. I wished to be entirely cool, but really there was very little to think about. My victims would, of course, admit me joyfully or with pretence of joy, and in a matter of moments I should have my revenge. I recalled my letter, addressed to Isabelle in her maiden name and in endearing terms. Would that put them to an embarrassment? I doubted it. I doubted much, even if I had written that letter. That lapse of time—which would be argued in their defence—tormented me. I ran into the hall, half fearing I should find it empty, save for the mouldering furniture. But there was my modest luggage and the sandalwood box. What was I to do with my precious plants? I took the box into the library and set it on the desk. Brooding over it, I imagined the dry anatomies it contained, spreading into a million stars or florets, like the glittering sparkles, like the diamonds worn by the tired dancers, like the reflection in the mirrors in the riverside ballroom. Was there not a virtue in this plant that made it almost a universal panacea?

"But now that I had lost Isabelle, I cared nothing for humanity.

"At one time I had thought that the heavenly powers had directed me in my perils and labours; now I was about to tear open the box and destroy the contents, when a knock sounded through the house.

"Already guilty in intention, I started fearfully. But I soon reassured myself. This could be no other than the stupid caretaker, who had lost his way in the wood, or forgotten something. I should soon be rid of him. So I went smoothly to the door, and there was an old fellow, a tramp or vagabond, hardly to be seen in the starlight or the gleam of the lamp I held.

" 'It is Christmas Eve,' he said. 'Can you give me a lodging?'

"I thought that I heard church bells in the distance, and this rather confounded me. As I hesitated, the old fellow had slipped into the hall. He looked so miserable that I said—what could the offer cost me?—'You may stay here with what hospitality you can find. As for me, I have an errand, I must abroad——'

" 'First show me the bed that in your great kindness you offer,' said he with a beautiful courtesy.

"I led the way to the library. I thought it odd that a stranger knocked at such an hour.

"I was a little jostled in my thoughts. Setting the lamp on the desk, I regarded him closely. Not only was he poor, dejected and old, but he seemed maimed as if beneath his ragged garments he was crushed or twisted. He shuffled along with difficulty to the bed in the alcove that I exposed by lifting the curtain. As he crept painfully under the coverlets, I said, 'I shall go down to the kitchen and heat you some wine.'

" 'Can your errand wait, then?' he asked softly.

" 'As long as that,' I replied.

"I took the lamp, leaving him in darkness, blew up the charcoal in the grate, heated the wine, and took it upstairs with some biscuits I found.

"As soon as the lamp was replaced on the desk, I glanced at the alcove. The curtain still hung in place. I forced myself to think of Isabelle and what I intended to do. 'How vexing,' I thought, 'that the coming of this stranger should have diverted me, for one single instant, from what I had planned so instantly and so positively.'

" 'Yes, I am right,' I declared aloud. 'I have been forsaken and betrayed.'

" 'Peace on earth to men of good will,' said my visitor.

" 'I thank you,' I replied, and I was surprised that there was anyone to give me this ancient greeting.

" 'Come and fetch your wine—I'll not pamper you,' I said roughly, in order to harden myself against him. I began searching for the knife, but I could not find it. Compelled to be quite composed, I sat down, took my head in my hands and tried to think it all out.

"First, I must find the knife. Perhaps I had left it in the kitchen. How foolish to allow myself to be disturbed by the fact that a stranger knocked.

"Perhaps it would be best to destroy the plants first. I could do that with my bare hands.

"I opened the sandalwood box.

"How often I had gloated over those dry twig-like objects and the benefits to humanity they contained. How often I had dwelt on Isabelle's rapture when she should bestow her name on the marvellous plant!

"Now hatred should destroy what love had found.

"I voiced that sentiment to myself, thinking how fine it sounded and seized the rootlets in their moss wrappings. They began to twist and swell in my grasp, as if they had been so many snakes.

"I dropped them in a rage and heard myself crying out: 'This is your doing!'

"There was no answer from the alcove, now lapped in shadow.

"Meanwhile the plants were becoming unmanageable. They twisted out of my hands, and flew upwards like rockets, into a shower of stars. Or so I thought—or so I thought! I retreated hastily from the desk, and pulled aside the curtain of the alcove. And there, calmly watching me, was the most beautiful, beautiful being——"

The old man shaded his eyes and whispered to himself: "Such wings!"

"You think it was a dream?" asked the master of the house kindly.

The old man smiled to himself and shook his head.

"It was morning. I put my sandalwood box under my arm. It was Christmas morning, and I called on my old friend with a present. She was pleased to see me, for she had thought me dead long ago. She accepted the plants, now dry again in their dry mosses—and with them some hope, for her husband was dying of a lung disease.

"The chemists compounded the roots and they cured my rival. I forgot that I had ever hated either of them; we always used to spend Christmas Day together."

"But who reposed in your alcove?" asked the master of the house. "It is he to whom you owe everything."

"I never saw him again," said the old man. "He might visit you any time. Especially I think when you feel most forsaken."

"He also was a dream," said one of the youths.

"No, sir, for look what I found on that humble pillow."

He pulled out his watch chain and they gathered round to see a feather that seemed to be of the finest gold, but delicate beyond all mortal workmanship.

Twilight of the Wise

JAMES HILTON

WE WERE talking, on Christmas night, about other Christmas nights. I had said that twenty years ago I was in the trenches somewhere in France. "And I," Middleton countered, "was somewhere in the Bavarian Alps."

It seemed a queer place for an Englishman to have been during the war years, until he explained, with a smile: "I was escaping. We managed it, you know—thanks to luck and Manny Stewart's German."

I guessed then that this fellow Middleton had deliberately stayed up to talk after the others had gone to bed; he knew I had known Manny from the conversation at dinner. I had quoted one of Manny's last poems, and we had all argued about what it probably meant—all of us, that is, except Middleton, who didn't seem the kind of person to argue much about a poem, anyway.

"You must have known him well?" I suggested.

"Not exactly. But it came as a personal loss when I read of his death last year, and again to-night when you quoted that poem. I suppose an experience of the kind he and I had, even if it only lasts a few days, counts for more than years of just 'knowing' somebody."

"Ordinarily, of course, Manny and I wouldn't have had much in common—even at the prison-camp he'd been with us at least a month before I exchanged more than a few words with him. He had his own friends—chaps interested in art and books and all that. Then one day he came up to me when I was alone and said: 'Is it true you nearly got away once?' It *was* true, and I told him all about it, how I'd been within a mile of the Dutch frontier when things went wrong, all because I didn't know that *Eisenstange* means a sort of iron rod. I was hiding in a railway wagon full of them . . . but that's another story. Manny laughed when I told it him. 'My German's pretty good,' he said. 'How would you like to have another try with me?' I looked at him and I knew damn well I'd like it, and he knew I knew, too—it was a sort of sudden contact between us that didn't have to be argued about."

"Yes," I said. "He made a good many of those contacts."

"So we fixed it right away, and began to make plans. Manny thought we ought to try an escape in midwinter, because of the long nights; and he had an idea that the third week of December might be lucky for us, because even in war-time Germany the Christmas spirit had its manifestations—feasting and jollification and a general slackening of vigilance. The food shortage wasn't too bad in our part of Bavaria, and the people were a comfortable lot compared with the Prussians—as I knew myself from experience. And then, too, he thought we might try to get across the mountains instead of keeping to lowland routes—the idea, you see, being to do just what nobody would expect. Actually, we could be among the mountains within a couple of hours of leaving camp—if we dared to risk it. Do you know the Bavarian Alps? I didn't, and neither did Manny, but we had a map, and we both found we'd had plenty of pre-war climbing experience in Switzerland. It was just a matter of nerve, endurance, food-supply, and luck with the weather. Well, we thought we had the first two, and we prayed for the others. We began to hide food till we had a store; then we collected warm clothing and white coats made of bed-linen, so that we shouldn't be spotted against a snow background. Then we had to make plans for the actual escape, but I needn't tell you about these, partly because they weren't very different from those of other escapes I've read of, and also because the get-away was pretty easy. We were six thousand feet above the camp when dawn broke. We had to put on dark glasses because of the snow dazzle, and we ate chocolate and chaffed each other and stared down at the camp below—just a few littered roofs amongst the pine forests.

"Of course, by that time the hue and cry must surely have been raised, but it didn't worry us much. You can't chase two men over high alps in midwinter, and *in* practice you don't consider it—because you don't believe the two men would ever be such fools. *We* were, though, and we were quite happy about it. I don't believe I've ever had a feeling of such almighty ecstasy as that morning as we climbed farther and higher up the snow-slopes till we reached the steep rocks.

"The day was glorious, and we lay out in the sun during the afternoon and slept, knowing that it would be bitterly cold at night, and that we should have to keep moving all the time. We didn't talk very much, except that Manny tried to brush up my German. We climbed an icy ridge, and descended the other side. There was no trace after that of any inhabited world—the mountains enclosed us on every hand. Manny led the way, and at nightfall the moon rose, so that we went on without a halt.

"Of course we might have known that it wouldn't be all as easy as that. The next day there was no sunshine at all, and a freezing wind blew; we were utterly exhausted and slept for odd minutes in any sheltered place we could find, until our stiffening limbs awakened us. We began to walk and climb in a daze; Manny recited poetry, and I told him, I remember, about my horses and dogs at home. We were really talking to ourselves—not to each other. That night we began to realize, though neither of us put it into words, the pretty awful chance we were taking. We ate our food, primed ourselves with brandy, smoked our pipes, and drew what consolation we could from the map. It was a good map, and Manny knew exactly the place he was making for. Nevertheless, our spirits sank lower, and lowest of all during the early hours of the morning. But afterwards, when the sun came out, we grew cheerful again.

"I won't try to detail each day as it passed—partly because I can't be sure how many days did pass. During the sunshine we lived; during the cold, dark hours we slipped into a kind of coma. I think there was an exact moment when we both felt that our number was up—though whether this came on the third or the fifth or the seventh day I can't be sure. We had come to the end of our food, we were chilled and utterly wearied,—and to make things worse—the comparatively fine weather broke down and snowstorms began. I think Manny saw the future as I did, for he said once, in that wry way of his: 'I'm afraid we've been guarding against the wrong sort of danger with these white coats of ours. The trouble's going to be that we *shan't* be found, not that we *shall.*' All the same, we kept going, though I believe I was the first to collapse, and had to be given what was left of the brandy. The next thing I recollect is a clearing sky and a valley vista opening at our feet, and far down, almost as if we could have jumped on skis to it, a cluster of lights. Rather like Lauterbrunnen seen from Wengenalp, if you happen to know that."

I said I did, and he went on: "There was no discussion about what we should do—we had planned it so many times in our heads. We'd comforted ourselves by thinking that as soon as we came to a house we'd wait till the occupants had gone to bed, break in, and take some food. So with this new and exciting hope we staggered down the slope, running when we came to the level of the pinewoods, and checking our pace by wild grabs from tree to tree. I can remember how dark it was in those woods, and rather terrifying; we kept stumbling and scratching our hands and faces. Then, just ahead of us—almost as if it hadn't been there before, if you know the feeling—we saw the lighted window of a house, shining out exactly like a Christmas card. Yes, and smoke curling up from the chimney. *Exactly* like a Christmas card. Warm and comforting and sentimental.

"But, of course, the light at the window meant that there were still people out of bed, so there was nothing for us to do but wait—and as it was Christmas night, we guessed we might have to wait a long time. Still, there would be some heavy sleeping afterwards, and that would help us. So we crouched down on a sort of grassy ledge, rather like a golf green, where the snow was half melted, and the moonlight lay over it like a sort of trembling sea. I suppose it was *we* who were trembling, really—you know how it feels when you've been hurrying downhill and you come to a level stretch again—your legs seem to sink under you. We were so exhausted we threw ourselves on the grass and rested a minute or two, and as I looked back at the pinewoods reaching up the side of the mountain, I noticed a star touching the dark edge of the tree tops—just one little star. I'm not much of a person for noticing things like that, but it's a queer thing—I can almost see those woods and that star now, if I shut my eyes.

"I dare say we waited a couple of hours—it seemed twice as long. What began to puzzle us was that there was no sound from the house. We were quite close, and the night was still—surely there ought to have been voices or a dog barking or something? But there wasn't. At last Manny whispered: 'I can't stand this hanging about any longer—I'm going to scout round!'

"We crept to the outside wall, and saw that the place was a mountain chalet, timbered and heavily gabled. We listened awhile but there still wasn't a sound—but I'll tell you what there was. There was a most luscious, and to us an infuriating smell of cooking. In the end that settled it. We groped round to the doorway, and Manny tried the handle. It turned—the door was unlocked. A gust of warm air reached us and—more overpowering than ever—a definite smell of sizzling meat and roasting poultry. I looked at Manny and my look meant: Let's take a chance. . . .

"We entered the house and tiptoed along a corridor. There was a room that had a strip of light under the door, but still no sound. Manny was trying to deduce where the larder was—we daren't strike matches. An then suddenly we heard footsteps on the inside of the lighted room, the door opened, and a young girl came walking straight into us—actually she'd have collided if we hadn't stepped away. I don't think my heart has ever jumped as much as it did at that moment. Manny had the presence of mind to say: 'Guten Abend.'

"The light from the doorway shone full on us then, and it suddenly occurred to me what a grim and frightening sight we must look—torn, scratched, dirty, eyes bloodshot, unshaven for days. But she didn't seem alarmed—she just said, in a tranquil voice: 'You are strangers?'

"Manny answered her, and they exchanged a few sentences in such rapid German that I couldn't properly follow it. Then I realized that we were being invited into the room. . . . That room . . . I shall never forget it. . . . It dazzled me, its firelight and lamplight, for the moment; then, as I gathered my wits, I saw a table set for two and food for a banquet warming in front of the log fire. Roast chicken, slices of veal, beans, potatoes. Cheese and a bottle of wine. A little Christmas tree. . . . I just stared and stared and left Manny to do the talking. It seemed to me we'd probably have to surrender and make the best of it—we certainly weren't prepared to terrorize a girl; and for myself, the thought of immediate things that surrender would bring—food, sleep, warmth—nearly outweighed the disappointment I knew I should feel afterwards. I wondered whether Manny felt the same, especially as the girl and he went on talking. At last she smiled and went out of the room. Then Manny turned to me and said: 'It's all right. You can sit down and make yourself at home.'

"I must have looked rather stupid about it, for he added: 'Draw your chair to the table and don't guzzle too much all at once.'

" 'But—have you—told her—who—who we are?' I whispered.

" 'Sssh,' he answered. 'I don't have to. Can't you see . . . she's blind.'

" 'Blind?'

" 'Simply the most incredible piece of luck,' he went on. 'She's alone here—her father's one of the frontier guards—he's out on the mountains with a search-party. The frontier's quite close, too—that's another piece of luck. There's a whole platoon of them looking for the two escaped Englishmen—apparently we've been well advertised.'

"I asked him who she thought we really were. He answered: 'Why, part of the search-party, of course—I've explained to her that we got lost, and are dead tired and hungry. And what's more to the point, my lad, she's going to give us our Christmas dinner!'

" 'But if her father returns?'

" 'Then we shall just be a little less in luck, that's all.'

"The girl came back then, and laid extra places at the table. She had a very serene face and beautiful hands. Now that the idea was put in my head, it seemed obvious that she was blind. Yet her movements were scarcely less quick and accurate than if she had had sight. She helped us to food and Manny carved the chicken. They talked and laughed a lot together, and though I could follow what they were saying more or less, sometimes they talked too quickly or used words I didn't understand. But the food—and the wine—and the fire! I've never had a dinner that was as good as that. I know now I never shall. . . . The girl showed us photographs of her father and her two brothers who were at the Front. We drank their healths and the healths of the German Army and —in our hearts—of the British Army, and of all brave men. Then she and Manny began an argument about the whole war business, and how damsilly it was that men should spend Christmas hunting other men over mountains instead of feasting at home. She agreed, and then added something that made my heart miss another beat. She said: 'I thought at first you were the two English prisoners.'

" 'That would have been awkward for you,' said Manny.

" 'Oh, no, I expect they would have wanted food, just the same.'

" 'They certainly would.'

" 'Because, after all, there's not as much difference between English and German as between tired and hungry people and those who aren't.'

" 'Other people mightn't see that,' said Manny, laughing.

" 'They see other things instead.' "

Middleton glanced round the room as if to reassure himself of privacy before he continued: "I remember this rather strange conversation, because at the time it scared me—I thought it was just the sort of too-clever-by-half stuff that a fellow like Manny would give himself away by, instead of sticking to the proper part of the simple German soldier. Because, you see, I was getting more and more panicky over an idea that had just struck me—that the girl was leading us on with all that sort of talk, that she already suspected who we were, and was deliberately trying to keep us till her father and probably some of the other searchers came back. As soon as she next went out of the room, ostensibly to fetch another bottle of wine, I whispered to Manny just what I felt about it. He seemed surprised, and told me then that the girl had offered to show us a short cut over the mountain that would lead us exactly where he wanted to go.

"I was scared again by that. 'I wouldn't trust a yard of that short cut,' I told Manny. 'She's obviously going to lead us straight into a trap.' He answered, in that dreamy way of his: 'Well, you may be right. Wisdom or cleverness—which are we up against?—that's the question, always.'

"That just irritated me—it didn't seem to be the right moment to be so damned philosophical. But he only kept on saying: 'You may be right, and I may be wrong—time will show.'

"But time never did—nor anything else. Because while we were still arguing we heard a commotion outside in the corridor, then the girl's sudden cry amidst men's voices. Both Manny and I took it that our number was up and that the girl was telling them all about us. But she wasn't. We could see what was happening through the gap in the hinge of the door. She was crying because they had brought her father home—on an improvised stretcher.

"Apparently he'd fallen pretty badly somewhere—had a nasty head-wound and an arm was limp. He was in a lot of pain, and we heard the girl imploring the men who had brought him in—there were two of them—to hurry down to the village and bring a doctor. And that would take them a couple of hours at least.

"Well, there isn't much more to tell you. Manny, as you may or may not know, was born to be a surgeon if he hadn't been a poet with a private income, and those soldiers hadn't done a good job with the broken arm. Manny refixed it, and we made the old boy as comfortable as we could before we left. He was semi-conscious and obviously didn't care a damn who we were—you don't, you know, if things are hurting and somebody's helping. . . . So we said

'Guten Abend' again, and made off into the woods. We didn't find the short cut, but we did, after sundry other adventures, manage to wriggle across the frontier. And that's the end of the story. I've no doubt Manny would have told it better."

"The odd thing is," I said, "that he never told it at all."

Middleton answered after a pause: "I wonder if he felt about it as I did afterwards—that it all happened in another sort of world? Mind you, it *did* happen—we escaped all right. That much is on record. And the roast chicken was real enough, I'll swear. And yet . . . oh, well, we were dazed with exhaustion, and sick with anxiety, and wild with hunger. And the girl was blind and her father half-crazy with pain. Things don't happen *to* you when you're like that—as Manny said, they happen *in* you."

I agreed, and we smoked awhile, and then he went on: "That's the worst and the best of war—you feel a brotherhood with the other side that you can't get away from, and equally that you can't give way to. I often wonder what became of the old boy—whether he got better; I hope he did. He was really quite a veteran—far too old and fat to be chasing youngsters like us over mountains. A few years after the Armistice, Manny was in Munich and tried to trace both the man and the girl, but he had no luck—couldn't even find the chalet on the hillside. Anyway, it's twenty years ago now—too late to hold an inquiry over it. But you can perhaps understand how . . . I felt . . . when you quoted that poem at dinner."

"Oh, the poem we were all arguing about?"

"Yes. As a matter of fact, I never knew Manny had written it—poetry, I must admit, isn't much in my line. But that poem . . . well, it reminded me."

I nodded. The volume of Manny Stewart's last poems, issued after his death, lay on the shelf at my elbow, and I reached for it, found the page, and leaned forward to catch the firelight as I read, in a sense for the first time:

You do not know our ways are strange
In war-perverted brotherhood;

How white the snow upon the range,
How warm the window in the wood.
You do not know, you have not seen
The moonlight trembling on the green;
Nor have you watched a single star
Rise over shades where terrors are.
Yet in that world whose beauty lies
Beyond the eye and in the mind,
Yours is the twilight of the wise,
And ours the noonday of the blind.

Christmas Honeymoon

HOWARD SPRING

We were married on December 22nd, because we had met on the 21st. It was as sudden as that. I had come down from Manchester to London. Londoners like you to say that you come up to London; but we Manchester people don't give a hoot what Londoners like. We know that we, and the likes of us, lay the eggs, and the Londoners merely scramble them. That gives us a sense of superiority.

Perhaps I have this sense unduly. Certainly I should never have imagined that I would marry a London girl. As a bachelor, I had survived thirty Manchester summers, and it seemed unlikely to me that, if I couldn't find a girl to suit me in the north, I should find one in London.

I am an architect, and that doesn't make me love London any the more. Every time I come down to the place I find it has eaten another chunk of its own beauty, so as to make more room for the fascias of multiple shops.

All this is just to show you that I didn't come to London looking for a bride; and if I had been looking for a bride, the last place I would have investigated would be a cocktail party. But it was at a cocktail party in the Magnifico that I met Ruth Hutten.

I had never been to a cocktail party in my life before. We don't go in much for that sort of thing in Manchester: scooping a lot of people together and getting rid of the whole bang shoot in one do.

From *The Queen's Book of the Red Cross* (published by Hodder and Stoughton). By permission of Ann Watkins, Inc., agents for the author.

It seems to us ungracious. We like to have a few friends in, and give them a cut off the joint and something decent to drink, and talk in a civilised fashion while we're at it. That's what we understand by hospitality. But these cocktail parties are just a frantic St. Vitus gesture by people who don't want to be bothered.

I shouldn't have been at this party at all if it hadn't been for Claud Tunstall. It was about half-past six when I turned from the lunatic illumination of Piccadilly Circus, which is my idea of how hell is lit up, and started to walk down the Haymarket. I was wondering in an absent-minded sort of way how long the old red pillars of the Haymarket Theatre would be allowed to stand before some bright lad thought what fun it would be to tear them down, when Claud turned round from reading one of the yellow playbills, and there we were, grinning and shaking hands.

Claud had something to grin about, because the author's name on the playbill was his. It was his first play, and it looked as though it wouldn't matter to Claud, so far as money went, if it were his last. The thing had been running for over a year; companies were touring it in the provinces and Colonies; and it was due to open in New York in the coming year. No wonder Claud was grinning; but I think a spot of the grin was really meant for me. He was the same old Claud who had attended the Manchester Grammar School with me and shared my knowledge of its smell of new exercise books and old suet pudding.

Claud was on his way to this party at the Magnifico, and he said I must come with him. That's how these things are: there's no sense in them; but there would have been no sense either in trying to withstand Claud Tunstall's blue eyes and fair tumbling hair and general look of a sky over a cornfield.

That's going some, for me, and perhaps the figure is a bit mixed, but I'm not one for figures at any time. Anyway, it explains why, five minutes later, I was gritting my teeth in the presence of great boobies looking like outsizes in eighteenth-century footmen, yelling names and looking down their noses.

We stood at the door of a room, and I was aware of the gold blurs of chandeliers, and a few dozen apparent football scrums, and a hot blast of talk coming out and smacking our faces, so I deduced this was the party all right. One of the boobies yelled: "Mr. Claud Tunstall and Mr. Edward Oldham," and from what happened it might just as well have been "The Archangel Gabriel and one Worm." Because, the moment we were over the threshold, all the scrums loosened up and girls descended on Claud like a cloud of bright, skittering, squawking parakeets, flashing their red nails at him, unveiling their pearly portals in wide grins, and bearing him off towards a bar where a chap in white was working overtime among all the sweet accessories of Sin. I never saw him again.

Well, as I say, I might have been a worm, no use at all to parakeets, but that lets in the sparrows. I was just turning slowly on my axis, so to speak, in the space that was miraculously cleared round me, when I saw a girl looking at me with an appreciative gleam in her brown eye. She was the brownest girl I ever saw—eyes, skin, and hair—homely as a sparrow, and just as alert.

As our eyes met, there came fluting out of one of the scrums a high-pitched female voice: "No, Basil, I'm teetotal, but I can go quite a long way on pahshun fruit."

The pronunciation of that *pahshun* was indescribable; it seemed the bogus essence of the whole damn silly occasion; and the brown girl and I, looking into one another's eyes, twinkled, savouring together the supreme idiocy. Instinctively we moved towards one another, the twinkle widening to a smile, and I found myself getting dangerously full of similes again, for when she smiled the teeth in her brown face were like the milky kernel of a brown nut.

We sat together on a couch at the deserted end of the room, and I said: "Let me get you something to drink. What would you like? Though whatever it is, it would taste nicer in civilised surroundings."

"I agree," she said simply. "Come on."

And so, ten minutes after I had entered the Magnifico, I was outside again, buttoning my overcoat warmly about me, and this girl was at my side. It was incredible. This is not the sort of thing I usually do; but it had happened so spontaneously, and to be out there in the street, with a little cold wind blowing about us, was

"Did that Christmas never really come when we and the priceless pearl who was our young choice were received, after the happiest of totally impossible marriages, by the two united families previously at daggers-drawn on our account?"

WHAT CHRISTMAS IS AS WE GROW OLDER

Story on page 479

such a relief after that gaudy Bedlam, that the girl and I turned to one another and smiled again. I could see she was feeling the same about it as I was.

Our eyes were towards the dazzle of Piccadilly Circus, when she turned and said, "Not that way," so we went the other way, and down those steps where the Duke of York's column towers up into the sky, and then we were in the park. To be walking there, with that little wind, and the sky full of stars huddling together in the cold, and the bare branches of the trees standing up against the violet pulsing of the night—this was indescribable, incredible, coming within a few minutes upon that screeching aviary.

Ruth Hutten was a typist—nothing more. Her father had been one of those old fogies who rootle for years and years in the British Museum to prove that Ben Jonson had really inserted a semi-colon where the 1739 edition or what not has a full-stop. Things like that. Somehow he had lived on it, like a patient old rat living on scraps of forgotten and unimportant meat. Ruth had lived with him—just lived, full of admiration for the old boy's scholarship, typing his annual volume, which usually failed to earn the publisher's advance.

When he died, the typewriter was all she had; and now she typed other people's books. She had been typing a long flaming novel about Cornwall by Gregoria Gunson; and Gregoria (whom I had never heard of before, but who seemed a decent wench) had said, "I'll take you along to a party. You'll meet a lot of people there. Perhaps I can fix up some work for you."

So there Ruth Hutten was, at the Magnifico, feeling as much out of it as I did, and as glad to escape.

She told me all this as we walked through the half-darkness of the park, and I, as naturally, told her all about myself. She was hard up, but I had never known anyone so happy. And I don't mean gay, bubbling, effervescent. No; you can keep that for the Magnifico. I mean something deep, fundamental; something that takes courage when you're as near the limit as Ruth was.

To this day I don't know London as well as Londoners think everyone ought to know the place. I don't know where we had supper; but it was in a quiet place that everybody else seemed to have forgotten. There was a fire burning, and a shaded lamp on the table. The food was good and simple, and no one seemed to care how long we stayed. I wanted to stay a long time. I had a feeling that once Ruth got outside the door, shook hands, and said "Good night," I should be groping in a very dark place.

I crumbled a bit of bread on the table, and without looking at her I said: "Ruth, I like you. I've never liked anyone so much in my life. Will you marry me?"

She didn't answer till I looked up, and when our glances met she said, "Yes. If you and I can't be happy together, no two people on earth ever could."

This was five years ago. We have had time to discover that we didn't make a mistake.

We were married at a registry office the next morning. The taxi-driver, who looked like one of the seven million exiled Russian princes, and the office charwoman, who had a goitre and a hacking cough, were the witnesses. I tipped them half a sovereign each. I cling to these practical details because I find them comforting in view of the mad impracticality of what was to follow. Please remember that I am an unromantic northerner who couldn't invent a tale to save his life. If I tried to do so, I should at once begin to try and fill it with this and that—in short with Something. The remarkable thing about what happened to me and Ruth was simply that Nothing happened. If you have never come up against Nothing you have no idea how it can scare you out of your wits. When I was a child I used to be afraid of Something in the dark. I know now that the most fearful thing about the dark is that we may find Nothing in it.

It was Ruth's idea that we should spend the few days of our honeymoon walking in Cornwall. Everything was arranged in a mad hurry. Not that there was much to arrange. We bought rucksacks, stuffed a change of underclothing into them, bought serviceable shoes and waterproofs, and we were ready to start.

Walking was the idea of both of us. This was another bond:

you could keep all the motor-cars in the world so far as we were concerned, and all the radio and daily newspapers, too; and we both liked walking in winter as much as in summer.

Cornwall was Ruth's idea. She had Cornwall on the brain. Her father had done some learned stuff on Malory; and her head was full of Merlin and Tintagel and the Return of Arthur. Gregoria Gunson's novel helped, too, with its smugglers and romantic inns and the everlasting beat of surf on granite coasts. So Cornwall it was—a place in which neither of us had set foot before.

We made our first contact with Cornwall at Truro. Night had long since fallen when we arrived there on our wedding day. I have not been there since, nor do I wish ever to return. Looking back on what happened, it seems appropriate that the adventure should have begun in Truro. There is in some towns something inimical, irreconcilable. I felt it there. As soon as we stepped out of the station, I wished we were back in the warm, lighted train which already was pulling out on its way to Penzance.

There was no taxi in sight. To our right the road ran slightly uphill; to our left, downhill. We knew nothing of the town, and we went to the left. Soon we were walking on granite. There was granite everywhere: grey, hard, and immemorial. The whole town seemed to be hewn out of granite. The streets were paved with it, enormous slabs like the lids of ancestral vaults. It gave me the feeling of walking in an endless graveyard, and the place was silent enough to maintain the illusion. The streets were lit with grim economy. Hardly a window had a light, and when, here and there, we passed a publichouse, it was wrapped in a pall of decorum which made me wonder whether Cornishmen put on shrouds when they went in for a pint.

It did not take us long to get to the heart of the place, the few shopping streets that were a bit more festive, gay with seasonable things; and when we found an hotel, it was a good one. I signed the book, "Mr. and Mrs. Edward Oldham, Manchester," and that made me smile. After all, it was something to smile about. At this time last night, Ruth and I had just met, and now "Mr. and Mrs. Edward Oldham."

Ruth had moved across to a fire in the lounge. She had an arm along the mantelpiece, a toe meditatively tapping the fender. She looked up when I approached her and saw the smile. But her face did not catch the contagion. "Don't you hate this town?" she asked.

"I can put up with it," I said, "now that I'm in here, and now that you're in here with me."

"Yes," she answered, "this is all right. But those streets! They gave me the creeps. I felt as if every stone had been hewn out of a cliff that the Atlantic had battered for a thousand years and plastered with wrecks. Have you ever seen Tewkesbury Abbey?"

The irrelevant question took me aback. "No," I said.

"I've never seen stone so saturated with sunlight," said Ruth. "It looks as if you could wring summers out of it. The fields about it, I know, have run with blood, but it's a happy place all the same. This place isn't happy. It's under a cold enchantment."

"Not inside these four walls," I said, "because they enclose you and me and our supper and bed."

We fled from Truro the next morning. Fled is the word. As soon as breakfast was over we slung our rucksacks on to our backs and cleared out of the granite town as fast as our legs would take us. December 23rd, and utterly unseasonable weather. The sky was blue, the sun was warm, and the Christmas decorations in the shops had a farcical and inappropriate look. But we were not being bluffed by these appearances. We put that town behind us before its hoodoo could reimpose itself upon our spirits.

And soon there was nothing wrong with our spirits at all. We were travelling westward, and every step sunk us deeper into a warm enchantment. Ruth had spoken last night of a cold enchantment. Well, this was a warm enchantment. I hadn't guessed that, with Christmas only two days ahead, any part of England could be like this. We walked through woods of evergreens and saw the sky shining like incredible blue lace through the branches overhead. We found violets blooming in warm hedge bottoms, and in a cottage garden a few daffodils were ready to burst their sheaths. We could see the yellow staining the taut green. We had tea at that cottage, out of doors! I thought of Manchester, and the fog blanketing Albert Square, and the great red trams going through it, slowly, like galleons, clanging their warning bells. I laughed aloud at the incredible, the absurd things that could happen to a man in England. One day Manchester. The next day London. The next marriage, Truro, and the cold shudders. The next—this! I said all this to Ruth, who was brushing crumbs off the table to feed the birds that hopped tamely round her feet. "It makes me wonder what miracle is in store for tomorrow," I said. "And, anyway, what is Cornwall? I've always thought it was beetling cliffs and raging seas, smugglers, wreckers and excisemen."

We entered the cottage to pay the old woman, and I went close up to the wall to examine a picture hanging there. It was a fine bit of photography: spray breaking on wicked-looking rocks. "That's the Manacles," the old girl said. "That's where my husband was drowned."

The Manacles. That was a pretty fierce name, and it looked a pretty fierce place. The woman seemed to take it for granted. She made no further comment. "Good-bye, midear," she said to Ruth. "Have a good day."

We did, but I never quite recaptured the exaltation of the morning. I felt that this couldn't last, that the spirit which had first made itself felt in the hard grey streets of Truro had pounced again out of that hard grey name: the Manacles. It sounded like a gritting of gigantic teeth. We were being played with. This interlude in fairyland, where May basked in December, was something to lure us on, to bring us within striking reach of—well, of what? Isn't this England? I said to myself. Isn't Cornwall as well within the four walls of Britain as Lancashire?

We breasted a hill, and a wide estuary lay before us, shining under the evening sun. Beyond it, climbing in tier upon tier of streets, was Falmouth. I liked the look of it. "This is where we stay to-night," I said to Ruth. "We shall be comfortable here."

A ferry took us across the harbour. Out on the water it was cold. Ruth pointed past the docks, past Pendennis Castle standing on the hill. "Out there is the way to Land's End," she said.

I looked, and low down on the water there was a faint grey smudge. Even a Manchester man would know that that was fog, creeping in from the Atlantic.

All night long we heard the fog-horns moaning, and it was very cold.

I hate sleeping in an airless room, but by midnight the white coils of fog, filling every crevice, and cold as if they were the exhalation of icebergs, made me rise from bed and shut the window. Our bedroom hung literally over the sea. The wall of the room was a deep bay, and I had seen how, by leaning out of the window, one could drop a stone to the beach below. Now I could not see the beach. I could not see anything. If I had stretched my arm out into the night the fingers would have been invisible. But though I could not see, I could hear. The tide had risen, and I could hear the plash of little waves down there below me. It was so gentle a sound that it made me shudder. It was like the voice of a soft-spoken villain. The true voice of the sea and of the night was that long, incessant bellow of the fog-horns. The shutting of the window did nothing to keep that out.

I drew the curtains across the window, and, turning, saw that a fire was laid in the grate. I put a match to it. Incredible comfort! In ten minutes we felt happier. In twenty we were asleep.

There seemed nothing abnormal about Falmouth when we woke in the morning. A fairly stiff wind had sprung up. The fog was torn to pieces. It hung here and there in dirty isolated patches, but these were being quickly swept away. There was a run on the water. It was choppy and restless, and the sky was a rag-bag of fluttering black and grey. Just a normal winter day by the seaside: a marvellous day for walking, Ruth said.

At the breakfast-table we spread out the map and considered the day's journey. This was going to be something new again. There had been the grey inhospitality of Truro; the Arcadian interlude; the first contact with something vast and menacing. Now, looking at the map, we saw that, going westward, following the coast, we should come to what we had both understood Cornwall to be: a sparsely populated land, moors, a rock-bound coast. It promised to be something big and hard and lonely, and that was what we wanted.

We put sandwiches into our rucksacks, intending to eat lunch out of doors. We reckoned we should find some sort of inn for the night.

A bus took us the best part of ten miles on our westward journey. Then it struck inland, to the right. We left it at that point, climbed a stile, walked through a few winter-bare fields, and came to a path running with the line of the coast.

Now, indeed, we had found traditional Cornwall. Here, if anywhere, was the enchanted land of Merlin and of Arthur—the land that Ruth dreamed about. Never had I found elsewhere in England a sense so overpowering both of size and loneliness. To our left was the sea, down there at the foot of the mighty cliffs along whose crest we walked. The tide was low, and the reefs were uncovered. In every shape of fantastic cruelty they thrust out towards the water, great knives and swords of granite that would hack through any keel, tables of granite on which the stoutest ship would pound to pieces, jaws of granite that would seize and grind and not let go. Beyond and between these prone monsters was the innocent yellow sand, and, looking at the two—the sand and the reefs—I thought of the gentle lapping of the water under my window last night, and the crying of the fog-horns, the most desolate crying in the world.

Southward and westward the water stretched without limit; and inland, as we walked steadily forward all through the morning, was now a patch of cultivation, now the winter stretch of rusty moor with gulls and lapwings joining their lamentations as they glided and drooped across it, according to their kind. From time to time a cluster of trees broke the monotony of the inland view, and I remembered rooks fussing among the bare boughs. Rooks, lapwings, and gulls: those were the only birds we saw that day.

It was at about one o'clock that we came to a spot where the cliff path made a loop inland to avoid a deep fissure into which we peered. In some cataclysm the rocks here had been torn away, tumbling and piling till they made a rough giant's stairway down which we clambered to the beach below. We ended up in a cove so narrow that I could have thrown a stone across it, and paved with sand of unbelievable golden purity. The sun came through the clouds, falling right upon that spot. It was tiny, paradisal, with the advancing tide full of green and blue and purple lights. We sat on the sand, leaned against the bottom-most of the fallen granite blocks, and ate our lunch.

We were content. This was the loveliest thing we had found yet. Ruth recalled a phrase from the novel she had typed for Miss Gregoria Gunson. "And you will find here and there a paradise ten yards wide, a little space of warmth and colour set like a jewel in the hard iron of that coast." Far-fetched, I thought, but true enough.

It was while we were sitting there, calculating how long that bit of sun could last, that Ruth said, "We wanted a lonely place, and we've found it, my love. Has it struck you that we haven't seen a human being since we got off the bus?"

It hadn't, and it didn't seem to me a matter of concern. I stretched my arms lazily towards the sun. "Who wants to see human beings?" I demanded. "I had enough human beings at the Magnifico to last me a very long time."

"So long as we find some human beings to make us a bit of supper to-night . . ."

"Never fear," I said. "We'll do that. There! Going . . . Going . . . Gone."

The sun went in. We packed up, climbed to the cliff top, and started off again.

At three o'clock the light began to go out of the day. This was Christmas Eve, remember. We were among the shortest days of the year. It was now that a little uneasiness began to take hold of me. Still, I noticed, we had seen no man or woman, and, though I kept a sharp lookout on the country inland, we saw no house, not a barn, not a shed.

We did not see the sun again that day, but we witnessed his dying magnificence. Huge spears of light fanned down out of the sky and struck in glittering points upon the water far off. Then the clouds turned into a crumble and smother of dusky red, as though a city were burning beyond the edge of the world, and when all this began to fade to grey ashes I knew that I was very uneasy indeed.

Ruth said: "I think we ought to leave this cliff path. We ought to strike inland and find a road—any road."

I thought so, too, but inland now was nothing but moor. Goodness knows, I thought, where we shall land if we embark on that.

"Let us keep on," I said, "for a little while. We may find a path branching off. Then we'll know we're getting somewhere."

We walked for another mile, and then Ruth stopped. We were on the brink of another of those deep fissures, like the one we had descended for lunch. Again the path made a swift right-hand curve. I knew what Ruth was thinking before she said it. "In half an hour or so the light will be quite gone. Suppose we had come on this in the dark?"

We had not found the path we were seeking. We did not seek it any more. Abruptly, we turned right and began to walk into the moor. So long as we could see, we kept the coast behind our backs. Soon we could not see at all. The night came on, impenetrably black and there would be no moon.

It was now six o'clock. I know that because I struck a match to look at the time, and I noticed that I had only three matches left. This is stuck in my mind because I said, "We must be careful with these. If we can't find food, we'll find a smoke a comfort."

"But, my love," said Ruth, and there was now an undoubted note of alarm in her voice, "we *must* find food. Surely, if we just keep on we'll see a light, or hear a voice, or come to a road——"

She stopped abruptly, seized my arm, held on to prevent my going forward. I could not see her face, but I sensed her alarm. "What is it?" I asked.

"I stepped in water."

I knelt and tested the ground in front of me with my hands. It was a deep oozy wetness; not the clear wetness of running water. "Bog," I said; and we knew we could go forward no longer. With cliff on the one hand and the possibility of stumbling into a morass on the other, there seemed nothing for it but to stay where we were till heaven sent us aid or the dawn came up.

I put my arm round Ruth and felt that she was trembling. I want to put this adventure down exactly as it happened. It would be nice to write that her nerves were steady as rock. Clearly they weren't, and I was not feeling very good either. I said as gaily as I could, "This is where we sit down, smoke a cigarette, and think it out."

We went back a little so as to be away from the bog, and then we plumped down among the heather. We put the cigarettes to our lips and I struck a match. It did not go out when I threw it to the ground. In that world of darkness the little light burning on the earth drew our eyes, and simultaneously we both stood up with an exclamation of surprised delight. The light had shown us an inscribed stone, almost buried in the heather. There were two matches left. Fortunately, we were tidy people. We had put our sandwich papers into the rucksacks. I screwed these now into little torches. Ruth lit one and held it to the stone while I knelt to read. It seemed a stone of fabulous age. The letters were mossy and at first illegible. I took out a penknife and scraped at them. "2 Miles——" we made out, but the name of this place two miles off we do not know to this day. I scraped away, but the letters were too defaced for reading, and just as the last of the little torches flared to extinction the knife slipped from my hand into the heather. There was nothing to do but leave it there.

We stood up. Two miles. But two miles to where, and two miles in what direction? Our situation seemed no happier, when suddenly I saw the stones.

I had seen stones like them on the Yorkshire moors, round about the old Brontë parsonage. But were they the same sort of stones, and did they mean the same thing? I was excited now. "Stay here," I said to Ruth, and I stepped towards the first stone. As I had hoped, a third came into view in line with the second, and, as I advanced, a fourth in line with the third. They were the same: upright monoliths set to mark a path, whitewashed half-way up so that they would glimmer through the dark as they were doing now, tarred on their upper half to show the way when snow was on the ground. I shouted in my joy: "Come on! Supper! Fires! Comfort! Salvation!" but Ruth came gingerly. She had not forgotten the bog.

But the stones did not let us down. They led us to the village. It must have been about nine o'clock when we got there.

Half-way through that pitch-black two-mile journey we were aware that once more we were approaching the sea. From afar we could hear its uneasy murmur growing louder, and presently threaded with a heart-darkening sound: the voice of a bell-buoy tolling its insistent warning out there on the unseen water.

As the murmur of the sea and the melancholy clangour of the bell came clearer we went more warily, for we could not see more than the stone next ahead; and presently there was no stone where the next stone should be. We peered into the darkness, our hearts aching for the light which would tell us that we were again among houses and men. There was no light anywhere.

"We have one match," I said. "Let us light a cigarette apiece and chance seeing something that will help us."

We saw the wire hawser: no more than the veriest scrap of it, fixed by a great staple into the head of a post and slanting down into darkness. I first, Ruth behind me, we got our hands upon it, gripping for dear life, and went inching down towards the sound of water.

So we came at last to the village. Like many a Cornish village, it was built at the head of a cove. The sea was in front; there was a horse-shoe of cliffs; and snuggling at the end was a half-moon of houses behind a seawall of granite.

All this did not become clear to us at once. For the moment, we had no other thought than of thankfulness to be treading on hard cobbles that had been laid by human hands, no other desire than to bang on the first door and ask whether there was in the place an inn or someone who would give us lodging for the night.

Most of the cottages were whitewashed; their glimmer gave us the rough definition of the place; and I think already we must have felt some uneasy presage at the deathly mask of them, white as skulls with no light in their eyes.

For there was no living person, no living thing, in the village. That was what we discovered. Not so much as a dog went by us in the darkness. Not so much as a cock crowed. The tolling from the water came in like a passing bell, and the sea whispered incessantly, and grew to a deep-throated threatening roar as the tide rose and billows beat on the sand and at last on the seawall; but there was no one to notice these things except ourselves; and our minds were almost past caring, so deeply were we longing for one thing only—the rising of the sun.

There was nothing wrong with the village. It contained all the apparatus of living. Bit by bit we discovered that. There was no answer to our knocking at the first door we came to. There was nothing remarkable in that, and we went on to the next. Here, again, there was no welcome sound of feet, no springing up of a light to cheer us who had wandered for so long in the darkness.

At the third house I knocked almost angrily. Yes; anger was the feeling I had then; anger at all these stupid people who shut down a whole village at nine o'clock, went to their warm beds, and left us standing there, knocking in the cold and darkness. I thudded the knocker with lusty rat-tat-tats; and suddenly, in the midst of that noisy assault, I stopped, afraid. The anger was gone. Plain fear took its place. At the next house I *could* not knock, because I knew there was no one to hear me.

I was glad to hear Ruth's voice. She said, surprisingly, "It's no good knocking. Try a door."

I turned the handle and the door opened. Ruth and I stepped over the threshold, standing very close together. I shouted, "Is there anyone at home?" My voice sounded brutally loud and defiant. Nothing answered it.

We were standing in the usual narrow passageway of a cottage. Ruth put out her hand and knocked something to the floor from a little table. "Matches," she said; and I groped on the floor and found them. The light showed us a hurricane lantern standing on the table. I lit it, and we began to examine the house, room by room.

This was a strange thing to do, but at the time it did not seem strange. We were shaken and off our balance. We wanted to reassure ourselves. If we had found flintlocks, bows and arrows, bronze hammers, we might have been reassured. We could have told ourselves that we had wandered, bewitched, out of our century. But we found nothing of the sort. We found a spotless cottage full of contemporary things. There was a wireless set. There was last week's *Falmouth Packet.* There were geraniums in a pot in the window; there were sea-boots and oilskins in the passage. The bed upstairs was made, and there was a cradle beside it. There was no one in the bed, no child in the cradle.

Ruth was white. "I want to see the pantry," she said, inconsequentially I thought.

We found the pantry, and she took the cloth off a breadpan and put her hand upon a loaf. "It's warm," she said. "It was baked to-day." She began to tremble.

We left the house and took the lantern with us. Slowly, with the bell tolling endlessly, we walked through the curved length of the village. There was one shop. I held up the light to its uncurtained window. Toys and sweets, odds and ends of grocery, all the stock-in-trade of a small general store, were there behind the glass. We hurried on.

We were hurrying now, quite consciously hurrying; though where we were hurrying to we did not know. Once or twice I found myself looking back over my shoulder. If I had seen man, woman, or child I think I should have screamed. So powerfully had the death of the village taken hold of my imagination that the appearance of a living being, recently so strongly desired, would have affected me like the return of one from the dead.

At the centre of the crescent of houses there was an inn, the Lobster Pot, with climbing geraniums ramping over its front in the way they do in Cornwall; then came more cottages; and at the farther tip of the crescent there was a house standing by itself. It was bigger than any of the others; it stood in a little garden. In the comforting daylight I should have admired it as the sort of place some writer or painter might choose for a refuge.

Now I could make it out only bit by bit, flashing the lantern here and there; and, shining the light upon the porch, I saw that the door was open. Ruth and I went in. Again I shouted, "Is anyone here?" Again I was answered by nothing.

I put the lantern down on an oak chest in the small square hall, and that brought my attention to the telephone. There it was, standing on the chest, an up-to-date microphone in ivory white. Ruth saw it at the same moment, and her eyes asked me, "Do you dare?"

I did. I took up the microphone and held it to my ear. I could feel at once that it was dead. I joggled the rest. I shouted, "Hallo! Hallo!" but I knew that no one would answer. No one answered.

We had stared through the windows of every cottage in the village. We had looked at the shop and the inn. We had banged at three doors and entered two houses. But we had not admitted our extraordinary situation in words. Now I said to Ruth, "What do you make of it?"

She said simply, "It's worse than ghosts. Ghosts are something. This is nothing. Everything is absolutely normal. That's what seems so horrible."

And, indeed, a village devastated by fire, flood, or earthquake would not have disturbed us as we were disturbed by that village which was devastated by nothing at all.

Ruth shut the door of the hall. The crashing of the sea on granite, the tolling of the bell, now seemed far off. We stood and looked at one another uneasily in the dim light of the hurricane lamp. "I shall stay here," said Ruth, "either till the morning or till something happens."

She moved down the hall to a door which opened into a room at the back. I followed her. She tapped on the door, but neither of us expected an answer, and there was none. We went in.

Nothing that night surprised us like what we saw then. Holding the lantern high above my head, I swung its light round the room. It was a charming place, panelled in dark oak. A few fine pictures were on the walls. There were plenty of books, some pieces of good porcelain. The curtains of dark-green velvet fringed with gold were drawn across the window. A fire was burning on the hearth. That was what made us start back almost in dismay—the fire.

If it had been a peat fire—one of those fires that, once lit, smoulder for days—we should not have been surprised. But it was not. Anyone who knew anything about fires could see that this fire had been lit within the last hour. Some of the coals were still black; none had been consumed. And the light from this fire fell upon the white smooth texture of an excellent linen cloth upon the table. On the table was supper, set for one. A chair was placed before the knife and fork and plates. There was a round of cold beef waiting to be cut, a loaf of bread, a jar of pickles, a fine cheese, a glass, and a jug containing beer.

Ruth laughed shrilly. I could hear that her nerves were strained by this last straw. "At least we shan't starve," she cried. "I'm nearly dying of hunger. I suppose the worst that could happen would be the return of the bears, demanding 'Who's been eating my beef? Who's been drinking my beer?' Sit down. Carve!"

I was as hungry as she was. As I looked at the food the saliva flowed in my mouth, but I could as soon have touched it as robbed a poor-box. And Ruth knew it. She turned from the table, threw herself into an easy chair by the fire, and lay back, exhausted. Her eyes closed. I stood behind the chair and stroked her forehead till she slept. That was the best that could happen to her.

That, in a way, was the end of our adventure. Nothing more happened to us. Nothing *more?* But, as you see, nothing at all had happened to us. And it was this nothingness that made my vigil over Ruth sleeping in the chair the most nerve-destroying experience of all my life. A clock ticking away quietly on the chimney-piece told me that it was half-past nine. A tear-off calendar lying on a writing-table told me that it was December 24th. Quite correct. All in order.

The hurricane-lamp faded and went out. I lit a lamp, shaded with green silk, that stood on the table amid the waiting supper.

The room became cosier, even more human and likeable. I prowled about quietly, piecing together the personality of the man or woman who lived in it. A man. It was a masculine sort of supper, and I found a tobacco jar and a few pipes. The books were excellently bound editions of the classics, with one or two modern historical works. The pictures, I saw now, were Medici reprints of French Impressionists, all save the one over the fireplace, which was an original by Paul Nash.

I tried, with these trivial investigations, to divert my mind from the extraordinary situation we were in. It wouldn't work. I sat down and listened intently, but there was nothing to hear save the bell and the water—water that stretched, I reminded myself, from here to America. This was one of the ends of the world.

At one point I got up and locked the door, though what was there to keep out? All that was to be feared was inside me.

The fire burned low, and there was nothing for its replenishment. It was nearly gone, and the room was turning cold, when Ruth stirred and woke. At that moment the clock, which had a lovely silver note, struck twelve. "A merry Christmas, my darling," I said.

Ruth looked at me wildly, taking some time to place herself. Then she laughed and said, "I've been dreaming about it. It's got a perfectly natural explanation. It was like this. . . . No. . . . It's gone. I can't remember it. But it was something quite reasonable."

I sat with my arm about her. "My love," I said, "I can think of a hundred quite reasonable explanations. For example, every man in the village for years has visited his Uncle Henry at Bodmin on Christmas Eve, taking wife, child, dog, cat, and canary with him. The chap in this house is the only one who hasn't got an Uncle Henry at Bodmin, so he laid his supper, lit the fire, and was just settling down for the evening when the landlord of the Lobster Pot thought he'd be lonely, looked in, and said: 'What about coming to see *my* Uncle Henry at Bodmin?' And off they all went. That's perfectly reasonable. It explains everything. Do you believe it?"

Ruth shook her head. "You must sleep," she said. "Lay your head on my shoulder."

We left the house at seven o'clock on Christmas morning. It was slack tide. The sea was very quiet, and in the grey light, standing in the garden at the tip of the crescent, we could see the full extent of the village with one sweep of the eye, as we had not been able to do last night.

It was a lovely little place, huddled under the rocks at the head of its cove. Every cottage was well cared for, newly washed in cream or white, and on one or two of them a few stray roses were blooming, which is not unusual in Cornwall at Christmas.

At any other time, Ruth and I would have said, "Let's stay here." But we now hurried, rucksacks on backs, disturbed by the noise of our own shoes, and climbed the path down which we had so cautiously made our way the night before.

There were the stones of black and white. We followed them till we came to the spot where we found the stone with the obliterated name. "And, behold, there was no stone there, but your lost pocket-knife was lying in the heather," said a sceptical friend to whom I once related this story.

That, I suppose, would be a good way to round off an invented tale if I were a professional story-teller. But, in simple fact, the stone *was* there, and so was my knife. Ruth took it from me, and when we came to the place where we had left the cliff path and turned into the moor, she hurled it far out and we heard the faint tinkle of its fall on the rocks below.

"And now," she said with resolution, "we go back the way we came, and we eat our Christmas dinner in Falmouth. Then you can inquire for the first train to Manchester. Didn't you say there are fogs there?"

"There are, an' all," I said broadly.

"Good," said Ruth. "After last night, I feel a fog is something substantial, something you can get hold of."

VII

WHAT IS THE CHRISTMAS SPIRIT?

☆

The time draws near the birth of Christ.
  The moon is hid, the night is still;
  The Christmas bells from hill to hill
Answer each other in the mist.

Four voices of four hamlets round,
  From far and near, on mead and moor,
  Swell out and fail, as if a door
Were shut between me and the sound;

Each voice four changes on the wind,
  That now dilate, and now decrease,
  Peace and goodwill, goodwill and peace,
Peace and goodwill, to all mankind.

ALFRED, LORD TENNYSON

What Christmas Is As We Grow Older

CHARLES DICKENS

TIME was, with most of us, when Christmas Day encircling all our limited world like a magic ring, left nothing out for us to miss or seek; bound together all our home enjoyments, affections, and hopes; grouped everything and every one around the Christmas fire; and made the little picture shining in our bright young eyes, complete.

Time came perhaps, all too soon, when our thoughts over-leaped that narrow boundary; when there was some one (very dear, we thought then, very beautiful, and absolutely perfect) wanting to the fulness of our happiness; when we were wanting too (or we thought so, which did just as well) at the Christmas hearth by which that some one sat; and when we intertwined with every wreath and garland of our life that some one's name.

That was the time for the bright visionary Christmases which have long arisen from us to show faintly, after summer rain, in the palest edges of the rainbow! That was the time for the beatified enjoyment of the things that were to be, and never were, and yet the things that were so real in our resolute hope that it would be hard to say, now, what realities achieved since, have been stronger!

What! Did that Christmas never really come when we and the priceless pearl who was our young choice were received, after the happiest of totally impossible marriages, by the two united families previously at daggers-drawn on our account? When brothers and sisters-in-law who had always been rather cool to us before our relationship was effected, perfectly doted on us, and when fathers and mothers overwhelmed us with unlimited incomes? Was that Christmas dinner never really eaten, after which we arose, and generously and eloquently rendered honour to our late rival, present in the company, then and there exchanging friendship and forgiveness, and founding an attachment, not to be surpassed in Greek or Roman story, which subsisted until death? Has that same rival long ceased to care for that same priceless pearl, and married for money, and become usurious? Above all, do we really know, now, that we should probably have been miserable if we had won and worn the pearl, and that we are better without her?

That Christmas when we had recently achieved so much fame; when we had been carried in triumph somewhere, for doing something great and good; when we had won an honoured and ennobled name, and arrived and were received at home in a shower of tears of joy; is it possible that *that* Christmas has not come yet?

And is our life here, at the best, so constituted that, pausing as we advance at such a noticeable milestone in the track as this great birthday, we look back on the things that never were, as naturally and full as gravely as on the things that have been and are gone, or have been and still are? If it be so, and so it seems to be, must we come to the conclusion that life is little better than a dream, and little worth the loves and strivings that we crowd into it?

No! Far be such miscalled philosophy from us, dear Reader, on Christmas Day! Nearer and closer to our hearts be the Christmas spirit, which is the spirit of active usefulness, perseverance, cheerful discharge of duty, kindness, and forbearance! It is in the last virtues especially, that we are, or should be, strengthened by the unaccomplished visions of our youth; for, who shall say that they are not our teachers to deal gently even with the impalpable nothings of the earth!

Therefore, as we grow older, let us be more thankful that the circle of our Christmas associations and of the lessons that they bring, expands! Let us welcome every one of them, and summon them to take their places by the Christmas hearth.

Welcome, old aspirations, glittering creatures of an ardent fancy, to your shelter underneath the holly! We know you, and have not outlived you yet. Welcome, old projects and old loves, however fleeting, to your nooks among the steadier lights that burn around us. Welcome, all that was ever real to our hearts; and for the earnestness that made you real, thanks to Heaven! Do we build no Christmas castles in the clouds now? Let our thoughts, fluttering like butterflies among these flowers of children, bear witness! Before this boy, there stretches out a Future, brighter than we ever looked on in our old romantic time, but bright with honour and with truth. Around this little head on which the sunny curls lie heaped, the graces sport, as prettily, as airily, as when there was no scythe within the reach of Time to shear away the curls of our first-love. Upon another girl's face near it—placider but smiling bright—a quiet and contented little face, we see Home fairly written. Shining from the word, as rays shine from a star, we see how, when our graves are old, other hopes than ours are young, other hearts than ours are moved; how other ways are smoothed; how other happiness blooms, ripens, and decays—no, not decays, for other homes and other bands of children, not yet in being nor for ages yet to be, arise, and bloom and ripen to the end of all!

Welcome, everything! Welcome, alike what has been, and what never was, and what we hope may be, to your shelter underneath the holly, to your places round the Christmas fire, where what is sits open-hearted! In yonder shadows, do we see obtruding furtively upon the blaze, an enemy's face? By Christmas Day we do forgive him! If the injury he has done us may admit of such companionship, let him come here and take his place. If otherwise, unhappily, let him go hence, assured that we will never injure nor accuse him.

On this day we shut out Nothing!

"Pause," says a low voice. "Nothing? Think!"

"On Christmas Day, we will shut out from our fireside, Nothing."

"Not the shadow of a vast City where the withered leaves are lying deep?" the voice replies. "Not the shadow that darkens the whole globe? Not the shadow of the City of the Dead?"

Not even that. Of all days in the year, we will turn our faces towards that City upon Christmas Day, and from its silent hosts bring those we loved, among us. City of the Dead, in the blessed name wherein we are gathered together at this time, and in the Presence that is here among us according to the promise, we will receive, and not dismiss, thy people who are dear to us!

Yes. We can look upon these children angels that alight, so solemnly, so beautifully among the living children by the fire, and can bear to think how they departed from us. Entertaining angels unawares, as the Patriarchs did, the playful children are unconscious of their guests; but we can see them—can see a radiant arm around one favourite neck, as if there were a tempting of that child away. Among the celestial figures there is one, a poor misshapen boy on earth, of a glorious beauty now, of whom this dying mother said it grieved her much to leave him here, alone, for so many years as it was likely would elapse before he came to her—being such a little child. But he went quickly, and was laid upon her breast, and in her hand she leads him.

There was a gallant boy, who fell, far away, upon a burning sand beneath a burning sun, and said, "Tell them at home, with my last love, how much I could have wished to kiss them once, but that I died contented and had done my duty!" Or there was another, over whom they read the words, "Therefore we commit his body to the deep," and so consigned him to the lonely ocean and sailed on. Or there was another, who lay down to his rest in the dark shadow of great forests, and, on earth, awoke no more. Oh, shall they not, from sand and sea and forest, be brought home at such a time?

There was a dear girl—almost a woman—never to be one—who made a mourning Christmas in a house of joy, and went her trackless way to the silent City. Do we recollect her, worn out, faintly whispering what could not be heard, and falling into that last sleep for weariness? Oh, look upon her now! Oh, look upon her beauty, her serenity, her changeless youth, her happiness! The daughter of Jairus was recalled to life, to die; but she, more blest, has heard the same voice, saying unto her, "Arise for ever!"

We had a friend who was our friend from early days, with whom we often pictured the changes that were to come upon our lives, and merrily imagined how we would speak, and walk, and think, and talk, when we came to be old. His destined habitation in the City of the Dead received him in his prime. Shall he be shut out from our Christmas remembrance? Would his love have so excluded us? Lost friend, lost child, lost parent, sister, brother, husband, wife, we will not so discard you! You shall hold your cherished places in our Christmas hearts, and by our Christmas fires; and in the season of immortal hope, and on the birthday of immortal mercy, we will shut out Nothing!

The winter sun goes down over town and village; on the sea it makes a rosy path, as if the Sacred tread were fresh upon the water. A few more moments, and it sinks, and night comes on, and lights begin to sparkle in the prospect. On the hill-side beyond the shapelessly diffused town, and in the quiet keeping of the trees that gird the village-steeple, remembrances are cut in stone, planted in common flowers, growing in grass, entwined with lowly brambles around many a mound of earth. In town and village, there are doors and windows closed against the weather, there are flaming logs heaped high, there are joyful faces, there is healthy music of voices. Be all ungentleness and harm excluded from the temples of the Household Gods, but be those remembrances admitted with tender encouragement! They are of the time and all its comforting and peaceful reassurances; and of the history that reunited even upon earth the living and the dead; and of the broad beneficence and goodness that too many men have tried to tear to narrow shreds.

Christmas in Possession

M. E. BRADDON

"But oh, Gus!" said a faltering voice as two little white hands clung about the captain's stalwart arm, "suppose that dreadful man should do what he threatened, and there should be an execution!" And Captain Hawthornden's pretty, pale-faced wife shuddered, as if she had been talking of one of those sanguinary performances which, in the good old times of English history, were wont to attract crowds to Tower Hill.

"Nonsense, my love! there's not the remotest chance of such a thing," cried the captain sturdily. "Do you suppose if there were I'd go away and leave my precious petsy-wetsy in danger of falling into the hands of the Philistines?"

"And Toodleums!" exclaimed Mrs. Hawthornden piteously. Toodleums was a pet name for that domestic miracle of beauty and genius, the first baby. "Imagine dreadful men taking away Toodleum's coral, that my own darling mother sent him!"

"I should like to see the bailiff that would put a finger on that coral!" cried the warrior fiercely. "But now let's talk dispassionately, my darling, for time's nearly up. It's half-past eleven. The express leaves King's Cross at 12:40, so my precious Clara must dry her pretty eyes and listen to her devoted Augustus."

The devoted Augustus looked very handsome and bright and cheerful as he bent over his tearful young wife, while two brisk little serving-maids scudded up and down stairs in quest of innumerable canes, overcoats, and courier bags, and a noble russia leather despatch-box, and skirmished with the cabman, who was groaning under the captain's portmanteau and gun-case in the hall.

"You see, my darling, all we have to do is to look things in the face. Absalom holds a bill of mine which he refuses to renew—having, in point of fact, renewed it two or three times already—which cursed bond falls due on the twenty-fourth, Christmas Eve; the idea of any bloodsucking-fellow having the heart to refuse to renew a bill falling due on Christmas Eve! and the black-hearted scoundrel swears if it isn't paid he'll put in an execution upon these goods before the day is out. Was there ever such a dastard?"

"But you do owe him the money, don't you, Gus darling?"

"Well, yes, I owe him *some* of it, of course; but you can't call compound interest at forty per cent. a just debt."

"But you knew what the interest was to be when you borrowed the money, didn't you, Gus darling?"

"Of course, the iniquitous rascal traded on my desperation. Women don't understand these things, you see, my love. However, scoundrel as I believe Absalom to be, I don't suppose him capable of putting in an execution on Christmas Eve, especially after the diplomatic letter I wrote him this morning. But I'll tell you what, Clara; be sure to let no stranger into the house on any pretence whatever. Sport the oak, my love, and tell your servants not to let a living creature cross the threshold."

"Yes, dear, I'll tell them. And there's the butcher, and the grocer, and the baker, and even the milkman, Augustus dear. You don't know how insolent their young men have been lately; and, you see, you won't answer their letters, and that makes them angry."

"Selfish bloodhounds!" cried the captain; "what the deuce do they want? Do they expect me to coin money? And upon my word, Clara, I don't think it's very generous on your part to torture me in this way, just as I'm off to spend Christmas with my uncle, Sir John Strathnairn—whose only son Douglas, a precious muff, by the way, stands between me and one of the oldest baronetcies and finest estates in North Britain—and am going to bore myself to death deer-stalking, and that kind of thing, entirely on your account; since this is about my only chance of squaring the old miser, and reconciling him to the idea of my imprudent marriage. It's positively selfish of you, Clara; and I hate selfishness."

At this the young wife's tears flowed afresh. She was very young, very inexperienced, the fifth daughter of a small gentleman farmer in Somersetshire, with no better fortune than her pretty face and bright winning manner. Augustus Hawthornden, late captain of hussars, had put the finishing stroke to a career of imprudence by falling in love with this bright hazel-eyed damsel, and marrying her off-hand, in his own impetuous way. This event had happened about eighteen months ago, immediately after the sale of the captain's commission, the price of which he had anticipated to the last penny by means of his friends the money-lenders. Since this time the captain and his wife had lived as mysteriously as the young ravens. They were now the inhabitants of a charming little villa at Kensington, prettily furnished by a crack West End upholsterer, and the proud and happy parents of an infant prodigy, whose laundress's account alone was no trifle, and whose baby-existence required to be sustained by the produce of one especial cow, charged extra in the dairyman's bill.

This was the aspect of affairs on the 21st of December, when Captain Hawthornden prepared to leave his Penates, on a journey to the extreme north of Scotland, where he was to spend some weeks at the grim feudal castle of a fabulously rich uncle, Sir John Kilmarnock Strathnairn, from whom he hoped to obtain a new start in life.

"That's what I want, Clara," he told his confiding little partner. "The army was a mistake for a man with nothing but a beggarly younger son's portion of three hundred a year. As if any fellow in the Eleventh could live on his pay and a paltry three hundred a year! So, of course, I got my poor little estate mortgaged up to the eyes; and there's nothing left but the reversion to Toodleums, which no doubt he'll dispose of to the Jews before he gets it."

Mrs. Hawthornden shook her head at this.

"Oh, yes, he will, or he's not the Toodleums I take him for," said the captain resolutely.

So it was that Augustus Lovat Hawthornden, scion of two good old Scottish houses, departed on his northern journey, with a view to softening the heart of his wealthy maternal uncle, and with a vague idea that Sir John Strathnairn would be induced to give him a start in some new profession—say the Church or the Bar. He knew some fellows who were doing wonders at the Bar, and he had heard of snug sinecures in the Church.

"Egad! if the worst comes to the worst, I suppose I must go in for a Government employment, and devote my mind to the investigation of the cattle plague, or the control of sewers, or some such low drudgery," said the captain.

So he caught his little wife in his arms, gave her a hearty kiss, and hurried off to the loaded cab that was to convey him on the first stage of his journey.

The tender young wife could not be satisfied with so brief a parting. She ran out to the cab, and there was a passionate clasping of hands, and murmured blessings made inaudible by the sobs. And at the last——"

"O Gus!" she cried, "*can* you go without kissing Toodleums?" And she beckoned to the little nurse who was holding the baby up to his parents' view at a first-floor window.

"Oh, d——!" exclaimed the captain, "I can't lose the train for this kind of tomfoolery. King's Cross, cabby, as hard as you can pelt!"

The cruel cab horse went tearing off, and Mrs. Hawthornden returned to the house with her pretty pale hair dishevelled by the bitter winter wind, and her face wet with more bitter tears. In the hall she met the cook, a fiery-faced young person, whom the inexperienced little wife always encountered with fear and trembling.

"Oh, if you please, ma'am," said this domestic, in a breathless, gasping voice that was very alarming, "did master leave the money for my wages—two quarters one month and three weeks azact—as you *said* you'd arst him?"

"No, Sarah," faltered Mrs. Hawthornden; "I'm sorry to say he could not settle *everything* this time; but directly he comes back from Scotland, he—I—I am sure all will be made right."

"Settle everythink, indeed!" cried the cook contemptuously. "I should like to see anythink as *he* has settled. Settling ain't much in his way. Here I have been slaving myself to death in his service—and to wait on a gentleman that wants devilled kidneys and briled bones promiscous, for hisself and his friends, up to twelve o'clock at night and later, is not what I've been used to—going on three-quarters of a year and never seen the colour of his money. And I can't stand it no longer. So, if you please, ma'am, I shall leave this afternoon; and if I can't get my doo by fair means, I must get it by foul; which summonsing at the County Court by his cook won't bring much credit on Captain Orthongding, I should think."

"Oh, and if you please, mum, I should wish to leave at the same time as cook," said the brisk young housemaid; "not that I've got anythink to say agen you, ma'am, which you have always been a kind missus; but flesh and blood can't bear to be put off, and to be sworn at into the bargain without no more consideration than if we was Injy slaves."

"Oh, very well, Sarah and Jane," replied Mrs. Hawthornden hopelessly, "you must do as you please, and go away when you please. I am sure my husband will pay to the last farthing if you can only wait patiently till his affairs are arranged; but if you can't—"

"No, mum, we can't," answered the cook resolutely. "We're tired of waiting. The line must be drawed somewheres; and when the tradespeople declines to call for orders the time has come to draw it."

Mrs. Hawthornden left the deserters and went upstairs.

"It was unkind of them to leave it till Gus was gone," she thought; and then, with a thrill of horror, she considered what would happen if the nurse should also revolt. "I can live without dinner, and I can do the housemaid's work myself," she thought; "but baby is used to Hannah, and if she went away——"

The picture was too awful for contemplation. The poor little woman ran straight to the nursery—the pretty chamber which had been so daintily furnished in the days when, rich in the sense of an open account at the upholsterers, the captain had given his orders with a noble recklessness.

Here she found the nursemaid, a good-tempered-looking girl of eighteen, bending over the pink-curtained bassinet.

"He's a little fretful with his teeth to-day, mum," she said.

"Oh, Hannah," cried Clara Hawthornden, casting herself on her knees before this homely young person, "you won't leave me, will you—you won't de-de-desert the baby?"

"Leave Toodleums, ma'am? Bless his dear little heart! I'd as soon cut my head off as leave him. Why, Mrs. Hawthornden, if you haven't been crying! Oh, do, please, mum, get up! What could have put such a notion into your pretty head? Oh, please, mum, don't take on so!"

"I can't help it, Hannah. The others are going, and I thought you would go too; and my darling would cry for you. Oh, Hannah, we shall be all alone in the house; and the tradespeople won't call anymore till Captain Hawthornden's affairs are arranged—and we shall have n-n-nothing to eat!"

"Oh, yes, we will, mum," replied the dauntless Hannah. "Don't you be downhearted, mum; we'll manage somehow, depend upon it."

"I don't know, Hannah. In the hurry of his going away I forgot to ask my husband for a little ready money; and I haven't so much as a shilling to buy baby's biscuits."

The girl looked aghast at this.

"Oh, how I wish mamma would send me a hamper this Christmas!" said Mrs. Hawthornden piteously. "She sends one to my married sister, Mrs. Tozer, every year; but papa was so angry when I married Captain Hawthornden—it was a runaway match, you know, Hannah—that he won't let my name be mentioned at home; and I haven't a friend in the world except mamma, who daren't be kind to me for fear of papa."

"Never you mind, mum," replied Hannah cheerfully; "we'll get biscuits for baby, somehow, or my name's not Hannah Giles. Isn't there anything in the house I could take to——"

Here this excellent girl made a discreet and significant pause.

"Yes, Hannah, you good and faithful creature, I know what you mean. My jewellery has gone ever so long ago; all but this poor little wedding ring, and I could scarcely part with that—unless Toodleums were starving. But there's my cashmere shawl, and the silver-grey moiré that I wear at dinner parties; and if you really wouldn't mind——"

"Lor' bless you, mum, not a bit! Wait till after tea to-night. I know where to take them."

"Bless you!" cried the disconsolate young wife; "you're a true friend, Hannah."

At this juncture mistress and maid were interrupted by the sudden awakening of Master Toodleums; and after this diversion they went downstairs to reconnoitre the enemy's country, Toodleums crowing and dribbling on his nurse's shoulder. Below all was desolation. Curiously they explored the snug little kitchen and offices, into which the timid young housekeeper had rarely ventured to intrude during the cook's stern dominion. Awful was the havoc revealed by the present investigation: broken crockery, bottomless saucepans, knife-blades without handles, forks without prongs, grease, rags, waste, ruin, were visible in every corner. The larder was bare of everything except the heel of a stale loaf and a box of sardines, the latter being a species of *hors d'oeuvres* which the lower powers had not affected.

"Oh, Hannah, what can have become of the sirloin of beef we had for the late dinner yesterday? Such a monstrous joint, too, as the cook ordered, though I told her a little piece of roast beef. Why, you and I could have lived upon it for a week!"

"And the cook has taken it off in her box, I dare say," cried Hannah. "Oh, the barefaced hussy!"

There was evidently nothing edible in the house except the sardines, so mistress and maid were fain to wait until the shades of evening should permit the faithful Hannah to execute the somewhat delicate transaction in relation to the silver-grey moiré and the cashmere shawl.

"If you don't mind taking care of the baby for an hour, mum,

I'll tidy up the kitchen a bit and get the tea things ready; and then, while the kettle's boiling, I can run around to where I spoke of; and get some tea and sugar, and a rasher or so of bacon, and the baby's biscuits, and a fancy loaf as I come back. I don't suppose you'll care much about dinner to-day, mum."

"Dinner!" cried Mrs. Hawthornden; "I feel as if I should never be able to eat anything more as long as I live. Oh, Gus, if you only knew what we have to go through! Oh, my precious popsy, when *you* grow up and marry, you must never leave your poor little wife alone at Christmas-time, with all the debts unpaid, and everybody angry."

This apostrophe was addressed to the six-months-old infant, who looked supremely indifferent to the fond appeal. Mrs. Hawthornden took the child in her arms and went to the drawing-room, where she sat in a low chair by the dull fire, and indulged in that dismal refreshment which women call "a good cry."

She was very desolate, very miserable. The short winter day was already darkening, the prospect without looked bleak; but in the windows of other villas the firelight shone cheerily and the lonely young wife thought sadly of happy families assembled in those rooms; families across whose hearth the dread spectre Insolvency had never cast his gloomy shadow. And then she thought of her own distant home. The good old-fashioned rooms, always made especially gay and pleasant at this season. The chintz room and the blue room, the oak room and the cedar parlour; the bright winter flowers, and ever-blossoming chintz curtains; the fires glowing red on every hearth; the noble Worcester punch-bowl brought from its retirement; the chopping and mincing, and cake- and pastry-making, and bustle and preparation in the housekeeper's room; the gardener coming into the kitchen with his pile of holly and mistletoe, laurel, and bay; the odour of Christmas that pervaded the house; and the dear friends with whom she might never spend that holy festival again.

"Oh, if papa could see me now, I don't think he could be angry with me anymore," she said to herself despairingly.

For nearly two hours she sat alone, singing softly to her baby, and crying more or less all the time. And then Hannah came in with the tea-tray, and lighted candles, and the daintiest little dish of fried bacon, and baby's biscuits, and a jug of milk for that young gentleman's consumption.

"It's all right, mum, one pound fifteen-fifteen on the shawl, and a pound on the moiré; but you'd never believe the trouble I had to screw him up to it. And he made me have a ticket for each. That's their artful way. I've heard father say they make mints of money out of the tickets alone. And now do cheer up, and take your tea, that's a dear lady."

The brisk little maiden stirred the fire, drew the curtains, arranged the table, and made all things as cheerful and pleasant as circumstances would permit. Her mistress insisted that she should share the meal; and the two took their tea together—the girl almost overcome by so great an honour, the young wife's thoughts speeding northward with the gallant captain, who sat in the *coupé* of an express train, smoking Henry Clays, at eighteenpence apiece.

"Now don't you be downhearted, mum," said the faithful handmaid, as she bade her mistress good-night. "I only spent three shillings this evening; one pound twelve will carry us on till master comes home."

This was comfort; but poor Clara had not forgotten the threatened horror of the twenty-fourth, Christmas Eve, that day to which she used to look forward at the dear old home, an old-fashioned festival enough, with its simple dissipations in the way of acted charades, snapdragon, and egg-flip.

"Oh, what a child I was!" she exclaimed; and she had been indeed a joyous and innocent creature in those days. If she had been a calculating person, given to weigh advantages, and not the most unselfish and devoted of wives, she might have asked herself whether the proprietorship of a dashing *cidevant* cavalry officer and his superb moustache was a privilege absolutely worth all it had cost her.

The dreaded twenty-fourth arrived, and the weary hours crept by with leaden feet. Every sound of a step in the street set Clara's heart beating. No ominous single knocks came to the door, except the faint appeal of a shivering dealer in boot-laces; for the angry tradespeople knew the captain was away, and did not care to torment his helpless young wife uselessly, any more than they cared to supply her with goods without hope of payment. Even that long day wore itself out at last; and the mistress and the maid took their tea and rasher again together before a cheerful fire, and discussed the probability that Mr. Absalom's stony heart had been melted by the softening influences of the season, and that there would be no execution.

"The very word is so dreadful," said Mrs. Hawthornden; "and yet that's better than calling a cruel thing that makes a man prisoner an 'attachment.' I remember Augustus telling me he had an 'attachment' out against him; and it didn't sound dreadful at all; but the very next week he was taken to Whitecross Street. I wonder what they are doing at home now?—at tea, I dare say. When I shut my eyes I can see them all sitting round the great fireplace. I wonder whether any one thinks of me? I do wish mamma had contrived to send me a hamper, with a home-made pound-cake, and some mince pies and one of our famous geese; not on my own account, but on yours, Hannah, for you've been so good to me; and I should like you to have a nice Christmas dinner, and something to take home to your poor mother to-morrow evening. But I'm a famous goose to think of such a thing; for mamma couldn't send me a hamper without papa's knowledge, and he is so *dreadfully* angry with me."

A sharp rat-tat, something between a single knock and a postman's sounded on the door at this moment, and gave maid and mistress a kind of galvanic shock.

"Don't let anyone in, Hannah," cried Mrs. Hawthornden. "My husband said we were not to admit a creature."

Hannah had skipped to the window-curtains, and was peering out at the doorstep. She jumped back into the room as if she had been shot.

"Oh, be joyful, mum!" she cried. "You've got your wish. It's a 'AMPER!"

"No!"

"Yes, mum; and *such* a big one! Ain't it lovely! And mince pies, and pound-cake, and gooses too, I'll wager. And baby shall suck a bit of roast goose to-morrow, bless him! My brother Joe's baby ain't five months old yet, and will suck the gravy out of anything as well as if he was a grown man. Oh, won't we have a merry Christmas, mum—you, and me, and baby? And ain't I glad that cross old cook's gone!"

"It's like magic!" exclaimed Mrs. Hawthornden, as the imitation postman's knock was repeated impatiently. "Run to the door, Hannah. You're sure it *is* a hamper?"

"Lor' bless your heart, mum, as if I didn't know a Christmas 'amper when I see one!" and the girl flew into the little hall.

It was a foolish thing to be moved, perhaps, by such a vulgar trifle as a Christmas hamper; but Clara Hawthornden wept tears of pleasure as she waited for the welcome basket. It was not of the famous home-reared goose or home-made mince pies she thought; but of the love that had contrived the gift, the tender motherly strategems and plottings and contrivings that must have been gone through in order to compass the seasonable surprise.

"God bless the dear mother!" she murmured as she went out into the hall, where the queer-looking little old man was just depositing a noble hamper, the very straw oozing from the interstices of which looked quite appetising. Mrs. Hawthornden was too much moved to remember that the little old man standing in the hall was there in direct disobedience of the captain's solemn mandate that no stranger should be admitted within that door.

"Here is sixpence for yourself, my good man," said Clara politely. "Good evening." She looked towards the open door, gently indicating that the little old man could depart; but the old man, instead of so doing, gave a little whistle, and beckoned to some one without.

In the next moment a portly stranger stood on the threshold, gaily attired in a drab overcoat and olive-green trousers, and with gold chains and lockets twinkling on his expensive waistcoat.

"Sorry to have recourse to stratagem, miss," said this gentleman, removing the newest of white hats from the blackest and curliest of *chevelures,* "but really, you see, the captain's one of those people with whom one must be deeper than Garrick. Here is my warrant, miss, all correct and regular, as you may perceive. Suit of Shadrach Absalom. This old gent and I will take an inventory, miss; and he can remain on the premises afterwards."

"What!" cried Clara, growing very white; "do you mean to say that hamper is not from my mother at Somerton Manor?"

"That hamper, my dear young lady, is like the wooden horse that went into Troy. Don't trouble yourself to open it, my good girl; there's nothing but straw inside, and a brickbat or two just to give it solidity. All stratagems are fair in love and war, and the recovery of a just debt, especially when a bill has been renewed three times, as this one has. Shadrach Absalom is my first cousin, miss, and as good a fellow as ever lived; but the captain has really been too bad."

"I'm sure my husband means to pay everything when he comes from Scotland, where he has gone to visit his uncle, Sir John Strathnairn," faltered the horror-stricken Clara.

"What, do you mean to say that Captain Hawthornden has got such a pretty young creature as you for his wife, and that he can have the heart to go away and leave you to bear the brunt of his difficulties?" cried Laurence Absalom, the sheriff's officer, with honest indignation.

"I beg, sir, that you will not remark upon my husband's conduct. He always acts for the best. Oh, Hannah, what are we to do?"

"I know what I should like to do," answered the handmaiden spitefully, "and that is to scratch that nasty, deceiving old man's face."

"If you could scratch some of the dirt off it you'd be doing him a service, my dear," said Mr. Laurence Absalom, with easy good nature, while the old man sat quietly on the delusive hamper, the picture of grimy meekness.

Mr. Absalom called for a candle, and proceeded to explore the house, attended by the meek old man, who wiped his dirty face upon the dingiest of blue cotton handkerchiefs, and breathed very hard as he followed his commanding officer. Together the two men ransacked drawers and wardrobes, peered into chiffoniers, and violated the sanctity of writing desks, and carefully catalogued furniture and bedding, books and electro-plate, china and glass, table linen and pictures. All Clara's pretty dresses, her dainty ribbons and laces, her coquettish little bonnets and innocent girlish jackets, were set down on a sheet of greasy foolscap, while the two women looked on, one of them utterly helpless and miserable, wondering what would come next.

At last the inventory was complete, and Mr. Absalom prepared to take his departure.

"Of course, you'll be writing to the captain, ma'am," he said; "and you'll please tell him that unless this business is squared in five days' time his property will go to the hammer. I'm sure I'm very sorry on your account; but, you see, the captain knew what he had to expect, and he really ought to have provided against it. Good evening, Mrs. Hawthornden. The old gent will stay till the sale. You'll find him very quiet."

"What!" cried Clara aghast, "is that dreadful old man to stop in the house?"

The dreadful old man gave a grunt of assent.

"Upon my word, ma'am, I wish I was the party," said Mr. Absalom gallantly; "I should consider it quite a privilege; but old Jiffins does that part of the work, and you'll find him as harmless as an old spaniel, if you don't mind his appetite; that is rather alarming, I admit. Good night."

And with an easy nod Mr. Laurence Absalom departed, leaving the mistress and maid staring in consternation at the man in possession, who was refreshing himself with a pinch of snuff out of a screw of paper. He certainly was by no means a prepossessing individual; indeed, it is impossible to imagine grubbiness more dingy than the grubbiness of this old man's aspect. He wore a long great coat, and of shirt or shirt collar there were no traces visible; but in lieu of these conventionalities he displayed a dirty wisp of neckerchief that had once been white, but which was now a sickly yellow. His boots seemed to have been the dress boots of a giant, and were wrinkled like the skins of French plums. On one hand he wore a roomy black glove, also of the texture of French plums. His grey hair straggled over the greasy velvet collar of his coat, in an eminently patriarchal fashion, and his bottle nose—nay, indeed, his complexion generally—was of that rubicund hue produced by copious consumption of malt and spirituous liquors, in conjunction with exposure to all kinds of weather. Such as he was, he seemed to Mrs. Hawthornden the living embodiment of a nightmare. She stood rooted to the ground, staring at him hopelessly and helplessly, and it was only the brisk Hannah who aroused her from the waking trance.

"Hadn't the old gentleman better step into the master's study?" suggested the girl. "He'll want to sit somewhere, you see, ma'am."

"To sit? Yes, and he is going to live here. Oh, Hannah, *what* shall we do?"

"Don't you be frightened, mum," whispered the girl; "I've lived where there's been a man in possession, and it's nothing when you're used to it. Step this way, if you please, sir," she added briskly, and she pointed to a little box of a room opposite the drawing-room.

The old man walked to the door of this apartment, then suddenly turned back and approached Mrs. Hawthornden, who quailed before him. To her horror he lifted his dirty hand and laid it—oh, so gently!—on her soft hair, patting her head as if she had been a child.

"Don't you be frightened, my pretty!" he said; "I've seen a deal of trouble in my time, and I can feel for them as have their homes broke up, though it *is* my business to break 'em. It's the business that's hardhearted, my pretty, not me. You bear that in mind, and don't worry yourself about old Jiffins no more than if he was an old tomcat. He'll keep his place, depend upon it, and won't give no trouble to no one."

"I'm sure you're very kind," murmured Clara, half crying; "but it does seem so dreadful!"

"Of course it do, to a sweet young creatur' like you. But Lor' bless you, mum, there's places I go to reg'lar, as you may say, and where I'm quite like one of the family. The children calls me uncle. 'Crikey, father!' cries one of the little chaps, 'if here ain't Uncle Jiffins come back agen!' and they're quite took aback to find their parents ain't over glad to see me. I suppose there ain't no objection to a pipe in this here room, ma'am?"

"Oh, no, no, no," cried Clara piteously, "you can smoke as much as you like; and there's some of my husband's Turkish tobacco in that jar on the mantlepiece which you can take if you please."

"Thank you, mum. Shag's more in my way; but if you could put your hand upon a little bit of Cavendish, I should take it very kind."

A piece of Cavendish tobacco was found, after some little trouble, and Mr. Jiffins ensconced himself in Augustus Hawthornden's easy chair—a charming chair, in which the captain had been wont to read the papers and ponder somewhat gloomily on financial questions; and Mr. Jiffins being duly established in this room, which was conveniently close to the hall door, and in a manner commanded the whole house, Mrs. Hawthornden and Hannah went back to the drawing-room, where Toodleums, happily unconscious of this domestic revolution, was still slumbering placidly in his bassinet.

Together the mistress and maid sat down to face life with its new responsibilities.

"I'll write to Augustus this very night, Hannah; but my letter can't go till to-morrow—perhaps not even then, as it's Christmas Day; and a letter takes such a time travelling to the Highlands; and then there would be the journey back; and oh, dear! when will Gus come to send that awful old creature away? He doesn't seem unkind, but oh, so dirty! And to think that he should be sitting in Gus's favourite chair, with his head against the antimacassar that I worked with my own hands!"

Happily the brisk little nursemaid was too cheery a creature to be altogether discomfited even by a man in possession. She gave the baby refreshment from a bottle furnished with a wonderful gutta-percha machine, which made the feeding business look very much like laying on gas; and then she reminded her mistress that it was getting late, and shops might be closed in the neighbourhood.

"There's to-morrow's dinner, you see, mum; and then there's the old gent's supper. I suppose I'd better get a bit of cheese?"

"Oh, good gracious me!" cried Clara, "will he want supper?"

"Lor' bless your innocence, mum, of course he will, and breakfast and dinner, and all his meals, and his beer. It's the rule, you see, mum: you finds 'em in everythink."

With this Hannah handed her mistress the baby, and departed.

The inexperienced girl-wife sat staring apathetically at the blackened coals in the pretty steel grate. She felt as some young mother of the antediluvian period may have felt, as she sat with her child in her lap, listening to the rising waters, and waiting for the end of the world.

Hannah came back by-and-by, with bread and cheese and beer for the old man, and a modest little joint of beef for the next day's dinner, and a quarter of a pound of tea, and other small matters, which altogether made a terrible hole in that one pound twelve shillings which alone stood between this household and destitution.

"We shall have to change the half sovereign for his beer to-morrow, mum," said the maiden; "but we shall hold out till the captain comes home, depend upon it."

Mrs. Hawthornden counted the hours that must elapse before the captain could possibly come home, and counted them over again, till her brain grew dizzy. Her only comfort next morning was to think that some of those weary hours were gone.

Hannah waited on Mr. Jiffins, taking his meals to the captain's snug little sanctum, and coming back to her mistress to report the awful havoc he had made with the loaf, or the alarming way he had slashed off slices from the joint.

"And I think if there was oceans of gravy, mum, he'd soak them up; for, let alone smashing his purtaters, he sops it up with his bread."

Oh, what a dreary Christmas Day! Cabs and carriages dashed up to other houses in the pretty suburban street; gaily dressed people went to and from the neighbouring churches; at night music sounded and lights gleamed from many windows, while Clara Hawthornden walked up and down with her fretful baby and thought of what they were doing at home—alas, her home no longer!

Toodleums had been fractious all day, and grew worse towards evening; and while Hannah went for the supper beer he took the opportunity of working himself into a paroxysm of crying that terrified the young mother out of her wits. She was pacing the room, trying in vain to soothe her infant, when the door was softly opened, and Mr. Jiffins appeared. Clara almost dropped the baby at sight of this apparition.

"Let me take him a bit," said Mr. Jiffins. "I'm used to babies, bless 'um."

"Oh, please don't!" cried Clara, as the dreaded intruder advanced his grimy hands; "indeed, indeed he wouldn't come to you."

But, to the mother's utter astonishment, Toodleums, the most particular and capricious of babies, did go to this grubby old man, and, after a few minutes' hushing and dandling and see-sawing in the air, did actually cease to cry.

"Bless their dear little hearts! they all come to *me*," said Mr. Jiffins complacently. "I've got a grandson just this one's size, and what that little dear do suffer with the wind on his stomach is only beknown to hisself and to me. It ain't temper, bless you, when they skreeks like that—it's wind; and you take my advice, and just let your gal fetch twopenn'orth of essence of peppermint—none of your Daffy for my money—and give him two drops on a lump of sugar melted in a spoonful of warm water, and he'll be quiet as a lamb."

Mr. Jiffins nursed the baby till Hannah came back with the beer and the change for that last half sovereign, which Mrs. Hawthornden had contemplated fondly as she parted with it forever. The girl stared aghast on beholding her charge in the arms of the intruder; but he despatched her to the chemist's for peppermint as coolly as if he had been the infant's favourite grandfather. Mrs. Hawthornden had sunk exhausted into her chair, and looked on with amazement while the man in possession developed a perfect genius for nursing, and entertained Toodleums with a broken tobacco-pipe and a latch-key, as that young gentleman rarely allowed himself to be entertained by the most elaborate inventions of the toy-maker.

"You seem to have a wonderful power over children," murmured Clara at last.

"I'm fond of 'em, ma'am, that's where it is; and they knows it. There's nothing gets over 'em like that—real rightdown fondness of 'em. Now, I'll wager while you was carrying this little chap up and down just now, your mind had wandered like, and you was thinking of your own troubles, and you felt him a drag upon you."

Clara nodded assent.

"*To* be sure!" exclaimed Mr. Jiffins triumphantly; "and that child knowed it—he knowed it as he hadn't got your whole heart; and you can't do nothing with a child unless you gives him your whole heart. They're the deepest little Garricks out for that, bless 'em!—— Ain't you now, ducksy? Yes, o' course; you knows you is."

Toodleums assented to this proposition with a rapturous crow.

"Bein' as it's Christmas night, mum," said Mr. Jiffins by-and-by, when the peppermint had been brought and administered, "and my disposition lively like, perhaps you wouldn't take it as a liberty if I asked leave to eat my bit of supper in here? It *is* rather lonesome in that there little room, and seems lonesomer being Christmas-time."

What could a helpless young wife and mother say to this startling request? Mr. Jiffins was master of the situation. There was something very dreadful in sitting down to supper with this dirty old man; but Toodleums was hanging on to one of his greasy coat-buttons with the affection of a life-time, and a man thus affected by Toodleums could not be utterly base. So Mrs. Hawthornden murmured a faint assent to the proposed arrangement. The tray was brought, modestly furnished with a piece of cheese, a loaf, a little glass dish of butter, and a jug of ale. Mr. Jiffins surveyed these simple preparations with an approving eye.

"Raw cheese is rather too cold to the palate in this weather," he said thoughtfully; "what would say now, mum, to a rabbit?"

"I am very sorry," faltered Mrs. Hawthornden apologetically, "but we haven't any rabbits in the house."

"Lor' bless you, ma'am, I means toasted cheese. If that good-tempered young woman of yours would get me the mustard-pot and a small saucepan, and then kneel down before the fire and toast a round or two of bread, I'd soon show you what I means by a rabbit."

Hannah ran off to procure these articles, and she was presently employed in toasting cheese under the old man's direction.

"A teaspoonful of mustard, and a good lump of fresh butter, and a tablespoonful of ale, and let it simmer by the side of the fire while you toasts the bread, my dear," said Mr. Jiffins, who had nursed the baby, and looked on approvingly while the handmaid obeyed him.

To poor Clara Hawthornden it seemed like some distempered dream. "If anybody should call!" she thought; and she had to tell herself over and over again that ten o'clock on Christmas night was not a likely hour for callers. She thought of the joyous party in her old home—the girls in white muslin and scarlet sashes, the matrons in their rustling silks: and then of the more stately festival at Strathnairn Castle, and the black oak buffets loaded with gold plate, which her husband had so often described to her; but from these bright pictures her fancy always came back to the old man superintending the simmering cheese.

Both he and Hannah persuaded her presently to taste this delicacy. She had eaten nothing at dinner, for the sense of the old man's presence in the captain's study had weighed upon her like an actual burden. He was not nearly so dreadful seated opposite her with her baby on his knee. Our skeletons are never so hideous when confronted boldly as when hidden away in some dark cupboard. Mrs. Hawthornden tasted the Welsh rarebit. It was really excellent. She remembered having heard Augustus talk of eating such things at Evans'. And presently she found herself eating this toasted cheese with more appetite than anything she had tasted since her husband's departure. Though familiar, Mr. Jiffins was not utterly wanting in reverence. He resigned the baby to Hannah, and insisted on taking his supper at the remotest corner of the table, where there was no tablecloth. The edge of the tablecloth he seemed to consider the line of demarcation; no persuasion could induce him to infringe upon it by the breadth of a hair. But at this uncomfortable corner he ate his supper with a relish that was almost contagious, and talked a good deal in a pleasant chirping manner, as he quaffed his ale. After supper he ventured upon a conundrum, and that being approved, upon another; and Mrs. Hawthornden found herself laughing quite merrily, but still with the sense that it was all a distempered dream. Dreadful as it was to be cheerful in the company of a nursemaid and of a broker's man, it was perhaps better for this lonely little wife than brooding over her woes. She slept quite soundly after the toasted cheese and the conundrums, and awoke next morning to find the cheerful Hannah at her bedside with a neatly arranged little breakfast-tray.

"It was Mr. Jiffins as told me to bring you up your breakfast, ma'am. 'Let her sleep a little late, poor pretty!' he said, 'and take her a cup of tea and a new-laid egg when she wakes'; and—*would you believe it*, mum? the old dear goes and fetches the egg hisself, while I biles the kettle, though he told me it was as much as his employment was worth to step outside our door! And if he hasn't been and hearthstoned the steps before I was up, mum, and swep' the kitchen beautiful—for a handier old man I never did see; and he says, if you could pick a bit of Irish stew for your dinner, he's a rare hand at one."

Mrs. Hawthornden did not care to pick a bit of Irish stew, nor did she affect any dish in the preparation of which the broker's man could be manipulatively engaged; but she fully appreciated his kind wish to help her and her faithful handmaiden, and thanked him prettily for his kindness when she encountered him downstairs. Before long she had still greater reason to thank him; for Toodleums suffered severely in the cutting of an upper tooth, and both nursemaid and mother profited by grandfather Jiffins' experience.

The days went by slowly, but no longer made hideous to Clara Hawthornden by her horror of Jiffins, who, instead of an incubus, had proved himself an elderly angel in the house. Her chief trouble now arose from her husband's silence. The fifth day must soon elapse, and then there would be a salc, and she and her child would be turned out of doors, homeless, shelterless. No, not quite. Here Providence interposed in the humble guise of Jiffins.

"My married daughter's got a room as she lets, and as is now empty; and if they've the heart to turn you out of here, you can go there and welcome," said the dingy benefactor. "There ain't no spring sofys, nor shiny steel grates; but it's that clean you might eat your victuals off the floor; and, if you don't mind a mews, it's respectable."

A mews! Where would not the desolate mother have gone to obtain shelter for her baby?

"Oh, Mr. Jiffins!" she cried, clasping one of those grimy hands, which had once inspired her with such aversion, "what should we do without you?"

What, indeed! The last shilling of that last half sovereign had been spent two days ago, and since then the little household had been sustained by money advanced by Jiffins.

"You'll pay me fast enough one of these odd days, I dessay," said Jiffins, when Clara deprecated this last obligation.

For the first time since she had left her home she wrote to ask a favour of her mother. The boon she demanded was a five-pound note, wherewith to pay and reward Jiffins. Never before had she allowed the home-friends to know that her Augustus left her with one wish ungratified.

The fifth day expired. The hour of doom was near. Strange men in paper caps came to take up the carpets. The dear little china closet, in which Clara had so delighted, when the housemaid would allow her to enter it, was rifled of its contents, and dinner services, tea services, and glass were spread on the dining room table. Bills were stuck on the outside of the house; within, nasty little bits of paper, with numbers on them, were pasted upon every article, even—oh, bitterest drop in this cup of bitterness—on the sacred bassinet of Toodleums, still a martyr to his teeth. Ignominy could go no further; and there were still no tidings of the captain. But for Jiffins and Hannah, Clara Hawthornden must surely have died of this agony.

It was the very morning of the sale. Mr. Absalom was there in all his glory. The auctioneer had arrived. Dingy men with greasy little memorandum-books pervaded the house. Clara sat with Hannah and the baby in the little study, where strange faces peered in upon them every now and then; and intending buyers made heartless remarks about the curtains, and informed the dingy commission agents how high they were disposed to bid for the captain's pet chair. There was no corner of the house sacred to the homeless woman's despair. Clara felt that it would have been almost better to sit in the street. The most unfriendly doorstep would have been a more peaceful resting place than this.

Alas! In this bitter crisis even the faithful Jiffins could no longer protect her. He was sent hither and thither by the higher powers, and could not yet snatch half an hour's respite in which to conduct Mrs. Hawthornden to the humble lodging he had secured for her.

"Oh, Hannah, I wish Mr. Jiffins would take us away from all these dreadful people!" Clara cried piteously. She had ceased to hope for rescue from Augustus. *That* ship had foundered, and Jiffins was the lifeboat of benevolence that must carry her to the shore of safety.

"Oh, Hannah, if he would only take us to his daughter's house in the mews!" she cried; and in the next moment a hansom tore up to the door, a stentorian voice broke out into exclamations of surprise and indignation, interspersed with execrations. A shrill scream burst from the young wife's pale lips.

"Gus!" she cried, while Toodleums set up a sympathetic shriek; "oh, thank God, thank God!" and she must have fallen but for Hannah's supporting arms.

Yes, it was the captain, dressed in black, and with a crape hatband. He distributed his anathemas freely as he strode into the villa. What the dash is the meaning of this dashed business? Take down those dashed bills and turn those dashed people out of the house; and so on. Mr. Absalom advanced politely, and suggested that if the captain would be so kind as to settle that little matter of 326*l.* 17*s.* 6*d.* the sale need not proceed. The captain pulled out a brand-new cheque book and signed his first cheque upon a brand new banking account, which document he handed to Mr. Absalom with an injured air.

"You ought to have known better, Absalom," he said, "after all our past dealing."

"To tell you the truth, captain, it was my experience of the past that made me rather sharp in the present," replied the other politely.

"Come, Clara, don't cry," exclaimed Captain Hawthornden to the poor little woman, who was sobbing on his shoulder. "I didn't get your letter till yesterday afternoon, and have been travelling ever since. I was away with a party in the mountains. And there's been a dreadful piece of work at Strathnairn—my cousin Douglas, Sir John's only son, killed by the explosion of his rifle. No one to blame but himself, poor beg—poor dear fellow! Sir John's awfully cut up, as well he may be; and I'm next heir to the title and estates. Yes, little woman, you'll be Lady Strathnairn before you die; for my uncle will never marry, poor old boy! Very dreadful, ain't it, poor Douglas' death? But of course, uncommonly jolly for us."

"Oh, Gus, how awful for Sir John! But, thank Heaven, you have come back! You can never understand what I have suffered; and if it hadn't been for Jiffins——"

"Jiffins! Who the deuce is Jiffins?"

"The man in possession. He has been so good to us—has lent us money, even; and but for him we must have starved."

"Good Heavens, Clara!" cried the captain, aghast, "you don't mean to say you've degraded yourself by borrowing money from a broker's man?"

"What could I do, dear? You left me without any money, you know," replied the wife innocently

"You really ought to have known better, Clara," said the captain sternly. "But where is Jiffins? Let me pay this fellow his confounded loan."

"I think you'd better let me pay it, dear. If you'll give me a ten-pound note, I can make it all right."

So Mr. Jiffins received about a thousand per cent. for his loan, which had been little more than a sovereign, and he spent New Year's Day very pleasantly in the bosom of his married daughter's household, No. 7½, Stamford Mews, Blackfriars. But perhaps at some future audit, when such small accounts are balanced before the Great Auditor, Mr. Jiffins may receive even more than a thousand per cent. for that little loan.

Christmas Eve—Polchester Winter Piece

HUGH WALPOLE

It was a seasonable Christmas that year. Enough snow fell, then enough frost came, and then the sun shone. If it did not shine, at least it rode a circle of crimson fire through the heavens and, before the frost but after the slime of preparatory fogs, fragments of its fire splashed the High Street and spread in pools across the Precincts floor.

As I have intimated in other chronicles, Polchester of the old days was an enclosed town. The Riviera was unknown to it and the Garden of Allah a dream with Omar. Though London might call to the richer citizens on one occasion or another, at Christmas time every one stayed at home and, more wonderful yet to our modern disillusion, enjoyed family parties with Christmas trees, plum puddings, stockings, and the waits invited into the hall. It is not true, however, that the weather was any more romantic then than it is to-day; there were just as many rainy and muggy and foggy and dirty and dismal skies, and Glebeshire, warmer than any other part of the British Isles, has never had an intimate acquaintance with crisp and shining snow. About once in twenty years there are snowfalls, frosts, and blue skies, and how happy then every one is and how eagerly every one hands down the year to an envious posterity!

This was such a year, and ten days before Christmas the frost came and held, the powdered snow remained jewelled and resplendent, the sun looked down from a sky as delicately blue as an egg-shell and laughed to see the fun. And fun there was!

Magnet's toy-shop in the Market Cloisters had a Father Christmas, a true and veritable Father Christmas to be seen with two crimson cheeks and long snow-white beard any afternoon between two and four. Jeremy Cole so beheld him, and his sisters Mary and Helen, and the Dean's son Ernest, and the Fisher girls, and little Tommy Chawner. He did not say much, but he moved between the dolls and the trains, the balls and the soldiers, as only Santa Claus could move, with an authority, a benignity, a ripe wisdom that no impostor could have been clever enough to feign!

Every one did their best. In the Market-place there was a Punch and Judy with a thick-set jolly-faced man in charge, and he might have been that very same Garrick, friend of Maradick, whose history has been elsewhere narrated. I don't say he was, and I don't say he wasn't. Half-way up the High Street, Gummridge's the stationers had a whole Christmas tree in their window. Here was a stumbling-block to the whole High Street traffic. It was quite impossible to get any child—any perambulator baby indeed—past that window. It was a tree frosted, coloured, and shining, hung about with every glittering bauble, shaped to a perfect pinnacle of exquisite symmetry. But best of all was the window of Hunt & Griffin, the General Store, for here, for the first time in Polchester history, was a whole front window given over to pageantry, to none other than the scene in the life of Cinderella when, despondent beside the fire, she is amazed by the sudden apparition of her peaked-hatted Godmother. There is the fire and there Cinderella, there the pots and pans, the brick floor, and the huge kitchen rafters, there the Godmother, and there beyond the snow-lined window-pane the vision of the gold coach and the snow-white ponies. So great was the confusion outside the window that had this occurred in these traffic-haunted times the show must have been forbidden, but in those lucky days nobody minded, nobody cared. Let the children have a good time, Christmas comes but once a year, and even Mrs. Sampson, although her neuralgia was at its height, could not but admit that the window made a happy display.

The town rang during those days with laughter. Propter Hill outside the town had just enough snow on it to allow of tobogganing, and Pol Fields, having been flooded, gave for a whole wonderful fortnight the most marvellous skating. The town rang with laughter and the ringing of bells. The Cathedral let itself go and burst into perpetual peals of merriment to the great annoyance of late sleepers, dyspeptics, and ruminating essayists. There was fun everywhere, apples and oranges in the Market-place, and carols up and down the streets after dark.

It was the best Christmas that Polchester had known for many a day past or would know for many a day to come.

Mrs. Amorest was one who had always enjoyed a seasonable Christmas. To her as to every old person Christmas was filled with sad memories, but she had a wonderful gift of enjoying fun at the moment of its occurrence, and being aware that she was so enjoying it, and because the fun in her life had been neither frequent nor extravagant very small occurrences amused and excited her.

This was the happiest Christmas known to her for many a day. Struggle as she might not to think of the money coming to her, she could not keep it out of her consciousness. She told herself again and again (and when she was alone in her room she repeated the words aloud sometimes) that she must not place too strong a reliance on her cousin's promise. "He may have altered his mind the next moment. It's silly to believe him." Nevertheless the solemnity of his words, the caress of his hand as it rested on her head—these things were difficult to dismiss.

And the happiness that came from the promise was also difficult to dismiss. She was naturally happy. Give her the least excuse and she must be happy. Although she believed that God did not intend human beings should be very happy because they were in this world for the training of their souls, and souls were better trained by sorrow than by joy, nevertheless an imp of happiness would continue to jump in her heart and stir her little world with his discordant cries of joy. Joy at what? A kindly action, a splash of sun across the street, a barrel-organ round the corner, a stained-glass window, an apple, and a piece of cheese. She *could* not keep down her spirits as, being a penniless, lonely old widow of over seventy, she should.

And, this Christmas, she lost completely her self-control. She adored above everything else in the world the spending of money, perhaps for the very reason that she never had very much to spend. She had never been able to believe that statement often written in the papers that millionaires did not know what to do with their money. Did not know! Why, she could spend a million pounds quite easily at Gummridge's alone! But there! The newspapers were never to be trusted. She liked greatly to be given things, but still better was it herself to make presents. The excitement of giving some one something he or she wanted was intense, to watch the opening of the parcel, to see the stare of pleasure and surprise, to hear the exclamation, to feel the affection flowing out—was there any luxury in life like it?

And it was a luxury that, of late, she had been compelled to deny herself. Last Christmas she had given Agatha Payne half a dozen pocket-handkerchiefs, Mrs. Bloxam a piece of ribbon, and her cousin a pocket-book. Worst sorrow of all, it was impossible to send Brand anything. No use to throw parcels out into the void. The best she could do was to write two letters, one a month in advance, and this she sent to the only address she had, something in California, and then one on Christmas Eve, such as she had always written to him at Christmas time. This she also sent out to California, but she wrote it because for a moment it brought him closer to her—she felt, with his photograph up there in front of her, as though she had him with her in the room. These were all but poor substitutes for reality, and, cheat ourselves as we may, our subconscious selves refuse to be deceived. Mrs. Amorest knew nothing about her subconscious self, but she did know that after last Christmas she had a miserable sense of inadequacy and frustrated purpose. She had made nobody happy. Even Mrs. Bloxam had disappeared into the intimacies of her family to emerge two days later with a black eye and a bruised cheek. This year she would fling her cap over the mill. She had prospects. She did not face them finally, those prospects, did not take them, hold them in front of her, look them in the eyes and say to them as one always ought to do to prospects, "Now, are you sound and healthy? Have you got heart and lungs and legs and arms and a good stiff back?" No, she merely reported on them—she heard that they were good and healthy and promised very well indeed! Then she went ahead.

The plan came to her in the middle of the night, or rather in one of those early morning hours when the first cock crows and the hidden despair raises its abominable head. Lying there in the early morning she drove her despairs away and considered Miss Beringer. Poor Miss Beringer! What a frightened, nervous, trembling creature she was! She would like to do something for her! She would like well to give her a happy Christmas! And Agatha Payne, too. It was then that the idea came to her.

At first she was frightened of it. It would demand energy and persistence. And *had* she money enough? Money in the future would not do. She examined her purse and found that she had sufficient did she use part of next quarter's rent. She trembled at that, but she was sure that kind Mr. Agnew, when he knew of the promise that her cousin had made to her, would not hesitate to advance her. . . .

She trembled. Her heart warned her. Her cheeks were flushed and she had a guilty air. But she held to her purpose, and once she had begun she did not look back. Once she had begun she *could* not look back. She moved, during those frosty coloured days, about the town, the very spirit of adventure. She found that she must go quietly. The excitement tired her, and sometimes she would, in a moment, feel so weary that she *could* not get to the top of the High Street, and on one occasion when she was at the top she could not go down again and had to take refuge in the shop of Mr. Bennett, the grand bookseller. There she sat, greatly alarmed, on a chair in the very middle of the shop with busts of Byron and Walter Scott looking down on her and a grand smell of Russian leather and old vellum in her nostrils, and the complete works of George Eliot at her elbow. Old Mr. Bennett was very kind to her although she told him at once that she was not there to buy anything, and who should come in at that very moment but Archdeacon Brandon himself, magnificent, handsome, superb, ordering somebody "on the Psalms" with the air of a king and a conqueror. She looked around her with the hope of seeing some of her husband's plays, and when she did not would have liked to ask Mr. Bennett whether he kept them in stock, but her courage failed her and she could only thank him very much and slip out of the shop as quietly as possible. Fortunately she did not hear the Archdeacon's question: "And who was that shabby little woman?" He asked out of all kindness, feeling it his duty as the father of the flock to keep his eye upon all the inhabitants of the town.

She tried to keep her head about her purchases. She found, as many another has found before and after her, that the best things were always the most expensive. And then when it came to the central purchase of all, to the core, the heart, the kernel, the pinnacle, the *pièce de résistance*, the *raison d'être*, and any other foreign phrase that you prefer, she found that *here* expense was inevitable. Try as you would, it must cost more than you had supposed. Of course she only wanted a small one, but even the small ones . . . And then at the last, two days before Christmas, she found in the Market-place, in a corner behind the old woman under the green umbrella, the very thing, a darling, a perfect specimen, a miracle, and, when she enquired of the nice round-faced man whose possession it was, she found that it was only . . . well, less than the experience of the last two days had led her to believe possible, although more, a good deal more, than she had originally intended. She bought it, and ordered that it should be sent to her room, blushing a little in spite of herself as she named the address. She gave her name very carefully, begging him to be watchful that it should not be sent to any other room by mistake, and he promised her, saying that he would himself bring it.

He did in fact arrive with it when she was there, and she liked him very much, holding him in conversation for quite a while, and then giving him an orange for the baby. After that she guarded her room like a dragoness and would not allow May Beringer, who was already forming a too constant habit of "dropping in," to cross her threshold.

Christmas Eve arrived, and Mrs. Amorest, awaking to the inspiring voice of Mrs. Bloxam, was delighted when she discovered how fine and clear it was; no wind, the smoke rising from the chimneys elephant grey against the blue, the thin rind of frost, the sparrows already chattering at her window for their crumbs.

After her little mid-day meal she sat down to the table, found her paper and envelopes, and wrote to Brand.

Her letter was as follows:

My dearest, darling Boy—I write to you as I always do, although I sadly fear that it will be a long time before you get this letter. The one that I wrote to you a month ago may reach you before Christmas, and I hope it will. This I am writing because it seems as though I am talking to you, and I don't wish to allow Christmas to pass by without having a word with my dear boy.

Perhaps you have been writing to me and still to the old address. I told them in Cheltenham to forward anything on, but they are so stupid at the post-office, although, as a matter of fact, I always think it wonderful, considering the sort of postmen one sees walking about, that they don't lose more letters than they do—quite boys some of them are, and they none of them have very intelligent faces, although I daresay they are good men.

Well, dearest boy, I try to imagine to myself the kind of Christmas you are having, but it is really difficult for me, because you told me in the last letter I had from you that it was quite hot at Christmas time. That seems to me very strange and not very nice, I think. Of course it is often warm here for Christmas. Both last year and the year before that we had rain and muggy weather, but this year it is delightful, with a hard frost and the sun shining, cold and seasonable. It's so pleasant for the children and more healthy for everybody, I am sure.

I am very well in health. That cough I had when I wrote to you last has quite gone away and I am sure it's those lozenges that I found at Cubitt's (He's our best chemist here in the High Street). If only I could hear that you are quite well and will come home soon for a visit I would be quite happy. You know, dear boy, I am an old woman now and can't expect to live for ever, so that I do hope you'll be able to come home soon. It's very nice here and I'm very comfortable. There's something else I'd like to tell you about, but I suppose that I must not just yet because it isn't quite settled. I think of you so much and pray for you night and morning. At this time of the year when God came down to earth and took upon Him our flesh and was a little baby in the manger, I think we should all make Him feel how thankful we are. I know that He is looking after you and so I don't worry about you. At least I know that you are warm. You used to be so careless about your underclothing when you were a little boy.

My dearest boy, you are always in my thoughts. Your loving

MOTHER.

She sat for a long time after she had written the letter with his photograph in front of her. She thought of him in all the ways that she had known him—as a baby at her breast, as a small boy in his first trousers, as a boy going to his first day-school and forgetting her so quickly in the new excitements of other boys and games and masters, as all right and proper boys must do, of course. And then, as he grew, her interest in the strange new personality that developed, as flower from the bud—a personality that was so strange because it was like neither herself nor his father, somebody quite new. And then his growing independence, his chafing at the literary and artistic interests of his father, his desire for the open-air life and complete independence. Then her own strange sympathy with him; and although she loved him so dearly she understood that he should want to get away and be free. She had felt it herself in her married life, and she realised that he *was* her own son, not by right of the quiet and domestic character that was most obvious in her, but by right of that secret independence and sharpness of judgment that her married life had subdued in her. He left her and at intervals returned to her. She had been a woman of forty when she had borne him, and he had been only twenty-seven when she had last seen him, still a boy although so strong and independent! She looked at the photograph until she seemed to draw him out of the frame and he came to her and put his arms round her and teased her in the old laughing way that he had always had. But she was not simply a sentimental woman; she was in fact scornful of emotion that led to nothing, and so she put the photograph back upon the mantelpiece, put on her bonnet and her coat, and, because it was already three o'clock and would soon be dusk, hurried off to take her present to her cousin.

This year she was giving him a picture, a photogravure in a nice black frame of Holman Hunt's "Carpenter's Shop." She had not been quite lately to visit him lest she should seem to be reminding him of his promise. She had not heard how his health was, but she hoped that this bright weather had helped him, and that he would perhaps see her. Nevertheless as she crossed the bridge and climbed the hill a little chilling wind, whence she knew not, breathed upon her heart. Rising out of the dark purple-hued river appeared the figure of Agatha Payne.

She saw, quite unexpectedly, reasons for May Beringer's terrors. There *was* something alarming about Agatha, something not quite normal and healthy, something odd and twisted. It came, perhaps, because the poor old thing lived so much alone, but Mrs. Amorest gave a little shiver and thought to herself that she would move from that house in the spring to somewhere brighter and more companionable. She could not drive the company of Agatha from her mind. All up the hill it kept pace with her, and then, in another flash of memory, she saw a picture of her childhood, something that had not come to her for many a year. It was a picture that used to hang in the dining-room, of a witch weaving her spells in a dark and lonely wood. Before her was a large iron pot into which she flung toads and snakes and strange purple-tinted leaves. From the cauldron came a blue thick smoke. It was true that the witch did not physically resemble Agatha. She was old and skinny, with a back bent double and long groping fingers, but there was something . . . something . . .

And then, pausing for breath before she entered her cousin's gate, she smiled at her folly. Her practical mind drove her fancies like mist into the frosty air.

The house, always ugly and forbidding, seemed simply not to

belong to the fresh and wonderful day. The woods that fringed the hill were marvellous in their mystery, the fragments of the river that gleamed among the brown folds of the sloping fields glittered like shreds of broken glass faintly amethyst, the powdered frost shone and twinkled in the sharp and friendly air, but the house was untouched by this beauty; aloof and hostile it seemed to deride and despise any spirit that could wish goodwill to men and friendship to all the world. To Mrs. Amorest especially, as she approached it, it seemed to say: "You aren't truly so sentimental as to believe that the human race is loving and kind. Rid yourself of your illusions. You should be ashamed of yourself at your age that you have any."

As she rang the bell and heard it clang defiantly through the house she felt again a dim and unhappy foreboding. She always disliked her meeting with the housekeeper. She felt that that woman despised and patronised her, and now to-day she wished that she might encounter no one who raised hostility in her heart. But one could only pass to her cousin over the housekeeper's body. There was no other way for it.

The woman herself opened the door and was more forbidding than she had ever been. Mrs. Amorest suspected that in some way she had learnt about her cousin's promise. Always before there had been a tacit recognition, however reluctant, that Mrs. Amorest had some right there. To-day she blocked the doorway with her peevish ill-natured body and showed no sign at all of moving. Mrs. Amorest felt a sudden, almost affectionate, pity for her gift. It had cost, as it seemed to her, a large sum, but in the eyes of this woman it would be simply another wheedling attempt on her part to extort more money from her cousin. She summoned her courage and smiled her friendliest smile.

"Good afternoon. How is my cousin to-day?"

"Not at all well, I'm afraid."

"Oh dear, I am sorry to hear that. I thought that this fine weather might have done him some good."

There was no answer to this, so after a little pause Mrs. Amorest, feeling the chill of the afternoon air, said:

"Of course it *is* cold, isn't it, but I thought that, being in bed, he might not notice it. Has the doctor been to-day?"

"Yes, the doctor has been."

Well, she might ask me into the hall, thought Mrs. Amorest. "Could I see him for a moment, do you think?"

"I'm afraid not, Mrs. Amorest. It was the doctor's orders that he was not to be disturbed."

"Not for a moment? I really would not bother him. Just to wish him a happy Christmas."

"I'm afraid not. Those were the doctor's orders."

"Would you not ask him whether he would not see me for a moment?"

"I'm sorry, but he is not to be disturbed by anybody."

There was a pause, and then Mrs. Amorest said cheerfully: "Oh, well, I'm sure that's quite right if the doctor says so. I only wanted to wish him a happy Christmas. I have a little gift." She produced it from under her arm. "I have written a little note in case I should not be able to see him. Would you kindly give it to him?"

"Certainly."

She took the parcel, looking neither at it nor at Mrs. Amorest, but forward into the brown and naked garden with a frown of determination as though she were forewarning some plant that was whispering hopefully about the spring that she was not going to stand any of that sort of nonsense.

There was another little pause, then Mrs. Amorest said: "Would you most kindly wish him a very happy Christmas for me? Of course I know that it can't be a *very* happy Christmas for him as ill as he is, but I always think it makes a difference if one knows that people are thinking of one, don't you?"

"I will certainly tell him."

"And I hope you'll have a happy Christmas too," said Mrs. Amorest, trembling with the cold, and wishing altogether in spite of her better feelings that the woman should herself know what it was to be kept out of a warm house on a cold day.

"Thank you very much, Mrs. Amorest. I wish you the same, I'm sure."

That was all. There was nothing more to be done. The door closed with a horrible final clang, and in some strange flash of vision she knew that she was never to enter that house again.

She walked down the hill, and in spite of all her courage, forebodings now crowded upon her. It was true that it was not her cousin's fault that he had not seen her. He had not known that she was there. But surely she had been foolish to build upon his idle word! And that woman. She had designs. She certainly had designs. She had looked at Mrs. Amorest with a hostility that could mean only one thing. And a sick man was so helpless, the worse his sickness the weaker he was. . . . As she crossed the bridge over the Pol it seemed to her that in another moment her courage would desert her. Because if that money did not come to her!

She summoned all her pluck, standing for a moment on the bridge and watching the river take on its evening colour, softly purple under the dark shadow of the rising hills.

Then, thinking of the evening that was coming and the fun that it would be, she smiled. Things always turned out better than you expected. The stars that were now breaking into the sky above her head were the eyes of God. She was watched over and cared for and protected. She had no need to fear.

The town as she passed up through the High Street was bubbling with merriment and gaiety. The shops blazed with lights; the street was crowded; every one was laughing and happy hurrying along loaded with parcels, stopping to speak, it seemed, to any one who was near that they might wish them good luck. This was the world that Mrs. Amorest loved. Why might it not always be like this? She stopped at the Cinderella window. How pretty and touching! She turned round to a stout man beside her and said, "Isn't it pretty?"

"Indeed it is, mum," he answered her, smiling. "My little girl wants to take it home. Don't you, Pansy?" and a diminutive child squeaked out "Yes."

"What a pretty little girl!" said Mrs. Amorest.

"Thank you, mum," answered the fat man. "A merry Christmas, I'm sure."

"And the same to you," said Mrs. Amorest.

The rest of the way home seemed easy.

Arrived in her room, she set about the development of her plan. She had asked Agatha Payne and May Beringer to come and visit her at eight o'clock. She had two hours for her preparations. The time flashed by and in a moment it was a quarter to eight. She hurriedly put on her silk dress, hung around her neck her thin gold chain with the locket that held Brand's portrait, brushed her lovely white hair, put on her lace cap fresh and crisp from the laundry, then her stiff white cuffs. Finished. Completed. She sat down to survey her work. A smile played about her lips. It was the most beautiful thing that she had ever seen in her life.

At five minutes past eight there was a knock on her door, and then another knock. Agatha Payne and May Beringer entered. They stood bewildered on the threshold.

It was indeed a pretty sight. The curtains were drawn and the far end of the rom was duskily shadowed, but at the fireplace end stood—THE TREE!

And what a tree! Of just the right size for the room, it had a shape and symmetry that surely no other tree in all Christmasdom could equal. It tapered gradually with exquisite shape and form to a point that quivered and flickered like a green flame. On the flame sturdily triumphed Father Christmas, diminutive in body, but alive in his smile, his stolidity, his gallant colour. It was the colour that entranced the eye. Mrs. Amorest had worked with the soul of an artist. She had not over-burdened the slender branches. The thin chains of frosted silver that hung from bough to bough seemed of themselves to dance in patterned rhythm. Balls of fire, emerald and ruby, amethyst and crystal, shone in the light of the candles. And at every place colour blended with colour. The tree was always the tree. The light that flashed from its boughs was not foreign to it, but seemed to be, integrally, part of its life and history. It had been placed on a long and broad looking-glass, into which it looked down as though into a lake of crystal water. The candles seemed to be the voices of the tree; it was vocal in its pleasure, its sense of fun at its own splendour, its grand surprise that after all it had come off so well.

In proportion, in blending of colour, in grandeur of spirit, it was the finest tree in England that night. On either side of the tree were two tables spread with white cloths. On one table were some parcels beautifully tied with coloured ribbons, and on the other sandwiches, a plum-cake with white icing, some saffron buns, and a dish of sweets and chocolates.

The two ladies stood amazed. So pretty was the room with its soft pink colours, its light dim save for the aureole of golden splendour shed by the tree, so utterly unexpected the display, that words would not come; only at last May Beringer cried, "Oh dear! Dear me! Dear me!"

Both ladies had dressed in their party best; May in her orange silk, that suited her, I fear, not too well, and Agatha in her dark purple, a dress of a fashion now forgotten, too small for her, but that nevertheless with her black hair finely brushed, her dark eyes flashing, gave her the air of older days, the air that had made Mr. Payne, thirty-five years ago, call her his "Gipsy Queen."

"Oh, I do hope you won't both think me too silly," said Mrs. Amorest, coming forward, "but I simply had to do something this Christmas. We've just done nothing the last two Christmases and it did seem too bad. Don't you think so? I do hope you don't mind?"

"Mind?" said May Beringer, coming towards the tree and gazing at it with her mouth open like a school-girl. "Why, Mrs. Amorest, it's lovely! It's the loveliest thing! Why, I can't speak. I can't, indeed. Words won't come. I can't say anything at all."

Agatha Payne was moved more deeply still. The colour possessed her as colour always possessed her, coming towards her like a living breathing person, holding out its arms to her, whispering to her, "You and I! We are the only ones here who understand. I have been waiting for you, and you alone."

Indeed it seemed to her that the tree belonged to her and was hers absolutely. The two other women vanished from her consciousness; she could see only the pale golden flame of the candles, so steady, so pure, so dignified, the balls of amethyst and ruby and crystal as they swung and turned and gleamed so slightly and yet always with a secret life and purpose of their own.

And the deep green of the tree, richly velvet under the light of the candles! She stood absorbed, entranced, waves of sensuous pleasure running through her body.

So silent were they both that after a minute had passed Mrs. Amorest was alarmed.

"I'm so glad you like it," she said almost timidly. "Shan't we sit down and look at it? I like to think of all the other trees there are tonight in everybody's homes and the children dancing round them and the presents——"

She broke off because a longing for Brand came to her so urgently that it was all she could do not to call out his name. For a moment it seemed to her foolish humbug, sham, and ridiculous sentiment, that the three of them, old, forgotten, not wanted by anybody, should indulge in this display. But looking up at the tree she was comforted. Anything so beautiful had its own purpose. She had made a beautiful thing. She felt the joy of the creator in her handiwork.

They sat in a row looking at the tree. May Beringer was, all in a moment, voluble. She had so much to tell them—of the trees that she had known, the trees that she had had in her own house, the trees that she and Jane Betts had decorated together, the Christmas festivities that they had had in Exeter (you would think to hear her that Exeter was the centre of all the splendour and gaiety of the world). Oh! she talked and laughed and was so wildly excited that she nearly cried.

Agatha Payne said very little. She only stared and stared at the tree.

The next part of the entertainment arrived. Mrs. Amorest picked up the parcels in their lovely white paper and coloured ribbon and, blushing a little (shell pink faintly colouring the ivory of her cheeks), said:

"These are little tiny things that I got. You mustn't laugh at me, please, for getting them. I think the chief part of a present is that it should be wrapped up in paper, don't you? But I hope you'll like them."

And they did like them. At least May Beringer liked hers. She had a case with three pairs of scissors and a book in a purple cover, *The Light of Asia,* by Sir Edwin Arnold. Agatha Payne said little about hers—only "Thank you, Lucy," in a deep hoarse-throated murmur. She had a box of coloured cottons and a purple blotter. She could not take her eyes away from the tree.

Then they cut the cake and ate the sandwiches, and Mrs. Amorest made tea and listened happily, cosily to May Beringer's reminiscences.

How happy it was with the blazing tree, the dim room, the bells pealing beyond the window, the crackling fire!

Each old lady forgot the other. They were lost in their own world of remembered and recaptured life—past joys, past sorrows, past desires, past regrets. The clock ticked on, the candles burnt with steady flame, the bells rang out.

Gradually Lucy Amorest closed her eyes. She heard May Beringer's voice from a vast distance. Then her own faintly replying, "How curious! Indeed. . . . In . . . deed."

Her head sank upon her breast. May Beringer also, bathed in the warmth of the room, comforted with tea and happiness, closed her eyes. Her head nodded—once and twice and thrice. She pulled herself up. Stared sharply at Mrs. Amorest. Saw two Mrs. Amorests, then three. Her head fell. She also slept.

Only Agatha Payne, her dark eyes fixed, sat, without moving, staring at the tree.

A Pint of Judgment

ELIZABETH MORROW

THE Tucker family made out lists of what they wanted for Christmas. They did not trust to Santa Claus' taste or the wisdom of aunts and uncles in such an important matter. By the first week in December everybody had written out what he or she hoped to receive.

Sally, who was seven, when she could only print had sent little slips of paper up the chimney with her desires plainly set forth. She had wondered sometimes if neatly written requests like Ellen's were not more effective than the printed ones. Ellen was eight. She had asked last year for a muff and Santa had sent it.

Mother always explained that one should not expect to get all the things on the list: "Only what you want most, dear, and sometimes you have to wait till you are older for those."

For several years Sally had asked for a lamb and she had almost given up hope of finding one tied to her stocking on Christmas morning. She had also asked for a white cat and a dove and they had not come either. Instead a bowl of goldfish had been received. Now she wrote so plainly that there was no excuse for misunderstandings like this.

Derek still printed his list—he was only six and yet he had received an Indian suit the very first time he asked for it. It was puzzling.

Caroline, called "Lovey" for short, just stood on the hearth rug and shouted "Dolly! Bow wow!" but anybody with Santa Claus' experience would know that rag dolls and woolly dogs were the proper presents for a four-year-old.

The lists were useful too in helping one to decide what to make for Father and Mother and the others for Christmas. The little Tuckers had been brought up by their grandmother in the belief that a present you made yourself was far superior to one bought in a store. Mother always asked for a great many things the children could make. She was always wanting knitted washcloths, pincushion covers, blotters, and penwipers. Father needed pipe cleaners, calendars and decorated match boxes.

This year Sally longed to do something quite different for her mother. She was very envious of Ellen, who had started a small towel as her present, and was pulling threads for a fringed end.

"Oh! Ellen! How lovely that is!" she sighed. "It is a real grown-up present, just as if Aunt Elsie had made it."

"And it isn't half done yet," Ellen answered proudly. "Grandma is helping me with cross-stitch letters in blue and red for one end."

"If I could only make something nice like that! Can't you think of something for me?"

"A hemmed handkerchief?" suggested Ellen.

"Oh, no! Mother has lots of handkerchiefs."

"Yes, but when I gave her one for her birthday she said she had never had enough handkerchiefs. They were like asparagus."

"They don't look like asparagus," Sally replied, loath to criticise her mother but evidently confused. "Anyway, I don't want to give her a handkerchief."

"A penwiper?"

"No, I'm giving Father that."

"A new pincushion cover?"

"Oh! no, Ellen. I'm sick of those presents. I want it to be a big—lovely—Something—a great surprise."

Ellen thought a minute. She was usually resourceful and she did not like to fail her little sister. They had both been earning money all through November and perhaps this was a time to *buy* a present for Mother—even if Grandma disapproved.

"I know that Mother has made out a new list," she said. "She and Father were laughing about it last night in the library. Let's go and see if it is there."

They found two papers on the desk, unmistakably lists. They were typewritten. Father's was very short: "Anything wrapped up in tissue paper with a red ribbon around it."

"Isn't Father funny?" giggled Ellen. 'I'd like to fool him and do up a dead mouse for his stocking."

Mother had filled a full page with her wants. Ellen read out slowly:

Pair of Old English silver peppers
Fur coat
("Father will give her that.")
Umbrella
Robert Frost's Poems
Silk stockings
Muffin tins
Small watering pot for house plants
Handkerchiefs
Guest towels
("Aren't you glad she asked for that?" Sally broke in.)
Knitted washcloths
A red pencil
A blue pencil
Ink eraser
Pen holders
Rubber bands
Hot water bag cover
A quart of judgment

This last item was scribbled in pencil at the bottom of the sheet.

As Ellen finished reading, she said with what Sally called her "little-mother air," "You needn't worry at all about Mother's present. There are lots of things here you could make for her. Couldn't you do a hot water bag cover if Grandma cut it out for you? I'm sure you could. You take a nice soft piece of old flannel . . ."

"No! No! Nothing made out of old flannel!" cried Sally. "That's such a baby thing. I want it to be different—and a great surprise. I wish I could give her the silver peppers. . . . That's the first thing on her list; but I've only got two dollars and three cents in my bank and I'm afraid that's not enough."

"Oh! It isn't the peppers she wants most!" cried Ellen. "It's the *last* thing she wrote down—that 'quart of judgment.' I know for I heard her tell Father, 'I need that more than anything else . . . even a pint would help.' And then they both laughed."

"What is judgment?" asked Sally.

"It's what the judge gives—a judgment," her sister answered. "It must be something to do with the law."

"Then I know it would cost more than two dollars and three cents," said Sally. "Father said the other day that nothing was so expensive as the law."

"But she only asked for a pint," Ellen objected. "A pint of anything couldn't be very expensive, unless it was diamonds and rubies."

"She wanted a *quart*," Sally corrected. "And she just said that afterwards about a pint helping because she knew a whole quart would be too much for us to buy."

"A hot water bag cover would be lots easier," cautioned Ellen.

"I don't want it to be easy!" cried Sally. "I want it to be what she wants!"

"Well, perhaps you could get it cheap from Uncle John," Ellen suggested. "He's a lawyer—and he's coming to dinner tonight, so you could ask him."

Sally was not afraid to ask Uncle John anything. He never laughed at her or teased her as Uncle Tom sometimes did and he always talked to her as if she were grown up. On any vexed question he always sided with her and Ellen. He had even been known to say before Mother that coconut cake was good for children and that seven-thirty for big girls of seven and eight was a disgracefully early bedtime. He thought arctics unnecessary in winter and when a picnic was planned, he always knew it would be a fine day.

Sally drew him into the little library that evening and shut the door carefully.

"Is it something very important?" he asked as they seated themselves on the sofa.

"Yes," she answered. "Awfully important. It's a secret. You won't tell, will you?"

"No, cross my heart and swear. What is it?"

"It's—it's . . . Oh—Uncle John—what *is* judgment? I must get some."

"Judgment? That *is* an important question, my dear." Uncle John seemed puzzled for a moment. "And it is hard to answer. Why do you bother about that now? You have your whole life to get it. . . . Come to me again when you're eighteen."

"But I can't wait so long. I must get it right away. Mother wants it for a Christmas present. She put on her list, 'A quart of judgment.' She said even a pint would help."

Uncle John laughed. He threw back his head and shouted. Sally had never seen him laugh so hard. He shook the sofa with his mirth and tears rolled down his cheeks. He didn't stop until he saw that Sally was hurt—and even then a whirlwind of chuckles seized him occasionally.

"I'm not laughing at you, Sally darling," he explained at last, patting her shoulder affectionately, "but at your mother. She doesn't need judgment. She has it. She always has had it. She's a mighty fine woman—your mother. She must have put that on her list as a joke."

"Oh no! Excuse me, Uncle John," Sally protested. "She told Father she wanted it more than anything else. Wouldn't it be a good Christmas present?"

"Perfectly swell," her uncle answered. "The most useful thing on earth. I've never heard of its being given for Christmas but it would be wonderful. If you have any left over, give me some."

"Why, I was going to ask you to sell me some," Sally explained. "Ellen said you would surely have it."

Just then Mother called, "Ellen! Sally! Bedtime. Hurry, dears. It's twenty minutes to eight already."

"Bother!" exclaimed Sally. "I'm always having to go to bed. But please tell me where I can get it. At Macy's? Delia is taking us to town tomorrow."

"No, my dear," he answered. "Macy sells almost everything but not that. It doesn't come by the yard."

"Girls!" Mother's voice again.

"Oh! Quick, Uncle John," whispered Sally. "Mother's coming. I'll have to go. Just tell me. What *is* judgment?"

"It is *sense,* Sally," he answered, quite solemn and serious now. "Common sense. But it takes a lot . . ." He could not finish the sentence for at this point Mother opened the door and carried Sally off to bed.

The little girl snuggled down under the sheets very happily. Uncle John had cleared her mind of all doubt. She had only time for an ecstatic whisper to Ellen before Delia put out the light: "It's all right about Mother's present. Uncle John said it would be 'swell.'" Then she began to calculate: "If it is just *cents, common cents,* I have ever so many in my bank and I can earn some more. Perhaps I have enough already."

With this delicious hope she fell asleep.

The first thing after breakfast the next morning she opened her bank. It was in the shape of a fat man sitting in a chair. When you put a penny in his hand he nodded his head in gratitude as the money slipped into his safety-box. Sally unscrewed the bottom of this and two dollars and three cents rolled out. It was not all in pennies. There were several nickels, three dimes, two quarters and a fifty-cent piece. It made a rich-looking pile. Sally ran to the kitchen for a pint cup and then up to the nursery to pour her wealth into it. No one was there in the room to hear her cry of disappointment. The coins did not reach to the "Half" marked on the measure.

But there was still hope. The half dollar and quarters when they were changed would lift the level of course. She put all the silver into her pocket and consulted Ellen.

Her sister had passed the penny-bank stage and kept her money in a blue leather purse which was a proud possession. Aunt Elsie had given it to her last Christmas. It had two compartments and a small looking-glass—but there was very little money in it now. Ellen had already bought a good many presents. She was only able to change one quarter and one dime.

"Let's ask Derek," she said. "He loves to open his bank because he can use the screwdriver of his tool set."

Derek was delighted to show his savings—forty-five cents—but he was reluctant to give them all up for one quarter and two dimes. It would mean only three pieces to drop into the chimney of the little red house which was his bank.

"They don't clink at all," he complained, experimenting with the coins Sally held out. "You'll take all my money. I won't have hardly anything."

"You'll have *just* as much money to spend," explained Ellen.

"Yes," Derek admitted, "but not to jingle. I like the jingle. It sounds so much more."

He finally decided to change one nickel and one dime.

Then Grandma changed a dime and Sally had sixty pennies all together to put into the pint cup. They brought the pile up about an inch.

When Father came home that night she asked him to change the fifty-cent piece, the quarter and the three nickels, but he did not have ninety cents in pennies and he said that he could not get them until Monday and now it was only Saturday.

"You understand, Sally," he explained looking down into his little daughter's anxious face, "you don't have any more money after this is changed. It only *looks* more."

"I know, but I want it that way," she answered.

On Monday night he brought her the change and it made a full inch more of money in the cup. Still it was less than half a pint. Sally confided her discouragement to Ellen.

"Are you sure," asked her sister, "that it was this kind of present Mother wanted? She never asked for money before."

"I'm sure," Sally replied. "Uncle John said it was *cents* and that it would take a lot. Besides she prayed for it in church yesterday—so she must want it awfully."

"Prayed for it!" exclaimed Ellen in surprise.

"Yes, I heard her. It's that prayer we all say together. She asked God for 'two cents of all thy mercies.'"

"But if she wants a whole pint why did she only ask for 'two cents'?" demanded the practical Ellen.

"I don't know," Sally answered. "Perhaps she thought it would be greedy. Mother is never greedy."

For several days things were at a standstill. Ellen caught a cold and passed it on to Sally and Derek. They were all put to bed and could do very little Christmas work. While Mother read aloud to them Sally finished her penwiper for Father and decorated a blotter for Uncle John—but sewing on Grandma's pincushion cover was difficult because the pillow at Sally's back kept slipping and she couldn't keep the needle straight. There seemed no way of adding anything to the pint cup.

"Mother, how could I earn some money quickly before Christmas?" Sally asked the first day that she was up.

"You have already earned a good deal, dear," Mother said. "Do you really need more?"

"Yes, Mother, lots more."

"How about getting 100 in your number work? Father gives you a dime every time you do that."

"Yes," sighed Sally, "but it's very hard to get all the examples right. Don't you think when I get all right but one he might give me nine cents?"

"No," said Mother laughing. "Your father believes that nothing is good in arithmetic but 100."

She did earn one dime that way and then school closed, leaving no hope for anything more before Christmas.

On the twentieth of December there was a windfall. Aunt Elsie, who usually spent the holidays with them, was in the South and she sent Mother four dollars—one for each child for a Christmas present. "She told me to buy something for you," Mother explained, "but I thought perhaps you might like to spend the money yourselves—later on—during vacation."

"Oh! I'd like my dollar right away!" cried Sally delightedly. "And," she added rather shamefacedly, "Lovey is so little . . . do you think she needs all her money? Couldn't she give me half of hers?"

"Why, Sally, I'm surprised at you!" her mother answered. "I can't take your little sister's share for you. It wouldn't be fair. I am buying a new *Benjamin Bunny* for Lovey."

Aunt Elsie's gift brought the pennies in the pint cup a little above the half mark.

On the twenty-first Sally earned five cents by sweeping off the back porch. This had been a regular source of revenue in the fall, but when the dead leaves gave place to snow Mother forbade the sweeping. On the twenty-first there was no snow and Sally was allowed to go out with her little broom.

On the twenty-second Ellen and Sally went to a birthday party and Sally found a shiny bright dime in her piece of birthday cake. This helped a little. She and Ellen spent all their spare moments in shaking up the pennies in the pint measure—but they could not bring the level much above "One Half." Ellen was as excited over the plan now as Sally and she generously added her last four cents to the pile.

On the twenty-third Sally made a final desperate effort. "Mother," she said, "Uncle John is coming to dinner again tonight. Do you think he would be willing to give me my birthday dollar now?"

Mother smiled as she answered slowly—"But your birthday isn't till June. Isn't it rather strange to ask for your present so long ahead? Where is all this money going to?"

"It's a secret! My special secret!" cried the little girl, taking her mother's reply for consent.

Uncle John gave her the dollar. She hugged and kissed him with delight and he said, "Let me always be your banker, Sally. I'm sorry you are so hard up, but don't take any wooden nickels."

" 'Wooden nickels,' " she repeated slowly. "What are they? Perhaps they would fill up the bottom—"

"Of your purse?" Uncle John finished the sentence for her. "No, no, my dear. They are a very poor bottom for anything—and they are worse on top."

"It wasn't my purse," said Sally. "It was—but it's a secret."

When Father changed the birthday dollar into pennies he said, "You are getting to be a regular little miser, my dear. I don't understand it. Where is all this money going to?"

"That's just what Mother asked," Sally answered. "It's a secret. You'll know on Christmas. Oh, Father, I think I have enough now!"

But she hadn't. The pennies seemed to melt away as they fell into the measure. She and Ellen took them all out three times and put them back again, shaking them sideways and forwards, but it was no use. They looked a mountain on the nursery floor but they shrank in size the moment they were put inside that big cup. The mark stood obstinately below "Three Quarters."

"Oh! Ellen!" sobbed Sally after the third attempt. "Not even a pint! It's a horrid mean little present! All my presents are horrid. I never can give nice things like you! Oh dear, what shall I do!"

"Don't cry, Sally—please don't," said Ellen, trying to comfort her little sister. "It's not a horrid present. It will look lovely when you put tissue paper around it and lots of red ribbon and a card. It *sounds* so much more than it looks," Ellen went on, giving the cup a vigorous jerk. "Why don't you print on your card 'Shake well before opening,' like our cough mixture?"

"I might," assented Sally, only partly reassured.

She had believed up to the last moment that she would be able to carry out her plan. It was vaguely associated in her mind with a miracle. Anything might happen at Christmas time but this year she had hoped for too much. It was so late now however that there was nothing to do but make the outside of her gift look as attractive as possible. She and Ellen spent most of the afternoon before Christmas wrapping up their presents. The pint cup was a little awkward in shape but they had it well covered and the red satin ribbon gathered tight at the top before Grandma made the final bow. It was a real rosette, for Sally had asked for something special.

Christmas Eve was almost more fun than Christmas. The Tuckers made a ceremony of hanging up their stockings. The whole family formed a line in the upper hall with Father at the head, the youngest child on his back, and then they marched downstairs keeping step to a Christmas chant. It was a home-made nonsense verse with a chorus of "Doodley-doodley, doodley-doo!" which everybody shouted. By the time they reached the living-room the line was in wild spirits.

The stockings were always hung in the same places. Father had the big armchair to the right of the fireplace and Mother the large mahogany chair opposite it, Lovey had a small white chair borrowed from the nursery. Derek tied his sock to the hook which usually held the fire tongs above the wood basket (it was a very inconvenient place but he liked it) and Ellen and Sally divided the sofa.

After the stockings were put up, one of the children recited the Bible verses, "And there were in the same country shepherds abiding in the field, keeping watch over their flock by night," through "And Mary kept all these things and pondered them in her heart." Sally had said the verses last Christmas—Ellen the year before—and now it was Derek's turn. He only forgot once and Ellen prompted him softly.

Then they all sang "Holy Night"—and Father read " 'Twas the Night Before Christmas." Last of all, the children distributed their gifts for the family—with a great many stern directions: "Mother, you won't look at this till tomorrow, will you? Father, you promise not to peek?" Then they went up to bed and by morning Father and Mother and Santa Claus had the stockings stuffed full of things.

It went off as usual this year but through all the singing and the shouting Sally had twinges of disappointment thinking of Mother's unfinished present. She had squeezed it into Mother's stocking with some difficulty. Then came Ellen's lovely towel and on top of that Derek's calendar which he had made in school.

There was a family rule at the Tuckers' that stockings were not opened until after breakfast. Mother said that presents on an empty stomach were bad for temper and digestion and though it was hard to swallow your cereal Christmas morning, the children knew it was no use protesting.

The first sight of the living-room was wonderful. The place had completely changed over night. Of course the stockings were knobby with unknown delights, and there were packages everywhere, on the tables and chairs, and on the floor big express boxes that had come from distant places, marked "Do Not Open Until Christmas."

Some presents are of such unmistakable shape that they cannot be hidden. Last year Derek had jumped right onto his rocking horse shouting, "It's mine! I know it's mine!" This morning he caught sight of a drum and looked no further. Lovey fell upon a white plush bunny. A lovely pink parasol was sticking out of the top of Sally's stocking and Ellen had a blue one. They just unfurled them over their heads and then watched Father and Mother unwrapping their presents.

The girls felt Derek and Lovey were very young because they emptied their stockings without a look towards the two big armchairs. That was the most thrilling moment, when your own offering came to view and Mother said, "Just what I wanted!" or Father, "How did you know I needed a penwiper?"

Mother always opened the children's presents first. She was untying the red ribbon on Ellen's towel now and reading the card which said "Every stitch a stitch of love." As she pulled off the tissue paper she exclaimed, "What beautiful work! What exquisite little stitches! Ellen—I am proud of you. This is a charming guest towel. Thank you, dear, so much."

"Grandma marked the cross-stitch for me," explained Ellen, "but I did all the rest myself."

Sally shivered with excitement as Mother's hand went down into her stocking again and tugged at the tin cup.

"Here is something very heavy," she said. "I can't guess what it is, and the cards say '*Merry Christmas to Mother from Sally. Shake well before opening.*' Is it medicine or cologne?"

Nobody remembered just what happened after that. Perhaps Grandma's bow was not tied tightly enough, perhaps Mother tilted the cup as she shook it, but in a moment all the pennies were on the floor. They rolled everywhere, past the chairs, into the grate, under the sofa and on to the remotest corners of the room. There was a terrific scramble. Father and Mother and Ellen and Sally and Derek, even Grandma and Lovey got down on their hands and knees to pick them up. They bumped elbows and knocked heads together and this onrush sent the coins flying everywhere. The harder they were chased, the more perversely they hid themselves. Out of the hubbub Mother cried, "Sally dear, what is this? I don't understand. All your Christmas money for me? Darling, I can't take it."

Sally flung herself into her mother's arms with a sob. "Oh! you must!" she begged. "I'm sorry it's not a whole pint. I tried so hard. You said—you *said*—you wanted it most of all."

" 'Most of all'?"

"Yes, judgment, *cents*. Uncle John said it was cents. You said even a pint would help. Won't half a pint be some good?"

Father and Mother and Grandma all laughed then. Father laughed almost as hard as Uncle John did when he first heard of Mother's list, and he declared that he was going to take Sally into the bank as a partner. But Mother lifted the little girl into her lap and whispered. "It's the most wonderful present I ever had. There's nothing so wonderful as sense—except love."

Country Christmas

PAUL HOFFMAN

I

All that day a thin mist hovered in the soft air, growing denser overhead until it blotted out even the gray-white patch behind which the sun stood and hung at last only a dirty, shallow dome close to the earth. Faintly shimmering, it clung to whatsoever it touched—to branch and bough and fence and field, against coat and cap and glove, and in the hair and brows—and like points, needle-fine, it stung the face gently. It settled upon the paltry blanket of snow not long since fallen, and penetrating what was so recently feathery pure, its crystals lightly lodged next one another, shrunk it to soddenness close-packed and large-pored. There was a sea smell upon the southwest wind that had come up slowly about midafternoon, so little windlike at first it barely stirred the least plumes of the pines and only faintly rattled the stiff clusters of longer grass thrusting through the snow. It might easily rain by nightfall, surely before tomorrow.

Although everyone hoped it wouldn't. Rain on a northern Christmas—and in Maine!—is somewhat more than a catastrophe. It is akin to disgrace.

Everyone had worked so hard too, to make this Christmas Eve a greater success than ever before. For days Seaver and Colby and Ernest had been cutting scrub evergreens—two hundred in all—

with which to bank the clearing, walling it about with a dense green fragrance to keep out whatever wind there might be; stripping yet more with which to build the lean-to that was to house the crèche; then weaving in the interstices of that framework of roof and three sides the lopped-off sprays of sweet-smelling cedar and spruce and tamarack; spreading what was left of these upon the ground to sit on, and over the planks as well which had long ago been placed between those few sturdier trees that still inhabited the clearing, rising proudly apart from the more crowded trunks and less shapely crests beyond this space. A terrifying heap of roots and stumps, gnarled and dry, stood ready for the oil which would be poured over it, then to be ignited. And in a sheltered spot a low wall of stones, charred from the fires of many Christmases, encircled a tent of small logs over kindling, an iron grating laid upon all. Here the rich creamy soup would be heated and the coffee brewed and the crisp buns, crescent-shaped, their tops glossy brown and thinly crusted, kept warm—the oven odor and that of yeast still in them. Last of all, the great tree—tallest and most perfect of fat-fingered firs—was cut and hauled by the oxen to its last proud stand, there to be richly trimmed and at the end to overcome in its splendid, final hour the swift-deepening winter twilight with soft, living flame.

All this had Seaver and his farmers accomplished. It must not rain.

II

But Marion had worked hard, too—perhaps even harder than the men—and not just for days either, but for weeks. For as Seaver was master she was mistress of this yearly ceremony. There would be about seventy people here and for each there must be a gift—nothing costly, to be sure, but withal practical and giftlike. Neither Aunt Minnie Bemis's Boston Store nor Southard's could yield all the objects of her fastidious search, so she had had to shop farther afield in Brunswick and in Bath. She had, in fact, begun the whole arduous business around Thanksgiving time in faraway

Boston while on a week-end visit there. And now each must be neatly wrapped in bright tissue and bound with gay ribbon or twine, each must be labeled. Nurse helped with this—Nurse, with her British competence and calm.

Then there were the costumes and properties for the tableau. But Susan, unfailing as usual in imagination and industry and because she was an oldest friend, was enlisted to help with these, and plundering the full store of her possessions, garnered against an occasion like this, she produced such fabrics, so rich a yield, as could only have been acquired in a life—as hers had been—of much travel. For Susan had ransacked the world for beauty. What was more, besides, she had always found it—and more often than not found it in a trifle, in those things which the unwise cannot treasure, failing in foresight and the deep, immediate enjoyment of impermanence. So that now the frail gauze, the brief and useless fragment whose deep tint recalled some hot Eurasian sky, the strip of red—these together were a Madonna's robe and wimple and soft enshrouding veil.

But Nurse felt that she must declare herself in the matter of this.

"I should like to see it all kept as simple as possible!" she asserted in her clipped way of speech.

Susan kept silent. Only afterwards she spoke of it bitterly to me, inveighing against that view which reduces the festive to its skeletal quantity.

"But what is life for," she cried, making an end of it, "if not to be adorned?"

And, of course, there was the matter of food. But Mary saw largely to that—under Marion's supervision and with Hilton's help. "Help" and Hilton—they were synonymous all through that winter. Because he had no steady work, he just helped—helped Mary, helped Marion and Seaver, and a butcher in town sometimes, on Saturdays and like that. And that morning he had helped Joan make great snow-men—three of them—to point the way to the edge of the woods where the path to the clearing began. They were strung across the western lawn and stretched each a stubby arm to the north, upon which a paper lantern was hung whose candle would be lighted at dusk. Planted solidly on their firm bases, one sporting side whiskers of feathery pine and another a goatee, an old and battered hat worn rakishly askew by the third, they stood pompous and mute, making an impressive trio, to say the least. The embellishments were Hilton's, and to Joan, just turned eleven, these were not short of—in truth surpassed—genius. When I had looked upon them and examined each in detail and admired and exclaimed, she turned her round ruddy face toward mine.

"Don't you really think," she pleaded, "now don't you *really*—that Hilton is a regular Praxiteles?"

And so the mist had served some happy purpose after all; for without its effect the snow could hardly have been made to bunch and cling for the creation of this stupendous statuary.

Yet there was not one of us but hoped hard it would not rain.

III

Then as that brief, dark afternoon became dusk and early evening, the wind was momently stilled and the mist thickened. It seemed that only a miracle could avert rain. But, for all that, each last preparation went forward with the impatient energy and haphazard skill of fatigue. In the farmhouse the Virgin and her midwives bore with good humor the pinpricks inflicted by hasty fingers as here a hem or there a fold was adjusted. In the silent barn Colby and Ernest led Star and Bright, the great oxen, from their stalls, driving them along the devious pathway to the clearing, returning then for Mooey, the sleek Jersey, and for Major, Joan's stoic donkey, who in his twenty-six years had been straddled and driven by two generations of children. For these, too, must each play a part in this modern mystery. And within the clearing itself Seaver kindled the great fire, touched with a taper the stubborn wicks of a hundred fat candles. While in the kitchen Mary, her clear-skinned, blue-eyed prettiness ruddied from the fierce heat there, spooned clotted yellow cream into the soup or thrust another stick under the glowing griddles. And as for Hilton, once he had lighted the snow-men's lanterns his presence was ubiquitous.

Then through the woods to the south and across the soggy fields came those who were afoot—the Colemans and Hamlins, the Dan Sortwells, the Rafters, and Frances. Along the treacherous, rutted road drove the Mareans, bringing Grandmother Sortwell—the Chases, the Nashes, the Whites, and Helena Bellas; and a score or two of others. Some there were among them who in all their lives had not ventured beyond the villages of Lincoln County, who had won a hard subsistence from small enterprises and from this bleak ground—and some who were rich and traveled, who had journeyed for this brief holiday from Boston, from New York and Washington, opening their fine houses to share this season's rare bounty and joy. But through many years each had known each, so that between them there was no ultimate barrier, only the kindly region of affection and respect.

IV

Slowly they made their way past those wondrous-fashioned sentries—now in the swiftly dimming light and in the fitful flicker from their lanterns at once terrifying and foolishly sad—but not without pausing before each to exclaim, to admire, to laugh a little. On they went into the woods toward the clearing, whose giant glow shone thinning above and round about, casting far-flung shadows along the path. The air here was heavy with dampness, and underfoot the feel of the needle-strewn earth was spongy. Everyone hurried a little.

But inside the clearing it was windless and warm. Wide pennants of blue and yellow flame were flung aloft from the spitting, hissing, crackling heap of roots and stumps, to fly off among the treetops in ragged fragments, for a moment flaring and then gone. In the strong, steady heat from these the encircling wall of massed evergreens had begun to thaw, their gray-green stiffness turned pliable and richly deep in tone, glossy with beaded moisture. A pungent, spicy smell was wafted inward from them and mingled with the faintly acrid one of smoke. Behind the lean-to, its fourth and open side now concealed by heavy curtains, the animals stirred restlessly in the airless darkness where Colby and Ernest held them in check. They tossed their heads and snorted uneasily.

But as each guest entered the clearing these things—sound, smell, fire—were all but lost to him before the soft dazzle and shimmer of the great fir rising there in its centre. Long strips of thick tinsel dipped in gentle festoons from its branches, were draped from crest to base, evening its contours. A thousand shining ornaments—multi-colored, great and small—were hung from its feathery fingers. And candy canes. And cornucopias stuffed with sweets. And each perfect candle flame burned silent and steadfast, save at the very top, where the freer air ruffled one or two. It was this sight which silenced each guest for an instant and made each stand in sudden and momentary wonderment as he came upon it. Here was Christmas, its chief symbol and reality.

V

There manifested itself then among these spectators a reaction and feeling as strange as it was unexpected. It was as if each wished to speak and none could, so that, without wanting it, the obstacle of chagrin came between, and all this glitter seemed no more than an empty function, planned and executed without feeling. A shyness possessed each and cut him off from his nearest fellow, made him even a little resentful—unreasoning though he knew himself to be.

And then out of their midst stepped Harry Nash.

"Come along, children!" he barked in that urgent voice which everyone knew only muffled his kindliness. "Ring round the Tree! Here, you, Dick and Shirley and Margaret Alexandra——"

Embarrassment vanished. For when Grandpa Nash gave orders, there was nothing for it but to obey—and that with no show of reluctance, either. Even grownups, remembering half-unconsciously when they too had been ordered about by him, came forward as well. And when they were solidly circled about the tree——

"All ready!" with forefingers raised, " 'O Christmas Tree——' "

His aging voice boomed—for all that the higher notes cracked a little and were sometimes flat. When that was finished we did "O Little Town of Bethlehem," "It Came Upon the Midnight Clear," and "Joy to the World."

And as I watched this little man with a mien and figure which, despite his years, were still sturdy and alert, I recalled what I knew of his brave life, and within me my heart swelled with admiration and sympathy so that the song on my lips was stopped. Born to wealth and position, the boyhood friend of statesmen, himself destined for a career of greatness—in his prime his health had broken and he had come here, never wholly to retrieve it, with his loyal wife and two children. Then, through the war years and afterwards, his inheritance had dwindled until now he was even grateful for the meagre stipend which his post as lay preacher in the village brought him.

But useless regret or embitterment had no part in his abundantly endowed nature. These simple creatures about him and their every want had become the whole concern of his and his wife's living. Scarcely a day passed that they did not deprive themselves to satisfy a need of one of these; and from his pulpit he exhorted their souls to valor. He was not unlike Saint Paul, I thought then, only perhaps more human.

VI

I looked toward Susan, who, like myself, stood a little apart watching. She too was being brave, but with more immediate gallantry. For, hard as her life had at times been, she had by her gayety and spirited enterprises outwitted ennui and drabness. Even with a purse slim as hers not uncommonly was, she had lived rich in friends, in places, and—more than all—in her own capacity for living. But now, under her seeming enjoyment of this moment, I knew she was sad. I knew that within her she felt "empty and dry as a pod rattling in the wind," as she herself was wont to say; for this Christmas she was alone. Her son was far away in South

America and ill with malaria; her daughter was kept in New York by her demanding work. And she was troubled, too, because she was herself unwell, and because for the first time the years of her life seemed many and the future chartless.

But, looking at her, I also knew that she was not letting her sadness be more to her than a vague aching, that she was seeing more beauty, more implications in this scene than all of us together. And I was reminded of what Helen had once said of her:

"Isn't Susan wonderful! She always makes things more attractive than they really are."

I wonder.

VII

During the last of the singing, Marion came up behind me to whisper that everything was at last ready, that the actors had made their way unseen from the farmhouse into the lean-to and had taken their places, so I moved nearer the firelight and turned, in the small Testament which I had been holding, to the second chapter of Saint Luke. A slow silence descended then and all eyes were upon the thick-curtained lean-to.

Mary, her hard, hot work in the kitchen now finished, slipped into the circle at the edge of the clearing, close beside Hilton.

"And it came to pass in those days, that there went out a decree from Caesar Augustus, that all the world should be taxed."

And as I read on of the shepherds and of the angel who summoned them to Bethlehem, the two midwives stepped out from the lean-to, holding high flaming torches of pitch pine. Gently they drew aside the curtains and stood, facing forward, one on either side of the holy pageant within. . . . There, in the foreground, bent tenderly over a simple manger, knelt little Joan, her round childish face rosy, reflecting the nimbus which glowed with a steady brilliance from the enshrouded figure on the fragrant hay. Beside her stood Seaver, who was now the kindly Joseph, his large figure dressed simply in a dark and flowing robe, its cowl thrown back upon his shoulders. A little behind and to one side were Colby and Ernest, the shepherds, their faces shadowed by coarse hoods save when a flicker from the midwives' torches played now and again for an instant across them, revealing their strong line and feature and the brown stubble of their beards. And, behind all, the four animals moved a little against each other and champed at their halters.

When I had finished, none stirred and all were silent for a time until, Harry Nash once more leading, each voice rose softly in "Silent Night, Holy Night." . . .

Turning aside, I looked over the rapt faces about me and at length found Mary's. And I thought of her name, and how soon she too was to be delivered, and that Hilton had no work. I remembered how at times in these past weeks her merry eyes had been turned inward with an unaccustomed look of fear. But now they were shining and moist and all unafraid, knowing that for her child, too, provision should somehow be made. Shyly then, without looking, and still singing, she moved closer to Hilton, while he in turn laid an arm across her shoulders.

I have since wondered whether the son who was born to them later was not named that night—Joseph.

". . . Sleep in heavenly peace."

The voices soared sweetly, then softly and slowly descended, and the thick curtains were drawn together. A last flare from the torches, a last glimpse of color and light, and it was over.

VIII

Now a low murmur rose on all sides and Hilton and Mary slipped back to the farmhouse, to return shortly with the great kettle of soup, with the trays of crisp buns smothered under fresh towels, and with the steaming coffee. Then cups were handed to each and spoons and bright paper napkins. A line began to form at the smaller fire—the one with the grating on which the food kept hot and savory.

Standing about in friendly groups, seated on the pine-covered planks and patches of ground, we talked much and ate our fill of this good fare and laughed. Joan and her two lovely cousins, who had been the midwives, walked among us in their costumes and we laughed to see under their skirts the incongruity of their clumsy galoshes. And when our eating was finished and we talked less because we were satisfied and a little tired, we looked again at the great tree, now mellowed by the night and by the shorter burning of its candles, and each thought his own long thoughts.

Suddenly a far cry and another rose from behind the woods.

"Gee!" it called. "Gee . . . haw-w-w!"

It came closer, was less muffled—the voice was Colby's. We were alert and silent, an excited suspense gripping each of us.

"Gee-haw . . . geeeeee!"

And into the clearing, through a wide opening, they came into the firelight. Their eyes rolling, the muscles of their large shoulders working nervously under the sleek hide, the small feet cautiously and deftly seeking a foothold in the slippery snow, came Star and Bright, the great oxen. Under a silver yoke they came, and with their long curving horns silvered. Behind them they brought a drag covered with gifts—those gifts for which Marion had shopped so hard and so carefully.

A shout went up. . . .

And when the excitement had abated a little Seaver came forward and distributed to each his gaily wrapped present. And none had been forgotten and none was passed over.

IX

At last it was finished. Little by little, singly and in groups, goodnights were said and we called "Merry Christmas" after those who left. . . . Now only a few remained—those who had helped and those who were oldest friends—like Susan and Frances and Grandmother Sortwell and Harry Nash. These alone sat on to watch the fires die down and the candles gutter, prolonging their old joy in each other which tonight had been renewed and confirmed. And none knew that for two among them this was to be a last Christmas together—for those perhaps best-beloved of them all. For in another year the gulls would be crying over Harry Nash's grave and faraway in New York Susan would rally from that last long illness to laugh and to plan a little, making even a deathbed gay. But for all that they did not know this, there was coupled with joy in each one's heart a little wistfulness, for none of them but had learned the wisdom which mistrusts tomorrow.

So, when Seaver had brought a tray of hot spiced drinks and they had drunk them, they went reluctantly out of the cosy clearing, now fast growing dim, and walked slowly into the open. Yet, parting, they made the night chime with pensive laughter.

Only then did the first rain fall.

Once on Christmas

DOROTHY THOMPSON

It is Christmas Eve—the festival that belongs to mothers and fathers and children, all over the so-called Western world. It's not a time to talk about situations, or conditions, or reactions, or people who emerge briefly into the news. My seven-year-old son asked me this evening to tell him what Christmas was like when I was a little girl, before people came home for Christmas in airplanes, thirty odd years ago. And so I told him this:

A long, long time ago, when your mother was your age, and not nearly as tall as you, she lived with her mother, and father, and younger brother, and little sister, in a Methodist parsonage, in Hamburg, New York. It was a tall wooden house, with a narrow verandah on the side, edged with curley-cues of woodwork at the top, and it looked across a lawn at the church where father preached every Sunday morning and evening. In the backyard there were old Baldwin and Greening apple trees, and a wonderful, wonderful barn. But that is another story. The village now has turned into a suburb of the neighboring city of Buffalo, and fathers who work there go in and out every day on the trains and buses, but then it was just a little country town, supported by the surrounding farms.

Father preached in his main church there on Sunday mornings

but in the afternoons he had to drive out to the neighboring village of Armor where there was just a little box of church in the middle of the farming country. For serving both parishes, he received his house and one thousand dollars a year. But he didn't always get the thousand dollars. Sometimes the crops were bad, and the farmers had no money, and when the farmers had no money the village people didn't have any either. Then the farmers would come to us with quarters of beef, or halves of pigs, or baskets of potatoes, and make what they called a donation. My mother hated the word, and sometimes would protest, but my father would laugh, and say, "Let them pay in what they can! We are all in the same boat together."

For weeks before Christmas we were very, very busy. Mother was busy in the kitchen, cutting up citron and sorting out raisins and clarifying suet for the Christmas pudding—and shooing all of us out of the room, when we crept in to snatch a raisin, or a bit of kernel from the butter-nuts that my little brother was set to cracking on the woodshed floor, with an old-fashioned flat-iron.

I would lock myself into my little bed-room, to bend over a handkerchief that I was hemstitching for my mother. It is very hard to hemstitch when you are seven years old, and the thread would knot, and break, and then one would have to begin again, with a little rough place, where one had started over. I'm afraid the border of that handkerchief was just one succession of knots and starts.

The home-made presents were only a tiny part of the work! There was the Christmas tree! Mr. Heist, from my father's Armor parish, had brought it from his farm, a magnificent hemlock, that touched the ceiling. We were transported with admiration, but what a tree to trim! For there was no money to buy miles of tinsel and boxes of colored glass balls.

But in the pantry was a huge stone jar of popcorn. When school was over, in the afternoons, we all gathered in the back parlor, which was the family sitting room. The front parlor was a cold place, where portraits of John Wesley and Frances Willard hung on the walls, and their eyes, I remember, would follow a naughty child accusingly around the room. The sofas in that room were of walnut, with roses and grapes carved on their backs, just where they'd stick into your back, if you fidgeted in them, and were covered with horse-hair which was slippery when it was new, and tickly when it was old. But that room was given over to visits from the local tycoons who sometimes contributed to the church funds, and couples who came to be married.

The back parlor was quite, quite different. It had an ingrain carpet on the floor, with patterns of maple leaves, and white muslin curtains at the windows, and an assortment of chairs contributed by the Parsonage Committee. A Morris chair, I remember, and some rockers, and a fascinating cabinet which was a desk and a book-case, and a chest of drawers, and a mirror, all in one.

In this room there was a round iron stove, a very jolly stove, a cozy stove that winked at you with its red isin-glass eyes. On top of this stove was a round iron plate, it was flat, and a wonderful place to pop corn. There was a great copper kettle, used for making maple syrup, and we shook the popper on the top of the stove—first I shook, until my arm was tired, and then Willard shook, until he was tired, and even the baby shook. The corn popped, and we poured it into the kettle and emptied the kettle, and poured it full again, until there was a whole barrel-full of popcorn, as white and fluffy as the snow that carpeted the lawn between the parsonage and the church.

Then we each got a darning needle, a big one, and a ball of string. We strung the popcorn into long, long ropes, to hang upon the tree. But that was only half of it! There were stars to be cut out of kindergarten paper, red and green, and silver, and gold, and walnuts to be wrapped in gold paper, or painted with gold paint out of the paint-box that I had been given for my birthday. One got the paint into one's finger-nails, and it smelled like bananas. And red apples to be polished, because a shiny apple makes a brave show on a tree. And when it was all finished, it was Christmas Eve.

For Christmas Eve we all wore our best clothes. Baby in a little challis dress as blue as her eyes, and I had a new pinafore of Swiss lawn that my Aunt Margaret had sent me from England. We waited, breathless, in the front parlor while the candles were lit.

Then my mother sat at the upright piano in a rose-red cashmere dress and played, and my father sang, in his lovely, pure, gay, tenor voice:

"It came upon the midnight clear
That glorious song of old,
From angels bending near the earth
To touch their harps of gold."

And then we all marched in. It is true that we had decorated the tree ourselves, and knew intimately everything on it, but it shone in the dark room like an angel, and I could see the angels bending down, and it was so beautiful that one could hardly bear it. We all cried, "Merry Christmas!" and kissed each other.

There were bundles under the tree, most alluring bundles! But they didn't belong to Christmas Eve. They were for the morning. Before the morning came three little children would sit sleepily in the pews of their father's church and hear words drowsily, and shift impatiently, and want to go to sleep in order to wake up very, very early!

And wake up early we did! The windows were still gray, and, oh, how cold the room was! The church janitor had come over at dawn to stoke the hot air furnace in the parsonage, but at its best it only heated the rooms directly above it, and the upstairs depended on grates in the floor, and the theory that heat rises. We shuddered out of our beds, trembling with cold and excitement, and into our clothes, which, when I was a little girl, were very complicated affairs indeed. First, a long fleece-lined union suit, and then a ferris waist dripping with buttons, then the cambric drawers edged with embroidery, and a flannel petticoat handsome with scallops, and another petticoat of cambric and embroidery, just for show, and over that a gay plaid dress, and a dainty pinafore. What polishing of cheeks, and what brushing of hair and then a grand tumble down the stairs into the warm, cozy back parlor.

Presents! There was my beloved Miss Jam-up with a brand new head! Miss Jam-up was once a sweet little doll, dears, who had become badly battered about the face in the course of too affectionate ministrations, and here she was again, with a new head altogether and new clothes, and eyes that open and shut. Scarfs and mittens from my mother's lively fingers. A doll house made from a wooden cracker box and odds and ends of wall paper, with furniture cut from stiff cardboard—and that was mother's work, too. And a new woolen dress, and new pinafores!

Under the tree was a book: *The Water Babies*, by Charles Kingsley. *To my beloved daughter Dorothy.*

Books meant sheer magic. There were no automobiles—none for Methodist ministers, in those days. No moving pictures. No radio. But inside the covers of books was everything, everything, that exists outside in the world today. Lovely, lovely words of poetry, that slipped like colored beads along a string; tales of rose-red cities, half as old as time. All that men can imagine, and construct, and make others imagine.

One couldn't read the book now. But there it lay, the promise of a perfect afternoon. Before one could get at it, one would go into the dining room. And what a dinner! This Christmas there was Turkey—with best wishes from one of my father's parishioners. And the pudding, steaming, and with two kinds of sauce. And no one to say, "No, dear, I think one helping is enough."

We glutted ourselves, we distended ourselves, we ate ourselves into a coma, so that we all had to lie down and have a nap.

Then, lying before the stove, propped on my elbows, I opened the covers of my Christmas book.

"Once upon a time there was a little chimney sweep, and his name was Tom. He lived in a great town of the North Country . . . in England."

How well I knew that North Country, with its rows on rows of dark stone houses, its mine pits, its poor workmen. From such a town my father had come, across the ocean, to this village in upstate New York. I forgot Christmas, forgot everything, except the fate of little Tom. What a book! It wasn't just a story. There was poetry in it. The words of the poems sang in my head, so that after all these years I can remember them:

When all the world is young, lad,
And all the trees are green;
And every goose, a swan, lad,
And every lass a Queen;
Then hey for boot and spur, lad,
And round the world away;
Young blood must have its course, lad,
And every dog his day.

The little girl lay and dreamed that all the world was wide and beautiful, filled only with hearts as warm and hands as tender, and spirits as generous as the only ones she had ever known . . . when she was seven years old.

I WISH YOU ALL A MERRY CHRISTMAS!
I WISH US ALL A WORLD AS KIND AS A
CHILD CAN IMAGINE IT!